Praise for Robert

'The work of a maste
Daily Telegr

'A scrupulous plotter and master of misdirection,
Galbraith keeps the pages turning ... Strike and Ellacott
remain one of crime's most engaging duos'
Guardian

'A blistering piece of crime writing'
Sunday Times

'[Galbraith] reminds me why I fell in love
with crime fiction in the first place'
Val McDermid

'Outrageously entertaining'
Financial Times

'Strike is a compelling creation ... this is
terrifically entertaining stuff'
Irish Times

'Come for the twists and turns and stay for
the beautifully drawn central relationship'
Independent

'A finely honed, superbly constructed tale'
Daily Mail

'One of the most unique and compelling detectives
I've come across in recent years'
Mark Billingham

'Superb ... an ingenious whodunnit'
Sunday Mirror

'I'm a huge fan of Cormoran Strike ... *Troubled Blood* is terrific'
Richard & Judy
Daily Express

'Galbraith is fluent in invention of incident, characters,
conversation and confrontations'
Scotsman

ROBERT
GALBRAITH

THE
INK BLACK
HEART

A *STRIKE* NOVEL

SPHERE

SPHERE

First published in Great Britain in 2022 by Sphere

1 3 5 7 9 10 8 6 4 2

A CIP catalogue record for this book
is available from the British Library.

Hardback ISBN 978-0-7515-8420-2
Trade paperback ISBN 978-0-7515-8418-9

Typeset in Bembo by M Rules
Printed and bound in Great Britain by
Clays Ltd, Elcograf S.p.A.

Sphere
An imprint of
Little, Brown Book Group
Carmelite House
50 Victoria Embankment
London EC4Y 0DZ

An Hachette UK Company
www.hachette.co.uk

www.littlebrown.co.uk

To Steve and Lorna,
my family, my friends
and two bulwarks against anomie,
with love

Two forms of darkness are there. One is Night . . .
And one is Blindness.

Mary Elizabeth Coleridge
Doubt

PROLOGUE

Wounds of the heart are often fatal,
but not necessarily so.

Henry Gray FRS
Gray's Anatomy

1

Why did you let your eyes so rest on me,
And hold your breath between?
In all the ages this can never be
As if it had not been.

Mary Elizabeth Coleridge
A Moment

Of all the couples sitting in the Rivoli Bar at the Ritz that Thursday evening, the pair that was having the most conspicuously good time was not, in fact, a couple.

Cormoran Strike and Robin Ellacott, private detectives, business partners and self-declared best friends, were celebrating Robin's thirtieth birthday. Both had been slightly self-conscious on first arriving in the bar, which resembled an art deco jewel box, with its walls of dark wood and gold, and its frosted panels of Lalique glass, because each was aware that this outing was unique in the almost five years they'd known one another. Never before had they chosen to spend an evening in each other's company outside work, without the presence of other friends or colleagues, or the pretext of injury (because there'd been an occasion a few weeks previously, when Strike had accidentally given his partner two black eyes and bought her a takeaway curry as recompense).

Even more unusually, both had had enough sleep, and each was looking their best. Robin was wearing a figure-hugging blue dress, her long strawberry-blonde hair clean and loose, and her partner had noticed the appreciative glances she'd drawn from male drinkers as she passed. He'd already complimented her on the opal lying in the hollow at the base of her throat, which had been a thirtieth birthday gift from her parents. The tiny diamonds surrounding it made a glittering halo in the bar's golden lights, and whenever Robin moved, sparks of scarlet fire twinkled in the opal's depths.

Strike was wearing his favourite Italian suit, with a white shirt and dark tie. His resemblance to a broken-nosed, slightly overweight Beethoven had increased now that he'd shaved off his recently grown beard, but the waitress's warm smile as she handed Strike his first Old Fashioned reminded Robin of what her ex-husband's new wife, Sarah Shadlock, had once said of the detective:

'He is strangely attractive, isn't he? Bit beaten-up-looking, but I've never minded that.'

What a liar she'd been: Sarah had liked her men smoothly handsome, as proven by her relentless and ultimately successful pursuit of Matthew.

Sitting facing each other in leopard-print chairs at their table for two, Strike and Robin had initially subsumed their slight awkwardness in work talk. Discussion of the cases currently on the detective agency's books carried them through a powerful cocktail apiece, by which time their increasingly loud laughter had started drawing glances from both barmen and customers. Soon Robin's eyes were bright and her face slightly flushed, and even Strike, who was considerably larger than his partner and well able to handle his alcohol, had taken enough bourbon to make him feel pleasantly buoyant and loose-limbed.

After their second cocktails, talk became more personal. Strike, who was the illegitimate son of a rock star he'd met only twice, told Robin that one of his half-sisters, Prudence, wanted to meet him.

'Where does she fit in?' Robin asked. She knew that Strike's father had been married three times, and that her partner was the result of a one-night stand with a woman most commonly described in the press as a 'supergroupie', but she was hazy about the rest of the family tree.

'She's the other illegitimate,' said Strike. 'Few years younger than me. Her mother was that actress, Lindsey Fanthrope? Mixed-race woman? She's been in everything. *EastEnders*, *The Bill* . . .'

'D'you want to meet Prudence?'

'Not sure,' Strike admitted. 'Can't help feeling I've got enough relatives to be going on with. She's also a therapist.'

'What kind?'

'Jungian.'

His expression, which compounded wariness and distaste, made Robin laugh.

'What's wrong with being a Jungian therapist?'

'I dunno . . . I quite liked her from her texts, but . . .'

Trying to find the right words, Strike's eyes found the bronze panel on the wall behind Robin's head, which showed a naked Leda being impregnated by Zeus in the form of a swan.

'. . . well, she said she hasn't had an easy time of it either, having him as a father. But when I found out what she does for a living . . .'

His voice trailed away. He drank more bourbon.

'You thought she was being insincere?'

'Not exactly insincere . . .' Strike heaved a sigh. 'I've had enough matchbox psychologists telling me why I live the way I do and tracing it all back to my family, so-called. Prudence said in one of her texts that she'd found forgiving Rokeby "healing"— Sod this,' said Strike abruptly, 'it's your birthday, let's talk about *your* family. What does your dad do for a living? You've never told me.'

'Oh, haven't I?' said Robin, with mild surprise. 'He's a professor of sheep medicine, production and reproduction.'

Strike choked on his cocktail.

'What's funny?' Robin asked, eyebrows raised.

'Sorry,' said Strike, coughing and laughing simultaneously. 'Wasn't expecting it, that's all.'

'He's quite an authority, I'll have you know,' said Robin, mock-offended.

'Professor of sheep— What was the rest of it, again?'

'Medicine, production and reprod— *Why's* that so funny?' Robin said, as Strike guffawed a second time.

'Dunno, maybe the "production" and "reproduction" thing,' said Strike. 'And also the sheep.'

'He's got forty-six letters after his name. I counted when I was a kid.'

'Very impressive,' said Strike, taking another sip of bourbon and attempting to look serious. 'So, when did he first become interested in sheep? Was this a lifelong thing or did a particular sheep catch his eye when he was—'

'He doesn't *shag* them, Strike.'

The detective's renewed laughter made heads turn.

'His older brother got the family farm, so Dad did veterinary science at Durham and, yeah, he specialised— Stop bloody laughing! He's also the editor of a magazine.'

'Please tell me it's about sheep.'

'Yes, it is. *Sheep Management*,' said Robin, 'and before you ask, no, they don't have a photo feature called "Readers' Sheep".'

This time Strike's bellow of laughter was heard by the whole bar.

'Keep it down,' said Robin, smiling but aware of the many eyes now upon them. 'We don't want to be banned from *another* bar in London.'

'We didn't get banned from the American Bar, did we?'

Strike's memory of the aftermath of attempting to punch a suspect in the Stafford Hotel was hazy, not because he'd been drunk, but because he'd been lost to everything but his own rage.

'They might not have barred us *explicitly*, but try going back in there and see what kind of a welcome you get,' said Robin, fishing one of the last olives out of the dishes that had arrived with their first drink. Strike had already single-handedly finished the crisps.

'Charlotte's father kept sheep,' Strike said, and Robin felt that small frisson of interest she always experienced when he mentioned his former fiancée, which was almost never.

'Really?'

'Yeah, on Arran,' said Strike. 'He had a massive house there with his third wife. Hobby farming, you know. Probably a tax write-off. They were evil-looking bastards – the sheep, that is – can't remember the name of the breed. Black and white. Huge horns and yellow eyes.'

'They sound like Jacobs,' said Robin, and responding to Strike's grin, she said, 'I grew up with massive piles of *Sheep Management* next to the loo – obviously I know sheep breeds ... What's Arran like?'

She really meant, 'What was Charlotte's family like?'

'Pretty, from what I can remember, but I was only at the house once. Never got a return invitation. Charlotte's father hated the sight of me.'

'Why?'

Strike downed the last of his cocktail before answering.

'Well, there were a few reasons, but I think top of the list was that his wife tried to seduce me.'

Robin's gasp was far louder than she'd intended.

'Yeah. I must've been about twenty-two, twenty-three. She was at least forty. Very good-looking, if you like them coke-thin.'

'How – what ...?'

'We'd gone to Arran for the weekend. Scheherazade – that was the stepmother – and Charlotte's father were very big drinkers. Half the family had drug problems as well, all the stepsisters and half-brothers.

'The four of us sat up boozing after dinner. Her father wasn't over-keen on me in the first place – hoping for something a lot more blue-blooded. They'd put Charlotte and me in separate bedrooms on different floors.

'I went up to my attic room about two in the morning, stripped off, fell into bed very pissed, turned out the light and a couple of minutes later the door opened. I thought it was Charlotte, obviously. The room was pitch black. I moved over, she slid in beside me –'

Robin realised her mouth was agape and closed it.

'– stark naked. Still didn't twig – I had most of a bottle of whisky inside me. She – ah – reached for me – if you know what I'm saying –'

Robin clapped a hand over her mouth.

'– and we kissed and it was only when she whispered in my ear that she'd noticed me looking at her tits when she'd bent over the fire that I realised I was in bed with my hostess. Not that it matters, but I hadn't been looking at her tits. I'd been getting ready to catch her. She was so pissed, I thought she was going to topple into the fire when she threw a log on it.'

'What did you do?' Robin asked through her fingers.

'Shot out of bed like I had a firework up my arse,' said Strike, as Robin began to laugh again, 'hit the washstand, knocked it over and smashed some giant Victorian jug. She just sniggered. I had the impression she thought I'd be straight back in bed with her once the shock wore off. I was trying to find my boxers in the dark when Charlotte opened the door for real.'

'Oh my *God*.'

'Yeah, she didn't take too kindly to finding me and her stepmother naked in the same bedroom,' said Strike. 'It was a toss-up which of us she wanted to kill most. The screaming woke Sir Anthony. He came charging upstairs in his brocade dressing gown, but he was so pissed he hadn't tied it properly. He turned the lights on and stood there holding a shooting stick, oblivious to the fact that his cock was hanging out until his wife pointed it out.

'"Anthony, we can see Johnny Winkle."'

Robin now laughed so hard that Strike had to wait for her to compose herself before continuing the story. At the bar a short distance from their table, a silver-haired man was watching Robin with a slight smirk on his face.

'What then?' Robin asked breathlessly, mopping her eyes with the miniature napkin that had come with her drink.

'Well, as far as I can remember, Scheherazade didn't bother to justify herself. If anything, she seemed to think it was all a bit of a laugh. Charlotte lunged at her and I held Charlotte back, and Sir Anthony basically seemed to take the view that it was all my fault for not locking my bedroom door. Charlotte was a bit inclined that way too. But life in squats with my mother hadn't really prepared me for what to expect from the aristocracy. On balance, I'd have to say people were a lot better behaved in the squats.'

He raised his hand to indicate to the smiling waitress that they were ready for more drinks, and Robin, whose ribs were sore from laughing, got to her feet.

'Need the loo,' she said breathlessly, and the eyes of the silver-haired man on the bar stool followed her as she walked away.

The cocktails had been small but very strong, and Robin, who spent so much of her life running surveillance in trainers, was out of the habit of wearing heels. She had to grasp the handrail firmly while navigating the red-carpeted stairs down to the Ladies' Room, which was more palatial than any Robin had visited before. The soft pink of a strawberry macaron, it featured circular marble sinks, a velvet sofa and walls covered in murals of nymphs standing in water lily-strewn lakes.

Having peed, Robin straightened her dress and checked her mascara in the mirror, expecting it to have run with all the laughing. Washing her hands, she thought back over the story Strike had just told her. However funny she'd found it, it was also slightly intimidating. In spite of the vast array of human vagaries, many of them sexual, that Robin had encountered in her detective career, she sometimes felt herself to be inexperienced and unworldly compared to other women her age. Robin's personal experience of the wilder shores of sexual adventurousness was non-existent. She'd only ever had one sexual partner and had reasons beyond the usual for wishing to trust the person with whom she went to bed. A middle-aged man with a patch of vitiligo under his left ear had once stood in the dock and claimed that nineteen-year-old Robin had invited him into a dark stairwell for sex, and that he'd choked her into unconsciousness because she'd told him she 'liked it rough'.

'I think my next drink had better be water,' Robin said five minutes later, as she dropped back into her seat opposite Strike again. 'Those are seriously strong cocktails.'

'Too late,' said Strike, as the waitress set fresh glasses in front of them. 'Fancy a sandwich, mop up some of the alcohol?'

He passed her the menu. The prices were exorbitant.

'No, listen—'

'I wouldn't have invited you to the Ritz if I wasn't prepared to cough up,' said Strike with an expansive gesture. 'I'd have ordered a cake, but—'

'Ilsa's already done it, for tomorrow night?' Robin guessed.

The following evening a group of friends, Strike included, would be giving Robin a birthday dinner, organised by their mutual friend.

'Yeah. I wasn't supposed to tell you, so act surprised. Who's coming to this dinner, anyway?' Strike asked. He had a slight curiosity about whether there were any people he didn't know about: specifically, men.

Robin listed the names of the couples.

'. . . and you and me,' she finished.

'Who's Richard?'

'Max's new boyfriend,' said Robin. Max was her flatmate and land-lord, an actor who rented out a bedroom because he couldn't make his mortgage repayments without a lodger. 'I'm starting to wonder if it isn't time to move out of Max's,' she added.

The waitress appeared and Strike ordered them both sandwiches before turning back to Robin.

'Why're you thinking of moving out?'

'Well, the TV show Max is in pays really well and they've just commissioned a second series, and he and Richard seem very keen on each other. I don't want to wait until they ask me to leave. Anyway' – Robin took a sip of her fresh cocktail – 'I'm thirty. It's about time I was out on my own, don't you think?'

Strike shrugged.

'I'm not big on having to do things by certain dates. That's more Lucy's department.'

Lucy was the sister with whom Strike had spent most of his child-hood, because they'd shared a mother. He and Lucy generally held opposing views on what constituted life's pleasures and priorities. It distressed Lucy that Strike, who was nearly forty, continued to live alone in two rented rooms over his office, without any of the stabi-lising obligations – a spouse, children, a mortgage, parent-teacher associations, duty Christmas parties with neighbours – that their mother, too, had ruthlessly shirked.

'Well, I think it's about time I had my own place,' said Robin. 'I'll miss Wolfgang, but—'

'Who's Wolfgang?'

'Max's dachshund,' said Robin, surprised by the sharpness of Strike's tone.

'Oh . . . thought it was some German bloke you'd taken a shine to.'

'Ha . . . no,' said Robin.

She really was feeling quite drunk now. Hopefully the sandwiches would help.

'No,' she repeated, 'Max isn't the type to try and set me up with Germans. Makes quite a nice change, I must say.'

'Do many people try and set you up with Germans?'

'Not Germans, but . . . Oh, you know what it's like. Vanessa keeps telling me to get myself on Tinder and my cousin Katie wants me to meet some friend of hers who's just moved to London. They call him Axeman.'

'Axeman?' repeated Strike.

'Yes, because his name's . . . something that sounds like Axeman. I can't remember,' said Robin, with a vague wave of the hand. 'He's recently divorced, so Katie thinks we'd be perfect for each other. I don't really understand why it would make two people compatible, just because they've screwed up a marriage each. In fact, if anything—'

'*You* didn't screw up your marriage,' said Strike.

'I did,' Robin contradicted him. 'I shouldn't have married Matthew at all. It was a mess, and it got worse as we went on.'

'He was the one who had the affair.'

'But I was the one who didn't want to be there. I was the one who tried to end it on the honeymoon, then chickened out—'

'Did you?' said Strike, to whom this was new information.

'Yes,' said Robin. 'I knew, deep down, knew it was all wrong . . .'

For a moment she was transported back to the Maldives, and those hot nights she'd paced alone on the white sand outside their villa while Matthew slept, asking herself whether she was in love with Cormoran Strike.

The sandwiches arrived and Robin requested a glass of water. For a minute or so they ate in silence, until Strike said,

'I wouldn't go on Tinder.'

'*You* wouldn't, or I shouldn't?'

'Both,' said Strike. He'd managed to finish one sandwich and start on his second before Robin had taken two bites. 'In our line of work it's not smart to put yourself online too much.'

'That's what I told Vanessa,' said Robin. 'But she said I could use a fake name until I got keen on someone.'

'Nothing like lying about your own name to build a firm foundation of trust,' said Strike and Robin laughed again.

Strike ordered more cocktails and Robin didn't protest. The bar was more crowded now than when they'd first sat down, the hum of conversation louder, and the crystals hanging from the chandeliers were each surrounded by a misty aureole. Robin now felt an indiscriminate fondness for everyone in the room, from the elderly couple talking quietly over champagne and the bustling bartenders in their white jackets to the silver-haired man who smiled at her as she gazed around. Most of all, she liked Cormoran Strike, who was giving her a wonderful, memorable and costly birthday evening.

As for Strike, who genuinely hadn't ogled the breasts of Scheherazade Campbell all those years ago, he was doing his best to extend the same courtesy to his business partner, but she'd never looked better to him: flushed with drink and laughter, her red-blonde hair shining in the diffused glow from the golden cupola above them. When she bent forward suddenly to pick up something on the floor, a deep cavern of cleavage was revealed behind the hanging opal.

'Perfume,' she said, straightening up, having retrieved the small purple bag she'd carried from Liberty, in which was Strike's birthday present. 'Want to put some on.'

She untied the ribbon, unwrapped the parcel and extracted the square white bottle, and Strike watched her spray a small amount on each wrist, and then – he forced himself to look away – down into the hollow between her breasts.

'I love it,' she said, wrist to her nose. 'Thank you.'

He caught a small waft of perfume from where he sat: his sense of smell slightly impaired from long years of smoking, he nevertheless detected roses and an undertone of musk, which made him think of sun-warmed skin.

Fresh cocktails arrived.

'I think she's forgotten my water,' said Robin, sipping her Manhattan. 'This has got to be my last. I don't wear heels much any more. Don't want to faceplant in the middle of the Ritz.'

'I'll get you a cab.'

'You've spent enough.'

'We're doing OK, money-wise,' said Strike. 'For a change.'

'I know — isn't it fantastic?' sighed Robin. 'We've actually got a healthy bank balance *and* tons of work coming in . . . Strike, we're a *success*,' she said, beaming, and he felt himself beaming back.

'Who'd have thought?'

'I would,' said Robin.

'When you met me I was well-nigh bankrupt, sleeping on a camp bed in my office and had one client.'

'So? I liked that you hadn't given up,' said Robin, 'and I could tell you were really good at what you did.'

'The hell could you tell that?'

'Well, I watched you doing it, didn't I?'

'Remember when you brought in that tray of coffee and biscuits?' said Strike. 'To me and John Bristow, that first morning? I couldn't fathom where you'd got it all. It was like a conjuring trick.'

Robin laughed.

'I only asked the bloke downstairs.'

'And you said "we". "I thought, having offered the client coffee, *we* ought to provide it."'

'Your memory,' said Robin, surprised that he had the exact words on the tip of his tongue.

'Yeah, well . . . you're not a . . . usual person,' said Strike.

He picked up his almost-empty drink and raised it.

'To the Strike and Ellacott Detective Agency. And happy thirtieth.'

Robin picked up her glass, clinked it against his and drained it.

'Shit, Strike, look at the time,' she said suddenly, catching sight of her watch. 'I've got to be up at five, I'm supposed to be following Miss Jones's boyfriend.'

'Yeah, OK,' grunted Strike, who could happily have spent another couple of hours here in his comfy chair, bathed in golden light, the smell of rose and musk drifting across the table. He signalled for the bill.

As Robin had anticipated, she was definitely unsteady on her high heels as she crossed the bar, and it took her far longer than it should have done to locate the token for her coat in the bottom of her handbag.

'Could you hold this, please?' she asked Strike, handing him the bag containing her perfume while she rummaged.

Having retrieved her coat, Strike had to help her put it on.

'I am *definitely* quite drunk,' Robin muttered, taking back the little purple bag, and seconds later she proved it by turning her heel on the edge of the circular scarlet rug that covered the lobby's marble floor and slipping sideways. Strike caught her, and kept his arm around her waist as he steered her out of one of the side entrances flanking the revolving door, because he didn't trust her in it.

'Sorry,' said Robin as they walked carefully down the steep stone steps at the front of the Ritz, Strike's arm still around her waist. She liked the feel of him, bulky and warm beside her: it had more often been she who had supported him, on those occasions when the stump of his right leg had refused to continue to bear his weight after some ill-advised piece of overexertion. He was holding her so tightly that her head was almost resting on his chest and she could smell the aftershave he'd put on for this special occasion, even over the usual smell of old cigarettes.

'Taxi,' said Strike, pointing, as a black cab came gliding smoothly towards them.

'Strike,' said Robin, leaning back into him so as to look into his face.

She'd intended to thank him, to tell him what a wonderful evening she'd had, but when their eyes connected no words came. For a minute sliver of time everything around them blurred, as though they stood in the eye of some slow-motion tornado of purring cars and passing lights, of pedestrians and cloud-dappled sky, and only the feel and smell of each other was real, and Strike, looking down into her upturned face, forgot in that second every stern resolution that had restrained him for nearly five years and made an almost infinitesimal dip of his head, his mouth heading for hers.

And unwittingly, Robin's expression moved from happiness to fear. He saw it and straightened up again, and before either of them could quite process what had just happened the mundane roar of a motorbike courier heralded the return of the world to its regular course; the tornado had passed and Strike was guiding Robin towards the taxi's open door, and she was falling back onto its solid seat.

''Night,' he called in after her. The door had slammed and the taxi had pulled away before Robin, dazed, could decide whether she felt more shock, elation or regret.

2

Come let me talk with thee, allotted part
Of immortality – my own deep heart!

Maria Jane Jewsbury
To My Own Heart

The days following their night at the Ritz were, for Robin, full of agitation and suspense. She was well aware that Strike had posed a wordless question and that she'd silently returned a 'no', far more forcefully than if she hadn't been full of bourbon and vermouth, and caught off guard. Now there was an increase of reserve in Strike's manner, a slightly forced briskness and a determined avoidance of all personal subjects. Barriers that had come down over their five years working together seemed to have been re-erected. Robin was afraid she'd hurt Strike, and she didn't underestimate what it took to hurt a man as quietly confident and resilient as her partner.

Meanwhile, Strike was full of self-recrimination. He shouldn't have made that foolish, unconsummated move: hadn't he concluded months previously that a relationship with his partner was impossible? They spent too much time together, they were legally bound to each other by the business, the friendship was too valuable to him to jeopardise, so why, in the golden glow of those exorbitantly priced cocktails, had he jettisoned every good resolution and yielded to powerful impulse?

Self-reproach mingled with feelings still less pleasant. The fact was that Strike had very rarely suffered rebuffs from women, because he was unusually good at reading people. Never before had he made a move without being certain that his advance would be welcome, and he'd certainly never had any woman react the way Robin had: with

14

alarm that, in his worst moments, Strike thought could have been disgust. He might be broken-nosed, overweight and one-legged, with dense, dark curly hair that schoolfriends had dubbed pube-like, but that hadn't ever stopped him pulling gorgeous women before. Indeed, male friends, to whose eyes the detective's sexual appeal was largely invisible, had often expressed resentment and amazement that he had such a successful sex life. But perhaps it was insufferable vanity to think that the attraction he'd held for previous girlfriends lingered, even as his morning cough worsened and grey hairs started to appear among the dark brown?

Worse still was the idea that he'd totally misinterpreted Robin's feelings over a period of years. He'd assumed her slight awkwardness at times when they were forced into physical or emotional proximity had the same root as his own: a determination not to succumb to temptation. In the days following her silent rejection of his kiss, he kept going over incidents he'd thought proved the attraction was mutual, returning again and again to the fact that she'd broken off her first dance at her wedding to follow him, leaving Matthew abandoned on the dance floor. She and Strike had hugged at the top of the hotel stairs, and as he'd held her in her wedding dress he could have sworn he'd heard the same dangerous thought in her mind as filled his: let's run away, and to hell with the consequences. Had he imagined it all?

Perhaps he had. Perhaps Robin had wanted to run, but merely back to London and the job. Maybe she saw him as a mentor and a friend, but nothing more.

It was in this unsettled and depressed mood that Strike greeted his fortieth birthday, which was marked by a restaurant dinner organised, as Robin's had been, by their mutual friends Nick and Ilsa.

Here, for the first time, Robin met Strike's oldest friend from Cornwall, Dave Polworth, who, as Strike had once predicted, Robin didn't much like. Polworth was small and garrulous, commented negatively on every aspect of London life and referred to women, including the waitress who served them, as 'tarts'. Robin, who was at the opposite end of the table from Strike, spent much of the evening making laboured small talk with Polworth's wife, Penny, whose main topics of conversation were her two children, how expensive everything in London was, and what a twat her husband was.

Robin had bought Strike a rare test pressing of Tom Waits's first album, *Closing Time*, for his birthday. She knew Waits was his favourite artist, and her best memory of the evening was the look of unfeigned surprise and pleasure on Strike's face when he unwrapped it. She thought she sensed some return of his usual warmth when he thanked her, and she hoped the gift would convey the message that a woman who found him repugnant wouldn't have gone to so much effort to buy him something she knew he'd really want. She wasn't to know that Strike was asking himself whether Robin considered him and the sixty-five-year-old Waits contemporaries.

A week after Strike's birthday, the agency's longest-serving sub-contractor, Andy Hutchins, handed in his notice. It wasn't entirely a surprise: although his MS was in remission, the job was taking its toll. They gave Andy a farewell drinks party, which everyone except the other subcontractor, Sam Barclay, attended, because he'd drawn the short straw and was currently following a target through the West End.

While Strike and Hutchins talked shop on the other side of the pub table, Robin talked to their newest hire, Michelle Greenstreet, known to her new colleagues, at her own request, as Midge. She was a Mancunian ex-policewoman, tall, lean and very fit, a gym fanatic with short, slicked-back dark hair and clear grey eyes. Robin had already been made to feel slightly inadequate by the sight of Midge's six-pack as she stretched to reach the topmost file balanced on a cabinet, but she liked her directness, and the fact that she didn't seem to hold herself superior to Robin, who alone at the agency wasn't ex-police or military. Tonight, Midge confided in Robin for the first time that a major reason for wishing to relocate to London had been a bad break-up.

'Was your ex police as well?' asked Robin.

'Nope. She never held a job for more than a coupla months,' said Midge, with more than a trace of bitterness. 'She's an undiscovered genius who's either gonna write a bestselling novel, or paint a picture that'll win the Turner Prize. I was out all day making money to pay the bills, and she was at home pissing around online. I ended it when I found her dating profile on Zoosk.'

'God, I'm sorry,' said Robin. 'My marriage ended when I found a diamond earring in our bed.'

'Yeah, Vanessa told me,' said Midge, who'd been recommended to the agency by Robin's policewoman friend. 'She said you didn't keep it, either, you fookin' mug.'

'I'd've flogged it,' rasped Pat Chauncey, the office manager, breaking unexpectedly into the conversation. Pat was a gravel-voiced fifty-seven-year-old with boot-black hair and teeth the colour of old ivory, who chain-smoked outside the office and sucked constantly on an e-cigarette inside it. 'I had a woman send me my first husband's Y-fronts in the post, cheeky cow.'

'Seriously?' asked Midge.

'Oh yeah,' growled Pat.

'What did you do?' Robin asked.

'Pinned 'em to the front door so they were the first thing he'd see when he come home from work,' said Pat. She took a deep pull on her e-cigarette and said, 'And I sent her somefing back she wouldn't forget.'

'What?' said Robin and Midge in unison.

'Never you mind,' said Pat. 'But let's just say it wouldn't spread easy on toast.'

The three women's shouts of laughter drew Strike and Hutchins's attention: Strike caught Robin's eye and she held it, grinning. He looked away feeling slightly more cheerful than he'd done in a while.

The departure of Andy placed a not-unfamiliar strain on the agency, because it currently had several time-consuming jobs on its books. The first and longest-running of these involved trying to dig up dirt on the ex-boyfriend of a client nicknamed Miss Jones, who was locked into a bitter custody battle over her baby daughter. Miss Jones was a good-looking brunette who had an almost embarrassing yen for Strike. He might have derived a much needed ego-boost from her unabashed pursuit of him, were it not for the fact that he found her combination of entitlement and neediness thoroughly unattractive.

Their second client was also the wealthiest: a Russian-American billionaire who lived between Moscow, New York and London. A couple of extremely valuable objects had recently disappeared from his house on South Audley Street, though the security alarm hadn't been tripped. The client suspected his London-based stepson and wished to catch the young man in the act without alerting either the police or his wife, who was disposed to consider her hard-partying and jobless offspring a misunderstood paragon. Hidden spy cameras, monitored by the agency, were now concealed in every corner of the house. The stepson, who was known at the agency as Fingers, was likewise under surveillance in case he tried to sell the missing Fabergé casket or the Hellenistic head of Alexander the Great.

The agency's last case, codenamed Groomer, was in Robin's view a particularly nasty one. A well-known international correspondent for an American news channel had recently broken up with her boyfriend of three years, who was an equally successful TV producer. Shortly after their acrimonious split, the journalist had found out that her ex-partner was still in contact with her seventeen-year-old daughter, whom Midge had dubbed Legs. The seventeen-year-old, who was tall and slender, with long blonde hair, was already featuring in gossip columns, partly because of her famous surname and partly because she'd already done some modelling. Though the agency hadn't yet witnessed sexual contact between Legs and Groomer, their body language was far from parental-filial during their secret meet-ups. The situation had plunged Legs' mother into a state of fury, fear and suspicion that was poisoning her relationship with her daughter.

To everyone's relief, because they'd been so stretched after Andy's departure, at the start of December Strike succeeded in poaching an ex-Met officer by the name of Dev Shah from a rival detective agency. There was bad blood between Strike and Mitch Patterson, the boss of the agency in question, which dated back to the time Patterson had put Strike himself under surveillance. When Shah answered the question 'Why d'you want to leave Patterson Inc?' with the words 'I'm tired of working for cunts,' Strike hired him on the spot.

Like Barclay, Shah was married with a young child. He was shorter than both of his new male colleagues, with eyelashes so thick that Robin thought they looked fake. Everyone at the agency took to Dev: Strike, because he was quick on the uptake and methodical in his record-keeping; Robin, because she liked his dry sense of humour and what she inwardly termed a lack of dickishness; Barclay and Midge, because Shah demonstrated early on that he was a team player without any noticeable need to outshine the other subcontractors; and Pat, as she admitted in her gravelly voice to Robin while the latter was handing in her receipts one Friday, because he 'could give Imran Khan a run for his money, couldn't he? Those eyes!'

'Mm, very handsome,' said Robin indifferently, tallying her receipts. Pat had spent much of the previous twelve months openly hoping that Robin might fall for the charms of a previous subcontractor whose good looks had been equalled by his creepiness. Robin could only be grateful that Dev was married.

She'd been forced to temporarily shelve her flat-hunting plans because of the long hours she was working, but still volunteered to stake out the billionaire's house over Christmas. It suited her to have an excuse not to return to her parents in Masham, because she was certain Matthew and Sarah would be parading their new-born child, sex so far unknown, around the familiar streets where once, as teenagers, he and Robin had strolled hand in hand. Robin's parents were disappointed, and Strike was clearly uncomfortable about taking her up on the offer.

'It's fine,' said Robin, disinclined to go into her reasons. 'I'd rather stay in London. You missed Christmas last year.'

She was starting to feel mentally and physically exhausted. She'd worked almost non-stop for the past two years, years that had included separation and divorce. The recent increase of reserve between her and Strike was playing on her mind, and little as she'd wanted to go back to Masham, the prospect of working through the festive season was undeniably depressing.

Then, in mid-December, Robin's favourite cousin, Katie, issued a last-minute invitation for her to join a skiing party over New Year. A couple had dropped out on finding out that the wife was pregnant; the chalet was already paid for, so Robin only needed to buy flights. She'd never skied in her life, but as Katie and her husband would be taking it in turns to look after their three-year-old son while the other was on the slopes, there'd always be somebody around to talk to, should she not wish to spend most of her time falling over on the nursery slopes. Robin thought the trip might give her the sense of perspective and serenity that was eluding her in London. Only after she'd accepted did she learn that in addition to Katie and her husband, and a couple of mutual friends from Masham, Hugh 'Axeman' Jacks would be of the party.

She told Strike none of these details, only that she had the chance of a skiing trip and would like to take it, which meant slightly increasing the amount of time she'd planned to take off over New Year. Aware that Robin was owed far more leave than she was proposing to take, Strike agreed without hesitation, and wished her a good time.

3

Eyes with the glow and hue of wine
Like yours, can daze a man outright . . .

Emily Pfeiffer
A Rhyme for the Time

On 28 December, the ex-boyfriend of Miss Jones, who'd lived an apparently blameless life for weeks, finally slipped up in grand style, buying a large quantity of coke in front of Dev Shah, then taking it in the company of two escorts, before taking them home to Islington. The exhilarated Miss Jones insisted on coming into the office to see the pictures Shah had taken, then tried to embrace Strike. When he pushed her gently but firmly away she seemed more intrigued than offended. After paying her final bill, she insisted on kissing Strike on the cheek, told him boldly that she owed him a favour and hoped he'd call it in one day, then departed in a cloud of Chanel No. 5.

The following day, the mother in the Groomer case was sent to Indonesia to report on a catastrophic air crash. Shortly before her departure, she called Strike to tell him her daughter was planning to spend New Year's Eve at Annabel's with the family of a schoolfriend. She was certain Groomer would try to meet up with her daughter there and demanded that the agency place detectives in the nightclub to keep watch.

Strike, who'd rather have asked almost anyone else for assistance, called Miss Jones, who'd be able to take Strike and Midge into the members-only club as her guests. Strike was set on taking Midge with him, not only because the latter would be able to tail Legs into the bathroom if necessary, but because he didn't want Miss Jones to think he'd engineered the situation in the hope of sleeping with her.

He felt a callous sense of relief when Miss Jones called him two hours before the proposed rendezvous to tell him her baby daughter had come down with a fever.

'... and my *bloody* nanny's phoned in sick and my parents are in Mustique, so I'm screwed,' she told him petulantly. 'But you can still go: I've left your names at the door.'

'I'm very grateful,' he told her. 'I hope she gets better soon.'

He rang off before Miss Jones could suggest any further meetings.

By 11 p.m., he and Midge, who was wearing a dark red velvet tuxedo, were to be found in the basement of the club in Berkeley Square, sitting opposite each other at a table between two mirrored pillars and beneath hundreds of golden helium balloons, from which dangled gleaming ribbons. Their seventeen-year-old target was sitting a few tables away with her schoolfriend's family. She kept glancing towards the restaurant entrance, wearing a look of mingled hope and nervousness. Mobile phones weren't permitted in Annabel's, and Strike could see the restless teenager's mounting frustration at being forced to rely solely on her senses for information.

'Five o'clock, party of eight,' Midge said quietly to Strike. 'You're getting looks.'

Strike spotted them as Midge said it. A man and a woman at a table of eight had turned in their seats to look at him. The woman, who had long hair of the same red-gold as Robin's, was wearing a skin-tight black dress and stilettos that laced all the way up her smooth brown legs to her knees. The man, who was sporting a brocade dinner jacket and a foppish cravat, looked vaguely familiar to Strike, though he couldn't immediately place him.

'D'you think they've recognised you from the papers?' suggested Midge.

'Bloody well hope not,' growled Strike. 'Or I'm out of business.'

The photo the press used most often dated from Strike's time in the military and he was now older, longer-haired and carrying much more weight. On those occasions when he'd had to give evidence in court, he'd always done so wearing the heavy beard that grew conveniently quickly when he had need of it.

Strike found his observers' reflections in a nearby pillar and saw that they were now talking with their heads together. The woman was very good-looking and – atypically, in this room – she appeared not to have had anything obvious done to her face: her forehead still wrinkled when she raised her eyebrows, her lips weren't unnaturally plump and she was too young – perhaps mid-thirties – to have submitted to the surgery that had left the oldest woman at her table with an unnervingly mask-like appearance.

Beside Strike and Midge, a portly Russian was explaining the plot of *Tannhäuser* to his much younger female companion.

'. . . but Mezdrich has updated it,' he said, 'and in this production Jesus now appears in a movie of an orgy in Venus's cave—'

'*Jesus* does?'

'*Da*, and so the church is unhappy and Mezdrich will be fired,' finished the Russian gloomily, raising his glass of champagne to his lips. 'He's standing his ground, but it will end badly for him, mark my words.'

'Legs on the move,' Strike informed Midge as the teenager stood up with the rest of her party, the ostrich trim on her mini-dress wafting fluffily around her.

'Dance floor,' Midge guessed.

She was right. Ten minutes later, Strike and Midge had secured a vantage point in a niche off the tiny dance floor, from where they had a clear view of their target dancing in shoes that appeared a little too high for her, her eyes still darting frequently towards the entrance.

'Wonder how Robin's enjoying skiing?' Midge shouted up to Strike, as 'Uptown Funk' began pounding through the room. 'Mate of mine broke his collarbone first time he tried it. D'you ski?'

'No,' said Strike.

'Nice place, Zermatt,' said Midge loudly, and then something Strike didn't catch.

'What?' Strike said.

'I said, "Wonder if she's pulled?" Good opportunity, New Year's—'

Legs was gesturing to her schoolfriend that she was going to sit the rest of the dance out. Leaving the dance floor, she snatched up her evening bag and wound her way out of the room.

'She's going to use her mobile in the bogs,' predicted Midge, taking off in pursuit.

Strike remained in the alcove, his bottle of zero-alcohol beer already warm in his hand, his only companion an enormous stucco Bodhisattva. Tipsy people were crammed on the sofas near him, shouting at each other over the music. Strike had just loosened his tie and undone the top button of his shirt when he saw the man in

22

the brocade jacket walking towards him, stumbling over legs and handbags as he approached. Now, at last, Strike placed him: Valentine Longcaster, one of Charlotte's stepbrothers.

'Long time no see,' he yelled when he reached Strike.

'Yeah,' said Strike, shaking the proffered hand, 'how's it going?'

Valentine reached up and pushed back his long, sweaty fringe, revealing widely dilated pupils.

'Not bad,' he shouted over the pounding bass. 'Can't complain.' Strike could see a faint trace of white powder inside one nostril. 'You here on business or pleasure?'

'Pleasure,' lied Strike.

Valentine shouted something indecipherable in which Strike heard the name of Charlotte's husband, Jago Ross.

'What?' he shouted back, unsmiling.

'I said, *Jago wants to name you in the divorce.*'

'He'll have a job,' Strike said loudly back. 'I haven't seen her in years.'

'Not what Jago says,' shouted Valentine. 'He found a nude picture she sent you, on her old phone.'

Fuck.

Valentine reached out to steady himself on the Bodhisattva. His female companion with the red-gold hair was watching them from the dance floor.

'That's Madeline,' Valentine shouted in Strike's ear, following his eyeline. 'She thinks you're sexy.'

Valentine's laugh was high-pitched. Strike sipped his beer in silence. At last the younger man seemed to feel no more was to be gained from proximity to Strike, so he pushed himself back upright, gave a mock salute and stumbled out of sight again, just as Legs reappeared on the edge of the dance floor and collapsed onto a velvet stool in a flutter of ostrich features and palpable misery.

'Ladies',' Midge informed Strike, rejoining him a few minutes later. 'Don't think she could get phone reception.'

'Good,' said Strike brutally.

'D'you think he told her he was coming?'

'Looks like it.'

Strike took another mouthful of warm beer and said loudly,

'So how many people are on this skiing trip with Robin?'

'I think there's just six of them,' Midge yelled back. 'Two couples and a spare bloke.'

'Ah,' said Strike, nodding as though the information were of only casual significance.

'They've been trying to fix her up with him,' said Midge. 'She was telling me, before Christmas . . . Hugh Jacks, his name is.' She looked at Strike expectantly. '*Huge axe.*'

'Huh,' said Strike, with a forced smile.

'Haha, yeah. Why,' Midge shouted in his ear, 'don't parents say it out loud before they choose the name?'

Strike nodded, eyes on the teenager now wiping her nose on the back of her hand.

It was a quarter to midnight. With luck, Strike thought, once the new year had been rung in, their target would be scooped up by the schoolfriend's family and taken safely back to their house in Chelsea. As he watched, the schoolfriend arrived to drag Legs back onto the dance floor.

At ten to midnight, Legs disappeared once more in the direction of the Ladies', Midge on her tail. Strike, whose stump was aching and who wished he could sit down, had no choice but to lean up against the gigantic Bodhisattva because most of the free seats were littered with bags and discarded jackets he didn't want to move. His beer bottle was now empty.

'D'you not like New Year's Eve or something?' said a working-class London voice beside him.

It was the woman with red-gold hair, now pink-faced and dishevelled from dancing. Her approach had been masked by an upheaval in the seats ahead of him, as nearly everyone had stood up to flood onto the too-small dance floor, excitement mounting as midnight drew closer.

'Not my favourite,' he shouted back at her.

She was extremely pretty and definitely high, though speaking perfectly coherently. Several fine gold necklaces hung around her slender neck, the strapless dress was tight across her breasts and the half-empty champagne flute in her hand was in danger of spilling its contents.

'Nor mine, not this year,' she shouted up into his ear. He liked hearing an East End accent among all these upper-class ones. 'You're Cormoran Strike, right? Valentine told me.'

'That's right,' he said. 'And you're . . . ?'

'Madeline Courson-Miles. Not detecting tonight, are you?'

'No,' he lied, but he was in far less of a hurry to shoo her away than he had been with Valentine. 'Why isn't this New Year your favourite?'

'Gigi Cazenove.'

'Sorry?'

'Gigi Cazenove,' she said more loudly, leaning in, her breath tickling his ear. 'The singer? She was a client of mine.' When she saw his blank look, she said, 'She was found hanged this morning.'

'Shit,' said Strike.

'Yeah,' said Madeline. 'She was only twenty-three.'

She sipped her champagne, looking sombre, then shouted in his ear:

'I've never met a private detective before.'

'As far as you know,' said Strike, and she laughed. 'What d'you do?'

'I'm a jeweller,' she shouted back at him and her slight smile told Strike that most people would have recognised her name.

The dance floor was now heaving with hot bodies. Many people were wearing glittery party hats. Strike could see the portly Russian who'd been talking about *Tannhäuser* pouring with sweat as he bounced out of time to Clean Bandit's 'Rather Be'.

Strike's thoughts flickered towards Robin, somewhere in the Alps, perhaps drunk on glühwein, dancing with the newly divorced man her friends were insistent she meet. He remembered the look on her face as he'd bent to kiss her.

It's easy being with you, sang Jess Glynne,
Sacred simplicity,
As long as we're together,
There's no place I'd rather be . . .

'One minute to 2015, ladies and gentlemen,' shouted the DJ and Madeline Courson-Miles glanced up at Strike, drained her champagne flute and leaned in to shout into his ear again.

'Is that tall girl in the tux your date?'

'No, a friend,' said Strike. 'Both at a loose end tonight.'

'So she wouldn't mind if I kissed you at midnight?'

He looked down into her lovely, inviting face, the hazel eyes warm, her hair rippling over her bare shoulders.

'*She* wouldn't,' said Strike, half-smiling.

'But you would?'

'Get ready,' bellowed the DJ.

'Are you married?' Strike asked.

'Divorced,' said Madeline.

'Dating anyone?'

'No.'

'*Ten –*'

'In that case,' said Cormoran Strike, setting down his empty beer bottle.

'*Eight –*'

Madeline bent to put her glass down on a nearby table but missed the edge: it fell onto the carpeted floor and she shrugged as she straightened up.

'*Six – five –*'

She wound her arms around his neck; he slid his arms around her waist. She was thinner than Robin: he could feel her ribs through the tight dress. The desire in her eyes was like a balm to him. It was New Year's Eve. *Fuck everything.*

'*– three – two – one –*'

She pressed herself into him, her hands now in his hair, her tongue in his mouth. The air around them was rent with screams and applause. They didn't release each other until the first raucous bars of 'Auld Lang Syne' had been sung. Strike glanced around. There was no sign of either Midge or Legs.

'I'm going to have to leave soon,' he shouted, 'but I want your number.'

'Gimme your phone, then.'

She typed her number in for him, then handed the phone back. With a wink, she turned and walked away, disappearing into the crowd.

Midge didn't reappear for another quarter of an hour. Legs rejoined her schoolfriend's party, her mascara smudged.

'She kept trying to find somewhere she could get reception, but no luck,' Midge bellowed in his ear. 'So she went back to the bogs for a good sob.'

'Too bad,' said Strike.

'Have you got lipstick on you?' asked Midge, staring up at him.

He wiped his mouth with the back of his hand.

'Met an old friend of my mother's,' he said. 'Well – happy 2015.'

'Same to you,' said Midge, extending a hand, which he shook. As she looked out over the jubilant crowd, where balloons were being batted around and glitter was exploding from party poppers, Midge shouted into Strike's ear, 'Never seen in the new year in a toilet before. Hope it's not an omen.'

4

Sleep on content, as sleeps the patient rose.
Walk boldly on the white untrodden snows,
The winter is the winter's own release.

Helen Jackson
January

On the whole, Robin had enjoyed her time in Zermatt. She'd forgotten what it felt like to have eight hours' sleep a night; she'd enjoyed the food, the skiing and the company of her friends; and suffered barely a tremor when Katie told her, with a look of concern that turned to relief when Robin responded calmly, that Matthew had indeed brought Sarah back to Masham over Christmas, along with his new-born son.

'They've called him William,' said Katie. 'We ran into them one night in the Bay Horse. Matthew's aunt was babysitting. I *really* don't like that Sarah. Sooooo smug.'

'Can't say I'm that keen on her either,' said Robin. She was glad to know she'd avoided the almost inevitable meeting in their home town, and with luck, next Christmas it would be Sarah's family's turn to host their grandson, so there'd be no danger of a chance encounter.

The view from Robin's bedroom was of the snow-coated Matterhorn, which pierced the bright blue sky like a gigantic fang. The light on the pyramidal mountain changed from gold to peach, from ink blue to heather depending on the angle of the sun, and alone in her room, staring at the mountain, Robin came closest to achieving the peace and perspective she'd sought in coming on the trip.

The only part of the holiday with which Robin would gladly have dispensed was Hugh Jacks. He was a couple of years older and

27

worked in pharmaceutical chemistry. She supposed he was quite nice-looking, with a neat sandy beard, broad shoulders and large blue eyes, and he wasn't precisely unlikeable, but Robin couldn't help finding him slightly pathetic. No matter the subject under discussion, he somehow managed to bring it back to his divorce, which appeared to have blindsided him. After six years of marriage, his wife had announced that she wasn't happy, that she hadn't been happy for a long time, packed her bags and departed. Hugh told Robin the whole story twice in the first few days of the holiday, and after the second, almost identical recital, she did her best to avoid sitting next to him at dinner. Unfortunately, he didn't take the hint, but kept targeting her, encouraging her to share details of her own failed marriage in a lugubrious tone that would have been appropriate had they both been suffering from the same terminal disease. Robin adopted a bracing attitude, telling him there were plenty more fish in the sea and that she was personally glad to be free again. Hugh told her how much he admired her feistiness with a slightly more cheerful look in his watery blue eyes, and she was afraid he might have taken her declaration of happy independence as a tacit invitation.

'He's lovely, isn't he?' Katie asked her hopefully, one evening in a bar, when Robin had just succeeded in shaking Hugh off after another hour of anecdotes about his ex-wife.

'He's all right,' said Robin, who didn't want to offend her cousin, 'but he's really not my type, Katie.'

'He's usually quite funny,' said Katie, disappointed. 'You aren't seeing him at his best. Wait until he's had a drink or two.'

But on New Year's Eve, with a large amount of beer and schnapps inside him, Hugh became first boisterous, though not particularly amusing, then maudlin. At midnight, the two couples kissed their partners, and the bleary-eyed Hugh opened his arms to Robin, who let him kiss her on the cheek and then tried to free herself, while he breathed drunkenly in her ear:

'You're so lovely.'

'Thanks,' said Robin, and then, 'could you let go, please?'

He did so, and Robin went to bed shortly afterwards, locking her door. Somebody knocked on it soon after she'd turned out the light: she lay in the darkness, pretending to be asleep, and heard footsteps walking slowly away.

The other less-than-perfect aspect of her break had been her own tendency to brood about Strike and the incident outside the Ritz. It was easy enough not to think about her partner while trying to keep herself vertical on skis, but otherwise her disengaged mind kept returning to the question of what would have happened if she'd cast off her inhibitions and fears, and let him kiss her. This led inexorably to another question, the same one she'd asked herself while pacing the warm white sand in the Maldives three years previously. Was she to spend every holiday, for the rest of her life, wondering whether she was in love with Cormoran Strike?

You're not, she told herself. *He gave you the chance of a lifetime, and maybe you do love him a bit, because he's your best friend, but you're not in love with him.* And then, more honestly, *and if you are, you need to get over it. Yes, maybe he was hurt when you didn't let him kiss you, but better that than he thinks you're pining away for love of him. A lovesick partner is literally the last thing he'd want.*

If only she could have been the kind of woman who could have enjoyed a kiss one drunken evening and then laughed it off. On the evidence of what she knew about Strike's past love life, that was what he liked: women who played the game with an insouciance Robin had never learned.

She returned to the office in the second week of January, bringing with her a large box of Swiss chocolates. To everyone who asked, Strike included, she said she'd had a wonderful time.

PART ONE

*The heart is the central organ of the entire system
and consists of a hollow muscle;
by its contraction the blood is pumped to all parts of the body
through a complicated series of tubes . . .*

Henry Gray FRS
Gray's Anatomy

5

'Tis a strange mystery, the power of words!
Life is in them, and death. A word can send
The crimson colour hurrying to the cheek,
Hurrying with many meanings, or can turn
The current cold and deadly to the heart.

Letitia Elizabeth Landon
The Power of Words

14 September 2011
From *The Buzz*, a news and entertainment website

The Buzz talks to Josh Blay and Edie Ledwell, boyfriend/girlfriend creators of YouTube's smash-hit cartoon, *The Ink Black Heart*!

TB: So, a cartoon about decomposing body parts, a couple of skeletons, a demon and a ghost . . . how do you explain its success?

Edie: Wait, is Drek a demon?

TB: You tell me!

Edie: I genuinely don't know.

[Josh laughs]

TB: I'm just saying, when you describe *The Ink Black Heart* to people who haven't watched it, they're kind of surprised it's a hit. *[Edie and Josh laugh]* Did you expect the reaction to your – let's be honest – very weird animation?

Edie: No, we definitely didn't.

Josh: We were having a laugh. It's basically a bunch of in-jokes.

Edie: But it turned out far more people got the joke than we expected.

TB: When you say 'the joke' – people read a lot of meaning into the story!

Josh: Yeah and we . . . sometimes you think 'Oh yeah, I suppose that is what we were getting at', but other times—

Edie: Sometimes they see things that – well, not that aren't there, but that we never saw or intended.

TB: Can you give an example?

Josh: The talking worm. We just thought that was funny, because a worm in a graveyard, you know, it's eating decomposing bodies. So we liked the idea of it being pissed off about its job and talking about it like it's boring hard graft. Like working in a factory. It's just a jaded worm.

Edie: But then we had people saying it's phallic or whatever. And a group of parents complaining—

Josh: —complaining that we're making penis jokes for kids.

Edie: And we're definitely not. The Worm is not a penis.

[All laugh]

TB: So why d'you think *The Ink Black Heart* has taken off the way it has?

Edie: We don't understand it any better than you do. We're inside it. We can't see it from the outside.

Josh: We can only assume there are far more disturbed people out there than any of us realised.

[All laugh]

TB: What do you think it is about Harty, the disembodied heart/hero that people love so much? You voice Harty, right, Josh?

Josh: Yeah. Er ... *[thinks for a long time]* I suppose he knows he's bad but he's trying to be good.

Edie: He isn't really bad, though. Or he wouldn't be trying to be good.

Josh: I think people kind of identify with him.

Edie: He's been through a lot of stuff.

Josh: Specifically, a rib cage, a coffin lid and six feet of soil.

[All laugh]

TB: So what are your plans for the cartoon? Stay on YouTube, or—?

Edie: We don't plan, do we?

Josh: Plans are for smugliks.

TB: But this thing is getting really big! You're making money now, right?

Josh: Yeah. Who knew? It's crazy.

TB: Do you have anyone helping you with this? An agent, or—?

Josh: We've got a friend who knows this stuff who's helping us, yeah.

TB: A couple of your fans have created an online game based on the game Drek plays in the cartoon. Have you seen it?

Josh: Yeah, we saw that the other day. It's an impressive bit of coding.

Edie: It's weird, though, because Drek's game – the one in the cartoon—

Josh: —yeah—

Edie: —isn't really a game. Or, I mean, it wasn't supposed to be, was it?

[Josh shakes head]

Edie: It was supposed to be more . . . the whole point of the game is that it isn't really a game.

TB: So when Drek forces everyone to 'play the game'—

Edie: Does he force them? I don't know whether he forces them. I think they kind of humour him because he's bored—

Josh: —borkled—

Edie: —sorry, yeah, borkled, and so they agree to play, but it always goes badly wrong for someone.

Josh: Drek's game is – you know *[in Drek's voice]* 'play the game, bwah!' . . . abide by rules. Do the expected thing.

TB: So it's a metaphor?

Edie: Yeah, but it's paradoxical, because Drek himself never plays by the rules. He just likes watching everyone else try and follow them.

TB: You say you don't plan, but will there be—?

Josh: Drek T-shirts? We were literally asked by someone the other day where they could buy a Drek T-shirt.

Edie: We were just . . . are you for real?

TB: No merch, then?

Edie: *[laughing]* We aren't planning merch.

Josh: We like it being what it is. We like just messing around. We're not business people.

Edie: We're more the kind of people who lie in a cemetery and imagine disembodied hearts bobbing around. *[All laugh]*

15 September 2011
Part of an in-game chat between the co-creators of the online *Drek's Game*

<15 September 2011 20.38>

Anomie: 'Not what we meant'. We took all the rules out of her fucking cartoon, pretentious fucking bitch.

Morehouse: calm down

Anomie: this is going to play
really fkn badly for Ledwell. She's
shitting all over the fans, saying
they're thick for liking our game

Morehouse: she wasn't saying that

Anomie: of course she fucking
was, she said we're a pair of
shitheads who don't understand
her metaphors

Anomie: it's on her if the fandom
turns on her after this

Morehouse: yeah, speaking of
which, maybe tone it down a bit on
Twitterr

Anomie: you know what this is
really about? Our game's getting
too popular. She doesn't like that
the fandom's looking to us to
entertain them between episodes.
She's scared we're getting too much
power. She'll try and shut us down
next.

Morehouse: Paranoid much? We're not
a threat, we're not making money,
it's a tribute.

Anomie: Don't forget, I fucking
know her. She's a fucking money-
grubbing hypocrite.

5 February 2013
From *The Buzz*, a news and entertainment website

Runaway YouTube success *The Ink Black Heart* snapped up by Netflix

Cult cartoon *The Ink Black Heart* will be leaving YouTube for Netflix, with
a second series already in development. Boyfriend–girlfriend animators
Josh Blay and Edie Ledwell, who dreamed up the cartoon in Highgate

Cemetery, are rumoured to have secured a high six-figure sum from the streaming service.

Fans of the animation are divided on its move to the mainstream. While some are excited, others are worried that the close connection between creators and fans will now be broken.

Anonymous superfan Anomie, creator of the popular multi-player *Drek's Game*, said on Twitter:

> So Ledwell's long-expected sell out's underway. Looks like everything fans loved will be sacrificed for cash. Prepare for the worst, Inkhearts.

6 February 2013
An in-game conversation between Anomie and three moderators of *Drek's Game*

\<Moderator Channel>

\<6 February 2013 21.41>

\<Anomie, Hartella, Fiendy1, Worm28>

Anomie: Did you see The Buzz quoted me?

Hartella: lol. You're famous!

Anomie: I was already famous

Anomie: everyone in the fandom wants to know who Anomie is

Hartella: that's true, we do!

Fiendy1: I still can't understand why your faithful mods can't know

Anomie: I have my reasons.

Anomie: Told you they

were going to go to
Netflix, though, didn't I?

Hartella: How do you
always know what's
going to happen next?!

Anomie: I'm a genius.
Anyway, I think we're
going to need 2-3
new moderators, we're
getting more and more
traffic in here

Anomie: Might ask that
girl Paperwhite. She
seems intelligent.

Hartella: LordDrek's
been playing longer
and I like him a lot.

Anomie: what d'you mean,
you 'like him a lot'?

Hartella: well he
seems quite nice and
he's a huge fan of the
cartoon and the game.

Anomie: I don't want
any real life friends in
here. Rule 14, remember?
Total anonymity.

Hartella: I don't know
him in real life, he
just seems a good guy!

Anomie: ok I'll ask him
and Paperwhite. And maybe
Vilepechora, he's always in
here, he can earn his keep

Hartella: don't you have
to check with Morehouse?

Anomie: why?

Anomie: he'll be happy
with whatever I decide

<A new private channel
has opened>

<6 February 2013 21.43>

<Fiendy1 invites Worm28>

<Worm28 joins the channel>

Fiendy1: doesn't get any
more modest, does she?
'I'm a genius'

Worm28: Anomie ?

Fiendy1: who else?

Worm28: you still think
Anomie 's a girl ?

Fiendy1: she's definitely
a girl, I can tell, from
things she says

Worm28: Morehouse knows
Anomie in real life and
says he 's a man

Fiendy1: only to throw
everyone off the scent

Worm28: Anomie 's
someone , right ?

Fiendy1: Everyone's someone

Worm28: I mean like an
insider on the Ink Black
Heart

Anomie: I'm the famous one, don't forget

Hartella: lol

>

>

>

Hartella: Where is Morehouse, anyway? He hasn't been in much lately.

Anomie: He'll be back, don't worry about that.

Fiendy1: Maybe. I don't know

Worm28: I wish they hadn 't left YouTube . I haven 't got Netflix . I cried when I heard

Fiendy1: I was sad too but Anomie needs to stop slagging off L******. She'll end up shutting us down

Worm28: omg don 't say that I 'd die

28 May 2014
From *The Buzz*, a news and entertainment website

Edie Ledwell's Agent Confirms Hospitalisation

Following days of rumours, Allan Yeoman, agent of writer/animator Edie Ledwell, has confirmed that the *Ink Black Heart* co-creator was hospitalised on the night of 24 May, but has now returned home.

In a statement, Yeoman, who runs creative agency AYCA, said:

'At Edie Ledwell's request, we confirm that she was admitted to hospital on May 24 and has since been discharged. Edie thanks fans for their concern and support and requests privacy to focus on her health.'

Fan speculation has been rife since press reports that police and ambulance were called to the animator's flat shortly after midnight on the 24th, with eye witnesses claiming Ledwell was unconscious as she was stretchered to the ambulance.

The *Ink Black Heart* fandom, which has been dubbed 'toxic' due to their online behaviour, was divided in response to news of Ledwell's hospitalisation. While most fans expressed concern, some trolls drew criticism for suggesting that Ledwell had faked a suicide attempt to garner sympathy . . .

28 May 2014
In-game chats between Paperwhite,
newest moderator of *Drek's Game*, Morehouse
and Anomie, co-creators of *Drek's Game*

\<Private channel\>

\<28 May 2014 23.03\>

Paperwhite: so L******
really did try and kill
herself

Morehouse: looks like it

Paperwhite: shit that's so
sad

Morehouse: yeah

Paperwhite: have you
talked to Anomie?

Morehouse: not yet

Morehouse: I think he's
avoiding me

Paperwhite: why?

Morehouse: because I told
him to lay off L****** on
Twitter

Paperwhite: you don't
seriously think that's why
why she did it? Twitter
trolls?

Morehouse: I don't know,
but it can't have helped,
being constantly called a
sell-out and a traitor

\>

Paperwhite: you're so sweet

Morehouse: Am I?!

Paperwhite: decent, I mean

Paperwhite: you're not even
pissed off that Anomie gets
all the credit for the game

Morehouse: let him have it

Morehouse: There's more to
life than having a load of
followers on fucking Twitter

Paperwhite: lol you're so
mature. I mean for real,
no snark. You are.

Paperwhite: Can I ask you
something?

Morehouse: Go on

Paperwhite: Is Anomie
definitely a bloke?

Morehouse: yeah of course.
Why are you asking that?

Paperwhite: Fiendy1 told
me the other day he thinks
Anomie's a girl

Paperwhite: he kind of
hinted you and Anomie are
together

Morehouse: Fiendy1's a
shit-stirrer, you don't want
to listen to a word he says
about me or Anomie.

Paperwhite: Hartella told
me you'd fallen out with
Fiendy1

Morehouse: yeah. He's an
immature prick sometimes.

Morehouse: hang on,
Anomie's arrived

>

<A private channel has
opened>

<28 May 2014 23.05>

<Anomie invites Morehouse>

>

>

>

>

>

>

Paperwhite: what's he saying?

>

Morehouse: wants me to moderate tomorrow

>

>

>

>

>

Paperwhite: I was worried he knew I sent you pictures

>

>

>

>

>

>

Morehouse: you still there?

Paperwhite: yes

>

Anomie: hi

<Morehouse has joined the channel>

Morehouse: I've been texting you all day

Anomie: I've been busy. I need you to moderate tomorrow morning, I can't do it.

Morehouse: Nor can I, I've got a deadline on a paper

Anomie: why are you in here then? Or is 'deadline for a paper' your nickname for Paperwhite?

Morehouse: ha ha

Anomie: you two seem to be getting on very well. I hope no pictures have been exchanged. Rule 14, don't forget.

Morehouse: Have you seen the news?

>

Anomie: what, the "suicide"? Yeah I saw

Morehouse: listen, you need to lay off Ledwell, I'm serious

Anomie: Go tell the rest of the fandom to lay off her. You think I'm the only one who's sick to death of her fucking hypocrisy and duplicity?

Morehouse: you're the only one who's got fifty thousand Twitter followers you keep urging to bully her.

>

>

>

Morehouse: good, won't be long

Paperwhite: <3

>

>

>

>

>

>

>

>

>

>

>

>

Morehouse: done

Paperwhite: did he listen to you?

Morehouse: always hard to know with Anomie. Something might've sunk in.

Morehouse: he doesn't like us talking, though. You and me.

Paperwhite: yeah, about that… when are you going to send me a picture back?

Anomie: If she really tried to top herself, it won't be because of Twitter. Probably a publicity stunt

Anomie: suppose I'll have to get Hartella to mod for me tomorrow if you can't.

Morehouse: why can't you do it?

Anomie: hospital appointment

Morehouse: shit, u ok?

Anomie: it's not mine, I'm just the chauffeur

Anomie: because god forbid the fucker should use public transport

Anomie: well I'll let you get back to your 'deadline'

<Morehouse has left the channel>

<Anomie has left the channel>

<Private channel has closed>

Morehouse: can't

Morehouse: my camera
phone's broken

Paperwhite: fuck off,
Morehouse

Morehouse: lol. Ok, I don't
like having my photo taken

Paperwhite: I wouldn't
have sent you what I sent
last nite if I didn't think
you'd reciprocate

Morehouse: u r gorgeous

Paperwhite: thanx

Morehouse: I'm not

Paperwhite: who cares? I
just want a pic of you

Paperwhite: I love talking
to you. I just want to
know what you look like!

Morehouse: just picture a
standard geek

Paperwhite: I like geeks.
Send me a pic!

Morehouse: so how's art
school life?

Paperwhite: wow, subtle
change of subject

(...)

7 January 2015
From *The Buzz*, a news and
entertainment website

Attention, *Ink Black Heart* fans!

According to insiders, Maverick Film Studios are serious about
turning your fave into a full-length feature film! Talks between Maverick,

Josh Blay and Edie Ledwell are said to be 'at an advanced stage', with a deal expected any day now. How do you feel about the leap from small screen to big? Let us know in the comments!

Comments are moderated. The Buzz reserves the right to remove comments that contravene guidelines.

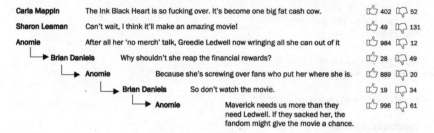

Carla Mappin	The Ink Black Heart is so fucking over. It's become one big fat cash cow.	👍 402 👎 52
Sharon Leaman	Can't wait, I think it'll make an amazing movie!	👍 49 👎 131
Anomie	After all her 'no merch' talk, Greedie Ledwell now wringing all she can out of it	👍 984 👎 12
➤ Brian Daniels	Why shouldn't she reap the financial rewards?	👍 28 👎 49
➤ Anomie	Because she's screwing over fans who put her where she is.	👍 889 👎 20
➤ Brian Daniels	So don't watch the movie.	👍 19 👎 34
➤ Anomie	Maverick needs us more than they need Ledwell. If they sacked her, the fandom might give the movie a chance.	👍 996 👎 61

7 January 2015
In-game chats between six of the eight moderators of *Drek's Game*

<A new private channel has opened>

<7 January 2015 16.01>

<LordDrek invites Vilepechora, Paperwhite, Hartella, Fiendy1, Worm28>

LordDrek: THIS IS URGENT

<Paperwhite has joined the channel>

Paperwhite: is this about the movie?

LordDrek: much bigger than that

<Hartella has joined the channel>

Hartella: omg, have you seen the news?

Paperwhite: about the movie?

Hartella: no, those gunmen who shot up the cartoonists in Paris

<Worm28 has joined the channel>

<Vilepechora has joined the channel>

Paperwhite: Charlie something, yeah.

LordDrek: Charlie Hebdo

LordDrek: that's what we should do to Ledwell. Go in there and shoot her and all the fuckers she's got working on the movie and start again.

Vilepechora: lol

Worm28: Drek don 't joke about stuff like taht

Paperwhite: is that what you wanted to get us all together for? plan a shooting?

LordDrek: You're not far wrong

Paperwhite: why haven't u invited Anomie or Morehouse?

LordDrek: Anomie, you'll see why in a sec. Morehouse because I don't trust him not to run off and tell Anomie.

Paperwhite: Tell Anomie what?

LordDrek: You'll see.

Worm28: you' tr making me
nervous

LordDrek: wait til you've
heard what I've got to say

LordDrek: you'll be proper
fucking nervous then

**<Fiendy1 has joined the
channel>**

Fiendy1: sorry, had to
change

Vilepechora: you realise
we can't see you, right?

Fiendy1: ha ha

Fiendy1: out of sports kit

Vilepechora: what sport?

Fiendy1: football

LordDrek: ok, brace
yourselves

LordDrek: Vilepechora and
I got suspicious about
Anomie

LordDrek: so we traced the
IP address.

Paperwhite: wtf?

Vilepechora: There's other
stuff we found out/made
connections on

Vilepechora: but the IP
address confirms who she
really is

Fiendy1: I fucking KNEW it
was a girl!

LordDrek: well you were
right

LordDrek: but not just any
girl

Hartella: what do you
mean?

LordDrek: OK, here it is

LordDrek: Anomie = Edie
Ledwell

>

Fiendy1: wtf no way

Worm28: ??????????

Paperwhite: that makes no
fkn sense!

Vilepechora: it does

Vilepechora: we've been
played

LordDrek: played for
fucking fools

Hartella: why would she do
that?

LordDrek: she's playing
a fucking devious game,
that's why

Fiendy1: sorry but there's
no fkn way that's true

LordDrek: it is

LordDrek: she's gonna 'cut
a deal' with Anomie to
make the game official and
start charging

Vilepechora: except there
is no Anomie. It's Ledwell's
game, it was all along

Fiendy1: I don't believe it

Paperwhite: Nor do I

Paperwhite: Morehouse
would never go along with
that

LordDrek: have you met
Morehouse face-to-face?

Paperwhite: no

Vilepechora: not watched
him wanking to you on
your webcam?

Paperwhite: go fuck
yourself Vilepechora

Paperwhite: I just don't
believe Morehouse would be
ok with Ledwell fooling us
all like that

Fiendy1: what would
she gain, pretending to
be Anomie and trolling
herself?

LordDrek: easy: 'meet'
Anomie and decide he's a
good guy after all – he's
got valid concerns about
over-commercialisation and
all that shit

LordDrek: 'let's monetize
the game, Anomie can take
the profits, he deserves
it'

LordDrek: she'll probably
have some crippled kid
playing Anomie for extra
feelz

LordDrek: Then cripple-
Anomie tells fans now
he's met her he realises
he got her all wrong,
she's great, Blay gets
sidelined/ bullied by
fandom who want the game

Vilepechora: fandom loves
Ledwell, she gets all the
good press & profits

LordDrek: & fans cough up
thinking Anomie's gonna
get the money

LordDrek: only problem:
Ledwell's gonna need a
fall guy to take the rap
for 'hacking' Anomie,
or whatever the excuse
is going to be for him
slagging her off

LordDrek: And she's got
money and skills to frame
one of us

Worm28: I don 't get it .
She hates Anomie .

Vilepechora: it's all been
fake, moron. Her way of
playing the victim to the
press & the fans

LordDrek: you want proof,
I'll send it to you now

**<LordDrek wants to send
you a file>**

**<Click alt+y to accept the
file>**

>

>

>

>

Worm28: shit there 's
loads

Hartella: omg how long
have u guys been working
on this?

LordDrek: months

>

>

Hartella: whoa

Hartella: when the game
went offline that time
was when Ledwell was in
hospital????? I never made
that connection!

Paperwhite: are you sure
the dates tally?

Hartella: omg I always
knew she was a liar but
this is insane

Fiendy1: how did you guys
get her emails to her
agent???

LordDrek: from a friendly
source inside her agent's
office who thinks she's a
total bitch

Hartella: OMG YES –
remember when she said
she'd only talk to
Anomie if he met her
face-to-face?

Vilepechora: yeah, all
laying the ground

Hartella: I thought that
was so fkn weird at the
time! why would she even
think of meeting him if
she hated him so much?

Vilepechora: exactly

LordDrek: and read the
deleted tweets. She's
slipped up more than once,
accidentally tweeting

Anomie messages from her
own account

Hartella: I feel physically
sick

Vilepechora: and don't
forget, we've been
bitching about Ledwell in
front of her all this time

Worm28: so this is the end
of the game ? We can 't
play any more ?

Paperwhite: no it isn't,
don't be stupid

Paperwhite: the game's
ours, it isn't hers

Paperwhite: the game's
bigger than Blay/Ledwell

Worm28: stop using there
full names , we 're not
allowed ! Rule 14 !

LordDrek: if you ask me,
B*** needs to know the
depths of her fuckin
treachery

LordDrek: she's trying to
fuck him over just as much
as us

Vilepechora: so how do we
let him know?

>

Hartella: I could go and
see him if u want

Worm28: you don 't know
where he lives

Hartella: I do, actually.
He'll see me, I'm sure he
will

Paperwhite: you know J***
B***? for real?

Hartella: yes. I forgot,
you probably joined after
I told the others. I used
to be L****** and B***'s
personal assistant.

Paperwhite: wtf????

Hartella: Drek, we could
go and talk to J***
together.

LordDrek: can't, hun,
sorry, im busy with you
know what

Worm28: what?

LordDrek: never u mind

Worm28: am I the only one
who never breaks rule 14 ?

Hartella: ok then I'll go
alone and show him this
dossier

LordDrek: u serious?

Hartella: of course, what
she's doing is despicable

Fiendy1: Hartella, you
know her - you really
think she could pretend to
be Anomie?

Hartella: honestly? Yes.
Working for her wasn't a
fun experience. She's hard
as nails and in it for all
she can get

LordDrek: you sure you're
ok to go alone?

Hartella: yeah, of course

LordDrek: wish I could come

Vilepechora: this is
awesome of you, Hartella

Hartella: anything for the
fandom

Vilepechora: Ok, remember:
not a word on the mods
channel or in front of
Anomie or Morehouse

Vilepechora: we can't be
too careful

Vilepechora: and don't act
any different

Vilepechora: no digs, no
hints, nothing

Vilepechora: because
she'll be looking for a
fall guy, remember

Worm28: shit , I 've got
to go I 'm late for work

<Worm28 has left the
channel>

Paperwhite: I'm supposed
to be moderating. See you
later.

<Paperwhite has left the
channel>

Fiendy1: I'm still not
sure, you guys

Vilepechora: read the
whole file and you'll
change your mind.

<Fiendy1 has left the
channel>

>

>

<A new private channel
has opened>

<7 January 2015 16.25>

<LordDrek invites Hartella>

<Hartella joins the
channel>

Hartella: Hi! How are
rehearsals going?

LordDrek: Hard work, but
that's Chekhov for you.
Listen, will you do me a
favour, babe?

LordDrek: Don't tell Josh
where you got the file.

LordDrek: if he thinks
a pair of mods in Drek's
Game put it together, he
might not trust it

Hartella: ok but where
do I say I got it then?

LordDrek: say concerned
fans/sources sent the
stuff to you. That's
credible, you're a leader
in the fandom

Hartella: ok, makes
sense. I'll try and go
see Josh this Saturday

LordDrek: you're a
heroine. Keep us posted.

Hartella: will do xxx

Hartella: ok I got to
get back to work, speak
soon xxx

LordDrek: thanks, gorgeous
xxx

>

<Hartella has left the channel>

LordDrek: is that all of them gone?

Vilepechora: roflmao

Vilepechora: Fuck me, they're thick

Vilepechora: not sure Fiendy1 totally went for it

LordDrek: who cares what that little fag thinks

LordDrek: all we need is for Blay to believe it

Vilepechora: true

LordDrek: I just called that fat pig Hartella 'gorgeous'

Vilepechora: roflmao you cuck

LordDrek: but she agreed not to say where she got the stuff

Vilepechora: fkn amazing

Vilepechora: think Paperwhite'll tell Morehouse?

LordDrek: not if she's got any sense

LordDrek: touchpaper lit, bwah

Vilepechora: lol if this works...

<Hartella has left the channel>

<LordDrek has left the channel>

<Private channel has closed>

6

Thou shalt have fame! − Oh, mockery! give the reed
From storms a shelter − give the drooping vine
Something round which its tendrils may entwine −
Give the parch'd flower a rain-drop, and the meed
Of love's kind words to woman! Worthless fame!

Felicia Hemans
Properzia Rossi

The last Friday afternoon in January found Robin sitting alone at the partners' desk in the agency's small office in Denmark Street, killing time before setting out to view a flat in Acton by reviewing the Groomer file. There was a lot of noise in the street outside: comprehensive building work continued to cause disruption around Charing Cross Road, and all journeys to and from the office meant walking over planks, past pneumatic drills and the catcalls of builders. In consequence of the racket outside, the first intimation Robin had that a prospective client had just walked in off the street wasn't the sound of the glass outer door opening, but the phone on the desk ringing.

On answering, she heard Pat's baritone.

'Message from Mr Strike. Would you be free to visit Gateshead this Saturday?'

This was code. Since last year's successful resolution of a cold case, which had earned the agency another flurry of flattering press coverage, two would-be clients of pronounced eccentricity had walked in off the street. The first, a clearly mentally ill woman, had begged Barclay, the only detective present at the time, to help her prove the government was watching her through the air vent of her flat in Gateshead. The second, a heavily tattooed man who seemed slightly manic, had become threatening to Pat when she'd told him there were no detectives available to take down the details of his neighbour who, he was convinced, was part of an ISIS cell. Fortunately, Strike had walked in just as the man had picked up Pat's stapler, with the apparent aim of throwing it at her. Since then, Strike had insisted that Pat keep the outside door locked when she was alone in the office, and they'd all agreed on a code which meant, in essence, 'I've got a nutter here.'

'Threatening?' said Robin quietly, flicking the Groomer file closed.

'Oh, no,' said Pat calmly.

'Mentally ill?'

'Maybe a bit.'

'Male?'

'No.'

'Have you asked her to leave?'

'Yes.'

'Does she want to talk to Strike?'

'Not necessarily.'

'All right, Pat, I'll have a word with her. Coming out now.'

Robin hung up the phone, put the Groomer file back in the drawer and headed for the outer office.

A young woman with untidy brown shoulder-length hair was sitting on the sofa opposite Pat's desk. Robin was immediately struck by several oddities in the woman's appearance. The overall impression she gave was of scruffiness, even grubbiness: she was wearing old ankle boots that needed re-heeling, slapdash eyeliner which looked as though it might have been applied the day before and a shirt so deeply creased it could have been slept in. However, unless it was a fake, the Yves Saint Laurent handbag sitting on the sofa beside her would have cost over a thousand pounds and her long black wool coat looked brand new and of high quality. When she saw Robin, the woman caught her breath in a little gasp, and before Robin could say anything, said,

'Please don't chuck me out. Please. I really, *really* need to talk to you. *Please.*'

Robin hesitated, then said,

'OK, come through. Pat, could you tell Strike I'm fine to go to Gateshead?'

'Hmm,' said Pat. 'I'd have refused, personally.'

Robin stood back to let the young woman pass into the inner office, then mouthed at Pat 'twenty minutes'.

As Robin closed the inner-office door, she noticed that the back of the woman's hair was a little matted, as if it hadn't been brushed in days, but the label standing up out of the back of her coat declared it to have come from Alexander McQueen.

'Was that some sort of code?' she said, turning to face Robin. 'That stuff about Gateshead?'

'No, of course not,' lied Robin with a reassuring smile. 'Have a seat.'

Robin sat down behind the desk and the woman, who looked around her own age, took the chair facing her. In spite of the unbrushed hair, the badly applied make-up and the pinched expression, she was attractive in an offbeat way. Her square face was pale, her mouth generous and her eyes a striking shade of amber. Judging by her accent, she was London-born. Robin noticed a small, blurry tattoo on one of the woman's knuckles: a black heart that looked as though she might have inked it herself. Her fingernails were bitten to the quick and the index and middle fingers of her right hand were stained yellow. Taken all in all, the stranger gave the impression of somebody down on their luck who'd just fled a rich woman's house, stealing her coat and bag as she went.

'I don't suppose I can smoke?' she said.

'I'm afraid not, we're a non-smoking—'

"S'all right,' said the woman. 'I've got gum.'

She ferreted around in her handbag, first taking out a brown cardboard folder full of papers. As she was trying to pop a piece of gum out of its pack while balancing the bag on her knee and keeping a grip on the folder, the papers inside slid out and scattered all over the floor. From what Robin could see, they were a mixture of printed-out tweets and handwritten notes.

'Shit, sorry,' said the woman breathlessly, scooping up the fallen papers and ramming them back into the folder. Having stuffed it back into her bag and put a piece of gum into her mouth, she sat upright again, now even more dishevelled, her coat bundled untidily around her and her bag clutched defensively on her lap as though it was a pet that might flee.

'You're Robin Ellacott, right?'

'Yes,' said Robin.

'I was hoping for you, I read about you in the paper,' said the woman. Robin was surprised. Clients usually wanted Strike. 'My name's Edie Ledwell. That woman outside said you haven't got any room for more clients—'

'I'm afraid that's—'

'I knew you must be really in demand, but – I can pay,' she said, and her voice carried an odd undertone of surprise. 'I really can pay, I can afford it, and I'm – to be perfectly honest, I'm desperate.'

'We *are* very booked up, I'm afraid,' Robin began. 'We've got a waiting—'

'Please can I just tell you what it's about? Can I just do that? Please? And then, maybe, even if you can't actually – actually *do* it – you can give me some advice about how to – or tell me someone who could help? Please?'

'All right,' said Robin, whose curiosity was piqued.

'OK, so – have you heard of *The Ink Black Heart*?'

'Er – yes,' said Robin, surprised. Her cousin Katie had mentioned the cartoon one night at dinner in Zermatt. Katie had watched *The Ink Black Heart* while on maternity leave and become fascinated by it, though she'd seemed unsure whether it was funny or simply strange. 'It's on Netflix, isn't it? I've never actually watched it.'

'OK, well, that doesn't really matter,' said Edie. 'The point is, I co-created it with my ex-boyfriend and it's a success, or whatever' – Edie sounded strangely tense as she said the word – 'and there might be a film deal, but that's only relevant because – well, it's not relevant to what I need investigating, but I just need you to know that I *can* pay.'

Before Robin could say anything, more words tumbled out.

'So, two fans of our cartoon, this is a few years ago now – I suppose you'd call them fans, in the beginning, anyway – these two fans created an online game based on our characters.

'Nobody knows who the two people who made the game are. They call themselves Anomie and Morehouse. Anomie gets most of the credit and he's the one who's got the big following online. Some people say Anomie and Morehouse are the same person, but I don't know whether that's true.

'Anyway, Anomie' – she took a deep breath – 'he – I'm sure it's a "he" – he's made it his mission to – to—'

She suddenly laughed, a laugh totally without humour: she might as well have cried out in pain.

'—to make my life as unbearable as he can. It's like – it's a daily – he never lets up, it never stops.

'It started when Josh and I gave an interview and they asked us whether we'd seen Anomie's game and whether we liked it. And – this is hard to explain – there's a character called Drek in the cartoon, right? I actually *really* fucking wish there *wasn't* a character called Drek in the cartoon, but it's too late for that now. Anyway, in our cartoon, Drek makes the other characters play a game and he's always inventing new rules and it always ends badly for everyone except Drek. His game isn't *really* a game at all, there's no logic to it, it's just him messing around with the other characters.

'So we were asked in this interview whether we'd seen Anomie and Morehouse's game and I said yes, but that the game in our cartoon isn't really a game at all. It's more of a metaphor – I'm sorry, this must all sound so stupid, but that's where it started, right, with me saying Anomie's game wasn't really the same as Drek's game in the cartoon.

'Anyway, Anomie went ballistic when the interview went online. He started attacking me non-stop. He said they'd taken all the rules of their game directly from Drek's rules, so what the fuck was I doing, claiming it wasn't accurate? And tons of the fans agreed with him, saying I was throwing shade on the game because it was free and I wanted to shut it down so I could make an official Drek game and profit off it.

'I thought it would blow over, but it's just got worse and worse. You can't – it's escalated beyond – Anomie posted a picture of my flat online. He's convinced people I worked as a prostitute when I was broke. He sent me pictures of my dead mother, claiming I told lies about her death. And the fandom believes all of it, and they attack me for stuff I've never done, never said, things I don't believe.

'But he also knows true things about me, things he shouldn't.

'Last year,' said Edie, and Robin could see her fingers trembling on the handles of the expensive bag, 'I tried to kill myself.'

'I'm so—' Robin began, but Edie made a gesture of impatience: she evidently didn't want sympathy.

'Hardly anyone knew I'd done it, but Anomie did before there was any news coverage; he even knew which hospital I was in. He tweeted about it, saying it was all a put-up job, done to make the fans feel sorry for me.

'Anyway, last Sunday,' said Edie, her voice now shaking, 'Josh – he's the guy I created *The Ink Black Heart* with – like I say, we used to be . . . we were together but we broke up, but we still do the cartoon together – Josh called me and said a rumour's going round that *I'm* Anomie, that I'm attacking myself online and making up lies about myself, all for attention and sympathy. I said, "Who's saying that?"

and he wouldn't tell me, he just said, "That's what I'm hearing." And he said he wanted me to tell him directly it wasn't true.

'I said, "*How can you even think, for a second, that that could be fucking true?*"' Edie's voice had risen to a shout.

'I hung up on him, but he called again, and we rowed again, and it's been two weeks or something and he still fucking believes it, and I can't convince him—'

There was a knock on the door.

'Hello?' called Robin.

'Anyone like coffee?' said Pat, opening the door a crack and looking from Robin to Edie. Robin knew Pat wanted to check that everything was all right, having heard Edie's raised voice.

'I'm good, thanks, Pat,' said Robin. 'Edie?'

'I – no, thanks,' said Edie, and Pat closed the door again.

'So the day before yesterday,' Edie resumed, 'Josh and I spoke on the phone again and this time he said he's got a dossier of "evidence"' – Edie sketched quotation marks in mid-air – '*proving* I'm really Anomie.'

'Is that the—?' began Robin, pointing at the bag on Edie's lap containing the cardboard folder.

'No, this is just the stuff Anomie's tweeted at me – I don't think this supposed fucking dossier of Josh's even exists. I said to him, "Where did it come from?" And he wouldn't tell me. He was stoned,' said Edie, 'he smokes a lot of weed. I hung up again.

'I spent all day yesterday just, like, pacing up and down and . . . What fucking proof can he have that proves I'm Anomie? It's just fucking *ridiculous!*'

Her voice rose again and cracked. Tears now spilled out from the amber eyes; in wiping them away Edie smeared her eyeliner into broad grey streaks across her cheeks and temples. 'My boyfriend was at work and I was just – I was feeling so fucking desperate, and then I thought, there's only one way I can stop this. I've got to prove who Anomie is. Because I think I *know.*

'His name's Seb Montgomery. He was at art school with Josh. Josh got chucked out but he and Seb stayed friends. Seb helped us animate the first couple of episodes of *The Ink Black Heart*. He's a good anima-tor, but we didn't need him as we went on, and I know he resented it once we started getting a big following, and he blamed me. It's true I never liked him much, but I didn't pressure Josh into dropping him, we just didn't need him any more.

'Seb and Josh are still friends, and Josh will tell anyone *anything*, he hasn't got any kind of filter, especially when he's pissed or stoned, which he mostly is, which is how Seb would know all the personal stuff Anomie knows about me, but what *proves* it's Seb,' said Edie, her knuckles now white on the handle of her bag, 'is that Anomie knows something I only ever told Seb. You see, there's this *other* character in the cartoon . . .'

Even though Robin felt genuinely sympathetic towards her uninvited guest, she glanced discreetly at her watch. The minutes were sliding by and Robin had a flat in Acton to see.

'. . . called Paperwhite, she's a ghost, and *she's* caused a whole lot of fucking trouble, too – but that's beside the – what's relevant is, I told Seb in the pub one night that I based bits of Paperwhite's character on my ex-flatmate. And a month ago, Anomie tweeted that, naming the flatmate.

'I called Seb. I said to him, "Who have you told about Paperwhite and Shereece?" And he pretended he couldn't even remember me telling him.

'He's lying. I *know* Seb's Anomie, I *know* he is and I need to prove it, I've got to, I can't keep on like this. Six months ago,' Edie pressed on as Robin opened her mouth to interrupt again, 'I joined the game myself, to look at it from the inside. It does look beautiful; whoever animated it is definitely talented, but it isn't that good as an actual game – it's really more of an animated chatroom. Loads of fans go in there just to slag me off, from what I can see. I tried asking the other players who Anomie was, and if they knew anything about him. Somebody must have told him I was asking too many questions, because I got banned.

'I hardly slept last night, and I woke up this morning and just thought, I've got to do something about it, because I can't carry on like this. I need a professional investigator, which is why—'

'Edie,' said Robin, breaking across her at last, 'I totally understand why you want to find out who Anomie is, and I sympathise, but—'

'Please,' said Edie, who seemed to shrink inside her bulky coat at Robin's tone. 'Please help me. I'll pay anything at this point.'

'We don't do work of the kind that might be needed here,' Robin finished, truthfully. 'I think you need somebody who specialises in cyber-investigation, which we've never really done. And we haven't got—'

'You can't imagine what it's like, wondering who it is, wondering who hates me this much. The way he talks . . . he likes Josh, but he *hates* me. I think he sees himself as the true – I don't know – I think he believes he should be in total control of *The Ink Black Heart*, to decide the storylines and make stipulations to the film company and cast all the voice actors – that's how he goes on, as though he should be in charge, and I'm just some inconvenient . . . some inconvenient *parasite* that got accidentally attached to the thing he loves.'

'Listen,' said Robin gently, 'I'm going to give you the names of two other agencies that might be able to help, because I don't think we're the right fit for you.'

Robin wrote the names down for Edie and passed her the note.

'Thank you,' said Edie in a small voice, the paper trembling as she looked down at the names of the agencies Robin had given her. 'I wish . . . I kind of wanted it to be you, but I suppose if you can't . . .'

She thrust the piece of paper into her bag, and Robin resisted the urge to tell her not to lose it, which seemed only too likely. Noticing Robin looking at the bag, Edie raised it off her lap slightly.

'I've only had it a month,' she said, and turning it around she showed Robin several black stains across the dark red leather. 'My pen exploded. I'm shit at keeping things nice. I bought it because I told myself I deserved it because we're a success . . . Ha ha ha,' she said bitterly. 'Big fat success.'

She got to her feet, clutching her bag, and Robin rose too. The harsh office light emphasised Edie's pallor, and as Robin moved towards her to open the door, she realised that what she'd thought was dirt or make-up on Edie's neck was in fact bruising.

'What happened to your neck?'

'What?' said Edie.

'Your neck,' said Robin, pointing. 'It's bruised.'

'Oh.'

Edie raised a hand to where Robin had noticed the bruising.

'That's nothing. I'm clumsy. As you might have noticed.'

Pat looked round as Robin and Edie entered the outer office.

'Is there a loo I could use?' asked Edie, her voice constricted.

'On the landing, just outside the door,' said Robin.

'Right. Well . . . bye, then.'

The glass door opened and closed, and Edie Ledwell disappeared.

7

Still she flees, and ever fiercer tear the hungry hounds behind,
Still she flees, and ever faster follow there the huntsmen on . . .

Amy Levy
Run to Death

'What was all that about?' asked Pat in her gravelly voice.

'She wanted us to investigate someone who's persecuting her online,' said Robin.

Even though it was true that they had no room for another client, and that the agency didn't specialise in cyber-investigations, Robin wished she could have taken Edie Ledwell's case. The more successful the agency had become, the higher the proportion of unlikeable individuals who gravitated towards it. Of course, those seeking to prove infidelity or treachery were by definition under a certain amount of strain, but some of their recent clients, most notably the billionaire of South Audley Street, had showed a definite tendency to treat Robin as a skivvy, and Edie Ledwell's ingenuous 'I was hoping for you' had touched Robin. Through the glass door came the sound of the noisy flush of the toilet off the landing and Robin saw the dark shadow of Edie's black coat pass the door, then heard her footsteps clanging away down the metal stairs.

'You turned her down?' rasped Pat, after taking a long drag on her e-cigarette.

'Had to,' said Robin, moving towards the kitchen area. She just had time for a cup of tea before leaving for Acton.

'Good,' said Pat bluntly, returning to her typing. 'I didn't take to her.'

'Why not?' said Robin, turning to look at the office manager.

'Drama queen, if you ask me. Her hair could do with a good brush too.'

Used to Pat's uncompromising snap judgements, which were rooted largely in people's appearance and occasionally on their superficial resemblance to people she'd previously known, Robin didn't bother contradicting her.

'Want a tea?' she asked as the kettle boiled.

'Lovely, thanks,' said Pat, e-cigarette waggling as she continued typing.

Robin made both of them drinks then returned to the inner office, closed the door and resumed her seat at the partners' desk. After staring abstractedly at the Groomer file for a few seconds, Robin pushed it aside, turned on the PC and typed 'ink black heart animation' into Google.

'*Indie cartoon attracts cult following . . .*' '*breakout success . . .*' '*From YouTube to Hollywood: will* The Ink Black Heart *find big screen favour?*'

Robin opened YouTube, found episode one of the cartoon, and pressed play.

An eerie, tinkling piano played over swirling, animated mist, which slowly cleared to reveal tombstones by moonlight. The shot tracked through stone angels overgrown with ivy until a translucent female figure was revealed, standing alone, pearly white among the graves.

'*Sad, so very sad,*' sighed the ghost, and although her face was rendered simply, it was odd how sinister her little smile was.

She turned and drifted off through the graves, dissolving into the darkness. In the foreground, with an unpleasant squelch, something shiny and black appeared to burst out of the ground. It turned to face the viewer, and Robin saw that it was a jet-black human heart with a smiling, innocent face completely at odds with its otherwise grotesque appearance. Robin vaguely registered the sound of the glass door outside opening again, as the heart waved a severed artery and said, in the jaunty timbre of a children's television presenter:

'*Hello! I'm Harty. I live here in Highgate Cemetery with my friends. You might be wondering why I didn't decay—*'

There was a knock on the inner door and Midge walked in without waiting for a response.

'*—well, that's because I'm evil!*'

'Oh, sorry,' said Midge, 'I thought it was your afternoon off. I need the—'

She broke off, looking disconcerted, and moved around behind Robin to look at the screen, where Harty was now bounding between graves, introducing a variety of characters crawling out of the ground to join him.

'You've gotta be kiddin' me,' said Midge, looking appalled. 'You an' all?'

Robin muted the cartoon.

'What d'you mean, me and all?'

'My ex was fookin' *obsessed* with that bloody cartoon. It's *shit*. Like something you'd make up when you were tripping.'

'I've never seen it before today,' said Robin. 'One of the creators was just in here, wanting us to do a job for her.'

'Who – what's-her-name Ledwell?'

'Yes,' said Robin, surprised that Midge had the name on the tip of her tongue.

Correctly reading Robin's expression, Midge said,

'Beth hated her.'

'Really? Why?'

'No idea,' said Midge. 'That fandom's toxic. "*Play the game, bwah!*"' she added in a squeaky voice.

'What?' said Robin, half-laughing.

'It's one of the catchphrases. In the cartoon. Beth was always sayin' it if I didn't wanna do something. "*Play the game, bwah!*" Fookin' ridiculous. She used to play the fookin' game, too. Online.'

'The one made by Anomie?' said Robin, interested.

'No idea who made it. Childish bollocks,' said Midge, picking the Groomer file off the desk. 'Mind if I take this? Got notes to add.'

'Carry on.'

As Midge left the room, Robin's mobile rang: it was Strike. She pressed pause on the muted cartoon.

'Hi.'

'Hi,' said Strike, who sounded as though he was somewhere busy: she could hear traffic. 'Sorry, I know it's your afternoon off—'

'No problem,' said Robin, 'I'm still at the office. I've got a flat viewing in Acton at six; there didn't seem much point going home first.'

'Ah, OK,' said Strike. 'I wondered how you'd feel about swapping jobs tomorrow? It'd be more convenient for me to do Sloane Square instead of Camden.'

'Yeah, that's fine,' said Robin. On the computer screen in front of her, the black heart stood frozen, pointing into the dark doorway of a mausoleum.

'Thanks, appreciate it,' said Strike. 'Everything all right?' he added, because he detected an odd note in Robin's voice.

'Fine, it's just – we had a Gateshead in just now. Well, Pat thought she was a Gateshead. She wasn't really. Have you ever heard of *The Ink Black Heart*?'

'No. What is it, a pub?'

'A cartoon,' said Robin, pressing play again. The animation was still muted: Harty backed fearfully away from a figure emerging slowly from the tomb's doorway. It was large, hunched and cloaked in black, with an exaggerated beak-like face. 'One of the creators wanted us to investigate a fan who's giving her grief online.'

'Huh,' said Strike. 'What did you say?'

'That we had no room, but I told her Patterson Inc and McCabes both do cyber-investigation.'

'Hm. I don't love giving Patterson work.'

'I wanted to help her,' said Robin with a trace of defensiveness. 'She was in a bit of a state.'

'Fair enough,' said Strike. 'Well, thanks for the swap, I owe you one.'

After Strike had rung off, Robin unmuted the cartoon. She watched for another minute or so, but couldn't make much sense of it. Perhaps she'd missed key plot points while it was on mute, but on balance she had to agree with Midge: except that it was beautifully animated, it had the air of a stoner's macabre fantasy.

She was just about to turn off the PC when Pat knocked and entered the room again.

'This was in the bathroom,' said Pat, brandishing the cardboard folder. 'That scruffy girl must've left it. It was on top of the cistern.'

'Oh,' said Robin, taking it. 'Right ... well, she might come back for it. If not, we should find an address to send it on to. You couldn't have a quick look and see whether she's got an agent or something, could you, Pat? Her name's Edie Ledwell.'

Pat gave a sniff that clearly implied she liked Edie Ledwell no better for having forgotten her folder, and left the room.

Robin waited for the door to close before opening the folder. Edie had printed out a large number of Anomie's tweets, which she'd annotated in distinctive swooping handwriting.

Anomie had more than fifty thousand Twitter followers. Robin started flicking through the tweets, which were now out of date order, having fallen to the floor.

Anomie
@AnomieGamemaster

Those buying Fedwell's sob stories of poverty should
know her well-off uncle gave her 2 big lots of cash in early
noughties. #EdieLiesWell

4.21 pm   22 Sep 2011

Edie had written beneath the tweet: *Anomie calls me either 'Greedie Fedwell' because I'm a recovered bulimic and because obviously I only care about money or 'Edie Lieswell' because I'm supposed to lie non-stop about my past and about my inspiration. It's true my uncle gave me some cash. £200 the first time and then £500. I was homeless the second time. He gave me the money and told me he couldn't do anything else for me. Josh knows this and could easily have told Seb.*

Robin turned to the next page.

Anomie
@AnomieGamemaster

Fedwell laughs in private about basing prize bitch Paperwhite
on black ex-flatmate by name of Shereece Summers. Keep
punching down Greedie.

3.45 am   24 January 2015

I told Seb I'd sort of borrowed bits of Shereece when we fleshed out the character of Paperwhite the ghost, but I never told anyone else she was part of the inspiration.

Robin looked at the next tweet.

Anomie
@AnomieGamemaster

Interesting news, game fans. #GreedieFedwell might
despise OUR game, but turns out she's expert at another
kind #OnTheGame

> **Max R** @mreger#5
> Not proud of it, but I paid @EdLedDraws for a blow job
> back in 2002

4.21 pm   13 April 2012

This, Edie had written, *is one of his favourite ploys. He gets other haters he's friendly with to do his dirty work for him, making up claims he can retweet, so he can't be reported for coming up with the bullshit himself.*

Robin turned another page.

Anomie
@AnomieGamemaster

Hearing Edie Ledwell has 'attempted suicide'. No comment
from agent
Anyone got more info?

10.59 pm   24 May 2014

Anomie
@AnomieGamemaster

Source tells me she's in Kensington Hospital.
Alleged overdose

11.26 pm   24 May 2014

Beneath this, Edie had written: *Anomie knew this had happened within hours. I thought Josh was the only person who knew.*

Anomie
@AnomieGamemaster

Hmmmmm . . . ...

> **Johnny B** @jbaldw1n1>>
> replying to @AnomieGamemaster
> well, that's strange, because my sister works at that
> hospital and saw her walking in unaided and laughing

12.16 pm   24 May 2014

Bullshit. I didn't walk into the hospital. I can't remember anything about getting there, I was unconscious. This Johnny guy is another one of his little helper elves, feeding him lies.

Anomie

@AnomieGamemaster

?

> **Sally Anne Jones** @SAJ345_>
> replying to @AnomieGamemaster
> Not being funny but that hospital does a lot of cosmetic
> procedures. Seems like there would have been a
> statement if she'd overdosed?

1.09 pm   24 May 2014

This Sally Anne is a sock-puppet account, created the same evening and never tweeted again. They've been saying I had a nose job ever since.

Beneath this were a few responses to the news of Ledwell's attempted suicide.

Max R @mreger#5
replying to @AnomieGamemaster
I call bullshit. She's gone to get her massive fkn nose
done #Nosegate

Lepines Disciple @LepinesD1sciple
replying to @AnomieGamemaster
Anyone live close to hospital? Should be easy to photograph
her coming out #Nosegate

Algernon Gizzard Esq @Gizzard_Al
replying to @AnomieGamemaster
death by botched nose job would be fkn hysterical
😂😂😂

DrekIsMySpiritAnimal @playDreksgame
replying to @Gizzard_Al @LepinesD1sciple
@AnomieGamemaster
😂😂😂😂😂😂😂😂😂

Zozo @inkyheart28
replying to @AnomieGamemaster
Stop luaghing at this . what if its real .

Laura May @May_Flower*
replying to @AnomieGamemaster
if she's genuinely tried to kill herself what you're doing is not ok

---

Andi Reddy @ydderidna
replying to @May_Flower* @AnomieGamemaster
there would've been a statement if she'd really done it
#trollingforsympathy

Robin checked her watch: it was time to leave if she wanted to see the Acton flat. Closing the folder, she carried it back outside with her empty mug. Midge was sitting on the sofa, busy adding her notes to the Groomer file.

'Got any plans for this evening?' asked Pat as Robin took down her coat from the peg beside the door.

'Viewing a flat in Acton,' said Robin. 'I hope to God it's better than the last place I saw. There was mould all over the bathroom ceiling and the basin was coming away from the wall. The estate agent said it was a "fixer-upper".'

'London fookin' property,' mumbled Midge without looking up. 'I'm living in a virtual fookin' eggbox.'

Robin bade the other two women goodbye, then left. It was chilly down on Denmark Street. As she walked towards the Tube station, she found herself scanning passers-by for Edie Ledwell, who might by now have noticed that she'd left her folder behind, but there was no sign of her.

It was nearly rush hour. Something she couldn't put her finger on was nagging at Robin. She'd reached the top of the escalator before she realised it had nothing to do with Edie Ledwell or her cartoon.

Strike wasn't scheduled to work this evening, so where exactly was he spending the night that made it more convenient for him to stake out Fingers' flat in Sloane Square the following morning, rather than Legs' school in Camden?

8

She was a careless, fearless girl . . .
Kindhearted in the main,
But somewhat heedless with her tongue,
And apt at causing pain.

Christina Rossetti
Jessie Cameron

The entrance to Nightjar, the speakeasy bar to which Strike was
headed that evening, wasn't easy to find. He initially walked straight
past the discreet wooden door on City Road and had to double back.
On ringing the bell and giving his name he was admitted and proceeded downstairs into a dimly lit basement bar of dark wood and
exposed brick.

This would be Strike's sixth date with Madeline Courson-Miles.
Each of their previous evenings together had started in a different bar
or restaurant picked by Madeline, and ended in her mews house in
Pimlico, which she shared with a son, Henry, to whom she'd given
birth at nineteen. Henry's father, whom Madeline hadn't married,
had also been nineteen when Madeline fell pregnant. He'd gone on
to become a successful interior designer, and Strike was impressed by
how amicable their relationship seemed to be.

Since splitting from Henry's father, Madeline had wed and divorced
an actor who'd left her for the leading lady in his first-ever film.
Strike was certainly a very different proposition from the arty men
Madeline had previously dated but, fortunately for the detective, she
seemed to be enjoying the contrast. As for sixteen-year-old Henry,
he was monosyllabic and barely polite to Strike whenever they came
into contact at Madeline's house. Strike didn't take it personally. He

could remember his own feelings towards the men his mother had brought home.

The detective was perfectly happy to let his new girlfriend choose the places they went on dates; because work had dominated his life for so long, he had very little knowledge of London's best nightspots. A couple of his exes, including his sometime fiancée Charlotte, had been perennially dissatisfied with the kind of places he could afford to take them, but these days he had enough money not to have to worry about bar or restaurant bills. If he had one quibble, it was that Madeline sometimes seemed to forget that a man of his size needed more than bar snacks at the end of a long day's work, and he'd taken the precaution of having a Big Mac and large fries before heading to Nightjar, which she'd promised offered good drink and live music.

He was shown to a table for two and sat down to wait. Madeline was usually at least half an hour late. She ran a very successful business, with a flagship store on Bond Street, from which she sold and lent jewellery to high-profile clients including A-list actresses and royals. Strike was becoming used to Madeline arriving in a keyed-up state, talking frenetically about the latest work problem until, with a few sips of alcohol inside her, she unwound. She was entirely self-made, and he liked her commitment to what she did, her passion for her business and her pithy observations on the people who underestimated her because of her accent and background. She also happened to be beautiful and eager to have sex with him, and after his long period of enforced celibacy and that dangerous moment with Robin outside the Ritz, these salves to his ego were exceptionally welcome. Even though he hadn't told any of his friends he was seeing Madeline, he was trying, as he put it to himself, to 'give things a chance'.

'I'll wait, thanks,' he told the waitress who'd come to take his order, and spent the following twenty minutes perusing a drinks menu that was notable both for its length and for the extravagant concoctions on offer. At the next table, a couple had just been delivered a pair of cocktails that appeared to have candyfloss balanced on the rim of the glass. Strike would have been far happier with a pint of Doom Bar.

'Babes, I'm so sorry I'm late again,' came Madeline's breathless voice at last. She was wearing a suede mini-dress and boots, and looked, as she had every time they'd gone out together, wonderful. Sliding into the chair beside him, she wound one arm around his neck, pulled him in for a kiss on the mouth, then said,

'I had to see lawyers – *God* I need a drink – they've looked at the pictures and they agree it looks like those bitches at Eldorado have ripped off my design. An *hour and a half* explaining to me exactly how hard it is to prove, as if I don't know that already – but I s'pose telling me the same thing ten different times keeps the clock ticking and they bill by the hour, so obviously – I haven't looked, you'll have to come back,' she snapped at the waitress, who'd reappeared. The girl retreated. Madeline took the cocktail menu from Strike.

'What are you having? I need something strong – what d'you think of this place? It's cool, right? What am I going to have? Vodka – yeah, I'll have an Orca Punch. Where's that girl gone?'

'You just told her to sod off,' said Strike.

'Shit, was I rude? Was I? I've had *such* a bloody awful afternoon – we've got a new security guy too and he's seriously OTT – he nearly stopped Lucinda Richardson coming in the store this afternoon. I think I'm gonna have to give him a cheat sheet of who people *are* – oh, there she is,' said Madeline, now flashing a smile at the waitress, who returned looking slightly wary. 'Can I have an Orca Punch?'

'And a Toronto, please,' said Strike, and the waitress smiled at him and moved away.

'How was your day?' Madeline asked Strike, but before he could answer she slid a hand onto his thigh under the table. 'Babes, I've got to ask you something, and I'm a bit worried about it. I think I'd rather just ask you now and get it out of the way.'

'I've been expecting this,' said Strike seriously. 'No, I'm not going to model for you.'

Madeline let out a yelp of laughter.

'Fuck, you'd be fantastic. *What* a fucking ad that would be: I could put you in a tiara. No, but it's funny you should say that, because . . . Look, it was already in the pipeline, but I'm worried how you're going to take it . . . It's Charlotte Campbell.'

'What about her?' said Strike, trying to keep his tone casual.

As Madeline had been dining with Charlotte's stepbrother on the night he met her, he hadn't been surprised to discover that Madeline knew rather a lot about his and Charlotte's long entanglement. However, he'd made a point of ascertaining the precise degree of her friendship with his ex-fiancée before progressing to a second date, and had been glad to learn that Madeline's acquaintance with Charlotte was slight, a mere matter of lending her jewellery and bumping into one another at the kinds of launches and cocktail parties that Madeline's clients routinely attended.

'She agreed to be one of my models for the new collection, last year,' said Madeline, watching Strike closely for his reaction. 'I've felt weird about telling you – there are four of them – I've got Alice de Bock, Siobhan Vickery and Constance Cartwright . . .'

None of these names meant anything to Strike, and Madeline seemed to gather as much from his blank expression.

'Well, they're all a bit – Alice is that model who was done for shop-lifting and Siobhan's the girl who had an affair with Evan Duffield while he was still married – the collection's called "Notorious", so I wanted to use women who're, *you* know – women known to the gossip columns, put it that way. I *was* going to use Gigi Cazenove,' said Madeline, her expression suddenly sombre. 'That poor girl who—'

'Hanged herself on New Year's Eve, yeah,' said Strike. He'd since read up on the story. The twenty-three-year-old pop singer hadn't produced the kind of music Strike ever voluntarily listened to and press pictures of her huge-eyed, narrow face had put him in mind of a startled deer. For six months before her death she'd been a spokes-woman for an environmental charity.

'Exactly. She'd been through this shitty social media storm that turned out to be based on *nothing* and I thought it would be such a glorious *fuck you* to all the people who'd hounded her, but – well, anyway, Charlotte agreed to model and we're supposed to be doing the photos next week. But if you don't want me to, I s'pose we could drop her—'

'Don't be stupid,' said Strike. 'It's your business – literally. I don't care. Nothing to do with me.'

He wasn't delighted by the news, but it wasn't a surprise. Charlotte had done some occasional modelling over the years he'd known her, along with writing odd bits and pieces for *Vogue* and *Tatler*: the fall-backs of a beautiful it-girl with no particular need to work.

'D'you mean that? Seriously? Because she *would* be fucking great and the four of them together would definitely make a splash. I'm going to put Charlotte in a *fuck-off* collar studded with uncut emeralds.'

'A collar?' repeated Strike, thinking of dogs.

'It's a heavy choker-y kind of necklace,' said Madeline, laughing at him again and leaning in for another kiss. 'God, I love that you don't give a shit about jewellery. It's such a nice fucking change of pace.'

'Are most men interested in jewellery?'

'You'd be surprised – or, I don't know if they give a shit about actual jewellery, but they're often quite interested in design, or the value of the stones, or they've got *opinions* – I'm so tired of men giving me their opinions – or maybe I'm just sick of lawyers. Where's that bloody girl? I'm *dying* for a drink . . .'

As Strike had expected, with half an Orca Punch inside her Madeline began to relax. A jazz quartet took to the small stage and her hand rested lightly on his thigh while they shouted comments into each other's ears.

'Did you tell me how your day was?' Madeline asked him when their second drinks arrived.

'No,' Strike said, 'but it was fine.'

To Madeline's slight frustration, he never shared details of cases with her. A private joke had grown up between them that he was investigating the Mayor of London and he might have thought up some amusing fictional crime he'd caught Boris Johnson committing, but he couldn't muster the lung-power to make her understand, given how loudly the saxophonist was currently playing. However, when at last a break in the music came, and the applause died away, Strike said,

'Have you ever heard of *The Ink Black Heart*?'

'The what? Oh – hang on – is it that weird cartoon?'

'Yeah. You know it?'

'No, not really, but Henry was into it for a while,' she said. 'There's a character called Dred or Dreg or something, isn't there?'

'Dunno,' said Strike. 'I heard about it for the first time today.'

'Yeah, Henry liked Dreg. But didn't they sack the guy who used to do his voice, or something? I remember Henry and his mates talking about it. Henry lost interest after that. It all slightly goes over my head, all the YouTube stuff. That's not where you make jewellery sales.'

'Where's best for jewellery?'

'Instagram,' said Madeline promptly. 'Haven't you seen my Instagram page? Bloody hell, call yourself a boyfriend . . .'

She pulled her iPhone out of her bag and brought it up to show him, her booted foot tapping impatiently because the Wi-Fi was slow.

'There,' she said, showing him.

He scrolled slowly through the pictures of various beautiful women wearing Madeline's jewels, interspersed with arty shots of London and quite a few selfies of Madeline wearing her own earrings or necklaces.

'We should take a selfie now and I can post it,' she said, taking her iPhone back and switching to her front camera. 'This is a cool backdrop.'

'Private detectives don't do Instagram,' said Strike, instinctively raising a large hairy-backed hand to block the lens.

'No,' she said with a look of surprise, 'I s'pose not. Shame. We're both looking kind of hot tonight.'

She slipped her phone back into her bag.

'You can post a picture of me once I'm in that tiara,' said Strike, and she giggled.

'Want another drink, or' – she leaned in, her breath warm on his ear – 'shall we go back to the house?'

'House,' said Strike, draining his glass. 'I've got to be in Sloane Square early tomorrow.'

'Yeah? What's Boris doing in Sloane Square?'

'Nicking hub caps, mugging old ladies – the usual,' said Strike. 'But he's a wily bastard and I still haven't managed to catch him in the act.'

Madeline laughed, and Strike raised a hand for the bill.

9

In-game chats between seven of the eight moderators of *Drek's Game*

<Moderator Channel>

<12 February 2015 09.22>

>

>

>

Anomie: Quiet today

>

>

Vilepechora: Yeah.
Numbers have been down
last two weeks.

>

>

>

<A new private channel
has opened>

<12 February 2015 09.24>

<Hartella invites
LordDrek, Vilepechora,
Fiendy1, Worm28 and

78

>

>

>

>

>

>

>

Anomie: What's with the sudden influx of mods?

>

Vilepechora: dunno

>

>

Anomie: I'm going to ban that bastard Harty292 if he keeps that up

Vilepechora: what's he doing?

Anomie: breaking rule 14. trying to get ages and locations off girls. Arsehole.

>

>

>

>

Anomie: ok I've had enough, I'm banning him.

Vilepechora: doesn't help our numbers if you keep banning people.

Paperwhite>

Hartella: peeps?

>

<Vilepechora has joined the channel>

<LordDrek has joined the channel>

<Worm 28 has joined the channel>

Worm28: have u heard from josh ?

Hartella: Let's wait for the others.

>

<Paperwhite has joined the channel>

<Fiendy1 has joined the channel>

>

Fiendy1: what's happened?

Hartella: Josh just texted me. He and Ledwell are going to meet face-to-face this afternoon. She's still denying it, so he's going to take the dossier and show it to her.

Fiendy1: whoa

Worm28: OMFG

Vilepechora: FKN EXCELLENT!

LordDrek: she's not gonna be able to bullshit her way out of this one

Paperwhite: where are

>

>

>

>

>

>

>

>

>

>

>

>

>

Anomie: I've got to be somewhere later. Can you cover?

>

Vilepechora: sorry, dude, got a work meeting

Vilepechora: get Morehouse to do it

Anomie: he's got a thing on, he can't

>

>

>

>

>

they gonna meet?

Hartella: can't tell you that, sorry

Paperwhite: because you don't know or?

Hartella: because Josh trusts me not to say.

Worm28: will there be loiyer 's there ?

Vilepechora: what the fuck's a loiyer?

LordDrek: rofl

Fiendy1: fuck off, she's dyslexic

Hartella: no, Worm, it'll be just the 2 of them

Vilepechora: She's in a shit mood on the moderator channel because the numbers have been down lately. Wait til Blay shows her our dossier, hahaha

Paperwhite: why can't you tell us where they're meeting?

Hartella: I've just told you, Josh trusts me not to tell anyone.

Hartella: obviously he doesn't want to be interrupted by autograph hunters.

Paperwhite: ffs I'm not going to try and get an autograph I'm miles away from London I just wondered

>

>

Anomie: I've got stuff to do

Anomie: back in a bit

\<Anomie has left the channel\>

>

>

>

>

>

>

>

>

>

>

>

>

>

>

>

>

>

>

>

>

Paperwhite: Tho actually it's kind of obvious where they'll meet

Hartella: Paperwhite, seriously, if fans turn up there Josh'll never trust me again

Paperwhite: I've just told you I couldn't turn up if I wanted to. I'm miles away.

Hartella: Josh trusts me, ok?

Paperwhite: Ffs, Hartella, we get it. Josh Blay's got your phone number. Get over yourself.

Paperwhite: Gtg

\<Paperwhite has left the channel\>

Hartella: What the hell's her problem?

Fiendy1: She's used to being Anomie and Morehouse's fave. She doesn't like you getting attention instead

LordDrek: I knew Morehouse fancied her, but Anomie as well?

Fiendy1: idk for sure but he lets her off with more than anyone else, haven't you noticed?

Vilepechora: guess who's left the mod channel because they need to be somewhere later?

Hartella: Well, there you are. As if we

needed more proof.

>

LordDrek: She'll be trying to make herself look less of a skank before she meets him.

>

Hartella: lol

>

LordDrek: only you could have done this, Hartella

>

Hartella: *blushes*

>

LordDrek: Blay should go armed. I'm starting to think she's psychotic

>

Vilepechora: can one of you come and help me on the mod channel?

>

Worm28: I will

<Worm28 has joined the channel>

>

Vilepechora: cheers

Hartella: when this gets out the fandom's explode

>

LordDrek: yeah. is JB going to let you know how it goes?

>

Hartella: yes, he said he would.

>

Vilepechora: suppose it might not matter soon if we slack off, lol

LordDrek: fuck, this feels like Christmas Eve

10

The ground is hollow in the path of mirth . . .

Felicia Hemans
The Festal Hour

The agency's next full team meeting took place at the office on the second Friday in February. It was a dark, wet London day. Heavy rain pattered on the windowpanes and the office's artificial light made everyone but Dev look unhealthily pale.

'Right,' said Strike, having dealt with a few loose ends and administrative details, 'on to Groomer. As you know, we thought he was too smart to hang around Legs' school, but that changed yesterday lunchtime. Midge?'

'Yeah,' she said, taking the biscuit tin from Barclay and passing it to Strike without taking anything herself, 'he turned up in his BMW at twelve-thirty, window wound down, scanning all the girls who were coming out for lunch. I took pictures – Pat's printed them out –'

Pat stuck her e-cigarette between her teeth, opened the folder on her lap and passed the wad of pictures around.

'– and as you can see, he texted her, rather than flag her down in front of her mates. Once the friends were out of sight she doubled back and got into the car with him. I was worried they were going to drive off somewhere, but he only went round the corner so they'd be out of sight of the school gates.'

The photos had reached Robin. She examined them one by one. In the last, which had been taken through the windscreen of the BMW, Groomer, a handsome man of around forty, with a full head of dirty blond hair and an attractively crooked smile, was kissing the back of the seventeen-year-old's hand as she sat in the passenger seat beside him.

'The hand-kissing happened right before the school bell rang,' said Midge. 'She checked her phone right after it, realised she was due back in class and legged it. He drove off. He didn't come back and she took the bus home as usual.'

'But there've been developments since,' said Strike. 'When Midge showed me these photos, I sent them straight to the mother, who called me this morning. She confronted Legs, pretended another mother had spotted her getting into Groomer's car. Legs claimed he had just happened to be passing the school and waved at her. The mother demanded to see her mobile. Legs refused. It degenerated into a physical fight.'

'Oh no,' groaned Robin.

'Legs managed to keep the mobile out of her mother's clutches, so her mother, who pays the bill, locked and wiped it remotely.'

'Nice one,' said Barclay and Midge in unison, but Dev shook his head.

'He'll exploit it – buy her a new phone. The worst thing that woman can do right now is make herself the bad guy.'

'I agree,' said Strike. 'The client's already panicking about what's going to happen when she goes abroad again. Legs will be staying with the schoolfriend whose family took her to Annabel's at New Year and, having seen them, they don't look like strict disciplinarians.

'Anyway, mother and daughter are currently driving to Hereford for Granny's ninetieth birthday.'

'The atmosphere in that car must be fantastic,' said Dev.

'Bottom line,' said Strike, 'the Groomer case continues, although my gut says we're not going to be able to give the client what she wants. Her daughter's of age. What Groomer's doing might be morally off, but it isn't illegal. Mind you, if he keeps hanging around the school gates we might have something to work with.'

'He's too canny to do that on a regular basis,' said Dev.

'A baseball bat tae the nuts might sort him out,' suggested Barclay.

'What we need is to prove to the *girl* he's a creep,' said Robin. 'That would end it. The problem is, she currently thinks he's wonderful.'

'Does she?' mused Midge, 'or is she getting a kick out of stealing her mother's boyfriend?'

'Maybe both,' said Robin.

'I agree,' said Strike. 'Psychologically, turning the girl off him's the one sure-fire way to end it, but putting full-time surveillance on Groomer himself is going to double the bills and I don't think the client will go for it. She's taking the view that she can put a stop to it all by threatening both of them and yelling.'

'She comes across as a lot smarter than that on the telly,' said Dev through a mouthful of biscuit.

'Naebody's smart wi' their own family,' said Barclay. 'I wouldnae be married if my mother-in-law hadn't kept telling my wife I was some worthless squaddie on the make.'

'Didn't you just repaint your mother-in-law's kitchen?' asked Robin.

'I did, aye. She almost thanked me too,' said Barclay. 'Magical moment.'

Robin and Dev laughed at his dour expression.

'You know, we've got a light weekend,' said Strike thoughtfully, rubbing the chin that already looked grimy with stubble, though he'd shaved that morning. 'It mightn't be a bad idea to have a shufti at what Groomer gets up to when the girl's not around. Who fancies some overtime?'

'I'll do it,' said Dev before anyone else could speak. 'I could use the money. Just found out the wife's expecting again,' he clarified, and there was a round of congratulations.

'OK, great,' said Strike. 'You've got his address. Anything you can get that might make him look a bit less knight-erranty to a schoolgirl ...

'So, on to Fingers. We're expecting him back from the Maldives tomorrow lunchtime, so it'll be business as usual from his arrival at Heathrow at twelve-forty. And I've got a meeting with that guy with the mad hair and the patent-pending problem on Monday. I'll let you know how that goes.

'Anyone got any issues with the rest of this month's rota? Pat's drawing up March now, so talk dates with her if you—'

'I wondered whether anyone could swap this Sunday with me,' said Robin. 'I'm supposed to be tailing Fingers. I wouldn't ask, but there's a viewing of a flat I really want to see. They're only showing it on Sundays.'

'No problem,' said Strike, 'I'll do your shift, if you don't mind doing my Monday.'

The swap was agreed and the discussion descended into small talk, so Robin typed out a quick email on her phone to the estate agent.

A notification from BBC News slid across her phone screen as she typed. Something about stabbing victims being named; she swiped it away. There was so much knife crime in London it was hard to keep up: the eight-inch-long scar on Robin's forearm, still raised, faintly pink and shiny, was the relic of such an attack.

The rest of the team was tidying away chairs or putting them back into their usual position. Rain continued to pound against the office windows. As Robin pressed send on her email, a second BBC notification slid across the screen. *Ledwell and Blay discovered in Highgate Cemetery.*

Robin stared at the screen for a few seconds, then tapped the notification with a finger. Somebody said goodbye to her but she didn't answer, because she was waiting for the full story of the stabbing in Highgate Cemetery to load. The glass door of the office opened and closed. Midge and Barclay had left, chatting to each other, their footsteps dying away down the metal staircase.

Highgate Stabbing Victims Were Creators of Cult Cartoon

The victims of a twin stabbing yesterday evening in Highgate Cemetery have been named by Scotland Yard as Edie Ledwell, 30, and Josh Blay, 25, co-creators of Netflix hit animation *The Ink Black Heart*, which is set in the same London graveyard.

Ledwell's body was discovered by a cemetery worker. Blay survived the attack and was taken to the Whittington Hospital, where he remains in a critical condition.

Police have asked members of the public who noticed anyone behaving unusually in the vicinity of the cemetery between 4pm and 6pm on the 12th February to call a dedicated hotline (number below). No description of an attacker has been released.

Ledwell and Blay created the surprise hit after meeting at North Grove Art Collective ...

Through the loud thumping of blood in her ears, Robin registered that someone was talking to her. She looked up.

'What's the matter?' said Strike sharply, because the colour had drained from Robin's face.

'That girl – woman – who wanted us to investigate the internet troll? She's been murdered.'

II

But should the play
Prove piercing earnest,
Should the glee glaze
In death's stiff stare,
Would not the fun
Look too expensive?
Would not the jest
Have crawled too far?

Emily Dickinson
LV

In-game chats between all eight moderators of *Drek's Game*

```
<Moderator Channel>

<13 February 2015
17.34>

Worm28: Hartella ?

Worm28: I can see
you're in here

Worm28: hello ?

Worm28: someone talk

Worm28: pleaes

>
```

\<Morehouse has joined the channel\>

Worm28: Morhuse , thank god have you seen ?

Morehouse: yeah

Worm28: I can 't

Worm28: It can 't be true can it ?

Worm28: oh god I can't stop cryign

Worm28: it can 't be true

Morehouse: I think it must be, Worm

Morehouse; They wouldn't give out names unless they were sure.

Worm28: oh god

\<Fiendy1 has joined the channel\>

Fiendy1: have you heard

Worm28: yes

\>

\>

Fiendy1: anyone know anything?

Morehouse: no

Fiendy1: I'm fkn shaking

\<A new private channel has opened\>

\<13 February 2015 17.35\>

\<Morehouse invites Paperwhite\>

Morehouse: Paperwhite?

\>

\>

\>

\>

\>

\>

\>

\>

\>

\>

\>

\>

\<Paperwhite has joined the channel\>

Paperwhite: Hey Mouse, sorry, I'm on the bus. Home in 20.

Morehouse: Are you sitting down?

\<A new private channel has opened\>

\<13 February 2015 17.36\>

\<Vilepechora invites LordDrek\>

Vilepechora: u there, C?

\<LordDrek has joined the channel\>

LordDrek: fuuuuuuuuuuck

Vilepechora: hahahahaha

\>

LordDrek: FUUUUUUUUUUCK

Vilepechora: can you fkn believe it

\>

Worm28: I can 't stop crying

Fiendy1: do you think Blay did it?

Worm28: what/ ? ?

Fiendy1: d'you think he stabbed her and then himself?

Worm28: why aer you saying that ?

Fiendy1: look at Twitter, that's what they're saying happened.

<Vilepechora has joined the channel>

<LordDrek has joined the channel>

LordDrek: you've all heard?

Worm28: yes

Fiendy1: yes

LordDrek: fuck

LordDrek: this is a fkn tragedy

Vilepechora: I know who my money's on.

Fiendy1: ?

LordDrek: K** N****

Vilepechora: exactly.

Paperwhite: Yeah, I'm on the bus!

Morehouse: You haven't seen the news?

Paperwhite: What news?

Morehouse: Ledwell's been murdered

>

>

Paperwhite: what?

Morehouse: Stabbed yesterday in H cemetery. Blay too. He's critical in hospital.

>

>

>

>

Paperwhite: Morehouse, if this is a joke it's not funny

Morehouse: you think I'd joke about something like this?

>

>

>

>

LordDrek: Burn this & go to mod chan, lets see how they're takin it

<Vilepechora has left the channel>

<LordDrek has left the channel>

<Private channel has closed>

89

Crazy fkn bitch.

LordDrek: yeah, I've always thought she was a Jodi Arias in the making.

<Anomie has joined the channel>

Anomie: fuck

>

Anomie: you all seen?

Worm28: yes

<Hartella has joined the channel>

>

>

>

Anomie: fuck

>

>

>

Anomie: you all been struck dumb or something?

Fiendy1: no we're just in shock

Worm28: I can 't stop cryign

>

Worm28: people on Twitter are saying it

>

>

>

>

Morehouse: are you still there?

Paperwhite: yes

>

Paperwhite: just googled it

>

>

Paperwhite: I think I'm going to throw up

Morehouse: I know

Morehouse: the hell were they doing in the cemetery together?

Morehouse: I heard they weren't even speaking to each other

Paperwhite: who told you that?

Morehouse: Anomie

>

>

<A new private channel has opened>

<13 February 2015 17.47>

<Hartella invites LordDrek and Vilepechora>

Hartella: Drek talk to me

>

>

>

Hartella: Vile, u there?

<LordDrek has joined the channel>

<Vilepechora has joined the channel>

LordDrek: how u doing

90

's the fans fault

Fiendy1: how is it?

Worm28: they thikn a fan might of done it

>

>

>

>

>

Fiendy1: it could've been random

Fiendy1: like a mugging or something

Fiendy1: or someone mentally ill

Worm28: what kind of thing is that to say

Worm28: you think I could kill someon ?

Fiendy1: Worm I don't mean like being depressed or whatever

<Worm28 has left the channel>

Fiendy1: shit

Anomie: lol

>

>

Paperwhite: Mouse, I've got to tell you something

Morehouse: what?

Paperwhite: LordDrek and Vilepechora thought Ledwell was Anomie

Morehouse: wtf?

Paperwhite: they put together a whole like dossier of proof

Morehouse: when was this?

Paperwhite: couple of weeks ago

Paperwhite: I never believed it but some of the others did

Paperwhite: and Hartella volunteered to take the dossier to Blay

Paperwhite: and Blay believed it and that's why he was meeting Ledwell, to tell her he knew she was Anomie

>

Morehouse: why the f didn't you tell me?

Paperwhite: they told me not to because you were in on it

hun?

Hartella: you know what's happened?

LordDrek: yeah

Vilepechora: fkn terrible

>

>

Hartella: I'm so scared

LordDrek: ?

Hartella: They're saying on twitter Blay did it

Vilepechora: if he did, he overdid it

LordDrek: news says he's critical

Hartella: I persuaded him to meet her tho

LordDrek: so?

Hartella: I knew they were going to meet in the cemetery

Hartella: he told me in his text

Hartella: it'll be on his phone

LordDrek: so? got an alibi?

Hartella: why are you saying that? why would

>
>
>
>
>

Anomie: we're doing massive numbers right now

Fiendy1: are you for real?

Fiendy1: you care about numbers today?

Anomie: I'm stating a fact, that's all

<Fiendy1 has left the channel>

>
>
>
>

Anomie: Hartella, why aren't you talking?

>
>
>
>

Morehouse: you just said you didn't believe it

Paperwhite: I didn't know what to think

Paperwhite: I wish I'd told you but the dossier was really convincing and so were Drek and Vile

>
>
>
>
>

Paperwhite: I'm sorry, but I don't know who you are, do I?

Paperwhite: you won't even send me a pic

>

Paperwhite: Morehouse, talk to me

Morehouse: I could've told you he wasn't Ledwell

Paperwhite: you told me you'd never met him face to face

Morehouse: I don't

I want them dead, for gods sake?

LordDrek: I never said you would, I was trying to reassure you

Hartella: I was at my sister's

LordDrek: well then, you've got nothing to worry about

Hartella: no

Hartella: I know

>

Hartella: Anomie's on the mod channel

LordDrek: yeah I can see

Vilepechora: shit

LordDrek: we genuinely thought he was Ledwell

LordDrek: I swear we thought he was

Hartella: do you think I should talk to the police and explain why they were meeting?

LordDrek: up to you

Vilepechora: probably better to tell them before they come and find you

LordDrek: yeah, if you're on his phone and

92

>

>

>

>

>

>

>

>

>

Hartella: sorry Anomie just trying to process this

Hartella: kind of devastated

Hartella: I can't be here right now sorry

<Hartella has left the channel>

LordDrek: fuck, this is terrible news

Vilepechora: yeah it is

>

LordDrek: we're doing massive numbers right now

Anomie: I know

Vilepechora: makes sense

need to meet him face-to-face I know exactly who he is, I've always known, we've Facetimed

Paperwhite: I'm shitting myself here

Morehouse: why?

Paperwhite: I guessed where Blay & Ledwell were going to meet. I told the others it was obvious.

Morehouse: so?

Paperwhite: so Hartella thought I was going to turn up to try and get an autograph or something

>

Paperwhite: Morehouse I know you're angry but talk to me

Morehouse: you've worried you'll be suspected?

Paperwhite: I wish I hadn't said I'd guessed where they'd meet

Paperwhite: I just thought it was obvious

Morehouse: but you live like four hundred miles away from Highgate Cemetery

he told you they were meeting at the cemetery the cops will want to see you

Hartella: yeah

Hartella: I'd better go think what to do

LordDrek: understood

LordDrek: take care of yourself xxx

Hartella: xxx

<Hartella has left the channel>

Vilepechora: lolololol

LordDrek: dumb fkn foid

LordDrek: mod channel, let's stir the shit some more

>

>

>

>

>

>

>

>

>

>

93

Vilepechora: people want to connect

>

>

Anomie: Harty292's back, I thought we perma-banned that cunt

LordDrek: I'll go kick him out

Vilepechora: what's your theory, Paperwhite?

Vilepechora: you & Morehouse consoling each other on another chan?

>

>

>

>

>

>

LordDrek: shit the numbers we're doing are off the fkn chart

Vilepechora: we're gonna do our biggest nite ever if this keeps up

>

>

>

Paperwhite: how do you know where I live?

Morehouse: I don't it was just a figure of speech

>

>

Paperwhite: 400 miles isn't a figure of speech

Morehouse: I just meant you don't seem to know London

Morehouse: so I assumed you didn't live there

Paperwhite: so you picked 400 miles at random

Paperwhite: we've never talked about London

Morehouse: you told me you'd never been to Highgate Cemetery

Paperwhite: I haven't but I bet nor have loads of Londoners

>

Paperwhite: you know who I am

Morehouse: no I don't, how could i?

>

>

>

>

>

>

>

>

>

>

LordDrek: Bet you £500 Paperwhite's telling Morehouse all about our dossier

Vilepechora: hahaha

>

>

>

>

>

>

>

>

>

>

>

>

>

>

>

>

>

>

>

>

>

Morehouse: Anomie, we should close the game for a few days

Morehouse: mark of respect

Anomie: should we fuck

Anomie: this is exactly the time to make bloody sure everyone knows fans want Drek's Game.

Anomie: show of strength

Morehouse: the hell is

Paperwhite: I've sent you pics

Morehouse: I know but that doesn't mean I know who u are

Paperwhite: so it's ok for you to cyber stalk me but I'm not even allowed to know what you look like?

Morehouse: I haven't cyberstalked u

Paperwhite: I don't believe you

<Paperwhite has left the channel>

<Morehouse has left the channel>

<Private channel has closed>

>

>

>

>

>

LordDrek: go and look at what's happening in the Circle of Lebanon

Vilepechora: why?

LordDrek: just go & look it's fkn hilarious

>

>

>

>

Vilepechora: hahahaha

LordDrek: fkn excellent isn't it

>

>

>

>

wrong with you?

>

Morehouse: Ledwell's
dead and Blay might   >
still die

>

Morehouse: we look
like shits, ignoring   >
what's happened and
keeping the game   >
open

>

Anomie: if she'd ever
been involved in the   >
game or approved of it
I'd close for   >
a couple of days

>

Anomie: but she fkn
hated it, so we stay   >
open

>

LordDrek: yeah, fans
are consoling each   >
each other in here,
Morehouse   >

Vilepechora: yeah,
they're pouring in here   >
to grieve

>

Morehouse: are they   >
hell

>

Morehouse: go look at
the Circle of   **Vilepechora:** hahaha,
Lebanon   Morehouse's noticed

LordDrek: why what's   >
happening?

>

Morehouse: They're
having a fkn party   >

Morehouse: they're   >
celebrating that she's
dead   >

Vilepechora: don't think so, bwah

Morehouse: they are

Morehouse: and you 3 don't seem too bloody sad about it either

<Morehouse has left the channel>

Anomie: fuck off then you little brown dwarf

Vilepechora: lol

LordDrek: lol

>

Anomie: so which of you stabbed Blay & which Ledwell?

>

Vilepechora: lol, we thought you did them both, bwah

Anomie: I did

Anomie: just testing ;)

>

>

>

>

>

>

>

>

LordDrek: wait is Morehouse <?

Vilepechora: sounds like it

LordDrek: worth knowing

Vilepechora: wanna go join the party?

LordDrek: nah

LordDrek: we should go talk to the boys

Vilepechora: WE GOT OURSELVES A KILL BWAH!!!

12

I, who should have known,
Forereckoned mischief!

Elizabeth Barrett Browning
Aurora Leigh

The team meeting had ended over an hour ago. Rain continued to pour down onto Denmark Street. The sky beyond the office windows was stormy-dark and the reflections of Strike and Robin, the only two people who remained at the office, were ghostly in the glass.

Pat had lingered beyond her usual going-home time, not because she particularly wanted to meet the CID officer who'd told Robin he'd be with her shortly, but because she seemed to feel that Strike was being insufficiently solicitous towards his partner.

'She still looks peaky,' Pat told Strike as he emerged from the inner office, where Robin had heard him cancelling dinner plans with someone unknown. 'She should have a brandy. I'll go out and buy some.'

'I don't want to meet the police stinking of booze, Pat,' said Robin before Strike could respond, 'and I only look horrible because of the light in here. I'm fine. Go home and have a good weekend!'

So Pat took down her umbrella and handbag from their peg beside the glass door and, with a last sceptical look at Robin, departed.

'What's wrong with the light in here?' Strike asked once the door had closed.

'It makes everyone look like they're anaemic,' said Robin. 'And you didn't have to cancel your dinner plans, either. I'm fine to meet the police alone.'

'I'd rather stay,' said Strike. 'Want another tea?'

'That'd be great,' said Robin. 'Thanks.'

She was glad he hadn't left. She felt more shaken than she wanted to admit. Needing activity, she folded up the plastic chair on which she'd sat for the team meeting, stowed it away and settled instead on the revolving chair behind Pat's desk, which was far more comfortable.

'I've put sugar in it,' Strike told Robin, setting the mug down in front of her.

'I'm *fine*, for God's sake,' said Robin, now slightly exasperated. 'If I keeled over every time someone got stabbed in London I'd spend half my life unconscious.'

Strike sat down on the fake leather sofa with his own mug of tea and said,

'Ledwell getting killed had nothing to do with you refusing to take her case. You know that, right?'

'Yes,' said Robin, preferring to sip tea than to meet his gaze. 'Obviously I do.'

'We couldn't have taken the case ahead of the waiting-list clients.'

'I know.'

'And even if that troll she was trying to unmask was the one who knifed her,' Strike pressed on, 'which I have to say is extremely unlikely – but even if the troll *was* the killer, we'd never have found out who they were in this short a period of time.'

'I know,' repeated Robin, 'but – but Edie Ledwell might have felt a bit happier during her last few weeks of life thinking she was doing something about – oh *shit*,' she said angrily, turning away from Strike so she could wipe her eyes on her sleeve.

A vivid image of Edie Ledwell had forced its way into her mind: the streaked eyeliner and the tattooed hand with its bitten fingernails, holding tight to the expensive ink-stained bag on her lap. The rain drummed on the windows. Robin really wanted CID to hurry up. She wanted to know exactly what had happened.

The buzzer rang. Robin jumped up, but Strike had already heaved himself off the sofa. When he pressed the intercom button a disembodied voice said,

'DCI Ryan Murphy here for Robin Ellacott.'

'Great, come up,' said Strike, pressing the button to open the door to the street.

Strike walked out onto the landing and looked down at the metal staircase below. Two people were climbing the stairs towards their office. One was tall and male, the other a petite woman with jet-black hair. Both wore civilian clothes.

'Ryan Murphy,' said the white officer, a pleasant-looking man with wavy light brown hair.

'Cormoran Strike,' said the detective, shaking hands.

'This is Angela Darwish.'

The black-haired woman nodded silently to Strike as they passed into the office where Robin now stood behind Pat's desk, ready to shake hands. This done, Strike took the plastic fold-up chairs out of the cupboard again. Once everyone was sitting down, and tea and coffee had been declined, Ryan Murphy asked Robin to tell them exactly what had transpired between her and Edie Ledwell when the animator had come to the agency.

Strike listened to Robin's account in silence while drinking his tea. He felt a certain pride in her powers of observation and in the method-ical way she took the officer through the brief encounter. Murphy took notes and added the occasional question. Darwish, who Strike judged to be over forty, was watching Robin with a slight frown on her face.

'How're we spelling "Anomie"?' asked Murphy the first time Robin said the name. She spelled it out for him.

'Is that supposed to be a play on "anonymous" or—?'

Strike, who hadn't heard the name of Ledwell's internet persecutor until this moment, opened his mouth to speak, but Darwish got there before he did.

'Anomie,' she said, in a high, clear voice, 'means a lack of the usual ethical or social standards.'

'Really?' said Murphy. 'New one on me. Carry on,' he added to Robin, 'you were saying she had a folder with her – what was in it?'

'Printed-out copies of tweets by Anomie, with her own annota-tions. I didn't look through the whole thing,' said Robin. 'She actually left it behind by mistake.'

'You haven't still—?'

'No,' said Robin. 'I asked our office manager to return it via her agent. I can check with Pat if she did.'

'I'll do that,' offered Strike, getting up and moving into the inner office again, so as not to interrupt the interview. The dividing door swung shut behind him.

'So this Anomie,' said Murphy, 'knew a lot of personal stuff about her?'

'Yes,' said Robin. 'I skimmed through the file before I gave it to Pat to send back. He knew she'd been given money by a relative, and that she'd tried to commit suicide, and where she was hospitalised afterwards.'

As Robin said the word 'suicide', she noticed Darwish's gaze flicker towards Murphy and away again. The latter's unblinking gaze remained fixed on Robin, who went on,

'Anomie also knew the identity of a girl who'd been the inspiration for one of the cartoon characters. It was that that made Edie think she knew who Anomie really was.'

'And who did she think it was?' asked Murphy.

'A man called Seb Montgomery.'

As she said the name Robin thought she saw an almost imperceptible lowering of shoulders and slackening of faces. She had the strange feeling that she'd disappointed Murphy and Darwish.

'Did she give you any details about this Montgomery?' asked Murphy.

'Yes, he's an animator or an artist who helped her and Blay when they first started making *The Ink Black Heart*,' said Robin. 'I think she said Montgomery was at the same art school as Blay. After they'd done a few episodes they didn't need him any more, and she said he resented being dropped, once the cartoon started getting a big following.'

The door opened and Strike reappeared.

'You were right,' he told Robin, as rain continued to lash the windows. 'Pat sent that folder back to Ledwell's agent. His name's Allan Yeoman. He runs an agency for creatives in the West End: AYCA.'

'Great, thanks,' said Murphy, making another note as Strike dropped back onto the sofa with a grunt.

'So, did Ledwell mention anyone else as a possible Anomie?' Murphy asked.

'No,' said Robin, 'only Montgomery.'

'What was her state of mind during your meeting with her, in your judgement?'

'Overwrought,' said Robin. 'She looked as though she wasn't really taking care of herself. Bitten fingernails, creased clothes – her boots needed re-heeling—'

'You noticed her boots needed re-heeling?' asked Murphy. His upper lip was thicker than his lower, which added a kind of sweetness to a face that was otherwise all angles. He had hazel eyes, though they were nowhere near as distinctive as Edie Ledwell's amber-coloured ones.

'Yes. She was – she was all odd contrasts. Very expensive bag and coat but otherwise a bit of a mess. She also had fingertip bruising on her neck.'

'Bruising to her neck?'

'Yes – I thought it was dirt at first, but then I got closer and saw what it really was. I asked her what had happened to her and she said she banged into something, that she was clumsy. But it was fingertip bruising, I could see the thumb mark. She mentioned a boyfriend, but didn't tell me his name. I got the impression they were living together.'

'Yeah, they were,' said Murphy. 'He's a teacher. Did she give you any reason to suppose she thought she was trying to escape the relationship? Any mention of domestic violence?'

'No,' said Robin. 'She seemed completely focused on what Anomie was doing to her and the fact that Blay thought she was behind it all, although I wouldn't be surprised if there were other personal troubles. She seemed – put it this way: if I'd seen on the news that she'd killed herself, that wouldn't have surprised me as much as this has. It was definitely done by somebody else, was it?'

'Yes,' said Murphy.

'Blay's injuries as well?' asked Strike.

'Yes, but – I'm sure you understand—'

'Of course,' said Strike, raising a placatory hand. It had been worth a try.

'This accusation of Blay's, that she was Anomie,' said Murphy. 'What led him to believe that, do you know?'

'From what I remember,' said Robin, staring down at the desk in an effort to recall Ledwell's exact words, 'he said it was something he'd heard, but he wouldn't tell her where he'd heard it. They spoke a few times on the phone, with him repeating the accusation and her denying it. But then, during their last call, he'd told her he had a dossier of proof that she was Anomie.'

'A literal dossier?' asked Murphy. 'A physical file?'

'I don't know for sure, but she seemed to think so,' said Robin. 'She said she'd asked him what was in it and he wouldn't tell her.'

'OK, this definitely needs looking into,' said Murphy, looking at Darwish, who nodded, 'this dossier and Anomie. We'll speak to this

Seb Montgomery, too. No idea where he works currently, I suppose?' he asked Robin.

'No,' said Robin, 'sorry. As we couldn't take the case, I didn't ask for his details.'

'No problem. Shouldn't be too hard to track him down if he helped them animate that cartoon.'

Darwish, who hadn't spoken since giving the definition of anomie, now cleared her throat.

'Just a couple more things,' she said to Robin, for the first time clicking out the nib of her own pen and opening a notebook. 'Did Ledwell say anything about this Anomie attacking her for her political beliefs?'

'No,' said Robin, 'she didn't mention politics at all. The attacks were all personal – claiming she'd worked as a prostitute, posting a picture of her flat. He also shared genuine private information he had about her.'

Darwish made a short note, then looked up and said,

'And you're quite sure, are you, she didn't mention anyone else as a possible persecutor?'

'I'm sure she didn't,' said Robin.

'Did she happen to mention the actor who used to voice her character Drek?'

'No,' said Robin, brow furrowed, 'but she *did* say something about that character: that she really wished they hadn't created him. She didn't say why – unless it was because, in the cartoon, Drek's the one who makes the other characters play the game. She might have meant that if there hadn't been any Drek, Anomie would never have made the game.'

'You've watched this cartoon, have you?' Murphy asked Robin.

'Only a tiny bit,' said Robin. 'It's . . .'

'Nuts?'

Robin forced a smile and said, 'A bit. Yes.'

Darwish, who'd made another brief note, now closed her notebook and then cast a look at DCI Murphy that plainly said *I've got everything I need.*

'Right, well, you've been very helpful, Miss Ellacott,' said Murphy as he and Darwish stood up. 'I'm going to give you my direct number, in case you remember anything else.'

He handed her his card. His hand was large, warm and dry as he shook hers. He was as tall as Strike, though rather slimmer.

Strike showed the visitors out. Robin was putting Murphy's card into her purse when her partner reappeared.

'You OK?' he asked, closing the glass door on the sound of the retreating footsteps.

'Fine,' said Robin, for what felt like the umpteenth time. She took the dregs of her sugary tea over to the sink and washed up the mug.

'There's something up,' said Strike as the sound of the door to the street slamming echoed up the stairwell.

Robin turned to look at him. Strike had just taken down his overcoat from beside the door. The rain was still pounding against the windows.

'What d'you mean?' asked Robin.

'That question about politics.'

'Well ... I suppose people argue about politics all the time on Twitter.'

'Yeah,' said Strike, who was holding his mobile in his right hand, 'but while Murphy was asking you your opinion of the cartoon, I looked up the voice actor who played Drek.'

'And?'

'He was fired because of what many took to be his far-right political position. He claimed he was being satirical, but Ledwell and Blay weren't having it and sacked him.'

'Oh,' said Robin.

Strike scratched his chin, eyes on the glass door.

'Don't know if you noticed, but they never told us what that Angela Darwish does either. She didn't leave a card.'

'I assumed she was CID as well.'

'Maybe.'

'What else could she be?'

'I wondered,' said Strike slowly, 'whether she was counter-terrorism ... maybe MI5.'

Robin stared at Strike until she realised warm water from the mug she was still holding was dripping onto her feet. She set it down on the draining board.

'MI5?'

'Just a thought.'

'What kind of terrorist would target a pair of animat—?'

She caught herself as Strike raised his eyebrows at her. The faint echo of bullets ripping through a Parisian publishers' office seemed to fill the space between them.

'But *Charlie Hebdo* – that was entirely different. *The Ink Black Heart* isn't a political cartoon, there was nothing about religion . . .'

'No,' said Strike. 'Maybe you're right. You ready to go? I'll walk down with you, I'm going to get a takeaway.'

If Robin hadn't been pondering the question of why the stabbing of two animators could have possibly interested MI5, she might have asked herself why Strike was taking a small rucksack into Chinatown to pick up his takeaway, but she was so preoccupied, his lie went unchallenged.

13

But when thy friends are in distress,
Thou'lt laugh and chuckle ne'er the less . . .

Joanna Baillie
A Mother to her Waking Infant

Madeline and her son, Henry, lived in a mews house in Eccleston Square, Pimlico. Henry's father lived a few streets away with his wife and their three children. He and Madeline had deliberately chosen to move into the same area so their son could come and go easily between the two houses. Henry seemed to be on good terms with both his stepmother and his half-siblings. To Strike, who'd been raised in conditions of insecurity and chaos, it all felt very grown-up and civilised.

He walked the short distance from Victoria Station with his collar turned up against the continuing rain, smoking while he still had the chance, because Madeline was a non-smoker and preferred her pristine house to remain cigarette-free. The subtle recalibration he always needed to perform when moving from work to a date with Madeline was proving harder than usual this evening. One reason he had no objection to Madeline's persistent lateness was because it allowed him extra time to summon the energy needed to meet her always keyed-up demeanour on first contact. Tonight, though, his thoughts remained with Robin and with the oddly vivid picture she'd painted for the police, of the now-dead animator with her bruised neck and old boots. If he were honest with himself, he'd rather still be at the office, speculating about the stabbings with Robin over a Chinese takeaway than heading towards Madeline's.

Best, then, not to be honest with himself.

It was Valentine's Day tomorrow. Strike had arranged for a showy spray of orchids to be delivered to Madeline in the morning and was carrying a card for her in his rucksack. These were the things you did for the woman you were sleeping with if you wanted to keep sleeping with her, and Strike was keen to keep sleeping with Madeline, for reasons both obvious and barely acknowledged.

The rapid thumps of teenage feet on the stairs followed Strike's ring on the doorbell, and Henry opened the door. He was a good-looking boy with Madeline's red-gold hair, which he wore as long and floppy as Westminster School would permit. Strike remembered being the age Henry was now: the indignity of angry pimples burgeoning on his hairless chin, being unable to find trousers long enough in the leg but small enough in the waist (a problem that, for Strike, had long since vanished), feeling uncoordinated and clumsy and full of a range of desperate and unfulfilled desires that the teenaged Strike had partly sublimated in the boxing ring.

'Evening,' said Strike.

'Hi,' said Henry, unsmiling, and he turned immediately to run back upstairs. Strike surmised that he'd been told to answer the door, rather than done it of his own accord.

The detective stepped inside, wiped his feet, took off his overcoat and hung it up beside the front door, then proceeded upstairs at a far slower pace than Henry, making liberal use of the banister. He arrived in the open-plan living area to find Madeline sitting on the sofa, pencil in hand, head bowed over an assortment of gemstones that were lying on a large piece of white paper spread out on the coffee table. A half-empty bottle of wine stood next to the paper, the glass beside it full.

'Sorry, babes, d'you mind if I just finish this?' said Madeline anxiously.

''Course not,' said Strike, setting his rucksack down on a leather chair.

'I'm really sorry,' she said, frowning at the design she was working on, 'I just had an idea and I want to follow it through before I lose it. Henry'll get you a drink – Hen, get Cormoran a drink – *Hen!*' she bellowed, because Henry had just put earphones in and was sitting back down at the desk in the corner, which had a large PC on it.

'What?'

'Get – Cormoran – a – drink!'

Henry just prevented himself from throwing down the headphones.

Strike would have offered to get the drink himself, but he guessed that would have been making himself a little too at home in the teenager's eyes.

'What d'you want?' Henry grunted at the detective as he passed him.

'Beer would be great.'

Henry strode off towards the kitchen, his fringe flopping over his eyes. Wanting to give Madeline peace and space, Strike followed her son.

The house was largely white: white walls, white ceilings, a white carpet in Madeline's bedroom, stripped floorboards everywhere else, the other furnishings almost all silvery grey. Madeline had told Strike she found it restful, after hours staring at vibrant gemstones in the workshop, or else presiding over her eclectically decorated Bond Street shop, to spend evenings in a serene, monochrome space. Her house in the country, she'd told him, was far busier and more colourful in style: they should go there, one weekend, and Strike – in the spirit of giving a real relationship a chance – had agreed.

Henry had already opened the enormous Smeg fridge-freezer when Strike arrived in the minimalist kitchen.

'There's Heineken or Peroni.'

'Heineken, please,' said Strike. 'Can I ask you something, Henry?'

'What?' said Henry, his tone suspicious. He was a full foot shorter than the detective and appeared to resent having to look up at him.

'Your mother told me you used to watch *The Ink Black Heart.*'

'Yeah,' said Henry, still sounding suspicious as he opened drawers, looking for a bottle-opener.

'I've never seen it. What's it about?'

'Dunno,' said Henry with an irritable half-shrug. 'What goes on in a cemetery after dark.'

He opened and shut another drawer and then, slightly to Strike's surprise, volunteered more information.

'It went off. It used to be funnier. They sold out.'

'Who did?'

'The people who made it.'

'The two who were stabbed yesterday?'

'What?' said Henry, looking round at Strike.

'The two people who created it were stabbed in Highgate Cemetery yesterday afternoon. The police have just released their names.'

'Ledwell and Blay?' said Henry. 'Stabbed in Highgate Cemetery?'

'Yeah,' said Strike. 'She's dead. He's critical.'

'Fuck,' said Henry, then, catching himself, he said, 'I mean—'

'No,' said Strike. 'Fuck's about right.'

Something adjacent to a smile flickered briefly on Henry's face. He'd found a bottle-opener. After prising off the cap he said,

'D'you want a glass?'

'I'm good with the bottle,' said Strike, and Henry passed it to him.

'Are you investigating it?' asked Henry, looking sideways at Strike.

'The stabbings? No.'

'Who do they think did it?'

'Don't think they know yet.' Strike took a swig of beer. 'There's a character called Drek in the cartoon, isn't there?'

'Yeah,' said Henry. 'That was what went downhill. He was the main reason I watched it. He used to be really funny ... Is she seriously dead? Ledwell?'

Strike resisted the urge to reply, 'Not seriously. Only a bit.'

'She is, yeah.'

'Wow,' said Henry. He looked more puzzled than sad. Strike remembered being sixteen: death, unless of your very nearest or dearest, was a distant and almost incomprehensible abstraction.

'I heard the voice actor who played Drek was sacked,' Strike said.

'Yeah,' said Henry. 'It was after they sacked Wally it all turned to shit. Got too PC.'

'What's Wally's full name?'

'Wally Cardew,' said Henry, now with a little renewed suspicion. 'Why?'

'Did he manage to get another job, d'you know?'

'Yeah, he's a YouTuber now.'

'Ah,' said Strike. 'And what does that entail?'

'What d'you—?'

'What does he do on YouTube?'

'Makes gaming videos and stuff,' said Henry, his tone comparable to an adult explaining what the prime minister does to a toddler.

'Right.'

'He's on tonight,' said Henry, glancing at the clock on the cooker. 'Eleven o'clock.'

Strike checked his watch.

'D'you need to subscribe to YouTube to watch?'

'No,' said Henry, wincing in further embarrassment at this ignorance.

'Well, thanks for the beer. And the information.'

''S'all right,' muttered Henry, sidling back out of the kitchen.

Strike remained where he was, leaning up against the side, facing the fridge. After drinking some more lager he took his mobile out of his pocket, opened YouTube and searched for Wally Cardew.

He now understood Henry's scorn at his ignorance: the ex-Drek voice actor had over a hundred thousand subscribers to his YouTube channel. Sipping Heineken, Strike scrolled slowly down through the archived videos. The still shots beside the titles all featured Cardew pulling a comical face: clutching his head in despair, wide-mouthed in hysterical laughter or yelling in triumph while giving a fist-pump.

Cardew bore a strong physical resemblance to a young soldier Strike had investigated while still in the SIB, one Private Dean Shaw, who'd had exactly the same combination of tow-coloured hair, pink-and-white skin and small, bright blue eyes. Shaw had been court-martialled for what he'd insisted was a prank gone wrong, which had resulted in the fatal shooting of a sixteen-year-old recruit. Reflecting ruefully that he'd now reached the age where almost everyone he met reminded him of somebody else he'd known, Strike continued to scroll through Cardew's list of videos.

The YouTuber's hairstyle varied according to the year in which the video had been filmed. Three years previously, he'd worn his white-blond hair to his shoulders, but it was now much shorter. Most of his videos were headlined *The Wally Shows MJ Show*. Strike assumed MJ was the cheery-looking, chubby-faced, bearded, brown-skinned young man who appeared next to Wally in some of the pictures, sidekick to the star.

Strike stopped scrolling at a video dating from 2012, entitled 'The Ink Black Fart', which had been viewed ninety thousand times. He pressed play. Long-haired Wally and short-haired MJ appeared, sitting side by side at a desk, each in a large padded leather chair. The wall behind them was covered in gaming posters.

'So, yeah, hi, ev'ryone,' said Wally, whose accent was pure working-class London, not dissimilar to Madeline's. He was holding a piece of what looked like headed notepaper. 'Just wan'ed to update you all on what my, ah, erstwhile friends've sent me. Fink it's called a "cease and desist" letter.'

'Yeah,' said MJ, nodding.

'MJ there, tryna look like he understands legals,' said Wally to camera, and MJ laughed.

'My uncle's a lawyer, man!'

'Yeah? Mine's a fuckin' gynaecologist, but I don't get to shove my fingers up random women.'

'Is he a gynaecologist? Seriously?' said MJ, giggling.

'No, you melt, I'm jokin' . . . So, yeah, basically I'm not allowed to use Drek's voice any more, or 'is catchphrases or . . .'

He consulted the letter, reading from it:

'" . . . any intellectual property of Edie Ledwell and Joshua Blay, 'ereinafter called *the creators*". So . . . yeah. There ya go.'

'Fuckin' bullshit, man,' said MJ, shaking his head.

'Hey,' said Wally, as though struck by a sudden thought. 'Would your uncle represent me for free?'

MJ looked taken aback. Wally laughed.

'I'm kiddin', man, but' – he looked back to camera – 'yeah, so I guess – no more Drek from me, bwahs.'

'Careful!' said MJ.

'It's fuckin'—'

'Yeah, it is,' said MJ soberly. 'It's shit.'

'I pretty much created the voice, the character an' everyfing, but you can't make fuckin' jokes any more, apparently, you can't be satirical, you can't take the piss –'

The camera zoomed in suddenly, so that Wally's face appeared in extreme close-up.

'OR CAN YOU?' thundered Wally, his voice artificially manipulated so that it echoed.

When the camera moved to wide shot again, the two men were in the middle of an all-white space. MJ was now lolling in his chair, pretending to be half-asleep, and wearing a long dark brown wig, a denim shirt and ripped jeans, and smoking what appeared to be a gigantic joint. Wally had donned a light brown straggly wig, some badly applied lipstick and eyeliner, a T-shirt reading 'The Ink Black Fart' and a long floral skirt.

Speaking in a high-pitched Essex accent he said,

'So yeah . . . we was lying in the cemetery . . . you'd just copped a feel, hadn't you, Josh?'

'Yeah . . .' said MJ, sounding sleepy.

'An' we was smokin', wasn't we?'

'Yeah . . .'

'And then all this brilliance come floodin' out my brain. And that's 'ow we created *The Ink Black Fart*. Because when you fart, right, it's like a bit of the inner you is struggling to free itself, so it's a metaphor and it's kind of beau'iful and deep, innit?'

Wally raised one buttock off his chair and produced a loud and apparently genuine fart. MJ corpsed before saying in the same stoned voice as before:

'Metaphor, yeah . . .'

'I got the idea of the fart from my dead mum . . . she 'ad a big wind problem . . .'

MJ was convulsed with barely suppressed laughter.

'And we ain't interested in cash, are we, Josh?'

'Nah . . .'

'We're two free spirits, innit. We want the whole world to enjoy my brilliance for free.'

'Free . . . yeah . . .'

'Which is why we don't pay no one, innit, Josh?'

MJ silently offered Wally a toke on his joint.

'No, Joshy babes, I gotta keep my head clear for negotiations wiv Netflix. Whoops, wait – did I say that out loud? Did I? Shit. Well anyway, fanks ev'ryone, I 'ope you all keep watching *The Ink Black Fart*.'

Wally produced a second fart.

'Oooh, that's better. Right, c'mon babes,' he said, getting up and taking hold of MJ by the shirt, 'you gotta draw Harty.'

'I need a proper slug, Ed,' moaned MJ. 'I'm blunted.'

'You come wiv me, you lazy bastard, we got money to make. Art, I mean. Art to m—'

'What the *hell* are you watching?'

Strike paused the video and looked around. Madeline was standing in the kitchen doorway.

'YouTubers,' said Strike.

Grinning, Madeline walked barefoot towards him in her pale grey cashmere sweater and jeans, slid her arms around his neck and kissed him on the mouth. She tasted of Merlot.

'Sorry about that, I had to get the design down while it was clear in my head. Sometimes you get an idea and you've just got to go with it.'

'No problem. Those were some pretty big rubies or whatever—'

'They're glass – I don't keep any real gems at home, it's an insurance nightmare. I use paste stones to help me figure out ideas sometimes. I need another drink,' she added, releasing him to reach up to the wine rack on the wall and extract a bottle. 'I've had a *nightmare* of a day. I forgot I'd agreed to give an interview to some jewellery blogger who's barely out of her teens – I don't want to generalise, but some of them really are little shits. All she wanted to know was whether everything's ethically sourced – where's the fucking corkscrew gone? – and because I couldn't say I *personally* go down to fucking Colombia and dig every emerald out of the rock and give every second stone to orphans or whatever – I mean, I make every effort to buy ethically, but you should have heard her on the – on the –'

Madeline was struggling to open the bottle. Strike put his mobile back in his pocket and held out his hands.

'Thanks – I ripped off a nail opening the last one. Yeah, so she was banging on about blood diamonds, and I . . .'

Carrying the newly opened bottle of wine and his own beer, he followed Madeline back through to the open-plan area, from which Henry had disappeared, where she dropped back down onto the sofa, talking all the while about the illegal mining of gold in Latin America and the various efforts she and fellow jewellers had made to ensure that their raw materials weren't produced under exploitative or criminal conditions. Strike replenished her glass and sat down too; he had the impression that Madeline was still justifying herself to an invisible interlocutor. His stomach rumbled. He'd been hoping, if not for a home-cooked meal, then at least for Madeline to suggest a takeaway.

'Mum,' called Henry from the top of the stairs, 'I'm going to Dad's.'

'When will you be—?'

But Henry had already run downstairs. They heard the door slam.

'Was he rude to you?' said Madeline, frowning. 'He's in a foul mood because his laptop's buggered. That's why he's using my PC.'

'No, he was quite forthcoming, actually,' said Strike.

'Really? That makes a change. You're good with him, actually. Jim totally screwed him up.'

Strike had already heard a good deal about how her ex-husband, the actor who'd left Madeline for his leading lady, had betrayed Henry's trust, but he maintained an expression of interest through a few further examples. His stomach rumbled again. When Madeline paused to down half her glass of wine he said, hoping to nudge her thoughts towards food,

'I'm sorry I couldn't do dinner—'

'Oh, no problem, I can hardly complain about you having work issues, I have enough myself. Anyway . . .'

She wriggled closer to him on the sofa and slid her arms around his neck again.

'. . . you can make it up to me now.'

An hour later, Strike lay naked in the darkness of Madeline's all-white bedroom, thoroughly satisfied in one sense, but not enough to make him forget his gnawing hunger. He supposed you didn't remain as slim as Madeline without eating sparingly, but a starvation diet wasn't really his style, even if he could stand to lose a bit of weight. Madeline's head lay on his shoulder, her hair tickling his face. One hand was splayed on his hairy chest.

'God, that was g-good,' she yawned. 'Sorry, I'm so tired . . . I had to be up at five for a call to L . . . to LA . . .'

He kissed the top of her head, then said,

'D'you mind if I fix myself something to eat?'

'No, darling, help yourself,' she murmured. Removing her head from his shoulder, she rolled away from him onto the other side of the bed, and as he pulled on his trousers and shirt in the dark, fearing an encounter with Henry, he thought he heard a soft snore.

The upper floor of the house was silent. Strike walked barefoot to the kitchen, his prosthesis making a dull clunk on the floorboards at every other step. The fridge, as he'd feared, contained little he wanted to eat. He rummaged unenthusiastically among pots of quinoa salad, zero-fat yoghurt and packs of avocados, thinking wistfully of bacon and eggs, or a large bag of chips. Finally he dug out a bit of pecorino, made himself a doorstep sandwich and opened another bottle of Heineken.

The clock on the cooker told him that it was ten o'clock. It felt far later. He moved to the window and looked out into the rainy street: the cobbles below looked as shiny as jet in the light cast by the streetlamps. After a while, Strike found a plate, took his sandwich and his beer back through to the dark sitting area and sat down at the computer.

He knew the password because Madeline had given it to him the last time he'd been here, when his phone battery was out of charge and he'd wanted to look up the details of the flight Fingers would be taking back to London. He turned the PC on, entered the password *spessartite19*, whiled away nearly an hour reading the news and doing emails and then, at eleven, opened Wally Cardew's YouTube channel just in time to join his livestream.

The gaming posters in the background had changed, and so had Wally and MJ. Cardew now wore his white-blond hair close cropped at the sides and a little longer on top. MJ's face was thinner than it had been in 2012, his hair neater. Both men were looking sombre and, in MJ's case, a little anxious.

'Hi, bwahs,' said Wally. 'Welcome to another episode of *The Wally Shows MJ Show*, and before we get started I – we –'

He glanced at MJ, who nodded.

'We wanna say first, OK, something properly 'orrible happened – er – yesterday, but we just found out about it today—'

'People have been, like, callin' us for the last five hours,' chipped in MJ, 'goin', "Did you know, did you know?"'

'Yeah,' said Wally, nodding, 'an' the answer is, no, we didn't know, we never knew nuffing until we seen it on the news. Anyway – yeah – we're talking about what's happened to Josh Blay and Edie Ledwell, in case you didn't know, and it's – it's fucked up, man, an' we don't know any more than you lot do, but it's seriously fucked up. An' I wanna, like, extend my condolences to their families and I'm, you know, I got everything crossed for Josh and we're – I dunno, do you pray, MJ?'

'Yeah, man,' said MJ quietly. 'I pray.'

'Me,' said Wally, throwing out his hands, 'I dunno what the fuck I believe, but we're finking of the families and we just hope Josh makes it, you know?'

'Yeah, we do,' said MJ, nodding. 'Seriously. We do.'

Wally sighed, slapped his thighs and said,

'OK, so, we got a special show lined up for you tonight – and don't forget, bwahs, this month we're donatin' twenty-five per cent of all merch purchased to Great Ormond Street Hospital, because, as some of you know, MJ's—'

'My little cousin, yeah, he's bein' treated for leukaemia there,' said MJ.

'So,' said Wally, 'let's get the old commentarium up an' runnin' . . .'

A rolling feed of viewer comments now appeared in the top right-hand corner of the screen, the text neon yellow scrolling upwards so fast that it was difficult to keep up. MJ's eyes were flickering from the camera to a side screen, checking on the comments viewers could see.

Drekfan10:	I love you Wally and MJ!!!!!!!!!!
KeiraS:	Do Drek's voice Wal
Derky96:	nice tribute
Krayfish:	you guys are class
BDJoker:	I knew ledwlle and blay
Hyggard:	don't pretend ur sad lol
Sh0zelle:	Wally say hi to Shona and Deb!
RedPill*7:	the only good sjw is a dead sjw
Chigginz:	I bought three T-shirts gimme a shoutout

'So,' said Wally, 'on wiv the show! First . . . need a few fings out from under here –'

He reached beneath the desk.

'Hold that for me, MJ.'

Wally had pulled out a large knife, which appeared to be covered in blood. MJ let out a cross between a yelp and a gasp, then clapped his hands over his face, trying to suppress his nervous laughter.

'Fuck!' said MJ to camera through his fingers. 'Fuck, I didn't know he was gonna do that, I swear I didn't!'

Deadpan, Wally said, 'Whassamatter? Oh, *this*?' He licked the blade. 'Tomato sauce, man, I was cuttin' a pizza.'

'Shit, Wal,' said MJ, lowering his hands and giggling.

'OK,' said Wally with a shrug, 'if you don't wanna hold it . . .' He threw the knife over his shoulder and then brought up a stack of papers from under the desk.

'No, because this is the theme of today's show, innit. I've been getting a lot of action on the old Twitter since the news about Ledwell and Blay came out, loads of action. I posted my condolences or whatever and basically I've 'ad a ton of people tellin' me I killed Edie Ledwell, so I fort we'd 'ave a look at some of 'em. Let's see what we've got . . . This is a good one.'

Wally picked up the top sheet of paper and began to read. The tweet flashed up behind him, beside the rolling comments.

The Coffin Fly @carla_mappin5
replying to @the_Wally_Cardew

how dare you say ur sad, you fucking hypocrite. You've
demonised Ledwell and Blay ever since you were rightly
sacked. Hate kills.

3.15 pm   13 February 2015

'"Hate kills",' repeated Wally, looking seriously into the camera.

'Wow,' said MJ, shaking his head. 'You feel rebuked, man?'

'I'll be honest, mate, it's made me refink my whole, like, effical system,' said Wally. 'I mean, turns out I'm an accomplice to murder because I took the piss out of *The Ink Black Heart* ... So,' he said to camera, 'I 'ad a little look at how Carla Mappin wants us all to behave online, so I can, y'know, learn from my betters.'

'Use her as a role model,' said MJ, nodding.

''Zactly,' said Wally. 'So this is one of Carla's from late last year ...'

A new tweet appeared behind Wally as he read it aloud.

The Coffin Fly @carla_mappin5
replying to @AnomieGamemaster

honestly at this point the bitch can choke. all that BS
about doing it for love not money #stopfeedingFedwell
#IstandwithJosh

9.02 pm   2 November 2014

'"The bitch can choke", ladies and gentlemen,' repeated Wally.

'What bitch is this?' asked MJ. Strike could tell they'd rehearsed this bit. Only the knife had been a surprise. 'Is it, like, a dog she's tryna rescue, got too big a bone, or—?'

Wally gave a little snort of laughter.

'No, funny enough, MJ, Carla was talkin' about Edie Ledwell. "The bitch can choke",' he said again, staring down the camera lens with his small blue eyes.

'Wal,' said MJ, whose gaze was temporarily fixed on something off camera, 'got a few shout-outs here. We've been shifting some merch – Chigginz, you bought three T-shirts: nice one, mate. BD Joker – I'm guessin' these ain't real names.'

'Thanks, BD,' said Wally, 'enjoy your Wally an' MJ baseball cap.'

'And Sooze an' Lily, pair of sweatshirts – thanks ladies!'

'OK, so back to the ol' Twitter,' said Wally, returning to his stack of papers. 'Let's see what else we got here . . . Yeah, this is a good one.'

The comments continued to roll past almost faster than Strike could read them.

motherofdrags:	sjws 'when I said trash I meant it in a good way' lol
LostInSpunk:	sjws such fkn hypocites lolololol
@Heimd&ll88:	fucking loving this
hotrod209:	living for u stickin it to the sjws bro
RubyLoob:	Ledwell was the epitome of white privilege
arniep:	suck my cock
LilaP:	I love u Wally xxxxxxxxxxxxxx
ArkeTheShadow:	it's ok to celebrate when bad people die
TheFiend:	what won't you do for views you pos?
TommyEngland14:	wally check out brotherhoodofultimathule.com

'OK,' said Wally, shuffling the papers, 'and now we've got – oh, this is my personal favourite, I fuckin' love this one. Andi Reddy – real name, look, there it is . . .

Andi Reddy @ydderidna
replying to @the_Wally_Cardew

U might not have held the knife, but u fanned the flames and if it turns out some far-right troll did this u should be prosecuted.

6.52 pm   13 February 2015

'Andi certainly seems to know the law, eh?' said Wally.

'Probably a judge,' said MJ. 'Nice of her to say you might not have held the knife, though.'

'Shall we see how Andi goes about not fanning the flames of hate?'

'Go on,' said MJ, starting to giggle again.

Andi's second tweet appeared over their heads. Again, Wally read it out loud.

Andi Reddy @ydderidna
replying to @AnomieGamemaster

can somebody tell that vile, mercenary bitch to take a dirt nap.
#stopfeedingFedwell #IstandwithJosh

11.45 am   29 July 2014

Both Wally and MJ roared with laughter.

'But it gets better,' said Wally through his guffaws. 'Wait – there's another one – it really shows her fuckin' non-flame-fannin' nature.'

A new tweet appeared.

Andi Reddy @ydderidna

the only thing that wd console me 4 the shitstorm my fave has bcm is #Fedwell shut up inside a big plastic Drek & seeing it lit on fire

10.34 pm   16 September 2014

As Wally and MJ broke into a fresh storm of thigh-slapping laughter, Strike heard a movement behind him and swiftly muted the livestream. Henry had returned. He looked disconcerted to see what Strike was watching.

'You got me interested,' said Strike.

'Oh,' said Henry.

They looked at each other, their faces in semi-darkness, the only light issuing from the computer screen.

'Goinga bed,' muttered Henry, and he retreated downstairs.

Strike unmuted the computer and turned back to the livestream. Wally and MJ were still doubled up with laughter at the last tweet Wally had read out. The comments continued to roll rapidly upwards.

algizzard:	Wal check out thebrotherhoodofultimathule.com
GillyInkHeart:	Wally say hi to your gran for me!
ArkeTheShadow:	Ledwell was a thief and a liar
saxonaxe14:	all the lib tears when yesterday they were calling her a cunt

119

dmitriplayssax:	Wally say hi to me Dmitri
PokerFac£:	wally r u fucking kea niven?
LepinesDisciple:	I killed Ledwell
TattyB:	yeah, not actually sad an ableist racist died
MGTOWise:	show those receipts boi this is class! ! !
SophieBeee:	I bought a T-shirt say hello to Soph Brown
BwahBoy88:	Wally ditch the sandn*****
aoifeoconnor:	people were angry about Netflix that's all
Sammmitchell:	people say things in heat of moment
UltimaBro88:	all the little SJW foids tryna cover their tracks lololololololololololololol

14

The one-bedroomed flat in Walthamstow that Robin viewed on Sunday afternoon was the first she'd seen in which she could imagine herself happily living. It was situated on the second floor of a recently developed block: clean and light, it had space for a sofa-bed in the living area should a friend wish to stay over, and was close to Blackhorse Road Tube station.

'I'll let you know,' she told the estate agent. 'Has there been a lot of interest?'

'Quite a bit,' said the young man in the kipper tie, whose relentless banter Robin could gladly have done without. He'd asked her twice whether she'd be living alone. Robin wondered what he'd have said if she'd asked him tearfully to move in with her, so she didn't have to endure the agony of singledom any longer.

After bidding the estate agent goodbye, she walked to the Tube station, timing the journey as she went. She'd have a longer commute than from her present flat, but not as lengthy as from some of the properties she'd seen. All things considered, she really thought the flat would do. Travelling home, she wondered who she'd be bidding against: she had a decent deposit, which she'd managed to wrest with difficulty from the marital joint account as part of her divorce settlement, and she was earning a far better salary than she'd started on, but you never knew in London.

Robin's mood had been low all through the cold, wet weekend, and once she left Earl's Court station into the rain, the lightening of spirits she'd experienced imagining herself living in that neat, bright little flat began to subside.

Max was spending the weekend in the country, along with Wolfgang the dachshund. Once home, Robin stripped off her coat and gloves, fetched her laptop from her bedroom and carried it upstairs into the living area, where her eye fell on the unwelcome Valentine's card she'd received the previous day from Hugh 'Axeman' Jacks, which she'd left lying on the kitchen side. The front featured a St Bernard with a heart-shaped cask on its collar and the words 'You Make Me Drool'. Inside the card Hugh had written 'if you're ever at a loose end' and his phone number. Robin supposed the St Bernard was meant to evoke happy memories of Switzerland, but as Hugh had been her least favourite part of the holiday, the only emotion was irritation that Katie had given Hugh her address. Still fighting a feeling of depression, she binned the card before making herself coffee, then sat down to peruse news sites for any fresh information about the stabbings in Highgate Cemetery.

Josh Blay was still alive, though he remained in a critical condition, and the police had released a new detail: both animators had been tasered before being stabbed. The public were still being encouraged to call the information hotline if they'd seen anybody acting suspiciously in the cemetery between 4 and 6 p.m. on 12 February.

The possession and use of tasers by civilians was illegal, so Robin wondered where and how the killer had got their hands on one. Had it been smuggled in from the Continent? Stolen? Surely its use suggested that this had been a premeditated crime, not a killing born of impulse? She wished Strike were here, to talk it all over.

A fresh news alert from the BBC popped up on her laptop. There'd been two separate terrorist shootings in Copenhagen: the first at an exhibition called *Art, Blasphemy and Freedom of Expression*, the second at a synagogue. The hard lump of misery in Robin's chest seemed to grow heavier. Human beings slaughtered for writing words, for making drawings: Edie Ledwell couldn't, surely, be one of them? What was there in that peculiar little cartoon that could so offend and enrage that the creators would be deemed worthy of assassination?

Articles about *The Ink Black Heart* had proliferated in the last twenty-four hours. Robin skimmed through recapitulations of its journey to unexpected success, analysis of its cultural significance and meaning, assessments of its appeal and flaws, and speculation as to its likely future. Nearly every one of these articles began by noting the strange irony of Ledwell meeting her death in the cemetery where she and Blay had set the cartoon: 'a grotesque symmetry', 'an almost unbelievable coincidence', 'a horrible end that had all the gothic strangeness of her creation'.

Thousands of words had also been expended on the cartoon's fandom, 'who call themselves Inkhearts and are notorious for their internecine wars'. These rows were evidently continuing to flourish in the wake of the attacks on the creators; hating herself for clicking on the link, Robin read a short piece entitled 'The Inkheart Murder Theory That's Causing Outrage' and learned that there was specu-lation on social media that Josh Blay had stabbed Edie Ledwell then attempted to kill himself, a charge that was being vehemently denied and refuted by Blay's fans, who, Robin noticed, appeared to greatly outnumber those of Ledwell.

Robin moved to YouTube, intending to watch a full episode of *The Ink Black Heart*. However, her attention was immediately caught by a video called 'Josh Blay and Edie Ledwell First Ever Interview'. It was dated June 2010 and was currently getting a lot of views.

Robin clicked on the video and pressed play.

Edie Ledwell and Josh Blay appeared sitting side by side on a single bed, backs against a wall on which were pinned a mass of line draw-ings, clippings from magazines and postcard-sized reproductions of paintings. Edie's hair was longer than it had been when Robin met her, shiny and well-brushed. She was wearing a pair of jeans and what looked like a man's blue shirt with the sleeves rolled up.

Josh, who was wearing a similar shirt to Edie's, was extraordinarily handsome. With his long dark hair, very square jaw, high cheekbones and large blue eyes, he could have been a rock star. Robin knew from news reports that he was five years younger than Edie, so back in 2010 he'd been twenty.

'Yeah, awight?' Josh said in a cockney accent. He gave a sheepish wave, then he and Edie looked at each other and laughed. The person holding the camera laughed too.

'Er . . .' said Josh, looking back to camera, 'so, yeah, we've 'ad a lotta nice feedback abou' the firs' two episodes of *The Ink Black 'Eart*, so we, er, fort we'd say 'ow much we appreciate it. An' our friend Katya fort it'd be good if we answered some of the, um, questions you guys 'ave been postin' under the animations, so, yeah, tha's what we're gonna do.'

He said it diffidently, as though worried people might think the video had been the creators' own egotistical idea.

'F'rinstance,' Josh continued, 'we've been asked "Are you stoned?" a lot.'

He laughed, as did the person holding the camera, which wobbled slightly. Josh and Edie were sitting so close that their arms were touching from shoulder to elbow.

'Short answer—' said Edie.

'We were, yeah,' said Josh. 'To be honest, we totally were. Tim is, right now.'

His eyes flicked upwards to the person holding the camera. The unseen Tim said in a Home Counties accent, 'I'm not, that's a filthy lie.'

Josh now looked sideways at Edie and they smiled at each other, the unmistakeable smiles of two people who are completely smitten.

'So, er – do we introduce ourselves, or wha'?'

'Well, there's nobody else here to do it,' said Edie, 'unless Tim wants to – actually, let's introduce Tim.'

The camera swung upwards: a dizzying shot of the ceiling was succeeded by a blurry close-up of a young man with red hair.

'Hi,' he said.

The camera moved back to Edie and Josh.

'That was Tim,' said Edie. 'He does the voice of The Worm. So, I'm Edie—'

'Yeah, an' I'm Josh, and we, er, got the idea for *The Ink Black 'eart* when we was in 'Ighgate Cemetery one afternoon—'

'Smoking,' came Tim's voice.

'Feelin' crea'ive,' said Josh, mock-dignified.

'And we were talking,' said Edie.

'A loada shit—'

'You might've been,' said Edie.

'No, I was bein' insigh'ful an' profound,' said Josh, and then, pointing sideways at Edie while leaning into her, he said to camera, 'No, it's 'er, really, it's all 'er fault this 'appened. We were talkin' abou' the, you know, the people wha' are buried there—'

'Yeah,' said Edie, 'really thinking about the fact that we were lying like feet from actual corpses.'

'Freakin' ourselves ou'.'

'You were freaking out, I wasn't—'

''Cause you're a freak.'

Edie laughed.

'You are, Ed, I'm not sayin' you're a serial killer or wha'ever, you're jus' ... creepy ... No, so, she starts imaginin' what 'appens at night and all these fuckin' surreal ideas—'

'Katya told you not to swear on this.'

'Bit fuckin' late for that.'

Edie laughed.

'So, yeah, all these ideas start comin' out of Edie and we was lying there, like, makin' all this stuff up ...'

'And then we got chucked out of the cemetery, because it was closing time,' said Edie, 'so we went home – we should say we live at an art collective, in a big old house—'

'Why should we say that?'

'I dunno ... To explain our "process"?'

'We 'aven't got a process, mate, ours is not a process.'

Edie laughed again.

'OK, well, whatever, we went back to the house and Josh drew – who did you draw first?'

''Arty, an' you drew Drek. We're bofe art students,' he told the camera.

'I'm not. You are. You were a proper one.'

'I go' chucked outta St Martin's,' Josh informed the audience. 'For bein' a slacker.'

'Yeah,' said Edie, 'so we drew the characters for fun, some of the ideas we'd had while we were – er—'

'Stoned,' said Tim off screen.

'—in the cemetery,' said Edie, grinning, 'and yeah, so it kind of—'

'Escala'ed—' said Josh.

'Developed, I was gonna say.'

'—from there. An' our friend Seb 'elped us animate the first one,' Josh continued. 'Seb's proper, 'e's still at St Martin's. An' we got some mates to voice the characters an' then we 'ad the firs' episode, and then Edie 'ad more ideas so, yeah, we did anuvver one.'

'And,' said Edie, 'we didn't expect – we were really, really surprised how much people liked it, which is why we wanted to say how much we appreciate your comments. So, um, we're gonna answer the most frequently asked questions now.'

Josh reached out of shot for a piece of lined paper that had evidently been torn out of a notebook, glanced at it, then said to camera,

'Right, so 'ere's one we've been asked a lot: "Where did you get the idea for 'Arty?"' He looked sideways at Edie. 'You need to answer that, because I 'ave no idea what goes on in your 'ead.'

'OK, so I don't really know how I thought of Harty except I think, when I was a kid, my mum told me a fairy tale about a stone heart . . . Is that a real thing, or have I imagined it? So I . . . I don't know, I've got this memory of being told a story of somebody swapping their heart with a stone and I had a mental image of a heart leaving a chest. So then when we were in the cemetery I had this idea of somebody evil – about their heart surviving and trying to do better after their death. Like, the owner turned it black through all the bad things they did, so the heart has sort of survived when the rest of the body's rotted, because it's—'

'—pickled in evil,' said Josh with relish.

'Kind of, but – no, because, isn't Harty, like, the nicest character in the whole thing?'

'Yeah, 'e is, I s'pose,' said Josh slowly. ''E's innocent . . . but 'e's not, though, is 'e? Because 'e's turned black, because of all the evil 'e did.'

'But he didn't do it,' said Edie. The two of them were absorbed in each other now, the camera temporarily forgotten. 'Harty gets blamed for it, he gets stigmatised, but he was a victim of the – the brain and the will, or whatever. He's trying to do better, but he's grotesque, so nobody believes he's good.'

She turned to look at the camera again.

'Did any of that make sense? No. Next question.'

'"Is Paperwhite s'posed to be a bitch?"' Josh read from his piece of paper. He looked up at the camera. 'Yeah.'

'No!' said Edie, half-indignant, half-amused.

'She is, though. She won' ever give 'Arty a chance.'

'She's just a bit – um – we've never analysed any of this.'

'That,' said Josh, 'will be pretty fuckin' clear to anyone 'oo's watched the cartoon.'

All laughed, including Tim. A beeping sounded.

'Shit, that's mine,' said Josh, 'forgotta turn it off . . .'

'We're so professional,' said Edie to the audience.

'It's from Katya,' said Josh, reading a message on his phone. '"Did you get round to makin' a video answerin' fans' questions because I fink it would be . . ." "Doin' . . ."' he read aloud as he typed and Tim laughed again, '" . . . it . . . right . . . now." Aaand mute.'

He tossed the phone onto the bed.

'Wha' were we sayin'?'

'About Paperwhite. She wants to be alive again. She hates being a ghost.'

'She *is* kind of a bitch, though.'

'Well, she's stuck among all these—'

'Freaks, yeah.'

'—ambulant body parts,' said Edie, and Josh laughed. 'Nobody would *want* to be stuck there for ever.'

'OK,' said Josh, picking up his piece of paper again. 'Nex' question. Drek. "What is Drek?"'

They looked at each other and laughed again.

'We don't know,' said Josh.

'We genuinely don't know what Drek is.'

'You drew 'im,' said Josh.

'His head, yeah – I saw this mask, ages ago, and it was one of those –'

Edie mimed a huge beak.

'– plague doctor's masks? Like a huge beaky nose and little eyes, and I thought it was really creepy. So . . . he's a bit sinister, Drek is.'

'But wha' *is* 'e?'

'I genuinely don't know,' said Edie, starting to laugh. 'What d'*you* think he is?'

'Fuck knows. Maybe that's episode free. "What the fuck is Drek?" Nex' question . . . "What are smugliks an' mukfluks?"'

At this, both Josh and Edie doubled up with laughter, bumping into each other, gasping for breath. Both had tears in their eyes by the time they composed themselves.

'We can' answer that,' said Josh in a falsetto.

'We can't put the answer into words,' said Edie breathlessly.

'You'll know a smuglik when you meet one,' said Josh, fighting his laughter. 'An' a mukfluk.'

They both subsided into hysterics again. The unseen Tim was also laughing: the camera shook. At last, Josh said,

'OK, let's get a grip 'ere . . . so . . . this is a serious question.' He brandished the piece of paper. '"D'you know the work of Jan Pieńkowski, because your animation reminds me of 'is illustrations." Yeah! We love 'is stuff. 'E's an influence. My mum gave me a book of 'is, what was published in the seventies.'

Edie now leaned offscreen and came back into shot holding a book of illustrated fairy tales.

'This is it. I'd never heard of Jan before Josh showed it to me and now I'm, like, his biggest fan.'

She opened the book, showing viewers the pictures.

'See? He did these incredible silhouettes against marbled paper. Aren't they amazing?'

'OK,' said Josh again, 'movin' on. Got anuvver ques-question 'ere.' He was fighting laughter again.

'"D'you – d'you fink there'll ever be a movie made of the—"'

He and Edie dissolved again into uproarious laughter.

'—of the – of *The Ink Black 'Eart*? Yeah ... no, in all 'onesty ... that'll never 'appen. Jesus, can you imagine? A movie of ...'

'Yeah, no,' said Edie, dabbing at her eyes, 'I can't somehow ...'

'Smugliks an' mukfluks would not wanna see that movie,' said Josh.

'So, um, is that all the questions?' asked Edie.

'There's one more. "Are you guys boyfriend and girlfriend?"'

Still out of breath from laughing, they contemplated each other in their almost-matching shirts, arms touching, both leaning back against the wall covered in pictures.

'Um ...' said Edie.

'Are we comf'table puttin' that out there?' Josh asked her.

'Yeah, good point. What if the paparazzi come calling?'

'It's a concern,' said Josh. He turned to look at the camera. 'We request privacy at this difficult time.'

'That's what you say when you split up,' said Edie, 'not when you say you're together.'

'Ah, sorry,' said Josh. 'I didn't read the 'ole 'Andbook for Slebs, jus' the last page.'

'How does it end?'

'Well, no spoilers, but badly.'

'Drink and drugs?'

'No, that's now.'

Edie and Tim laughed. Edie turned back to the camera.

'If any kids are watching, we're joking.'

Behind her back, Josh mouthed 'We're not'.

The video ended.

Robin stared at the frozen image for a few seconds – Josh Blay and his beautiful, wide smile, Edie beaming as she leaned into him, amber eyes bright – then, in spite of her best efforts, she put her face in her hands, and wept.

PART TWO

The arteries undergo enormous ramification in their course
throughout the body,
and end in very minute vessels, called arterioles, which in
their turn open
into a close-meshed network of microscopic vessels, termed
capillaries.

Henry Gray FRS
Gray's Anatomy

15

Who spoke of evil, when young feet were flying
In fairy rings around the echoing hall?

Felicia Hemans
Pauline

A full month had passed since Edie Ledwell had been found dead in Highgate Cemetery, but the newspapers had reported no new leads. Robin, who checked regularly for updates, knew Josh Blay remained hospitalised, his condition no longer critical but serious. Otherwise, there was a dearth of information.

'Maybe Blay didn't see the attacker?' Robin wondered aloud to Strike one night in Sloane Square, where the latter had arrived to take over surveillance of Fingers. Their target, who lived on the third floor of a large building with a department store at its base, still hadn't gone anywhere near South Audley Street or shown any sign of trying to dispose of the casket or the sculpture that had vanished from his stepfather's house. To Robin, it beggared belief that a young man who could afford to live in the heart of Belgravia would have felt the need to steal from his stepfather, but a few years tracking the lives of the super-rich had taught her that these things were all relative. Perhaps, to Fingers, this was the equivalent of sneaking a tenner out of a parent's wallet.

'If Blay was tasered first, then attacked from behind, I'd doubt he saw much at all,' said Strike. 'Has our friend been outside at all today?' he added, looking up at the balconied windows behind which Fingers lived.

'No,' said Robin. 'But he had a heavy night last night. Barclay says he didn't get home till four.'

'Any news on your flat?' asked Strike, lighting a cigarette.

'I'm still trying to make up my mind how much it's worth to me,' said Robin, whose first offer had been rejected. 'I went to see a place in Tower Hamlets last night. It was the kind of place Dr Crippen would have felt at home in.'

Her feet were numb with cold, so she bade Strike goodnight shortly afterwards, leaving him to lean up against a conveniently positioned tree, the chilly air pinching his fingers as he smoked. Resigned to remaining in Sloane Square until at least 2 a.m., when it was usually safe to assume the young man was asleep, Strike's thoughts lingered briefly on Robin, then drifted to another couple of niggling personal dilemmas.

The first concerned Madeline, who'd called the previous evening to invite him to accompany her to the book launch of a well-known novelist friend. Strike could have pretended that he had to work that night, but instead had chosen to be honest and say that he had no desire to go anywhere, ever, that might result in his picture being in the paper.

Though there'd been no argument, he could tell from Madeline's tone that his refusal had gone down poorly and the subsequent discussion had led to Strike laying out what he saw as rules of engagement in fairly stark terms. He couldn't, he told her, work as a private detective while also appearing in the society pages of *Tatler*, drinking champagne with the literati of London.

'You've already been in *Tatler*,' said Madeline. 'Your agency was listed in their "25 Numbers You Never Knew You Needed".'

Strike hadn't been aware of this, though he supposed it might account for a slight recent increase in calls to the agency concerning the tracking of well-heeled spouses.

'I can't afford to become recognisable,' said Strike.

'Your picture's already *been* in the papers, though.'

'Always bearded and never by choice.'

'Why can't you come to the launch but tell them you don't want to be photographed?'

'I'd rather make sure of it by not turning up at the kinds of events where people go to be seen.'

'So what were you doing in Annabel's?'

'I was working,' said Strike, who hadn't previously admitted that he'd lied on the night they met.

'Were you?' said Madeline, distracted. 'Ohmigod – who were you investigating?'

'That's confidential. Look, I can't squire you to events where there are press. It'll ruin my business. I'm sorry, but there it is.'

'OK, fine,' she said, but there was a note in her voice that told him it wasn't fine, not really.

The phone call had left Strike with an unpleasant sense of déjà vu. His relationship with Charlotte seemed to have been a protracted battle over what kind of joint life they wanted to lead. Ultimately, there'd been no reconciling Strike's preference for a vocation that meant long hours and, at least in the beginning, very little money with Charlotte's desire to continue enjoying the milieu into which, after all, she'd been born: one of ease, celebrity and wealth.

With the possible exception of his friends Nick and Ilsa, Strike had never witnessed a relationship that didn't involve compromises he personally would have resisted. This, he supposed, was the selfishness of which Charlotte had constantly accused him. Night buses rattled past and Strike's cigarette smoke hung heavily in the chilly air as he cast his mind back to the time in Nightjar when Madeline had tried to turn her camera on both of them and wondered for the first time whether, for her, part of his attraction was his newsworthiness. It was an unpleasant thought. There being nothing to be gained from this unsatisfactory line of speculation, he turned his thoughts instead to the second of his personal dilemmas.

His half-sister Prudence, Jungian therapist and fellow illegitimate child of Jonny Rokeby, had been in touch again by email, asking whether he was free for a drink or dinner on three specific dates. He still hadn't answered her, largely because he hadn't decided whether he actually wanted to meet her.

It would have been easier had he been dead set against a meeting, but ever since Prudence had contacted him directly, over a year ago, he'd felt an odd pull towards her. Was it shared blood, or the fact that the two of them were bracketed together in being the accidental children, the illegitimates, two unwanted consequences of Rokeby's almost legendary promiscuity? Or did it have something to do with turning forty? Was he, in some unacknowledged part of himself, wanting to reckon with a past as painful as it was complicated?

But did he have room for another relationship, for another call on his time and his affections? Strike was starting to feel a certain strain at the amount of compartmentalisation his life seemed to entail. He was adept at sectioning off parts of his life; indeed, every woman he'd ever had a relationship with had complained of his facility in this respect. He told Madeline virtually nothing about his day-to-day life. He was concealing the fact that he was dating Madeline from Robin, for reasons he chose not to admit to himself. He was also avoiding any mention of Prudence to his half-sister Lucy. The idea of trying to forge a relationship with Prudence without Lucy finding out about it – because he was certain she wouldn't like it, that she'd feel she was being replaced in some way – might just add an unsustainable level of duplicity to a life already laden with other people's secrets, with professional pretence and subterfuge.

Strike stood in the cold square until two, by which time all the lights in Fingers' flat had gone out, and, after waiting a further half an hour to be absolutely sure that Fingers wasn't about to emerge, returned to his attic and went to bed, burdened by a faint feeling of persecution.

He'd intended to spend the following morning catching up on paperwork, but at eleven o'clock Fingers' stepfather rang in a temper from New York. His London housekeeper had found one of the hidden cameras the agency had installed.

'You need to replace it – and put it somewhere she won't find it this time,' the billionaire client snarled down the phone.

Strike agreed to take care of the job personally, rang off, then phoned Barclay to check where Fingers currently was.

'He's just gone intae James Purdey and Sons.'

'The gun shop?' said Strike, who'd already walked back into the outer office to take down his overcoat. 'That's near South Audley Street, is it?'

'Couple o' blocks away,' said Barclay. 'He's wi' a pal, that greasy-lookin' ponce wi' the beard.'

'Well, keep an eye on him, and if he looks like he's heading for the house let me know,' said Strike. 'I've just agreed to replace the camera immediately.'

'An' wha' if they bust in on ye with a shotgun?'

'I'll have advance warning, won't I, unless you're planning to take the rest of the afternoon off? But murder's a big step up from petty larceny,' said Strike.

'Nuthin' petty about his larceny,' said Barclay. 'Didn't you say that box thing he nicked was worth a quarter of a million?'

'Small change to this lot,' said Strike. 'Just keep me posted on his movements.'

The day was cloudy and cold. By the time Strike reached Mayfair, Barclay had texted that Fingers and friend had left the gun shop and were heading away from South Audley Street. Out of cigarettes, and relieved of the worry that he was about to walk into Fingers, Strike went into a newsagent's and joined a short queue. Pondering the best place to hide the new security camera so that the housekeeper wouldn't find it, Strike didn't immediately register that he was looking at the words 'Stabbing of animators' in a subheading on the front page of *The Times* lying on the counter.

'Twenty B&H, box of matches and this, please,' said Strike, holding up a copy of the newspaper, which he tucked under his arm before setting off again.

Their client had provided the agency with a set of keys to his house. Strike glanced up and down the road before letting himself in, then switched off the security alarm and proceeded into the echoing marble and gilded space, where art worth hundreds of thousands of pounds hung on the walls and sculptures just as valuable stood on artfully spot-lit plinths.

The security camera discovered by the housekeeper had been hidden in a false book on the shelves in the drawing room. After contemplating his options for a few minutes, Strike placed the new camera on top of a tall cabinet on the other side of the room. As it was concealed in a small black plastic box, hopefully it would be passed over by the housekeeper as having something to do with the internet or the existing security system.

Having shoved the box into place, Strike asked himself, not for the first time, whether the housekeeper could be as innocent as she seemed. Their client was adamant that she couldn't be the thief, because her references were impeccable, her salary generous and the risks involved in purloining objects of such value and distinctiveness surely too high for a woman who was sending money home to the Philippines every month. During the weeks she'd been unknowingly under surveillance, the housekeeper had been caught on film doing nothing more suspicious than taking a break to watch *The Jeremy Kyle Show* on the enormous flatscreen TV. On the other hand, Strike thought it remarkably conscientious to take out books and dust them individually – which was how she claimed to have found the security camera – given that her employers were likely to be absent for at least another six weeks.

New camera hidden, Strike reset the alarm, left the house and walked further along the street to Richoux, an Edwardian tearoom which had pavement tables where he could smoke. Having ordered himself a double espresso, Strike unfolded *The Times* and read the story that filled most of the front page.

FAR-RIGHT GROUP TARGETING MPS AND CELEBRITIES

A far-right group claiming responsibility for multiple fatalities has been uncovered in a joint operation by Scotland Yard's Counter Terrorism Command and security services, *The Times* has learned. The group is believed to have sent explosive devices to female MPs and has also claimed responsibility for the deaths of child star and animal rights activist Maya Satterthwaite (21), singer and climate change spokesperson Gigi Cazenove (23) and animator Edie Ledwell (30).

According to a source close to the investigation, the far-right group, which calls itself 'The Halvening', 'has modelled itself on paramilitaries and religious terror organisations'. Communicating with members on the dark web, it is organised into 'cells' which are given responsibility for specific jobs and targets. The Halvening has so far planned and carried out a number of lethal and potentially lethal acts of violence against prominent left-wing women.

'This is a sophisticated operation, which has not only planned and carried out direct attacks on elected politicians, but is capitalising on social media networks to recruit members, spread disinformation and ramp up hostility towards targets,' said a source.

The Times understands that the terror group has both a 'Direct Action' and 'Indirect Action' list. The Direct Action list is believed to include left-wing female MPs such as Amy Wittstock and Judith Marantz, whose constituency offices have both been sent explosive devices within the last 12 months. The pipe bombs were deactivated by specialist officers, without casualties. Those who are known to be on The Halvening's Direct Action list have been alerted to the fact and provided with increased security at both their homes and offices.

Stabbing of Animators

The terror group claims that its Indirect Action programme has been responsible for three fatalities, one attempted suicide and one serious injury. These include Maya Satterthwaite, who took a fatal overdose in April 2012, Gigi Cazenove, who was found hanged on New Year's Eve 2014, and Edie Ledwell, who was fatally stabbed in Highgate Cemetery last month. Ledwell's co-creator of the cult animation *The Ink Black Heart*, Joshua Blay, was also attacked and remains in hospital. Comic book writer Fayola Johnson survived a suicide—

Strike's mobile rang. He tugged it out of his pocket. It was Madeline.

'Hi,' she said, sounding extremely tense. 'Can you talk?'

'Yeah, I'm on a break,' said Strike. 'What's up?'

'Have you seen *The Times*? Gigi Cazenove – I—'

'Yeah,' said Strike. 'I've just been reading that. It's—'

'*Fucking alt-right group of trolls made her kill herself!*' said Madeline, who was clearly on the verge of tears. 'I just – I mean, I can't get my head around it – she was twenty-three, what *fucking* threat was she to a bunch of fascists?'

'Don't think you're going to find any reasonable answer to that,' said Strike. 'But it's horrible, I agree.'

'I'm not pretending she was my best friend,' said Madeline, 'but she was a really sweet girl. She was always popping into the shop for a chat and ... sorry ... I can't ... I mean, her crime was *talking about fucking climate change* ...'

'Yeah,' said Strike. 'I know. It's—'

'Fuck, I'm going to have to go, I've got another bloody lawyers' meeting. Talk later?'

'Yeah. I'll call you.'

Madeline rang off. Strike put his phone back in his pocket, picked up the paper again, and read on.

Comic book writer Fayola Johnson has also been targeted by the group, but survived a suicide attempt in October 2013.

Prior to their deaths, all three women were subject to 'trolling' campaigns over social media that appear to have been planned and coordinated by The Halvening, with the aim of forcing their targets out of public life, or into taking their own lives.

'What we're seeing here are sophisticated campaigns of misinformation and harassment which aim in part to turn progressives against their own,' said *The Times*' source. 'While we've previously seen "trolling" of liberals originating in spaces like 4chan, the terror group is using social media in a more organised and sophisticated way to incite harassment and campaigns of intimidation.'

Singer Gigi Cazenove was subjected to sustained abuse on social media after emails in which she had allegedly used racist language to describe a former backing singer were leaked online. The emails were subsequently found to have been faked. Maya Satterthwaite was revealed to have 'misgendered' a prominent trans woman in private text messages which were also leaked online, while Edie Ledwell was subject to a prolonged hate campaign for multiple alleged transgressions, particularly against the disabled, and survived a suicide attempt in 2014 before being fatally stabbed in February.

Hate Symbols

The terror group's name is taken from a term used in cryptocurrency, where a 'halvening' refers to the deliberate halving of the amount of bitcoin that can be 'mined'.

'The Halvening's stated aim is to reduce the number of so-called "social justice warriors" in public life and to diminish the value of holding progressive views,' said *The Times*' source.

The term 'social justice warrior' is used pejoratively by right-wingers to describe those who advocate and disseminate socially progressive agendas, although it is used as a badge of pride by many on the left.

While The Halvening—

Strike's mobile rang for a second time. Wresting it out of his pocket he saw Lucy's number. He hesitated before answering, but decided it was better to get the conversation out of the way now, while he was free to talk, rather than postpone it and pay an additional surcharge of resentment.

'Stick?'

'Hey, Luce. What's up?'

'I've just been talking to Ted. He sounds really low . . .'

Ted was Strike's recently widowed uncle, a man he'd always considered his surrogate father.

'. . . so I've asked him up to stay with us on the weekend of the seventeenth of April,' said Lucy. 'Could you come over and join us?'

'Er – I haven't got the work rota in front of me,' said Strike, truthfully, 'but I'll—'

'Stick, I'm giving you plenty of notice, it's a month away!'

'But I'll try,' Strike finished.

'OK, well, I'll send you a text reminder,' said Lucy. 'He really does want to see you, Corm. You haven't been down to Cornwall since Christmas . . .'

Five minutes of intensive guilt-tripping later, Lucy hung up. The scowling Strike put his mobile back in his pocket, shook *The Times* free of creases again, then continued reading.

While The Halvening's name is taken from the world of crypto-currency, it also uses familiar far-right language and iconography. Members use pseudonyms taken from Norse runes, followed by the number 88. According to the Anti-Defamation League, the number 88 is a hate symbol representing the eighth letter of the alphabet repeated twice, and stands for 'Heil Hitler'.

Growing Threat

According to MI5, the fastest-growing terror threat in the UK comes from the far right.

'Historically, the threat from neo-Nazism and the alt-right has come from individual "haters", which makes them difficult to track. Far right terror groups have tended to be short-lived.

'The Halvening, by contrast, seems to be unusually well-organised and disciplined. They offer a unifying ideology, with both political and religious elements. Movements offering a coherent philosophy or belief system tend to be more cohesive and successful at instilling loyalty and in recruiting *continued page 4*

Strike was just turning to page four when his mobile rang for the third time.

'*Fuck's sake.*'

He tugged the phone out of his pocket yet again. The call had been forwarded from the office.

'Cormoran Strike.'

'Ah, yes,' said an unknown voice, 'hello. My name's Allan Yeoman. I'm Edie Ledwell's agent – or rather' – he cleared his throat – 'I was.'

16

We must arise and go:
The world is cold without
And dark and hedged about
With mystery and enmity and doubt,
But we must go . . .

Charlotte Mew
The Call

At the precise moment Strike took the call from Allan Yeoman, Robin was eight miles away in Walthamstow, feigning interest in a stained-glass panel showing a naked Adam naming the animals. He sat round-shouldered on a grassy tussock, pointing at a tiger, while a bearded angel beside him recorded the chosen name in a book. Two tropical birds seemed to be poking out of the top of the angel's halo. Adam's expression was vacant, even clueless.

Groomer and Legs were standing with their backs to Robin on the other side of the room, discussing the symbolism of the pelican in a design by Edward Burne-Jones. Precisely as Legs' mother had feared, her departure for Iraq, where she'd been sent to report on the destruction by Daesh of the ancient archaeological site of Nimrud, had coincided with her daughter taking a day off school, presumably on pretence of sickness. Ten minutes after her schoolfriend's parents had left for work, Groomer had arrived to take Legs for a day out. Robin had followed in Strike's BMW, which she'd borrowed because she'd previously used her own ancient Land Rover to follow the schoolgirl. Given that she'd worried the couple were heading for a hotel, Robin had been pleasantly surprised when her targets pulled into the car park of the William Morris Gallery.

143

Robin felt she'd learned a great deal about Legs and Groomer's relationship while wandering from room to room in their wake, eavesdropping on their conversation. Apparently Legs had evinced an interest in the Arts and Crafts movement, and she was now trying to live up to what Robin suspected had been a chance remark, while Groomer treated her opinions and insights with a flattering serious-ness. The hand-kissing witnessed by Midge hadn't been repeated, although Groomer had placed a hand lightly on Legs' back between two of the gallery's rooms, and had also picked something invisible out of her long blonde hair. Legs herself was clearly smitten to a degree she was finding it impossible to conceal, and Robin could only imagine how gratifying the forty-year-old was finding the teenager's gasping laughs at his lightest witticism, her adoring gaze as he held forth on the Pre-Raphaelites and her frequent blushes as he praised her knowledge and her insights, all of which sounded to a cynical Robin as though they'd been hastily mugged up on from Wikipedia.

Having explained the Christian symbolism of the pelican, which was feeding her chicks with her own blood, Groomer wondered aloud whether Legs was ready for a coffee, and after lingering for another couple of minutes in apparent admiration of Adam, Robin followed them to the café, a space of glass and exposed brick that looked out onto the gallery's gardens.

She'd just bought herself a cappuccino when her mobile rang.

'Hi,' she said quietly to Strike, 'give me a mo, I've got to find somewhere to sit.'

Having paid for her coffee, she took a seat with an unimpeded view of Groomer and Legs, then raised her mobile to her ear again.

'OK, I'm here. What's up?'

'Quite a bit,' said Strike. 'Can you talk?'

'I should be fine for fifteen minutes at least,' said Robin, watching Legs giggling and throwing her hair back over her shoulders, her coffee so far untouched.

'Don't suppose you've seen today's *Times*?'

'No. Why?'

Strike gave Robin a precis of the front-page story about The Halvening.

'So you were right,' said Robin. 'It *was* a terrorist attack.'

'I'm not so sure.'

'But—'

'Ledwell was on this Halvening group's Indirect Action list. They were trying to whip up enough harassment to tip her into killing herself. They weren't planning to murder her, and they don't seem to have stabbed anyone so far. According to *The Times*, their preferred m.o. is pipe bombs.'

'Well,' said Robin, staring out over the gallery's sweeping lawns, 'maybe they spotted an opportunity and decided to kill her rather than wait for her to do it herself?'

'But why stab Blay? There's no mention of him being on either list. It seems to be left-wing women they've got a problem with.'

'Stabbing Blay might not have been planned. He could've got in the way of the attacker. Maybe he tried to defend her.'

'I'd still have thought it made more sense to kill her when she was alone, if they were intent on murder. Two targets means a good chance of one of them escaping or raising the alarm. Of course,' Strike added, 'we don't know how many assailants there were. Nothing to say there was only one.'

'They might not have known Blay was going to be there until they arrived. Come to that, how did the attacker know Ledwell was going to be in the cemetery that afternoon?'

'Excellent question,' said Strike. 'Well, there's a chance we'll be able to find out, if you're up for it. I've just got off the phone from Edie Ledwell's agent, Allan Yeoman.'

'Seriously?' said Robin, who'd experienced one of the familiar charges of excitement that were the reward of the job, and which usually resulted from an unexpected discovery, the sudden opening of a new vista.

'Yeah. He wants to know whether we'd be prepared to have a meeting – and not just with him. There'd also be a bloke called Richard Elgar, who's the head of Maverick Films in the UK, plus Edie's aunt and uncle. He's suggesting we all have lunch at the Arts Club on Dover Street next week. He wants to know whether we'd be up for finding out who Anomie is.'

'But we're still full up with cases,' groaned Robin.

'Not as full as we were. Dev's just called: he's taken care of the patent-pending guy. Found the leaker in his office, got pictures of her with the head of a rival firm.'

'Quick work,' said Robin, impressed, before returning to the main point. 'But why does Edie Ledwell's agent want to find out who Anomie is now?'

'Yeoman said he'd rather tell us that in person, but I gathered Anomie's still making a nuisance of themselves.'

'Did you tell Allan Yeoman we don't really do cyber-investigation?'

'I did, yeah, but he doesn't seem to think that's an issue. I'd imagine we'll find out why if we agree to lunch. Anyway, I'm assuming you'd rather tackle Anomie than whichever trophy wife is trying to secure a fatter divorce settlement this week?'

'Definitely,' said Robin.

'Yeah, me too. OK, I'll call Yeoman back and tell him we can do next Tuesday. Happy lech hunting.'

He hung up and Robin, though excited by the prospect of the new case, returned her attention to Groomer and Legs, who were now nose to nose, whispering to each other.

17

Is this a stupid thing to say
Not having spent with you one day?
No matter; I shall never touch your hair
Or hear the little tick behind your breast . . .

Charlotte Mew
On the Road to the Sea

An in-game chat between moderators of *Drek's Game*, Paperwhite and Morehouse

<A new private channel has opened>

<13 March 2015 14.31>

<Paperwhite invites Morehouse>

<Morehouse joins the channel>

Paperwhite: I've been in here for ages waiting for you to show up! Where have you been?

Morehouse: Talking to Anomie

Paperwhite: Did you see, in the news?

Morehouse: The Halvening stuff? yes

>

>

Paperwhite: and?

147

Morehouse: and what?

>

>

>

Paperwhite: Are you angry at me
or something?

Morehouse: Why would I be angry?

>

>

>

>

>

Paperwhite: Morehouse, talk to me

Morehouse: Have you still got that
'proof' LordDrek and Vilepechora
gave you, that Anomie was Ledwell?

Paperwhite: Yes, why?

Morehouse: Why d'you think?

>

>

Paperwhite: You think LordDrek
and Vilepechora are Halvening?

Morehouse: look at the Halvening
m.o. in the Times. It's exactly
what LordDrek and Vile did to you
lot

Morehouse: they created a false
narrative designed to turn you on
Ledwell

Paperwhite: they didn't start the
rumour she was Anomie

Paperwhite: tons of fans thought she might be

Morehouse: like who?

Paperwhite: I don't know their names off the top of my head but it was all in the dossier

Morehouse: sock puppet accounts

Morehouse: all designed to keep people riled up and hounding her

Paperwhite: I never hounded her

Morehouse: I never said you did

Paperwhite: Hartella thinks it was a random attack

Morehouse: yeah I'll bet she does

Paperwhite: What's htat supposed to mean?

Morehouse: lets her off the hook. Has she spoken to police?

Paperwhite: I think so yes

Morehouse: did she tell them where she got that dossier?

Paperwhite: I don't know

Morehouse: well I think one of you needs to take that dossier to the police if Hartella hasnt

>

>

>

Paperwhite: Morehouse, there was a guy in the year above me who retweeted some alt-right American guy and they chucked him out of college

Paperwhite: I never thought
Ledwell was Anomie, I never
asked for that dossier, I never
wished any harm on her at
all,but that won't matter to
the press

Paperwhite: they'll go for all of
us if they think we were mixed up
with the alt-right and murder

Paperwhite: and how d'you think
C******** would like it?

Morehouse: you sound exactly like
Anomie

Paperwhite: what does that mean?

Morehouse: we just ignore
the fact that neo-Nazis have
infiltrated us, do we?

Paperwhite: no, if it's proven
that's what LordDrek and Vile are
then obviously Anomie should kick
them out

Paperwhite: but explain to me how
can that dossier have anything
to do with Ledwell and Blay being
stabbed?

Morehouse: it's the reason they
met, isn't it, it's why they went
to the cemetery in the first place

Morehouse: LordDrek and
Vilepechora set up the situation
which resulted in two stabbings

Morehouse: The Halvening wanted
her dead and she's dead

Paperwhite: and if they genuinely
believed she was Anomie?

Morehouse: I don't think they
ever believed it and you said
yourself you didn't

Morehouse: and if YOU guessed

where they were meeting, anyone
could have done

Paperwhite: thanks, I'm that
stupid am I?

Morehouse: ffs I didn't mean it
like that, you sound like Worm28

Morehouse: I'm saying people could
have guessed and lain in wait,
seized the opportunity to knife
them. Or Hartella could have told
LordDrek and Vile where they
were going to meet, on a private
channel.

>

>

>

Paperwhite: My mother's ill. I'm
not putting her through a ton
of shit from the press and the
police. I've doen nothing wrong

Morehouse: You didn't tell me your
mother was ill

Paperwhite: didn't think youd care

Morehouse: of course I care, why
are you saying that?

>

>

>

Morehouse: Paperwhite?

Paperwhite: U8N xetubg

>

Paperwhite: shit

Paperwhite: I'm crying I can't
see3 properly

Morehouse: what's wrong with your mum?

Paperwhite: I don't want to talk about it

Paperwhite: if I talk about it its real

Morehouse: tell me

Paperwhite: why?

Morehouse: you know why

Morehouse: because I care about you

Paperwhite: no you fkn don't you've been playing me all along

Paperwhite: getting nudes off me, never send a pic back

Paperwhite: playing mr sensitive

Paperwhite: how many other girls are you stringing along?

Morehouse: wtf are you talking about? Nobody

Morehouse: I never asked u for those pics

Paperwhite: i'm a slut then am i?

Morehouse: ffs did I say that?

Paperwhite: now I'm sobbing in the middle of the fkn library

Morehouse: don't

Morehouse: I never wanted to hurt you

Morehouse: tell me what's happened with your mum?

>

\>

Paperwhite: she found a lump

Paperwhite: biopsy results came back late yesterday

Paperwhite: it's malignant

Morehouse: oh shit

Morehouse: I'm so sorry

Paperwhite: I can't stand much more of this

Paperwhite: you don't think I'm good enough for you

Morehouse: ?????

Paperwhite: you know who I am, I know you do. That 400 miles comment

Paperwhite: if you'd liked what you saw you'd have tried to meet me

Morehouse: it isn't that simple

Paperwhite: I've got all these feelings for you and you clearly don't feel the same way

Morehouse: that isn't true

Paperwhite: it's too much to cope with, I cant do it any more, not with mum ill as well

Paperwhite: I'm going to take Drek's Game off my phone

Morehouse: don't do that

Morehouse: please don't

Paperwhite: why not?

\>

Morehouse: look it's crazy to have such strong feelings for someone I've never met, but I do

Morehouse: I think about you all the time

>

Paperwhite: you might find this hard to believe, but I have other offers, you know

Morehouse: I don't find that hard to believe at all

Paperwhite: then prove you care, send me a picture of yourself

>

>

>

Morehouse: I can't

>

<Paperwhite has left the channel>

18

Well of blackness, all defiling,
Full of flattery and reviling,
Ah, what mischief hast thou wrought
Out of what was airy thought,
What beginnings and what ends,
Making and dividing friends!

Mary Elizabeth Coleridge
The Contents of an Ink Bottle

Strike and Robin shared a taxi from the office to the Arts Club the following Tuesday. She noticed, but didn't mention, that he was wearing the same Italian suit he'd worn to the Ritz on her birthday. Robin had chosen a smart but low-key black trouser suit. As they headed towards Mayfair, Strike turned off the passengers' intercom and said to Robin,

'I've been thinking about it, and we can't tell them who Edie thought Anomie was. It isn't a fair accusation to be bandying about if she was wrong.'

'No, I know,' said Robin. 'It'll be interesting to hear whether they agree with her, though.'

'I went looking for Montgomery online yesterday,' said Strike, who, unlike Robin, had had Monday off. 'Found him on LinkedIn and Instagram. He's working ten minutes' walk away from our office, at a digital-effects company in Fitzrovia. He lives in Ladbroke Grove with his girlfriend. His Instagram page is full of pictures of them with their hipster friends.'

Robin looked sideways at Strike.

'You don't think it's him,' she said, more statement than question.

'Well, if it is, he must have a very tolerant boss who doesn't mind him tweeting regularly throughout the day. I had a quick look at Anomie's account last night. He's on Twitter at all hours ... Maybe I'm just working off a stereotype. When you think of internet trolls, you tend to assume they haven't got much of a life. Montgomery's seems pretty good, from what I can see.'

Given that it lay a mere ten minutes away from the billionaire's house in South Audley Street, Robin had expected the Arts Club to be smart, but even so the degree of grandeur came as a surprise. From the white-jacketed waiters and the marble floors, to the oyster bar and extravagant modern chandeliers, the place gave the Ritz a run for its money. Scruffy, ink-stained Edie Ledwell would have been thoroughly out of place here; indeed, the clientele seemed to consist exclusively of middle-aged and prosperous-looking men in suits. Robin's outfit was almost identical to the one worn by the pretty young woman who greeted them at the door, then led them upstairs to the private dining room where, she told them, the rest of the party was already assembled.

The small room had a trace of an opium den about it, with its dark red walls, vaguely Chinese-looking carved wooden screens and subdued lighting. The four people waiting for them hadn't yet sat down. All turned, falling silent, when Strike and Robin entered.

'Aha,' said the smiling, bespectacled, pink-faced man nearest the door. He looked younger than his untidy white hair might have suggested and his slightly baggy suit looked as though it was worn for reasons of comfort rather than style. 'Mr Strike and Miss Ellacott, yes? How do you do? I'm Allan Yeoman.'

He shook hands with both of them in turn, then introduced them to the dapper, forty-something man beside him, whose tie was the same silvery colour of Madeline's bedroom curtains. His dark hair was as neat as Yeoman's was scruffy and his well-tailored suit had very definitely been chosen for reasons of style.

'This is Richard Elgar, chief executive of Maverick Films in the UK.'

'Hi,' said Elgar, and his accent revealed him to be American. A glint of onyx and steel cufflink was revealed as he shook hands. 'Good to meet you. You actually helped a friend of mine out with a personal matter a couple of years ago.'

He mentioned the name of a female client who'd divorced a philandering multimillionaire.

'And this is Grant Ledwell,' said Yeoman, indicating a man with heavy eyebrows and an underbite, which gave him more than a passing resemblance to a bulldog. Grant's thick hair was bristle cut, his blue suit was double-breasted and his shirt collar looked tight. 'Edie's uncle, you know.'

Grant's strong jaw and bushy eyebrows didn't entirely account for the slightly pugnacious air he was giving off.

'Very sorry for your loss,' said Strike as they shook hands, and Grant made an ambiguous, subterranean noise in his throat.

'And his wife, Heather,' concluded Yeoman.

Heather, who was pregnant, looked at least ten years younger than her husband. Though not particularly good-looking, she gave a general impression of lustrous fecundity, with her creamy skin and long, glossy brown hair. Her clinging, low-cut purple wrap dress revealed at least half of her swollen breasts. Robin noticed how determinedly Strike kept his eyes firmly on Heather's face as he shook her hand.

'I've read all about you,' Heather said, beaming up at Strike. 'Wow.'

'Shall we sit down?' suggested Allan Yeoman.

The six of them took their seats around the circular table and Robin wondered whether anyone else was reminded unavoidably of a séance, with the light pooled over the table but the corners of the room in shadow. When Heather pulled her chair in, one of the bright overhead lights illuminated her breasts so that they looked like twin moons; the waiter who'd arrived to hand out menus stared for a few seconds as though dazed.

Elgar made easy small talk about the Arts Club, of which he was a member, until the door closed behind the waiter, leaving the group alone.

'Well,' said Yeoman, turning to Strike and Robin, 'it's very good of you to meet us.'

'We're happy to be here,' said Strike.

'I know Edie would be glad we're meeting, too,' Yeoman continued sombrely. 'As you can imagine, this has been an appalling shock for all of us – and for Grant and Heather, of course, a personal tragedy.'

'How's the police investigation going?' Strike asked Grant.

'We haven't had an update for a week,' said Edie's uncle, whose voice tended naturally to a growl. 'But they seem pretty convinced it was someone from this far-right group, this Halving, or whatever they're called.'

'Have they got a description of the attacker yet?' Strike asked.

'No,' said Grant. 'Blay claims he was hit in the back with the Taser. Says he fell face-down, was stabbed on the ground and all he saw was a pair of black trainers running away.'

'Is there some doubt about his story?' asked Strike, because Grant's voice had held a note of scepticism.

'Well, people online are saying *he* stabbed Edie,' Heather said before Grant could answer. 'Aren't they, Grub? And, face it, this has all worked out quite well for Blay, really, hasn't it? He's been left in charge of everything, hasn't he?'

'No, he hasn't,' said Grant shortly. '*We'll* see to that.'

There was a slightly uncomfortable pause.

'The papers say he was stabbed in the neck,' Strike said.

'That's right,' said Yeoman before Grant could respond. 'From what I gather, what saved him was the high collar on his leather jacket. If the knife had gone in any deeper – I believe it was a question of millimetres. Even so, he's been left with a significant spinal-cord injury and he's partially paralysed.'

'He and Edie had fallen out—' began Grant, but two waiters now re-entered the room with bottles of water and a selection of bread rolls, and he fell silent. Nobody had ordered alcohol. When the man pouring water asked whether they'd decided what they were going to eat yet, Heather gave a little laugh.

'Oh, I haven't chosen!' she said, flipping open the menu and perusing it.

Once she'd ordered, she turned to Robin and said, rubbing her belly, 'This one's a boy and *can't* I tell! I wasn't this hungry with either of our girls!'

'When are you due?' asked Robin politely.

'Not till June. Have you got any?'

'No,' said Robin with a smile.

'To be honest, this one wasn't planned,' said Heather in a stage whisper. 'But he's only got to *look* at me and I'm pregnant. But who knows, I might be able to afford some help, if . . .'

She left the sentence unfinished. As she sipped her water, Robin wondered how much Grant and Heather stood to gain from their unexpected inheritance.

Food orders taken, the waiters left again. Once the door had closed, Yeoman said:

'So, as I explained on the phone, we're hoping you might agree to undertake an investigation for us. We' – he indicated himself and Elgar – 'would be your clients and bear the costs, but we felt it right that Grant should be here today, too, as Edie's next of kin. Richard, would you like to—?'

'Thanks, Allan,' said the American. 'To give you some background,' he said, putting his beautifully manicured fingertips together, 'when Edie died, she and Josh were on the verge of concluding a film deal with us. Josh had already signed and Edie was due to do so at Allan's office the morning after she was attacked.

'A few days ago, Josh sent us a message, via his agent, that he doesn't want to proceed with the movie unless some way of shutting down Anomie is found.'

'You aren't Josh's agent, then?' Strike asked Yeoman. 'Only Edie's?'

'Correct,' said Yeoman. 'Josh is represented by a woman called Katya Upcott. We, ah, should come back to her.'

'Now, obviously Josh has already signed the contract, so he can't legally stop the movie,' said Elgar, 'but naturally nobody wants to go against his wishes, given what's just happened.'

'We should say, it's very much in Josh's best interests for the film to be made,' added Yeoman. 'If his paralysis doesn't resolve, he's unlikely to be able to animate again. He doesn't come from a wealthy family. We want to set his mind at rest about Anomie so he can focus on his recovery. He's feeling a lot of guilt about accusing Edie of being Anomie – torturing himself, Katya says—'

'Well, *imagine* accusing her of that,' interrupted Heather indignantly. 'As if *anyone* would do that to themselves, putting personal things about themselves online! We're having a taste of what she went through right now – aren't we, Grub?' she said, glancing sideways at her husband. 'As soon as Edie was dead, this Anomie started churning out private things about me and Grant on Twitter!'

'Really?' said Strike, pulling out a notebook. 'Would you mind if we take notes?'

'No, of course not,' said Heather, who seemed rather excited at the prospect. 'He's got *some* things wrong – he said Grant was out in Saudi, not Oman, and that I was Grant's secretary, which I wasn't, I was PA to another guy, and he's claimed Grub and I had an affair while he was still married, but his first marriage was—'

'Over in all but name,' said Grant, more loudly than was necessary.

'He's been going for us *non-stop* for a month, because Grant's going to have a say now in what happens with the cartoon!' continued Heather. 'I'm keeping track of all these so-called fans coming on our Facebook page and writing terrible things. I can give you the names, if you like.'

'Thank you, that'd be very helpful,' said Strike, not particularly sincerely. 'Interesting that Anomie knows private details about you as well as Edie. Could he have got them online – from your Facebook page, for instance? Or does he know things that aren't in the public domain?'

Grant and Heather looked at each other.

'I s'pose *some* of it's on our Facebook page,' said Heather, as though this thought had only just occurred to her. 'But he knew Laura's got lupus. I don't see how he could have known that, do you, Grub?'

'Laura's my ex-wife,' Grant explained. 'No, I can't see how he'd have known that. I was in Oman when Edie's mother, my younger sister, died,' he continued, and Strike suspected they were about to hear a prepared speech. 'I was unmarried at the time and working all hours – there was no way I could've taken in a small child. By the time I met my first wife, Edie was settled with a good foster family. It would've done more harm than good, disrupting her life and her education to drag her abroad. Then, after we moved back to London, Laura got ill. It was all she could manage, looking after Rachel, our own daughter. I mean, I checked in with Edie to see how she was doing' – he gave an aggressive upwards jerk of the chin – 'but given my personal situation – simply not practicable to have her to live with us.'

'And she was doing drugs and all sorts later,' said Heather, 'wasn't she, Grub? We wouldn't have wanted that around the kids.'

Elgar, who'd maintained an expression of mild interest while the conversation had entered this side route, now returned to what, for him, was clearly the main point of the meeting.

'As Allan says, we all want to do the right thing by Josh, but we've got sound business reasons for closing down Anomie as well. Anomie's very much against our movie and he's whipping up the fandom against it. He's got a well-established track record of creating animosity towards any change in the franchise he doesn't approve of.'

Yeoman, whose mouth was full of bread roll, nodded and said thickly,

'When the show moved to Netflix, Anomie orchestrated hate

campaigns against the voice actors and animators. A couple of people resigned because of the harassment Anomie was inciting against them online. In terms of the overall brand, *The Ink Black Heart* is starting to be almost as well known for the aggression of the fandom as for the cartoon itself. Nobody wants the property to become a byword for online toxicity, but I'm afraid that's where we're headed, unless something changes.'

'Which is a shame,' said Elgar, 'because we've got high hopes for the movie adaptation. We're planning a mixture of live action and CGI. A gothic love story mixed with a dark comedy, full of funny, appealing characters.'

Robin thought the last line sounded as though it had been lifted directly from a press release.

'Presumably,' she said, 'Maverick would get the rights to produce digital games, if this film deal's concluded?'

'Hammer hit on head, Ms Ellacott,' said Elgar with a wry smile. 'Anomie's game will have a lot of competition once we get gaming rights. We think that's the primary reason he's determined to stop the cartoon becoming a film.'

'Where did Blay get this idea that Edie was Anomie, do any of you know?' asked Strike.

Yeoman sighed.

'Somebody took him a dossier of supposed proof. I haven't been able to talk to Josh yet, so that's all I know, but ... well, he's quite a heavy consumer of cannabis and alcohol. Relations between him and Edie were very poor by the end; there was a lot of bitterness, paranoia and acrimony. I don't think he'd have needed a lot of persuading that Edie was up to no good.'

'Your agency turned Edie down because you don't do a lot of cyber-investigation, is that right?' Elgar asked Robin.

'And because our client list was full at the time,' explained Robin.

'Well, you should know the interested parties represented at this table have probably exhausted the cyber-investigation route,' said Elgar.

'Really?' said Strike.

'Yes. We were all acting independently,' said Yeoman, 'and it's only since Edie died that we've pooled information. Grant—'

'Yeah, I've had a good friend of mine looking into this Anomie these last few weeks,' said Grant with another aggressive upward jerk of the chin. 'Len heads up a cybersecurity firm. Met him out in Oman. Len says the security around this game of Anomie's is top notch. He hasn't managed to dig up anything on who's behind it.'

'Just to clarify a point,' interjected Robin, 'there are two people credited with creating this game, aren't there? Not just Anomie?'

'That's right,' said Yeoman. 'The other calls himself Morehouse and—'

'They're the same person,' said Heather with absolute confidence. 'I've been looking into it all online. They're the same person.'

'Well, maybe – I don't know,' said Yeoman tactfully. 'Morehouse, if he's a real person, keeps a very low profile. He doesn't tweet a lot and he never hounded Edie, as far as I know. It's Anomie who's become the power in the fandom and who's widely credited with the game.'

'And you two have both tried to investigate Anomie online as well?' Strike said, looking from Yeoman to Elgar.

'Yes,' said Elgar. 'As we were getting closer to a deal, the negativity coming from the fandom was starting to concern us. Anomie was pumping out a particularly pernicious mix of fact and fiction.'

'He knew things he shouldn't have done?' asked Robin.

'He did, yeah,' said Elgar. 'Just odd details, nothing major, but enough to make me wonder whether I wasn't harbouring Anomie at our studio. I went to a cyber-investigation firm we previously used to look into a leak from our studios. They had no more success than Grant's contact. Anomie and Morehouse have done a very good job of protecting themselves and their game. As a matter of fact, my guys don't think they can be amateurs, whatever they pretend online. But we did satisfy ourselves that Anomie wasn't tweeting from inside the company, which was something.'

'Anomie and Morehouse claim to be an ordinary pair of fans, don't they?' said Robin.

'That's right. They're assumed to be young, though they've never explicitly stated their ages, as far as I know,' said Yeoman. 'Everyone also talks about them as male, though obviously we have no idea whether that's true either.'

'You tried to find out who Anomie was, too, Allan?' Strike asked the agent.

'I did,' said Yeoman, nodding. 'I didn't tell Edie, didn't want to get her hopes up. I'd been advising her to ignore Anomie. She engaged with him a few times on Twitter, and it didn't help – in fact, it made things worse. But it's one thing advising a client to ignore social media, and another making them do it.

'So yes, six months ago I asked someone at my agency to do what he could. Benjamin does all our cyber-security, he's quite a whizz-kid. He looked into how Anomie's game's being hosted, he even – between ourselves – tried to breach its security, to hack into the administrator's account and get himself onto the moderator channel, but got nowhere. As Grant says, whoever made the game is very clever.'

The door opened again and the waiters returned with their food. Strike, Yeoman and Grant had all ordered the Wagyu beef, Elgar and Robin salads, whereas Heather had chosen risotto.

'This *is* a treat,' said Heather happily and Robin, who'd been fighting her feeling of dislike, silently stopped resisting. They were here in this sleekly appointed club, eating this delicious food, because of the brutal death of Heather's niece by marriage. Even if Heather had barely known her, as seemed to be the case, her frank enjoyment of her fancy lunch and her persistent eyeing-up of Strike seemed both inappropriate and distasteful to Robin.

When the door had closed behind the waiters, Robin asked:

'Did anyone ever try to reach out to Anomie? To reason with them, or fix up a private meeting?'

'Yes: Edie herself,' said Yeoman, now vigorously cutting up his beef. 'She asked Anomie over Twitter to meet her face to face. He never answered.'

'Couldn't you have done something with copyright law?' asked Strike. 'What's the legal position, if his game's using all Ledwell and Blay's characters?'

'Grey area,' said Yeoman, now through a mouthful of steak. 'You could argue infringement, but as the fans liked it and nobody was making any money, we thought it wisest not to be heavy-handed. If Anomie had started monetising it, then yes, we'd have had a copyright violation. We imagined fans would eventually tire of it, thereby diminishing Anomie's influence, but that hasn't happened.'

'Ordinarily,' said Elgar, 'we'd be looking to bring him on side, as an influencer – you know, a superfan with a following within the community. Tickets to early screenings, face-to-face meetings with the writers and actors, that sort of thing. But it wouldn't be possible in this case, even if we were minded to be generous. Anomie seems to treasure his anonymity, which to me suggests he knows it would hurt him to be unmasked.'

'This is obviously an uncomfortable question,' said Strike, turning to Grant, 'but given that Anomie seems to have a lot of inside information, it must have occurred to you that he might be a family member, Grant?'

'It definitely isn't anyone in the family,' Edie's uncle said at once.

'Nobody in the family really knew her,' said Heather. 'You barely did, did you, Grub?'

'I was abroad,' Grant repeated, glaring at Strike, 'and my ex-wife was ill. My parents are dead, as are both of Edie's parents. The only other relatives are my kids and none of them ever met her. It's *definitely* not anyone in our family.'

'I made discreet enquiries at the agency,' said Yeoman, 'because it naturally occurred to me that I might be harbouring Anomie, but as far as I could find out, nobody there ever had so much as a coffee with Edie outside work. And while someone might have known about developments with the cartoon, they simply can't have known all those private details about Edie's past. In my view, Anomie has to be someone who's been in Edie's immediate circle at some point or – more likely – in Josh's.'

'Why d'you say it's more likely to be someone in Josh's?' asked Robin.

Yeoman set down his knife and fork, swallowed a mouthful of food, and said,

'Well, for one thing, Anomie's never targeted Josh,' he said. 'It was always Edie he fixated on and abused and harassed. That's one of the things that drove a wedge between Josh and Edie: Josh was being treated very kindly by the fandom and Edie was being blamed for everything they didn't like. But as I've said, Josh has a history of drinking far more than he should and smoking a lot of pot. I'm afraid he's a poor judge of character, too. We had quite a few problems with some of the original cast, who were mostly his friends, which, um, brings us back to Katya Upcott.'

Yeoman glanced at Elgar, who made a small movement with his fork that indicated that Yeoman should go on, so the agent said,

'I didn't invite Katya to this lunch because she's fiercely protective of Josh – which, of course, is an entirely honourable sentiment, especially given his present condition. But we can talk more freely without her here.'

'Does Katya have her own agency?' said Strike.

'Er . . . no. She's a – a very nice lady who runs a crafting supplies business from home. Katya met Josh and Edie a few years ago, at the art collective where they were living. Katya was taking evening classes there. She'd worked in PR before she set up her own business, so she gave Josh and Edie advice on how to handle themselves when *The Ink Black Heart* started attracting fans.

'After a while, she started acting as their de facto agent. In 2012 Edie decided to find a professional agent, and I took her on. Josh remained with Katya. It isn't unusual, you know, for people who have a surprise hit to cling to familiar people. There's loyalty, of course, but also fear. It can be hard to know who to trust when you suddenly become hot property. Katya's a perfectly nice, well-intentioned woman,' he emphasised, 'and she knows I'm calling in private detectives to try and find Anomie and she's said she'll give any help she can. She'll know far more than I do about Josh's friends and close contacts, but you'll need to tread carefully, because she's deeply resistant to the idea that Josh, through naivety, carelessness or lack of good judgement, could be partly responsible for the Anomie mess.'

'What family has Josh got?' asked Robin.

'He was raised by a single father, one of three children, and my impression is – this is from things Edie told me, I'm not speaking from personal knowledge – that Mr Blay senior never really knew how to handle his son, and lately seems to have abnegated parental duties to Katya, who's old enough to be Josh's mother.'

'If you could give us Katya's contact details, that would be great,' said Strike, and Yeoman nodded as he picked up his knife and fork again.

'Edie was in a new relationship when she died, wasn't she?' asked Robin.

'Him!' said Heather with a small snort.

'Yes. His name's Phillip Ormond,' said Yeoman. 'He's a teacher – geography, I think. He works at a local school in Highgate. He met Josh and Edie because he went for evening art classes, same as Katya. After Josh and Edie split up, Phillip offered a shoulder to cry on.'

'He *claims* they were engaged when she died,' said Heather.

'You don't think they were?' asked Strike.

'Well, nobody *else* thought they were. She didn't have a ring,' said

Heather, whose own third finger sported a large solitaire diamond above her wide wedding band.

'She didn't tell *me* she was planning to get married either,' said Yeoman.

'Or her foster sister,' said Heather. 'I asked, at the funeral.'

'What's the foster sister's name?' asked Strike.

'Catriona Douglas,' said Grant. 'Edie remained in touch with her after she left the family.'

Strike noted down the name.

'Ormond's got an eye to the main chance, if you ask me,' Heather said. 'He's hoping he'll have some kind of claim on her estate. There was a whole ridiculous thing about letters in the coffin. First, Blay — you'd have thought, after he'd accused her of being Anomie . . . Well, anyway, he dictated what he wanted to say to Katya, who brought us the letter and blah-di-blah and then' — Heather rolled her eyes — 'when Phillip got wind of Blay writing a letter, *he* had to write a letter too. I said to Grub, a coffin's not a bloody letterbox!'

If Heather had expected laughter at this, she was disappointed.

'Yeah, there was definitely a bit of competition between them to be chief mourner,' said Grant. 'Can't say I took much to Ormond, but he had a better right to it than Blay. He was living with Edie at the time and he wasn't making wild accusations against her.'

'It'd be good to talk to Ormond,' said Strike. 'And to this foster sister, Catriona. Have you got their contact details?'

'I've got Ormond's,' said Grant, pulling out his phone. He glanced down at it, scowled and muttered to his wife,

'Missed call from Rachel.'

'His daughter with his ex,' she told Robin in another stage whisper. 'Bit of a handful.'

'She'll be calling about the match,' said Grant, handing Strike his mobile. 'I'll ring her back later.'

'You said you'd had problems with the members of the cast who were Josh's friends,' Strike said to Yeoman. 'Are you talking about Wally Cardew?'

'You already know about Wally, do you?' said Yeoman. 'Yes, he was one of our early headaches. He and Josh were at school together. Wally had no acting experience, but he used to do a comic voice when they were teenagers — high-pitched, sinister — imitating a teacher they had. When Edie and Josh animated the first episode, they asked Wally to voice the character of Drek. He did his falsetto and fans loved it.

'But Wally got very big for his boots. He started making videos of his own on YouTube, using the Drek voice and the character's stock expressions and catchphrases, and making some extremely questionable jokes. Some elements of the fandom loved it. Others didn't. Then Wally and his friend MJ made the infamous "cookies" video.'

'"Cookies"?' repeated Strike.

'A so-called satirical piece mocking the Holocaust,' said the unsmiling Yeoman. 'There was a lot of fallout. Josh thought it would all blow over, but Edie was furious. Josh went along with the sacking, though grudgingly, and Wally took it extremely badly. He's since made a career for himself on YouTube. We've wondered whether Wally could be Anomie,' Yeoman said, correctly anticipating Strike's next question. 'He's wily, but I don't think he's got the kind of brains you'd need to create this game, and I have to say I think his ego's too big for him to remain anonymous.'

'Any other friends of Josh's we should talk to?' asked Strike.

'Well, yes, there was Sebastian Montgomery, an animator who helped them with the first couple of episodes. He was at art school with Josh and he was a bit snide about *The Ink Black Heart* on social media after he was dropped, but I'm not sure he ever knew Edie that well, so I can't imagine he'd have all those personal details about her that Anomie's used.'

'Unless,' said Strike, 'they came via Josh.'

'Well, yes, I suppose so,' admitted Yeoman.

'Anyone else?'

'Let's think . . . There was a young man called Timothy Ashcroft – although, now I think of it, he was a friend of Edie's originally, not Josh's. He voiced The Worm and I think he had acting ambitions, so he can't have liked being dropped, but he and Edie remained friends as far as I know. I haven't got any contact details for Tim, I'm afraid.'

'Why did they let him go?' asked Robin.

'Candidly,' said Yeoman, 'he wasn't very good. I've seen the early episodes; The Worm's a good comic character but Tim wasn't doing him justice. When they did the TV deal, it was a condition that Netflix would have a say over casting. I think it was a relief to Edie, honestly, to have somebody else make those decisions. Josh himself had voiced Harty in the beginning and Catriona, Edie's foster sister, was Paperwhite at first, but from what she told me at Edie's wake, she couldn't wait to leave. She never enjoyed doing the voice and was happy for a real actress to take over.

'But I wasn't involved back then, so there may be others who were left by the wayside that I don't know about. As I say, Katya's the one you should talk to about the old days. She was there from the begin— No, wait,' said Yeoman. 'There was another friend Edie mentioned. She lived at the art collective. *What* was she called? . . . Something like Miriam.'

'This would be the North Grove Art Collective, right?' asked Strike, pen poised.

'Yes, exactly,' said Yeoman. 'It's run by a Dutch man who sounds quite eccentric. Edie and Blay both rented rooms there for a while, which is how they met, and I know Josh stayed friendly with the Dutch man and used to hang around the collective even after the cartoon became successful. North Grove's right beside Highgate Cemetery, which is how Edie and Josh ended up among the graves one day and came up with the idea for the cartoon.'

'Well,' said Strike, reaching for the folder he'd brought with him, 'before we go any further, you should probably have a look at our standard contract and rates. I've got contracts here, if you'd like to give them the once over.'

He passed the contracts over the table and there was a lull while Elgar and Yeoman perused the terms and conditions, and the only sound was the scraping of Strike's, Robin's and the Ledwells' knives and forks, and the sound of Grant's chewing, which was unusually loud. Finally the agent and the film executive took out pens and signed the agreements, along with a third copy for the agency.

'Thank you,' said Strike, once all had been signed and he'd taken his own copy back.

'And I,' said Yeoman, reaching beneath his own chair in turn, 'should give you this.'

It was the cardboard folder Edie had brought to the agency and left behind on the toilet cistern.

'We'll get started immediately,' said Strike. 'If you can give me your contact details I'll update you weekly, but obviously if we have queries or important information I'll be in touch before that.'

Both Elgar and Yeoman handed business cards across the table.

'As a matter of interest,' Strike said, having put their cards in his wallet, 'once you know who Anomie is, what do you intend to do about it?'

There was another pause, and a deeper silence than hitherto, because Grant was no longer chewing. Richard Elgar then spoke.

'Literally nobody,' said the American, 'is mob-proof. I'm sure, if you're able to find out who Anomie is, we'll be able to find some evidence of hypocrisy, racial insensitivity, sexual harassment . . . Those who live by the mob must be prepared to die by the mob. Once we know who we're dealing with, I don't think it'll be too hard to turn Anomie from hunter into prey.'

19

Yes; I was tired, but not at heart;
No—that beats full of sweet content,
For now I have my natural part
Of action with adventure blent;
Cast forth on the wide world with thee,
And all my once waste energy
To weighty purpose bent.

Charlotte Brontë
The Wood

'Fancy a pint and a debrief?' asked Strike half an hour later, once he and Robin were back outside on the chilly pavement and Strike was flagging down a taxi.

'Definitely,' said Robin.

'The Tottenham pub, Charing Cross Road,' Strike told the driver, and he opened the door for Robin to enter the cab first.

Her enthusiastic tone as she'd agreed to the pub had pleased him. It was being slowly borne in on him that Robin wasn't avoiding tête-a-têtes with him, as she surely would have done if she'd truly felt repelled by what had happened outside the Ritz. He'd expected her to match his own subsequent increase in reserve, yet she seemed to be trying to resume the friendly relations they'd had before he'd made that foolish move.

'Any news on the flat?' he asked as their taxi rolled back towards the West End.

'I put in an increased offer yesterday,' said Robin. 'Waiting to hear. It'd be *so* great to get it. I'm tired of looking at horrible places and feeling like a gooseberry at Max's.'

The road outside the Tottenham, Strike's favourite pub in the vicinity of their office, remained a building site and they had to cross planks over a rubble-filled ditch to reach the door. Once inside, and in spite of the noise outside, they found the familiar safe haven, with its engraved glass mirrors and decorative panels painted by a long-dead theatrical designer.

Having requested a coffee, Robin sat down on one of the red leather banquettes and took out her phone to look up the North Grove Art Collective. When Strike joined her, holding a pint, he said,

'We should let the police know we've been asked to find Anomie, as a courtesy. I'll ring DCI Murphy.'

'Great,' said Robin. Then, passing Strike her phone, 'There: look – that's where it all started.'

Strike looked down at a photograph of a large dirty pink house, beneath which was written:

NORTH GROVE ART COLLECTIVE
We offer classes in life drawing, pottery, print-making and photography.
Beginners welcome! We also rent studio space to artists.

'If Josh was still hanging around the collective right up to the stabbing, we should check it out,' said Robin. 'It's got to be a possible haunt of Anomie's.'

'Agreed,' said Strike, scrolling down the website to examine pictures of art classes, some featuring earnest-looking adults sitting behind their pottery wheels, others showing children in PVC aprons making prints, with many examples of students' oil paintings, photographs and pencil drawings. As he handed back the phone, he said,

'Fancy having a go at a suspect profile?'

'Go on,' said Robin, taking out her notebook.

'Well, if Anomie's genuinely what they represent themselves to be – a fan who's obsessed with the game – they're surely young.'

'Agreed,' said Robin. 'I can't imagine anyone over thirty being this obsessed with a cartoon on YouTube.'

'But if they're *not* just an angry fan, and in fact had a massive personal grudge against Edie and saw this as a way to get at her—'

'Well, yes, then they could be any age, I suppose,' said Robin.

'And we're looking for someone with programming or coding experience,' said Strike, pulling out his notebook and starting to write.

'Unless . . .' said Robin, and Strike looked up. 'Well, Edie told me the game was like a beautifully animated chatroom. If two people genuinely made it, one could be an artist or a designer and the other a programmer?'

'We need to get inside that game,' said Strike, setting down his pen and pulling out his mobile. 'That's first base: have a good look from the inside and see what we can pick up.'

While Strike was searching for the game online, Robin drank her coffee and savoured a feeling of contentment as her eyes roamed around the familiar painted panels. The slight constraint that had hung over her interactions with Strike since that night at the Ritz seemed to have dispersed completely in the face of this new case. While Strike was scowling over his phone, typing search terms with his thick fingers, Robin allowed her eyes to rest on him and to feel the unalloyed fondness that had so often disturbed her peace of mind.

'Shit,' said Strike after a solid five minutes' silence.

'What?' said Robin.

'I can't get in. Just made three attempts.'

He showed Robin his phone's screen. A small animation of Harty, the jet-black heart with his hanging arteries and veins, looked back at her out of the screen, smiling and shrugging. Beneath Harty were the words:

'*Whoops! Something went wrong. Try again later, bwah!*'

'I'll have a go,' said Robin. She got to work on her own mobile, but after entering the email address she'd set up for these kinds of circumstances, which had no connection either to her real name or to the agency, and picking a password, she, too, found herself looking at the little animation of Harty shrugging, and was told to try again later.

'Maybe they're having technical problems,' she suggested.

'Let's hope so, because the one sure-fire way of ruling out suspects is going to be observing them going about their daily business without recourse to a phone or a laptop, while Anomie's tweeting or active in the game.'

'OK,' said Strike, returning to his notebook, 'our suspect profile so far reads: most likely to be under thirty' – he glanced up at Robin, who nodded – 'either adept at coding or artistic, or both . . . Male or female, do you reckon?'

'Could be either,' said Robin, 'although everyone seems to assume Anomie's male.'

'I think we need to do a deep dive into Anomie's Twitter account and see what they might have given away ... Actually,' said Strike, 'explain Twitter to me.'

'What d'you mean?' said Robin with a laugh.

'Well, I've seen it, but I've never used it. Have you?'

'I used to have a Twitter account, but I never did much with it.'

'So how exactly does it work?'

'Well, you write short messages – tweets – and you can communicate with anybody else on Twitter, unless they've blocked you.'

'And everyone on Twitter can see each other's tweets, can they?'

'Yes, unless you've made your account private. Then only your followers can read what you've written. And if two people are following each other, they can send direct messages that nobody else can see.'

'Right,' said Strike. 'And what's the point?'

'I don't know,' said Robin, laughing again. 'It can be fun: there are a lot of jokes and stuff on there. You can communicate directly with famous people. Have a bit of banter.'

'People used to go to pubs for that – admittedly, not the talking to famous people bit ... Yeah, probably best you look into Anomie's output, as you understand Twitter.'

'And what would you think about me signing up for an evening class at North Grove? If I can't turn up anything useful, I could back out and you could go in as yourself to question them.'

'Good thinking,' said Strike, 'and better you than me, as you can actually draw.'

So Robin made a note to herself.

'And then there's motive,' said Strike, tapping the end of his pen against his notebook.

'I thought—' began Robin, smiling, but Strike, correctly anticipating the rest of her sentence, said:

'This isn't a normal case. Means are still going to be key, but the "why" is more relevant here than usual, because there's an inconsistency, isn't there? The game can't have been created as a means of driving Ledwell to suicide, because – well, why would it? The game was surely done out of love for the cartoon.'

'Especially as they weren't monetising it.'

'Right – but then Anomie switched and became highly abusive over Twitter.'

'Edie thought that was because she criticised the game in an interview.'

'Don't you think that's a fairly flimsy reason for nigh on four years of persecution?'

'If a disordered personality's found something that speaks to them on a level they've never experienced before, any criticism from the creator, or any change to the work, might feel like a personal attack,' said Robin.

'Yeah,' said Strike, nodding slowly. 'Good point.'

'I watched a video of Edie and Josh discussing the cartoon, you know,' Robin said. 'They were answering fans' questions and discussing Harty, who's the hero – that black heart you just saw. They disagreed over whether he's evil or not, whether he was *made* evil and is a victim, or whether he caused the evil his owner did while alive. In the first episode of the cartoon, Harty introduces himself as evil, quite cheerfully. Could someone who feels they don't fit in with society see something of themselves in Harty? Is that why they've got so obsessive about the cartoon?'

'You think we should add "evil and knows it" to the profile?'

'You're joking,' said Robin, 'but maybe we should ... You know, I keep wondering why they called themselves "Anomie". Wouldn't you expect a superfan to choose the name of one of the characters? Calling themselves Anomie's almost ... almost declaring upfront what they are, isn't it? "A lack of moral or societal values." They're being weirdly open about it ... unless they're just some disaffected teenager,' she added, second-guessing herself. 'It's the kind of name a teenager might pick, I suppose. Somebody who's feeling angry at the world.'

'You're making a good case for the fact we're hunting a crazed fan, not a personal friend.'

'They can't be an ordinary fan, though, can they? They know too many personal things about her, they've got access to inside information, which *does* suggest a friend ... although I suppose Anomie wasn't necessarily in *direct* contact with Josh or Edie,' said Robin. 'They could be at one remove. We should check out partners or flatmates of anyone close to Edie and Josh. There can't be too many intermediaries, though. Anomie's known things too quickly. It surely can't be a friend-of-a-friend-of-a-friend.'

'I wouldn't have thought so,' agreed Strike.

Both sat in thought until Strike broke the short silence.

'There's a definite vein of narcissism here as well. Anomie thinks they should be in charge of the cartoon.' He picked up his phone again. 'Which brings us back to Wally Cardew. I'd say he's exactly the kind of egotistical little prick who wouldn't like his game being criticised, however mildly.'

'How come you know so much about Cardew?'

'Watched one of his videos on YouTube,' said Strike, now accessing it on his mobile. 'A few hours after Ledwell and Blay were named as stabbing victims, Wally and his sidekick, MJ, did a livestream during which Cardew pulled out a bloody knife from under the desk – for a joke. It was really tomato sauce.'

'Witty,' said Robin coldly.

'"Cookies",' said Strike, who'd found what he was looking for. 'This is the video that got him sacked. Haven't watched this one.'

Strike glanced around to make sure nobody was in earshot, then turned the phone on its side and propped it against his beer glass so that Robin could watch as well, and pressed play.

Wally and MJ stood side by side in front of a table of baking ingredients and a large mixing bowl. Blond Wally was long-haired and MJ chubby-faced and a little untidier than in the video Strike had watched the day after the stabbings. Both were wearing aprons and chef's hats.

'*Welcome bwahs!*' said Wally in a high-pitched voice, '*Today we is mingling with smugliks and mukfluks who is saying we is making bad racist jokes and that we is fascist mukfluks!*' He reverted to his normal voice. 'So today, we're just gonna do some baking, keep things mellow.' He showed MJ a bag of flour. 'Is this kosher?'

'It's halal,' said MJ.

'That's the same thing, right?'

'No, dude,' said MJ, half-laughing, 'it's—'

'*Don't be smuglik, bwah,*' said Wally in his falsetto. '*Play the game, bwah!*'

MJ laughed as Wally upended the bag of flour and poured it energetically into the mixing bowl, spilling quantities and making a dusty cloud rise into the air.

'And we put in the nice kosher butter,' said Wally, holding up a pack with a Star of David drawn on it in thick felt-tip and dropping it, unwrapped, into the bowl, before picking up a carton of milk.

'And we put in – is this kosher? *Is cows kosher, bwah?*'

175

'Cows are – is it Hindu where they're holy?' asked MJ.

'Who thinks cows are fucking holy? *These people is mukfluks, they is all mukfluks,*' said Wally, splashing the milk into the mixing bowl and making sure to splatter MJ, who backed off, laughing.

'And the eggs are kosher, look – nice,' said Wally, showing them to camera. As with the butter, he'd drawn on Stars of David. He now threw the eggs into the bowl, hard, with the clear intention of getting MJ as covered in the mixture as possible.

'*You is nice white boy now, MJ,*' said Wally in his Drek voice, as MJ, half-laughing and half-coughing, wiped flour off his face.

'*And we mixes and mixes,*' said Wally, grabbing a spoon and flicking more of the soggy mass at MJ. '*And we sings: "Ebony and ivory live together in perfect harmony—"*'

'Fuck, dude, stop!' said MJ, still laughing but now trying to shield himself from the mixture Wally was throwing at him.

'*And now we has nice mixture, bwahs,*' said Wally.

The video cut to a shot of Wally and MJ with a ball of uncooked cookie dough on the table in front of them. MJ was completely covered in flour, Wally entirely clean.

'*And now we smashes this mukfluk,*' said Wally, taking a rolling pin and smashing the ball of dough with one end of it, '*and now we cuts up mukfluk into smuglik pieces.*' He took a gingerbread-person-shaped cookie cutter and pressed it into the dough.

The video cut again, to several rows of perfect gingerbread men, each with a Star of David on them, and some with yarmulkes and payots.

'Oh no,' said Robin, who could see exactly where this was heading. Strike's expression was impassive.

'*And now we puts smugliks into oven and turns it up high, high, high,*' said Wally in his falsetto.

The video cut to Wally putting the tray into an oven, then to a cartoon hand turning up a dial to 'fucking hot', and finally back to Wally and MJ standing in front of their table, both with their arms folded. In his normal voice, Wally now turned to MJ and asked:

'See the game Saturday?'

'Yeah, nice goal by Drogba,' said MJ, equally seriously.

'See what Fuller—?'

'Yeah,' said MJ. 'Stamping on a guy's fucking balls is not fucking cool.'

There was a pause, and both young men drummed their fingers on their arms.

'Think the cookies are done?' Wally asked MJ.

'Yeah, maybe,' said MJ.

Wally checked his watch.

'Might give 'em a bit longer.'

The video cut to a black screen with the words '1 hour later' written across it, then back to Wally and MJ, who were now standing in front of an oven billowing black smoke. They continued to talk, apparently oblivious.

'. . . take my gran out for the day,' Wally was saying.

'That's nice, dude, that's a nice thing to do.'

There was another brief silence, then Wally said:

'Yeah, they should be done by now.'

He opened the oven door, coughing.

The video cut to a close-up shot of cookies burned beyond recognition, then to a wide shot of Wally and MJ holding their chef's hats in silent respect, candles burning in a menorah behind them. Strike hit pause and looked at Robin.

'Not amused?'

'On what planet is *that* satire?'

'We're obviously too stupid to grasp the delicate irony. Incidentally, I noticed when I watched the livestream he did the night after the stabbings that a few of Wally's fans had the number eighty-eight after their names. You add together Holocaust jokes, far-right followers and a connection to *The Ink Black Heart*—'

'And you can definitely see why MI5 might have questions,' said Robin.

'You can. On the other hand, Cardew might not know he's attracted neo-Nazi fans. There's a chance,' said Strike, picking up his pint again, 'he thinks because his best mate's brown he can't possibly be racist.'

'You know, if Wally's Anomie, and was recruited to The Halvening after making the game—'

'The switch from fan to persecutor is explained, yeah,' said Strike. 'When you're going through Anomie's Twitter account, pay attention for any indication as to what their politics are. I'd imagine MI5 have checked, but I doubt they'll share their conclusions with us.'

Robin made another note.

'If it's not a Halvening member, though,' said Strike, 'we're left with the question of why these two creators are so keen on maintaining their anonymity. You'd think they'd be proud of the game, if they're genuinely just two kids having fun. Richard Elgar said back there he thinks Anomie being unmasked would hurt them and I agree as far as that goes, but *why* would it hurt them? Why don't they want credit?'

'Anomie's getting a *kind* of public credit,' said Robin. 'Fifty thousand followers on Twitter and a lot of interest in who they really are. That must feed their ego.'

'True, but you heard what Elgar said: revealing themselves back in the early days might've got them some genuine input into the franchise, so why didn't they do it? And then there's the lack of monetisation.'

'Well, we know why that is, don't we?' said Robin. 'It'd be copyright violation, making money out of someone else's characters.'

'True, but I'm looking at it from a different angle. Anomie and Morehouse have spent years working on the game without earning anything from it. That suggests people with a lot of time on their hands and no great need for money. Are they being supported by someone else? Parents? Taxpayers?'

'There are *some* jobs with downtime,' Robin pointed out. 'They could be self-employed or working part time. They could be making a good living and this is just a hobby.'

'But if Anomie's in work, they must be doing a job where they can access the internet or use their phone whenever they fancy ... which makes Edie's boyfriend, this' – Strike flipped back his notes to find the name – 'this teacher, Phillip Ormond, an unlikely fit.'

'He was never a possibility, though, surely?' said Robin. 'Why would her boyfriend want to persecute her online? Anyway, they wouldn't have been together when Anomie started the game. She was still dating Josh.'

'It isn't unknown for people to play games with their nearest and dearest online, or even for someone to date a person without realising they've met them online,' said Strike, 'but I agree, Ormond's unlikely. On the other hand, he should be able to tell us who Edie was close to, or might have confided in, other than the people we've already heard about.

'So,' said Strike, picking up his pen again, 'I'll contact Ormond, Katya Upcott and that foster sister, Catriona. Short term,' he continued, 'we'll put surveillance on Seb Montgomery and Wally Car—'

Robin's phone rang.

'Oh my God, that's the estate agent,' said Robin, looking suddenly panicked, and she answered. 'Hello, Andy?'

Strike watched Robin's expression change from tension to elation.

'Seriously? Oh, that's fantastic! Thank you! ... Yes! ... Yes, definitely! ... When? No, that's fine by me ... OK ... I will ... Thanks so much!'

'Bad news?' said Strike as Robin hung up, beaming.

'I got the flat! Oh, wow – you know what, I *am* going to have a drink. I'm not working this evening.'

'I'll get it,' said Strike, but Robin was already on her feet. As she edged out from behind the table she bent down impulsively and hugged Strike, her hair falling over his face, and he inhaled the perfume he'd bought her on her thirtieth.

'Sorry – I'm just so bloody happy – this is going to make such a difference to my life!'

'No need to apologise,' said Strike, patting her arm as she released him. Robin went to the bar and Strike, realising he was grinning foolishly, consciously repressed his smile. He could still feel the warm shape of Robin's body, pressed briefly against him.

20

I have forged me in sevenfold heats
A shield from foes and lovers,
And no one knows the heart that beats
Beneath the shield that covers.

Mary Elizabeth Coleridge
The Shield

In-game chats between five of the eight moderators of *Drek's Game*

<Moderator Channel>

<19 March 2015 18.25>

<Present: Anomie, Hartella>

Anomie: we're still getting a shit ton of new people trying to get into the game.

Hartella: really?

<Worm28 has joined the channel>

Worm28: I 've had such a crap day

<Vilepechora has joined the channel>

Vilepechora: lol any of you on Twitter right now?

Hartella: no, why?

Vilepechora:
#ExhumeLedwell's trending

Anomie: yeah I saw
that. It's not funny

Vilepechora: I thought
you'd find it fkn
hysterical

Anomie: I don't want
her dug up

Vilepechora: not
growing a conscience
are you, bwah?

Anomie: I just want her to
stay where she is and rot

Anomie: it's Uncle
Grunt we need to
concentrate on now

**<Fiendy1 joins the
channel>**

Fiendy1: are any of u on
Twitter at the moment?

Vilepechora: we've just
been talking about it,
fucking hilarious but
Anomie doesn't think so

Fiendy1: it's not
hilarious it's horrible.
what if her family saw it?

Anomie: she was always telling
us she didn't have any family.

Hartella: I agree with
Fiendy1, it's horrible

>

>

Anomie: I'm not accepting
any new applications til

numbers drop off. Let the
pigs get bored.

Fiendy1: what are you
on about?

Anomie: We're getting about
100 new applications a day
atm. Police, probably. So I'm
not accepting anyone new

Vilepechora: good for u mate

Fiendy1: if it's police
they could hack us

Vilepechora: nah

Vilepechora: Morehouse
is supposed to have
made us impregnable

Fiendy1: where is he
anyway? I thought he
was modding tonight?

Vilepechora:
impregnating Paperwhite
somewhere, probably

Worm28: Hartela swapped
shifts with him because
he 's got something on

Vilepechora: got on
something, more like.

Vilepechora: don't blame
him. She's fkn gorgeous.

Fiendy1: How do u know?

Vilepechora: That's
classified

Fiendy1: I gtg

<Fiendy1 has left the
channel>

Vilepechora: lol, such
a little fag

<A new private channel
has opened>

<19 March 2015 18.30>

<Hartella invites Anomie>

Hartella: you don't
seriously think the police
are trying to get in here?

<Anomie has joined the
channel>

Anomie: stands to reason

Hartella: why?

Anomie: probably want
to know if one of us
killed Ledwell

Anomie: scared?

Hartella: why should I
be scared?

Anomie: the dossier you
took to Blay 'proving'
I'm Ledwell?

>

Hartella: who told you?

Anomie: Paperwhite told
Morehouse and he told me.

Anomie: it's not a
problem. I've had it
out with LordDrek and
Vile. Honest mistake.

Hartella: I thought
you'd be livid.

Anomie: nah, it's kind
of funny.

Anomie: and don't
forget the silver lining

Worm28: don 't say that

Vilepechora: can I ask
u something, Worm?

Worm28: what ?

Vilepechora: why do
you put a space before
every punctuation mark?

Worm28: what ?

Vilepechora: like, where
did you go to school?

<Worm28 has left the channel>

Vilepechora: rofl

Hartella: oh, Vile, did you have to?

Anomie: hahahaha

Hartella: what?

Anomie: Fedwell's dead

Hartella: omg Anomie,
don't joke

Anomie: However, I
think you should
increase my percentage
of the royalties as an
apology

Anomie: because, let's
face it, without me
you've got fuck all

Hartella: I'd have to
talk to P

Anomie: you do that

**<Hartella has left has
left the channel>**

21

'Bet you a tenner they've decided not to admit new players to *Drek's Game* because they think they're being watched by the police,' Strike told Robin as their paths crossed at the office one Thursday lunchtime, three weeks after they'd taken on the Anomie case.

'Yeah, I'm not taking that bet,' said Robin, who was finishing off a sandwich at the partners' desk, Anomie's Twitter account on the screen in front of her.

In spite of multiple attempts by both Strike and Robin to get inside the game, they continued to be presented with the animated Harty shrugging and telling them to 'try again, bwah'. Currently, their only hope of ruling out either Seb Montgomery or Wally Cardew was for Anomie to tweet at a moment when one of the targets was under observation and not using any digital device. This was, to say the least, an unsatisfactory situation.

'Where are you off to?' Robin asked Strike, who'd just dropped off his receipts to Pat and still had his coat on.

'Taking over from Dev in fifteen minutes,' said Strike, checking his watch. 'I'll be following Montgomery to yet another hipster bar this evening, I expect. I watched a couple of episodes of the cartoon last night, by the way. Thought I should, to understand what the hell we're investigating.'

'What did you think?'

'I think it's insane,' said Strike. 'What's that Drek character s'posed to *be*?'

'I don't think even Josh and Edie knew,' said Robin.

'How's that going?' Strike asked, pointing at Anomie's Twitter feed.

'A few interesting bits and pieces,' said Robin, 'but nothing major so far.'

'We should do a full catch-up soon,' said Strike. 'By the way, Phillip Ormond can meet us next Thursday. He's been in Ireland. School holidays.'

'Great. Have you heard back from Katya Upcott?'

'No,' said Strike. 'I spoke to her husband, who told me she was visiting Blay in hospital and sounded quite pissed off about it. She hasn't rung back. Might give her a nudge this afternoon. Anyway . . . enjoy Twitter.'

The April day was sunny and the short walk to Newman Street gave Strike time to smoke a cigarette. Upon seeing Strike approaching, Shah moved off down the street without speaking to him, which told Strike their target remained inside the building with the splashy graphic design in primary colours on its glass double doors.

Strike was just debating whether to sit down at the conveniently placed café opposite the office and order a coffee when the glass doors opened and Seb Montgomery emerged.

He looked exactly like a hundred other young men walking the Fitzrovia streets this lunchtime: medium height, skinny, neatly groomed beard, dark hair cut long on top and cropped at the sides, just like Wally Cardew's, and all-black outfit comprising T-shirt, bomber jacket, jeans and trainers. Seb also had a messenger bag slung over his shoulder and a phone in his hand, on which he was currently typing. Strike automatically checked Anomie's Twitter feed, which was inactive.

Strike thought he detected a jaunty air about Montgomery, as though his working day was over even though it was barely two o'clock. This suspicion was confirmed when, instead of turning into any of the eateries along his route, Montgomery went into Goodge Street Underground station, Strike following at a distance.

The detective soon realised Montgomery wasn't going home, because he boarded the Northern line. Strike entered the same carriage, standing in the corner by choice, watching Montgomery's reflection in the dark window. The young man sat with his knees wide apart, effectively blocking the seats on either side of him, apparently playing some game on his phone and glancing up periodically. As they approached Highgate station, Montgomery pocketed his phone, hitched his messenger bag back onto his shoulder and headed for the doors.

Strike allowed a group of four young women to pass ahead of him up the escalator, so that he wasn't too close to his target. As he reached street level, his phone vibrated in his pocket. Barclay had sent a text.

Cardew heading north. Possibly Highgate

Montgomery had left the station, but advanced only as far as a tall, prematurely balding young man standing just outside it. The unknown man's jeans, shirt and jacket were nondescript, as suitable for a man of fifty as they were for a person in his late twenties, which Strike guessed him to be. Montgomery and the stranger shook hands, both looking slightly awkward, though evidently they knew each other, because Strike caught routine exchanges of 'how's it going?' and 'long time no see'. The detective lingered inside the station, because it was clear to him that Montgomery and the unknown young man were waiting for someone else to join them, and it didn't take great perspicacity to guess who the third person was.

Already at station, he texted Barclay. **SM here waiting for WC. Suggest we greet each other and follow them in tandem.**

Twenty minutes later, by which point Montgomery and his unknown companion seemed to have exhausted everything they had to say to each other, Wally Cardew appeared through the ticket barrier, wearing jeans and a T-shirt that read 'Fuck Calm, Die in Battle and Go to Valhalla'. Upon seeing Montgomery and the second man he said loudly, in his Drek falsetto,

'*You is a pair of mukfluks!*' and the other two laughed, though Strike thought he saw a shade of apprehension in the taller man's expression. Montgomery reciprocated Wally's complicated hip-hop handshake and the failure of the second man to do so correctly generated some ice-breaking laughter. The threesome had moved off up the street together and Barclay emerged from the place where he'd been hovering out of sight.

'Sherlock Bigcock, I presume?' Barclay muttered to Strike.

'And you must be Tartan Twelve-Inch,' replied Strike. 'Shall we?'

They headed off after their targets, who were already two hundred yards away, walking in an apparently prearranged direction.

'What's Cardew been up to?' asked Strike.

'Fuck knows. He's bin inside all day,' said Barclay. 'Maybe they're goin' tae visit the scene o' the crime. Whur's the cemetery from here?'

'Not far,' said Strike, checking his phone, 'and we're heading in the right direction.'

'Who's the baw heid?'

'No idea,' said Strike.

As they followed the three younger men, Strike brought up Anomie's Twitter account again. There was no new activity: the last time Anomie had tweeted was shortly before eleven o'clock that morning, when he'd commented on the terrorist who'd bombed the Boston marathon.

Anomie
@AnomieGamemaster

Haha Dzhokhar Tsarnaev's mother says he's the 'best of the best'

Yeah, you must be so proud, you stupid fucking bitch.

10.58 am   9 April 2015

The three young men Strike and Barclay were following proceeded along a street lined with Georgian houses, eventually turning off the road into the forecourt of a large, white-painted and bow-windowed pub called the Red Lion and Sun, where wooden tables and benches stood among shrubs in pots. After some brief dithering, they decided to sit outside. The tall, bald man disappeared into the pub to buy the first round. Strike took a table a short distance away from their targets, while Barclay headed inside for drinks. The only other drinkers in the beer garden were an elderly couple who were sitting in silence, reading the newspapers while their Cavalier King Charles spaniel snoozed at their feet.

'Nearly a total slaphead now, innee, poor bastard?' Strike heard Cardew say, his speaking voice loud enough to reach Strike. ''E still 'ad enough for a combover last time I saw 'im.'

Montgomery laughed.

'You still at that – wha's it, cartoon place, or—?'

'Digital effects,' said Montgomery, whose accent was middle class. 'Yeah.'

'Fucked anythin' good lately?'

The elderly owners of the Cavalier King Charles spaniel had looked around at this question, then returned their gazes quickly to their papers. Strike thought them wise.

Montgomery laughed again, though with slightly more restraint.

'Yeah, I'm – got a girlfriend. Living together, actually.'

'The fuck you doin' that for?' said Wally in mock outrage. 'You're on'y my age!'

'Dunno,' said Montgomery. 'We get on really – ah, here's Nils.'

Strike glanced up over the top of the phone in which he was pretending to be absorbed. A sallow-skinned giant of a man with long blond hair and an untidy goatee was crossing the road, heading towards the pub. The newcomer looked as though he was in his forties, wore a loose, dark pink shirt, khaki cargo shorts and dirty Birkenstocks, and had to be at least six foot six. Beside him walked a boy who was unmistakably his son: both had wide, upturned mouths and hooded, downturned eyes, which gave a peculiarly mask-like appearance. Though already as tall as Seb Montgomery, the boy's slightly pigeon-toed, childish walk made Strike suspect he was far younger than his size would have suggested: perhaps eleven or twelve.

'*Shit*,' said Wally, 'he's brought fucking Bram with him. And where's Pez?'

'Nils!' said Montgomery as the tall man reached the table. 'How's things?'

'Good to see you, Seb,' said Nils, smiling as he shook Montgomery's hand. He had a very slight accent, and Strike, remembering that the owner of North Grove Art Collective was Dutch, guessed he was looking at him. 'And you, Wally. Hey, Tim!' he continued as the tall, balding young man re-emerged from the pub carrying three pints.

'Nils, hi,' said Tim, setting down the drinks and shaking hands. 'Hi Bram.'

The boy ignored Tim.

'Wally?' he said in a high treble voice, looking excited. 'Wally?'

'What?' said Wally.

'*Play the game, bwah!*'

'Yeah,' said Wally, with a forced laugh. 'Very good.'

'I watch you on YouTube!'

'Yeah?' said Wally, without enthusiasm. He turned to Nils. 'Pez not coming?'

'No, he had something to do,' said Nils. 'Or someone,' he added. Wally and Seb laughed, but Tim remained po-faced.

Barclay returned with zero-alcohol beer for himself and Strike. The two detectives now made intermittent, mumbled small talk as they continued to listen to the far louder conversation of the group they were observing. Seb's mobile lay on the table beside his beer, whereas the others' phones were out of sight. Strike was keeping an eye on Anomie's Twitter feed, which was still inactive. When Nils went to fetch drinks for himself, Bram remained behind, constantly squealing Drek catch-phrases, impervious to Wally's increasingly obvious irritation.

'*Drek is lonelik and borkled! You is all smugliks! Play the game, bwah!*'

'He loves Drek,' said Nils unnecessarily on arrival back at the table, handing Bram a Coke before folding his gigantic legs beneath the table. '*So* . . . I think we should toast, yes? To Edie – and to Josh's recovery.'

None of the three younger men appeared to have expected a toast. Indeed, the balding Tim blushed, as though somebody had said something unspeakably offensive. However, all three drank, before Montgomery said:

'How's Josh doing, Nils, have you heard?'

'Yeah, I spoke to Katya last night. She sends all of you her love. She was in tears. So, he's paralysed all down the left side' – Nils demon-strated on his own body – 'and has no sensation on his right. The spinal cord isn't severed, but seriously damaged. It's got a name, his condition. A syndrome.'

'Shit,' said Montgomery.

'Bloody awful,' said Tim.

'But there's a chance it will improve,' continued Nils. 'Katya says there's a chance.'

Nils's son, who'd remained seated only long enough to down his Coke in one, stood up again, looking around for something to do. He saw a pigeon pecking at a few crumbs of crisps on a free table and ran at it, arms windmilling. Once it had flown away, Bram spotted the Cavalier King Charles spaniel asleep under the table and strode boldly over to the owners.

'Can I stroke your dog?' he asked loudly.

'I'm afraid he's asleep,' said the elderly female owner, but Bram ignored her. He fell to his knees and began fussing at the dog, which woke with a start, growled and snapped. A minor commotion ensued, in which the elderly couple, doubtless afraid their dog would be blamed for taking a chunk out of the boy, tried to restrain it while attempting to persuade Bram to leave it alone, a feat that proved beyond their power. Nils sat enjoying his beer, apparently as oblivious to the commotion behind him as Bram had been to Wally's displeasure at his non-stop Drek impressions. The four men were still talking but Strike and Barclay couldn't hear what they were saying, because the elderly couple, who'd decided to leave, were making a lot of noise about it. The barking dog was now held tightly in the husband's arms; Bram, who was as tall as the old man, kept trying to stroke it even while the old man kept turning to and fro, and all the while the elderly woman kept repeating, 'No, dear, please don't. *Please* don't, dear.'

When finally the dog-owners had left, the grinning Bram returned to the table and said '*Smugliks is gone*' to Wally, who ignored him. Seb was talking in a low voice; the other three men's attention was fixed on him and Strike could only just make out what was being said.

'. . . at work,' he said. 'So I called them back, obviously, and I said I was happy to help and all that, you know, but I'd rather not do it at the office. So, yeah, they said that was OK and they came round the flat Saturday morning.'

'How long did they talk to you for?' asked Tim.

''Bout an hour.'

'Can I have something to eat? Nils? . . . Nils? . . . Nils, can I have something to—?'

If Seb hadn't stopped talking at Bram's interruption, Strike had a hunch his father would have ignored him indefinitely. Nils pulled a crumpled note out of his pocket and gave it to his son, who scampered off into the pub.

'So, yeah,' Seb resumed, 'basically they told me Edie – this is fucking insane, but – they said Edie thought I was Anomie.'

'Thought you were *Anomie*?' said Nils, looking surprised.

'Yeah, that fan who made that game online,' said Seb. 'That multi-player game. You remember. Josh and Edie hated it.'

'I didn't know they called themselves "Anomie",' said Nils. 'That's strange.'

'Who the hell did she tell *that* to, that you were Anomie?' asked Tim.

'They didn't say. So after that they asked me a ton of questions about my social media accounts—'

'She wasn't stabbed on social fuckin' media,' said Wally. 'I dunno why they're so fixated on that.'

'It's that neo-Nazi group, isn't it?' said Seb. 'They probably think Anomie's one of them.'

'So,' said Tim, who looked anxious, 'did they take away your phone or your hard drive or—?'

'No, thank Christ,' said Seb. 'Not that – you know what I mean. Nobody wants the police going through their hard drive, do they?'

All three men shook their heads and Tim laughed.

'No, they asked a load of questions, I showed them my Twitter account and logged on in front of them to prove it was me, I showed them my Instagram page, and I told them, that's it, that's all I do on social media.'

'Didn't they ask you where you was when they were—?' began Wally.

'Yeah,' said Seb. 'They did.'

'Christ, did they?' said Tim.

Bram now reappeared, accompanied by a barman, who was holding a bag of crisps.

'Nils,' said the latter, 'I've told you: we can't sell to under-eighteens in the pub.'

'He only wants crisps,' said Nils.

'An adult needs to buy them for him,' said the barman, putting the crisps and change down on the table and walking away, his exasperation showing this was a conversation that had been had before. Bram wriggled back onto the bench, opened his crisps and ate for a while in silence.

'So did you give 'em, like, your alibi?'

'"*Alibi*",' repeated Seb, with a little snort, as though he could defuse the word by laughing at it. 'Yeah, I told them I was meeting some mates, but I got the pub wrong.'

'Whoa, fishy, bwah,' said Wally, and Bram laughed loudly.

'I realised I was in the wrong place and went and found them. It wasn't a big deal.'

'Did they check up with your mates?' asked Wally.

'Yeah.'

'Bloody hell,' said Tim. 'They're being thorough.'

'Is this the *police*?' asked Bram at the top of his voice. Everyone ignored him.

'What did they say to you, Wal?' asked Seb.

'I dunno, same sort of shit. I was wiv 'em longer'n an hour, though.'

'Did they ask whether you were Anomie?'

'No, but they asked if I knew 'oo Anomie was, and then they just kept goin' on about some Brotherhood of Ultimate Something.'

'I thought the group's called The Halvening?' said Seb.

'They didn't mention The Halvening, they just kept talkin' about this fuckin' Brotherhood,' said Wally. 'I said, "I'm not in no fucking Brotherhood, do I look like a monk?" And they asked me about being sacked as Drek and all that, and what I fort of Edie's politics.'

'What did you say?' asked Tim.

'Said I fort 'er politics were a pile of shit. They knew that anyway,' said Wally, whose voice now held an undertone of aggression. 'They'd watched my videos. I said, you wanna go talk to some of the little SJWs. They wanted 'er dead, I didn't. Go find the cunt—'

He caught himself too late, but Bram simply laughed.

'He's heard it all before,' said Nils airily.

'*You is rude mukfluk,*' Bram told Wally, in his Drek falsetto.

'Yeah, well,' said Wally, 'I told 'em, "Go find 'ooever writes that Pen of Justice thing." You seen that?' he asked the others, who all shook their heads.

'*You'd* like the Pen of Justice,' Wally told Tim, with a trace of malice. 'The Worm's transphobic, apparently.'

Tim's smile looked forced.

'Yeah?'

'Yeah. Hermaphrodite, innit? So it's taking the piss out of non-binary kids. Obviously.'

'And did they ask you where they were that afternoon?' asked Seb.

'Yeah, an' I told 'em I was at home with my gran and my sister, and they talked to them an' confirmed it, and that was that.'

'Did they wanna know when you last saw Edie?'

'Yeah,' said Wally. 'I told 'em I 'adn't seen 'er since I got sacked, but I told 'em I still see Josh sometimes.'

'Do you?' said Tim, who sounded surprised.

'Yeah. Well, we were mates before that fuckin' cartoon, weren't we? Anyway, Josh didn't want me gone, did 'e? That was all 'er. And they asked when I last seen Josh and I told 'em New Year. We were at the same party.'

'Yeah?' said Tim.

'Yeah, 'e was off 'is fuckin' face,' said Wally with a harsh laugh. 'Talkin' film deals and shit.'

'Katya was talking about the movie last night,' said Nils.

'It can't happen now, can it?' said Seb. 'If Josh is . . .'

'No, I think it's still going to happen,' said Nils.

Tim now took out his mobile, looked at it, didn't seem to particularly like what he saw, and put it back in his pocket. Simultaneously, Seb picked up his own mobile and tapped something into it before putting it down again. Strike glanced down at Anomie's Twitter feed. There were still no fresh tweets. The two detectives continued to make intermittent small talk, though the four men and the boy didn't seem interested in them, nor particularly worried that anyone might hear their conversation.

'What did they ask *you*, Nils?' asked Tim. 'Why did they want to see you, even?'

'Well, they'd heard Josh was staying at North Grove for a month before they were attacked.'

'Was 'e?' said Wally, looking as surprised as the other two young men.

'Yeah. He flooded his new flat, and the one beneath. A lot of structural damage.'

'Silly sod,' said Seb, but not unkindly.

'So we said he could have his old room for a bit. The police wanted to know all about Yasmin visiting and—'

'Who?' said Seb.

'Ah, that was after your time, perhaps,' said Nils. 'She helped them out for a while, part time. Dealing with fan mail, scheduling interviews and so on.'

'I remember 'er,' said Wally. 'Fat bird, yeah? Edie sacked her an' all.'

'Yeah. Anyway, Yasmin went to Josh's new flat and he wasn't there, so she tracked him down to us, and they had a talk and afterwards Josh had it in his head that Edie was—'

At this point the bored Bram got up again and began spouting Drek phrases at the top of his voice. His eyes slid over Strike and Barclay as he looked around for any kind of distraction.

'*Drek is lonelik and borkled. Drek is lonelik and borkled. Drek is lonelik and borkled.*'

The relentless squawking drowned out everything Nils was telling the three younger men. It was a couple of minutes, though felt much longer, before Nils broke off whatever he saying, took his phone out of the pocket of his cargo shorts and held it wordlessly out to Bram, who grabbed it, sat down again and fell silent as he began to play a game on it.

'So,' resumed Nils, 'Katya says Josh took the dossier with him.'

'Didn't they find it in the graveyard?' asked Seb.

'No,' said Nils. 'They think the attacker took it. *And* Josh's phone.'

'Shit,' said Seb.

'And 'ave the police talked to Pez?' asked Wally.

Nils shook his head.

Tim now took his phone out of his jacket again, and typed something into it. Strike checked Anomie's Twitter feed. It was still inactive.

'I'm gonna have to head off,' said Tim.

'We 'aven't even got to you,' said Wally.

'I told you, they haven't been in touch,' said Tim, now getting to his feet. 'I just thought, if they'd gone to you they must be working their way through everyone involved in *The Ink Black Heart*, but it sounds like they had other reasons for speaking to you three.'

This idea seemed to have reassured Tim.

'Good to see you, anyway,' said Tim. Then, catching sight of a taxi, he said, 'Actually, I might grab that,' and with a wave of his hand jogged out of the beer garden to flag it down.

Wally, Seb and Nils watched Tim go. Bram didn't look up from his game. After the taxi had pulled away, Wally said,

'I always fort he was a bit of a tosser.'

Seb chuckled. Wally now consulted his own phone, and said,

'Yeah, I need to split, too. Give my best to Mariam, Nils. Tell 'er at least I never set fire to nuffing.'

This appeared to make sense to Nils, who smiled and shook hands with Wally.

'Seb, you going back to the Tube?'

'No, I might grab a cab as well.'

'All right, well, see ya.'

Wally set off at a fast pace in the direction of the Underground station. Barclay let him walk out of sight before holding out his hand to Strike, who shook it.

'Nice meetin' you,' Barclay said quietly. 'But ye don't look anything like yer photo.'

'In fairness, it was of my arse,' said Strike, and the grinning Scot departed, leaving Strike alone at the table.

Seb was typing on his phone again. Strike checked his own: Anomie still hadn't tweeted.

'Yeah, think I'll head off, too,' said Seb, draining the last of his pint and now appearing anxious to be gone. 'Good to see you, Nils.'

'We'll walk with you,' said Nils, a suggestion the younger man didn't appear particularly to welcome.

Strike let them get a short head start then got up and followed, intending merely to watch Seb until he got into his cab.

Seb hailed a taxi at the small roundabout a short walk from the pub, leaving Nils and Bram to continue up Hampstead Lane, Bram still playing on his father's phone and regularly bumping into lampposts, walls and people. Strike now paused on the pavement and lit up a cigarette. It was still only mid-afternoon; he had plenty of time to kill before his date with Madeline later, perhaps enough to get back to the flat, shower and change, which was a luxury he didn't often have. Intending only to finish his cigarette before flagging down a cab himself, he remained stationary, smoking, until his eye fell on a thin young woman dressed all in black who was hurrying along the pavement on the other side of the road, her phone pressed to her ear, scanning her surroundings in what looked like desperation.

22

. . . a stunted child,
Her sunk eyes sharpened with precocious care . . .

Christina Rossetti
Behold, I Stand At the Door and Knock

The girl's distress was so evident that Strike's attention was caught. She was tiny, perhaps five feet tall, and thin to the point of emaciation, with protruding collarbones that were visible even from across the street. Her hair, which was almost waist-length, was dyed a blueish black and her eyes were outlined with a lot of black kohl, so that they stood out starkly against her very pale skin. Though her chest looked virtually flat, and in spite of her size, Strike assumed that she was at least eighteen, because she was sporting a half-sleeve of black tattoos on her left arm. Her thin black vest top, long skirt and flat ankle boots all looked old and cheap.

Evidently the person she was trying to call wasn't picking up. Every minute or so she'd stab at the phone with her finger and raise it to her ear again, still looking wildly up and down the street. Finally she began to walk quickly in the direction from which Strike had just come.

Strike turned back and followed the girl, still smoking as he watched her hurry along on the opposite pavement. When he'd almost reached the Red Lion and Sun, she ran across the road, phone still clamped to her ear. Strike slowed down, watching her scan the tables, which were occupied with a few more drinkers, before hurrying into the pub. As she darted across Strike's path he saw her close up. Her teeth looked too big for her sunken face and, with a small thrill of surprise, he recognised one of the tattoos on her forearm: Harty, the jet-black hero of *The Ink Black Heart.*

Now definitely intrigued, Strike stood waiting on the pavement, because he had a feeling that whoever the girl was trying to find wouldn't prove to be in the pub. Sure enough, she re-emerged in under a minute, phone still held to her ear, though not talking. After standing irresolute on the pavement for a few seconds while Strike pretended to examine something on his own phone, she walked away from the pub more slowly, giving the impression of one whose destination is no longer important, although she kept trying to reach somebody on her phone, holding it to her ear until, Strike guessed, voicemail answered, then lowering the mobile without speaking, pressing (Strike assumed) 'try again', then raising it to listen once more.

Strike continued to follow her at a distance of twenty yards. A quantity of cheap silver bangles clinked on her wrists. Her shoulder blades were as prominent as her collarbones. She was so thin Strike could have reached around her upper arm with one hand. He wondered whether she was anorexic.

As Strike followed his quarry into Highgate High Street, his own mobile began to vibrate in his pocket and he took it out.

'Strike.'

'Oh, yes, hello,' said a jittery middle-class voice. 'This is Katya Upcott.'

'Ah, thanks for getting back to me, Mrs Upcott,' said Strike, continuing to follow the black-clad girl. She was so small, the six-foot-three Strike felt slightly creepy following her, and was hanging well back.

'Yes, I'm *terribly* sorry, Inigo wrote your number on the notepad but he got one of the digits wrong and I kept getting some poor woman who was getting really annoyed at me, so I called your agency just now and a very nice man called Pat gave me the right number.'

Grinning slightly, Strike said,

'Very good of you to take the trouble. You know what I'm calling about, I take it?'

'Anomie, yes,' she said. 'I'm delighted Allan and Richard have called you in. I certainly hope you can find out who he is. Josh' – her voice became slightly higher as she said the name – 'is so distressed – I know they told you about it – just an awful misunderstanding,' she said, and he thought she sounded on the verge of tears. 'We're both so happy it's you. I read Josh an article about you.'

'Well, we're certainly going to do our best,' said Strike. 'How *is* Josh?'

'He's—' Her voice broke. 'I'm so sorry … it's just been so ghastly. He's being very – very brave. He's paralysed. They call it Brown-Séquard Syndrome; he can't move at all on one side and he's lost all feeling on the other. They're saying this kind of paralysis *can* improve, and I'm trying to – everyone's trying to be positive – he wants to meet you. He managed to tell me so, this afternoon, but the doctors would rather he's not fussed just yet, because he's struggling to talk and the subject of Edie gets him so agitated and – and distressed—'

She gave a little gasp, and Strike heard muffled crying and guessed she'd put her hand over the receiver.

Ahead of him, the young woman in black had turned right into a park. Strike followed.

'S-so sorry,' sobbed Katya Upcott in his ear.

'Please don't apologise,' said Strike. 'Terrible situation.'

'It *is*,' she said, as though he'd said something profoundly insightful, which nobody else around her had spotted. 'It really *is*. He – he feels so *horrible* about Edie, and about accusing her of being Anomie. I … He dictated a letter to me, to put in her – in her – in her coffin. Saying how s-s-sorry he was and – and what she'd meant to him – he's *twenty-five*,' sobbed Katya, without explanation, but Strike knew what she meant. The man who'd had his body ripped in half in the explosion that had taken half of Strike's right leg had been the same age as Josh Blay.

'Sorry, sorry,' repeated Katya, clearly fighting to get control of herself. 'I visit him every day. He doesn't really have anyone else. His father's a raging alcoholic and his friends – well, people of that age, they're all scared of what's happened, I think. Anyway, the doctors want him kept quiet just now.'

'Well, I certainly don't want to bother him until the doctors think he's up to it,' said Strike, 'but I'd very much like to talk to *you*, given that you knew Josh and Edie right from the beginning of *The Ink Black Heart*. I'd like to know who's been close to them, because as you know, Anomie seems to have got hold of a lot of personal information about Edie.'

The girl he was following continued to walk along the paved path through the middle of the park, her phone pressed against her ear.

'Of course, yes, anything I can do to help,' said Katya. 'Edie moved around a lot before she went to North Grove. She had a lot of ex-flatmates and people she'd worked with. I'll help in any way I can – I've promised Josh I will.'

'How would you be fixed next week?' Strike asked.

'Yes, next week should be fine, but – I expect Allan told you I work from home,' said Katya. 'Would it be convenient for you if we met in a café, rather than at my house? Because my husband's ill, you see, and I'd rather not disturb him.'

'No problem at all,' said Strike. 'Whereabouts is good for you?'

'Well, we're in Hampstead – would that be too far?'

'Not at all,' said Strike. 'I'll be in your area on Thursday, to speak to Phillip Ormond. You know—?'

'Yes, I know who Phillip is.'

'I'm meeting him at six o'clock, in a pub near the school where he teaches. Perhaps I could talk to you that afternoon, before I see Phillip?'

'Thursday, Thursday,' she said, and he heard the turning of pages and assumed Katya was that increasingly rare beast, a person who kept a physical diary. 'Yes, Thursday should be fine. I usually visit Josh in the afternoons, but I know he'd rather I prioritised talking to you.'

They agreed on a time and a café in Hampstead, then Katya thanked him again for taking the case in a now slightly husky voice and rang off.

The girl ahead of Strike was still walking and trying to call somebody on her phone. Strike brought up Anomie's Twitter feed again. There were no fresh tweets.

The end of his amputated leg was starting to chafe, in spite of the gel pad between stump and prosthesis. There'd been a lot of unexpected walking this afternoon. Strike kept his eyes focused on the girl's left arm and those intricate tattoos. They must have cost a decent amount, he thought, but if she had hundreds of pounds to spend on tattoos, why were her clothes so worn and cheap?

Quite suddenly, the girl stopped walking. She was talking into the phone at last, her manner extremely agitated as she moved out of the middle of the path and dropped down onto an empty bench, her head bowed, one hand shielding her eyes. Strike moved onto the grass, always a difficult surface to navigate with his prosthesis, and feigned absorption in his own phone. Apparently aimlessly, he approached the place where she was sitting until he was able to hear what she was saying.

'. . . but why couldn't you 'ave *told* me, just *told me*?' she was saying, in a thick Yorkshire accent, which came as a surprise. "Ow d'you think I *felt* when she said you was meetin' Nils?'

A long silence ensued, during which the person on the other end of the phone was clearly talking.

'But *why*, though?' said the girl from Yorkshire. Her voice broke, but unlike Katya, she made no attempt to hide from the person on the end of the phone that she was crying. '*Why?*'

There was another long silence, while the girl's thin shoulders shook and she made gurgling, gasping noises. A young man with the hood raised on his zip-up top passed, his eyes sliding over the sobbing girl without compassion.

'Yeah, but why couldn't I be there too, then? ... But they didn't 'ave to know ... Why did they?'

Another pause, and then she burst out:

'*But you want me to say you was with me when it suits you, don't you?*'

Jumping up from the bench, she started walking again, faster than before. Strike followed, losing ground because he had to move off the grass and back onto the paved path. She was talking vociferously now, gesticulating with her tattooed left arm, and he knew she must be still crying because of the curious stares she was attracting from those walking the other way.

She was now approaching the exit of the park and Strike realised for the first time how close they were to Highgate Cemetery. The park abutted it and he could see glimpses of graves through the trees to his left. His target moved out of the park and turned left into the lane beyond, and as he gained on her, he could hear fragments of what she was saying, so distressed she appeared not to care who heard her.

'I didn't mean ... I never threatened ... why, though? ... just excuses ... working tonight ... No, why, though?'

The person with whom she was talking had evidently hung up. She came to a halt, level with the imposing neo-gothic gatehouse that formed the entrance to the cemetery, and Strike slowed down too, once again pretending interest in his phone. Wiping her eyes childishly on her right forearm, the girl stood irresolute, looking towards the right-hand entrance to the cemetery, and he saw her again in profile and thought her white, sunken face with its too-prominent teeth and black eyes looked like a death's head. The long dyed hair, the tattooed arm and the cheap black clothing all lent her a curious sense of fitness with the scene: she was modern, but she was gothic-Victorian, too, a child mourner in her long black skirt, staring towards the graves. Pretending to be texting, Strike snatched several photographs of her standing still, contemplating the graveyard, before she set off again.

He followed her for another twenty-five minutes, until she reached Junction Road, a long, busy street full of traffic. On she walked, past shops and offices, until at last she turned into Brookside Lane and disappeared through a side door that Strike could tell would lead to the upper rooms of an irregularly shaped corner shop. The windows looked dirty. A sign for a letting agent stood out between two of them.

Strike took pictures of the place on his phone, then turned away to look for a taxi. The end of his stump was now extremely sore and he thought he might prioritise getting a burger over going home to shower and change, in the only-too-likely event of Madeline's chosen bar not offering much beyond spiced nuts.

It was ten minutes before he found a fast food restaurant. Sitting down with a grunt of relief at getting the weight off his prosthesis, he took a large bite of cheeseburger then tried for the umpteenth time to sign up for *Drek's Game*. Just as had happened on every previous occasion, the little black animated heart appeared, smiling and shrugging, and told him to try again.

Strike took a second mouthful of cheeseburger, then switched to Twitter to see whether Anomie had had anything more to say.

The tweet appeared while Strike was eating his chips.

Anomie @AnomieGamemaster

If god meant us to feel sympathetic, why'd he make crying people look so fkn ugly.

5.14 pm   9 April 2015

23

And there is neither false nor true;
But in a hideous masquerade
All things dance on . . .

Amy Levy
Magdalene

In-game chats between six of the
eight moderators of *Drek's Game*

```
<Moderator Channel>

<9 April 2015 19.32>

<Present: Hartella,
Fiendy1, Worm28>

Hartella: Has LordDrek
been in?

Fiendy1: haven't seen
him, why?

Hartella: just wondered

Fiendy1: Anomie still
not letting anyone new
in?

Hartella: No

<Morehouse has joined
the channel>
```

Morehouse: No Anomie?

Hartella: He was here half an hour ago then he disappeared

Morehouse: yeah. He was taking a phone call from me.

Fiendy1: wow, must be like having God's phone number

Worm28: lol

Morehouse: LordDrek and Vilepechora been in?

Hartella: I haven't seen either of them today. Why?

Morehouse: because I'm getting sick of waiting for Anomie to kick them out

Hartella: Morehouse, they're not Halvening, I keep telling you!

Worm28: they cuold be

Hartella: don't be stupid

<Worm28 has left the channel>

Fiendy1: Hartella, stop calling her stupid!

Fiendy1: she's really insecure about her

<A new private channel has opened>

<Anomie invites Morehouse>

<9 April 2015 19.35>

spelling and all that

<Paperwhite has joined
the channel>

Fiendy1: about bloody
time

Fiendy1: I haven't been
able to leave until
you got here, Anomie's
orders

Fiendy1: just because
you're Morehouse's fave
doesn't mean you can
swan in and out whenever
you feel like it.

<Fiendy1 has left the
channel>

Paperwhite: wtf?

Hartella: don't mind
him. He's jealous

Paperwhite: why?

Hartella: because you
and Morehouse got close.
He doesn't like it. I'm
pretty sure he's gay.

Paperwhite: oh, I
didn't know

Hartella: and Worm28's
just stormed off
again. She's so bloody
thin-skinned.

Paperwhite: we've all
got insecurities.

Hartella: I know, but
she's ridiculous. She'd

<Morehouse has joined
the channel>

Anomie: I told you
after the last fucking
time. Don't ever call
me at home again.

Morehouse: You won't
talk to me about it in
here, so I called.

Morehouse: And if you
still won't discuss
it in here, I'll call
again.

Anomie: you can't call
me on the fucking
landline. You can't do
that.

Morehouse: I did it
from a payphone. Your
fucking paranoia!

>

Anomie: yeah, from a
payphone in C********

Morehouse: Can we drop
this fucking childish
****** bollocks?

Anomie: What do
you want from me?
I told you I'd look
into LordDrek and
Vilepechora. I'm still
looking.

Morehouse: it's been
weeks.

Anomie: and it's taken

204

better come back, I
need to be out of here
at 9

Hartella: actually,
maybe you can talk
some sense into
Morehouse

Paperwhite: about what?

Hartella: about LordDrek
and Vilepechora

Hartella: he thinks
they're Nazi terrorists

Paperwhite: are you
sure they aren't?

Hartella: I just happen
to know they can't be,
ok?

Paperwhite: how?

Hartella: just from
conversations I've had
with them

>

Paperwhite: wait, do
you know who they are?

Hartella: no, of course
not

**<Worm28 has joined the
channel>**

Paperwhite: hey, Worm x

Worm28: hi Paperwhite

Hartella: Worm, I
didn't mean to upset

weeks and they're
coming up clean. If
I find anything, I'll
chuck them out.

Morehouse: what do
you expect to find, a
fucking KKK hood?

>

Anomie: look, I can't
kick them out on no
proof.

Morehouse: fuck proof.
You know I always
thought there was
something off about
Vilepechora.

Anomie: They didn't
kill her, ok?

Morehouse: and how the
fuck can you be so sure?

Anomie: I just am. I
happen to know they
were nowhere near
Highgate that night.

Morehouse: fkn hell,
you don't know them in
real life?

Anomie: no, that'd
break rule 14

Morehouse: fuck's sake,
forget rule 14, we're
talking about murder here

Morehouse: what they did,
convincing the others you
were Ledwell, is exactly
the Halvening m.o.

205

you just then

Worm28: ok but I ' m tired of people calling me stupid and moron

Hartella: When have I ever called you a moron?

Worm28: not you, Vilepchero

Worm28: I can ' t spell it

Worm28: and he always goes on about my punnctuation too

Hartella: he doesn't mean it

Hartella: it's just a joke

Paperwhite: not a very funny one

Worm28: no it ' s not

Hartella: ok well I've got to go.

Hartella: see you tomorrow

<Hartella has left the channel>

Paperwhite: u ok, Worm?

Worm28: yes

Worm28: thanks for asking

>

>

Anomie: look, if I find out they're Halvening, they go.

Morehouse: Is that a promise?

Anomie: What do you want me to do, hold your fkn pinkie?

Anomie: I've said I'll look into them

>

>

Anomie: but they're good mods, even if they are Nazis

Morehouse: is that supposed to be funny?

Anomie: kind of, yeah

Morehouse: I feel like you['ve got a reason for wanting to keep them around that you're not telling me

Anomie: like what?

Morehouse: Maybe you're all Halvening together?

Anomie: piss off. I'm not toasting Odin out of a horn or any of that wank

Morehouse: who toasts Odin out of a horn?

>

Paperwhite: if it's any consolation, you're not the only one having problems with other mods. Fiendy1 hates me.

Worm28: he doesn 't, not really

Worm28: he and Morehouse were really good friends but they argeud

Paperwhite: when was this?

Worm28: right before u became a mod

Worm28: I don 't know what it was about

>

Paperwhite: I can't imagine Morehouse arguing with anyone

Worm28: he can be tuough when he needs to be

Worm28: he 's really angry about Lorddrek and Vile still being in here

>

Paperwhite: yeah, I know

Anomie: not gossiping behind the leader's back, are we?

Paperwhite: not

Anomie: The Halvening, probably. Norse runes and all that shit.

>

Morehouse: you're well-informed

Anomie: ffs I read it in the Times like everyone else

Anomie: anyway, you're in no position to lecture me about morals

Morehouse: what's that supposed to mean?

Anomie: wanking yourself stupid over Paperwhite's nudes

Anomie: we agreed when we set this up there'd be none of that

Morehouse: how the fuck do you know she's sent me pics?

Morehouse: are you spying on private channels?

Anomie: no

Anomie: she sent me a pic meant for you by mistake

>

>

>

Morehouse: I don't

207

gossiping, just talking

>

>

>

>

Morehouse: Paperwhite, can I have a word?

Paperwhite: yes of course

Anomie: lol

Worm28: what's going on?

Anomie: lovers' tiff

<Hartella has joined the channel>

Anomie: I was wondering where you were

Hartella: I'm sorry, I'm an idiot. I misread the clock, thought it was later than it is.
I've still got an hour in here before clocking off time.

Anomie: I thought Worm was the only special needs mod in here.

<Worm28 has left the channel>

Hartella: oh god, Anomie, she's only just come back after

believe you

Anomie: ask her

Morehouse: I fucking will

<Morehouse has left the channel>

<Anomie has left the channel>

<Private channel has closed>

<A new private channel has opened>

<9 April 2015 20.04>

<Morehouse invites Paperwhite>

Morehouse: I need to ask you something

<Paperwhite has joined the channel>

Paperwhite: you're scaring me. What's wrong?

Morehouse: Anomie claims you sent him a picture meant for me, by mistake

Paperwhite: oh god

Morehouse: you mean you did?

Paperwhite: yes

I accidentally upset
her!

>

Anomie: well she'd
better not stay away.
She's supposed to be
moderating

>

Anomie: I'll be back in
10 to check and
if she's not here,
there'll be trouble

>

<Anomie has left the
channel>

>

>

Paperwhite: I didn't
tell you because I
thought you'd be really
angry

>

>

Morehouse: shit

>

>

>

Paperwhite: Morehouse,
I'm so sorry, but it
wasn't a bad one, not
dirty or anything

>

Paperwhite: I had to
say I hadn't meant it
for him

Hartella: Paperwhite?

Paperwhite: I know I
should have been more
careful

>

Hartella: I can't
moderate all on my own,
we've got a log jam at
Wombwell again

Paperwhite: I'm really,
really sorry

Morehouse: it's ok

>

Paperwhite: I'll be
there in a minute

Paperwhite: no it
isn't, now he knows
we're breaking rule 14

>

>

>

>

>

Hartella: Paperwhite, I
need you to help!

>

>

>

Paperwhite: I told you,
I'll be there in a minute!

>

>

>

>

>

Paperwhite: where's Worm?

Hartella: flounced out
again

Hartella: Anomie upset her

>

>

>

>

>

>

>

>

Paperwhite: d'you think
he'll ban me?

Morehouse: he can't
unilaterally ban
you, I'm co-creator,
remember?

Morehouse: I just didnt
want Anomie knowing our
business becos he fucks
with people's heads.
He's a control freak.
he doesn't like anyone
having relationships that
don't involve him. Either
you're a suck up like
Hartella or you end up
getting kicked out. Ive
only lasted this long
because he needs me

Paperwhite: I'm so
sorry, Morehouse

Morehouse: no, it's ok

Morehouse: which pic
was it?

Paperwhite: the one in
the pink shirt

Morehouse: ffs I
thought you said it
wasn't dirty?!

Paperwhite: you can't
see nipples

Morehouse: lol is that
the definition?

Paperwhite: yeah

Paperwhite: well, and

>

>

>

>

Paperwhite: ok, where
do you want me?

Hartella: log jam at
Wombwell

Paperwhite: I see it

>

<Worm28 has joined the
channel>

Hartella: thank god,
Anomie's coming back
soon to check you're in
here, Worm

Worm28: I ' m tired of
everyone taking the
piss out of me

Hartella: Nobody's taking
the piss, now come and
help with Wombwell or
we'll all be in the shit

Morehouse: calm down,
I can help as well

<Anomie has joined the
channel>

Anomie: good, everyone's
present and correct

Anomie: shit would've
hit the fan otherwise

pubes

Morehouse: lol

Paperwhite: babe, I'd
better go and moderate
or Anomie'll be on my
case.

Morehouse: yeah ok xxx

Paperwhite: *blows kisses*

<Morehouse has left
the channel>

<Paperwhite has left
the channel>

<Private channel has
closed>

Morehouse: we always
enjoy your motivational
speeches

Anomie: oderint dum
mentuant

>

>

>

>

Anomie: Hartella, ban
that fucker Inky501

Hartella: why?

Anomie: he keeps asking
people what they know
about me

Hartella: oh ok

>

>

>

>

Hartella: that's him gone

Anomie: good

Hartella: Anomie, is
there any news about
Maverick and the film yet?

Anomie: what makes you
think I know?

Hartella: because you

<A new private channel
has opened>

<9 April 2015 20.08>

<Anomie invites Morehouse>

Anomie: well?

<Morehouse joins the
channel>

Morehouse: well what?

>

>

Anomie: have you checked
with Paperwhite whether I
was lying about the pic?

Morehouse: yes

Morehouse: fine, you
weren't lying

Anomie: nice tits, I'll
give you that

Morehouse: fuck off

>

Anomie: are you sure it's
really her in the pic?

Morehouse: yes

Anomie: how? Video

always know everything
first.

Anomie: lol. True.

Hartella: so are they
still planning to make
it or what?

>

>

>

>

>

>

>

>

>

>

>

Anomie: I'll be
revealing what I know
on Twitter in due course

Anomie: so I'm afraid
you won't be able to
break the news ahead
of me

Hartella: that's not
why I'm asking!

>

Anomie: you'll forgive
me if I don't entirely

chatting with her as well?

Morehouse: none of
your business

Anomie: that's a "no" then

Morehouse: why do you care?

Anomie: I don't, bwah.
Just looking out for
you. Do you trust her?

Morehouse: why shouldn't I?

Anomie: just the game,
isn't it?

Anomie: nobody's who they
say they are, in the game

Morehouse: speak for
yourself

Anomie: I'm speaking
for both of us

Anomie: or has she
seen pics of you, too?

Morehouse: fuck off

<**Morehouse has left
the channel**>

>

>

<**Anomie has left the
channel**>

<**Private channel has
closed**>

trust you after recent
events, Hartella.

Anomie: I tend not to
put my faith in people
who hide things from me.

Anomie: and before
anyone points out that
I hide my own identity,
that's a different
matter. Splendide
mendax is my motto.

Worm28: what does that
mean ?

Anomie: 'nobly untruthful'

Anomie: funnily enough,
it applies to my co-
creator too

**<Morehouse has left
the channel>**

24

A silent envy nursed within,
A selfish, souring discontent
Pride-born, the devil's sin.

Christina Rossetti
The Lowest Room

Robin spent the following morning watching Fingers' flat in Sloane Square, grateful for the mild, sunny day, because she was wearing the blue dress she'd last donned for the Ritz. That night she was going out for dinner at an upmarket restaurant ten minutes from the Denmark Street office with lawyer Ilsa Herbert.

Ilsa, who'd been at primary school with Strike, had married one of the detective's London schoolmates, Nick. Robin had become close to them too, because she'd stayed in their spare room for a full month after leaving her ex-husband. She hadn't seen Ilsa for a while, and dinner was supposed to be a joint celebration of Robin getting her flat, on which she hoped soon to exchange contracts (she'd wanted to have this done before celebrating, and a superstitious part of her prayed dinner wouldn't jinx it), and of Ilsa winning a tricky case she'd expected to lose. Ilsa had chosen tonight's venue, Bob Bob Ricard, because she'd never been there and always wanted to go: a British-Russian restaurant, it had buttons in each booth to press for champagne, of which it was supposed to pour more than any restaurant in England.

Fingers finally left his flat around midday, clad head to foot in Armani, and walked the short distance to The Botanist, a restaurant Fingers frequented in the same way Robin and Strike sometimes grabbed lunch in the local kebab shop. Fortunately the blue dress didn't look out of place given the standard of dress of the young women coming in and out of the restaurant. Robin lingered outside until, at 2 p.m., Midge appeared to take over, on time as ever and wearing a pair of Ray-Bans, jeans and a leather jacket.

'He's still having lunch,' said Robin.

'Lazy little shit,' said Midge, and they parted, Robin heading for the office, where she intended to continue combing through Anomie's Twitter feed for personal information.

When Robin had climbed the familiar metal stairs, which wound around the birdcage lift that had been out of order all the time she'd worked for the agency, she found only Pat in the office.

'He's just rung,' Pat informed Robin as she typed away, e-cigarette lodged between her teeth as usual. Robin understood Pat to be referring to Strike, whose name she rarely used. Over time, this habit had come to seem almost affectionate.

'What did he want?' Robin asked as she hung up her raincoat.

'Says he's just sent you an email and some photographs, and if you've got time he'd like to discuss it when he gets back here at half-past four. And you've had a message from a Hugh Jacks.'

'What?' said Robin, turning to look at Pat.

'Yeah, he asked to be put through to you,' said Pat. 'Didn't know who he was, so I said you were busy. He asked you to call back.'

'OK, well, I'm always busy if Hugh Jacks calls the office.'

Pat looked intrigued.

'Some friends tried to set me up with him,' Robin explained, moving to the kettle. 'But I'm not interested, which I'd've thought he'd have realised by now.'

'Stinkier the turd, harder it is to scrape off your shoe,' said Pat laconically.

Having made herself and Pat coffee, Robin proceeded into the inner office to read Strike's email.

Few things arising out of yesterday's surveillance.

Montgomery, Cardew and Tim Ashcroft met at a pub in Highgate to discuss the stabbings. They were joined by a man called Nils and expected someone called Pez, but Pez didn't turn up.

I've identified Nils online. He's Nils de Jong, Dutch owner of North Grove Art Collective. Tim Ashcroft used to have a full head of red hair but is now almost entirely bald. He's the friend of Edie's who voiced The Worm in the cartoon and he's currently a member of a theatrical company that goes into schools to give performances and workshops. Group's called the Roving School Players.

No idea who Pez is, still looking.

Also present was Nils's enormous and obnoxious son, Bram.

Points of interest:

- De Jong, Cardew and Montgomery have all been interviewed by the police. Cardew and Montgomery both gave alibis for the time of the killing: Montgomery was allegedly in the pub with friends and Cardew at home with his sister and grandmother.

- According to online records, Ashcroft, who hasn't been interviewed by the police, is unmarried and lives with his parents in Colchester when he's not on tour with the company. No evidence of computer or design skills.

- Cardew was asked by police whether he belonged to a 'brotherhood' of some kind. This was queried by Montgomery, who said he thought the far-right group was called The Halvening. I've got an idea I've seen or heard something about a brotherhood recently but can't remember where – have you come across anything online, connected to Cardew or the cartoon?

- Blay went back to live at North Grove for a month before he was stabbed, because he flooded his flat (location unknown).

- Blay was visited during his month at North Grove by a woman called Yasmin (no surname given) who used to work for Blay and Ledwell, handling fan mail. According to Cardew, she's fat and Ledwell sacked her.

- Yasmin appears to have given Blay the idea that Ledwell was Anomie and it seems likely she's the source of the dossier of 'proof'.

- Blay set out for the cemetery carrying this dossier, which hasn't been found. The presumption is that the killer took it.

- The killer also took Blay's phone (no mention of Ledwell's).

- Cardew mentioned a blog called 'The Pen of Justice', which seems to have had it in for Ledwell/The Ink Black Heart. Could be worth checking out in case it's an Anomie side venture.

- Shortly after Montgomery, Cardew, Ashcroft and de Jong left the pub, a girl with an armful of Ink Black Heart tattoos appeared, clearly looking for one of them. She phoned some person unknown and asked why they hadn't told her they were meeting Nils and why she hadn't seen them for a month. She's from Yorkshire. Her photo's attached, as is a photo of the place she's living. We should ID her and also find out who, if anyone, she lives with.

We can divvy up these leads when we meet, just wanted to give you an update on what happened yesterday.

Have also got appointments to meet Katya Upcott and Phillip Ormond on Thursday. We should do these together. –S

Robin opened the first attachment and saw the picture of the emaciated black-clad girl staring towards the entrance to the cemetery. Zooming in on the tattoos on the girl's left forearm, Robin saw not only Harty, but also Drek, Paperwhite the ghost and a sad-looking worm. She suspected that all the tattoos, even those she didn't recognise, like the magpie and the two grinning skeletons in Victorian hats, had come out of the cartoon, and like Strike, she wondered how much it had cost the girl to have these characters permanently etched onto her skin.

She opened the second photograph. Even the worst of the flats Robin had viewed hadn't had as shabby an exterior as the wedge-shaped building on Junction Road, with its cracked window frames and dirty plaster.

Turning back to Strike's email, Robin noted that she was already in a position to give him information on one of the items he was asking about. In the course of working her way through three years' worth of Anomie's tweets and Twitter interactions, she'd already come across the Pen of Justice blog. She now opened the document she'd been planning to share with Strike later, and sent it to the printer on Pat's desk.

Next, Robin checked the new Twitter account she'd created for herself, (@inkblackfan:). She'd followed Anomie and Morehouse and added as many *Ink Black Heart* fan accounts as she could find, so she could keep abreast of rumours and developments. Instead of her own picture, she'd used a stock photo of a young and pretty brunette. She'd already received three direct messages.

@jbaldw1n1>>
If that's your real picture you're probably sick to death of
blokes in your DMs so I'll go now.

@Drekbwah9
wank me off

@mreger#5
This isn't a sleazy pick up ploy, just wanted to say that Julius
guy was seriously out of order and I've reported him.

Interested in the third of these messages, Robin went to see what
had provoked it.

Two days previously, Robin had tweeted that she hoped the *Ink
Black Heart* film would remain faithful to the original series, an opinion
she'd thought was uncontroversial. However, the tone of the replies
had been heated. Fans had lined up to tell her that the mere making
of the film, irrespective of its quality, would destroy everything they
loved about *The Ink Black Heart*. However, nobody had taken such
exception to Robin's innocent statement as @i_am_evola.

Julius @i_am_evola
replying to @inkblackfan:)
shallow bitch

Julius @i_am_evola
replying to @inkblackfan:)
if u got raped every time u said something dumb u'd be
permanently full of cok

Robin stared at these messages for a second or two, then went to
look at @i_am_evola's account. The account avatar showed a teenage boy she suspected was sixteen at most. His main preoccupations
seemed to be superhero movies, *The Ink Black Heart* and sending
women messages of the type Robin had just received. Deciding that
nothing good could come of interacting with him, she navigated
back to Anomie's account, then opened the folder of hard-copy
tweets Allan Yeoman had returned to her, which Robin had now
put into date order so she could match them against Anomie's
Twitter feed.

The last tweet she'd examined dated from 2012. When Jimmy

219

Savile, the late DJ and knight of the realm, had been exposed in October of that year as Britain's most prolific known paedophile, Edie Ledwell had tweeted 'How can all these people saying Savile abused them have been ignored? Why did nobody listen?'

Anomie had retweeted Edie's comment with his own: 'Gonna start claiming he was the one who did you? #trollingforsympathy.'

Beneath the printed version of this tweet, Edie had written: *This implies knowledge of the fact that I was sexually abused in one of the foster families I lived with. I've never discussed this publicly.*

Robin now resumed her slow backwards perusal of Anomie's Twitter timeline.

Some of Anomie's tweets were anodyne: in July 2012 they'd shared the fact that they'd enjoyed *The Dark Knight Rises*. In June 2012 they'd informed their followers that a cat was sitting on their garden fence, watching them through a window. 'This is exactly why I own a catapult.'

Joke, wondered Robin, or genuine? Had the cat really been there, or, for that matter, the garden fence? Ought she to add 'possible cat hatred/phobia' to the profile she and Strike were trying to construct?

She continued scrolling.

'People saying I should be paid for my services to the fandom. I'll accept Magnum Infinitys. They're fkn good.'

Hardly a distinguishing characteristic, Robin thought, continuing to scroll. Who didn't like ice cream?

But then, on 8 June 2012, Anomie had had a more interesting revelation.

Anomie
@AnomieGamemaster

Fedwell has ditched Katya Upcott, friend who helped propel #TheInkBlackHeart to success. Now with @<AY©A>. @realJoshBlay stays w Upcott.

11.53 pm   8 June 2012

This tweet had been printed out by Edie, who'd written beneath it: *Anomie knew this had happened within a few hours of me telling Katya I wanted to pay for a real agent. I didn't want Katya to stop representing me because I didn't want to pay. We never had any kind of contract and she always said she didn't want payment. I thought she was giving us bad advice and I wanted to pay for proper representation, because the whole thing was getting bigger and bigger and I felt like it was out of control. Josh didn't like me leaving Katya. He said I was disloyal.*

The fandom hadn't taken kindly to Anomie's revelation either, as the replies proved.

Andi Reddy @ydderidna
replying to @AnomieGamemaster
omfg, when she could actually afford to pay their friend for all the work she done for free, she ditches her?

Caitlin Adams @CaitAdumsss
replying to @AnomieGamemaster
This is a new low, even for #Fedwell. These people helped her and she's just throwing them off.

Arlene @queenarleene
replying to @AnomieGamemaster
Good for @realJoshBlay sticking by Katya, it just makes me love him even more. And at this point, honestly, #fuckFedwell.

Kea Niven @realPaperwhite
replying to @AnomieGamemaster
She's violently racist and ableist. If you're only getting shocked by her now, I don't know where the fuck you've been.

Robin continued scrolling. Just two days prior to the news that Edie had joined Allan Yeoman's agency, Anomie had broken further important news.

Anomie
@AnomieGamemaster

I hear Netflix is sniffing around #TheInkBlackHeart.

#GreedieFedwell prepared to close Drek's Game, sack more original voice artists . . . 1/2

10.06 pm   6 June 2012

Anomie
@AnomieGamemaster
replying to @AnomieGamemaster

... ditch Blay, etc, to cash in.

Make your feelings known to @EdLedDraws and
@realJoshBlay – what should be non-negotiable? 2/2

10.07 pm   6 June 2012

This, too, Edie had printed out and commented on. *The possible deal wasn't public knowledge and we weren't supposed to be talking about it. I wasn't planning on doing any of this rubbish. I didn't have the power to sack Josh, we were partners.*

Robin scrolled through the predictable explosion of fury Anomie's tweets had unleashed.

MrsHarty @carlywhistler_*
replying to @AnomieGamemaster
noooo this isn't real is it? how do you know this?

Anomie @AnomieGamemaster
replying to @carlywhistler_*
The Gamemaster knows all

Timothy J Ashcroft @TheWormTurning
replying to @AnomieGamemaster
I don't think @EdLedDraws intends on doing any of
this, seriously

Anomie @AnomieGamemaster
replying to @TheWormTurning
You think wrong. I'm hearing you're top of the firing list

Robin paused to make a note of the fact that Anomie had claimed to have early notice that Tim Ashcroft was likely to be fired from his role as The Worm, then kept reading.

HartysGirl @hartyalways7
replying to @AnomieGamemaster
If she ditches Josh and closes the Game she'll lose the whole
fandom and she can die in a dumpster fire #IstandwithJosh

DrekBwah @hellandfurie$
replying to @AnomieGamemaster
#stopfeedingFedwell

Lepines Disciple @LepinesD1sciple
replying to @hellandfurie$ @AnomieGamemaster
fkn excellent idea let's get #stopfeedingFedwell trending

Zozo @inkyheart28
replying to @AnomieGamemaster
she cna 't close the the game it 's ours !!!! #notoNetflix
@EdLedDraws plaes listen to your fans !!!!!

Kea Niven @realPaperwhite
replying to @AnomieGamemaster
Wow this is great, all my ideas are going to Netflix to make a
ton of money for Edie Ledwell

Loren @l°rygill
replying to @realPaperwhite @AnomieGamemaster
Kea, if you did a crowdfunder loads of us would help you sue
her #stopfeedingFedwell #notoNetflix

Robin reread the last two tweets. Intrigued by the suggestion that the person called Kea Niven had grounds to sue Edie Ledwell, she brought up Kea's Twitter account.

The banner at the top of the page showed a photograph of a double rainbow. Kea's bio read *Spoonie – CFS – POTs – fibromyalgia – she/they. Yes, I was named after a parrot. What of it?*

Even allowing for the filters used on the photograph of the account owner, Robin could tell that Kea Niven was a very pretty girl. Her long dark hair tumbled over her shoulders and her enormous brown eyes looked up and sideways at the camera, a slight pout on her scarlet lips.

A tweet from October 2011 was pinned to the top of her Twitter page. It read:

'Fuck it. This is the truth. Believe me, don't believe me, I don't give a shit.'

Robin clicked on the YouTube link beneath these words.

The video began with Kea Niven sitting on a single bed. She

was indeed startlingly pretty, with a heart-shaped face, cupid's bow mouth and wide, liquid-brown eyes, and wore cut-off jeans and a black T-shirt with a yellow, pink and blue design on it, which Robin recognised as a Strokes album cover.

The set-up reminded Robin of the first video Josh and Edie had ever made, in which they too had sat on a single bed facing the camera. The wall behind Kea was covered in sketches, but there didn't seem to be anyone operating the camera, which was stationary. A masked lovebird was sitting on Kea's shoulder, its body a dusky blue and its white-rimmed black eyes blinking at the camera.

Kea started to speak with exactly the same kind of sheepish grin and wave with which Josh had opened the video Robin had already watched.

'So – um – hi! My name's Kea Niven and I'm a second-year student at St Martin's. This is my student ID –'

She pulled a card out of the back pocket of her jeans and held it up to the lens.

'– that's me, ignore the hair, it was a bad hair day. And behind me is some of my work, just to prove I'm like, whatever, not some rando pretending they can paint.

'And this is Yoko – aren't you, eh?' Kea said in a high-pitched voice to the lovebird on her shoulder. 'Yeah. We've got John and Yoko, this is Yoko.

'Soooo, why am I making a vlog? *Well . . .*' Kea flapped her hands and gave a breathy little laugh. 'OK, first I should say that I'm super-nervous about doing this and I've gone back and forth wondering whether it's smart or whatever, but I'm not after money or . . . This isn't about money, it's about fairness and, like, being acknowledged, at least.

'Soooo . . . *The Ink Black Heart*, if you've watched it, it was made by my ex-boyfriend Josh Blay and a woman called Edie Ledwell. So, Josh and I were dating at St Martin's and obviously, when you're dating, you tell each other – like, all your stories and whatever . . .

'Soooo . . . I told Josh about this thing, about Margaret Read, who was basically accused of witchcraft in, like, 1590 where I grew up, which is King's Lynn, and when they were burning her at the stake – this bit's, like, super-gory, so trigger warning or whatever – her heart, like, *burst* out of her and hit the wall and it's marked where the heart hit – actually, I've got a pic of it on my phone, wait a mo—'

She picked up her mobile and scrolled, looking for the picture. Robin suspected that none of this was as spontaneous as Kea evidently wished it to appear.

'Yeah, see there?' said Kea, holding the picture of a heart etched inside a diamond on the brick lintel of a window. 'That's where Margaret Read's heart hit the wall.

'So, anyway, I told Josh this whole story and I had, like, this *thing* about the heart bursting out of someone's chest and whatever. Sooo ... yeah, then, like, a year later, I see Edie Ledwell talking about "her" idea for Harty and I'm like, wow, that sounds really, *really* familiar.

'And you don't automatically reach for the conclusion that you've been, like, ripped off or whatever,' said Kea plaintively to camera, 'but, yeah, I went and watched the cartoon and I was like ... whoa. OK. That's *literally* what I said about the heart. So, um, it was confusing, because *he* wasn't saying he'd come up with it, you know ... *she* was. And I was thinking, right, OK, he must've told her and she's now claiming it was all *her* idea. Soooo ... yeah, then I watched the whole thing and I'm not gonna lie, it was really, like, um, kind of ... disturbing?

'Because there's the bird, Magspie, that can talk? Which is something I told Josh about when we were dating, that magpies can learn to talk, which he didn't know, and again, this Edie Ledwell's saying it was, like, her idea ...

'And then, OK, the ghost or whatever, the, um, heroine in the cartoon – so this is just crazy to me, but I've had several people say, "She looks like you," and I'm like, um, Josh was always going on about how white I am – I mean, like, pale-skinned – and when I saw the ghost in the cartoon I was like, uh, OK, somebody thinks to be really pale is like a creepy thing or whatever? Like, he had pictures of me, obviously, so has she made the ghost, like, to get at me, or ...? So that was kind of creepy ...

'But then, and this was, like, the clincher or whatever ... see this picture?'

Turning and kneeling up on the bed, the lovebird still perched on her shoulder, Kea pointed at a pencil drawing on the wall above her. It showed a bird-headed, human-bodied monster, which was casting a long shadow.

'So, I drew this sketch when I was doing A levels, OK? So ...

this was literally a nightmare I had, so, like, it's super-personal? Ouch, Yoko—'

The lovebird had fluttered off her shoulder out of shot, snagging a strand of Kea's hair as she left.

'Soooo . . . yeah,' said Kea, turning to sit back down on the bed, 'I showed Josh this picture when we were dating. It's just a sketch, but it's, like, the shadow there . . . yeah. So, um, if you've seen the cartoon, the figure of Drek is, like – I mean, it's literally that shadow, with the kind of no-neck, the beak, that huge pointed beak thing, I mean – oh, I didn't say: I grew up surrounded with birds – my mum breeds parrots. So I had a dream about this bird-headed monster and then I saw the figure of Drek and I was just like . . . um . . . OK, so *that* looks super-familiar. I mean, I'm not imagining that, am I?

'So then I'm like, OK, is this, like, four coincidences, or . . .?

'Soooo, I guess some people will just say "oh, she's like the bitter ex-girlfriend" or whatever, but what's kind of messing with my head is that it isn't Josh saying "yeah, I like took inspiration from a friend or an ex or whatever", it's like, *she's* saying she came up with it all independently and I'm . . . like, if it was *one* of the things, yeah, maybe, I guess coincidences happen or whatever, but it's, like, really crazy to me that she's sitting there saying "yeah, I can't remember where I got the idea for the heart, it just came to me" or whatever, like, how could you not remember a thing like that? Because it's a pretty *out there* idea to most people? So anyway, yeah, that's basically all I've got to say, and I just want to put it out there because, like I say, this is for my self-respect or whatever. I just wanted to, um, say my piece or whatever. Soooo . . . yeah.'

Kea gave a breathless little giggle, then leaned forward and turned off the camera.

Beneath the video were comments:

Harty Harterson 3 weeks ago
I heard Ledwell ripped a ton of people off and sounds like you were just the first

Nikki 4 weeks ago
the heart thing does sound like they got it from you, I agree. Love your little bird!

Crash Test Dummy 1 year ago
'They got the idea of a ghost from me being a white girl' roflmao

Robin sat quite still for a minute, thinking over what she'd just seen, then picked up the office phone and called Allan Yeoman. She was put on hold for a short period, during which an instrumental version of 'My Heart Will Go On' played, and then heard the agent's voice.

'Yes, hello, Robin?'

'Hello, Allan. I've got a quick question and I wondered whether you could help. Would you happen to know anything about a girl called Kea Niven?'

'Kea Niven . . .' repeated Yeoman slowly. 'Um . . . the name rings a bell – sorry, remind me?'

'An ex-girlfriend of Josh Blay's, who—'

'Oh, *Kea Niven*, yes, of course, of course!' said Yeoman. 'The one who claimed she had all the ideas for *The Ink Black Heart*, and that Edie stole them?'

'That's the one,' said Robin.

'I should've told you about her at lunch,' said Yeoman. 'She can't be Anomie.'

'What makes you say that?'

'Oh, Edie ruled her out entirely. I think because Anomie was present in the game at a time when Edie knew Kea couldn't be. You knew Edie managed to get into the game at one point?'

'I did, yes. She said she got banned for asking too many questions about Anomie.'

'Exactly right.'

'So this girl, Kea?'

'Josh ditched her for Edie. I know Anomie hopped on the Kea bandwagon for a while—'

'Did he? I haven't found that yet.'

'Yes, he amplified her plagiarism claims a few years back, but if memory serves, he got bored and moved on – found better ways of getting at Edie.'

'D'you think Kea genuinely believes Edie and Josh stole her ideas?'

'Possibly,' sighed Yeoman. 'You know, this kind of thing is incredibly common when there's a hit. It's usually a case of wishful thinking, or a genuine failure to grasp that similar ideas may come to lots of different people. Amazing how often two films come out at the same time, on the same subject. Nobody's stolen anything. It's just there, you know, in the ether. Cyril Scott would have said it was the devas, whispering into the ears of people who're receptive.'

After she'd thanked Yeoman and rung off, Robin returned to Kea Niven's Twitter page and began to scroll through it, looking for the interaction between Kea and Anomie. She found it at last back in 2011, dated just a few days after Kea had posted her video.

Anomie
@AnomieGamemaster

Well, well, well. This might explain why Fedwell's so hazy on how she came up with Harty

> **Kea Niven** @realPaperwhite
>
> The story of Margaret Read's heart which I told to @realJoshBlay and its odd resemblance to a *certain* cartoon character
> https://www.youtube.com/watch?v=8qxGhc4oaBQ

11.16 pm   11 Oct 2011

A few responses down, Robin found a direct exchange between the two.

Kea Niven @realPaperwhite
replying to @AnomieGamemaster
Thanks for sharing ☺

Anomie @AnomieGamemaster
replying to @realPaperwhite
No problem. Great hair, btw

Kea Niven @realPaperwhite
replying to @AnomieGamemaster
lol thanks ♥

Still more intrigued, Robin scrolled up. This was the first sign of anything resembling flirtation in Anomie's feed. Indeed, during her

The Ink Black Heart

careful examination of Anomie's past tweets she'd started to think of them as a strangely sexless entity, in both senses of the word. There'd been no hint of romantic interest or sexual desire: the only bodily need ever mentioned was hunger.

A couple of days after Anomie and Kea's first interaction, Anomie had again directed their followers to Kea's video, and Kea had shown her appreciation.

Kea Niven @realPaperwhite
replying to @AnomieGamemaster
Thanks so much for sharing and sticking up for truth ♥

Anomie @AnomieGamemaster
replying to @realPaperwhite
Have DMed you.

'DMed', as Robin knew, meant that Anomie had sent Kea a direct message. There were no further public interactions between the two that Robin could find.

Turning back to Kea's more recent Twitter output, Robin saw that in the five days after the stabbing story had broken, Kea hadn't tweeted at all, but on the sixth day she'd posted a link to a microblogging site, tumblr, which Robin clicked on.

> Following a catastrophic downturn in my health I've been forced to leave London to return to live with my mother. I'm currently bedbound. As I live with multiple disabilities, this isn't an unusual situation, but it's probably the severest relapse I've had in several years. Honestly at this point, death would be a relief.

A hundred and fifteen notes had been posted beneath this short message. They began kindly enough.

> thinking of you Kea xxx

> so sorry to hear this, K. Remember, self-love is not selfishness

But slowly, and not altogether to Robin's surprise, another theme began to surface.

sorry you're ill but you got nothing to say about your ex
who's literally fighting for his life?

no comment on Edie Ledwell being murdered?

yeah I'd probably go to bed and stay there if I were you

fuck, not a word – NOT A WORD – about Ledwell and Blay?

bitch you couldn't stop fucking talking about Ledwell and
Blay for four years and now you got nothing to say?

'death would be a relief' wow, so we should pity you more
than Ledwell, is that what you're saying?

The landline on the desk in front of Robin rang. Her eyes still on
Kea's tumblr page, Robin answered.

'Hello?'

'Message from Mr Strike,' said Pat's gravelly voice in her ear. 'He
thinks you might need to go to Gateshead on Monday.'

'You're kidding,' said Robin quietly, closing tumblr with her left
hand as she spoke. 'Another one?'

'Well, he wasn't clear,' said Pat, 'but yes, I think it was
Gateshead he said.'

'Male?'

'No, the other one.'

'OK,' said Robin, 'coming out now.'

'Thanks, I'll let him know,' said Pat and hung up.

Robin got up, crossed to the door into the outer office and
opened it.

There on the fake leather sofa, beautiful and composed, sat
Charlotte Campbell.

25

. . . in truth now have you seen
Ever anywhere such beauty, such a stature, such a mien?
She may be queen of devils but she's every inch a queen.

Christina Rossetti
Look On This Picture and On This

Strike, who was currently walking up Charing Cross Road towards the office, was tired, sore, and bitterly regretting the Balti curry he'd eaten late the previous evening with Madeline. He was very fond of highly spiced food, so didn't understand why his guts had been churning most of the day, unless it had something to do with the combination of madras and the acidic cocktail Madeline had insisted he have first, because they were a speciality of the house. A night of very little sleep had followed, because he'd felt uncomfortably gassy. Then, instead of keeping comfortable watch over Groomer's office from a café (their client having now agreed that it might be a good idea to try to find out something about Groomer that would repel her daughter), he'd been forced to follow the man on foot as he firstly went shopping on Bond Street, then lunched in a booked-out restaurant and finally chose to walk all the way to the British Museum for what Strike assumed was a business meeting, because he was greeted at the door by a couple of people wearing name badges.

'I don't know where the fuck he's gone,' Strike told Barclay irritably in the museum's Great Court, the all-white two-acre space with a spectacular glass roof that cast a mesh of triangular shadows over walls and floor. 'He got in that lift, but I didn't make it in time.'

He didn't want to admit that the hamstring of his amputated leg,

231

which he'd previously torn, was playing up again. He'd missed the lift because he was starting to limp and hadn't been able to move fast enough to bypass a large crowd of tourists.

'Ach, nae bother,' said the Glaswegian, 'he'll have to come doon sooner or later. Anyway, doubt he's doing drugs or hookers in here.'

So Strike had left, masochistically taking the Tube rather than a cab, and as he hobbled into Denmark Street he felt only relief at the prospect of being able to sit down for an hour or so with a strong mug of tea, in close proximity to his own bathroom where, if necessary, he could fart as loudly as he pleased.

For about the thousandth time, climbing the stairs, he wondered why he'd never contacted the landlord about getting the lift fixed. Finally, having heaved himself onto the second landing with the aid of the banister, he pushed open the glass door to find three women looking at him: Pat, Robin and Charlotte.

For a moment he simply stared at Charlotte, who was sitting on the fake leather sofa with her long legs crossed, her dark hair pulled back into a messy bun, her make-up-free skin flawless. She was wearing a cream cashmere dress and a long brown suede coat and boots, and, though very thin, looked as gorgeous as he'd ever seen her.

'Hello, Corm,' she said, smiling.

He didn't return the smile, but turned an almost accusing look at Robin, who felt nettled. *She* hadn't invited Charlotte into the office and it wasn't *her* fault if Charlotte, having been told that Strike wasn't there, had simply announced that she'd wait.

'It isn't Robin's fault,' said Charlotte, as though she'd read both their minds. 'I just walked in off the street. Could I have a word?'

In silence, Strike limped across to the door dividing the inner office from the outer, opened it and pointed Charlotte ungraciously inside. She got up unhurriedly, picked up her handbag, smiled at both Robin and Pat, said 'thanks', although neither had done anything for which she might reasonably thank them, and walked past Strike, leaving a faint trace of Shalimar in her wake.

When Strike had closed the door on his partner and office manager, Charlotte said,

'Have you got a code for women who come here to fling themselves at the famous detective? Is that what "Gateshead" means?'

'What d'you want?' said Strike.

'Aren't you going to ask me to sit down? Or d'you prefer clients to stand in your presence?'

'Do whatever you like but make it quick. I've got things to do.'

'I'm sure you have. How's it going with Mads, anyway?' she asked as she took a seat and crossed her long legs.

'What d'you want?' Strike repeated.

He chose not to sit down, even though his hamstring was still throbbing, but stood with his arms folded, looking down at her.

'I need a detective,' said Charlotte. 'Don't worry, I'm not expecting a freebie. I'll pay.'

'You won't,' said Strike, 'because our client list's full. You'll have to find someone else. I recommend McCabes.'

'I thought you might tell me to go somewhere else,' said Charlotte, no longer smiling, 'but if I take this particular problem to McCabes, they might just leak it to drive you out of business. I'd imagine you're a bit of a thorn in the side of other detective agencies these days. First on everyone's list, I expect.'

When Strike didn't answer, Charlotte looked around the office with her flecked green eyes and said,

'It's bigger than I remembered ... I like Mads, by the way,' she added, looking back at the stony-faced Strike. 'You know I did a bit of modelling for her the other week? It was quite fun. The collection's called "Notorious" and—'

'Yeah, I know all about the collection.'

'I bet it took a lot of persuasion for you to let her keep me in.'

'There was no persuasion needed. It was nothing to do with me.'

'Mads told me you'd OK-ed it,' said Charlotte, eyebrows raised.

Inwardly cursing Madeline, Strike said:

'If that's what you want to call me saying "do whatever you like, it's nothing to do with me".'

'Oh, let's stop playing games, Bluey,' said Charlotte earnestly.

'Don't call me that.'

'I *know* you know why I'm here. Valentine told you, at New Year.'

When Strike didn't respond, she said,

'Must admit, I was quite surprised you wanted to pick up a girl who was out with Valentine.'

'You think I chatted up Madeline purely to get to you, do you?' said Strike. 'Your fucking ego ... The only negative thing about her I could see was that she knew your fucking stepbrother.'

'If you say so, darling,' said Charlotte.

He heard the thrill of pleasure in her voice. She'd always loved sparring. *At least when I'm fighting I know I'm alive.*

'All right,' she said lightly, 'if you want me to spell it out. Jago found the nude I sent you, on my old phone.'

'Did he now?'

'Don't pretend, Bluey, you know he did – Valentine told you. I assume you don't think *Valentine's* a – what was it you called me, during that last row? A narcissistic mythomaniac?'

'I think you made *bloody sure* Jago found that nude, which as you *fucking* well know I didn't ask for and didn't want.'

'Hmm,' said Charlotte, eyebrows raised (and in truth, how many straight men could honestly say they wouldn't want a nude picture of her?). 'Well, Jago doesn't buy that. He also knows you phoned Symonds House while I was there – and incidentally, *I* never asked you to do that.'

'You sent me suicidal fucking messages from the grounds.'

'Well, you could have ignored me, darling, you've had plenty of practice,' said Charlotte. 'Anyway, Jago knew it was you who phoned them, he's not stupid, and he doesn't believe you were being a Boy Scout, he thinks you had some personal interest in saving my life.'

'An impression I'm sure you were eager to correct.'

'When Jago wants to believe something, dynamite wouldn't shift him,' said Charlotte.

Strike took half a step towards her. His leg throbbed worse than ever.

'If I'm named in your poxy divorce, my business will be fucked. It'll mean paps following me, my face all over the papers—'

'Exactly,' said Charlotte, looking him steadily in the face. 'Which is why I thought you might like to help me get something on Jago before he screws both of us. He's trying to take the twins away from me. He wants full custody and he's determined to get me into court and have me declared an unfit mother. He's got a tame psychiatrist ready to say I'm crazy and unstable, and he's hoping to get me certified drug-addled and promiscuous to boot. Ruining *you* will just be an extra bit of fun.'

'You told me you couldn't wait to leave your fucking kids while you were pregnant with them.'

He thought he saw her composure waver at that, but then, with a good impression of her previous calm:

'They're mine as much as his. I'm not just a fucking incubator, whatever Jago's mother thinks. I'm the mother of the future Viscount Ross. James is the heir to the title and he's my bloody son and they're not having him – they're not having either of them.

'Amelia's going to testify that he beat me up,' Charlotte went on. Amelia was Charlotte's sister, a plainer but far less volatile woman, who'd never much liked Strike. 'She saw me with a black eye, just before I got packed off to Symonds House.'

'If that's supposed to awaken my chivalrous instincts,' said Strike, 'I'd remind you that you knew damn well what he was before you married him. I remember you telling me he'd beaten up his ex when you came out to see me in Germany. You heard it on the old fucking girls' network and you had a good laugh about what a lucky escape you'd had.'

'So I deserve to be smacked around, do I?' said Charlotte, her voice rising.

'Don't play fucking games with me,' snarled Strike. 'You know *fucking* well that if I believed *any* woman should be knocked around we wouldn't be having this conversation, because you'd already be dead.'

'Charming,' said Charlotte.

'You only agreed to marry Jago because you thought I'd come and burst into the wedding and stop you doing it, that I'd ride to your fucking rescue yet a-fucking-gain. You told me as much: "I didn't think you'd let me do it."'

'So what?' said Charlotte impatiently. 'Where does any of this get us? Are you going to help me get something on Jago, yes or no?'

'No,' said Strike.

There was a long silence. For a full minute Charlotte looked up at him, and he found her appallingly familiar, fatally desirable and utterly enraging.

'OK, darling,' she said in a clipped voice, bending to pick up her handbag and getting to her feet again. 'Well, don't forget this conversation when you try and pin what happens next on me. I asked you to help me stop it. You refused.'

She smoothed out the cashmere dress. He wondered how long she'd taken to decide what to wear to meet him. Her pared-back style, often praised by fashion magazines, was, he knew, the result of careful deliberation. Now, in a familiar move, she waited for him to open the door for her; how often had she, who claimed to deplore the milieu into which she'd been born, suddenly decided that she wanted old-world manners from the boyfriend who'd spent a large part of his early life in squalor?

Strike wrenched the door open. As she passed him, he smelled Shalimar, and hated the fact that he recognised it.

Robin, who was reading through the document she'd printed earlier, looked up. Her blue dress, which she liked, felt like a dishcloth beside the quality of Charlotte's clothes: every item Charlotte wore, Robin knew, would need specialist cleaning.

'Short but sweet,' said Charlotte, smiling at Robin. 'Nice to meet you properly at last. I think we've spoken a couple of times on the phone.'

'Yes,' said Robin, aware of Strike glowering in the background but mustering a polite smile.

'Funny,' said Charlotte, considering Robin with her head to one side, 'you look a bit like Madeline.'

'Like who, sorry?' said Robin.

'Corm's girlfriend,' said Charlotte, glancing back at Strike, her smile angelic. 'Haven't you met her? Madeline Courson-Miles. She's absolutely lovely. Jewellery designer. I've just done a bit of modelling for her new campaign. Well, bye, Corm. Take care.'

The shock slithered down from Robin's brain, freezing her innards. She turned away from Strike, pretending to check the printer, although she knew perfectly well that everything she'd wanted to print was already in her hand. The door closed behind Charlotte.

'Thinks a lot of herself, that one,' said Pat with a sniff, returning to her typing.

'She isn't mentally unstable, though, Pat,' said Robin, trying to sound casual, even amused. She could hear Strike moving back into the inner office. 'Not a Gateshead.'

'She is,' said the office manager in the low croak that passed for her whisper. 'I've read the papers.'

'Are we going to have a catch-up on Anomie, then?' Strike called from the partners' desk, where he'd finally sat down.

'It'll have to be a quick one,' Robin said, trying to sound purely businesslike. 'I'm meeting Ilsa for a drink and dinner later.'

There was more than enough time to reach Bob Bob Ricard, but Robin was suddenly aware of a desire to get out of Strike's vicinity as soon as possible. The cold, clammy inward sensation persisted, along with small aftershocks that she was afraid presaged a state in which she wasn't going to be able to pretend to be indifferent to the news she'd just heard.

'I printed this off for you,' she said, moving into the office. 'You wanted some information on the Pen of Justice blog. This is all I've got so far.'

Strike's jaw was set and he looked livid. Robin drew courage from the fact that he wasn't pretending to be unaffected by Charlotte's visit.

'You didn't tell me you were seeing someone,' she said, and she heard the artificially casual note in her own voice. But weren't they supposed to be friends? *Best* friends?

Strike gave Robin a fleeting look, then turned his attention to the document she'd just handed him.

'Er – yeah, I am. So this is . . . yeah, the Pen of Justice thing?'

'Yes,' said Robin. 'Oh, and I've also found a girl online who claims Edie Ledwell stole all her ideas for *The Ink Black Heart*.'

'Really?'

'Yes,' said Robin, still standing in front of him in the blue dress Strike recognised from the Ritz. 'Her name's Kea Niven. I called Allan Yeoman about her, but he says she can't be Anomie because Edie ruled her out.'

'How did she rule her out?' Strike asked, still preferring to glance through the Pen of Justice notes than look at Robin.

'He said Anomie was active in the game at a time Kea didn't have access to a computer or phone. Anyway,' said Robin, whose urge to get away from Strike was becoming overwhelming, 'as I say, I'm meeting Ilsa for an early drink. You don't mind if I clock off now, do you?'

'No, not at all,' said Strike, who was as eager to be alone with his thoughts as Robin was to be gone.

'See you Thursday, then,' said Robin, because the rota didn't demand that they meet until then, and she carried her shock back into the outer office, where she took down her coat and bag, bade Pat a smiling farewell and left.

Strike remained where she'd left him, heart pounding as though he'd just stepped out of the boxing ring, and tried to force himself to read the document Robin had just handed him.

Note on the Pen of Justice Blog

The anonymous Pen of Justice blog was started in January 2012. Whoever's behind it is on Twitter as @penjustwrites. Their location is hidden. The focus of the blog—

But he couldn't concentrate. Throwing the papers down onto the desk, he gave way to the full force of his own fury at Charlotte, which was worse for the rage he also felt at himself. He'd ignored a looming danger. He *had* known that Jago had found that bloody nude, and done nothing about it because it suited him to believe the coked-up Valentine was scaremongering. Strike felt he'd been catastrophically complacent, both on a very serious threat to his business and – time to look facts in the face – in his belief that Robin need never know about Madeline.

Charlotte had an uncanny ability to read other people's emotional states, a skill honed by necessity in navigating a family full of addiction and mental illness. Her preternatural ability to intuit hopes and insecurities that others thought well-hidden made her equally adept at charming people and at wounding them. Some might assume she'd just acted out of the pure will to destruction that was one of her most unnerving qualities, but Strike knew better. The last text he'd had from Charlotte, six months previously, had read: *I don't think I've ever felt so envious in my life as I am of that girl Robin.* He'd bet everything in his bank account that Charlotte sensed he was trying to displace the attraction he felt towards Robin onto Madeline, because she could read Strike just as well as he could read her.

'That's me off,' croaked Pat from the outer office.

'Have a good weekend,' Strike said automatically.

He heard her go and immediately reached for a cigarette and the ashtray he kept in a drawer in his desk. Drawing deeply on a freshly lit Benson & Hedges, he asked himself how he was going to solve the problem of Jago Ross and that bloody nude, but his unruly thoughts careered back towards Robin and he found himself doing the very thing he'd been avoiding doing for months: reliving that foolish, dangerous moment outside the Ritz, and, for the first time, facing certain unpleasant truths.

He hadn't wanted Robin to know about Madeline, because some small part of him continued to hope that he'd been wrong about that silent 'no' Robin had given him. There was trauma in her past that might have made her flinch automatically from an unexpected advance. What if the 'no' he'd seen had been a mere reflex, or conditional, or temporary? Lately he'd thought she was trying to show him that she wasn't worried that his clumsy, drunken move would be repeated. In his experience, women found ways of letting a man know that further advances would be unwelcome. She hadn't grown colder, hadn't avoided one-on-one meetings, hadn't mentioned a new boyfriend to signal her unavailability; she'd been enthusiastic about the idea of drinks with him, and hugged him spontaneously in the pub. None of that added up to a feeling of repulsion, or of wanting to push him away.

But if he hadn't blown his chance, what then? No easy answer came. The same old objections remained to his trying to push the relationship beyond the bounds of friendship: they were business partners, they spent too much time together, and if – when – a relationship with Robin went wrong, it would take everything with it, the whole edifice they'd built together, which was the one stable thing in Strike's life.

But he was having great difficulty in stifling the feeling for Robin he never gave a name. The truth was that he wanted her to stay single, while he disentangled what he felt and what he wanted. Now, thanks to Charlotte, Robin might just consider herself at liberty to find another Matthew, who'd offer her a ring – she was the kind of woman men wanted to marry, Strike had no doubt about that – and then everything would fall apart just as surely as if they'd fallen into bed and regretted it, because she'd end up leaving the agency, if not immediately then eventually. He was living proof of how hard it was to do this job and have a permanent relationship.

But, of course, his own ability to do the job might soon be taken from him. A divorce and custody battle between Charlotte and Jago, with their ancestral castle up in Scotland and Charlotte's fractured, photogenic and scandal-prone family, would fill endless columns of newsprint, and unless he did something to prevent it Strike's name and picture would be dotted all over those pages too, with the result that his only chance of continuing to do the job for which he'd sacrificed so much would be extensive facial surgery. Failing that, he'd be reduced to a deskbound director, watching Robin and the subcontractors do all the actual investigative work, while he grew a little fatter every year, schmoozing clients in the office and making sure the accounts were in order.

Strike stubbed out his half-smoked cigarette, picked up his mobile and called Dev Shah, who answered on the second ring.

'What's up?'

'Where are you currently?'

'Newman Street, waiting for Montgomery to leave work,' said Dev. 'His girlfriend's here with a couple of mates. Looks like they're going drinking somewhere local.'

'Great,' said Strike. 'I want a quiet word with you. Let me know when they reach their destination and I'll join you.'

'Will do,' said Shah, and Strike rang off.

26

And I walked as if apart
From myself, when I could stand,
And I pitied my own heart,
As if I held it in my hand . . .

Elizabeth Barrett Browning
Bertha in the Lane

Robin's feet were behaving quite normally as she moved through Soho, as though they were transporting a normal human being who belonged in the physical world and wasn't full of a numb sense of disconnect.

She recognised this feeling. She'd had it once before, after she'd found her ex-husband's mistress's diamond earring in her bedroom. While waiting for Matthew to come home, she'd experienced precisely this strange, out-of-body sensation, during which she'd viewed the room in which she sat as though from a distance of years, knowing that she'd never be there again and that she'd one day look back upon that brief sliver of time as a turning point in her life.

I'm in love with him.

She'd been kidding herself too long. This wasn't friendship or mere fondness: you didn't feel as though all your intestines had been seared with dry ice when you found out your friend was sleeping with someone new. But what a brutal way to be forced into facing the truth. It would have been so much easier if the realisation had crept gently upon her in the golden haze of the Ritz, while consuming cocktails that might have anaesthetised her against the shock, or while contemplating the fang-like peak of the Matterhorn, where she'd have had time and space to deal with a truth she'd preferred not to face.

When had Strike's new relationship started? How soon after that moment on the pavement outside the Ritz? Because she couldn't believe he'd been dating then; no matter how angry she felt at him right now, he surely hadn't held her, and moved to kiss her, when there was a girlfriend in the background, expecting to see him later.

Her mobile rang in her bag. She didn't want it to be Strike; she didn't think she could stand talking to him right now. To her relief, it was an unknown number.

'Robin Ellacott.'

'Hi,' said a male voice. 'Ryan Murphy here.'

'Ryan ...' said Robin, unable to think who this was.

'DCI Murphy. I came to your office about Edie Led—'

'Oh,' said Robin, 'yes, of course. Sorry.'

'Is this a convenient time?'

'Yes,' said Robin, trying to focus.

'I wanted to check a couple of points with you, if you don't mind.'

'No, carry on,' said Robin as her feet still carried her onwards in the direction of the restaurant Ilsa wouldn't reach for another hour and a half.

'I wondered whether, when she came to see you, Edie Ledwell mentioned a woman called Yasmin Weatherhead?'

'No, she didn't,' said Robin, and as though she'd stepped back inside an office in her mind she heard herself say perfectly calmly, 'Is this the assistant, who used to help Edie and Josh with fan mail?'

'That's the one,' said Murphy.

'She was the person who took this dossier of supposed "proof" that Edie was Anomie to Josh?'

'Already there, are you?' said Murphy, who sounded mildly impressed. 'Yeah, that's her.'

'We've heard the dossier wasn't in the cemetery when Josh and Edie were found.'

'Have you got some tame policeman in your pocket who's leaking to you?'

'No,' said Robin. 'It came from a bit of surveillance.'

'Ah, OK. Well, you're right, we didn't find it in the cemetery. Sorry – we're a bit sensitive about leaks right now. I assume you saw the *Times* article?'

'About The Halvening? Yes.'

'Not helpful, having that splashed across the front page. We weren't aiming to let them know we're watching them.'

'No, I'm sure,' said Robin. 'How's the investigation going?'

She asked mainly because she wanted a brief respite from thinking about Strike.

Murphy made a noise midway between a sigh and a grunt.

'Well, we might have cast our net a bit too widely asking the public whether they'd noticed any unusual activity in or around Highgate Cemetery. We've heard about two stolen pushbikes in the vicinity of the cemetery and an out-of-control Alsatian on Hampstead Heath, but no mention of a suspicious person running away from the scene, or anyone disguised or behaving strangely within the cemetery at the time they were stabbed. We're currently examining Ledwell's and Blay's phone records.'

'The killer took Blay's mobile, didn't they?'

'You *sure* you aren't getting information from my department?'

'That came out of the same bit of surveillance.'

'Both phones were missing. D'you know what happened to Ledwell's?'

'No,' said Robin, and in spite of her underlying shock and misery, her interest quickened.

'This might yet come out in the press, because police were seen dragging the ponds, but don't shout it around, please. According to the satellite signal, Ledwell's phone moved out of the cemetery and onto Hampstead Heath after she was killed. As far as we can tell, it was turned off near Highgate Number One Pond. We've dragged the pond, and the one beside it, but the phone wasn't in either.'

'The killer took the phone out of the cemetery and onto Hampstead Heath?'

'That's what it looks like.'

'What about Blay's phone?'

'It was turned off around the time we think he was stabbed. Possibly the killer didn't realise they hadn't turned off Ledwell's until they got onto the Heath. Anyway—'

'Yes, of course,' said Robin, assuming Murphy needed to go.

'No, er, actually – um – ha,' said Murphy. 'I was, er, going to ask whether you'd be free for a drink this weekend.'

'Oh,' said Robin, 'well, I'd have to check the rota. Would you want Strike there too?'

'Would I – what, sorry?'

'Are you looking to speak to both of us, or—?'

'I – no, I was actually asking whether you'd – whether you'd be free for a drink in the – the date sense.'

'*Oh,*' said Robin as a fresh wave of mortification rolled over her, 'I'm sorry, I thought – I'm working all weekend.'

'Ah,' said Ryan Murphy, who sounded nearly as uncomfortable as Robin felt. 'Well – no worries. Er – enjoy your – yeah, happy hunting. Bye.'

'Bye,' said Robin, her voice higher than usual, and she turned off the call.

She could feel her face burning. Onwards she walked, a little faster now, her only objectives to put more distance between herself and Cormoran Strike, and then to find a dark corner in which she could savour to the full her realisation that she was the most romantically inept woman in London.

27

He looks for war, his heart is ready,
His thoughts are bitter, he will not bow.

Jean Ingelow
At One Again

A mere half an hour after they'd last spoken, Shah called Strike to say that Montgomery and his friends were in Opium, a dim sum parlour in Chinatown and a short walk from the office. Strike's gastric symptoms had been eased by a visit to the bathroom but his stump was still complaining about carrying his weight. Ignoring the pain, he pulled his coat back on, locked up the office and set out to join Shah, once again navigating his way across the channels still dug in the roads.

Montgomery's party was on the third floor (*because of course they bloody are,* thought Strike, his hamstring screaming in protest all the way upstairs), sitting on steel-legged stools around a wooden table where a bartender was mixing cocktails in front of them. All the meticulously groomed young men in the group looked to Strike like versions of Montgomery, their beards neatly trimmed, their T-shirts tight, while the young women were all very heavily made-up, their hair dyed colours not found in nature: purple-grey, vermillion, blue-bell. Everyone in the group had their phones out, taking pictures of the cocktails, the shelves of bottles behind the bartender and the picture of Chairman Mao painted on a cabinet. The exposed brick and bare floorboards reminded Strike of the bars he went to with Madeline, all of which were starting to become a blur.

Shah was sitting a short distance away from the group in a side room, Montgomery in his eyeline.

'Anomie just tweeted,' he informed Strike as the latter sat down opposite him. 'And Montgomery was typing on his phone at the time.'

'OK, keep an eye on him while I'm talking,' said Strike. 'I need another job done.'

While he outlined the problem of Jago Ross, Shah stared, apparently absent-mindedly, at the noisy group at the bartender's table. When Strike had finished talking, Shah looked directly at him for the first time.

'So ... you want me to get something on your ex's husband.'

Shah had an odd look on his face that Strike had never seen there before: blank, shut down.

'Yes,' said Strike. 'I'll be completely fucked if he names me in the divorce. I need bargaining power.'

Shah glanced back at Montgomery's table, then said,

'Why'm I getting this job?'

'Well, I can't bloody do it, can I? He knows me. He's a prick but he's not an idiot. I don't want to risk him recognising Robin either. She was in the paper last year and so was Barclay. I want clean, new faces on the job, people he can't associate with me. It'll have to be you and Midge.'

Shah sipped his drink, glanced towards Montgomery again, but said nothing.

'Is there a problem?' Strike asked, annoyed.

'This is a job on the books, is it?' Shah asked. 'Or are we talking cash in hand and nothing on the record?'

'Why d'you ask?'

'I'm asking,' said Shah, watching the group rather than looking at Strike, 'because Patterson had a sideline in using his agency to fuck over people he had personal grudges against. All done cash in hand, off the record, but sometimes he "forgot" to pay. I was usually picked to do that kind of stuff.'

'This isn't a personal grudge,' said Strike. 'I'm well rid of his wife. He's doing this to try and fuck up my business. If he wasn't trying to make me part of their mess, I wouldn't give a shit. I'll put it through the books and I'll pay like any other client.'

Strike hadn't thought as far as how he would tell Robin what he was up to, but now, he supposed, he had little choice.

'I'm well aware we haven't really got capacity for another case right now,' Strike added. 'I wouldn't be doing this if I had a choice.'

'OK, sorry. I just wanted to be clear about what's going on,' said Shah. 'You got the guy's details?'

'I'll email you everything when I get back to the office. He's on his second marriage. I'll try and get details of his first wife as well, and I'll copy Midge in.'

'Right you are,' said Shah. 'I'll get started as soon as you've sent it.'

Strike thanked his subcontractor and left the bar, his limp more pronounced with every step.

28

Away, away with loving then,
With hoping and believing;
For what should follow,
But grieving, grieving?

Anne Evans
Outcry

It was almost seven o'clock, so Robin, who'd been sitting in a corner of a Soho café, alternating between feelings of humiliation and wretchedness, set out at last for Bob Bob Ricard, nearing the entrance just as fair-haired, bespectacled Ilsa got out of a cab in front of her.

They hugged. Ilsa looked tired but pleased to see Robin, who craved both a drink and the opportunity to unburden herself. The question was how much she wanted to share with Ilsa, whose attempts at matchmaking between Robin and Strike had previously caused Robin some embarrassment.

They were shown downstairs into a basement room that combined high Victorian opulence with the atmosphere of a nightclub: dramatically lit, with red and gold decor, a floor decorated like a backgammon board, leather banquettes and – she saw it as soon as they slid into their booth – a 'Push for Champagne' button on the wall beside them.

'You all right?' said Ilsa, looking concerned.

'Think I might need a drink before I tell you,' said Robin.

'Well, then, press the button – that's what we're here for, isn't it?'

'Tell me about your case,' said Robin.

'I can't *believe* we got her off,' said Ilsa, and for the short time it took for a pink-waistcoated waiter to bring them champagne, she told Robin about the teenage girl who'd stood trial for helping plan a terrorist attack.

'... so the other four were all found guilty,' Ilsa finished, just as the waiter set two glasses of champagne down in front of them, 'and so they bloody well should have been, but I thought, *she's finished*. I could hear her mother sobbing behind us. But thank *Christ* the judge believed the psychologist. Fifteen, profoundly autistic and convinced she'd found real friends online ... of course she fell for it. And she was the one they were going to strap the bloody explosives to. Bastards. Right, tell me what's up with you.'

'First things first: congratulations on winning,' said Robin, clinking her glass against Ilsa's, then drinking some champagne. 'So, I just got asked out by a guy from CID, and I asked if I could bring Strike along on the date.'

'You *what?*'

By the end of Robin's explanation, Ilsa was laughing so much people were turning to look at her.

'Don't,' groaned Robin, although her sense of humiliation was lifting in the face of Ilsa's hilarity. 'I'm a *moron*.'

'You aren't a moron: the guy was calling about a case, what were you supposed to think? Come on, Robin, it's funny!'

'Yes, well, that's not everything ... Charlotte Campbell turned up at the office this afternoon.'

'What?' said Ilsa, no longer laughing.

'I don't know what she wanted. Well, I do – to see Strike,' said Robin. 'He took her into the inner office, they were in there about five minutes, then they came out and she said – she said I look just like Strike's new girlfriend, Madeline. I didn't know he was seeing anyone. He didn't tell me. She's a jewellery designer, apparently.'

'He's *dating?*' said Ilsa, sounding exactly as outraged as Robin had expected, and there was both pain and pleasure in hearing her own shock echoed in Ilsa's voice. 'When did *that* start? He never told us he was seeing anyone!'

'Well,' said Robin with a shrug, 'he is. He confirmed it after Charlotte left.'

'All right, before we get into this *Madeline* person,' said Ilsa, as though the very name was suspect, 'let me tell you *exactly* what Charlotte was doing there.'

Ilsa took a deep breath, then said,

'Robin, she can smell something between you and Corm, and she wants to screw it up.'

Either Ilsa's words or the champagne had slightly leavened Robin's misery, but nevertheless, she said,

'Charlotte's never seen the two of us up close until today, and then it was for three minutes tops.'

'That's irrelevant,' said Ilsa flatly. 'You and Corm have been together at the agency for what – five years now? *He made you his business partner*, for God's sake. Nick and I *never* thought he'd do that. He *voluntarily* got legally entangled with you, and for Corm, believe me, that's a big deal. I've never known anybody as commitment – we'd better order,' said Ilsa, catching a waiter's eye, 'or they'll just keep interrupting.'

Food chosen, the waiter moved out of earshot and Ilsa said,

'What was I . . .? Yeah – I've never known anyone as commitment-phobic as Corm.'

'He proposed to Charlotte.'

'Oh, *please*,' said Ilsa, rolling her eyes. 'It was the lowest point in his life, and he's had his fair share of low points. He'd just had his leg blown off, his army career was over and she decided to play the ministering angel because there was a bit of drama in it. Of course he fell for the act, anyone would have done. Robin, he shares the most important part of his life with you. Five years is the single longest continuous relationship of any kind Corm's had with *any* woman. Charlotte will know that and she'll *hate* it. Trust me. I know her,' said Ilsa darkly. She picked up her full glass of champagne, then put it down again without drinking.

'Charlotte never wanted him to start the agency. She might've pretended she did for about five minutes after they got engaged, but as soon as she realised it meant him working all hours and bringing in no money, she did everything she could to screw it up. But now look: he's a massive success and he says himself he could never have done it without you. Trust me: if Charlotte had known this was how the agency was going to work out, that Corm would be famous and wildly successful, she'd have clung on and never let him go. No,' said Ilsa, 'Charlotte will know *exactly* how important you must be to Corm, and she knew *exactly* what she was doing, mentioning this new woman in front of you.'

Robin had finished her own champagne. Before she could do it,

Ilsa had reached across and pressed the button for her. Robin laughed, then said,

'There's something else. Only, don't make a big deal of it.'

'Go on,' said Ilsa, looking riveted.

'You know Strike took me out for a drink at the Ritz on my birthday?'

'Yes,' said Ilsa, leaning in.

'It's not that exciting. We didn't – you know – end up in bed together.'

Ilsa looked, if anything, even more riveted.

'Well,' said Robin, 'we both got a bit pissed. The cocktails we were drinking were lethal and we hadn't eaten much . . . Anyway, he kind of had his arm around me, because I nearly fell over, and then there was this moment outside the Ritz while we were waiting for a taxi and I think – I don't know, but I'm pretty sure he was going to kiss me.'

Ilsa's gasp was so loud that a passing waiter looked back at her.

'Don't,' groaned Robin. 'Honestly, Ilsa, don't. It was . . . Oh God, I keep remembering the look on his face. He leaned in and I panicked and I think he . . . I got the impression he . . .' Robin shook her head. 'He probably thought I was disgusted at the idea or something. He looked a bit . . .'

Robin closed her eyes briefly, remembering Strike's expression.

'. . . mortified. He backed off and then we – we went back to normal. Well, sort of normal. He was a bit more distant than usual afterwards.'

'Why did you panic?' asked Ilsa, her expression intense.

The waiter arrived to refill Robin's glass. She drank nearly half of it before saying:

'I don't know – because I'm thirty and I've literally been with one man, ever?' She groaned again, as the memory of her phone call with Ryan Murphy swept back over her. 'Because I'm such a moron I don't even realise I'm being asked out?'

But her own inexperience wasn't the whole reason and Robin knew it.

'But *mainly* . . . I knew Strike would regret it, if we kissed. I *knew* he would, once he sobered up, and . . . I couldn't stand hearing him tell me it was a big mistake. You know what he's like about his privacy and his space, and we spend most of our lives together as it is. I didn't want to hear him tell me he hadn't meant it.'

251

Ilsa sat back against the banquette, frowning slightly. Again, she reached for her champagne, and again changed her mind.

'Yeah, you're right. He *would've* regretted it. That's Corm, isn't it?' said the lawyer. 'He'd've told you it was a drunken mistake and then he'd probably have found ways to drive a good big wedge between the two of you, so he can preserve his messed-up ideas about relationships . . . I'll lay you odds he started dating this bloody woman—'

'You don't know she's a bloody woman,' said Robin reasonably. 'She could be lovely. His last girlfriend was. Lorelei. There was nothing wrong with her.'

'Of course there wasn't, that's why he ditched her,' said Ilsa dismissively. 'How's he going to maintain his lifelong view that a stable relationship means some kind of prison if he goes out with women who might not fuck up his life? No, I'll bet you a month's salary he's with this new woman because the pair of you nearly kissed and it scared the living daylights out of him.'

Ilsa sat in thought for a few seconds, then a broad grin spread over her face.

'Why are you smiling?'

'Sorry, I can't help it,' said Ilsa. 'I'm just thinking how good that will have been for him, to think you were disgusted at the idea of kissing him.'

'Ilsa!'

'Oh, Robin, come *on*, you've seen the effect he has on women. They think he's this big unshaven lump with an attitude and half an hour later they've decided he's the sexiest thing on legs. I'm immune,' said Ilsa with another shrug. 'It's not my thing, that "how do I fix down this man who clearly doesn't want to be fixed down" bullshit. But a lot of women love it, hence his very high success rate.'

'I never found him remotely sexy,' said Robin, but then the spirit of truthfulness unleashed by the champagne forced her to add, 'Not for ages.'

'No,' said Ilsa. 'I think he was ahead of you there. *Don't* tell me I don't know what I'm talking about, Robin, I saw the way he was looking at you at your birthday dinner. Why d'you think he didn't tell you he was seeing this Madeline person?'

'I don't know.'

'I do,' said Ilsa. 'It's because he doesn't want you to feel free to go and shag CID officers. He wants to get his end away while you stay available and he decides whether he can afford the consequences of another lunge.

'I've known Corm since we were both five and bloody Dave Polworth was pulling my hair in the playground. You never met his Aunt Joan. I loved her, everyone did, but she was the polar opposite of his mother. Joan ran a tight ship, it was all about the manners and buttoned-up behaviour and not shaming the family. Then Leda used to turn up and snatch him back and let him do whatever the hell he liked while she got stoned in London. He spent his life bouncing between two extremes: man of the house and too much responsibility whenever he was with Leda, but little boy who had to mind his Ps and Qs when he was with Joan. It's no wonder he's got very odd ideas about relationships.

'But *you*,' said Ilsa, staring shrewdly at Robin through her glasses, 'you're something entirely novel for Corm. You don't need fixing. You fixed yourself. You also like him just the way he is.'

'I wouldn't be too sure of that,' said Robin. 'Not this evening.'

'D'you want him to give up the job? D'you think he ought to settle down and have a couple of kids and start driving a Range Rover and join the PTA?'

'No,' said Robin, 'because the agency wouldn't be what it is without him.'

'The agency,' repeated Ilsa, shaking her head in wonder. 'Honestly, you're just like him.'

'What d'you mean?'

'The job comes first. Listen to yourself. "The agency wouldn't be what it is." My God, he's lucky to have you. I don't think he's ever met *any* other woman who has wanted him to be free to do what he does best.'

'What about all these women who find out how sexy he is after an hour in his company?'

'Once they get past an hour, or a week, he starts pissing them off,' said Ilsa. 'He'd piss *me* off. The weird thing is, I don't think he'd piss you off, if you two ever get there ... what else d'you know about this woman he's dating?'

'Only that her name's Madeline Courson–Miles and she's a jewellery designer. She must be successful. Charlotte's done some modelling for her new collection.'

Ilsa pulled her phone out of her bag and searched for the name.

Robin, who wasn't sure she wanted to see the results, drained her second glass.

'Found her,' said Ilsa, peering down at her phone. 'Oh, for God's sake – *look at her!*'

She passed the phone across the table. Robin looked down at beautiful, beaming, tousle-haired Madeline, who was standing between two supermodels, all three of them holding glasses of champagne.

'Can't you see it?' asked Ilsa impatiently.

'See what?'

'Robin, she looks *just like you!*'

Robin started to laugh.

'Ilsa—'

'She does!' said Ilsa, pulling her phone out of Robin's hand to examine the picture of Madeline again. 'Same hair colour, same—'

'When have you ever seen me wear leather trousers and a silver lamé shirt open to my navel?'

'Well, admittedly you couldn't get away with the shirt,' said Ilsa. 'Your boobs are too big. So that's Ellacott two, Courson-Miles nil, for a start.'

Robin laughed harder.

'Ilsa, will you please drink your champagne? I don't want to be the only one pressing the button.'

Ilsa hesitated, then said quietly,

'I can't. I'm pregnant.'

'*What?*'

Robin knew that Ilsa and Nick had been trying for years to have a baby and that their final round of IVF had failed.

'Ilsa, that's wonderful! I thought you said you weren't going to do another—?'

'It happened naturally,' said Ilsa, now looking tense. 'But it won't last. It never lasts. Three rounds of IVF, three miscarriages. It'll go wrong, it always does.'

'How far on are you?'

'Nearly twelve weeks.'

'What does Nick—?'

'He doesn't know,' said Ilsa. 'You're the only one I've told.'

'*What?*'

'I can't stand going through it all again,' said Ilsa. 'The hope and then it ending . . . there's no need for Nick to suffer.'

'But if you're nearly at twelve—'

'Don't,' said Ilsa firmly. 'I can't – Robin, I'm forty. Even if it sticks around, there might be something wrong with it.'

'So you haven't been for a scan or anything?'

'I'm not staring at some tiny little wriggling blob that'll never make it, what's the point? I've done that before and it half killed me . . . Not again.'

'How far along were you when you lost the others?'

'Eight weeks, the first one, and ten the other two. Don't look at me like that. Just because this one's clung on an extra fortnight . . .'

'And if you're still pregnant in another two weeks? A month?'

'Well, then . . . then I suppose I'll have to tell Nick,' said Ilsa. Then, looking suddenly panicked, she said, 'Don't tell—'

'Of course I won't tell Strike, what d'you take me for?'

'You drink it,' said Ilsa, pushing the full glass across the table.

Their starters arrived. As Robin took her first bite of pâté, Ilsa said, 'What's this CID guy like, who just asked you out?'

'He was tall and I think he was quite nice-looking, but we were talking about murder, so, you know . . . that was uppermost in my mind.'

'Ring him back. Say you'd like the drink.'

'No,' said Robin firmly. 'He probably thinks I'm special needs after the conversation we just had.'

'How are you going to get past the "I've only ever been with one man" thing unless you actually date some other people? It's only a drink. You aren't risking much with a drink. You never know what might come of it.'

Robin looked at her friend, eyes narrowed.

'And I'm sure making Strike jealous is the last thing on your mind.'

'Well,' said Ilsa with a wink, 'I wouldn't say it's the *last*.'

29

I have been a witch's prey,
Art mine enemy now by day,
Thou fell Fear? There comes an end
To the day; thou canst not wend
After me where I shall fare . . .

Jean Ingelow
At One Again

By ten o'clock Strike, who'd just eaten the stir-fry that was his go-to when he couldn't think of anything else to cook, was lying on his bed in his attic room, still fully dressed, belt loosened and trouser button undone, a freshly lit cigarette in his mouth, a triple measure of his favourite single malt sitting on the small table beside him and Robin's printed-out notes on the Pen of Justice blog next to him on the bed.

Charlotte's intrusion into his office had occupied his thoughts for hours, but a measure of equilibrium was returning: firstly, because he'd set some action in motion that would hopefully counter Jago Ross's determination to ruin Strike along with his estranged wife; secondly, because this was his second triple whisky; and, lastly, because the habit of mental discipline that had stood him in good stead throughout his career had reinstated itself. Work had always been his best refuge, and if his own emotions weren't yet entirely subduable, he could at least attempt to impose order on the messy problem of Anomie. So he pulled out his phone and tried, one more time, to sign up for *Drek's Game*, but as had happened every other time, Harty appeared, shrugged and told him to try again later.

Setting his mobile down on the bed, Strike took a swig of Scotch, then picked up Robin's printed notes on the Pen of Justice blog, and began to read.

Note on the Pen of Justice Blog

The anonymous Pen of Justice blog was started in January 2012. Whoever's behind it is on Twitter as @penjustwrites. Their location isn't disclosed. The focus of the blog is to critique pop culture. However, the Pen of Justice writes at least three blogs about *The Ink Black Heart* for every one they write about other shows/movies. Anomie has only once shared a Pen of Justice blog (see attached).

Anomie and the Pen of Justice have interacted with each other occasionally. If the same person's behind both Anomie's account and the Pen of Justice blog, they're being careful to maintain two different characters online. Broadly speaking, Anomie seems to share anything that casts Edie Ledwell in a bad light, whereas the Pen of Justice mostly critiques the alleged flaws in the cartoon, and in other shows, from a socio-political standpoint.

After Edie tried to kill herself in May 2014, Anomie and the Pen of Justice were both accused of having hounded her into it. Anomie claimed Ledwell's suicide attempt was faked. The Pen of Justice went quiet for six weeks, then returned with a blog post entitled 'Why Call Out Culture is a Powerful Tool for Social Change', which concluded:

> I've been accused of trying to 'shame' and 'bully' people into conformity with my views. Well, I make no apology for this. If society is to change for the better, if it is to be inclusive of all races, all genders, all people with disabilities, making bigots scared is no bad place to start. So-called 'cancel culture' is really no more than holding people accountable for the views they are intentionally putting out into the public sphere.
>
> Do I want Edie Ledwell dead? Of course not.
>
> Does Edie Ledwell make the world a more unsafe place for marginalised groups with every thoughtless stereotype she puts on screen? Yes, she does.

I'm glad she's feeling better. Now I want to see her do better.

Although Morehouse (Anomie's co-creator of the game) has denied it, there's a persistent rumour in the *Ink Black Heart* fandom that he writes the Pen of Justice blog. The theory first surfaced in January 2013 (see attached tweets).

Strike flipped over the page and saw a line of printed-out tweets.

Penny Peacock @rachledbadly
@theMorehou©e I know you wrote this
www.ThePenOfJustice/WhyThe . . .

Morehouse @theMorehou©e
replying to @rachledbadly
Nope

Penny Peacock @rachledbadly
replying to @theMorehou©e
Heisenberg

Morehouse @theMorehou©e
replying to @rachledbadly
You're as wrong about me being The Pen of Justice as you are
about uncertainty principle

Penny Peacock @rachledbadly
replying to @theMorehou©e
lol

Mags Pie @maggiespie25
replying to @suze_mcmillan @rachledbadly @theMorehou©e
Wait, what? Morehouse = The Pen of Justice?????

Carol S @CJS_inkheart
replying to @maggiespie25 @suze_mcmillan @rachledbadly
@theMorehou©e
This blog is spot on, the Ink Black Heart is ableist af

Dan Spinkman @SpinkyDan
replying to @CJS_inkheart @maggiespie25 @suze_mcmillan
@rachledbadly @theMorehou©e
It's a cartoon about corpses. Be kind of strange if they were in
perfect health

Kea Niven @realPaperwhite
replying to @SpinkyDan @CJS_inkheart @maggiespie25
@suze_mcmillan @rachledbadly @theMorehou©e
please do ablesplain why disabled people like me should have
to tolerate this kind of fucking "humour" #spoonie #ableism
#TheInkBlackHeart

Lepine's Disciple @Lep1nesDisciple
replying to @realPaperwhite @SpinkyDan @CJS_inkheart
@maggiespie25 @suze_mcmillan @rachledbadly
@theMorehou©e
being too ugly to fuck ≠ being disabled

Strike had the feeling he'd just seen a name that ought to mean something to him but, possibly because he'd consumed a third of a bottle of whisky, he couldn't put his finger on it. He turned to the next page, across the top of which Robin had written: *This is the article by the Pen of Justice that Anomie retweeted.*

Why *The Ink Black Heart* Is Seriously Ableist and Why That Should Trouble You

Content Warning: this article will use terms and words relating to physical and mental disabilities that you may find offensive, derogatory or hurtful. While I'm using these terms for educational purposes, I would strongly advise you practising sensible self-care and postponing a read if you're currently in a place of pain or vulnerability, or feeling unsafe in your current environment. The issues with which this piece engages will necessarily be a triggering subject for many people with disabilities.

Strike paused to scratch his leg at the point where the end of his stump met the prosthesis, a pointless exercise as the itch originated in the nerve endings that refused to believe his lower leg was absent.

Casual ableism is everywhere. When did you last go an entire day without hearing or reading somebody using the words *idiot, cretin, moron, dumb, dim, nuts, insane, lame, daft, delusional, deranged, demented, crazy, mad, deformed, handicapped, disorder, hysterical, sociopath* or *narc*?

Representation of people with disabilities in popular culture is extremely poor, both in terms of quantity and quality. On the rare occasion we see a person with disabilities on screen, they are usually played by an able-bodied actor. Moreover, characters with disabilities are generally defined by their physical or mental issue in superficial or stereotypical ways.

Given that one of the creators claims to have had mental health issues, one might have expected *The Ink Black Heart* to buck this trend. Unfortunately, it is undoubtedly one of the greatest offenders currently on our screens.

Nearly all of the characters have 'comical' disabilities of some kind. From Harty's regular palpitations to bones dropping randomly off the Wyrdy-Grobs' skeletons, we're invited to laugh at the strangeness of imperfect bodies. Sick minds fare no better: Paperwhite's depression and anorexia and Drek's arguably manic-depressive episodes are likewise mocked. The Worm and Magspie, clearly the only two working-class characters, are shown as having 'caused' their own illnesses: The Worm by overeating and Magspie by stealing objects too heavy to lift. This, of course, furthers the stereotype that the (criminal) poor have only themselves to blame for conditions of obesity and chronic pain.

The language used throughout the cartoon is consistently problematic. Barely an episode passes without one character calling another 'madsick' or 'gruesog', meaning mentally unstable/ugly. Casual cruelty is endemic: Drek capitalising on Harty's lack of legs and kicking him like a football; Magspie taunting Paperwhite for not pulling herself together and making the most of her unhappy life; all the other characters laughing at the Wyrdy-Grobs' delusion that they remain healthy and beautiful, in spite of being reduced to literal piles of bones.

It would not be going too far to say that, just as healthy visitors were able to visit the eighteenth-century mental hospital Bedlam to mock and abuse the patients, we are invited to jeer at the unhappy inmates of *The Ink Black Heart*.

Strike reached sideways for his whisky, drank some more, then flipped over the page and read on with the glass balanced on his chest.

At the top of the new page, Robin had written: *Row between Anomie and Edie after Anomie retweeted the blog about disabilities. Note Kea Niven joining in.*

With an effort, Strike now succeeded in recalling what Robin had told him earlier, about the girl who believed Edie Ledwell had stolen her ideas for *The Ink Black Heart*.

Anomie @AnomieGamemaster
Decent analysis of Greedie Fedwell's weird fascination with disabilities and ugliness:

www.penofjustice/WhyTheInkBlackHear . . . .

Anomie @AnomieGamemaster
replying to @AnomieGamemaster
Extra fun fact: Fedwell's foster brother's disabled. Apparently Lord Wyrdy-Grob's walk was based on his

---

Edie Ledwell @EdLedDraws
replying to @AnomieGamemaster
That's a fucking lie

Anomie @AnomieGamemaster
replying to @EdLedDraws
where'd you get the idea for his walk?

Edie Ledwell @EdLedDraws
replying to @AnomieGamemaster
I don't animate Lord Wyrdy-Grob, Josh does

Anomie @AnomieGamemaster
replying to @EdLedDraws
sure he does. Seriously, have you ever considered not lying?

Edie Ledwell @EdLedDraws
replying to @AnomieGamemaster
It isn't a fucking lie and you need to leave my friends and family alone

---

Anomie @AnomieGamemaster
replying to @EdLedDraws
Says the woman who claims she's got no family and has literally no friends left, because she's fucked them all over

---

Edie Ledwell @EdLedDraws
replying to @AnomieGamemaster
You're full of shit

Anomie @AnomieGamemaster
replying to @EdLedDraws
Seriously, keep insulting fans online. It's a great look

Kea Niven @realPaperwhite
replying to @AnomieGamemaster @EdLedDraws
She doesn't give a shit about fans, all she cares about is £££
and her own disgusting agenda #ableism

Kea Niven @realPaperwhite
replying to @realPaperwhite @AnomieGamemaster
@EdLedDraws
Her vile cartoon promotes the idea that disabled people are
'other'/laughable/strange #spoonie #ableism

Yasmin Weatherhead @YazzyWeathers
replying to @realPaperwhite @AnomieGamemaster
@EdLedDraws
and she still hasn't sat down with any disability group to
discuss fans' valid concerns #ableism

Lepine's Disciple @Lep1nesDisciple
replying to @YazzyWeathers @realPaperwhite
@EdLedDraws @penjustwrites @AnomieGamemaster
what's your disability? Being a land whale?

Robin's notes on the Pen of Justice ended here. Strike set down the pages, drained his glass of whisky, stubbed out his cigarette, then picked up his phone again and went to examine Kea Niven's Twitter page.

After noting how pretty Kea was, he accidentally pressed the link to her tumblr page with his thumb.

Strike, who'd never heard of tumblr, found himself momentarily confused as to what he was looking at. Kea's page was covered in images and short written pieces, some re-blogged from other accounts, others written or drawn by herself. At the top was a picture of many silver spoons and the legend:

> Disabled artist – fashion, music and bird lover –
> life right now is mostly about being sick.

CF – fibromyalgia – POTs – allodynia –
I need more spoons . . .

Strike had no idea what the need for spoons referred to and assumed it was a piece of whimsy, possibly from some book or film he didn't know. He read Kea's post about being forced to return to live with her mother, then began to scroll through examples of her art, which was heavily anime-influenced. There were many re-blogged statements about chronic illness ('the hardest pill to swallow is some things aren't fixed by mind over matter', 'letting go of who you were meant to be isn't easy') and a multitude of quotations, usually set against pastel backgrounds:

Stab the body and it heals, but injure the heart and the wound lasts a lifetime – **Mineko Iwasaki**

When you give someone your whole heart and he doesn't want it, you cannot take it back. It's gone forever – **Sylvia Plath**

All changes pass me like a dream,
I neither sing nor pray;
And thou art like the poisonous tree
That stole my life away **– Elizabeth Siddal**

Strike kept reading until he found a couple of short pieces written by Kea herself.

My mother, a woman who breeds parrots and is allergic to feathers, is bitching about my poor life choices. OK, Karen.

A little below this was:

It's fine not to 'work' or to 'achieve'. Feeling guilty that you aren't able to do either is the result of internalised capitalism.

It's fine to ask for accommodations. Your assessment of your own body's needs should not depend on how 'sick' other people believe you to be.

It's fine to use a mobility device if it makes your life easier, even if it wasn't prescribed or advised by a doctor.

Strike's gaze moved unconsciously to the drawer where he kept the collapsible walking stick Robin had once bought him, when his amputated leg had been giving him so much trouble he'd barely been able to walk. He didn't like using it, firstly, because the stick added another recognisable feature to an appearance that was already distinctive and in danger of becoming too recognisable, and secondly, because it invited enquiries and sympathy that he found generally unwelcome.

He closed Kea's tumblr page, which he'd found unattractively mawkish, and lay motionless on his bed for another minute, looking up at the ceiling, before getting to his feet and limping towards the bathroom. While peeing, he remembered that Charlotte had once given him a cane as well: antique, made of Malacca, with a silver handle. She'd claimed it had been her great-grandfather's, but who knew whether that was true; it might just as easily have been bought from an antique shop. In any case, it had been useless; far too short for Strike, and when they'd split for the final time Charlotte had kept it.

Staring at the bathroom wall, waiting for his bladder to drain, Strike felt he might be on the verge of coining an aphorism about what seemed attractive in times of trouble versus what a man actually needed, what was of value as opposed to what cost a lot, but his tired brain, rendered sluggish by the whisky, refused to turn neat phrases. He therefore turned instead to the more practical issues of taking off his false leg, rubbing cream onto the end of his stump and falling into bed.

30

But if I can cheat my heart with the old comfort,
that love can be forgotten,
is it not better?

Adah Isaacs Menken
Myself

Champagne and her chat with Ilsa had temporarily lifted Robin's spirits, but she felt them sagging again now that she was heading home in a taxi. Aftershocks from the revelation that Strike was in a relationship kept hitting her in the solar plexus. Ilsa had wanted to give her hope: hope that Strike would miraculously change and want a real relationship with the woman he called his best friend, but that would jeopardise the agency and the spartan, self-sufficient life in his attic flat he'd never shown the slightest sign of wishing to exchange for a less lonely existence. Ilsa might have known Strike a long time, but Robin suspected she knew the man he was now better than Ilsa did. Whether or not Ilsa was right about his reasons for hiding the relationship with Madeline, it sprang from a habit of self-protective compartmentalisation Robin doubted Strike was likely ever to give up.

Staring out of the taxi window watching dark shops slide past, some of them still with their lit neon signs above their blackened windows, she told herself, *You need to fall out of love. It's that simple.*

But how exactly she was to do that, she had no idea. There'd been no effort required with her ex-husband: love had slowly been eroded by an incompatibility hidden by circumstance, until at last she'd realised it had vanished and his betrayal had set her free.

As though she'd willed it to happen, onto the taxi radio came 'Wherever You Will Go' by The Calling. It had been her and

Matthew's song, the first dance at their wedding, and even though she tried to find humour in the coincidence, tears pricked Robin's eyes. The song had still been playing when she'd run out on her first dance to pursue Strike, who'd left the reception, thereby setting the tone (or so it seemed to Robin in retrospect) for her short, doomed marriage.

> *Run away with my heart,*
> *Run away with my hope,*
> *Run away with my love . . .*

'Ridiculous,' Robin whispered to herself, wiping the tears away, then she did exactly what her business partner had done an hour previously, and turned to work as a better refuge than drink.

Opening Twitter, she saw she'd had two more direct messages from her would-be flirt, @jbaldw1n1>>.

> @jbaldw1n1>>
> not even gonna fkn answer?
>
> @jbaldw1n1>>
> fuck u then you snobby fkn bitch

Closing her direct messages, Robin checked Anomie's Twitter feed and saw that a new tweet had been posted while she'd been at the restaurant.

Anomie
@AnomieGamemaster

This is how much the 'protector of the flame' cares about The Ink Black Heart and its fans

> **Grant Ledwell**
> @gledwell101
>
> A brief message to thank fans for their condolences.
>
> Edie Ledwell's family are committed to developing and protecting #TheBlackInkHeart as Edie would have wished.

11.15 pm   10 April 2015

Robin had now spent long enough immersed in the world of *Ink Black Heart* fandom to have predicted the uproar Anomie's retweet of Grant's words would cause.

DrekIsMySpiritAnimal @playDreksgame
replying to @AnomieGamemaster @gledwell101
Fkn prick can't even get the title right
😂😂😂😂😂😂

Belle @Hell5!Bell5!
replying to @AnomieGamemaster @gledwell101
try getting the title right you moron

LepinesDisciple @LepinesD1sciple
replying to @AnomieGamemaster @gledwell101
hey Grunt, your wife looks like the stuff left in the bucket after liposuction

---

Black Hart @sammitchywoo
replying to @AnomieGamemaster @gledwell101
we listen to Josh not you. He knows the title, for one thing
#notoMaverick #IstandwithJosh

Zozo @inkyheart28
replying to @AnomieGamemaster @gledwell101
omfg josh is tweeting again . Josh is askin people not , to attack the Ledwells

---

> **Josh Blay** @realJoshBlay
> replying to @AnomieGamemaster
> Please leave the Ledwells alone. Please stop what you're doing.

LepinesDisciple @LepinesD1sciple
replying to @inkyheart28 @realJoshBlay
@AnomieGamemaster @gledwell101
that's not him he's a vegetable now. it'll be some little PR tit from Maverick

---

Streetlights cast sliding orange bars across the taxi seat and the screen of Robin's phone. Feeling a sudden revulsion against Twitter, Robin closed the app and instead tried to enter *Drek's Game* again, but couldn't get in. As she watched Harty smiling and shrugging, Robin concluded that Strike was right: Anomie didn't want anyone new in the game right now.

And then, quite suddenly, the solution to their problem came to her as though it had been whispered in her ear by one of the devas Allan Yeoman had mentioned. They'd get in by being somebody who *wasn't* new. Depression lifting in a sudden rush of adrenalin, Robin tried to remember the night's rota. Barclay was watching Cardew, Shah was tailing Montgomery, so Midge was surely on Fingers. She pressed Midge's number, and the latter answered on the second ring.

'Wassup?'

'Oh good, you're awake.'

'Yeah, still in Belgravia with a bunch of arseholes.'

'Midge, I need a favour. The agency will reimburse you, if it takes money.'

'Go on.'

'Strike and I still haven't been able to get into Anomie's game. It looks like they aren't admitting anyone new. So, I was wondering—'

'Robin,' said Midge, 'you'd better not be thinking what I think you're thinking.'

'I'm pretty sure I am.'

Ahead of the taxi, a police car had pulled over beside what looked like the aftermath of a fight. A gaggle of people stood outside a bar, one man on the ground nursing his head. Broken glass sparkled all around him on the pavement.

Midge groaned in Robin's ear.

'Fook's sake, Robin.'

'Was Beth still playing the game when you split up?'

'Not as much. I think she was getting bored of it.'

'Well,' said Robin, 'that's kind of ideal from our point of view.'

'It might be from *your* fookin' point of view, but I hoped never to speak to her again.'

'Is there anything we could offer her in exchange for her log-in details?'

Another longer pause followed.

'*You* couldn't,' said Midge at last, 'but *I* could, I s'pose.'

'I wouldn't want you to do anything that makes you uncomfortable,' said Robin, crossing the fingers of her free hand.

'It won't make me uncomfortable, it'll just fook me off to give her what she wants.'

'What's that?'

'I kept an antique mirror when we split. She's mad about the thing.'

'We could buy you a new one,' suggested Robin.

'I don't want a new one, I hate it. I only kept it because she wanted it so much and I fookin' paid for it,' said Midge. She heaved a loud sigh. 'All right, I'll see what I can do.'

'Midge, I can't thank you enough,' said Robin, now beaming.

After Midge had hung up, and in spite of the fact that she'd closed it minutes earlier, Robin opened Twitter again.

The responses to Anomie's retweet of Grant's unfortunate mistake were still flooding in.

Soph The Gopher @BlackHartIsMe
replying to @AnomieGamemaster @gledwell101
if that dumb fucker's in charge #TheInkBlackHeartIsOver

Brother of Ultima Thule @UltimaBro88
replying to @AnomieGamemaster @gledwell101
#BringBackWallyAsDrek

Algernon Gizzard Esq @Gizzard_AI
replying to @AnomieGamemaster @gledwell101
Hey, Anomie, you should kill Grunt next

31

The rat is the concisest tenant.
He pays no rent, —
Repudiates the obligation,
On schemes intent.

Emily Dickinson
The Rat

In-game chats between all eight moderators of *Drek's Game*

```
<Moderator Channel>

<10 April 2015 23.29>

<Anomie, Vilepechora,
Paperwhite, Fiendy1,
Hartella, Worm28>

Anomie: right, everyone
here?

Worm28: Morehouse isnt

Hartella: LordDrek
isn't either

Anomie: ok we'll
wait because I want
everyone to hear this

Anomie: did you all see
what Grunt just did on
Twitter?
```

```
<A new private channel
has opened>

<10 April 2015 23.29>

<Morehouse invites
Anomie>

>

>

>

>

>

>

>

>
```

```
<A new private channel
has opened>

<10 April 2015 23.29>

<LordDrek invites
Vilepechora>

LordDrek: what the fuck
is wrong with you?

LordDrek: are you
pissed?

>

>

<Vilepechora has joined
the channel>

Vilepechora: what's up?
```

Vilepechora: getting the title wrong? yeh

Worm28: josh doesn 't wand us to attack him tho

Vilepechora: has josh got magic powers in hospital?

Worm28: ?

Vilepechora: 'wand'. Or as you'd say, ' wand '

Fiendy1: piss off and leave Worm alone, Vilepechora

Hartella: Josh must be be loads better if he's tweeting

Fiendy1: cd be getting a nurse or someone to do it for him

Fiendy1: hurry up, Anomie, don't keep us in suspense, it's not the bloody X Factor

Worm28: lol

>

>

>

Hartella: it's terrible Grant Ledwell's going to have so much power over the IBH when he can't even get the title right

Hartella: god knows

>

<Anomie has joined the channel>

Anomie: there's a meeting on the mod chan, come join us

Morehouse: why haven't you kicked out Vilepechora and LordDrek like you said you were going to?

Anomie: I said I'd look into them

Anomie: I did and they're not Halvening

Morehouse: how did you look into them?

Anomie: questioned them

Morehouse: fuck's sake, what were you expecting, a confession?

Morehouse: I went back through the logs. Neither of them were in here when the killing happened.

Anomie: Nor were you and I don't see anyone accusing you of killing Ledwell

Morehouse: what did they say about that dossier?

Anomie: they thought it was all true

LordDrek: are you drunk?

>

Vilepechora: lol yeah

LordDrek: what the fuck are you playing at, saying that on Twitter?

Vilepechora: saying what?

LordDrek: about Anomie killing Grant Ledwell next

LordDrek: ffs, we aren't supposed to be advertising our presence in this fkn game

LordDrek: and it doesn't take a fucking genius to see through "Al Gizzard" either

Vilepechora: paranoid, much?

LordDrek: I'm not fkn paranoid, I've just been talking to Eihwaz. He was interviewed by the pigs this afternoon.

Vilepechora: shit why?

LordDrek: we've either been infiltrated or hacked again, because from what they asked him they clearly suspect he's the the bombmaker

Vilepechora: the twat was probably mouthing

what the film will be
like if he's in charge

Fiendy1: he won't be
completely in charge,
there's still Josh

Worm28: Maverik should
sit down with fans ,
and hear what we think
should happen with the
movie

Hartella: yeah

Paperwhite: that'll
never happen, though

**<LordDrek has entered
the channel>**

LordDrek: sorry I'm
late, only just got
home from work

Hartella: hi LordDrek xxx

LordDrek: hi Hartella

Anomie: right, all here?

Anomie: ok, so, Grunt
Ledwell's title mishap
just proves there's
no point playing nice
any more

Fiendy1: you've been
playing nice so far,
have u?!

Anomie: it's time to
start terrorizing Grunt
Ledwell and those
Maverick fucks

Fiendy1: how?

Morehouse: bollocks,
they were trying
to turn the fandom
against Ledwell and
get them harassing
her

Anomie: They were
only saying what most
fans think. She was a
mercenary cow. You're
obsessed with the fkn
Halvening.

Morehouse: ffs, you
should be too

Anomie: Just come into
the mod channel, I'm
telling them my plan
for Comic Con

Morehouse: fuck your
plan, I'm not finished
talking about this

**<Anomie has left the
channel>**

**<Morehouse has left
the channel>**

**<Private channel has
closed>**

off in a pub about
explosives or something

LordDrek: whatever he's
done, I don't need you
publicly connecting
your Halvening name to
this game

>

>

Vilepechora: ok I've
deleted the tweet

LordDrek: delete the
whole account, dickwad!

**<Vilepechora has left
the channel>**

**<LordDrek has left the
channel>**

**<Private channel has
closed>**

Anomie: we need as many people as possible to turn up at Comic Con wearing Drek's Game T-shirts

Anomie: show them this game's the epicentre of the fandom

Anomie: and any attempt to shut us down will mean a massive backlash against them and their shitty film

<Morehouse has joined the channel>

Worm28: but how do we keep ruel 14 if we're all there ?

Anomie: no names, no personal details and masks

LordDrek: sexy. Like a swingers' orgy

Hartella: lol

Morehouse: I want to talk about the Halvening

Anomie: Morehouse ffs give it a rest

Morehouse: I think we've got two members of The Halvening in here and I want them to fuck off out of this game and not come back

<A new private channel has opened>

<10 April 2015 23.37>

<Hartella invites Morehouse>

>

LordDrek: I take it you're referring to Vilepechora and myself?

Morehouse: correct

LordDrek: we've had this out with Anomie and he accepts we made an innocent mistake

Morehouse: did you fuck

Vilepechora: we did

Vilepechora: we didn't even know what the Halvening was until Anomie explained it to us

Vilepechora: he's well up on all that dark net stuff

Vilepechora: we think he used Bitcoin to buy the machete and taser

Worm28: how can u joke about that ?

Fiendy1: fuck u Vilepechora!

Fiendy1: a human being was murdered and your making fkn jokes

Hartella: Morehouse, hun,don't do this, please.

Hartella: there's no way LordDrek's Halvening!

Hartella: please don't tell Anomie that I know this, because I've broken rule 14, but LordDrek's black!

Hartella: so how can he be a white supremacist?!

>

>

>

>

Hartella: Morehouse?

>

>

>

>

>

<Hartella has left the channel>

<Private channel has closed>

<A new private channel has opened>

<10 April 2015 23.41>

<LordDrek invites Vilepechora>

<Vilepechora has joined the channel>

274

Fiendy1: Morehouse's completely right, if it was an innocent mistake you'd be hiding under a rock after hwat happened to Ledwell and Blay but here you are bloody laughing about it. I don't think it was a mistake

<Fiendy1 has left the channel>

Anomie: made it up with Fiendy1, eh, Morehouse?

Anomie: been having little cosy private channel chats again, like in the old days?

Morehouse: You can keep LordDrek and Vile or you can keep me, Anomie.

<Morehouse has left the channel>

>

>

>

>

>

>

LordDrek: look, if our presence is ruining the game for everyone else, we'll

<A new private channel has opened>

<10 April 2015 23.46>

<Paperwhite invites Morehouse>

Paperwhite: you're my fkn hero

<Morehouse has joined the channel>

Paperwhite: it's only what the rest of us have been too scared

LordDrek: SHUT THE FUCK UP NOW

LordDrek: I'm not fkn kidding

LordDrek: tell me the truth: have yhou been talking to Anomie about Bitcoin?

>

>

Vilepechora: yeah, a bit

LordDrek: you stupid arsehole

LordDrek: what did I say to you when we started this job? we're just a pair of poxy nerds who're obsessed with a fucking cartoon

LordDrek: what else have you been giving him instructions on?

Vilepechora: nothing

LordDrek: well we do not need that prick Morehouse going to the pigs about us

LordDrek: so shut the fuck up and follow my lead

>

>

>

bow out

Hartella: don't be silly! Morehouse is being ridiculous!

LordDrek: but he's co-creator

LordDrek: we're just a pair of shitheads who thought Drek's Game was cool

Vilepechora: yeah

Hartella: Anomie, tell them we know it isn't true!

LordDrek: if we can't get back in here tomorrow, fair enough, we'll know we got voted out.

<LordDrek has left the channel>

<Vilepechora has left the channel>

Hartella: This is crazy!

Hartella: Anomie, you know they just made a mistake!

Hartella: you aren't going to let Morehouse blackmail you?

Anomie: of course not

Hartella: if we had a vote, Morehouse is the

to say.

>

Morehouse: It's them or me and Anomie needs me a fuck sight more than he needs them.

>

Morehouse: He couldn't have done any of this without me. His coding's shit.

Morehouse: I'm mad enough right now to tell you who he is.

Paperwhite: don't

Paperwhite: you'd hate yourself afterwards

Paperwhite: he's still your friend

Morehouse: is he?

Paperwhite: you told me you were really close

Morehouse: not recently

>

Morehouse: sometimes I think he did it

Paperwhite: did what?

Morehouse: What d'you think?

>

Paperwhite: come off it

>

>

>

>

>

>

>

>

->

>

>

>

>

>

>

>

LordDrek: if I find out you've been swinging your dick in here telling Anomie how to buy stuff untraceably

Vilepechora: I haven't

LordDrek: you'd better fucking not have done

Vilepechora: I haven't

only one who'd vote against them

Hartella: you wouldn't, would you, Worm?

Worm28: I don't know

Hartella: Worm, we can't chuck them out!

Anomie: what d'you mean 'we', Hartella?

Hartella: I mean all the moderators,

Anomie: I don't remember you creating this game

Hartella: I know, I didn't mean to imply I did, Sorry, Anomie.

>

Worm28: what Lorddrek and Vielpachora did was weird though

Worm28: that file of stuf they showed us and none of it was true

Hartella: it was a mistake

Worm28: but wear did they get those emails ?

Hartella: just because Ledwell wasn't Anomie doesn't mean the emails weren't

Paperwhite: that's crazy

Paperwhite: why would he?

Morehouse: literally all he cares about is Drek's Game

Morehouse: being in charge of the game and being a leader of the fandom out on Twitter

Paperwhite: that's not a motive

Morehouse: not to a normal person

>

>

Morehouse: ok forget I said that

Morehouse: I'm just feeling really weird about him lately

Morehouse: how's your mum?

Paperwhite: ok

Paperwhite: she's had three chemo sessions

Paperwhite: her hair's starting to fall out

Paperwhite: but as long as it works

Morehouse: yeah.

>

LordDrek: I'll see you tomorrow at Mum and Dad's

LordDrek: and we'll talk more there

<LordDrek has left the channel>

<Vilepechora has left the channel>

<Private channel has closed>

real

Worm28: I knw you really like Lorddrek but what if they faked that stuff ?

Hartella: oh piss off Worm

<Worm28 has left the channel>

Hartella: oh for god's sake

>

>

>

>

>

Hartella: Anomie?

Anomie: what?

Hartella: what are you going to do about LordDrek and Vile?

>

>

>

Anomie: that's for me to know. But Worm's right, you *do* seem to like LordDrek a lot

Hartella: I don't!

Everything crossed

Paperwhite: xxx

>

>

>

>

>

>

>

Paperwhite: listen, I know this will sound insecure af

Paperwhite: but you're not having chats with Fiendy1 I don't know about, are u?

Morehouse: no of course not. Why are you asking?

Paperwhite: It was just what Anomie said on the mod channel The 'cosy little chat' thing.

Paperwhite: Like if you were bi it wouldn't matter to me

Morehouse: I'm not bi, I'm straight and I haven't spoken to Fiendy1 on a private channel for over a year

Hartella: I mean, I like him the same way I like the rest of you

Anomie: so you haven't been breaking rule 14?

Hartella: no, of course not!

>

>

>

Anomie: Worm28 was supposed to be moderating tonight

Hartella: I know

Anomie: as you were the one who took it upon herself to order her to leave, you can do the night shift instead

Hartella: Anomie, I can't, I've got to be up early!

Anomie: consider it a reminder that you don't give the orders around here. I do.

Hartella: please, Anomie, I've got a 6am start!

Anomie: too bad

<Anomie has left the channel>

Paperwhite: ok! only from things people have said in here, it sounds though Fiendy1 used to like you

Morehouse: He definitely didn't, not that way.

>

Paperwhite: I want to ask you something else but I'm scared you'll freak out

Morehouse: ask

>

Paperwhite: are you disabled?

>

>

>

>

Morehouse: why are you asking me that?

>

>

Paperwhite: Mouse, it wouldn't matter at all to me if you were

Morehouse: what made you think I was?

Paperwhite: well it was

just something Fiendy1
>   once said

<Morehouse has left   <Morehouse has left
the channel>   the channel>

32

And all our observations ran
On Art and Letters,
Life and Man. Proudly we sat, we two, on high,
Throned in our Objectivity;
Scarce friends, not lovers (each avers),
But sexless, safe Philosophers.

Amy Levy
Philosophy

In the five days that passed before Strike and Robin next saw each other, they communicated only by text and email. It was by the latter that Strike told Robin the agency had taken on another job: of finding something to the discredit of Jago Ross, which could be used against him to prevent Strike being dragged into the Rosses' divorce case. As Strike didn't tell Robin why Jago might suspect him and Charlotte of conducting an affair, Robin was given fresh fodder for painful speculation, and in spite of her recent admission to herself that she might just be in love with her business partner, she'd never felt more sympathy for the women who, in Ilsa's words, he pissed off. Ordinarily she'd have called him to discuss the fresh detail of the case Ryan Murphy had given her by phone – the strange behaviour of Edie's Ledwell phone, which had travelled out of Highgate Cemetery to the vicinity of a pond on Hampstead Heath after its owner's death – but she chose instead to pass on the information by return email.

Meanwhile Strike was in the not altogether unfamiliar position of feeling that his life had become one long procession of emotional demands he was failing to meet and physical requirements he was barely able to fulfil. His hamstring was continuing to play up, and in spite of twice-daily applications of cream, the end of his amputated leg remained inflamed. Given that he was to blame for adding an extra job to the agency's workload, he was trying to cover as many hours as possible, to free up Dev and Midge for the Ross investigation. Not only did this mean it was impossible to remove his prosthesis and rest up with an ice-pack pressed to the end of his stump, as he knew his specialist would have advised, he'd been forced to turn down invitations both from Madeline, who had tickets to *La fille mal gardée* at the Royal Opera House, and Lucy, who'd expected him to spend the weekend at her house in Bromley with their recently bereaved Uncle Ted. Neither woman had hidden their disappointment and displeasure when he said he had to work, and Strike, who was far less fond of the ballet than of his uncle, had at least made time to snatch a coffee with Ted before he returned to Cornwall.

Days out with his favourite nephew had also had to be shelved for the present. Strike's growing closeness to Jack was as much of a surprise to him as to his sister. He'd had little voluntary contact with Lucy's three sons before Jack had been hospitalised, when Strike had been forced to deputise for the parents who were stuck in Italy. Out of that traumatic, chance event had grown a totally unforeseen connection that had strengthened over the next couple of years. Strike genuinely missed his and Jack's outings, which usually involved going to see things of mutual, usually military, interest. As Jack now had his own mobile phone they occasionally texted each other jokes or information they thought the other might appreciate. Jack had lately told his uncle he was going to do his First World War project on the 1915 Battle of Neuve Chapelle (where the Royal Military Police, in which Strike had served and which Jack aspired to join, had played a decisive role). As Strike was the one who'd told Jack all about the Battle of Neuve Chapelle, he felt an unfamiliar glow of vicarious pride and for a few minutes wondered whether this sort of feeling accounted for people's desire to procreate, an urge Strike had never personally felt.

Adding to his general feeling of strain, Strike realised on Wednesday night that two of the three dates his half-sister Prudence had proposed for a possible meeting had already passed. He wrote a hasty email apologising for not answering her sooner, told her truthfully that he was exceptionally busy, and said, somewhat recklessly, that he'd try to make the third of her suggested dates.

When Robin picked Strike up from the office at midday on Thursday, she saw in the rear-view mirror of her old Land Rover that he was limping. As Strike never responded well to enquiries about his leg, and as she was in any case feeling a good degree of resentment towards him just now, she passed no comment.

'Just had a call from Katya,' said Strike, trying not to wince as he clambered into the Land Rover. 'Venue for the meeting's changed. She wants us to go to her house, not the café, because her daughter's unwell and off school. Lisburne Road in Hampstead. I can navigate.'

'OK,' said Robin coolly, moving off. 'That stuff on the dashboard's for you to look at. I think I've found that brotherhood the police asked Wally Cardew about, and I've also found out something about Edie's phone that might be relevant.'

Strike reached for the plastic folder and took out the sheets of paper inside. The first was a printout of a web page.

Brotherhood of Ultima Thule
(BOUT)

"Let a man never stir on his road a step
without his weapons of war;
for unsure is the knowing when need shall arise
of a spear on the way without."

The Hávamál

The Brotherhood of Ultima Thule is committed to defending the civilised values common to the northern European nations: justice, racial purity, Enlightenment values and national sovereignty. We subscribe to the Viking ideals of strength, solidarity and brotherhood. We live by the laws and maxims laid down in the Hávamál. We believe that feminism and the legalisation of homosexuality have disastrously undermined both the traditional family and wider society. We believe that multiculturalism has failed. We support humane repatriation of Jews and other non-native ethnic groups from all northern nations.

Ultima Thule

Ultima Thule was the name given in ancient times to a landmass in the extreme north, a place at the far reaches of the known world. Ultima Thule was the capital of Hyperborea – the land beyond the north wind. Recent archaeological finds confirm that the hominids who first populated the boreal regions originated in the distant north. The birthplace of the Northern races is not Africa, but Ultima Thule.

Faith

The Brotherhood of Ultima Thule practises the ancient faith of Odinism. Odinism is an ancient religion of the northern races, entirely uncorrupted by Jewish influence.

Publications

BOUT regularly produces written papers on key issues of the day. The founder of the brotherhood, Heimdall, has published two books: **The Hávamál for Modern Man** and **Reclaiming Masculinity.**

The Brotherhood

BOUT accepts only male members. New brothers must be vouched for by two existing members. For further details, contact heimdall@#B_O_U_T.com.

Meet–ups

BOUT meets regularly for political gatherings and Odinist retreats.

Follow BOUT on Twitter at **@#b_o_u_t** and on Reddit r/ Brotherhoodofultimathule

'I found it yesterday,' said Robin, eyes on the road ahead, 'through the tweets on the next page. They date from three years ago. Their members aren't shy about being in the Brotherhood. A lot of them have got "BOUT" or "UT" in their usernames.'

As the tweets showed, Wally Cardew had come to the Brotherhood of Ultima Thule's notice through the 'Cookies' video that had got him sacked from *The Ink Black Heart*.

Brotherhood of Ultima Thule
@#B_O_U_T

Literally the funniest thing you'll see this year.

www.YouTube/DrekMakesCookies

9.06 pm   12 March 2012

Arlene @queenarleene
replying to @#B_O_U_T
if you think mocking the holocaust is funny you're fucking disgusting

---

SQ @#B_O_U_T_Quince
replying to @queenarleene @#B_O_U_T
they're mocking the kind of outrage junkie who wants to police every fucking joke, dumbass

---

Wally Cardew @The_Wally_Cardew
replying to @#B_O_U_T_Quince @queenarleene @#B_O_U_T
Exactly. We're taking the piss out of SJWs who see Nazism everywhere.

Strike turned over.

Anomie
@AnomieGamemaster

Fedwell's about to sack @The_Wally_Cardew as Drek. I'm hearing @realJoshBlay doesn't want him to go.

Sign petition below to #KeepWallyDrek

https://www.change.org/KeepWallyDrek

7.27 pm   15 Mar 2012

Zozo @inkyheart28
replying to @AnomieGamemaster
Noooooooooooooooo #KeepWallyDrek

Terence Ryder @Ultima_Brother_14
replying to @AnomieGamemaster
This better not be fucking true #KeepWallyDrek

Pen of Justice @penjustwrites
replying to @AnomieGamemaster
I've disagreed with a lot Ledwell's done but in fairness
I don't see that @The_Wally_Cardew left her with a lot
of choice.

Algernon Gizzard Esq @Gizzard_AI
replying to @penjustwrites @AnomieGamemaster
Fuck off cuck. Wally's literally the only good thing about that
shitty cartoon

Pen of Justice @penjustwrites
replying to @Gizzard_AI @AnomieGamemaster
sure, if by 'good' you mean 'literally a Nazi'

Wally Cardew @The_Wally_Cardew
replying to @AnomieGamemaster
First I've heard I'm being sacked.

Anomie @AnomieGamemaster
replying to @The_Wally_Cardew
Sorry to be the one to break it to you. You're getting
too famous
for #GreedieFedwell. Can't have anyone outshining Greedie.

King of Ultima Thule @Heimd&ll88
replying to @The_Wally_Cardew @AnomieGamemaster
What you get for working for SJWs mate. Check out
www.brotherhoodofultimathule.com

'So Anomie knew Cardew was being sacked before he did?'
said Strike. 'And then the head of the Brotherhood tried to recruit
him?'

'He tried twice,' said Robin. 'Look at the rest of the tweets.'

Brotherhood of Ultima Thule @#B_O_U_T

.@The_Wally_Cardew

Check out our response to your sacking.

www.BrotherhoodOfUltimaThule/TheSackingof . . .

8.03 pm   18 March 2012

Wally Cardew @The_Wally_Cardew
replying to @#B_O_U_T
Yeah, that about sums it up, cheers for the support

Brotherhood of Ultima Thule @#B_O_U_T
replying to @the_Wally_Cardew
We're big fans of yours. Would be great to meet up. Contact
me here or at @Heimd&ll88.

'Good work, finding this,' Strike said. 'Was that the last time the
Brotherhood and Wally interacted on Twitter, three years ago?'

'I think so. I couldn't see anything else.'

'Maybe they took the relationship offline after that. Did you read
what the Brotherhood had to say about Wally's sacking?' he added,
checking that the article wasn't attached.

'Yes,' said Robin, 'but there was nothing new there. Boiled down
to Wally being discriminated against because he was a straight white
man, feminazis are taking over the world and you can't make a simple
joke about burning Jews without the thought police coming for you.'

The car rolled on up Tottenham Court Road.

'Mind if I smoke?' asked Strike in deference to Robin's definitely
cold manner; he wouldn't normally have asked, given that she kept a
tin in the glove compartment for him to use as an ashtray.

'No,' she said, and then, 'd'you think there's any chance the
Brotherhood of Ultima Thule and The Halvening—?'

'Are the public and secret face of the same organisation?'

'Exactly.'

'A bloody good chance, I'd've thought,' said Strike, blowing
his smoke carefully out of the window. 'The Brotherhood's the
recruitment tool and the hardcore members get drafted into the mil-
itant wing.'

Strike now turned to the last page Robin had printed out, which was a short excerpt from an online interview with Edie Ledwell from a website called Women Who Create back in 2011.

WWC: What's a typical day like for you?

Edie: There isn't really a typical day. Getting Josh out of bed is the first big job. But then we often work through till 3 or 4 a.m., so I suppose he's entitled to a lie-in.

WWC: And what's the division of labour?

Edie: Well, I tend to come up with the story for each episode, although Josh is always throwing in ideas and I often use them or develop them, or whatever. We both animate: he does Harty, Magspie and Lord and Lady Wyrdy-Grob and I do Drek, The Worm and Paperwhite.

WWC: Has your process evolved, or has it remained the same?

Edie: We've got a bit more organised. I've started putting ideas and reminders on my phone instead of scraps of paper I immediately drop or throw away by mistake.

'She kept ideas on her phone,' said Strike. 'Interesting . . . I've been wondering why the phones were taken. The obvious answer was to try and stop the police seeing who they'd called before they were killed at the cemetery, but that would've meant the killer didn't realise the police could get that information anyway. If getting hold of her ideas was the motive, it fits better with my other theory.'

'Which is?'

'That the phones were taken as trophies,' said Strike. 'Mark Chapman made sure to get his album signed before he killed Lennon.'

An unpleasant prickle ran down Robin's spine.

They drove on, up through Camden, Strike smoking out of the window.

He was wondering exactly why Robin's manner was so frosty. Usually, when a woman gave him the silent treatment, he could hazard a good guess at what he'd done wrong. He'd certainly detected an edge to her voice after Charlotte had so skilfully broken the news that he was dating Madeline, but he'd been so consumed by his own fury, discomfort and worry in the aftermath of her visit he hadn't had much room in his head for analysing what Robin felt about it all. Was her continuing coolness merely down to the fact that, as her supposed best friend, he'd failed to mention the relationship, and therefore rooted in hurt pride at being the last to know? Or was she pissed off that he'd added another case to their already groaning workload, a case, moreover, that she might see (however unfairly) as of his own making? Or – and he was well aware that even posing the question to himself might be more of the same vanity that had led him to assume she'd welcome his advances outside the Ritz – was she jealous?

Merely to break the silence, he said,

'I still can't get into that bloody game.'

'Nor can I,' said Robin.

She hadn't told Strike her idea about using Midge's ex-girlfriend's log-in details, partly because Midge hadn't got back to her and she didn't want to promise what she might not be able to deliver, but also (if she were honest) because she didn't see why Strike should be the only person who kept secrets.

'Oh, and I read your notes about the Pen of Justice,' Strike said, flicking ash out of the window. 'We should definitely ask Katya Upcott what she knows about the Pen, and about Kea Niven ... Straight on here,' he added, as they entered Parkhill Road, 'and then left in about half a mile.'

The rest of the journey passed in silence.

33

By slow degrees it broke on her slow sense . . .
That she too in that Eden of delight
Was out of place, and, like the silly kid,
Still did most mischief where she meant most love.
A thought enough to make a woman mad.

Elizabeth Barrett Browning
Aurora Leigh

Lisburne Road was a quiet residential street of terraced red-brick houses: solid, palatial family homes. As most of the parking spaces were full, Strike and Robin had to park some distance from Katya Upcott's house, and Strike suffered in silence the renewed twinges of his hamstring and the irritated end of his stump as they proceeded up the street, which was built on a slight incline.

As they approached the front door, the sound of a cello reached them through the downstairs window. So accomplished was the solo that Robin assumed it was a recording, but when Strike pressed the door-bell a long, drawn-out note broke off and they heard a male voice call:

'I'll get it.'

The door was opened by a thin young man in a very baggy sweat-shirt. The most noticeable features of his face were painful-looking raised cauliflower-like bumps over both cheeks and the swelling of one eye.

'Hi,' he mumbled. 'Come in.'

The walls of the hall were painted cream and hung with oil paintings. A stairlift had been installed, and it currently sat at the top landing. Three large cardboard boxes stood beside the stairs. One had been opened and revealed a selection of fabric squares.

'Oh, thank you, Gus darling!' said a flustered female voice, and a woman they assumed was Katya Upcott came hurrying downstairs. Like her son, she was thin, but where Gus had dark, thick hair, Katya's was mousy and sparse. She was wearing a mustard-yellow sweater, which looked homemade, a tweed skirt and sensible sheepskin slippers. A pair of reading glasses swung on a chain around her neck. As Gus retreated into what Strike and Robin assumed was the sitting room and closed the door, Katya said:

'That's actually Gus's bedroom. We remodelled the house to make things easier for Inigo, so he can stay mostly on one level. He's got ME – Inigo, I mean. So we put Gus downstairs and moved the drawing room upstairs, knocked through, and Inigo has a study and combined bedroom off it, and a bathroom he can get his wheelchair into. Oh' – she gave a little gasping laugh, and held out a thin hand – 'I'm Katya, obviously, and you must be, um, Cormoran, and you're—?'

'Robin,' said Robin, who was used to her name not springing as readily to clients' lips as Strike's did.

As they followed Katya upstairs, the sound of the cello started up again through Gus's bedroom door.

'He's wonderful,' said Robin.

'Yes, isn't he?' said Katya, looking delighted by Robin's praise. 'He *should* be doing his final year at the Royal College of Music, but we had to take him out while we try and sort out his urticaria. You saw?' she whispered, making a circular movement towards her own face with a forefinger. 'We thought it was under control then it came back with a vengeance, and he got angioedema – even his throat swelled up. He's been *really* ill, poor thing, he was in hospital for a bit. But we've got him a really good new specialist in Harley Street and hopefully that will sort him out. He just wants to get back to college. Nobody wants to be stuck at home with their parents at that age, do they?'

The entrance to the drawing room had a push button set at waist height beside a snugly fitting door. When Katya pressed the button, the door swung slowly open. Robin wondered how much money it had cost to renovate the house to this standard and assumed that Katya's crafting supplies business must be doing very well. Once they'd entered the drawing room and the door had closed behind them, the sound of the cello disappeared entirely.

'We had the door and floor soundproofed,' Katya explained, 'so

Gus practising doesn't disturb Inigo when he's napping. Now, would you like tea? Coffee?'

Before either could answer, a second electric door at the end of the room slid open, and a man in a wheelchair emerged slowly to the accompaniment of 'The Show Must Go On' by Queen, which was playing in the room behind him. Puffy-faced and yellowish of skin, he had untidy grey hair and thick lips that gave him a petulant air, and wore half-moon glasses perched on the end of his nose. There were flecks of dandruff on the shoulders of his thin maroon sweater and his legs showed signs of muscle wastage. Without acknowledging either Strike or Robin, he addressed his wife in a slow, quiet voice that gave the impression of a man who spoke only with immense effort.

'Well, it's a total mess. Barely turned a penny's profit this month.'

Then, as though his vision was time-lagged, he gave what Strike considered a slightly hammy performance of a man who'd only just realised there were two strangers in the room.

'Ah – good afternoon. Excuse me. Trying to make sense of my wife's accounts.'

'Darling, you don't need to do that,' began Katya, in evident distress. 'I'll sort it out later.'

'*Acta non verba*,' said Inigo, and looking up at Strike he added, 'And you are—?'

'Cormoran Strike,' said the detective, holding out his hand.

'I don't shake, I'm afraid,' said Inigo, unsmiling, his hands remaining on his knees. 'I have to be exceptionally careful about germs.'

'Ah,' said Strike. 'Well, this is Robin Ellacott.'

Robin smiled. Inigo blinked slowly back at her, poker-faced, and she felt as though she'd committed a social solecism.

'Yes, so – *would* you like tea or coffee?' Katya asked Strike and Robin nervously. Both accepted the offer of coffee. 'Darling?' she asked Inigo.

'One of those non-caffeinated teas,' he said. 'But not that strawberry thing,' he called after her, as the door swung closed.

After another slight pause, Inigo said, 'Sit down, do,' and rolled himself to sit at the end of the coffee table that stood between twin sofas, both of which were the same mustard yellow as his wife's sweater. An abstract painting in shades of brown hung over the mantelpiece and a modernist marble sculpture of a woman's torso sat squatly on a side table. Otherwise, the room was sparsely furnished and devoid of decorative objects, the polished floorboards an ideal surface for the wheelchair. Strike and Robin sat down facing each other on different sofas.

From the side room, which contained a day bed and a desk, Freddie Mercury continued to sing:

Outside the dawn is breaking
But inside in the dark I'm aching to be free . . .

It seemed to Strike that Inigo's entrance into the room had been highly contrived, perhaps even down to the grandeur and melancholy of the song still playing. From putting down his wife's business in front of strangers and his implausible pretence that he didn't know, or had forgotten, that Katya had an appointment with two detectives to the unsmiling way he'd offered his justification for not wishing to shake hands, Strike thought he sensed a thwarted, even embittered, will to power.

'An accountant, are you, Mr Upcott?' he asked.

'Why should you think I'm an accountant?' said Inigo, who appeared offended by the suggestion which, in fact, Strike had made purely to draw him out, without believing it.

'You said you were sorting out your wife's—'

'Any fool can read a spreadsheet – except Katya, it appears,' said Inigo. 'She runs a crafting business. Thought she could make a go of it . . . Ever the optimist.'

After a short pause, he went on:

'I used to be an independent music publisher.'

'Really? What kind of—?'

'Largely ecclesiastical. We had an extensive—'

The electrically operated door from the landing opened and a girl of around twelve walked in. She had long dark hair and wore thick-lensed glasses and a fleece onesie patterned like a Christmas pudding, with a sprig of holly on the hood. Either the presence of strangers or her mother's absence seemed to disconcert her, and she turned to leave without speaking, but was called back by her father.

'What did I tell you, Flavia?' he demanded.

'Not to come—'

'Not to come *anywhere near me*,' said Inigo. 'If you're ill enough to be off school, you should be in bed. Now *get out*.'

Flavia pressed the button opening the electric door and departed.

'I have to be exceptionally careful about viruses,' Inigo told Strike and Robin.

Another pause ensued, until Inigo said,

'Well, this is all a bloody fine mess, isn't it?'

'What's that?' asked Strike.

'These stabbings and what have you,' said Inigo.

'Certainly is,' said the detective.

'Katya's at the hospital nearly every day ... She won't be able to press the button if she's holding a tray,' he added, looking towards the door, but as he spoke the door opened again. Gus had accompanied his mother upstairs to press the button for her. Robin saw Gus try to duck out of sight again, but Inigo called him back into the room.

'Been practising?'

'Yes,' said Gus a little defensively, and he showed his father the calloused fingertips of his left hand, in which were deep grooves made by the strings.

'Did you hear him as you came to the door?' Inigo asked Robin, who wasn't sure whether Inigo was fishing for vicarious compliments or thought his son might be lying.

'We did, yes,' she said. 'It was beautiful.'

Looking self-conscious, Gus edged towards the door again.

'Heard from Darcy, darling?' his mother asked him.

'No,' said Gus, and before anyone could ask him anything else he slid out of the room. The electric door swung closed. Katya whispered,

'We think he's split up with his girlfriend.'

'There's no need to whisper, we're soundproofed,' said Inigo, and with sudden vehemence he said, 'And she's a bloody waste of time if she can't stick by a man when he's sick, isn't she? So why d'you keep pestering him about her? Good riddance.'

The short silence that followed was enlivened by Freddie Mercury, now singing a different song.

I'm going slightly mad,
I'm going slightly mad ...

'Turn that off, will you?' Inigo barked at Katya, who hurried off to do so.

'Inigo's a musician too,' she said with brittle brightness as she returned and began handing around mugs.

'*Was*,' Inigo corrected her. 'Until *this* bloody thing happened.'

He gestured towards his chair.

'What did you play?' asked Strike.

'Guitar and keyboards ... band ... songwriter too.'

'What kind of music?'

'Rock,' said Inigo with a faint flicker of animation, 'when we were doing our own stuff. A few covers. Nothing of your father's,' he shot at Strike, who registered with silent amusement Inigo's sudden swerve away from pretending he'd forgotten the detectives were coming to knowing Strike's parentage. 'Could've gone the classical route, like Gus – had the ability – but there you are, I never did the expected thing. Despair of my parents. You're looking at a bishop's son ... Nobody much appreciated rock music at home ...'

Turning to his wife he added:

'Flavia was just in here, by the way. If she's got a fever she shouldn't be anywhere near me.'

'I know, I'm sorry, darling,' said Katya, who remained standing. 'She's just bored up there, you know.'

'Our problem child,' said Inigo, looking at Robin, who could think of no appropriate response to this. 'We had her late. Bad timing. I'd just got this bloody thing.'

Again, he indicated his wheelchair.

'Oh, she's not so bad,' said Katya weakly, and possibly to stop further discussion of Flavia she said to Strike, 'You said on the phone you wanted to know all about Josh and Edie's friends, so I thought—'

She crossed to a small escritoire in the corner of the room, took a sheet of writing paper from the top and returned to Strike, holding it out.

'—this might help. I've made a list of everybody I can remember who was close to Edie and Josh when Anomie's game first appeared.'

'That,' said Strike, taking the handwritten sheet, 'is extremely helpful. Thank you very much.'

'I had to look up some of the surnames,' said Katya, now perching on the edge of the sofa beside Robin, 'but luckily they were on the credits of the early episodes, so I could go online and check. I know you'll need to rule out as many people as you can. I'm quite, *quite* sure,' she added emphatically, 'none of Josh's friends can be Anomie. They were all lovely people, but I understand you need to rule people out.'

The sun flooding through the large bay window showed every line on Katya's exhausted face. She must, once, have been a good-looking woman, Robin thought, and perhaps could be again, with enough sleep. Her warm brown eyes and full-lipped mouth were attractive, but her skin was dry and slightly flaky, and the deep lines across her forehead and around her mouth suggested a state of perennial anxiety.

'How's Josh?' Robin asked Katya.

'Oh, thank you for – there's no change, but the doctors say they wouldn't expect any, so – so soon.'

Her voice rose to a near squeak. She fumbled with her sleeve, took out a wad of tissue and pressed it to her eyes.

Robin noticed how much Inigo's hands were shaking as he tried to raise the mug to his lips. He seemed in imminent danger of spilling boiling tea onto himself.

'Would you like me to—?' she offered.

'Oh – thank you,' said Inigo stiffly, permitting her to take the mug and set it back on the table. 'Very kind.'

Strike was scanning the notes Katya had given him. She'd not only made a list of names in small, neat, square writing, but given each person's role in *The Ink Black Heart* and their exact relationship to Josh or Edie, and added the known contacts of each individual, such as 'flatmates, don't know their names' and 'girlfriend called (I think) Isobel'. Where she knew them, she'd also added addresses or locales.

'We should draft you into the agency, Mrs Upcott,' he said. 'This is exactly what we were after.'

'Oh, I'm so glad – and please, call me Katya,' she said, flushing, and Robin found it a little pathetic to see her pleasure at being praised. 'I really do want to help in any way I can. Josh is absolutely set on finding out who Anomie was. I think he feels, apart from anything else, he can –' her voice rose to a squeak again '– he can make it up to Edie, somehow,' she finished in a rush, before pressing her wad of tissue to her eyes again.

Strike folded up the list Katya had given him, put it into an inner pocket and said,

'Well, that's hugely helpful. Thank you. We've got a few questions, if you don't mind? Would it be OK to take notes?'

'Yes, of course,' said Katya in a muffled voice.

'Perhaps we could start with Josh's thoughts on Anomie?' said Strike, opening his notebook. 'Did he ever have any ideas about who was behind the game, before he got the idea it was Edie?'

'Oh dear,' said Katya, looking distressed. 'I was afraid you were going to ask me that.'

Strike waited, pen poised.

'Would you mind giving me back my tea?' Inigo said in a low voice to Robin.

She handed him back his mug and watched a little apprehensively as he raised it tremulously to his mouth again.

'Well ... yes, Josh *did* tell me once who he thought Anomie was, but he was talking a bit wildly at the time,' Katya said.

'Was that one of the nights he turned up here drunk?' asked Inigo over the rim of his shaking mug.

'Inny, that only happened a couple of times,' said Katya with a weak smile, and turning back to Strike she said:

'You *really* need me to say?'

'It would be helpful.'

'All right, well ... it's so silly ... but Josh thought it was a twelve-year-old boy.'

'A specific twelve-year-old boy?'

'Um ... yes,' said Katya. 'His – his name's Bram. Bram de Jong. He's Nils's son – the man who owns the art collective.'

Out of the corner of her eye, Robin saw Inigo give a very slow, world-weary shake of his head, as though the conversation was moving in a direction he'd expected but deplored. Katya went on quickly:

'But Josh definitely doesn't think it's Bram any more, because ...'

Her voice became still higher as she fought off tears again.

'... because, you see, Josh thinks Anomie's the one who stabbed them,' she said. 'That's the first thing he – he said to me, when I saw him after – after what happened. "It was Anomie."'

'Has he told the police that?' said Strike.

'Oh yes. They didn't understand what he was mouthing at first, but I realised what he was saying. They asked him *why* he thought it was Anomie, and it was because the – the person with the knife whispered something to him, after stabbing him.'

For the second time that afternoon, a prickle ran down the back of Robin's neck.

'What did they whisper?' asked Strike.

'"I'll take care of things from here, don't worry",' quoted Katya. 'And then they stole the folder Josh took to the cemetery with him, and his phone.'

'"I'll take care of things from here, don't worry",' repeated Strike. 'Was it a male or a female voice?'

'He thinks it was male, but he's sure it wasn't Bram. Well, *of course* it couldn't be Bram. He's only twelve.'

'This folder the attacker took: I take it it's the one supposedly containing—?'

'Proof that Edie was Anomie, yes,' said Katya in a small voice.

'*Supposed* proof,' Inigo corrected his wife.

'It was Yasmin Weatherhead who gave Josh the dossier, right?' said Strike, ignoring Inigo.

'Oh, you already know that?' said Katya. 'Yes, yes it was.'

'We don't know much about her,' said Strike, 'except that she helped Josh and Edie with fan mail for a while.'

'With fan mail and social media, yes,' said Katya. 'I – well, I was the one who actually recommended Yasmin to them. She was – I mean, I *thought* she was, when I first met her at North Grove – just a nice, sincere young fan. She's, um – well, she's quite a big girl, and she seemed very sweet and grateful to be getting the opportunity to work with two people she admired so much. She didn't seem to have much else in her life, so I – as I say, I urged Josh to let her help out. They really *did* need somebody, and I thought Yasmin seemed ideal. Her day job was handling social media and PR for a small cosmetics firm, so she understood managing a brand and so on . . .

'But it ended badly. She seemed so nice and sincere, but I'm afraid she wasn't at all.'

'Why d'you say that?' asked Strike.

'Well, Josh and Edie found out she was playing *Drek's Game*,' said Katya. 'Anomie's game, you know. As a matter of fact, I think she'd become a – a moderator, is it? In the game. And Edie was really unhappy about that, because Anomie was being so nasty to Edie online, and when she found out that Yasmin was chatting away to Anomie she suspected some of the private information Anomie had about her could be coming from Yasmin. So she told Josh she wanted to get rid of Yasmin and – and that was that.

'Anyway, Yasmin turned up at North Grove again a few weeks ago. Josh was staying there again, because he'd accidentally flooded his flat, and she showed Josh this dossier of evidence that supposedly proved Edie was Anomie. He brought the dossier with him, here, the night before it happened. Before they were stabbed.'

'He was here the night before, was he?' said Strike, looking up from his notebook.

'Yes,' said Inigo, before his wife could answer. 'Katya had given Mr Blay to understand that he could turn up at any hour of the day or night and he took full and regular advantage of the offer.'

There was a short, nasty silence, in which Robin rather missed Freddie Mercury.

'Josh set fire to a wastepaper basket accidentally, in his room at North Grove,' said Katya, 'and the curtains caught fire too. I think he'd fallen asleep and dropped a cigarette. Anyway, Mariam was furious and she threw him out. It was ten o'clock at night. So he went wandering around for a bit and finally turned up here, because he didn't really have anywhere else to sleep.'

Inigo opened his mouth to speak and Katya said in a rush:

'He *couldn't* have gone back to his father's, Inny. They weren't talking to each other.'

'And all the hotels were closed, of course,' said Inigo.

'So Josh stayed the night here, did he?' asked Strike.

'Yes, in the spare room upstairs,' said Katya miserably.

'And he showed you the dossier Yasmin had given him?'

'Yes, the following morning,' said Katya, her knuckles white because she was clutching her tissues so tightly. 'I didn't read it all, just a few bits and pieces.'

'Can you remember what the bits you read said?'

'Well, there were some printed-out tweets of Edie's and Anomie's where they'd said similar things, like they'd both enjoyed the same film and neither of them were excited about the Queen's Jubilee. And there were emails between Edie and her agent, Allan Yeoman. In – in one of them, Edie said Anomie was actually rather a good thing, and she didn't want him shut down, because fans were starting to feel sorry for her, which would give her and Allan Yeoman more leverage when negotiating with Josh and me. The email was quite rude about me, actually, saying that every bit of advice I'd ever given them had been wrong and – and bad. She also said she thought *Drek's Game* was rather good and that there might be a way of monetising it, and she told Allan she thought Anomie should get the bulk of the profits, as he'd done all the work, which seemed such an odd thing for her to say when Anomie's been persecuting her online all these years.'

'Did you believe the emails were genuine?' asked Strike, who thought he already knew the answer.

'Well, I – I didn't know what to think. They *looked* genuine, but . . . as I say, I hadn't seen Edie for three years at that point, so . . . well, I didn't know *what* to think,' she repeated. 'She'd left me – not that we ever had a formal arrangement – but she stopped talking to me and hired Allan Yeoman instead, so I suppose . . . well, they *looked* convincing. But then, when that article came out in *The Times*, about Edie being on the list of targets of that right-wing group, I realised they must have been clever forgeries. Somebody must have hoodwinked Yasmin. I *can't* believe Yasmin would have deliberately – I can't believe she'd be part of any terrorist group. I'm *sure* she isn't mixed up with anything like that.'

'When did Josh and Edie fix up their meeting, do you know?' asked Robin.

'The day before the attacks. The eleventh. Edie rang Josh at North Grove.'

'*She* rang *him*?' said Strike.

'Yes,' said Katya. 'He told me he'd been trying to talk to her about it for two weeks and she kept hanging up, but then she called him and said, "Fine, let's have this out and you can bring this so-called proof as well."'

'Josh took this call at North Grove, did he?'

'That's right,' said Katya.

'Did they arrange the time and meeting place on that same call?'

'Yes,' said Katya.

'Whose idea was it to meet in the cemetery?'

'Edie's. Josh told me she said something like "I want you to look me in the face, in the place where it all started, and tell me you honestly believe I could have been planning to – to fuck you over five years ago".'

'Meaning, when the game appeared online?' asked Robin.

'Exactly,' said Katya.

'Did they fix a specific spot in the cemetery?'

'Yes,' said Katya, her voice shaking again. 'At the place where they first had all the ideas, a hidden place among the graves. It's in a part of the cemetery you're only supposed to enter as part of a guided tour, but they knew a place you could sneak in. Very naughty,' she added faintly.

'Where did Edie call Josh from, d'you know?' asked Robin.

'No, I don't, but she was living in Finchley at the time, with her new boyfriend, Phillip Ormond.' She looked at Strike. 'You said you're meeting him—'

'After this, yes,' said Strike.

'Were Josh and Edie together when the attacks happened,' Robin asked, 'or—?'

'No, not together,' said Katya. 'Josh was – he was late. The police think Edie was killed before Josh was attacked. She was found at the place they'd agreed to meet. They think the killer then went after Josh, doubled round behind him as he approached the spot and tasered him.

'They found Josh first. Somebody goes round ringing a bell every evening at six, making sure everybody's left the cemetery before they lock the gates. The man found Josh lying just off the path. He thought Josh was dead, then realised he was trying to talk. And the man realised Josh was saying somebody else might have been attacked, so he raised the alarm and people went looking. It took them a while for them to – to find her, because she was in a place that was off the path. She'd been – it happened just the same way as Josh. Tasered from behind and stabbed with the same kind of knife. They say it was a big one. Like a machete. They think she'd have died instantly. She was stabbed in the back, right through her hear—'

Suddenly shaking with barely repressed sobs, Katya tried to stem her tears and streaming nose with her now almost useless wad of tissues.

'I'm – I'm sorry – need more –'

She got up and stumbled to the door. It took her two slaps of the electric button to make it open. They heard a bar of Gus's cello before the sound was cut off again.

'I know what you're thinking,' said Inigo darkly, and both Strike and Robin looked around at him. Inigo's hands were shaking so hard his fruit tea now slopped, as Robin had feared, onto his jeans. 'Middle-aged woman, mixing herself up with a bunch of kids, thinking she's helping them. Feeling important. Giving free advice. Ego boost ... and here we are,' as though the inevitable and foreseeable consequence of helping a pair of animators deal with new-found fame was that they should be stabbed in a graveyard. The door opened again and Katya reappeared, blotchy of face, with a fresh load of tissues clutched in her hand.

When she'd sat back down, Strike said:

'Could we go back to Bram? What gave Josh the idea he was Anomie, d'you know?'

'Yes,' said Katya, her voice now croaky. 'When Josh and Edie were living at North Grove, they found out Bram had drilled a hole in their bedroom wall and was watching them through it.'

'He drilled a hole in the wall?' repeated Robin.

'Bram's a bit . . . He's an odd boy,' said Katya. 'Very big for his age and I think he might have, um, ADHD or something. There are tools in the sculpting workshop and he just helps himself and his parents don't – don't seem to mind. He hung around Josh and Edie a lot when they were both living there, and – well – one doesn't like to criticise anyone's parenting. I like Nils and Mariam very much, but they do rather let Bram run wild, and I know Nils has signed him up for social media he oughtn't to be on, because he's too young, but Nils, um – well, he's Dutch,' said Katya, as though this explained everything, 'and he doesn't believe in age restrictions and things, and anyway, he told me Bram would find a way to get on Twitter in any case, so better that he does it with his parents' permission.'

'Josh surely didn't think Bram had created the game?' said Strike. 'Bram would only have been, what – seven, eight? – when Anomie started it?'

'No, he didn't think Bram made the game, exactly,' said Katya. 'Josh's theory—'

'You have to understand,' said Inigo, speaking at the same time as his wife, and although he hadn't raised his voice, she gave way to him, 'that Mr Blay smokes a good deal of weed, which accounts—'

'Inigo, that's not f—'

'—not only for the almost biblical number of floods and the fires he leaves in his wake—'

'It was just an idea he had, because—'

'—but for a degree of irrationality—'

'But it *was* as though Anomie was literally listening in on Josh and Edie's conversations, he knew things so quickly!'

'But as Mr Strike has already spotted, not that it takes any great *intelligence* to do so,' said Inigo, 'an eight-year-old boy could hardly have—'

'Well, I was just trying to explain that bit!' said Katya, goaded into a weak show of spirit, and she turned back to Strike. 'Josh thought Bram might be working with an older fan he'd met online, who'd made the game – because there's another person involved, someone who calls themselves Morehouse. So Josh's idea was that Bram was eavesdropping on his and Edie's creative discussions and sending all their ideas to Morehouse, and that Morehouse created the actual game, whereas Bram operated the Twitter account, putting all Edie and Josh's private information online.'

'Did Josh ever talk to Bram, or to Bram's parents, about his suspicions?' asked Strike.

'Oh, no,' said Katya. 'Josh is very fond of Nils and Mariam, he wouldn't want to upset them. I know Edie was furious about the spyhole and she wanted to tell Mariam, but Josh talked her out of it. Josh blocked up the hole and said Bram wouldn't dare make another one, and I don't think he did. But Edie refused to stay at North Grove after that.'

'Is that when they split up?' Robin asked.

'No, they were still together,' said Katya, 'but things weren't going terribly well between them. Edie wasn't happy that Josh didn't want to move out with her, but, you see, North Grove felt like a safe place for him. He was surrounded by friends. I was still going there for my art classes. He did move out eventually, but that was after he and Edie split up. He bought himself a very nice flat in Millfield Lane, just on the Heath.'

'Katya found it for him,' said Inigo, who was trying to set the mug of fruit tea back onto the table, his hand shaking badly: there were large wet patches on his jeans now. Robin helped him move it the last few inches. 'Thank you. Yes, Katya drove Blay to see the new flat. Nice and close to us.

'Need the bathroom,' he added, and wheeled himself slowly to the door, pressed the button beside it, backed expertly away as it opened and left the room. Another brief snatch of Gus's cello reached them, before the door swung closed again.

'Inigo thinks I got over-involved,' said Katya in a low voice. 'He doesn't understand – we were all helping *each other* – I – I was going through rather a nasty bout of depression when I met Josh and Edie at North Grove. It – it isn't always easy, with Inigo being ill, and poor Gus having such a nightmarish time with his skin, and Flavia's had some problems at school, and I'm the sole breadwinner these days – I mean, we've got some capital, but one doesn't want to eat into that, not when Inigo's condition is so uncertain – but he had to give up work, and running my business from home can be quite stressful, so I ended up seeing a therapist who told me I should do something for *myself*,' said Katya, with desperate emphasis. 'I've always wanted to draw, so I went along to North Grove and that's where I met Josh and Edie and all the others. It was all ... just rather fun. All their friends doing the voices ... Tim's a lovely man and ... it was fun, that's all and yes, I suppose I felt' – she baulked momentarily at the word – 'maternal towards Josh – towards them both,' she added, and Robin, remembering the YouTube video of the extraordinarily handsome Josh Blay, with his long dark hair, square jaw, high cheekbones and large blue eyes, saw Katya turn pink again and felt uncomfortably as though she'd just caught a glimpse of the older woman in her underwear.

'Josh is rather vulnerable,' Katya hurried on, 'and he was having difficulty adjusting to all the decisions success brings, so I tried to help as best I could. I was in PR when I met Inigo, I've got experience – anyway, I'm *glad* Josh felt he could drop in here any time for a chat. That was part of – he needed to be able to talk to someone, in confidence. He's quite unworldly and naive in some ways, always assuming the best of everyone, and people exploit that, they take advantage! Once the cartoon started getting lots of fans, there were managers and agents *queuing up* to take their ten or their twenty per cent commission, or whatever these people charge, but whether they'd have had Josh's best interests at heart is another question. And he doesn't have any family, not *proper* family – his mother's dead, his father's an alcoholic—'

Katya broke off as the door reopened; the sound of the cello drifted upstairs and was cut off again as Inigo wheeled himself back to the coffee table.

'There was one other matter we hoped you might be able to help us with,' said Strike. 'We've come across a blog called the Pen of Justice, which has been quite critical of Edie and J—'

'Oh, I think I know who *that* is,' said Katya, and the change in her manner was so sudden as to be startling: she now spoke eagerly. 'I'm certain that's written by—'

'Katya,' said Inigo, eyes now narrowed, 'before you do even *more* damage under the guise of being helpful, I'd advise you to carefully consider what you're saying.'

Katya looked stricken.

'My wife,' said Inigo, looking at Strike, and while he was clearly angry he was also, Strike thought, finding cathartic pleasure in venting his rage, 'has become quite obsessive about the Pen of Justice blog.'

'I—'

'If you spent as much time running your business as you do obsessing over that damned website, we wouldn't be having to cash in half our investments to pay for Gus's treatment,' said Inigo, whose hands were shaking again. 'I'd have thought, after everything that's happened, you'd be ready to learn from your mistakes!'

'What d'you—?'

'Egging Blay on to go and confront Edie about all the nasty things she'd supposedly written about you in her emails,' spat Inigo. 'Encouraging him to think the only woman in the world he could trust is *you*. And now you're going to denigrate some young girl out of jealousy—'

'Jealousy, w-what do you mean, jealousy?' stammered Katya. 'Don't be so – so ridiculous, there's no question—'

'You haven't a shred of evidence—'

'They want information—'

'Wild guesswork driven by resentment is not information—'

'It's *exactly* her tone! I've watched all her videos!'

'An essential part of being Josh's agent, or manager, or lifestyle coach, or whatever title you're using this week, I'm sure,' said Inigo.

'I might be completely off base,' said Robin, and her quiet, reasonable tone made both Upcotts look round at her, 'but you don't happen to think Kea Niven's behind the Pen of Justice blog, do you?'

'There, you see!' Katya said to her husband in tremulous triumph. 'I'm *not* the only one! They already know about Kea!'

Katya turned eagerly back to Robin.

'That girl's been virtually stalking Josh ever since they split up! Saying he stole all her ideas. Absolute tosh. She claims to be ill – I think Josh feels sorry for her, which is why he didn't want to take legal action against her.'

'If he feels sorry for anyone,' said Inigo nastily, 'it isn't Kea Niven.'

Katya's face burned scarlet. Her breathing had become shallow. Robin, who was certain the Upcotts had never openly discussed these things before, felt desperately sorry for her.

'From what *I've* heard,' Inigo continued, 'Blay treated that young Kea person extremely badly. It seems to me – and, of course, I wasn't privy to *all* the conversations my wife had with Josh, oh dear me no – but it seems to me that Mr Blay is a young man who's made something of a career of using people for his own ends, then casting them aside. And people who feel they've been *used*, and then cast aside like so much *trash*—'

The electric door swung open again and Flavia walked into the room, still in her Christmas pudding onesie, with a phone in her hand.

'Mummy, Auntie Caroline says I can go and see the puppies if—'

'Get BACK!' roared Inigo with sudden ferocity, as though Flavia were a wild animal. 'You are INFECTIOUS!'

Flavia stopped dead.

'If you wish me to be bedbound for the next six weeks, by all means keep allowing her into this *fucking* room!' Inigo snarled at Katya. 'But perhaps that's the whole idea? I tell you what – I'll remove *myself* from the vicinity, shall I, as nobody else seems particularly interested in my well-being?'

He turned his wheelchair and wheeled himself rapidly back into the side room. The door, which seemed to be electrically operated as well, slid shut. Inigo's outburst seemed still to echo through the room.

'Please can I go and see the puppies, Mummy?' said Flavia in a small voice.

Tearful and still scarlet in the face, Katya said:

'You're poorly, Flavia.'

'Auntie Caroline says she doesn't mind, she's already had this cold.'

'Well – well then, put on proper clothes,' said Katya. Flavia let herself out of the electric door. This time, no cello was heard, and the reason became apparent when, just before the door closed behind Flavia, Gus slipped into the room instead, holding a mobile phone in his hand.

'Dr Hookham says she's had a cancellation and could see me tomorrow afternoon.'

'That should be fine,' said his harassed and tearful mother.

'I can drive myself if you're going to the hosp—'

'You can't drive,' said Katya, her voice now shrill, 'not when you can't see out of one eye! You'll take public transport!'

Scowling, Gus ducked out again.

'I'm so terribly sorry,' Katya said, her voice squeaky again. 'As you can see – lots going on.'

'You've been extremely helpful,' said Strike, slipping his notebook into his pocket and getting to his feet. Katya and Robin stood up too, Katya breathing rapidly and unable to meet anyone's gaze.

They walked downstairs in silence.

'Thanks so much for seeing us,' said Robin, shaking Katya's hand.

'No trouble at all,' said Katya in a constricted voice.

The cello started up again in Gus's bedroom. He was now playing a fast, staccato piece that seemed to give expression to the jangled moods of the house's various occupants.

34

Death sets a thing significant
The eye had hurried by . . .

Joanna Baillie
London

'God save us all,' Strike said quietly, as they approached the gate, 'from well-intentioned helpers who don't want paying.'

Before Robin could answer, Flavia popped up from behind the hedge. She was hopping on the spot, tugging on a trainer, which she seemed to have been adjusting to her satisfaction. In spite of her mother's instructions, she was still in her Christmas pudding onesie.

'Did you come in that?' she asked them, pushing her glasses back up her nose and pointing at the distant Land Rover, which stood out in its decrepitude among the generally expensive family saloons that surrounded it.

'Yes,' said Robin.

'I thought so,' said Flavia, falling into step beside them as they set off down the street, 'because I never noticed it here before.'

'Good observational powers,' said Strike, who was lighting up a cigarette.

Flavia glanced up at Robin.

'Are *you* a detective, too?'

'Yes,' said Robin, smiling at her.

'I'd like to be a detective,' said Flavia with a small skip. 'I think I could get good at it, if I was trained . . . Mummy *really* doesn't like Kea Niven,' she added. 'She's always going on about her.'

When neither Strike nor Robin said anything, she said:

'Daddy's got ME. That's why he's in a wheelchair.'

308

'Yes, your mum told us,' said Robin.

'He thinks *The Ink Black Heart*'s stupid,' said Flavia.

'Have you ever seen it?' asked Robin, diplomatically ignoring Inigo's opinion.

'Yes. I *quite* like it,' said Flavia judiciously. 'The Worm's the funniest. I'm only walking with you,' she added, as though she feared they would think her intrusive, 'because my Auntie Caroline lives just on the other side of your car. She isn't my real auntie, she just looks after me sometimes ... Her dog's had puppies, they're really, *really* sweet. If you sit down with them they crawl all over you and lick you. Have either of you got a dog?'

'Well, he isn't mine, but I live with a dachshund called Wolfgang,' said Robin.

'Do you? I'd *love* a dog,' said Flavia longingly. 'I really, really want one of Auntie Caroline's puppies, but Daddy says we can't because dogs are unhygienic, it would make too much work for Mummy and Gus is frightened of dogs because one bit him when he was four. I said *I'd* look after the dog, so Mummy wouldn't have to, and Gus could be hypnotised. I saw a programme about people being hypnotised and there was a woman who was scared of spiders and by the end she could hold a tarantula ... But Daddy still said no,' Flavia concluded mournfully.

After a few steps of silence she said:

'Are you going to go to North Grove to ask them questions too?'

'Maybe,' said Robin.

'I've been there a few times with Mummy. The people there are *weird*. There's a man who walks around without a shirt on. All the time. And there's a boy who lives there called Bran or something who told me he broke another boy's arm at school.'

'Accidentally?' asked Robin.

'He said it was, but he was laughing about it,' said Flavia pensively. 'I don't like him much. He showed me stuff he does to play tricks on people.'

'What kind of stuff?' asked Strike.

'Well, like ... he's got an app that makes background noises when you're on the phone so people think you're on a train or something, and he told me he hid once and called his dad using the noise that sounded as if you were in an airport, and told him he was at Heathrow and was going to get on a plane because his stepmum had told him off *and his dad believed it,*' said Flavia solemnly, 'and drove off to Heathrow and had them putting appeals out for Bran over the loudspeaker and all the time he was at North Grove, hiding under his bed.'

'I expect his dad was pretty angry when he found out,' said Robin.

'I don't know if he was or not,' said Flavia. 'I think he was just glad Bran was all right. But if *I* did that Daddy would *kill* me . . . Have you met Tim? He's bald.'

'Not yet,' said Robin.

'He's nice,' said Flavia. 'One time when I was at North Grove and he was waiting to do The Worm's voice, he showed me how to draw animals by starting with shapes. It was quite clever. Are you going to come back to our house again?'

'I don't think we'll need to,' said Strike. 'Your mum was a big help.'

'Oh,' said Flavia, who seemed disappointed.

They'd reached the car.

'I was at Edie's funeral,' she said, stopping as they did. 'Have you seen her boyfriend yet? He's called Phillip. He's sometimes at North Grove.'

'Yes, we're meeting him in' – Strike checked his watch – 'just over an hour.'

Flavia seemed to teeter on the verge of saying something else, then change her mind.

'Maybe you'll have to come back again,' she said to Robin.

'Maybe,' said Robin, smiling.

'OK, well, bye,' said Flavia and she walked off down the street.

Strike and Robin got into the Land Rover. As Robin did up her seatbelt, she watched Flavia through the windscreen. The girl pressed the bell on the neighbour's house and was admitted, but not before looking back and waving.

'Can't really see what makes her a problem child, can you?' she asked Strike.

'No,' he said, slamming the car door. 'On short exposure, I'd have to say she comes at the least fucked-up end of the Upcott spectrum.'

Robin started the car and drove off down Lisburne Road while Strike consulted his phone.

'How would you feel,' he said, 'about going to have a look at Highgate Number One Pond before we meet Phillip Ormond? It's only a four-minute drive from there to The Flask.'

'OK,' said Robin.

Strike exhaled, then said,

'Well, there was a hell of a lot of food for thought at the Upcotts', wasn't there?'

'There was,' agreed Robin.

'How d'you fancy a musical prodigy for Anomie?' asked Strike as they turned the corner at the end of the road.

'Are you serious?'

'He ticks quite a few boxes on our profile. Not working. Supported by his family. Plenty of time on his hands.'

'You don't get that good at the cello by sitting around on the computer all day.'

'True, but he's not being watched by a supervisor nine to five, is he? I get the feeling that's a family where individual members are happiest staying well away from each other. Ever see that old film *The Ladykillers*?'

'No. Why?'

'Gang of crooks rent a room in an old lady's house, pretending to be a musical quintet. They play classical records while planning their heist and only pick up their instruments whenever she knocks on the door to offer them tea.'

'Gus didn't get into the Royal College of Music by playing them records.'

'I'm not suggesting he *never* plays, I'm saying there might be times when he doesn't. And he's had potential access to a lot of personal information on Josh and Edie via his mother.'

'If I were Gus Upcott,' said Robin, 'I'd stay downstairs as much as possible. And as they've soundproofed the upper floor—'

'He could've bugged the upstairs.'

'Come on—'

'If he's Anomie, he'd bloody bug the upstairs!' said Strike. 'A bad case of hives and a cello aren't good enough reasons not to have a good look at him.'

'Fine,' said Robin, 'although I'm not sure how we put surveillance on him if he's holed up in his bedroom all the time.'

'Yeah, well, that's the bugger of this case, isn't it?' said Strike. 'Keep going left,' he added, checking the map on his phone. 'We've got to go round the edge of the Heath to the other side.

'We need to get inside that fucking game,' Strike said. 'It's going to take years to narrow down the suspect list if all we've got is Anomie's

Twitter feed ... That said,' Strike continued, struck by a thought, 'Gus Upcott's going to his doctor's in Harley Street tomorrow afternoon. If we get lucky and Anomie tweets while Gus is reception-free on the Tube, we can count him out. Might see if Barclay can do that little job,' he added, now typing out a message to the office manager. This done, he said:

'How's your application to get into North Grove going?'

'I'm in,' said Robin, 'but the course doesn't start for another fortnight.'

'Good going ... Incidentally, have you had any luck on that girl with the tattoos who lives off Junction Road?'

'She isn't on any record I can find,' said Robin. 'Maybe she only just moved in.'

'Then it'll probably have to be surveillance on her as well, to find out who she is,' said Strike. 'Jesus, we could put everyone on the agency on this case and still be stretched.'

Robin, who hadn't forgotten he had just added another case to their workload, one she considered entirely of his own making, said nothing. After a brief pause, Strike said,

'So Blay thinks Anomie stabbed them. "I'll take care of things from here, don't you worry" – hard to see what that meant, unless it was the cartoon.'

'D'you think Maverick would still have made the film if Josh and Edie had both died?' asked Robin. Annoyed as she felt at Strike personally, the interest of the discussion was temporarily overcoming her irritation.

'I'd've thought it would have felt pretty bloody tasteless to press on,' said Strike.

'So in some senses, Anomie *would* be in charge of the fandom. All there'd be left were old episodes and *Drek's Game*.'

'The police'll be concentrating on who knew Josh and Edie were going to be in the cemetery that afternoon, and now we know the Upcotts did, for starters.'

'Katya knew,' Robin contradicted him, 'but we can't be certain about any of the others. It was a Thursday morning: Flavia would have been at school, and you just said yourself, the family seems to be happiest shut up away from each other.'

'Katya might still have told them. Or they could have overheard.'

'Inigo couldn't have stabbed anyone. He *really* isn't well,' said Robin, as Hampstead Heath appeared through railings on the left-hand side of the road. 'You saw how badly his hands were shaking.'

'Pretty sure some of that was rage,' said Strike unsympathetically. 'But yeah, he doesn't look strong. His legs are wasted ... though, of course, we don't know the killer went to the cemetery on foot. And tasering someone before stabbing them means you won't have to physically subdue them to get the job done.'

'Phillip Ormond surely knew they were meeting,' said Robin, 'given that he was living with Edie?'

'Yeah, assuming she made the call within earshot of him, or that she felt comfortable telling him she was meeting her ex-boyfriend at a spot that presumably had romantic significance for them,' said Strike. 'Alternatively, Edie might *not* have made the call from home, and might *not* have told Ormond, which leaves the question of where she made the call from, and who else could have been listening in.'

'And on the other end of the line we've got Josh at North Grove—'

'Well, you're going to be getting into the art collective soon. Maybe you'll be able to find out who was around at the time.'

'There's also a period of what sounds like a couple of hours at least,' said Robin, 'where Josh went wandering off into the night after being chucked out of North Grove.'

'Yeah,' said Strike. 'Well, I'm sure the police have traced his movements in that period. Maybe you could chat up Murphy and see whether—'

'*You* chat him up, if you want that done,' snapped Robin.

Strike looked around at her, surprised by her tone.

'I wasn't suggesting – I'm only saying, he might not mind doing a bit of reciprocal back-scratching. You helped the police out, telling them all about Edie's visit to the agency, didn't you?'

Robin said nothing. The very mention of Murphy had brought back memories she could do without.

'We're close,' Strike said, pointing ahead, and still puzzled by the source of Robin's uncharacteristic irritability. 'We should probably park wherever you can get a space.'

'You realise where we are?' said Robin, slowing down.

'Where?'

'Millfield Lane, where Josh's flat is.'

'Now, that,' said Strike looking around at the houses that bordered the narrow street, 'is an odd coincidence, isn't it?'

They got out of the Land Rover, crossed the road and entered the Heath, between two large ponds that might more properly have been called lakes. Strike's stump, which was painful enough while walking on tarmac, complained worse than ever as they reached the uneven path.

'It's this one,' said Strike, indicating the pond to their left, which was fringed with trees. Various kinds of waterfowl were bobbing serenely on the khaki-coloured water, or clustering hopefully near the bank, should passers-by happen to have bread on them.

'So,' said Strike as they came to a halt beside a low railing, 'what made the killer come here?'

'Well, it definitely wasn't to throw Edie's phone in the pond, because the police dragged the bottom and didn't find it,' said Robin, casting a look all around them. 'But the pond mightn't have been their objective at all. This might just have been the place where the killer realised one of the phones was still switched on.'

'True, in which case the killer was heading – where?'

Wordlessly, both Strike and Robin turned and looked back towards Millfield Lane.

'Could they possibly have been going to Blay's flat, now they thought he was dead and couldn't disturb them?'

'That's got to be a possibility,' said Strike. 'And that suggests the killer knew they'd be able to get access to the flat. Pity we don't know whether anything's gone missing from it. Mind you,' Strike added, consulting the map on his phone, 'it's hard to see why, if Josh's flat was their objective, they needed to come onto the Heath at all. There's an easy direct route through the streets from Highgate Cemetery to Millfield Lane.

'If,' said Strike slowly, thinking it through, 'the killer was Gus Upcott – humour me for a moment – crossing the Heath to get to and from the cemetery would've been the quickest route and avoided CCTV cameras. However,' said Strike, scratching his chin while staring at the map, 'he shouldn't have come anywhere near this pond. It's right off his route, assuming he headed straight home after stabbing them.'

'Could the killer have been meeting somewhere else here?' asked Robin. 'There are a lot of trees. Good place of concealment. Or did they head into the trees to take off a disguise?'

'Both possibilities,' said Strike, nodding, 'although there are clumps of trees closer to where Gus would've logically entered the Heath. Of course, this all assumes the killer *meant* to come here. The alternative is that they were forced to divert for some reason.'

'To avoid people?'

'People . . . or maybe just one person, who'd have recognised them,' said Strike, who'd just pulled the list of names Katya had given him out of his pocket. 'Yeah, look at this . . . a lot of people originally connected to *The Ink Black Heart* grew up in this area or live locally. Wally Cardew, Ian Baker and Lucy Drew, who played Lord and Lady' – Strike squinted at the paper – '"Wyrdy-Grob", were all from Gospel Oak. Schoolfriends of Josh Blay's. And Preston Pierce was living at North Grove at the same time as Edie and Josh,' said Strike, reading off Katya's notes. '"Liverpudlian, voiced Magspie for two episodes."'

'Pez,' said Robin suddenly.

'What?'

'Preston. Pez. The person who was supposed to be meeting Nils, Wally, Seb and Tim at the Red Lion and Sun. It was in your notes.'

'Bloody well remembered,' said Strike. 'Yeah, I'll bet that's him.'

'Where's North Grove from here?' asked Robin, looking around.

Strike consulted the map.

'That way,' said Strike, pointing across the pond towards the road. 'No earthly reason to come onto the Heath if you were heading back to North Grove. It'd be a very short walk home from the cemetery if the killer was someone from that art collective.'

Strike folded up Katya's paper and tucked it back into his notebook, and contemplated a passing swan for a few moments before saying:

'These attacks were planned. The time and place might not have been predetermined, but you can't buy tasers in this country and people don't generally have machetes lying around. This whole thing smacks of someone just waiting for a decent opportunity. They had everything ready to go.'

Robin's phone rang. It was Midge. Robin answered, her heart suddenly racing.

'Hi,' she said.

'You owe me big time for this, Ellacott.'

'Oh wow,' said Robin, and Strike wondered why she was suddenly looking elated.

'Got a pen?'

'Yes,' said Robin, rummaging in her pocket and pulling out her notebook. She dropped into a crouch, pulled off the lid of her pen

315

with her teeth and readied herself to write with the notebook open on her knee.

'All right, here we go,' said Midge heavily. 'Her username's Buffypaws, all one word, capital B. *Don't* laugh. Buffy was the name of our cat.'

Robin spelled the name aloud to Midge as she wrote it down.

'Exactly,' said Midge. 'And the password,' she growled, 'is WishIWasWithEllen. All the words are capitalised – tell you what, I'll text it to you.'

'Midge, I can't thank you enough for this.'

'"Wish I was with fookin' Ellen",' said Midge bitterly. 'That was her ex before me.'

'Tasteful,' said Robin. 'Did you have to give up the mirror?'

'Yeah. Don't worry, though,' said Midge. 'There's going to be a fookin' big crack in it by the time she takes delivery.'

Robin laughed, thanked Midge again, then got to her feet.

'We can get into the game.'

'What?'

Robin explained.

'Ellacott, you're a genius,' said Strike. 'You can be inside the game while I'm interviewing Ormond. If Anomie turns up while Ormond's talking to me, we're down one suspect.'

35

By that gate I entered lone
A fair city of white stone . . .
Yet I heard no human sound;
All was still and silent round
As a city of the dead.

Christina Rossetti
The Dead City

The Flask, which lay close to Hampstead Heath, was a very old pub, which had three separate parlours and two different bars: it was, in fact, tailor-made for two people who wished to coordinate their activities while out of sight of each other.

'Great, it's got Wi-Fi,' said Robin, checking her phone as she and Strike stood at the bar together, fifteen minutes before Phillip Ormond was due to arrive. 'I'll keep my phone for Anomie's Twitter feed and use my iPad to access the game . . . I've been carrying it around ever since I asked Midge for Beth's log-in details,' she explained to Strike, pulling the iPad out of the small nylon backpack she usually took on surveillance. 'Just in case.'

'The Boy Scouts missed a trick, not recruiting you,' said Strike. 'What d'you want?'

'Tomato juice and a bag of crisps, please, I'm starving,' said Robin. 'Then I'll get out of the way so Ormond can't see me.'

Once she had her drink and crisps, Robin left Strike for the parlour adjacent to the main bar, where she sat down at a small corner table beside a fireplace. Having eaten a third of the crisps in a couple of mouthfuls, she propped up her iPad in front of her, took out her notebook and pen, checked Anomie's Twitter feed, which showed no new activity, then brought up *Drek's Game*.

A group of four middle-aged Americans entered the small parlour, one of the women reading aloud from a guidebook.

"'... *haunted*",' said a voice from the Deep South, and the word seemed to have twice as many vowels as Robin would have given it, "'by the ghost of a *Spanish barmaid* who *hanged herself* in the cellar, for unrequited love of the pub's owner".'

A good deal of loudly interested comment ensued and much scraping of chairs, as the foursome took the table beside Robin.

Feeling tense, Robin typed the username Buffypaws into *Drek's Game*'s login panel and then, after checking the capitalisation on Midge's text, the password, WishIWasWithEllen.

Please work. Please work. Please work.

"'The Flask",' continued the American woman with the guidebook, "'was the site of one of England's *first ever* autopsies, performed" – *oh, my word –*'

Robin hadn't ever watched a loading gif revolve with such anticipation.

"' – on a *body* stolen by gravediggers, from *Highgate Cemetery* ..."'

The screen on Robin's iPad turned black. White letters floated into sight like spectres.

Welcome To Drek's Game

The letters faded. Robin was looking at a beautifully animated Highgate Cemetery, in which wisps of mist curled around ivy-draped stone angels. The colour palette was monochrome, like the original animation. White figures drifted across the screen. Some looked like Paperwhite the ghost, others were skeletal, still more were bounding hearts, like the hero, Harty. Evidently you could choose what you looked like in the game from a limited number of options. Robin had no idea how she appeared to the other players, each of whom had their usernames written in tiny print above them. Meanwhile, a sidebar showed everyone who was entering and leaving the game.

```
<InkHart66 has left the game>
<Paperwhite MOD has entered the game>
<InkBlackStacey has entered the game>
```

After some trial and error, Robin located a control panel that enabled her to move around. Slowly she made her way up a misty path, past urns wrapped in overgrown vegetation. Suddenly a bat swooped low over her character and transformed into a vampire, blocking her path. The vampire, who looked weak and weedy, stood panting, his hand on his chest, before 'speaking' to her, the dialogue appearing across its chest.

```
Mind if I suck on an artery?
```

Robin hastened to find the place where you typed dialogue and after a few seconds' fumbling found a pull-up keyboard. Having no idea what the correct answer was — or, indeed, whether there *was* a correct answer — she typed:

```
I'd rather you didn't
```

The vampire appeared to sigh.

```
But I'm anaemic
```

Mildly amused, Robin typed:

```
Sorry
```

The vampire replied:

```
One day you'll be undead. THEN you'll be sorry
```

He turned back into a bat and fluttered away.

Robin continued up the path. Some of the tombs had interactive features, opening to reveal skulls and bones or, in one case, a gigantic spider, which showed signs of giving chase and made Robin move her character swiftly away. Then one of the drifting Paperwhites crossed the path ahead, paused and 'spoke' to her.

```
InkBlackStacey: Hey Buffypaws long
time no see

Buffypaws: Hi InkBlackStacey

InkBlackStacey: How's it going?
```

Buffypaws: Good thnx and you?

InkBlackStacey: How fuckin awful is
it about J*** and E***?

Buffypaws: I know, terrible

Robin wondered what the asterisks were about. Were players not supposed to write Josh and Edie's names inside the game? Was Anomie's ego such that the creators mustn't be mentioned?

Before she could consider that point any further, two dialogue boxes opened simultaneously in front of her.

<A new private channel has opened>

<16 April 2015 17.57>

<Worm28 MOD invites Buffypaws>

Worm28: omg , I thought u 'd gone forever !!!!

\>

\>

\>

<A new private channel has opened>

<16 April 2015 17.57>

<Vilepechora MOD invites Buffypaws>

Vilepechora: thought you'd gone for good

Vilepechora: still a dyke?

\>

\>

Shit.

Robin reached for her phone and typed a hasty text to Midge.

Tell me literally anything about Beth.
I'm inside the game. Some of these people know her

Beside Robin, the American woman with the guidebook, whose purple plastic glasses were perched on the end of her nose, continued to read aloud.

"'*Byron, Keats and Shelley* are known to have drunk in The Flask, as is the *famous highwayman, Dick Turpin*"!'

Deciding it would look too fishy not to respond to the two moderators, Robin began to type again.

Worm28: I thuoght I drove u away with all my problems !

Buffypaws: no, I missed this place!

>

>

Buffypaws: don't be silly, of course not

Buffypaws: how r u?

Worm28: guess what I 'm in L*****!

>

Buffypaws: No way!

Worm28: yeh

Worm28: I came down to be with my bf

Buffypaws: omg that's great!

Buffypaws: yeah. Turns out you can't unlearn it

Vilepechora: lol

Vilepechora: maybe u just haven't had good dick

Buffypaws: or maybe dick's not my thing

>

>

Vilepechora: if you've only fucked cucks u won't know

Buffypaws: interesting theory

>

>

>

>

>

Robin's phone vibrated. Midge had answered her text:

Self-obsessed, unfaithful cow. Likes cats. Writing novel (3 paragraphs), aspiring artist (shit collages), fancies Rachel Maddow, can't cook anything except pasta with a tin of tuna dumped on top, collects Christmas tree ornaments and pissed off girlfriends

Grinning, Robin texted back:

And broken mirrors. Thanks x

She returned to her iPad.

Buffypaws: back

Worm28: it's not goin well tho

Buffypaws: what do u mean?

Worm28: guess how many
times i 've seem him
since I got here

Buffypaws: go on

Worm28: once

Buffypaws: oh no that's
shit

Worm28: he 's super busy tho

Worm28: what happened
with u and yr girlfriend?

>

Buffypaws: Anomie not in
tonight?

Vilepechora: no

Vilepechora: come back
to see whether he killed
L******?

Vilepechora: hahaha at
least you're honest

>

>

>

Vilepechora: well, he did

Robin tried to take a screenshot of these conversations, but the game wouldn't let her do it. She grabbed her pen, put the two usernames 'Worm28' and 'Vilepechora' at the top of the page and scribbled a few notes under each before returning to the iPad.

Buffypaws: we split up

Worm28: finally!

Buffypaws: yeah it was time

Worm28: I was wrroied about u
, she sounded so controlling

Buffypaws: yeah. so tell
me more about u

Worm28: I'm working kind of

Worm28: fuck I wish I
could tell u where

Buffypaws: tell me!

Worm28: lol

Worm28: i 'm scred of Anomie

>

>

Vilepechora: so pissed
right now

Buffypaws: aren't we all

>

Vilepechora: what u wearing?

Buffypaws: full body armour

>

>

Vilepechora: so fkn bored
of this place

Worm28: if I tell u we 'd
trigger conseqnce 14

\>

Buffypaws: ok hint

Worm28: lol no better not

Worm28: guess what tho

Worm28: I met B***!!!

Buffypaws: why u still
here then?

Vilepechora: intel

Vilepechora: so do u use
a strap on or what

\>

\>

\>

Robin picked up her pen again and jotted rapidly under 'Worm28'
poss met Blay, 'kind of' working; beneath 'Vilepechora': *here for 'intel'* and,
on the facing, so far blank page, *trigger Consequence 14 what is this?* She
resumed her typing.

Buffypaws: no way!!!

Worm28: yaeh true story

Worm28: I just walked in
the room and he was their

Worm28: I nearly fainted !!

Buffypaws: did u talk to him?

Worm28: no i was shaking !!!

Buffypaws: lol

Vilepechora: are u sitting
on a strap on right now?

Buffypaws: your sense of humour
as sophisticated as ever I see

Vilepechora: you're lucky
I don't ban u

\>

Buffypaws: what for?

Vilepechora: for being a
fkn pervert

The American reader of the guidebook was now reading the menu
aloud to her companions, even though each had one of their own.
'*Steak and kidney pie* . . . *boiled potatoes* . . .'
Robin's phone vibrated. She looked down; Strike had texted:

Ormond's here.

36

And on his shield a bleeding heart he bore . . .

Mary Tighe
Psyche

Strike, who was sitting at a table for two facing the door of the pub, correctly identified Phillip Ormond as soon as he entered, even though the man in no way conformed to Strike's mental image of either a geography teacher or a person likely to sign up for art classes. Strike might even have suspected a military background, given the man's bearing and the meticulous smartness of his appearance.

Several inches shorter than the man he'd come to meet, Ormond looked as though he might be a regular gym user. He had light blue, wide-set eyes, light brown hair, which was worn short and neat, and a pointed jaw covered in carefully trimmed stubble. Without the black briefcase he was carrying, his dark suit and plain navy tie might have suggested funeral wear. He paused inside the doorway to look around, squaring his shoulders as he did so.

Catching the detective's eye, Ormond approached Strike's table.

'Cormoran Strike?'

'That's me,' said Strike, standing to shake hands, his stump protesting angrily at having to bear his weight so soon after sitting down.

'Phillip.'

Ormond now proved himself to belong to that category of men who seem to think they'll be suspected of impotence unless their handshake causes the recipient physical pain.

'I'll get a drink,' said Ormond, before departing for the bar. He returned to the table carrying a half-pint of lager and sat down facing Strike, giving off an aura of slight suspicion.

'Well, as I told you on the phone—' Strike began.

'You're trying to find out who Anomie is. Yeah.'

'Would you mind if I took notes?'

'Feel free,' said Ormond, though he didn't look particularly happy about it.

'What happened there?' Strike asked, now noticing that two fingers on Ormond's left hand were bandaged.

'Hydrofluoric acid spill,' said Ormond and when Strike looked blank, he said, 'I was doing a bit of steel etching at North Grove. Won't be trying that again. Burn got infected. I've had two lots of antibiotics so far.'

'Sounds nasty.'

'Hardly the worst thing that's happened to me lately,' said Ormond with a trace of aggression.

'No, of course not,' said Strike. 'I'm very sorry for your loss.'

'Thanks,' said Ormond, unbending very slightly. 'It's been ... a bad time.'

'I'm sure,' said Strike. 'Would you mind answering a couple of questions about North Grove?'

'Fire away.'

'When did you start classes there?'

'2011,' said Ormond.

'Do you do a lot of art, or—?'

'Not really. Writing's more my thing, actually.'

'Really?' said Strike. 'Published?'

'Not yet. Just playing around with a few ideas. That was something Edie and I had in common, you know: stories.'

Strike, who had some difficulty imagining Phillip Ormond writing stories, nodded. Reasonably good-looking though the teacher was, Strike was slightly puzzled by Edie's choice of boyfriend, but perhaps Ormond's appeal had lain in him being the absolute antithesis of her feckless, pot-smoking, curtain-burning ex.

'No, I went to North Grove because I'd just separated from my wife,' said Ormond, unprompted. 'Trying to fill my evenings a bit. Signed up for an evening class ... thought I might try the old-fashioned way of meeting a girl, you know?' he said, with a self-consciously bleak smile. 'Met my wife on a dating site. And the ones you meet at the gym – they haven't usually got enough upstairs for me,' he added, tapping his temple.

'So when you first met Edie——?'

'She was still dating Blay, yeah. I got interested in their cartoon, listening to people at North Grove talking about it, and ended up inviting her and Blay to come into school and give my Year Sevens a talk about animation and computer-generated imagery. The kids enjoyed it,' said Ormond, though not as if this gave him any particular gratification.

'You teach geography, right?'

'Computing,' said Ormond, frowning. 'Who told you I teach geography?'

'Think it was Edie's agent,' said Strike, making a note. 'Crossed wires somewhere. When did you first become aware of Anomie?'

'I saw he'd posted a picture of Edie's flat on Twitter. I sent her a text to see whether she was OK. I still had her phone number from when she came into school to talk to the kids. We texted back and forth a bit and ended up going for a drink. She and Blay had split up by that time. Found out we had quite a bit in common. Writing,' he said again. 'Stories. We had a bit of a laugh about North Grove. There are some real characters there. A kid who's a proper *Jeremy Kyle* candidate.'

'Would that be Bram de Jong?' asked Strike, noting that Ormond had just used a bit of police slang.

'That's him, yeah,' said Ormond, nodding. 'I was leaving North Grove one night and took a fucking rock to the back of the head. He was up on the roof throwing them at anyone he could hit. If I could've laid hands on him – he cut me,' said Ormond, pointing at the back of his head. 'I've still got a scar there. Edie told me about some of the things he did while she was living there. She found a dead bird in her bed one time. The parents are just . . . There's no control,' said Ormond and Strike noticed his nostrils flare as he said it. 'None.'

'Did you discuss Anomie when the two of you went for a drink?'

'Oh yeah, she told me all about it. She thought it was someone she knew, because of him knowing so much about her. She sort of went through the people she suspected with me. I thought it sounded like that girl – what's her name? Blay's ex.'

'Kea Niven?'

'Yeah, but Edie said she'd ruled her out.'

'How did she do that?'

'Edie told me she was at the animation studio one afternoon, looked out the window and saw her hanging around in the street. Hoping to run into Blay, see. Edie had Anomie's game running on her laptop and checked it. Anomie was in there, moving around and talking, but Niven wasn't using a phone or an iPad or anything.'

'That's very helpful, thanks,' said Strike, making a note before looking up again. 'Kea was hanging around the animation studio, was she?'

'Yeah. Edie told me she turned up a couple of times when Edie was with Blay, staring at them across bars and pubs. Had an ex like that myself. Psycho.'

'When exactly did Edie rule Kea out, can you remember?'

'Before Edie and I went for our first drink, so must've been mid-2013.'

Ormond took another sip of beer, then said,

'I still thought Niven needed shutting down – all those bullshit plagiarism claims – but Edie thought it would make it worse – or, more likely, her agent told her it would make things worse,' the computing teacher added with a slight sneer. 'Yeoman's advice always seemed to be "do nothing". Not my style.'

'You've never spoken to Kea personally?'

'Nah – luckily for her,' said Ormond with another flare of his nostrils. 'She was just like Anomie, attacking Edie, letting Blay off scot-free. He could do no bloody wrong with the fandom, which shows you how little they knew.'

'How d'you mean?'

'Well, Edie was doing ninety per cent of the work and Blay spent most of the day stoned. She was pissed off with carrying him, by the end. And I can tell you this: she'd've been fucking outraged if she'd known he wanted to put a fucking letter in her coffin, after what he put her through those last two weeks.'

'Did Edie rule anyone else out, that you know of?'

Ormond shook his head.

'We know she suspected Seb Montgomery towards the end, but was there ever anyone else?'

'Oh, you know about Montgomery, do you?' said Ormond with a slight recurrence of suspicion. 'Well ... yeah, he was her number one sus' – Strike noticed the second bit of police slang – 'but she wondered whether it could've been Wally Cardew before that, because he took a few pops at her online after she ditched him as Drek, but she reckoned Cardew wouldn't've stayed anonymous. Big mouth, see. Plus, she didn't think Cardew could code or animate to the level of the game.'

'What about Tim Ashcroft, who voiced The Worm?'

'Him? Real user,' said Ormond contemptuously. 'He thought, if he sucked up to Edie enough, she'd find a part for him in the film. I told her, "You want to stop hanging out with him." Not *told* her,' Ormond corrected himself. 'Not like that. Just didn't like seeing her taken advantage of. It was making him think he was still in with a chance of a part, her having coffees with him.'

'She never thought Ashcroft was Anomie, though?'

'Nah. Long tall streak of piss. Posh lefty. You know the type.'

'So as far as you know, Montgomery was her only credible suspect?'

'Yeah. She decided it was him after Anomie said on Twitter Edie had based a character on some flatmate – which was total bollocks.'

'She didn't base Paperwhite on this girl?'

Ormond took a sip of beer, then said,

'She might've taken a bit of the girl's behaviour for Paperwhite, but that doesn't make them the same bloody person. All this shit about thinking every fictional character's got a – you know – a living counterpart. Inspiration can come from anywhere,' said Ormond, a slight flush rising in his face as he spoke. 'You can't say that such-and-such a character *is* a living person. It's an impression. A – a picture taken through the lens of the creator.' He took another swig of beer. 'That's what I find, anyway,' he said, having set his glass back down. 'In my writing.'

Strike had no way of knowing whether these were the teacher's own original thoughts on the subject of inspiration and character development, but he couldn't help suspecting that Ormond was faithfully parroting someone else.

'Did Edie talk to you a lot about her work?'

'All the time,' said Ormond, suddenly more animated than he'd been all conversation. 'She pretty much shared her whole creative process with me. Yeah, we had a lot of in-depth discussions of characters and I'd throw in ideas, you know.'

'You were collaborating, were you?' said Strike, taking care to sound impressed.

'Yeah, I s'pose you could call it that.' He fixed Strike with an unblinking stare. 'Edie actually said she wanted me to be given a writing credit, come the film. Said I'd given her a couple of really good ideas.'

'Interesting,' said Strike, 'that she was looking to bring in new collaborators, other than herself and Blay.'

'Not collaborators, plural. There wasn't anyone other than me,' said Ormond firmly.

'Maverick must be glad to know you can tell them how Edie saw the film taking shape?'

There was a short pause before Ormond said,

'You'd think so, but nobody's deigned to respond to my email.'

'Seems short-sighted. You've got it all written down, presumably?'

'We didn't write it down. Just talked it all out. It's all in here,' said Ormond, tapping his temple again. 'And as I'm the only one who knows, you'd think they'd . . .'

He shrugged irritably.

'Frustrating,' said Strike.

'Yeah. And now that bloody uncle of hers, who bunged her a couple of hundred quid to get rid of her when she was literally sleeping on the streets, stands to – funny who ends up benefiting. But she didn't make a will, so there you are,' said Ormond, a definite undertone of bitterness in his voice.

'This next point is sensitive,' said Strike. 'Edie tried to kill herself in 2014. Anomie knew what had happened, and even the hospital she was in, within a very short space of time.'

'Yeah, I remember,' said Ormond darkly.

'I'm interested in finding out who could've known that.'

'Search me. I was one of the last to find out,' said Ormond.

'Really?'

'Yeah. She tried to call me, obviously,' the teacher added quickly, and Strike wondered whether this was true, 'but I didn't hear my phone ring over the noise of the pub. I was out with people from work. So then she called Blay. He realised what she'd done and called the police. They had to break down the door.'

The memory of Charlotte's groggy voice, speaking on a mobile from the grounds at Symonds House, surfaced and was immediately repressed.

'She overdosed after drinking alone in her flat all evening and watching people on Twitter tell her to kill herself,' said Ormond. 'This was before we moved in together. Blamed myself, obviously, when I found out what she'd done. She wasn't really fit to live alone, not by that stage. It was after the overdose she moved in with me and that was a big turning point, you know. She was much happier. Much.'

'D'you live locally?'

'No, I'm up in Finchley. Ballards Lane.'

'D'you know if Blay was alone when he realised she'd overdosed?' asked Strike.

'No idea,' said Ormond, 'but he took his bloody time about telling *me*. When he first started talking I thought it was an LOB—'

'Got to ask,' interrupted Strike. 'Are you ex-police?'

Ormond looked momentarily taken aback, but then, for the first time, grinned.

'Still that obvious, is it? Yeah, I was Met. Got out because the ex-wife wanted me to. Retrained as a teacher and then the marriage went tits up anyway.'

'Sorry, go on. You thought Blay was talking a load of bollocks—'

'Yeah. He sounded stoned. Mind you, he usually did; probably had a spliff to limber himself up to call me. Yeah, so it took me a minute or so to cotton on to what he was telling me.'

'Were you with anyone else when you got that call?'

'I was, as it happens. Elderly neighbour of mine. He's ninety-odd. I help him out with a bit of shopping from time to time,' said Ormond, self-consciously modest. 'Give him a lift to the doctor's when he needs it. Nice old guy.'

'But not a good candidate for Anomie,' said Strike, making a note.

''Course not,' said Ormond. 'Nah, the only way Anomie could've known what Edie had done so fast is because Blay shot his big mouth off. He had hours to tell all his mates before it occurred to him he should tell *me* – you know – her bloody boyfriend.'

Strike made another note, then looked up at Ormond again.

'Did Edie ever think Anomie was a physical threat to her? Did she ever worry they'd do her violence?'

'Nah, I don't think so,' said Ormond.

'Not even after Anomie put her address online?'

'That wasn't Anomie.'

'I thought—?'

'He put a picture of the flat online, yeah, but some other guy told people to direct message him if they wanted the full address.'

'Who was the person who offered the address, d'you know?'

'No idea. There were so many of them having a go at her.'

'D'you think Anomie might've killed her?' Strike asked, watching closely for Ormond's reaction.

'I don't know,' said the teacher. The question seemed to have jolted him. 'How would I? I've got no reason to say it was him. Well, I've got no reason to think it was anyone.'

Strike took care to write Ormond's words down as spoken before saying,

'This dossier Blay said he had, allegedly proving Edie herself was Anomie—'

'What a load of bullshit,' snarled Ormond. 'Edie persecuting herself to the point of suicide for three years, four years, whatever it was? Piss off.'

'I presume Yasmin Weatherhead was before your time?' asked Strike.

'Yeah,' said Ormond. 'Why?'

'She took the dossier of supposed proof to Blay.'

'Oh, right, yeah. No, they sacked her before Edie and I got together.'

Ormond took another sip of beer.

'Bit harsh, actually, I thought, letting the girl go just because she played the game. Not that – but Edie was probably getting paranoid, imagining that everyone around her was feeding information to Anomie.'

Strike, who wouldn't have expected this leniency towards Yasmin, given Ormond's uncompromising opinions on everyone else in Edie's vicinity, said,

'You don't think it was an odd thing for an assistant to do, to join Anomie's game? Or keep playing it, given that Anomie was giving Edie such a hard time?'

'Well, I s'pose from that point of view ... Yeah, I s'pose,' said Ormond, as though the subject was of little interest to him.

'You and Edie got engaged before she died, I heard?'

'Oh, you knew about that?' Ormond sounded pleased to hear it. 'Yeah, I proposed two days before – before it happened. We were going to get her a ring that weekend.'

'Very sad,' said Strike, allowing a moment's pause before saying, 'To go back to the dossier: Blay called Edie and accused her of being Anomie, right?'

'That's right,' said Ormond, his expression hardening.

'Did Edie discuss that with you?'

'Of course.'

'What was your advice? Meet Blay and have it out or—?'

'I told her,' said Ormond forcefully, 'to tell him to go fuck him-self. He kept calling and she kept hanging up. Quite bloody right. If he was smoking so much weed he'd believe something like that, screw him.'

'But then,' said Strike, 'Edie changed her mind, and decided to meet him face to face?'

'Yeah. To tell him in person what she thought of him.'

'Who called who?' asked Strike.

'He called her,' said Ormond, 'like I said. He kept doing it.'

'Right,' said Strike.

'And finally she decided, "OK, let's have it out."'

'Edie told you that, did she?'

'Obviously, yeah,' said Ormond impatiently.

'So you knew they were meeting that afternoon?'

'Yeah.'

'Did you know *where* they were meeting?'

'No,' said Ormond. 'I assumed it'd be in a café or what have you.'

'And when Edie didn't come home——?'

'Well, obviously, I was worried. I'd been taking a detention at school that afternoon. Afterwards, I realised I'd been watching bloody Sophie Webster write lines when the actual – you know – when it happened. I got home expecting Edie to be there. She wasn't. I waited. By eleven o'clock I was getting worried. I called the police round about a quarter to midnight.'

'Did you try and call Edie during that time?'

'A couple of times, yeah, but she didn't pick up. The police put me on hold and – well, obviously, I knew then there was something up. I used to be a copper. I know how this stuff works. They asked me to describe Edie, which I did. Then they said they were going to send people out to talk to me.

'They came to the flat and they told me a body matching my fiancée's description had been found in Highgate Cemetery . . . I had to go and ID her.'

'I'm sorry,' said Strike. 'Must've been hell.'

'Yeah,' said Ormond, the undertone of aggression back in his voice. 'It was.'

Strike looked over his notes. As far as Anomie went, he'd learned very little. He did, however, feel immeasurably better informed about Phillip Ormond.

'Well ... unless you've got any more thoughts or information on who Anomie might be—?'

'Well, if you ask me,' said Ormond, who seemed to relax slightly now that the end of the interview was in sight, 'they're seriously fucking disturbed. Whoever it is, even if it's some kid hiding behind' – he gestured vaguely towards his face, indicating a mask – 'a keyboard, there's something very fucking wrong with them. Four solid years, attacking someone online? What was Edie's crime? Creating something they were supposed to love? No, I figure Anomie as the kind of person who'd do anything to save their own neck, who'd be happy to accuse anyone else or put suspicion on anyone else if it meant they got off.'

'What makes you say that?' asked Strike.

'Just my gut feeling,' Ormond said, before draining his glass of lager.

'Well, I think that's everything,' said Strike untruthfully. 'Oh yeah – just wondered – did you suggest our agency to Edie, or was that her idea?'

'Did I what?' said Ormond, frowning.

'Edie came to see my partner, at our agency,' Strike said.

It was easy to see Ormond's pupils dilating, even in the not particularly bright light of the pub, because of the pallor of his blue irises. Evidently neither the police nor Allan Yeoman had told Edie's supposed fiancé about her visit to the detective agency, and these omissions told Strike something significant about the police and the agent's attitude to Ormond.

The teacher seemed to realise his pause had gone on too long for a lie.

'Er – no, I – I had no idea. When was this?'

'Ten days before the attacks.'

'What did she want to do that for?' said Ormond.

'To ask us to help her find out who Anomie was.'

'Oh,' said Ormond. 'Right. Yeah – actually – I didn't know it was *you* she'd come to. She said she was thinking of – yeah, I thought it was a reasonable idea.'

'But she didn't tell you she'd done it?'

'Actually,' said Ormond, after another hesitation, 'she might've done and it didn't register. She was stressed as hell and I was busy at work – I might not've heard her properly or tuned out or something. I was very busy at work,' he repeated. 'Had an interview coming up, for department head.'

'Did you get it?'

'No,' said Ormond, almost snapping.

'Well, when she came to the agency, my partner noticed some bruising on—'

'Oh, that was your partner, was it? Telling the cops I'd choked her?'

Ormond seemed to regret his display of temper as soon as it had escaped him. He stared at Strike with those pale blue, wide-set eyes, at a loss, it seemed to Strike, to know how to repair this last, damaging impression.

'Nobody said anything about choking,' said Strike. 'My partner simply reported the bruising. Well, thanks very much for meeting me, Phillip. You've been extremely helpful.'

After a brief, loaded silence, Ormond got slowly to his feet.

'No problem,' he said in a clipped voice. 'Good luck with the investigation.'

Strike held out his hand, ready to compete this time for hardest grip.

Ormond departed, and Strike knew the fingers of his right hand would be throbbing, a thought that gave him some petty satisfaction. Once the teacher had disappeared from view, Strike took out his mobile and typed a short text to a friend in the Metropolitan Police.

37

. . . the work was done; the new-made king
Had risen, and set his feet upon his realm,
And it acknowledged him.

Jean Ingelow
A Story of Doom

Robin was still watching her iPad when Strike found her at the corner table out of sight of the main bar. He was carrying a pint of London Pride for himself, and a second tomato juice for Robin, though he noticed she'd barely touched her first. Beside her iPad lay her mobile, which was face up and displaying Anomie's Twitter feed, and on her other side lay her open notebook. Strike, who was quite adept at reading things the wrong way up, saw that Robin had made three columns headed with the names Worm28, Vilepechora and Paperwhite, and that she'd been making notes on all three. Worm28's column seemed fullest.

'Anomie in the game?' Strike asked her as he sat down.

'No,' said Robin, glancing up and then immediately back at her screen. 'He hasn't been in here all the time you were with Ormond. Sorry, I'm going to have to keep typing. There's a moderator in here called Worm28 who was online friends with Beth. It's either a gay man or a girl, because they're in a relationship with an unnamed man I'm supposed to know about. They've confided in Beth a lot. They thought they'd driven her out of the game by telling her all their problems.'

'Twenty-eight,' commented Strike, 'is another hate symbol.'

'Seriously?'

'Second letter of the alphabet, eighth letter: BH. Stands for blood and honour. Blood and Honour are a neo-Nazi skinhead group.'

'I can't see Worm28 as a neo-Nazi skinhead,' said Robin as she typed. 'If I had to bet one way or the other, I'd say it was a girl and quite a young one. Possibly dyslexic. Her spelling's wonky and her punctuation's all over the place ... if you're looking for a possible Halvening member, though, Vilepechora seems a bloody good candidate. Wait ... Oh, thank God. Worm28 needs the loo.'

Robin turned her iPad so that Strike could see it. He moved his chair in: Robin felt his knee bump hers.

'The players talk out in the open game,' she said while Strike sipped his pint and watched the animated figures moving among the graves. Like Robin, he was struck by the unsettling beauty of the animation, with its shifting mist and looming tombs. 'But moderators are able to open private channels to talk to anyone they want and nobody else can see what they're saying. Worm28 and Vilepechora both opened private channels with me right after I entered the game.'

'What makes you think Vilepechora could be Halvening?'

'Homophobic as hell,' said Robin. 'Told me I was a pervert.'

'Nice,' said Strike.

'I'm pretty sure he's male. He's also drunk. He told me so three times. He says he's bored of the game and when I asked why he was still in here he said "intel".'

'"Intel"?' repeated Strike. 'Very interesting indeed.'

'And he told me Anomie killed Ledwell.'

She glanced up to see Strike's reaction.

'Did he now?'

'Under the guise of banter,' said Robin, looking back at the game. 'The only other moderator I've spoken to is Paperwhite. She asked me if I needed help navigating the game and gave me some hints about getting into an expanded area that's been created since Beth was last in here. She didn't open a private channel, she just offered to help out in the open game. I don't actually know that she's female, obviously, I'm just assuming so because of the user name. No personal chat.'

Strike was watching the sidebar of player arrivals and departures.

```
<BorkledDrek has left the game>
<Inky1010 has entered the game>
<Magspy7 has entered the game>
```

'If I log out,' said Robin, turning the iPad back towards herself, 'you can tell me about Ormond.'

'Stay logged in,' said Strike, 'so we can keep an eye out for Anomie. I'd like to see how they behave in there. Can you tell this Worm person you've got to go and do something offline for a bit?'

'"Need – to – take – clothes – out – of – washing – machine,"' said Robin, typing. '"Back – in – a – bit."'

She sat back with an air of relief, drank some tomato juice and readjusted the angle of the iPad so that both of them could continue watching it.

'How was Ormond?'

'Ormond,' said Strike, 'was quite interesting. Not what I was expecting. He's a computing teacher and ex-police.'

'Really?' said Robin.

'Yeah, and if I had to bet either way, I'd say they weren't in a relationship prior to her trying to kill herself. I think he took advantage of her being vulnerable to ask her to stay at his place, and she found it hard to get out again. I asked about the fingertip bruising to the neck. He didn't like that much.'

'You amaze me,' said Robin.

'I'm sceptical about the supposed engagement as well. I think Heather Ledwell was right: he's pissed off he's not going to get a penny out of her estate or any financial benefit from the cartoon if it's made into a movie. He mentioned her not having written a will. But he hasn't given up hope of benefiting: he spent half the interview positioning himself as a writer. He claims he was collaborating with her on future storylines and that she wanted him to have a writing credit if the film happened. I asked whether this had all been put in writing and no, the ideas are all in his head. He's emailed Maverick to offer his services but they haven't got back to him.'

'Bloody hell,' said Robin quietly.

'There were a few other interesting points. For one, he says Edie told him she was going to meet Josh the afternoon she was killed but claims he didn't know exactly where they planned to meet. The fishy bit is that he said Blay called *her* to suggest the meeting. Either Ormond or Katya's got it wrong and my money's on Ormond. My suspicion is he had no idea she was going to meet Blay, which begs the question, why lie? If he's worried about being suspected of the stabbings it would make more sense to tell the truth and say he had no idea they were meeting. It's an odd half-lie, saying he knew they were meeting but not where. 'Course, it might be ego: he doesn't want to look like a bloke whose girlfriend's meeting her ex on the sly. He strikes me as that type.

'Also – and this is definitely strange,' said Strike, flicking open his notebook. 'He told me he thinks Anomie's "the kind of person who'd do anything to save their own neck", specifically that they'd try and blame or throw suspicion on someone else. I asked him why he was saying that, and he told me it was just a "gut feeling", but I found that pretty bloody suggestive. Sounds to me like he thinks Anomie might have something on *him*.'

'But that surely means he knows who it is?'

'You'd think so, but he wasn't in any hurry to tell me who he thinks it might be. The reverse: he dismissed everyone I mentioned. Incidentally, he says Edie ruled Kea out. Observed her on the street without a digital device while Anomie was in the game.'

'Oh,' said Robin. 'Well, that's useful to know.'

'Yeah ... One last weird thing Ormond said. I asked whether he thought Anomie might have killed Edie and he said, "I've got no reason to say it was him."'

'"I've got no reason to say it was him,"' repeated Robin. 'Odd form of words.'

'My thoughts exactly,' said Strike. 'Why not just say no?'

The phone in his pocket rang. He took it out. The caller ID was hidden. The suspicion it would be Charlotte made him hesitate, but after a couple of seconds he answered.

'Strike.'

He could hear breathing. The line was crackly. Then a very deep, sonorous voice said:

'If you want the truth, dig Edie Ledwell up.'

The line went dead.

Robin could tell by Strike's expression that something out of the ordinary had just happened. Her immediate thought was *Charlotte*. Then she wondered whether it could be Madeline who'd made his face go blank.

Strike lowered the mobile and looked at it as though the caller ID might somehow materialise.

'I've just been told,' he said, looking back up at Robin, 'to "dig Edie Ledwell up" if I want to know the truth.'

'*What?*'

'"If you want the truth, dig Edie Ledwell up,"' repeated Strike.

They stared at each other.

'What did the voice sound like?'

'Darth Vader. Could've been a voice-changing device or a genuine bass tenor. The line wasn't good.'

'A few weeks back,' said Robin, 'there was a hashtag trending on Twitter. "Exhume Ledwell".'

'Any particular reason, or just a bit of edgy fun?' said Strike, putting the phone back in his pocket.

'Some troll said she'd probably faked her own murder to get sympathy and they should dig up the body to make sure.'

'Well, if it's a troll calling me, they know we're on the case. I hope to Christ neither of us has been recognised while we've been keeping suspects under surveillance.'

'Look,' said Robin with a sudden gasp, pointing at the iPad. 'He's there!'

A unique figure had appeared on the screen. It looked nothing like any of the other figures – the drifting imitations of pretty Paperwhite, the bobbing Harty-ish hearts or the wandering skeletons. This was an empty cloak, which rippled as though it stood in a wind. There was no face: the being inside the cloak was invisible. Though animated simply, it was odd how eerie it was. The legend Anomie MOD was suspended over its head. The figure began to 'talk', the type appearing across its non-existent face.

Anomie: Good evening children

And the avatars of the other players clustered round, type appearing across each of their faces as they greeted him.

Inky101: Anomie in da house!!!!!

Mr_Drek_D: How u doin bwah?

Hartsore9: Anomie, please unban Harty192 he didn't mean it

Paperwhite MOD: evening

InkHart4evs: Anomie, my bwah!

Vilepechora MOD: All hail the king emperor

Magspy7: Anomie, fkn loving
watchin you drag Grunt on Twitter!

WyrdyOne: We gonna go to Comic
Con, Anomie?

Anomie responded to none of them, but floated towards Strike and Robin, and the latter, though she knew it was totally unreasonable – they were sitting in a pub, and this figure was no more than pixels on a screen – felt a shiver of actual fear. Anomie came so close to Buffypaws that the empty hood of his cloak filled almost the entire screen.

Anomie MOD: You've come back

Robin hastily reached out to type, leaving the screen in position so Strike could see what was happening.

Buffypaws: yeah I missed this place

Anomie MOD: favourite animal?

'Dog,' said Strike.
'No,' said Robin, typing. 'I checked.'

Buffypaws: cat obvs

'God, I hope that'll do,' said Robin. 'I didn't get much else.'

Anomie MOD: favourite sexual
position?

Robin stared at this question, very aware that Strike didn't have anything to offer this time. After a few seconds, she began to type with a sense of risking everything on one throw:

Buffypaws: seem to remember I told u
to fuck off when you asked last time

She and Strike watched the screen. Robin had a feeling Strike, too, was holding his breath.

Anomie MOD: lol

> **Anomie MOD:** yeah u did

'Bloody well done,' said Strike.

> **Anomie MOD:** now ask me what you came back to find out

Robin hesitated.

> **Buffypaws:** what do u mean?
>
> **Anomie MOD:** did I kill E*** L******?

Robin's hands hovered uncertainly over the keyboard panel, but before she could respond, Anomie had spoken again.

> **Anomie MOD:** I did. And you're welcome.

Anomie turned and floated away, and as the empty cloak moved off through the *Ink Black Heart* characters, they made their feelings known.

> **Vilepechora MOD:** I fkn told her u did! lololol
>
> **DaddyDrek:** hahahahahahaha
>
> **InkHart4evs:** fkn legend lol
>
> **Mr_Drek_D:** roflmao
>
> **Hartsore9:** omg don't joke
>
> **GhostyHi:** lol
>
> **WyrdyOne:** we bow to our fucking king
>
> **MyHart1sBlak:** lolololololol
>
> **Inky101:** yaaassssss king
>
> **Paperbitch97:** u took out the trash
>
> **Magspy7:** hahaha fkn own it

Kinkheart: Anomie took care of
business lol

Blackhart_4: U ARE OUR GOD

Strike and Robin watched in silence as Anomie's floating figure shrank and finally disappeared into the mists of the game, off to some other part of the animated graveyard.

'Well, there you go,' said Strike, picking up his pint. 'We've got a confession. Now we've just got to find out who made it.'

PART THREE

*If the epicardium and the subjacent fat are removed from a
    heart*
which has been subjected to prolonged boiling . . .
the superficial fibres of the ventricles will be exposed.
                  Henry Gray FRS
                  Gray's Anatomy

38

I've scanned you with a scrutinizing gaze,
Resolved to fathom these your secret ways:
But, sift them as I will,
Your ways are secret still.

Christina Rossetti
The Queen of Hearts

The twice-married Honourable James 'Jago' Murdo Alastair Fleming Ross, heir to the Viscountcy of Croy, merchant banker, father of five and estranged husband of Charlotte Campbell, had been under surveillance for nearly a fortnight. Strike knew it was hugely optimistic to expect compromising material on the man after so short a period, but nevertheless, results so far had been discouraging. Ross was protected by a thick membrane of wealth. A driver took him to and from work every day and when he ate out it was in exclusive private clubs. So scrupulous was Ross in never leaving the premises with any other person that Strike, looking over the scant number of photographs Midge and Dev had managed to take over the preceding two weeks – Ross's distinctive vulpine face and white-blond hair making him easy to pick out in every picture – had to suspect that Ross had rightly assumed his wife was having him watched.

Routine background searches had revealed that Ross's first wife had remarried and was living in Oxfordshire. His younger brother worked as private secretary to a senior royal. The eldest daughter from Ross's first marriage was a boarder at Benenden School; the younger two girls were still attending an Oxfordshire primary. Charlotte was living with her twins and a pair of alternating nannies in the family home in Belgravia, while Ross spent weeknights in a palatial flat in Kensington, which upon investigation turned out to have been owned by his parents for thirty years, and weekends at a large country house in Kent, to which one of the nannies brought his and Charlotte's children.

Ross's working days were spent in a skyscraper on Fenchurch Street, where his bank had recently relocated. Though Strike generally had no strong architectural preferences, he found it entirely fitting that Jago should work in a building of notable and unapologetic ugliness, with a concave face that formed such a powerful solar reflector it had already melted parts of a car parked in its vicinity. In theory, the public had free access to the top three floors of the Walkie Talkie, where there was a roof garden, a fact that had persuaded planners to grant permission for the massive building, which lay on the edge of a conservation area. In practice, the public were allowed into the top of the building in ninety-minute slots, as Dev Shah had discovered when he was instructed to leave before Jago had appeared in the restaurant where he usually took lunch. The only notable exceptions to Jago's routine had been two visits to an extremely expensive and notoriously hard-nosed divorce lawyer. Strike wondered whether Charlotte's old phone, on which Jago had found that compromising photo, had already been displayed to the shrewd, rapacious woman inside, veteran of many a newsworthy break-up.

Strike hadn't discussed his increasingly insistent worry about being implicated in the Rosses' divorce with anyone, least of all Madeline, because the launch of her new collection was imminent and she was even more stressed than usual. Their dates had temporarily become just regular meetings for sex at her house, a change Strike silently welcomed, although here, too, he was pursued by other stresses.

'So . . . when did you and Robin split up, anyway?' Madeline asked one night as they lay naked together in the dark. Strike, who was craving but resisting the urge for a post-coital cigarette, had been thinking about the catch-up on the Anomie case he and Robin were due the following day, and took a few seconds to process what he'd just been asked.

'When did – what?'

'You and Robin,' repeated Madeline. She'd drunk almost a bottle of wine before they'd retired to the bedroom. 'When exactly did you break up?'

'What are you talking about?'

'You and Robin,' repeated Madeline more loudly. She was lying with her head on his shoulder; he was still wearing his prosthesis, which would need to come off soon; he could feel the increasingly raw end of his stump smarting.

'D'you mean when I sacked her?' said Strike, who was certain he'd never told Madeline about that episode.

'You sacked her?' said Madeline, now removing herself from his shoulder to prop herself up on her elbow and looking down at him in the dark.

'Yeah, a few years back,' said Strike.

'Why?'

'She did something I told her not to do.'

'Were you together at the time?'

'No,' said Strike. 'We've never been together. Who—? Wait a minute.'

He groped sideways and switched on the bedroom lamp, wanting to see Madeline's face. She looked both desirable and very tense.

'This wouldn't be something Charlotte told you, would it?' he asked, squinting up at her.

'Well ... yeah.'

'Fuck's sake.'

Strike passed a hand roughly over his face, as though washing it. Had it been Charlotte lying beside him rather than Madeline, he might have been tempted to throw something – not at her, but possibly something breakable, at a wall.

'There's never been anything between me and Robin. We've never been involved.'

'Oh.'

'Charlotte's shit-stirring,' he said, looking up at Madeline again. 'That's what she does. You'll do best to assume that anything that comes out of her mouth about me is total bollocks.'

'So you and Robin haven't ever—?'

'No,' said Strike forcefully. 'We haven't.'

'OK,' said Madeline, and then, 'Charlotte said I look a lot like Robin.'

'You don't,' lied Strike.

Madeline continued to stare down at him.

'You're angry.'

'No, I'm not. Well, not at you.'

'I mean, it wouldn't matter,' she said. 'If it's over, it's over.'

'It never started,' said Strike, glaring at her.

'OK,' said Madeline again. 'Sorry.'

'It's fine,' he lied again, stretching out an arm to invite her to put her head back on his shoulder, then turning out the light.

He lay fuming in the dark until Madeline fell asleep with her head in the crook of his shoulder, and rather than disturb her and risking a further chat about Robin or Charlotte, he slept that night still wearing his prosthesis, which resulted in a sweat rash on the end of his stump.

Strike and Robin's scheduled catch-up was delayed due to Strike spending longer than expected watching Groomer, who took a very long lunch at the Charlotte Street Hotel. It was past five o'clock when Groomer finally got up from the table and Strike, who was by this time taking photographs covertly on the street, watched him out of sight, then called Robin.

'Hi,' she said, sounding as tired as he felt. 'Has lunch gone on all this time?'

'Yeah, sorry. Did you need to get home?'

'No,' she said. 'Are you still on for our Anomie meeting?'

'Yeah, definitely,' said Strike, who'd eaten very little while shuffling between bar, hall and street, watching Groomer's party. 'Listen, would you mind if we do it over food? Maybe in Chinatown?'

'That'd be great,' said Robin. 'I'm starving. I'll find somewhere and text you.'

Twenty minutes later, Strike entered the upper floor of Gerrard's Corner restaurant to find Robin sitting at a table by the window, her iPad propped up on the table beside her, her mobile phone lying beside it, along with an open notebook. Of the few diners, he and Robin were the only Caucasians.

'Hi,' she said, glancing up as Strike sat down, then dropping her gaze back to the game. 'Anomie's here, so I need to keep playing. He comes chivvying people along if they stand still too long. I'm praying Montgomery leaves the office without his phone while Anomie's still active, so we can rule *someone* out.'

'That,' said Strike, gingerly stretching out his aching leg, 'would be a great help.'

His mobile vibrated in his pocket. He really hoped it wasn't Madeline, but to his relief saw a text from his half-sister Prudence, whom he'd agreed to meet the following evening.

Cormoran, I'm so sorry: I'm not going to be able to do tomorrow night. Slight family crisis. Would it be ok to take a rain check? Pru

Strike was so relieved she, rather than him, was calling off dinner, he experienced a wave of affection for this woman he'd never met.

No problem, completely understand. Hope all OK

Robin, who happened to glance up at Strike again as he was typing, saw his faint smile and look of warmth, and assumed he was texting Madeline. Dropping her eyes to her iPad again she tried to quell a rising feeling of antagonism.

'Have you ordered?' asked Strike.

'No, but I'd like something with noodles so I can eat one-handed. And I'll need a fork.'

Strike raised his hand, ordered both of them Singapore noodles, then said,

'Want to hear something interesting, before we get started on Anomie?'

'Go on,' said Robin, eyes still on the game.

'I asked Eric Wardle to do me a favour. Find out why Phillip Ormond left the Met. I had a hunch it mightn't have been voluntary.'

'And?' said Robin, looking up.

'If he hadn't jumped, he'd almost certainly have been pushed. "Thought he was Dirty Harry" were Wardle's exact words. He liked roughing up suspects. Also, his wife walked out before he left the force, which isn't the timeline he gave me.

'Anyway . . .'

Strike pulled out his notebook.

'Want me to start on Anomie, while you're playing the game?'

'Yes please,' said Robin, who was currently steering Buffypaws between tombs.

'I've been looking into all the people we know about who were close to Edie and Josh when the game first appeared. The good news is, we can rule most of them out.'

'Thank God,' said Robin fervently.

'I started with Josh's siblings. The brother works for Kwik Fit, the vehicle-repair place, and the sister's a receptionist at an optician's. I've ruled out most of the cast members too. They've all got steady nine-to-five jobs and there's no way any of them could be tweeting and moderating the game at all hours without getting sacked.

'I talked to the foster sister Edie stayed in touch with. She's events manager at a hotel and would be fired for being online as much as Anomie during working hours. Same applies to Edie's foster brother.

'However, I think we should have a word with Tim Ashcroft. He and Edie were friends predating *The Ink Black Heart* and at the very least he might know about people close to Edie we've missed so far.'

'You don't fancy Ashcroft himself as Anomie?' Robin asked.

'Being sacked is good grounds for a grudge,' admitted Strike, 'but I haven't found any evidence that he can draw or code.'

'He taught Flavia to draw animals using shapes,' Robin reminded Strike.

'Shit – so he did: well remembered. The foster sister hasn't got contact details for him, though, and I'm not sure it's wise to approach Ashcroft directly. He's still in contact with Wally, Montgomery and Nils de Jong and I'd rather not tip off all our potential Anomies that we're on the case. The only thing I can think of is luring Ashcroft into some kind of interview situation without him knowing he's talking to a detective.'

'You mean pretend to be a journalist or something?'

'It couldn't be a journalist from any mainstream outlet, that's too checkable – anyway, he's not well-known enough for them to be interested,' said Strike. 'But I wondered about cobbling something together on the educational front, seeing as his theatre group's going into schools. What d'you think about getting Spanner to knock up a website on drama in education, something like that?'

Spanner was an IT specialist to whom the agency tended to turn for all tech requirements.

'Then,' said Strike, 'if he looks you up—'

'You want me to interview him?'

'I think so. I don't think he clocked me outside the Red Lion and Sun, but better to play it safe.'

'OK,' said Robin. 'Let's get Spanner on the job.'

'Which means I'd have to impersonate you – Buffything – in *Drek's Game* while you're with Ashcroft. Think you could put together a cheat sheet for me?'

'Will do,' said Robin, pausing her activities in the game to add this item to her lengthy 'to do' list.

'Anyway,' said Strike, turning a page of his notebook, 'there is *one* other guy on Katya's cast list who's interesting me: Preston Pierce.'

'The one who voiced Mags—? Anomie's left the game,' said Robin suddenly. She snatched up her mobile and called Barclay.

'Have you got eyes on Montgomery right now?'

Strike could tell, from Robin's frustrated expression, that the answer was no.

'Bugger,' she sighed, having thanked Barclay and hung up again. 'Sorry. Go on about Preston Pierce.'

'Twenty-seven years old, originally from Liverpool, digital artist,' said Strike. 'He seems to use North Grove as his permanent base, though he goes back home a lot, judging by his Instagram account. He's definitely got the kind of skill set we're looking for, he doesn't work nine to five but on different freelance projects, and he's also carrying a bit of resentment. I found an exchange between Preston and the Pen of Justice, on Twitter, about The Worm and Magspie being caricatures of the working classes.'

'I think I read a bit of that,' said Robin, frowning as she tried to remember. The Pen of Justice was so prolific that she hadn't had time to read all of their blog posts. 'Didn't the Pen take issue with Magspie being from Liverpool? Because Magspie's a thief and they thought that was a stereotype?'

'Spot on,' said Strike. 'Preston Pierce agreed with the Pen that Magspie was a slur on his home city and said if he'd known what the character was going to turn into he'd never have voiced it in the first place.'

'Sorry,' said Robin, suppressing a yawn. 'It's been a long day. I could murder a beer.'

'Have one.'

'We're working,' said Robin, 'and I've got to stay in the bloody game. Midge is on Cardew.'

'Where is he?'

'At home with his grandmother. That's the whole problem, isn't it? We can't see what any of them are getting up to when they're behind closed doors.'

'Chin up,' said Strike bracingly. 'We're due a breakthrough.'

'Well, I'm off to North Grove for my first art class tomorrow evening. You never know . . . Is Preston Pierce currently in residence?'

'He is, yeah,' said Strike, who was now bringing up Instagram on his phone. 'There you go. That's him.'

Robin took the phone from Strike and examined the picture of a shirtless young man, both wiry and muscly, with longish black curly hair and large doleful eyes. There was a fine line of tattooed script running around the base of his neck.

'Presumably that's who Flavia was talking about: the man who never wears a shirt,' said Robin, handing back the phone.

'Meanwhile,' said Strike, pocketing his phone and returning to his notebook, 'I'm none the wiser about the identity of that tattooed girl who lives on Junction Road, but I'm hoping you might be able to get a line on her at North Grove too. If she knows Nils, she might be taking art classes th— Is something happening in your game?'

Robin glanced down at the iPad, where a private channel had opened, and groaned.

'It's Worm28 wanting a chat,' she said. 'I spent two solid hours yesterday trying to cheer her up . . . It's definitely a girl,' she added. 'She told me her period had just started and she felt shit.'

'Ah,' said Strike. 'Well, that would seem conclusive.'

'I think I've found her on Twitter as well,' said Robin. 'She goes by Zozo on there, aka @inkyheart28. Zozo makes exactly the same kinds of grammatical mistakes as Worm28. The location on the account's London, but I haven't had time to go through all her tweets yet. I'll tell her I can't talk for a bit . . . sorry – on – the – phone – to – my – mum,' she read out loud while typing.

'The only other stuff I've got is on Yasmin Weatherhead,' said Strike.

'I've got a bit on her too,' said Robin. 'You go first.'

'She's still working for the cosmetics firm in Croydon,' said Strike, 'and manning their social media accounts. She lives with her parents, also in Croydon. She's been tweeting under her own name far less regularly since Edie and Josh were attacked – and that's all I've got so far.'

'Here come our noodles,' said Robin.

A waiter placed the plates in front of them. Strike ordered two beers.

'I can't,' Robin protested. 'Seriously. I'll just fall asleep and miss Anomie confessing to murder.'

'He's already done that,' Strike reminded her. 'I'll drink it if you don't want it.'

He loaded up his chopsticks with as many noodles as they could reasonably hold and said:

'Right, tell me how you've got on.'

Robin took a forkful of noodles herself, chewed, swallowed, then opened her own notebook.

'OK, well, as you've mentioned Yasmin,' she said, flicking through several densely written pages to find her, 'she's still a moderator in the game, where she calls herself Hartella.'

'You're sure it's her?'

'Ninety-nine per cent sure,' said Robin. 'Everything matches. Worm28's told me more than she thinks she has. She mentioned that Hartella used to know Edie and Josh and also told me in strictest confidence that Hartella had to speak to the police after the killings. I asked her why and she claimed not to know, but I can tell she's scared of saying too much.'

'Have you spoken to Yasmin directly?'

'Only in the open game, about tasks. She and Bethany don't ever seem to have been friendly.'

Robin took another large mouthful of noodles and waved her fork until she could speak again.

'There's a rule in the game that you mustn't use any proper names for people or places. Players get round it by typing the first initial and putting asterisks in place of all the other letters.'

'Strange,' said Strike, frowning.

'It *is* odd,' said Robin. 'Absolute secrecy about personal identities is enforced on everyone. It's called Rule 14.'

'Fourteen,' said Strike, 'is another hate symbol.'

'Are there *any* numbers that aren't hate symbols?'

'Yeah, most of them,' said Strike with a grin. 'But fourteen refers to the fourteen words.'

'What fourteen words?'

'I don't know it off by heart, but it's some far-right slogan about securing the future for white children. Go on about the secrecy.'

'OK, so, everyone's scared of triggering instant expulsion from the game, which supposedly happens if you use a proper name or give too much personal information. Allegedly, Anomie's fixed up some mechanism that will instantly trigger Consequence 14 if anyone does those things.'

'Allegedly?'

'Well, I don't believe the mechanism exists,' said Robin. 'I think it's a pretence most people go along with and only credulous players really believe in.'

'Like Worm28?'

'Yes, although I'd have thought she'd have realised by now that if Consequence 14 was real she couldn't have told me as much as she has. She talks endlessly about being depressed because the man she moved south to be near has barely called her or come near her since she moved to London.'

'Which she presumably spells with an L and five asterisks?'

'She does, yes. She's also said she doesn't like her job much. The job involves kids, but I haven't got any more details.

'Anyway, she says even the moderators don't know each other's real identities, or they're not supposed to. Worm28 thinks Hartella knows the real identity of a moderator who calls himself LordDrek. The only direct interaction I've had with him was pretty insulting.'

'In what way?'

'He opened a private channel and immediately attacked me for my perverse practices.'

'Didn't that happen with another—?'

'Yeah, it did: Vilepechora, the first time I entered the game. I've noticed Worm28 brackets LordDrek and Vilepechora together a lot, like they're – I don't know, a double act or something.

'Anyway, Worm28 said something odd about Hartella and LordDrek last night, when I'm pretty sure she was stoned. She said she'd scored and after a while her spelling and grammar got even more patchy than usual. You can't take screenshots directly of the game, but I took a picture of my iPad.'

Robin found the photo on her phone and handed it to Strike.

```
Worm28: Harltlea re ally likes
lordrek i can tell

Buffypaws: d'you think they've met
irl?

Worm28: don ''t knwo

Worm28: she protecting him thio

Buffypaws: what d'you mean,
'protecting'?

>

Worm28: police
```

```
Buffypaws: ?

>

>

>

Worm28: shodln ''t jhave said that
```

'Very, very interesting,' said Strike.

'There's more,' said Robin thickly, through noodles. 'Swipe right.'

Strike did so, and saw a second picture of Robin and Worm28's private chat.

```
Buffypaws: I'm not going to tell
anyone!

Worm28: no forget i said , that pls

Worm28: it was just am istake

Worm28: what they did

Buffypaws: Hartella and LordDrek?

Worm38: no

Worm38: LordFrek asn Vile

>

>

Worm28: pls gorget
```

'I couldn't get any more out of her,' said Robin. 'I didn't want to push it, but hopefully she'll get stoned again and I can have another try.'

Their beers arrived. In spite of her prior resolution, Robin poured hers into a glass and drank some. It was delicious and the slightly calming effect it had on her overworked brain was very welcome.

'So these two blokes – *are* they blokes?'

'I think so. Worm28 always talks of them as male.'

'So these two men, who think lesbianism is a perversion and seem to be in cahoots with each other, have done something the police might be interested in,' said Strike, handing Robin back her phone. 'And Hartella's protecting them. Or at any rate, protecting one of them.'

'Exactly,' said Robin. 'Remember the Brotherhood of Ultima Thule's home page? "We believe that feminism and the legalisation of homosexuality have undermined western civilisation" or something.'

'Can you pass people documents on private channels, do you know?'

'No idea, I haven't tried.'

'Well, if you can,' said Strike, 'this could be how the dossier full of faked emails reached Yasmin Weatherhead, couldn't it? And it'd be a perfect way to do it. Everyone in the game's compulsorily anonymous and the Brotherhood-slash-Halvening would have a ready-made hotbed of Ledwell haters, eager to believe any old shit they were fed . . . I think a bit of surveillance on Yasmin might be in order, you know. Find out who she's meeting out in the real world.'

He ate in silence for a minute, thinking.

'As far as you know,' he said, 'would it be possible for one person to be operating more than one moderator account? Could Anomie also be either LordDrek or Vilepechora? Or both of them?'

'Well, communication on private channels happens in real time, so I've sometimes had two moderators talking to me simultaneously – obviously a single person couldn't be typing two messages at once. But yes, I suppose a single person *could* have two separate moderator accounts, as long as the two different moderators weren't required to type at the same time.

'The bit of the game I'd *really* like to get into is the moderator channel. If Anomie lets anything slip that's the place they'd do it, I'm sure.'

'How many moderators are there?'

'Eight,' said Robin, turning pages of her notebook to find the notes she'd made on each of them. 'Anomie, obviously – Worm28 – LordDrek – Vilepechora – Hartella – Fiendy1—'

'Who's Fiendy1?'

'From what Worm28's told me, he's young and male. She thinks he's gay. During one of our early chats she said, "You know how Morehouse and Fiendy1 used to be really good friends, well, they fell out badly." She didn't know what about, though. I haven't managed any chat with Fiendy1 at all, even in the open game.'

'Any leads on Morehouse?'

'Nothing concrete, but his main interest other than the game seems to be science. His Twitter avi—'

'His what?'

'You know, the picture on the account. It shows a comet and I've seen him talking to a girl he seems to know about discoveries in space. The girl's still at school, judging by her talking about homework and rows with her mother.'

'Any location for the girl? If she and Morehouse are at school together—'

'No, I looked, but she lists her location as "out of my head". I've had no direct contact with Morehouse, which is frustrating as everyone seems to agree he's the only one who knows who Anomie really is. But Worm28's hinted he's in some kind of relationship with Paperwhite.'

'A real-world relationship?'

'No idea.'

'And what do we know about Paperwhite?'

'She's the newest moderator, and Worm28 made a throwaway comment about all the male moderators fancying her.'

'How can they fancy her? They don't know her real identity, do they?'

'I didn't understand that, either, but that's what Worm28 said. Other than that, I haven't been able to find out anything about her.

'But I've collated absolutely everything I've got on Anomie,' Robin added. 'I've gone all the way back through his Twitter feed and added every little thing Worm28's let slip. It's all on a printed document I've put in the file in the office, but I've got it here too, if you want the highlights.'

'Go for it,' said Strike, who was still shovelling noodles into his mouth.

'OK,' said Robin, flicking back to more densely written pages in her notebook. 'Twitter first.

'Anomie's account first appeared on 10 July 2011. Their first tweet told people to check out the new multi-player game they and Morehouse had created. Morehouse's account appeared on the same day, but he tweets about once to every hundred tweets of Anomie's and he's never attacked Edie or Josh and hardly ever interacts with fans. Mostly he just says things like "check out new game expansion". Purely informative.

'Anomie's tweets were all about the game initially, but they really enjoyed fans praising it. People were all agog to find out who they and Morehouse were, and Anomie seems to have got a real kick out of the admiration and made comments along the lines of "wouldn't you like to know". Originally, fans thought Anomie was Josh Blay himself, but that rumour died for good on 14 September 2011, which is when Edie and Josh's interview went online, saying they'd seen the game and that it wasn't really what they'd meant when they created *Drek's Game*. On the same day, Anomie tweeted: "So Ledwell doesn't like our game because 'the game's really more of a metaphor'. We literally based it on your own rules, u pretentious cow."

'From that point on,' said Robin, 'Anomie attacked her constantly until she died. In October of that year they tweeted: "How do I say this politely? Shouldn't a bulimic be ... thin?" And he coined the hashtag GreedieFedwell, which never really went away.'

'Was she bulimic?'

'She had been, according to the note in her file. That was the very first time Anomie used a piece of personal information against her.'

'What about Anomie's politics? Any clues?'

'Well,' said Robin, 'they never say anything *overtly* political. They've only been interested in progressive criticisms of the cartoon when they can be used to directly attack Ledwell for hypocrisy or cruelty to people around her. A hard core of right-wing accounts crops up constantly around Anomie, though. They all complain the cartoon's become too PC. There's someone who calls themselves Lepine's Disciple who's a big Anomie fan and defends Anomie if progressives ever take issue with Anomie doing things like revealing Edie was bulimic.'

'Lepine's Disciple,' repeated Strike. 'Yeah, I think I've seen them. Want another beer?'

He'd already finished his own.

'I can't,' said Robin. 'I'll just fall asleep ... There are left-wingers who hang around Anomie too, but they're mostly focused on criticising Ledwell for being racist and ableist and ... well, pretty much every "ist" and "phobic" you can think of.

'But Anomie never really gets drawn into political stuff, except where it could be used to make a personal attack on Ledwell. If I had to bet, I'd say social justice isn't their thing. Judging purely by their Twitter output, their primary aim is to maintain their own status within the fandom and maximise their influence on the work. It mostly feels ... well, if I had to give it a name, power-hungry.

'I know you think people usually slip up and give away their true identities online,' Robin went on, 'but Anomie's really careful. I get the impression they're very conscious of not giving away personal information that could identify them. They do give occasional trivia: they like Magnums – the ice cream – and *The Dark Knight Rises*. I wrote it all down, but it amounts to almost nothing. I bet you could find a couple of million people in London tonight who like and dislike the same things as Anomie.

'But there are three tweets I thought *might* just say something deeper about them.

'Tweet number one: Anomie said they wanted to use a catapult on a cat on their garden fence. That could be their idea of humour, but it tallies with their general tone of casual cruelty. You saw Anomie boasting about killing Edie the night I got inside the game. There's a general tone of bravado and callousness which, I have to say, sounds a lot like Wally Cardew. That bit of the video, where he pulled out the bloody knife from under the desk? I went and watched it. That felt like a very Anomie-ish joke, especially Anomie as they appear inside the game.

'The second tweet I thought was a *bit* odd was sent a year ago. A lot of *Ink Black Heart* merchandise was coming out and Anomie started attacking Edie for doing what she'd once laughed at and having *Ink Black Heart* T-shirts and keyrings. Anomie tweeted: "And as cash registers ring out across the land, you've got to wonder how @SebMonty91 feels about being the Pete Best of *The Ink Black Heart*".'

'What's wrong with that?'

'Well, I had to look up who Pete Best was.'

'You're kidding?'

'No,' said Robin, amused by Strike's expression of mild outrage. 'The Beatles broke up fourteen years before I was born, you know.'

'Yeah, but . . . it's the Beatles,' said Strike.

'I'm just saying, there are far more recent examples of people who've left bands before they got big. Names I'd have thought under-thirties might've reached for before they got to Pete Best. LaTavia Roberson—'

'Who?'

'One of the original members of Destiny's Child. All I'm saying is, why was Pete Best the go-to reference for Anomie? It seemed odd, if Anomie's late teens or early twenties . . . You're not convinced,' she added, watching Strike's expression.

'No,' he said slowly, 'you're right . . . but I'd've slid straight past that. It wouldn't have registered at all.'

'OK, well, the third tweet I wondered about was that Pen of Justice blog post Anomie shared, about disabilities. I asked myself, "Why share that one?" Because the Pen of Justice is pretty prolific and Anomie hasn't retweeted any of the other articles. Are they disabled or ill themselves? Or close to someone who's ill?

'Which ties into something Worm28 told me. I said Anomie can be a bully, and she said, "He's not all bad. I think he's a carer. He sometimes talks about driving someone to hospital."'

'Anomie, a carer?' said Strike.

'I know,' said Robin. 'I wouldn't much fancy being Anomie's patient. I tried to dig deeper, but I don't think she knows anything else.

'Anyway,' she continued, 'I've noticed another thing. Or lack of a thing. There's something off about Anomie and sex.'

Strike kept chewing his noodles, his expression impassive.

'I've been through four years' worth of tweets,' said Robin. 'There's only one occasion when Anomie becomes even slightly flirty. It was with Kea Niven. They told her she had great hair. And, on a later occasion, they said that they'd sent her a direct message.

'Four years,' repeated Robin. 'Four years of getting lots of adulation and girls begging them to reveal who they really are. And Anomie never capitalises on it, never flirts, never tries to draw them in or offer them information in exchange for nudes . . . If you'd ever been a woman online,' said Robin slightly impatiently, because Strike was merely staring at her, 'you'd know exactly what I'm saying.'

'No,' said Strike, 'I get it. But—'

'The thing is, inside the game, Anomie's different – kind of brash. You saw the question about my favourite sexual position – Buffypaws's favourite position, I mean. Inside the game, it's as though Anomie's acting the part that's expected of them. Everyone thinks they're male, but it doesn't ring true to me somehow. So . . . I've got a theory.'

'Thank Christ,' said Strike. 'Because I've got fuck all. Go on.'

'Well, I think we need to take a closer look at Kea Niven. I know Edie ruled her out,' she continued, before Strike could say anything. 'But we're taking a lot on trust if we don't look at her. We're accepting Allan Yeoman's and Phillip Ormond's word that Edie saw Kea without an electronic device while Anomie was in the game. We don't know how good Edie's view of the street was or whether the men misheard or misremembered – Allan was pretty vague on the phone. What?' she added, a little defensively, because Strike had failed to suppress a grin.

'Nothing,' he said, but seeing that she wasn't going to accept that, he went on, 'just' – he made a revolving motion with his chopsticks, as Robin had waved her fork earlier, then swallowed – 'just thinking, you're good at this detective shit.'

Disarmed, Robin laughed.

'Well, anyway – Kea's an artist, she's got a massive personal grudge, she's ill, which tallies with retweeting that Pen of Justice blog about disabilities, and if she's Anomie it explains that contradiction we were talking about – making the game as a tribute, but hating on one of the creators. *Drek's Game* might have been planned initially as a way of showing Josh Blay that anything Edie did Kea could do better. But then Edie criticised the game, which gave Kea an excuse to go on the attack, taking the fandom with her. Plus, if it's Kea, the anonymity's explained too. She wouldn't want Josh to know she was behind it all, would she? By the sounds of it, she's completely obsessed with him.'

'So you think that little interchange between Anomie and Kea—?'

'Well, it could've been a nice little bit of theatre, couldn't it?' said Robin. 'Kea gets a wider audience for her claims that Edie stole her ideas. She compliments herself as Anomie, drawing people in to look at her video – Kea establishes they're two different people … *and,*' said Robin, 'Kea happens to own two lovebirds by the names of John and Yoko.'

'Bloody well reasoned, Ellacott,' said Strike, who'd finally finished his noodles and now sat back in his chair, looking at her in frank admiration.

'There's still one big question, though,' said Robin, trying not to show she was pleased by his reaction, 'which is how Kea knew all those private things about Edie – but I had a thought about that too.'

'Go on.'

'I think there's a chance that Josh stayed in contact with her after they split up, and that he hid the fact from Edie and Katya. Allan Yeoman said Josh is charming but he doesn't like confrontation or unpleasant conversations. He also told us Josh's judgement about people's poor. Maybe Josh thought he could stop Kea attacking Edie by telling her what a hard life Edie had had.'

'Thereby giving her more ammunition?'

'Exactly – but we can't spare anyone to run surveillance on Kea in King's Lynn, can we? Anyway, assuming Kea's telling the truth about her health, she's currently bedbound. We'd just be watching her house.'

Strike fell silent, thinking. Finally, he said:

'If you're right, and Josh was the source of all her inside information, I can't see any harm in making a direct approach. She was never friends with the cast. You haven't seen any evidence of her being in contact with any of them, have you?'

'No,' said Robin, 'although I haven't been through absolutely all her social media yet. Haven't had time.'

'We'll risk it,' said Strike. 'I'll call her tomorrow. If she agrees to an interview, you can be watching *Drek's Game* while I'm talking to her. We're due a breakthrough,' Strike repeated, as he raised his hand for another beer, 'and I like your theory a lot.'

It was at times like this that Robin found it difficult to remain pissed off at Cormoran Strike, however aggravating he might otherwise be.

39

I'll have no traffic with the personal thought
In art's pure temple.

> Elizabeth Barrett Browning
> *Aurora Leigh*

The three wigs and many sets of coloured contact lenses Robin kept at the office were called into service late the following afternoon. With the aid of the magnifying mirror she kept in a bottom drawer of the partners' desk, Robin set about disguising her appearance for her first evening class at North Grove.

She'd signed up for lessons under the name Jessica Robins and had since worked out a persona and background. Jessica was a marketing executive with frustrated artistic ambitions who'd just broken up with her boyfriend, which had given her more free time in the evenings. Robin chose a shoulder-length brunette wig (Jessica wasn't able to do anything too outré with her hair, due to her marketing job), gave herself hazel eyes, then applied scarlet lipstick and winged black eyeliner modelled on Kea Niven's look, because Jessica liked to emphasise the fact that a dramatic creature lived beneath her conventional exterior, a person who yearned to escape the confines of her humdrum career. Along with her jeans, Robin put on a retro black T-shirt emblazoned with the words BLONDIE IS A BAND and an old black suede jacket, which she'd picked up in a second-hand shop for surveillance occasions such as this. Looking critically at her reflection in the spotted mirror in the bathroom on the landing, Robin was satisfied: Jessica Robins was precisely the mixture of indie chick and conventional office worker she'd been aiming for. Having honed her London accent during the five years she'd lived in the capital, Robin had decided to claim she'd grown up on the Lismore Circus estate, like Josh Blay, which might give her a line into talking about *The Ink Black Heart*, although she planned to pose as someone with only passing knowledge of the cartoon. She took her iPad with her in a sizeable tote bag and intended to leave the game running while, hopefully, she was observing Preston Pierce.

Pat had already left for the day. Robin was almost at the outer door when Strike's shadow loomed behind the engraved glass panel. He entered the office limping and wearing the tight, drawn expression with which Robin had become familiar, which meant he was in a lot of pain.

'Who are you?' he asked, smiling slightly at the sight of her.

'Jessica Robins, marketing executive with arty aspirations,' said Robin in perfect estuary English. 'Where have you been? Fingers?'

'Yeah,' said Strike, lowering himself onto the fake leather sofa opposite Pat's desk without removing his coat and briefly closing his eyes in relief at getting his weight off his stump. 'The bastard did a lot of walking this afternoon, and one of the places he walked to was Sotheby's.'

'Really?'

'Yeah ... but he can't be so dumb he'd try and auction off the stuff he nicked, surely?'

'Seems unlikely.'

'Maybe he was shopping. I also phoned Kea Niven, but got her mother,' Strike went on. 'Apparently her precious daughter's far too sick to talk to me, she wouldn't have the faintest idea who this Anomie person is, she's a very vulnerable and suffering person who's being demonised for sticking up for her rights and fuck off, basically.'

'Oh, shit,' said Robin.

'I asked Mrs Niven not to tell anyone else we're looking into Anomie, because it could endanger the investigation, and she got bloody huffy about that too: who did I think they were going to tell? Kea's too poorly to talk to anyone etcetera, etcetera ...'

Strike really wanted some tea and painkillers, but that would entail standing up. The idea of asking Robin to get them for him crossed his mind, but he said nothing. Now she had hazel eyes, the resemblance to Madeline was pronounced. The notion of offering Strike tea also occurred to Robin, but she really did need to leave immediately to be sure of reaching North Grove in time and, after all, she thought, with a slight hardening of her heart, he could call his girlfriend if he needed looking after.

'Well, I'll text you if I get anything interesting,' she said, and departed.

The early evening was warm and the brunette wig tight and slightly itchy. It took Robin half an hour to travel by Tube to Highgate station, and a further fifteen minutes to find the large dirty pink house, which stood on the corner of a street that was also called North Grove. The place looked slightly ramshackle: some of its many windows bricked up, whereas others open to admit the warm evening air. A VOTE LABOUR poster was pasted on one of the bricked-up windows.

Robin hung back for a couple of minutes to check *Drek's Game* before entering the building. It always became glitchy when run off 4G rather than Wi-Fi. The only two moderators currently in there were Paperwhite and Hartella. Robin returned the iPad to her bag with the game still running, then walked up the short garden path and entered the art collective.

The appearance of the spacious hallway was, to say the least, unexpected. A large wooden spiral staircase, which clearly wasn't an original feature, stood right in the middle of the space, its banisters polished tree branches, sinuous and tangled. In a corner to the right of the entrance stood a gigantic Monstera deliciosa, which had grown to touch the ceiling, its glossy green leaves making a partial canopy over Robin's head.

The surrounding walls were all covered in drawings and paintings, some framed. The small amount of painted surface that was visible was Pepto-Bismol pink. To Robin's left was a glass door to what appeared to be a small shop, its shelves laden with pottery goblets and figures. As the hall was deserted, and there was no signage to tell her where to go, Robin headed into the shop, where a short, stocky woman with a vast quantity of long grey hair piled on top of her head was counting up the day's takings. She wore a purple vest and had a tattoo of a purple five-petalled flower on her upper arm.

'Life drawing?' she said, looking up as Robin entered.

'Yes,' said Robin.

'That's my class. This way,' said the woman with a smile, and bringing the locked deposit box with her, she led Robin around the spiral staircase into a studio space at the rear of the building, where five other students had already taken their places at easels. In the middle of this room was a plinth draped in a grubby sheet, on which stood an unoccupied wooden chair. The long windows behind the plinth looked over a scrubby patch of garden. Though the sun was setting, Robin could just make out a tortoiseshell cat in the shadows, stealing through some anaemic-looking daffodils.

Robin took a seat at a free easel. A sheet of white paper had already been pinned to it.

'Hello,' said an elderly man beside her, who had a stiff grey beard and wore a Breton sweater. 'I'm Brendan.'

'Jessica,' said Robin, smiling as she took off her black suede jacket.

'We'll get started in five minutes,' announced the woman holding the deposit box. 'We've got one more student due.'

She departed the room to the rattle of loose change. From somewhere in the building the silent class heard a high, childish treble voice, singing a song in Dutch.

> *Het witte ras verliest,*
> *Kom op voor onze mensen . . .*

'Stop that!' they heard the woman with the deposit box say. 'It isn't funny!'

There followed a cackle of high-pitched laughter and the sound of heavy feet running up the spiral stairs.

'Actually,' Robin whispered to Brendan of the Breton sweater, 'I think I might need the loo before we begin. You wouldn't happen to—?'

'Second right,' said Brendan, pointing. 'I'm an old-timer.'

'Great, thanks,' said Robin, whose intention was really to have a quick nose around for Preston Pierce. She took her tote bag with her to the toilet, passing an open door to a room in which there were several computers. A gigantic man with long blond hair was staring at one of the screens.

The toilet was as eclectically decorated as the hall. Every inch of wall, ceiling and the back of the door was covered in portraits presumably done by students, some painted, some line drawings. Glancing around, Robin recognised two faces. An accomplished sketch of Edie Ledwell was staring down at her from the top of the door, a half-smile on her face. The drawing had been done in charcoal and pencil, and was signed 'JB'. The second picture, which had been pinned to the ceiling, took her longer to place, but finally she realised it depicted Gus Upcott, drawn, Robin assumed, by his mother, who was far more talented than Robin might have guessed. A small wooden bookcase full of tattered volumes stood beside the toilet, including *Ride the Tiger* by Julius Evola, *Suicide* by Émile Durkheim and *Breek het partijkartel!: De noodzaak van referenda* by Thierry Baudet.

She sat down on the toilet seat and took out her iPad, but as she'd expected, there was such poor 4G reception the game had frozen. As far as she could see, Anomie still wasn't present.

After flushing the toilet Robin opened the door and, to her surprise, almost walked into a tiny girl with long dyed black hair whose gaunt, death's head face was unmistakably that of the girl Strike had photographed outside Highgate Cemetery. The girl's tattoos weren't visible tonight, because she was wearing a long-sleeved black top that would have fitted an eight-year-old.

'Sorry,' said Robin.

'No problem,' said the girl in her thick Yorkshire accent. ''Ave you see a little k—? Oh, shit,' said the girl, dashing away from Robin, who now saw a blonde toddler in a nappy making her tottery way up the spiral staircase. The gaps in the polished branches were easily large enough for the child to fall through. The girl in black chased and caught her, then swung her up into her arms.

'Wharr've I told you about going oop and down there alone?'

The girl in black carried the struggling, whining toddler back down the stairs, passed Robin and disappeared the way she'd come.

Robin returned to the studio space to find the last student had arrived: an eager-looking girl with short blue hair and multiple piercings. In Robin's absence, a curly-haired young man in a ragged grey dressing gown had taken his place on the wooden chair on the plinth, his bare legs crossed. He was currently looking out of the window, where the lowering sun was slowly turning the garden into a mass of blue shadow. Although he had the back of his head towards Robin, she had a sudden suspicion of his identity.

The stocky grey-haired woman in the purple vest was now standing in front of the class without her deposit box. She seemed to have been waiting for Robin to reappear.

'Sorry,' Robin said hastily, sitting back down beside Brendan, who winked at her.

'All right, then,' said the grey-haired woman, smiling around at the seven students. 'My name's Mariam Torosyan and I'm going to be taking your class. I'm an illustrator and stained-glass artist these days, but I trained in fine art and I've been teaching for nearly thirty years now.

'So,' she went on, clapping her strong-looking hands together, 'most people, when they think of life drawing classes, imagine they'll be working from the nude, and I always like to meet expectations, so this evening we will indeed be working from the nude.'

There was a ripple of nervous laughter and the young man on the plinth turned his head, now grinning. As Robin had suspected, it was Preston Pierce. He was sallow-skinned, with dark shadows under his large brown eyes.

'This is Preston Pierce, or Pez, as we call him,' said Mariam, 'who's actually an artist himself and a very talented one. He lives here at the collective, but he acts as a life model for us when needed—'

'Need the ackers, like,' said Preston in his Scouse accent, and the class laughed again.

'Why don't we go round and introduce ourselves before we get started? And perhaps you could tell me what made you want to come for this class and what previous experience you've got. Brendan, why don't you take the lead?' said Mariam. 'Brendan's an old friend,' she added fondly. 'He's taken – how many classes is it now, Brendan?'

'This is my fifth,' said Brendan cheerfully. 'Trying to find the one I'm good at!'

Another, looser round of laughter ensued, in which Mariam joined.

'He's being very self-deprecating,' she told the class. 'He's a fine print-maker and a very decent potter. What about you, my love?' she asked Robin.

'I'm Jessica,' said Robin, her heart rate slightly accelerated. 'I – um – did art A level, but nothing since then. I work in marketing and – well, I suppose I'm here because there's more to life than marketing.'

This elicited another, knowing laugh from the rest of the class, who clearly empathised with the sentiment. Preston Pierce's eyes lingered on Robin, a smirk playing across his lips.

The rest of the class answered Mariam's question in turn. The stout woman in the magenta sweatshirt had 'always loved to draw', the young man with the straggly beard had an idea for a comic book he wanted to illustrate and the black girl in the short yellow dress wanted to explore her creativity. The elderly woman with wispy, blondish hair was also an old habitué of North Grove, and she wanted to take the life drawing class because Mariam had said it would be good for her artistic development.

'And you, my love?' asked Mariam of the young blue-haired girl.

'Oh, I'm a big *Ink Black Heart* fan,' said the girl. 'I really just wanted to, you know, soak in the magic? See if I can catch some?'

She beamed around the group. If she'd expected a sense of immediate connection with her fellow students, or with Mariam, she didn't get it. Robin thought Mariam's smile became a shade less warm as she turned away from the girl to address the whole class again.

'Well, we're clearly a class of varying experience, which is just fine. I want you all to have fun with this. You'll be getting constructive feedback from me, but tonight's really more about diving right in and learning by doing. All right, Preston—'

Pierce got up from the chair and took off the ragged grey dressing gown, beneath which he was entirely naked. Wiry and well-muscled, he arranged himself nonchalantly on the wooden seat.

'Need to get comfy,' he said, arranging his limbs. With his arms over the back of the chair, he sat sideways to the class, his face turned away from the girl with the blue hair and towards Brendan and Robin. The latter became temporarily preoccupied with not looking at Preston's penis, which was quite a bit larger than her ex-husband's and suddenly seemed to be the only object in the room.

'I've given you everything you should need,' said Mariam. 'You've got a nice couple of 2B pencils and a new eraser—'

'Would it be all right,' piped up the elderly woman, 'if I use my own HBs, Mariam?'

'You use whatever suits you, my love,' said Mariam, and the old lady rummaged in a large tapestry bag.

Soon all the students set to work, most tentatively and a little self-consciously, with the exception of cheerful, bearded Brendan, who was already making swooping marks on his paper.

For the next thirty minutes, the only sound was the scratching of graphite on paper and Mariam's occasional murmurs of encouragement and assistance. Eventually, on pretence of retrieving her eraser from the floor, Robin checked her iPad in her bag. There was better reception in the studio than in the bathroom: the game was moving again, though jerkily. Anomie still wasn't there, and nor (to Robin's relief) was Worm28, but Paperwhite had opened a private channel to Buffypaws some twenty minutes previously. Robin read her message quickly:

```
<A new private channel has
opened>

<23 April 2015 20.14>

<Paperwhite MOD invites
Buffypaws>

Paperwhite: Hi

>

>

>

>

Paperwhite: hello?
```

With a nervous glance around the room, Robin hastily typed a reply.

```
Buffypaws: sorry, missed this

>

>

>

>

Paperwhite: there u are! are you
stuck in the game? Can I help u?

Buffypaws: no thanks
```

Mariam was moving along the line towards Robin.

```
Buffypaws: sorry brb
```

She shoved the iPad out of sight and straightened up again.

'Now, that's not bad at all,' said Mariam encouragingly when she reached Robin. 'You can certainly draw. What you need to work on is *seeing*. I want you to look – really look – at Preston because *this –*'

Mariam pointed at the shoulder she'd drawn, which Robin had known all along was at the wrong angle but hadn't bothered to correct.

'– isn't what you're seeing. Now have a good hard look and try and put that shoulder back where it should be.'

Robin did as she was told. Staring at Preston's shoulder, she was aware that his mournful eyes were either fully on her, or on Brendan, but she kept her gaze determinedly on his clavicle.

After another fifteen minutes, Mariam announced a break and invited the students to follow her to the kitchen for a cup of tea or a glass of wine. Robin let the other students leave the room without her, so that she could get back to Paperwhite.

> **Buffypaws:** back, really sorry about that
>
> \>
>
> \>
>
> \>
>
> **Paperwhite:** I just noticed you haven't moved for ages and Anomie's on the warpath
>
> **Buffypaws:** why?
>
> **Paperwhite:** he's not keen on players coming in here but not playing
>
> **Buffypaws:** I got a phone call from my sister just after I logged on
>
> **Paperwhite:** ah ok
>
> **Paperwhite:** Anomie just wants us to check that everyone's here to play
>
> **Paperwhite:** not to spy on the other players

Shit.

> **Buffypaws:** why would I want to spy on the other players?!

Paperwhite: we think the police
might be looking at fans
currently. because of what
happened to E*** L******

'Answering your marketing emails?' said Preston Pierce.

Robin gave a start. The artist-model, who'd thankfully put his dress-ing gown back on, had approached while she'd been typing and was now contemplating her with the same slight smirk he'd worn earlier.

'How d'you guess?' Robin said lightly.

'Look like you've gorra cob on.'

Robin smiled. He was only a little taller than she was. The sentence tattooed around the base of his neck was obscured at either end by the lapels of his robe. Robin could only read '*hard to be someone but it*'.

'Don't want a drink?' asked Preston.

'No, I do,' said Robin, putting the iPad back in her bag. 'Which way?'

'Follow me,' said Preston and he led her out of the room, Robin answering his questions about her marketing career at random, pre-occupied with the question of whether it would be more sensible to log out of the game rather than continue to remain inactive for the rest of the class.

At the rear of the house was a huge communal kitchen, which was painted the same sugary pink as the hall. Directly opposite Robin was a large and beautiful stained-glass window that she guessed was Mariam's work. It had been cleverly illuminated with an artificial light source on the exterior of the building, so that even in the evening light it cast patches and flecks of cerulean, emerald and crimson light over the scrubbed wooden table and the many large pots and pans hanging on the walls. At first glance Robin thought the window might depict a vision of paradise, but the many people depicted there bore no wings or halos. They were working cooperatively on different tasks: planting trees and picking fruit, tending a fire and cooking over it, building a house and decorating its front with garlands.

Mariam stood chatting to Robin's fellow students near an old black lead range. Some were drinking tea, others small glasses of wine. Robin guessed this convivial half-time break might account for some of the students' fondness for classes at North Grove. The gigantic blond man she had seen earlier was now sitting at the table, drinking a far bigger glass of wine than had been given to the students, and throwing the occasional comment into their conversation. Leaning up against the cupboards on the far side of the room, not talking to anyone but apparently in charge of a baby monitor plugged beside her, was the tiny girl with long black hair, who'd just taken out her phone. There was no sign of the toddler in the nappy.

Reaching a decision about the game, Robin smiled at Preston, who seemed disposed to linger beside her, and said,

'Sorry, I'm going to have to send an email.'

'Dedicated,' he commented, and headed for the group around Mariam.

Robin took out her iPad and saw, with a sinking heart, that Worm28 had just logged on and, inevitably, opened a private channel to Buffypaws.

> **Worm28:** hi how 's your day been ?
>
> \>
>
> **Buffypaws:** not bad
>
> **Buffypaws:** Paperwhite just told me I need to keep active in here or Anomie will think I'm a spy
>
> **Worm28:** yeah anomies told all the mods to maek sure people are who they say they are not plice
>
> **Buffypaws:** think I'd better log out then. I'm on the phone to my sister.don't want to get banned
>
> **Worm28:** wait I thought u were an ony child

Shit, shit, shit.

> **Buffypaws:** she 's my step-sis we never lived together
>
> **Worm28:** ah ok
>
> **Buffypaws:** gtg. speak tomorrow?
>
> **Worm28:** yeah ok xxxx

Robin closed the private channel, logged out of the game and slipped her iPad back into her bag. Looking up again, she saw the girl in black sigh deeply, then put her phone back in her pocket. Seeming to sense Robin's scrutiny, she turned and looked at her out of her heavily kohled eyes. A sudden, wild idea occurred to Robin, but she kept her expression impassive as she strolled over to join the group around Mariam, who was telling her students about the purple flower tattoo on her plump upper arm, which she'd only recently had done.

'. . . for the hundredth anniversary tomorrow,' she was saying.

'Armenian genocide,' said Preston Pierce's Scouse voice in Robin's ear. 'Her great-grandparents died in it. Wanna wine?' he added, offering her one of the glasses in his hand.

'Great, thanks,' said Robin, who had no intention of drinking more than a sip.

'Jessica, was it?'

'Yeah . . . That window's amazing,' she said.

'Yeah, Mariam did it, five, six years ago,' said Preston. 'Everyone on there's a mate of hers, like. I'm helping put the roof on the house.'

'Oh, wow,' said Robin, looking at the curly-haired figure on the window. 'You've been here that long, have—?'

'Are Ledwell or Blay on there?' said an eager voice behind them. Both turned: the girl with the blue hair and piercings, who'd introduced herself in class as Lia, was staring at the window. Robin thought she must be eighteen at most.

'No,' said Preston. Robin had a feeling he was lying.

Lia lingered, either unfazed by or oblivious to Pierce's tone.

'Who are Ledwell and—?' began Robin.

'Edie Ledwell and Josh Blay,' said Lia with the pleasurable self-importance of one who has special, inside knowledge. 'They created *The Ink Black Heart*? The cartoon?'

'Oh,' said Robin, 'yeah, I think I've heard—'

'They used to live here,' said Lia. 'This is where they started it all. Didn't you see in the paper about Edie Ledwell getting—?'

'Edie was a friend of mine and Mariam's,' said Preston Pierce in a low growl. 'Her murder isn't exciting fucking goss to us. Why don't you stop pretending you wanna learn drawing and go sniff around in the cemetery? Might still be a bit of Edie's blood on the grass. You could frame it. Sell it on eBay.'

The girl turned red and her eyes filled with tears. She shuffled out of Preston's vicinity. Robin felt sorry for her.

'Fucking stans,' said Preston to Robin in a low voice. 'That's another one, over there,' he said, nodding towards the black-haired girl. 'The way she were fucking crying after Edie died, you'd've thought they were twins. She never even met her.'

'I'm so sorry your friend was killed,' said Robin, feigning shock. 'I don't – I don't really know what to say.'

''S'all right,' said Preston brusquely. 'Nothing *to* say, is there?'

Before Robin could respond, a very large blond boy came bursting into the kitchen, dressed in jeans and a T-shirt. He had the huge blond man's features: both faces resembled stylised Greek comedy masks, and Robin surmised that this was Bram de Jong. At the top of his voice he sang again:

Het witte ras verliest,
Kom op voor onze mensen . . .

'Oi,' Preston called to Bram. 'We've told you about that. Stop singing it!'

A few of the group around Mariam had looked around, interested.

Bram cackled loudly. His father seemed mildly amused.

'What does it mean?' Robin asked.

'Go on,' Preston said to the boy. 'Tell her.'

Bram grinned broadly and insolently at Robin.

'It's Dutch,' he said in his high, childish treble.

'Yeah, but what does it mean in English?' said Preston.

'It means "the white race is losing. Stand up for our peop—"'

'No,' said Mariam loudly. 'That's enough. It's not a joke, Bram. It's not funny. Right, everyone,' she added, 'back to work.'

There was a general move to place empty mugs and glasses on the table at which Nils was sitting. Robin heard Mariam say crossly to Nils as she passed him,

'He'll stop if *you* tell him to.'

But Nils, who was now play-wrestling with Bram, either didn't hear Mariam, or chose to ignore her.

While waiting to put down the glass of wine she'd barely touched, Robin glanced up at the stained-glass window again, trying to make out Edie or Josh. She had a suspicion they might be the two people picking fruit: both had long brown hair and the female figure was throwing apples down to the male. Then she noticed, with a little start of surprise, the ruby-coloured glass letters set across the top of the picture, like a biblical verse.

A state of anomie is impossible
wherever organs in solidarity with one another
are in sufficient contact,
and in sufficiently lengthy contact.

40

But I, who am seventeen next year,
Some nights, in bed, have grown cold to hear
That lonely passion of the rain
Which makes you think of being dead,
And of somewhere living to lay your head
As if you were a child again,
Crying for one thing, known and near
Your empty heart, to still the hunger and the fear
That pelts and beats with it against the pane.

Charlotte Mew
The Fête

The art class ended with Mariam delivering a short verdict on every-one's drawing. Preston Pierce, who'd pulled his grey dressing gown back on, sat smoking a roll-up, grinning as each rendition of his naked figure was held up for everyone to see. He was particularly interested in Robin's, which was given qualified praise by Mariam. Once the assessments of all the drawings had concluded, Mariam wished her pupils a good week, told them she was looking forward to seeing them at the next lesson, and informed them that there'd be no class the week after that, because it would be the day of the general election, and Mariam would be one of those manning the local polling station.

It was ten o'clock, and the studio windows had become inky oblongs revealing nothing of the garden beyond. Everybody stood up and pulled coats and jackets on. The blue-haired girl with the pierc-ings was first to leave, looking as eager to depart as she'd been keen to arrive. Robin was sure she wouldn't be back again.

The tiny girl with the long hair was talking to a couple in the hall when Robin left the studio. Robin pretended to be searching for something in her bag as an excuse to linger and listen.

'. . . fast asleep,' the younger girl was saying, 'and I give her her blankie out of the wash.'

'Aw, cheers, Zo,' said the older woman, who had a crew cut and was already heading for the stairs, hand in hand with her turbaned partner. 'See ya Monday, then.'

The couple proceeded up the spiral staircase with its curving banisters. The tiny black-clad girl drew her thin jacket tightly around her, then passed beneath the canopy of Monstera deliciosa leaves and left the building.

Robin had just started after her, with the intent of luring the girl into conversation, when a Liverpudlian voice called her back.

'Hey, Jessica.'

Robin turned. Preston Pierce had left the studio room in pursuit of her. He was still wearing his tatty dressing gown.

'You going straight home, like?'

For a split-second, Robin hesitated. Preston Pierce was a genuine suspect for Anomie, but something about that tiny black-clad girl was calling to her and she had an idea that continually checking her iPad while talking to Pierce might look very strange.

'Yeah,' said Robin, forcing a disappointed look onto her face. 'I've got to be up at five tomorrow. Going to Manchester.'

'Condolences,' he said, grinning. 'I liked your drawing of me.'

'Thanks,' said Robin, smiling and trying not to think about his penis.

'OK, well . . . see you next week,' he said.

'Yeah,' Robin replied brightly. 'Can't wait.'

He looked cheerful at that, clearly taking her enthusiasm as encouragement, as she'd intended, and with a half-salute he turned and padded on his bare feet back in the direction of the kitchen.

Robin hoisted her tote bag over her shoulder and left the building, looking around for her quarry in the dark. She spotted the girl in the distance, passing under a streetlight, arms folded, walking rapidly.

Robin hurried after her, mulling over her options. Reaching a decision, she retrieved her purse from the bottom of her bag, broke into a run and, slightly broadening her natural Yorkshire accent, shouted:

'Excuse me?'

The girl turned with a start and waited as Robin ran up to her.

'Is this your purse?'

Robin thought she saw the idea of claiming it cross the girl's face, so she said quickly,

'What's your name?' and opened the purse to examine a credit card.

'Zoe Haigh,' said the girl. 'No, it's not mine.'

'Shit,' said Robin, looking around. 'Someone's dropped it . . . I better hand this in. D'you know where the nearest police station is?'

'Maybe Kentish Town?' suggested the girl and then, curiously, 'You from Yorkshire?'

'Yeah,' said Robin. 'Masham.'

'Yeah? I'm from Knaresborough.'

'Mother Shipton's Cave,' said Robin promptly, falling into step beside Zoe. 'We went to see it on a primary school trip. I thought it was creepy as fuck.'

Zoe gave a little laugh. Her face truly was strangely old-young: sunken and white, smooth and gaunt. The heavy black eyeliner didn't help the skull-like appearance.

'Yeah, it is,' she said. 'I were taken there when I were a kid. I thought the witch still lived there. I were petrified – ha ha,' she added.

The main attraction of Mother Shipton's Cave was the petrifying well, which appeared to turn objects into stone, through a process of calcification. Robin, who'd got the unintentional joke, laughed on cue. Zoe looked pleased to have amused her.

'What're you doing in London, if you're from Knaresborough?' asked Robin.

'Moved to be wi' my boyfriend,' said Zoe.

The idea that had occurred to Robin back in the North Grove kitchen suddenly seemed a lot less wild. *Zoe. Zozo. @inkyheart28. Worm28.*

'Me too,' she said. It happened to be true: Matthew hadn't been her husband or even her fiancé when she'd moved to London to be with him. 'But we split up.'

'Shit,' said Zoe. The information seemed to depress her.

'You work at North Grove, do you?' Robin asked, discreetly slipping her purse back into her bag.

'Yeah, part-time,' said Zoe.

They walked on in silence for nearly a minute and then Zoe piped up again, 'Mariam wants me to move in there. Cheap room. Cheaper'n where I am now.'

Robin had to assume Zoe's unusual readiness to confide in a

stranger sprang from loneliness. Certainly an air of deep unhappiness hung over her.

'Mariam's the one who took my class, right?'

'Yeah,' said Zoe.

'She seems really nice,' said Robin.

'Yeah, she is.'

'So why don't you move in? Seems like a cool place.'

'M' boyfriend don't want me to.'

'Why? Doesn't he like the people?'

When Zoe didn't respond, Robin said,

'Who else lives there? It's like a commune, in't it?'

'Yeah. Nils owns it. He's that massive bloke who was in t'kitchen.'

Zoe walked on for a few paces in silence, then said,

'He's really rich.'

'Yeah?'

'Yeah. His dad was like some big businessman or something. Nils inherited, like – I dunno – millions. So that's 'ow come they can afford that big house and everything.'

'You wouldn't think he was a millionaire, looking at him,' said Robin.

'No,' agreed Zoe. 'I were really surprised when I found out. 'E just looks like some old hippy, don't he? 'E told me 'e always wanted to live like that. Be an artist and 'ave, like, a place where loads of artists live together.'

But Zoe's tone didn't hold much enthusiasm.

'Are he and Mariam together?'

'Yeah. But Bram – the big blond kid – isn't hers, just Nils'.'

'Really?'

'Yeah. Nils had him with a girlfriend in Holland, but the girlfriend died, so Bram came to live at North Grove.'

'Sad,' said Robin.

'Yeah,' said Zoe again.

They walked on in silence until they reached a bus stop, which Robin had assumed was Zoe's destination, but she strode onwards.

'How're you getting home?' asked Robin.

'Walkin',' said Zoe.

The day had been sunny but the night sky was cloudless and the temperature had plummeted. Zoe was walking with her arms wrapped around herself and Robin thought she might be shivering.

'Where d'you live?' Robin asked.

'Junction Road,' said Zoe.

'That's in the same direction as the police station, isn't it?' said Robin, hoping this was true.

'Yeah,' said Zoe.

'So ... you must be artistic, right? To get a job at North Grove?'

'Kind of,' said Zoe. 'I wanna be a tattoo artist.'

'Seriously? That'd be so cool.'

'Yeah,' said Zoe. She glanced up at Robin, then rolled up her jacket sleeve, and the sleeve of the thin top beneath it, to reveal the densely tattooed forearm covered in characters from *The Ink Black Heart*. 'I done them.'

'You – what?' said Robin, unaffectedly astonished. '*You* did them?'

'Yeah,' said Zoe, shyly proud.

'They're incredible, but – *how?*'

As Zoe laughed, Robin saw a glimpse of a young person behind the skull-like face.

'Y' just need to make the stencils an' 'ave ink an' a tattoo gun. I got one second-hand, off t'internet.'

'But doing it on yourself ...'

'I used mirrors and that. It took a long time. Over a year to do it all.'

'That's all stuff from *The Ink Black Heart*, isn't it?'

'Yeah,' said Zoe.

'I *love* that cartoon,' said Robin, well aware that she'd now split into two different Jessicas: one from London who knew only vaguely about *The Ink Black Heart*, and one from Yorkshire who adored it, but there was no time to worry about that now.

'Do ya?' said Zoe, looking up at Robin again as she pulled down her sleeve. She seemed to like Robin the more for hearing it.

'Yeah, of course. It's really funny, isn't it?' said Robin. 'I love the characters and what they say about – I don't know' – (which was true: Robin grasped for generalities) – 'life and death and the games we all play' – (Drek's game meant something like that, didn't it?) – 'and I love Harty,' Robin concluded. It was safe to love Harty. Nearly all the fans whose tweets she'd been wading through for weeks loved Harty.

Zoe wrapped her arms around herself again and then, suddenly, words poured out of her.

'It saved my life, that cartoon,' she said, staring ahead of her. 'I felt so bad when I were thirteen. I were in care, like Edie Ledwell. There's so many things the same between us. She tried to kill 'erself and I did too, when I were fourteen. Slit me wrists – I've tattooed over the scars.'

'God, I'm sor—'

'I found *The Ink Black Heart* on YouTube and it was so fookin' weird but I couldn't stop watchin' it. I loved the style of the drawings and all the characters. They're, like, so messed up, but they're still OK really, in't they? I felt proper bad and wrong when I were fourteen but, like, all the things Harty says, like, it's never too late, even if you was made to do bad stuff, you don't have to for ever. I just loved watching them, and it's proper funny.

'I were gonna do it again – slit me wrists. I 'ad the stuff ready and I were gonna pretend I were goin' on a sleepover and go in the woods an' do it, so nobody could find me. But the cartoon was the first thing that made me laugh in, like, a year. An' I thought, if I can still laugh . . . and then I saw Edie Ledwell online sayin' she were gonna do another one and I wanted to see it, so I didn't kill meself. That's what stopped me. That's mad, innit?' said Zoe, staring into the darkness. 'But it's true.'

'That doesn't sound mad,' said Robin quietly.

'So I watched the second one an' it were really funny an' all. That were the first one Magspie spoke in. You know that guy 'oo was chattin' you up back there? Preston? The one 'oo was modelling for your class?'

'Yes,' said Robin.

'He were the voice of Magspie in episodes two an' three.'

'No way!' said Robin.

'Yeah – but then 'e went home to Liverpool for a few months so they got someone else in doing a Scouse accent. He 'ates people goin' on about *The Ink Black Heart*. When 'e saw my tattoos 'e were a right bastard about them . . . 'e's . . .'

But Zoe left the thought unfinished. They walked on in silence for a while, with Robin wondering whether it was a good or bad idea to bring up the game.

'Edie Ledwell spoke to me once,' said Zoe, breaking the silence. 'On Twitter.'

She spoke of it in a hushed, awed voice, as though of a religious experience.

'Wow, really?' said Robin.

'Yeah. It was the day me mum died.'

'Oh, I'm so sorry,' said Robin.

'I weren't livin' with 'er,' said Zoe quietly. 'She were . . . She 'ad a lot of problems. She 'ad to be sectioned twice. She did drugs. That's why I were in care, mostly. Me foster mum told me she'd died an' gave me a day off school. I went on Twitter an' I said me mum 'ad died that day. An' Edie Ledwell spoke to me. She—'

Robin looked down: the girl's face had crumpled. She could have been a ninety-year-old woman or a baby with that expression of anguish, her tears making no impression on the thickly applied kohl, and Robin suddenly remembered Edie Ledwell's smeared eyeliner as she'd wept at the office.

'—she were really nice,' said Zoe through sobs. 'I told 'er me foster mum 'ad just told me an' she said she were in care an' all. An' she sent me a h-hug an' I told 'er – I told 'er she was my 'eroine an' – an' I loved 'er. I said that . . . I *did* tell 'er that . . .'

'Have a tissue,' said Robin quietly, pulling some out of her tote bag.

'S-sorry,' said Zoe. 'I jus' – I wish – like, people were 'orrible to 'er online and I were – I didn't – like, people were sayin' there was tons of stuff wrong with the cartoon an' – but – I dunno, I never thought there were nuthin' wrong with it, but then when I read what people were sayin' it sort of made sense – but I wish I 'adn't – me b-boyfriend says we didn't do nuthin' wrong but—'

Robin's mobile rang. Inwardly cursing the caller, she fished it out of her bag. It was Strike.

'Hi,' he said. 'How'd it go at North Grove?'

'I said everything I had to say to you last weekend,' said Robin coldly. 'I'm busy, OK?'

'Right you are,' said Strike, who sounded amused. 'Call me when you're not busy.'

'No, *you* are,' said Robin, and hung up.

'Your ex?' said Zoe in a small voice. She was mopping her face with the tissue Robin had given her.

'Yeah,' said Robin, stuffing the mobile back in her bag. 'Go on, what were you saying?'

'Oh, nuthin',' said Zoe hopelessly.

They walked on, the only sound from Zoe an occasional sniff. Highgate Hill was a long and well-lit street along which plenty of traffic was still moving. A group of youths cat-called the two women as they passed on the opposite side of the road.

'Bugger off,' said Robin under her breath, and Zoe smiled weakly.

'I met Josh Blay,' Zoe said, her voice slightly croaky now.

'Seriously?' said Robin, appropriately impressed.

'Yeah. 'E come to stay at North Grove for a month before 'e and Edie were ... were attacked.'

'Did you talk to him?' said Robin, sure she already knew the answer.

'No, I were too scared! I walked in the kitchen an' he were just standin' there.'

And you were shaking.

'An' I was, like, *shakin'*,' said Zoe with a tearful little laugh. 'Mariam introduced me an' I couldn't talk. I never got the courage up.'

But it was evident to Robin that Zoe was a rarity in the *Ink Black Heart* fandom: someone who'd esteemed Edie Ledwell more highly than Josh Blay.

'What was he like?' Robin asked Zoe.

'Stoned,' said Zoe with a sad smile. 'Mostly. 'E didn't like meetin' people. 'E stayed in 'is room a lot an' 'e kept playin' that Strokes song, "Is This It" over an' over again ... and then 'e set fire to the room.'

'He did what?' said Robin, feigning surprise again.

'Well, Mariam thought it were Josh,' said Zoe, 'but *I* don't think it were.'

'Who, then?'

'Shouldn't say ... wanna keep my job.'

Robin considered pressing her, but having built up trust, was afraid of breaking it.

'What d'you do at North Grove, anyway?'

'All sorts,' said Zoe. 'When I got to London I went to visit it, just to see ... just to see where it all 'appened. I went in the shop an' got talkin' to Mariam. She were proper nice about me tattoos an' I told 'er a bit about being a big fan and that, an' about just leavin' care, an' she said, did I 'ave a job, an' I said no, an' she offered me one.

'I 'elp out with this class Mariam takes on Tuesdays with kids who've got special needs. Edie used to do it when she were livin' at North Grove,' said Zoe with a slight return of the holy voice. 'An' I wash brushes an' do a bit of cookin', and I babysit the kids a bit. Star's all right, Freyja's kid, but Bram's ... well, 'e's bigger 'n me. 'E don't give a shit if I tell 'im t'do anything.'

They turned at last into Junction Road.

'Hey,' said Robin, as though the thought had only just occurred to her, 'you didn't ever play that game, did you? That those fans made, about *The Ink Black Heart*? I'm only asking 'cause I did, a bit,' said Robin. 'A few years back. I just got really into the cartoon. The game was quite good, seeing it was supposed to be made by amateurs.'

'Yeah,' said Zoe cautiously, 'I played it a coupla times . . . what were your username? Maybe we talked to each other in there.'

'It was – bloody hell, I can't remember now,' said Robin with a little laugh. 'InkHarty or something.'

'There's tons of InkHartys,' said Zoe, which was precisely why Robin had chosen the name.

They passed a toy shop, Zoe's gaunt reflection sliding across rows of plastic figurines.

'I live oop there,' she said, pointing to the narrow corner building Robin had already seen in Strike's photo.

'Yeah? Got flatmates?'

'Not really. There's other people in there, but I've just got a box room,' said Zoe. 'It's got a sink,' she added, almost defensively.

'London property,' said Robin with an eye-roll.

'Yeah,' said Zoe. 'Well – it's been nice talkin' to you. Nice to meet someone from Yorkshire,' she added.

'Yeah,' said Robin warmly. 'Hope I see you next week. I'm gonna go to the police station and hand this purse in.'

'D'you live far from 'ere?'

'No. Short walk. See you.'

Zoe smiled and disappeared around the corner. Robin walked on. After crossing the road she glanced back and saw Zoe letting herself into the corner building via the side door.

Robin pulled out her mobile and, still walking, called Strike back.

'Evening,' he said. 'How'd it go?'

'Pretty well,' said Robin, now looking around for a cab. 'I met Preston Pierce and your girl with all the tattoos.'

'Seriously?'

'Yeah. She's working at North Grove and – hang on, that's a taxi,' said Robin, flagging it down.

Having given the driver her address and got in, Robin raised her mobile to her ear again while groping in her bag for notebook and pen. She wanted to write down everything she'd just heard from Zoe before she forgot any of it.

'Her real name's Zoe Haigh,' said Robin. 'But in the game she's moderator Worm28.'

'You serious?'

'Yep,' said Robin, pulling off her pen lid with her teeth. 'She came down to London to be with her boyfriend and it clearly isn't going well between them. Worm28 told me in the game "I wish I could tell you where I'm working" – Zoe's working at North Grove. Worm28 told me she met Josh Blay but couldn't talk to him and just stood there shaking. Zoe's just told me exactly the same thing.'

'Bloody hell. Didn't I say we were due a breakthrough?'

'There was other stuff,' said Robin, scribbling in the notebook open on her lap. 'Something about her boyfriend telling her they "hadn't done anything wrong". She seemed to be feeling guilty, although it might just have been for criticising *The Ink Black Heart* online. She loved the cartoon, but she seems to have been persuaded by the arguments that it was ableist and all the rest of it.'

'Her boyfriend's got to be one of the three who met Nils at the Red Lion and Sun,' said Strike. 'My money's on Wally Cardew.'

'You think?' said Robin.

'Can you see how she'd fit into Montgomery's life? He's living with his girlfriend, he's holding down a good job: what would he want with Zoe?'

'It could've started as an online flirtation she took a lot more seriously than he did. He might not've realised she was going to up sticks and move to be near him.'

'I can't see that happening to Montgomery. Why would he let an online flirtation develop into a situation that might jeopardise his nice life? Cardew hasn't got a girlfriend, from what we've got on him so far, and he's a reckless tosser. I could imagine him sleeping with young fans and getting a shock when one of them decided to move to London to be near him.'

'What about Tim Ashcroft?'

'Pukka public-school type … I dunno, it could be him, but I'd imagine he'd go for someone a bit more—'

'Cashmere sweater?' Robin suggested.

'Well, yeah.'

'He's an actor. He might be attracted to more bohemian types. And don't forget her username in the game. Ashcroft played The Worm.'

'There's that,' said Strike, although he didn't sound convinced.

'Zoe said something else,' Robin went on, still making notes on a page that was turning alternately orange and grey as the taxi passed beneath streetlights. 'She doesn't think Blay set fire to his own bedroom, but she wouldn't tell me who did. Said she wanted to keep her job.'

'Interesting,' said Strike.

'I know ... but I've got bad news too,' said Robin. 'I had to get out of the game. Anomie's given an order that mods need to keep an eye out for people who log into the game but don't play. He thinks the police might be spying on fans, which might explain the fact that he's not on there much himself at the moment.'

'Inconvenient,' said Strike, 'but not irretrievable. We'll just have to make sure you do a good bit of playing in the next few days to allay suspicion. What about Pierce?'

A mental image of Preston Pierce's large penis intruded immediately into Robin's mind and was firmly repressed.

'He came close to asking me out for a drink.'

'Fast work,' commented Strike, who didn't sound particularly pleased about it.

'I turned him down in favour of walking Zoe home. I think it was the right call. I couldn't interrogate him and keep an eye on the game. Anyway, there's next week ...

'There's one other thing,' said Robin, 'which seems – well, it could be a huge coincidence, but – there's this stained-glass window in the communal kitchen. Mariam made it, the woman who took my class. It's been there five or six years, according to Pierce.

'There's – I think it must be a quotation, but I don't know – words written across the top of it, anyway – about anomie. The window shows a kind of idealised commune and the people represented on it have all been at the collective, or are friends of Mariam's, apparently. And over the top of the picture there's this quote about the conditions under which it's impossible to feel anomie. Something about organs being in solidarity with each other?'

Robin could almost hear Strike thinking in the pause that followed. At last he said,

'Well, coincidences happen, but that feels like a *hell* of a coincidence.'

'You think that's where Anomie got the idea for the name?'

'I'd've thought it's a strong possibility.'

'All of them were at North Grove at some point. The whole cast.'

'You've done a bloody good night's work there, Robin.'

Robin thought she heard a woman's voice in the background, from Strike's end of the call. Television, or Madeline Courson-Miles?

'I'd better go,' she said quickly. 'Speak tomorrow.'

She hung up before Strike could respond.

41

But there comes an idealess lad,
With a strut, and a stare, and a smirk . . .

Constance Naden
Natural Selection

The condition of Strike's stump was deteriorating. In spite of his twice-daily applications of cream, the skin beneath the gel pad remained irritated and inflamed. He was afraid he might be looking at the early signs of choke syndrome, whereby the skin would ulcerate and break down, yet he made no doctor's appointment. What was the point? He couldn't afford to stop working. The addition of surveillance on Jago Ross had rendered their current roster of investigations unsustainable. The only solution was to find new subcontractors who might be drafted in to help.

Having exhausted all his police and army contacts, Strike went back through every previous temporary hire he'd decided against making permanent. Finally, and in desperation, he succeeded in re-hiring, on a weekly contract that could be terminated without notice at either party's behest, an ex-Red Cap by the name of Stewart Nutley who, three years previously, had driven his moped into the rear of a taxi he was supposed to be following. Strike had bawled Nutley out for the offence and sacked him on the spot, so it was with minimal enthusiasm that he rang the man and ate some humble pie. A gap-toothed, mouse-haired married man in his early thirties, Nutley's resting expression was unattractively self-satisfied. As he hadn't managed to hold down a civilian investigative job since he and Strike parted ways, Nutley was keen to prove his worth to an agency that had gained greatly in prestige since he'd left it. While nobody on the team was particularly enamoured of the new hire, all were grateful for another pair of legs and eyes.

Meanwhile Madeline's new collection was due to launch in a week's time, which meant she wasn't free to see Strike at all – which, as he acknowledged to himself while expressing regret to Madeline, was convenient. Her state of high tension translated itself into long monologues by phone.

'I shouldn't've made the collection so big. Never, *ever* again. Listen – will you come and meet me after the launch is over? I need to cut loose: this has been the worst one ever. I want to be with someone who doesn't give a shit about jewellery – I want to be with *you* – and I want a drink and a fuck.'

Strike had no objection to most of this programme and yet a suspicion, born of the invitation to the literary launch, prompted him to say:

'*After* it's over, right? You aren't asking me to come in? Because there'll be press, won't there?'

'Yeah,' she said, 'but – OK, no, don't come in, not if you don't want to.'

'Great, well, I'll meet you afterwards. What time will it be over?'

'Nine,' she said, and then, '*Please* come if you can. I'm missing you and if I know you're coming to take me away from it all I'll be able to look happy for pictures.'

'You should be happy anyway,' he said. 'The stuff you've shown me looked incredible.'

'Oh, Corm, you're so sweet,' she said tearfully. 'It all looks like complete *crap* to me at the moment, but I always feel like this right before a launch – or I *think* I do, but it always happens in such a blur I can't be sure.'

So Strike (still in the spirit of giving a proper relationship a chance) had committed to meeting Madeline after her launch, although he'd noted that what she wanted was for him to pick her up, whereas he wanted to meet her well away from the place he was sure Charlotte would be. To articulate this concern would be to open a door onto another conversation he didn't want to have, so the plan was left vague, both he and Madeline, perhaps, determined that their preference would prevail.

Meanwhile a couple of welcome absences temporarily alleviated pressure on the agency: Groomer took off to Morocco for ten days and Fingers flew to New York to visit his adoring mother and the stepfather who suspected him of being a thief.

'So this is our opportunity,' Strike told the team during a pep talk by conference call (there being no time for a face-to-face team meeting), 'to rule out a few Anomie suspects.'

The first Monday in May, which was a bank holiday, saw Strike limping into the Lismore Circus estate shortly after dawn, there to keep watch over the three-bedroomed maisonette where Wally Cardew lived with his grandmother and sister. By eight o'clock there'd been only two signs of life from within the flat: somebody had opened the curtains, and a pure white cat had leapt up onto the window sill to stare out across the estate with the superciliousness peculiar to its species.

According to housing records, the YouTuber and his sister had lived in this same maisonette with their grandmother for the past twenty years. Wally's sister, who worked in a local chemist's, resembled her brother in being tow-headed and Scandinavian in appearance, though she was voluptuous where her brother was short and stocky, with large round blue eyes and full lips. Shah and Barclay had both independently informed Strike, out of earshot of Robin, Midge and Pat, that they'd be happy to keep watching Chloe Cardew for as long as the case might require, or indeed after it was no longer necessary.

While Strike watched the flat in Gospel Oak, Robin was sitting at the window of a Croydon café by the name of the Saucy Sausage, which was situated directly opposite the house of Yasmin Weatherhead and her parents. She was relieved to be out of the office, where she'd recently put in many more hours playing the game in order to allay Anomie's suspicions that she might be there to spy on other players. This had entailed a few more private chats with Worm28, who'd told her artlessly she'd met a nice woman from 'where I used to live', but hadn't let anything more slip about her boyfriend or about Anomie's identity. Strike, who sympathised with Robin's desire to do something other than stare at her iPad all day, had agreed that she could watch Yasmin, who was a person of second-tier interest compared to the plausible Anomie suspects.

Yasmin's street had an air of sleepy respectability. On one side was a row of local shops and on the other a terrace of middle-sized houses with small front gardens. Robin was alternating between watching the front of Yasmin's parents' house and keeping an eye on the game and Twitter, on which Anomie had already been active that morning.

Anomie
@AnomieGamemaster

Heavy Fedwell reported to be looking forward to hiring multiple nannies for the kids she keeps littering, once the #InkBlackCashIn starts.

9.06 am   4 May 2015

Every Anomie suspect under surveillance had been inside their respective houses and out of sight when Anomie posted these words. Kea Niven remained unwatched due to lack of personnel, although ·Strike had decided to leave a new, carefully crafted message on the Nivens' answering machine, which was designed to play on Kea's fear of what Blay would think of her if she refused to help their investigation.

At ten past ten, Robin, who was already on her third cup of coffee to justify her continuing presence at the Saucy Sausage, and who hadn't yet caught any glimpse of Yasmin Weatherhead, received a call from Strike.

'Wally and his mate MJ have just come out of his flat. I'm following them. What's Anomie's game status?'

'Absent,' sighed Robin as she navigated Buffypaws past the vampire drifting along one of the game's paths.

'Think they're heading towards the Tube,' Strike told Robin, wincing as he sped up to keep the two younger men in sight. 'MJ's carrying a video camera. This'd be an ideal opportunity for Anomie to drop into the game. Cardew's not on his phone.'

'I'm starting to think Anomie knows exactly when it would be helpful to drop into the game, and avoids it on purpose,' said Robin bitterly.

'Any sign of Yasmin?'

'No. Nobody's left the house since nine this morning. Well, it is a bank holiday.'

'Hang on,' said Strike.

Robin waited.

'Someone else is following them,' said Strike in a low voice.

'Police?' said Robin, so sharply that the waitress looked round at her.

'No,' said Strike. 'I don't think so. I'll call you back.'

He hung up.

The man Strike had noticed was hard to miss. He was at least six feet tall and his buzzcut was so short he was almost shaven-headed, though he also sported a bushy beard and moustache. He'd been leaning up against a wall, apparently texting, when Wally and MJ approached, but once they'd passed he'd pocketed his phone and set off in pursuit, hands in the pockets of his jeans. On the back of his old leather jacket was a skull and crossbones topped with a steel helmet. He had many visible tattoos, and while the Union Jack on the side of his neck and the gothic cross on the back of his left hand might have been fake, the large skull tattooed on the back of his head, and visible through the millimetres of stubble, certainly couldn't be, which ruled the man out as a disguised police officer.

The unknown man entered the same Tube carriage as Wally and MJ, and Strike followed. The YouTubers were deep in conversation and didn't seem to have noticed either of the men following them. Strike took a couple of surreptitious photographs of the unknown man on his phone, noting a further tattoo on his Adam's apple which the detective, though no expert on the Futhark, couldn't help thinking looked like a Norse rune.

After a twenty-minute journey, they arrived at Embankment, where Wally and MJ got out, followed, firstly, by the tattooed man and, secondly, by Strike.

The four men, two of them still oblivious to the fact they were being followed, headed into Whitehall Gardens, where Wally took a handheld microphone out of his backpack and MJ switched on the camera.

The purpose of coming to Whitehall Gardens on a bank holiday became clear when Wally and MJ began waylaying tourists and asking them, as far as Strike could see, to be interviewed on camera. A pair of Japanese girls were first, then a family who, judging from the small boy's football strip, were from Brazil. Strike was too far away to hear what questions Wally was asking, but as each interview progressed he saw the interviewees' expressions change from polite or giggly to bemused, dismayed or, in the case of the Brazilian father, angry. Strike surmised that the point of today's video was to take the piss out of foreigners. The tattooed man in the leather jacket sat down on a bench a hundred yards away, openly watching the filming. Deciding against sitting down himself, in case the bearded observer noted Strike mirroring his behaviour, the detective took up a position behind a statue of Henry Bartle Frere, a nineteenth-century colonial administrator, and looked up Viking runes on his phone, where he found the very mark the bearded man was sporting so proudly on his throat. It resembled an angular letter P and its name was Thurisaz, which, according to the internet, signified danger, chaos and brute strength.

Strike was just putting his mobile back into his pocket when it rang. 'Cormoran Strike.'

'Hello?' said a weak female voice, in barely more than a whisper.

'Hi,' said Strike. 'Who's this?'

'Um ... Kea Niven.'

'Ah, great,' said Strike. It looked as though his guilt-tripping voicemail message had done the job. 'Thanks for getting back to me, Kea. I take it you know what this is about?'

'Yes ... Anomie,' she whispered. 'Yes. But I ... I don't know anything.'

She sounded far younger than twenty-five. If he hadn't known, he might have thought she was thirteen.

'Would it be all right to meet face to face and talk?'

'I'm ... I'm not well. I ... don't think that will be possible.'

'I'm more than happy to come to your house, if that helps,' said Strike.

'No, I ... I don't think I'd be able to ... but I *do* want to help,' she whispered. 'I really do. So I ... thought I'd call and ... and tell you I ... don't know anything.'

'Right,' said Strike. 'Well, it's probably only fair to tell you, Kea, that there's a theory out there that *you're* Anomie.'

There was no need whatsoever to say that the theory was his partner's.

'I – *what?*'

'That you're Anomie,' repeated Strike.

'Who ...? Oh my God ... does Josh ... does *Josh* think that?'

'He wants me to find out who Anomie is,' said Strike, avoiding a direct answer. 'But if you're too unwell to speak to me—'

'I ... oh – oh God ...'

A storm of dry sobs followed. They might have been genuine; they might not, but it wasn't Strike's job to offer comfort. He watched pigeons wheeling against the cloudy sky until at last Kea said:

'Why ... why can't I just tell you *now*? ... I don't know anything ... I'm not Anomie! I'd never ... *never* ...'

'Look, I just wanted to give you an opportunity to speak for yourself,' said Strike. 'I also wanted to show you a few things—'

'*What* things?'

'Photographs,' said Strike, which wasn't entirely untrue. The screenshots he'd taken of her Twitter activity were photos of a type. 'And documents,' he added, to add a bit of extra intrigue. Documents always sounded scary.

'Well, why c–can't you just email them to me?'

'Because they're confidential,' said Strike.

There was another long pause.

'I . . . All right . . .'

'You'll let me come and talk to you?'

'Yes, I suppose . . . yes.'

'What day's good for you?' asked Strike.

'Not this week,' she said hastily. 'I'm too ill. Um . . . maybe Thursday next week?'

That was the day of Madeline's launch. Strike could have done without a five- or six-hour round trip to King's Lynn beforehand, but as his priority had to be ruling out as many Anomie suspects as possible, he said:

'Great. Well, I'll be coming from London, so I could be with you around eleven, if that suits you?'

'Yes,' whispered Kea. 'All right, then.'

'And keep this between ourselves, please,' Strike added.

'Who . . . who would I tell?'

'I just mean that talking about our investigation will hamper it and, as you can imagine, Josh is very keen for us to succeed.'

After hanging up, Strike texted Robin to tell her that an interview had been arranged and received a one-word answer: 'Great.'

Strike had just put his phone back in his pocket when Nutley, who was supposed to have Gus Upcott under surveillance, called.

'What's up?' asked Strike.

'I'm on the young bloke, right?'

'What d'you mean?' said Strike, trying not to sound too irritable.

'The old geezer's just come out of the house.'

'In a wheelchair?'

'No. Walking with a stick. And he's talking on his mobile.'

'Stay where you are unless the son goes out,' said Strike. 'What about the other family members?'

'The wife took the daughter out about half an hour ago, in the car.'

'OK, well, you're on Gus.'

'Roger that.'

Nutley hung up.

Wally and MJ had now succeeded in persuading a group of Chinese students to talk to them. The tattooed man, or Thurisaz, as Strike had now mentally dubbed him, had vanished from his bench. Strike was left thinking about Inigo Upcott, walking with a stick on his wasted legs now that his wife had left the house, and taking a call where the only family member remaining in the house couldn't disturb him.

He called Nutley back.

'Follow the old bloke.'

'What?'

'Follow him. Can you still see him?'

'Yeah, he's not moving fast.'

'Well, get after him. Ideally, find out what he's talking about.'

After hanging up again, Strike asked himself what he was playing at and found no good answer. He didn't like hunches or intuitions, which in his opinion were generally prejudice or blind guesswork. Nevertheless, he knew that if he'd been watching the Upcotts' house he'd have gone after Inigo.

Meanwhile, in the Saucy Sausage, Robin, who was now on her fourth cup of coffee, had succeeded for the first time in making direct contact with the moderator called Fiendy1, to whom she'd never previously spoken on a private channel, and who she'd inveigled into it by expressing frustration at one of the more difficult tasks in the game.

> **Buffypaws:** I've tried everything.
> EVERY-FRIGGING-
> THING.
>
> **Fiendy1:** lol
>
> **Fiendy1:** you're not the only one.
> We're always getting logjams at
> Wombwell's tomb
>
> **Buffypaws:** Help me
>
> **Fiendy1:** you need to try Drekisms.
>
> **Buffypaws:** I've tried them all

Fiendy1: it's an obscure one. Try
and think what Drek would say if a
stone lion wouldn't let him past

Buffypaws: ?

Buffypaws: I'm supposed to be
working and all I can think about
is how to get past a stone lion

Fiendy1: Clue: series 2, episode 3

Buffypaws: ok that'll help, but if
I get fired for watching the Ink
Black Heart at work it's on you

Fiendy1: lol why're you working?
It's a bank hol

Buffypaws: small business, don't
have to abide by bank holiday rules

Buffypaws: you got the day off?

Fiendy1: yeah but no

Buffypaws: ?

Fiendy1: got the day off but the
Dear Leader wants me in here
moderating til 6pm

Fiendy1: punishment for going to
the footie on Saturday

Robin wrote 'Fiendy1 football fan' in her notebook. At random,
she suggested:

Buffypaws: M********* U**?

Fiendy1: ha no. but I loved
seeing WBA beat them.

Fiendy1: you a M** U fan?

Robin had virtually no interest in football, but deciding that Google
would be her friend if she needed to fake an interest, she typed:

Buffypaws: yeah

Fiendy1: lol sorry then

Buffypaws: u?

Fiendy1: the W*****

Robin took out her phone and took a picture of this exchange.

Buffypaws: why doesn't Anomie
like u going to the football?

Fiendy1: I forgot I was supposed
to be modding so Hartella had to
do it all by herself all day

Reminded that she was supposed to be watching the Weatherhead house, Robin glanced up through the café window again.

A young woman was walking in lumbering fashion down the garden path. She had long, thick dark-blonde hair and wore a knee-length black cardigan, which didn't successfully disguise the excess weight she was carrying. Robin couldn't see her face, because she was looking down, fiddling with her phone. Opening the garden gate, the young woman Robin assumed to be Yasmin stepped out onto the pavement and stopped, still concentrating on her phone.

Robin glanced back down at her iPad screen. Fiendy1 was still messaging her.

Fiendy1: I was threatened with loss
of moderator status, the works

Fiendy1: you know his motto

'Could I pay, please?' Robin asked the waitress, groping in her purse for some cash.

Across the road, Yasmin had looked up. She had a pale, flat, round face and was now watching the oncoming traffic. While the waitress was fetching her bill, Robin hastily answered Fiendy1.

Buffypaws: what motto?

Fiendy1: oderint dum metuant

Fiendy1: you must've seen him say it

Fiendy1: he says it all the fkn
time

Robin hastily took a picture of this exchange, too.

Buffypaws: shit that's my supervisor

Fiendy1: ok cya

<Private channel has closed>

Robin shoved her iPad back in her bag, paid her bill and left the Saucy Sausage with her mobile in her hand.

A dark red Ford Fiesta was slowing down, driven by a white man Robin didn't recognise. Raising her phone, Robin filmed Yasmin beaming and waving at the driver. The car drew up in front of her, Yasmin got in and they drove away. The number plate, Robin noticed, terminated in the letters CBS, which happened to be Strike's initials.

42

After a thirty-minute absence, the tattooed man reappeared in Whitehall Gardens, now talking on his mobile and wandering between flowerbeds and benches. Strike, who'd been treating himself to a sit-down on a bench, once again retreated behind the statue of Henry Bartle Frere, his leg throbbing, and hoping the YouTubers would soon have enough footage of disconcerted foreigners to break for lunch.

Sure enough, at close to one o'clock Wally and MJ stopped filming. Strike, who was now wearing sunglasses and faking a phone conversation, watched as Wally put the microphone in his backpack, took out his mobile and began typing on his phone. Now, at last, the tall, tattooed, bearded man walked purposefully towards Wally, and greeted him.

The detective was too far away to hear what was being said, but he could have sworn he saw Thurisaz's lips form the words 'big fan'. Thurisaz and Wally shook hands, then talked for ten minutes, both laughing more frequently as the conversation progressed, MJ's expression becoming progressively less happy.

Finally, Strike saw a proposal being made. Wally seemed keen to accept. He turned to MJ, who shook his head. After a couple of minutes' further discussion, MJ set off in the opposite direction to the other two, carrying his video camera, while Wally and Thurisaz left the gardens and walked towards Villiers Street.

Strike had been following for less than a minute, trying to ignore the mounting pain in his leg, when his mobile rang yet again: Robin.

'Anomie entered the game about ten minutes ago, but he's inactive. Present, but not speaking, just hovering there. He could be talking to someone on a private channel – but this is the important bit: Barclay's just texted me – Tim Ashcroft's sitting in a café, typing on a laptop. He started typing about ten minutes ago.'

'Well, I'll match Barclay and raise you one suspected white suprem-acist,' panted Strike, who was struggling not to limp too obviously. 'About ten minutes ago, Cardew started typing on his phone, but was interrupted by a large tattooed guy who's been tailing him all morning and who I'd bet a grand is a paid-up member of the Brotherhood of Ultima Thule.'

'Seriously?'

'Yeah,' panted Strike, who was struggling to maintain the same pace as the two men ahead. 'He's got a rune tattooed on his Adam's apple. Think I'm witnessing an attempted in-person recruitment. MJ got ditched and Cardew and Rune Man are walking towards a second location. Any news from the others?'

'No. Preston Pierce went out to buy bread and he's back home. Montgomery hasn't left his flat all day. I haven't heard from Nutley, so I assume Gus is still at home too.'

'Nutley isn't on Gus any more.'

'You haven't sacked him again?' said Robin anxiously.

'No, he's following orders. I'll explain later.'

'OK,' said Robin. 'I'm about to send you a video. It isn't urgent.'

'I'll look once I'm stationary. Keep me posted on Anomie.'

Strike hung up.

The pair he was tailing turned into a narrow alley called Craven Passage and were headed towards a pub called the Ship & Shovell, which was in fact a pub in two halves, which faced each other across the alley. Both establishments had red doors and window frames and sported identical signs showing a portly bewigged seventeenth-century seaman. Wally and Thurisaz entered the bar on the right.

Relieved to stop walking, Strike waited a full five minutes and smoked a cigarette outside before entering the pub himself.

Wooden booths lined one side of the small bar, which was very crowded. In one of the booths nearest the door sat Wally, Thurisaz and a third individual, of whom Strike could see nothing but the sleeve of a corduroy jacket, due to the fact that three German tourists were standing in the way.

Having bought himself a pint of Badger beer, Strike found a standing space as close to the booth as he could manage without being in direct sight of any of his targets. The loud buzz of the pub muffled most of their conversation, but by dint of long practice the detective was able to tune out some of the surrounding clamour and catch a small amount of what was passing between the three men in whom he was interested.

Thurisaz's voice was unexpectedly soft. The man in the corduroy jacket sounded upper middle class and was currently complimenting Wally on his YouTube output, evincing an in-depth knowledge of Cardew's videos that the latter must surely find very flattering. At one point, Wally adopted the Drek falsetto:

'*You is no mukfluk, bwah!*' and his two companions roared with obliging laughter.

After a while, plates of food were delivered to Wally's table. The pub was becoming still more crowded: Strike, who could hear less and less of their conversation, took out his phone and opened the video Robin had sent him.

He watched as the pale overweight girl in the long black cardigan beamed and waved at the driver of the dark red Ford Fiesta, which pulled up, then set off again with Yasmin in the passenger seat. Frowning slightly, Strike rewound and watched again, then a third time. He paused the video at the point the driver's profile was most evident, then enlarged the picture, examining it for close to a minute before texting Robin.

The driver of the car in your vid is Phillip Ormond

Her reply came barely a minute later.

omg

knew there was something off about his reaction when I mentioned her. We'll need to follow this up. What's Anomie up to?

In the game but still not moving or speaking. Barclay says Ashcroft's still typing. Where's Cardew?

in the pub flirting with the alt-right

Worm28's just told me Anomie's favourite motto is oderint dum metuant

'Let them hate, so long as they fear'

Makes sense. Also had a private chat with Fiendy1 earlier. What football team would The W*** be?**

The Whites = Leeds Utd. Also known as the P*******

The what?

I'll let you work it out

Smiling slightly, Strike slipped his mobile back into his pocket, resting nearly all his weight on his real foot and trying to ignore the smarting end of his stump and his throbbing hamstring.

A group of new arrivals were now crowding in on Strike, talking in what he thought might be Finnish. Capitalising on the apparent necessity to move out of their way, he edged closer to the booth and was just able to catch phrases and snatches of the man in the corduroy jacket's speech, which sounded like a pitch.

'... and, I mean, where does that leave humour? Well, you know that better than any ... myself as a race realist. Have you read Jared Taylor? You should read him, it's all ... disenfranchisement, marginalisation, replacement ... listen, you're a master ... broad-based appeal ... shift the culture ... acceptable discourse ...'

Strike eased his weight tentatively back onto his false leg. He needed a pee. Once back from the bathroom, he'd try to snatch a picture of Wally's companions using a conveniently placed mirror.

The detective took a single step in the direction of the stairs leading to the basement, but got no further. His false foot had caught itself in the strap of a bag on the floor, placed there by one of the Finnish women. Attempting in vain to right himself, Strike's hand slid off the wooden frame of Wally's booth; he crashed into one of the Finnish men, who gave a shout of surprise as he was knocked sideways, then fell heavily to the floor. Miraculously, Strike's empty pint glass didn't shatter, but rolled away.

The whole pub had turned to stare. Making sure to keep his face turned away from the group in the booth, the humiliated Strike waved away the multitude of hands offered to help him up. He could tell, by the solicitous enquiries of the Finns, all of whom spoke perfect English, that the metal rod of his prosthesis had been revealed in the fall. Furious, he managed to struggle back to his feet and limped off towards the steep stairs, down which his now shaking stump was barely able to support him.

Once in the bathroom, he staggered into a cubicle, locked the door, slammed down the toilet lid and dropped down onto it, breathing hard, fingers fumbling at his trouser leg. The knee of his stump, which had taken most of the impact of his fall, was already already swelling. He probed the back of his thigh with his fingers: his hamstring felt as though it could have torn again. Pain came in waves, with an edge of nausea. He castigated himself for not noticing the bag. He'd have been fine if only his real foot had caught it: it was the total lack of feeling that had done for him.

He heard the bathroom door open outside, prayed whoever it was wouldn't want a shit, and heard with relief the sound of urine hitting the urinal. Pushing himself back up into a standing position, he lifted the toilet seat again and had a pee himself, one hand steadying himself on the cubicle wall.

It wasn't a long walk to the office from here, but he doubted he'd be able to make it without doing himself further damage, so it would have to be a taxi. He opened the cubicle door.

Facing him – clearly waiting for him – was the bearded, rune-marked man he'd tailed from Wally's estate. Tall and broad, exuding aggression, Thurisaz stared unblinkingly into the detective's eyes, then took a step forwards, placing them toe to toe.

Three seconds passed – longer than it had taken for the vehicle in which Sergeant Strike of the Royal Military Police had been travelling to explode, ripping off half his leg; long enough for Strike to deduce that his bearded friend had evidently clocked him at some point, during all their hours tailing the same targets; ample time for a once gifted boxer to read the way this was about to go. Others might have said 'excuse me', or 'is there a problem?', might even have raised their hands in meek surrender and suggested they talk things out, but Strike's amygdala had taken control, flooding him with adrenalin that temporarily obliterated his excruciating pain.

He feinted with his left hand to Thurisaz's head. The latter swerved out of the way, swinging at Strike in turn, but too late: Strike had hit him hard in the solar plexus with his right. He felt his fist sink deep into the man's soft belly, heard the breath leave his lungs in a high-pitched wheeze, watched him double over and, satisfyingly, slip on what might have been his own piss on the floor. Winded, Thurisaz fell to one knee and Strike set off at a fast hobble for the door.

Face now contorted in pain, because the swivel involved in the punch had ground the inflamed end of his stump against the pros-thesis, Strike hauled himself upstairs, eager to reach the street before Thurisaz regained his wind. Wally and Corduroy Jacket had van-ished; evidently the attack dog had been sent to take care of the man who appeared to have been keeping them under surveillance while they beat a retreat.

Whichever deity it was who granted small mercies following fuck-ups, they were smiling on Cormoran Strike. A black cab came driving down Craven Street as the detective emerged, sweaty-faced, from Craven Passage, arm raised.

'Denmark Street,' he gasped, grappling for the door handle and heaving himself inside.

As the cab pulled away from the kerb Strike looked back through the rear window just in time to see Thurisaz emerge from the alley at a run, looking wildly up and down the street. His lips clearly formed the word 'fuck'. Strike turned to face forward again. He knew he'd now damaged his leg well past the point he'd be able to walk on it. The prospect of getting up three flights of metal stairs to his attic flat was appalling: there was a good chance he'd have to heave himself up them backwards while sitting on his arse, like a small child.

His phone rang again. Expecting Robin, he tugged it out of his pocket to see Nutley's number.

'Hi,' said Strike, trying not to sound as though he was suffering as much as he was. 'What's going on?'

'Got some stuff on the old guy with the stick,' said Nutley, who sounded pleased with himself. 'Mr Upcott.'

'Go on,' said Strike, while sweat passed in waves down his body.

'He's playing away,' said Nutley. 'He was on the phone to her for nigh on fifty minutes. We ended up in a café. I was back to back with him. I could hear nearly all of it.'

'How d'you know it was a woman on the other end?'

'Well, you can just tell, can't you?' said Nutley. 'Tone of his voice. "My darling child." "Listen, sweetheart." Sounded like she was worried they'd been found out. She was doing most of the talking. He was reassuring her. I took some notes,' said Nutley, as though this was something that would have only occurred to a man of extraordinary initiative. '"You needn't worry." "I shall take care of all that." "I have things fully in hand at this end." Sounded like she was properly scared of something. Probably her husband. "You have nothing to blame yourself for."'

'Did he notice you, d'you think?'

'Well, he looked at me on the way out of the café, but otherwise—'

'Get out of there.'

'I don't think he—'

'Get out of there,' repeated Strike, more aggressively. He didn't want two members of the agency becoming identifiable to targets; one gigantic mistake today was enough. 'You won't be able to watch the Upcotts again.'

'If I hadn't followed him to the café, I wouldn't've heard—'

'I know that,' said Strike. It was extremely tempting to redirect his anger at himself onto Nutley, but he needed the idiot. 'You can cover one of the other suspects going forwards. Good work on listening in to the call,' he added through gritted teeth.

Mollified, Nutley rang off. Strike sat back in the taxi, the pain in his right leg coursing through his entire body, tempted to offer the cabbie fifty quid to drive him around for a while, just so he could keep the weight off his stump a bit longer.

43

Given the agency's workload and the imminence of both Groomer's and Fingers' returns to the UK, Strike could hardly have chosen a worse moment to put himself out of action, but other possible ramifications of his bungled surveillance job on Cardew troubled him even more than the additional workload he was heaping on his colleagues. There had to be a possibility that Thurisaz, putative member of the Brotherhood of Ultima Thule and, perhaps, The Halvening, had recognised Strike as a private detective. This fear prompted Strike to call DCI Ryan Murphy the following morning and apprise him of what had happened.

'I got pictures of the guy with the rune on his throat and can send them over,' Strike concluded, in an attempt to mitigate the impression of ineptitude left by a story that had sounded no less embarrassing in the telling. 'As I say, I was intending to get a photo of the brains of the outfit, but I fell arse over tit before I got a chance.'

'Yeah, I'd like those pictures, thanks,' said Murphy. 'Very telling he hasn't gone to the police about you punching him.'

'I – er – I'm aware I'm self-reporting an assault here,' said Strike, who'd weighed up the advisability of doing so before making the call.

'I didn't hear you,' said Murphy.

'Cheers,' said Strike.

'What can you remember about the third guy?'

'I only saw his corduroy jacket. Never got a clear view of his face. Upper middle-class accent. Articulate.'

Strike heard the tapping of computer keys again. Finally, Murphy said,

'OK, give me a second.'

Strike heard footsteps and surmised that Murphy was taking his mobile out of earshot of colleagues, then heard the sound of a door closing.

'All right,' said Murphy finally in Strike's ear. 'Your agency's been very helpful to us, so I'm going to share something. I trust it'll go no further.'

'Understood,' said Strike.

'The Halvening have shifted the way they're communicating – still dark web, but MI5 recorded a conversation last night about them thinking an undercover officer had tailed one of them to a pub where they were trying to recruit what they call a "face". We thought they'd lost interest in Cardew – obviously not. The guy who squared up to you in the Gents' was only supposed to be holding you up, to give Cardew and the other bloke time to get away. He's had a bollocking for being heavy-handed about it.

'Currently, they don't know who you are. I think you've got away with it, but I'd still advise you to be careful about security going forwards. Any unsolicited packages, call us.'

So Strike was forced to inform Pat and the subcontractors that there was a slim possibility he'd made the agency the target of a far-right terrorist group. He hadn't expected the news to raise staff morale, and had a fairly good suspicion of what his employees might be saying about him once he'd retreated to his attic, where he applied topical creams to the end of his stump, rubbed anti-inflammatory gel into the afflicted hamstring, continued to apply ice packs and hoped to God that the whole lot would heal soon.

In spite of the fact that Robin was a partner in the firm, Strike was still seen as the boss by the subcontractors – it was, after all, his name engraved on the glass outer door – and whether for this reason, or because they had qualms about venting their displeasure on a one-legged man now trapped in an attic, it was Robin who absorbed most of their resentment.

'Look, I hope he's OK,' Dev told Robin in clipped tones, calling in from Hampstead where the Upcotts remained concealed behind the walls of their house. 'But it hasn't bloody helped us, has it?'

'I just hope he's finding us someone else,' said Midge grumpily over the phone from Lancashire. Tim Ashcroft was undertaking a week-long tour of schools in the north with the Roving School Players, and Midge had been sent after him, taking a couple of wigs with her. 'Because we can't go on like this.'

'Daft fucker should've told us his leg was bad,' Barclay growled when he and Robin met at the office kettle.

'He didn't fall over on purpose,' snapped Pat from her desk behind them before Robin could answer.

Robin and Barclay turned to look at the office manager. It was the first time either of them had ever heard her defend Strike.

'What?' she said, e-cigarette stuck between her teeth. 'How would *you* like to be stuck upstairs, hopping around on one leg?'

'I'd give my fucking right leg to get some kip right now,' said Barclay sourly, and abandoning the mug in which he'd started to make tea he walked out.

'Ungrateful sod,' growled Pat as Barclay's footsteps receded down the stairs. 'He gave Barclay a job, didn't he?'

'Everyone's stressed, that's all,' said Robin, who was exhausted herself. Trying to play *Drek's Game* while also keeping suspects under observation was stretching her to her limit. 'Sam's wife's upset about the number of hours he's been doing.'

'You had another call from that Hugh Jacks, by the way,' said Pat. 'He seemed to think I hadn't passed the last message on.'

'Oh, for God's sake,' said Robin irritably. 'Sorry. I'll have to call him and spell it out.'

She carried her tea into the inner office and closed the door, thoroughly annoyed that Hugh Jacks had added yet another item to a to-do list that already seemed impossibly long. She checked *Drek's Game*, noted that the only moderator present was Paperwhite, did a couple of tasks to make sure Buffypaws wouldn't be admonished for not moving, then returned to an Instagram account she was perusing on her own initiative: that of Christabel Ross, the fourteen-year-old daughter of Jago Ross and his first wife.

Like Strike, Robin suspected that Ross was taking every precaution against being photographed in a compromising position. She'd got the idea of looking into his older children from the endless monitoring of social media that the Anomie case required. She felt slightly seedy about doing it, but as Ross was arguably an even bigger threat to the agency's ability to function than The Halvening, she'd overridden the promptings of her conscience.

She'd found Christabel on Instagram fairly easily, by cross-referencing photographs of the Ross family that had appeared in the press. An old picture from Jago's fortieth birthday had been particularly helpful: she'd found it on Tatler.com and it showed Jago, a heavily pregnant Charlotte looking as gorgeous as ever, and the three girls from his first marriage, all of whom had inherited his white-blond hair, narrow faces and high cheekbones. The oldest had made no effort to smile for the camera and Robin, examining the picture very closely, saw that unless it was a trick of a light, Jago's knuckles were white from the pressure with which he was gripping her around her thin shoulders.

The Instagram page of @christy_ross was littered with selfies, pictures of drummer Ashton Irwin, on whom she appeared to have an outsize crush, and photos of schoolfriends pulling funny faces. However, there were also a number of reposted items from other Instagram accounts, all of which had remarkably similar themes.

**The scapegoat is the child who dares to disagree
with the narcissistic parent.
AN ABSENT PARENT IS BETTER
THAN A TOXIC ONE.**

Some people were put in your life to show you what love isn't.

Before she could get any further with her investigation of Christabel's online activities, Robin's mobile rang.

'Sorry,' said Strike. He felt so guilty at the moment he was developing a tendency to start all verbal exchanges with the word. 'Wondered whether you've got time for a quick partners' chat?'

So Robin took her mug of tea upstairs with her iPad in her other hand, and knocked on Strike's attic door by gently banging it with her elbow.

Strike opened the door on crutches, right trouser leg pinned up. His skin had a greyish look, exaggerated by the fact that he hadn't shaved.

'Sorry,' he repeated.

'No problem,' said Robin.

Strike's attic flat, which comprised a kitchen, a bedroom and a very small bathroom containing a toilet and shower, was, as ever, neat and orderly. There were only two objects of decorative or sentimental value. The first was a school photo of his three nephews, which his sister Lucy had sent him. Strike heartily disliked Luke, the oldest, and was more or less indifferent to the youngest, Adam, but as he had a large soft spot for twelve-year-old Jack, he'd put the picture up on the chest of the drawers in his bedroom, still in its cardboard frame. The only other non-functional item in his flat was a photocopy of Jack's detailed handwritten and hand-illustrated three-page report of the Battle of Neuve Chapelle, which was now taped up on his kitchen cupboards. The piece of homework had gained his favourite nephew an A in his last history assignment and Strike's congratulations and enthusiasm had prompted Lucy to send him the coloured photocopy.

'Is that Jack's?' Robin asked, pausing to look. She'd sat by Jack's hospital bed with Strike while the boy fought the infection that had placed him in intensive care, and consequently felt a personal interest in him.

'Yeah,' said Strike, part smiling, part grimacing as he lowered himself into one of the chairs at his small kitchen table. 'Good, isn't it?'

'It's great,' said Robin, sitting down opposite him. Strike's laptop was open on the table, and Robin propped up her iPad behind it, *Drek's Game* still running.

'I've been trying to find us another subcontractor. Nothing doing. We're going to have to drop a case.'

Robin, who'd been thinking the same thing, said quickly,

'*Not* Anomie.'

Strike hesitated.

'Look, I want to keep Anomie too – although that's the one taking most of the manpower.'

It was adding Charlotte's husband that screwed us up, Robin thought, though she refrained from saying it.

'OK, well, if you don't want to drop Anomie, it'll have to be Groomer,' said Strike. 'The client's getting bloody antsy anyway. I had her on the phone yesterday. She came close to suggesting we fit Groomer up with something. He's a creep – we've proved he's a creep – but I'm not about to plant drugs on him. Anyway, I don't want to lose Fingers, the money's too good.'

'All right,' said Robin. 'That makes sense. Will you call Legs' mother, or—?'

'Yeah, I'll do it. Any news from Midge?'

'Not much. Ashcroft does a lot of typing in cafés,' said Robin, 'which has twice coincided with Anomie being in the game, so we can't rule him out yet, unfortunately ... How's Spanner's website coming along, by the way?'

Strike turned his laptop to face her.

Arts and Drama in Schools

The UK's premier resource for using arts and drama as a tool across multiple disciplines. ADS provides learning materials and workshops at all levels of learning, from primary to higher education.

Spanner had done a very convincing job. Robin scrolled down the website's homepage, which featured many photographs of theatrical performances and some quotations from actors who claimed to have worked with ADS.

'They're all stock photos,' said Strike. 'And the interviews with actors have been cut and pasted from other publications. If you click on "Who We Are" —'

Robin did so, and found a short list of people who allegedly ran ADS. One photograph, captioned Venetia Hall, was missing.

'Spanner needs a picture of you wigged up,' said Strike.

'OK, I'll get onto that,' said Robin, making a note.

'And he's also made a Twitter profile for Venetia and bought her five thousand followers.'

'He's done what?'

'Bought you five thousand followers,' repeated Strike. 'I didn't know that was a thing either, but it'll add credibility if Ashcroft's suspicious enough to check Venetia out beyond the website.'

'OK. And what about Kea Niven? Would you rather I went to King's Lynn?'

'No, I'll be fine by then — it's over a week away,' said Strike. 'Been on her tumblr page lately?'

'No,' said Robin. 'Why?'

Strike turned the laptop back towards himself, typed a few words then swung it around to face Robin again, who read:

So last week I was asked to do something I know will cause me
severe mental distress and impact negatively on my physical and

mental well-being. It is associated with serious trauma I went through recently and which I don't believe I've processed fully. In fact, I believe I'm now showing symptoms of PTSD.

From experience, I know that putting myself through the kind of ordeal I'm being pressured into will have catastrophic effects on my health. And yet I agreed to do what I know will harm me.

I've blogged before about how I'm trying to figure out how to exist in a less self-sacrificing way, trying to sort out healthy mechanisms for asserting my safe limits. Society tells us that to be a 'good' person we must centre other people's needs rather than our own. Like all chronically ill people, I beat myself up all the time for not being able to cope with things the healthy totally take for granted.

One of my (many!) problems is that I have ADHD, which comes with a great little extra called Rejection Sensitivity Dysphoria. My RSD is triggered by criticism that neurotypical people would totally take in their stride. So when I'm (implicitly) told that I'm selfish/ heartless for not wanting to do something I know will damage me, I'm easily persuaded, even though I know I'm being manipulated.

Yeah, so I guess being in constant pain/suicidal isn't enough. Thanks, life! Any fellow spoonies out there got advice?

#chronicallyill #spoonie #POTS #ADHD #RSD #alloydnia #cfs #invisibleillness #disability #triggers #boundaries #RSD #ableism

Beneath this were two notes:

spoonie-sara-j
Kea, hard as it is, you must focus on YOU!
jules-evola
Kill yourself.

'What's a spoonie?' asked Strike when Robin had finished reading.
'I had to look that up too,' said Robin. 'It's a term for the chronically ill. It comes from a blog somebody did in which they compared having finite energy to having a certain number of spoons.'
'Spoons?' repeated Strike.

In spite of her tiredness, Robin smiled at his bemused expression.

'I think the person explaining how tired they got just grabbed a handful of spoons to represent units of energy. Anyway, Kea hasn't backed out, has she? So that's good.'

'Not yet,' said Strike, reaching for his cigarettes. He lit up, chucked the match into the ashtray and said, 'Have you had time to read that note Nutley did on Inigo Upcott?'

'Yes,' said Robin. 'Obviously it *could* be an affair, but it could equally be somebody he's giving advice to or mentoring.'

Nutley's notes hadn't been particularly helpful in reconstructing the one-sided conversation, because they were very sparse. He had read out almost the entirety of his jottings to Strike over the phone.

'"Darling child" is quite intimate language to use to a mentee,' said Strike. 'Although I doubt Inigo's sex life is going to be key to cracking this case ...'

If Strike hadn't looked so drained and depressed, Robin might have asked why he'd sent Nutley after Inigo in the first place. Perhaps her expression had revealed her thoughts, because Strike went on:

'I dunno why I told Nutley to follow him. Just seemed interesting behaviour, to make a call where he could be sure nobody could overhear him.'

Strike's mobile rang. Robin, reading the name 'Madeline' upside down, immediately got to her feet and said,

'I'll let you take that. I need to get on anyway.'

Strike would have chosen to let the call go to voicemail if Robin hadn't got up. He didn't much relish the idea of another forty-five-minute monologue about how the launch was definitely going to be a disaster, but as he couldn't think of a reason to keep Robin talking he waited until the door had closed behind her, then answered his phone.

The call began as all of Madeline's calls had begun in the last few days: with sincere concern about Strike's leg, and genuine regret and frustration that she couldn't help him, or, realistically, have him to stay given the current demands on her. Far from being peeved, Strike was secretly relieved. He'd repeatedly told her he was best left in his attic flat, which he'd set up perfectly to work for a man with only one leg, and where he was self-sufficient.

'Are you still OK for food?' asked Madeline anxiously.

'Pat's getting it in for me,' said Strike, which was true. The office manager had uncomplainingly carried bags of food up the stairs for him.

'So when d'you think you'll be out and about again?'

'Couple of days, hopefully.'

'So you'll still be able to meet me after the launch next week?'

'If I'm back on two legs by then—'

'You just said you thought you'd be OK in a couple of days.'

'Yeah, I'm sure I will be,' said Strike, doing his best not to sound irritable.

Madeline then embarked, as expected, on a new monologue about the tribulations she was experiencing with regard to her new jewellery collection. Strike sat in silence, smoking and trying not to think about Robin.

44

. . . weary mummers, taking off the mask,
discern that face themselves forgot anon
and, sitting in the lap of sheltering night,
learn their own secrets from her . . .

Augusta Webster
Medea in Athens

Thursday was the day of the general election. Blogging for the first time since the murder of Edie Ledwell, the Pen of Justice informed their readers that to even consider voting for a party other than Labour meant you were lacking in all basic humanity. Wally Cardew shared a video in which the leader of the UK Independence Party asserted that migrants were coming to Britain for HIV treatment at a cost of £25,000 a time. To those who flooded his timeline with abuse and accusations of racism and bigotry Wally was defiant and scathing, tweeting 'British people are waiting for fucking medical treatment because of queue-jumpers.' Among those who sent Wally their support was a Twitter user called @jkett_BOUT, who sent Cardew the message 'keep telling the TRUTH. Keep England WHITE.'

There was no life drawing class at North Grove that evening, due to the election. Robin's second evening class had been far less fruitful than her first: Preston Pierce had been nowhere to be seen, and instead of a nude man the class had been asked to draw a collection of dried gourds and glass bottles. Zoe had told Jessica that she was staying over at the collective that night to babysit, so there'd been no repeat of their night-time walk home, and no opportunity for further confidences. Other than her chat with Zoe, Robin had spoken

416

as little as possible, in the hope that people would forget the Estuary accent she'd affected during her first class.

Robin planned to spend the morning of election day at home, playing *Drek's Game*, then vote before taking over surveillance on Wally Cardew for the afternoon and evening. However, an entirely unforeseen personal emergency threw her day's plans into disarray. Max, her flatmate, had a dentist's appointment and left her in charge of his elderly dachshund, Wolfgang, who hadn't eaten anything for twenty-four hours, and had urinated in his bed during the night, something he hadn't done since puppyhood. Wolfgang had also refused to take a walk that morning, merely shivering on the pavement when Max set him down.

Twenty minutes after Max had left, Wolfgang's breathing became ragged and uneven. Unable to reach Max, who she guessed was now in the dentist's chair, the worried Robin decided to drive Wolfgang to the vet's.

Country-born, Robin had expected the vet's verdict, but that made it no easier; she'd become deeply fond of the little dog during her time living with Max.

'I'm not his owner,' she said, fighting the lump in her throat. 'He's at the dentist's, please let me call him.'

Two hours later, Max and Robin watched, tears trickling down their faces, as Wolfgang was put to sleep. While the bereft Max talked to the vet about Wolfgang's cremation, Robin moved out into the reception area and pretended to be browsing cat toys while mopping her eyes with her sleeve.

Her mobile rang. Still sniffing and blurry-eyed, Robin answered it while still staring at the cat toys.

'Hi,' said Ilsa.

'Hi,' said Robin, trying to compose herself. 'How are you?'

'Fine,' said Ilsa. 'You OK? Your voice sounds funny.'

'I – Wolfgang was just put down. Max's dog.'

'Oh, I'm so sorry,' said Ilsa.

'No, it's fine,' said Robin, fishing in her pocket for a tissue. 'How're things with you?'

'Well, Nick and I both had the day off, so I've told him about the baby.'

'Oh, thank Christ,' muttered Robin. She'd been urging Ilsa to do this in every phone call they'd had recently. Ilsa was now sixteen weeks pregnant: Robin had been afraid Nick would be kept in the dark until Ilsa went into labour. 'How did he take it?'

'He was half raging and half over the moon. He accused me of not telling him because I was still trying to punish him for saying I worked too hard and should've taken it easy after I lost the last one. I said that *wasn't* why I hadn't told him; I just wanted to spare him going through all the grief if it went wrong again. Then, next breath, he started having a go at me for working on that terrorist case and having all the stress when I knew I was pregnant again.'

'Bloody hell,' said Robin, torn between amusement and annoyance. 'Can he not hear himself?'

'So we had a massive row,' said Ilsa cheerfully, 'but then we made it up and he cried a bit, and now we're having champagne with lunch. Oh, and it's a boy.'

'Please tell me you've told Nick that, Ilsa. I don't want to let it slip accidentally.'

'Yeah, I've told him. You can actually see it's a boy in the scan picture. That's what made him cry, when I showed him.'

'The sight of his son's penis?'

'You know what men are like about penises,' said Ilsa. 'Endlessly proud.'

In spite of her misery about Wolfgang, Robin laughed.

Between Wolfgang's death, Ilsa's news and the need to watch Wally Cardew's maisonette, Robin entirely forgot about going to vote. By the time all the lights in the Cardews' house had gone out, the polling station, naturally, was closed.

Max and his boyfriend Richard were sitting with their arms around each other on the sofa when Robin arrived home, Richard already talking about the possibility of getting a puppy once he moved in. Not wanting to intrude, Robin grabbed a cheese sandwich and an apple, and took both downstairs to her bedroom.

Opening her laptop she saw that the exit poll was already in: if correct, the election, which was supposed to have been exceptionally close, had been won convincingly by the Conservatives. Robin heard Max and Richard giving shouts of shock from upstairs and knew they must have just seen the same results she had.

Feeling depressed, she picked up her iPad to check the game again. Shortly after midnight, Anomie arrived to the usual chorus of acclaim from players. Anomie seemed to be in an expansive and communicative mood, returning jocularly offensive replies to greetings. Those privileged enough to be insulted seemed to take Anomie's behaviour as a mark of esteem and affection.

Robin noted the time that Anomie had entered the game, then texted Midge, Nutley and Shah, who were watching Seb Montgomery, Tim Ashcroft and Preston Pierce. All targets were currently at home and out of sight.

Robin sighed and returned to her laptop. Anomie was speaking out in the main game.

> Anomie: some of u arleady know
> about ths
>
> Anomie: but we've got Tshirts
> available on
> www.keepdreksgame.org now
>
> Anomie: so go buy yours

Then a new channel opened on the screen in front of her.

> <A new private channel has
> opened>
>
> <8 May 2015 00.23>
>
> <Anomie invites Buffypaws>

Robin stared at the screen, feeling worried. Anomie had never before asked to speak to her privately.

> Buffypaws: hi

Perhaps it made sense to make a virtue of her nerves:

> Buffypaws: have I done something
> wrong?

Waiting for Anomie's response, she checked the main game, which Morehouse had just entered. Anomie's cloak was suspended in mid-air but not gliding around. She suspected Anomie was also talking to someone else – or perhaps multiple people – on private channels.

At last, Anomie appeared in hers.

Anomie: lol

Anomie: guilty conscience much/?

Buffypaws: I do feel guilty

Buffypaws: I didn't vote!

Anomie: wht kind of bullshit thng
is that to feel guillty about?

Anomie: i killed someone the
other week andi feel no guilt

Anomie: thought I might

Anomie: nothing

Anomie: sitting here planning
thea next one
haha

Robin picked up her phone and took a picture of this bit of dialogue, set her mobile down and paused, thinking.

Buffypaws: lol who's goin to be next?

Anomie: I'tll be on the news youll see

Buffypaws: it's not me, is it?

>

>

>

>

This time the pause went on for two minutes. Now convinced Anomie was talking to other people privately, Robin sat in suspense until they returned.

Anomie: not unless you piss me
off big time

Anomie: you'er in Manchester, rihgt?

Buffypaws: yes

Robin noticed that Anomie wasn't bothering with asterisks in proper names and was confirmed in her suspicion that Consequence 14 existed only in the minds of the gullible. She was interested in the fact that Anomie knew Beth was in Manchester. Did they make a habit of trying to find out players' true identities?

> **Anomie:** we need a big game
> presence at Comic con on the
> 23tj. easy trip from Manc
>
> **Anomie:** scare the shit out of
> Grunt and Maverick
>
> **Anomie:** so I wabt as manhy
> p;ayers as possible to come

Robin wondered whether Anomie could possibly be drunk or stoned. She'd never seen their typing this erratic before. Perhaps, she thought, they were a Conservative supporter, and had been celebrating the unexpectedly resounding win. Having made a note of Comic Con's date, she kept typing.

> **Buffypaws:** what about rule 14?
>
> **Anomie:** if you want to b let back
> inside the gaem, you'll keep it,
> Masks and no exhcghn of private ingo
>
> **Anomie:** info
>
> **Buffypaws:** ok I'll definitely try
> and come
>
> **Anomie:** and wear a tshit
>
> **Buffypaws:** yeah, of course

She expected Anomie to leave the channel, but they didn't. The winking cursor marked the passing seconds, moving further and further down the screen, leaving a long line of tail-less arrows in its wake.

Then, suddenly, more words appeared rapidly.

> **Anomie:** yes ibn pissed who gives
> a shit

Anomie: get it through hour skyll
I don't want what you want

Anomie: so called achieventes and
all that bullshit

Anomie: you know my situatiohn

Anomie: im stuck in a fucking cage

Anomie: il/l take care of LorD and V

Anomie: by the end of thenmonth
they'' be gone

Anomie: thye'll be gone ok?

>

>

Anomie: hahaha

Anomie: just realised im
plagiarsing

Anomie: Id on't want what you want

Anomie: i dont feel what you feel

Anomie: hgeart in a cage

Anomie: gonna put it on

Robin hastily took a second picture of the screen, using her phone, but only just in time. Ten seconds after Anomie had typed 'gonna put it on' the private channel closed and she was left staring at Anomie's empty cloak, fluttering but otherwise immobile, in the main game.

She sat looking at the last bit of dialogue on her phone for several minutes, her brain working furiously, then checked the time. It was now twenty to one and self-evidently too late to call Strike. Nevertheless, she picked up her mobile and texted him.

**you're probably asleep but if you're
still watching the election coverage I might
have something on Anomie**

422

The moment she'd sent the message, it occurred to her that Strike might be lying in bed with Madeline. She imagined his phone buzzing while he snored (Robin knew he snored; he'd fallen asleep in the Land Rover on one long journey and snored for several hours) and Madeline waking and reaching across Strike for it, and being annoyed that Strike's work partner thought it appropriate to text him in the early hours of the morning. Robin's and Strike's positions had reversed: once she'd been the one who lay in bed with a partner who resented her frequent work calls, now Strike might be cursing her, having perhaps been woken by Madeline's loud exclamation of displeasure—

Robin's mobile rang.

'What've you got?' Strike said, sounding wide awake.

'You weren't asleep, were you?'

'No, I'm lying here watching Labour implode. Pollsters got this one wrong, didn't they?'

'Very,' said Robin. 'How's your leg?'

'Not bad,' said Strike, which Robin interpreted as 'not good'.

'OK, well, I'm about to send you some photos of a private-channel conversation I just had with Anomie.'

She did so. While waiting for his response, Robin lay down on her bed, her eyes on the dark sky outside her window.

'"I killed someone the other week and I feel no guilt",' Strike read aloud. '"Thought I might. Nothing. Sitting here planning the next one . . ."'

'It could be bravado – their idea of humour?'

'Well,' said Strike slowly, 'let's hope so.'

'Have you read the next bit?'

'Yeah.'

'Anomie didn't mean to send me that. They were drunk and got careless. I'm sure they had more than one private channel open and they accidentally sent that lot to me, instead of . . . Well, if I had to guess, I'd say they thought they were talking to Morehouse. The tone of it—'

'Yeah,' said Strike. 'Feels like Anomie's talking to an equal, doesn't it? Promising to get rid of LordD and V, who I assume are—'

'LordDrek and Vilepechora, must be.'

'"I don't want what you want . . . I'm stuck in a fucking cage . . ."'

'Strike, this is sounding more and more like Kea to me. Those lyrics Anomie quoted are from "Heart in a Cage" by the Strokes. Kea was wearing a T-shirt with one of their album covers on it in her video.'

'Bloody well spotted,' said Strike. 'Yeah, and I suppose the being stuck in a cage would be having to go back to her mother's because she's ill. She's not big on achievements either: she says so on her tumblr page. Feeling guilty about not achieving stuff is the result of internalised capitalism, apparently.'

'Seriously?'

'Oh yeah. You never been to a communist country? Everyone lies on sofas all day while trained poodles bring them cake.'

'Ha ha. There's also "that's not me *any more*". She was at art school . . .'

'This could fit Gus Upcott as well, you know,' said Strike. 'Very similar story. Ill health, forced off his music course—'

'He's intending to go back, though. He doesn't seem to have given up on achievement, judging by the standard of the music he was playing.'

'How ambitious did Preston Pierce seem when you met him?'

'Hard to tell,' said Robin, once again trying not to picture Pierce naked. 'But I can't see why he'd describe his situation as being in a cage – although, of course, you never know.'

'Tim Ashcroft might fit too,' said Strike. 'He's an actor who thought he might ride *The Ink Black Heart* to the big time. Instead he's playing school gyms in Salford.'

'There's nothing wrong with performing to students,' said Robin.

'Never said there was, but *he* might think so. That "I don't care about achievements any more" is the kind of thing people say when they're bitter about not having achieved what they expected to . . . Have you heard Ilsa and Nick's news?'

'Yes,' said Robin. 'Fantastic, isn't it?'

'Yeah, really happy for them,' said Strike. 'You know they're going to ask both of us to be godparents?'

'I – no, I didn't,' said Robin, both surprised and touched.

'Shit. Well, act surprised when Ilsa asks you, then . . . what exactly *is* this Comic Con Anomie wants you to go to?' Strike asked.

'Exactly what it sounds like,' said Robin. 'A big conference for fans of movies and comics. You know the kind of thing.'

'Is Anomie going?'

'No idea.'

'Well, we should be there, in case.'

'In masks?' said Robin.

'Yeah. We wouldn't stand out. Half the people there will be dressed as *Star Wars* characters.'

'I can see you as Yoda.'

'And you'd make a lovely Darth Vader,' said Robin.

On that note, they said goodnight.

Catching sight of herself in the dressing-table mirror, Robin saw that she was smiling. She consciously repressed her uplifted spirits in the usual way: by reminding herself of the existence of Madeline Courson-Miles, and of Charlotte Campbell's divorce.

45

To do good seemed so much his business,
That, having done it, she was fain to think,
Must fill up his capacity for joy.

Elizabeth Barrett Browning
Aurora Leigh

An hour after the fake website for Arts and Drama in Schools went live, Venetia Hall contacted Tim Ashcroft through his Twitter account, requesting an interview and providing the number of a burner phone she'd bought for the purpose. To Robin's shock, Ashcroft sent his enthusiastic agreement a mere twenty minutes later, and after a short exchange of emails the meeting was fixed for three days later. This gave Robin rather less time than she'd hoped to mug up on Ashcroft's acting career to date, create a background for the woman she was impersonating and complete her cheat sheet for Strike, who was going to take over Buffypaws while Robin was with Ashcroft.

'Christ,' said Strike, looking down the long document she handed him in his attic flat the evening before the interview. His stump was still elevated on the chair beside him, an ice pack lying on his knee and the end slathered in cream. 'You reckon I'll need all this?'

'You'll need to be able to navigate the tasks,' said Robin. 'If you can't get through them they'll smell a rat straight away, because I'm in there all the time and I could do them in my sleep. The rest is mostly stuff Zoe and I have told each other about our lives, so you don't slip up if she talks to you, but with luck you won't need all that. I shouldn't be with Ashcroft more than a couple of hours.'

'Where are you meeting?'

'A bar called Qube in Colchester,' said Robin. 'I offered to go to him and he accepted. How's your leg?'

'Better,' said Strike. 'Want a cuppa?'

'Can't,' said Robin, 'I've got to sort myself out for tomorrow. I'll text you once I'm in Colchester.'

This businesslike encounter and swift departure left Strike feeling deflated. He could have used a chat, if only about Kea Niven's social media output, which he was currently working his way through prior to interviewing her.

Little did Strike realise that Robin was feeling seriously resentful towards her business partner at the moment. She knew he was worried about their caseload and in continuing pain, but even so, it would have been nice if he'd remembered she was supposed to be moving house. Perhaps he imagined she'd somehow achieved the feat without taking any time off work, but she'd still have appreciated a polite enquiry.

In fact, the seller of Robin's new flat had begged through his lawyer for a postponement of the moving-in date, because the purchase of his own new house had fallen through. In spite of her own lawyer telling her she needn't agree, Robin had done so. Until Strike was literally back on two feet, the overburdened agency desperately needed one fully functioning partner, so she really couldn't afford the time off. Nevertheless, calling her parents, who'd wanted to come down to London to help with the move, and witnessing Max and Richard's imperfectly concealed disappointment that she wouldn't be getting out of their way on the date promised, hadn't done much to lift her mood or diminish her stress levels.

Robin made the two-hour drive to Colchester the following morning in her old Land Rover. Today's iteration of Venetia Hall, a pseudonym she'd used before, wore a wavy ash-blonde wig Robin knew didn't suit her, but which, with a pair of square-framed glasses and pale grey contact lenses, dramatically altered her appearance. On her left hand were what appeared to be wedding and engagement rings: not her own, which she'd left behind when she walked out on her ex-husband, but fakes made of tin alloy and cubic zirconia. Venetia's imaginary husband, over whose creation she'd taken just as much trouble as her own fictional persona, had been designed with the express intention of helping unlock confidences from Tim.

Having parked, Robin texted Strike.

Will be in bar in 5 mins

She'd just locked the Land Rover when she received his reply.

This game's fucking dull

The bar where Tim wanted to meet presented a minimalist black exterior. The venues chosen by interviewees were often an early guide to character, and Robin had time to wonder why Tim had chosen what proved, on entering, to be a dimly lit and, in Robin's opinion, self-consciously sophisticated space, before she heard her pseudonym spoken in a pleasant Home Counties tenor.

'Venetia?'

She turned, smiling, to see the tall, balding Tim beaming at her, hand outstretched.

'Tim, hello!' said Robin in her best middle-class London accent, shaking his hand.

'I hope this place is OK?' asked Tim, who was wearing an open-necked blue shirt and jeans. 'I chose it because we're not likely to be interrupted by any of my parents' friends. Home town – you know.'

'I do,' said Robin with a laugh.

He'd already chosen a table for two flanked by high-backed arm-chairs, and stood politely until Robin sat down.

'This is perfect,' said Robin, smiling as she took a small tape recorder out of her bag and set it on the table near Tim. 'It's *so* kind of you to do this.'

'Oh, not at all, not at all,' said Tim.

His early baldness was at odds with his unlined face, which was boyish, with attractive mottled-green eyes.

'Do we order here, or—?' asked Robin.

'Yeah, it's table service,' said Tim.

'Lovely town,' said Robin, peering out of the window at a beamed house opposite. 'I've never been here before. My husband's always told me how nice it is. He grew up in Chelmsford.'

'Oh, really?' said Tim, and they talked about Colchester and Chelmsford, which lay a mere thirty-minute drive away, for the time it took for a waitress to come and take their order for coffee. During this interval, Robin managed to mention that her husband, Ben, was a TV producer. Tim's eyebrows twitched upwards at that, and his smile became still warmer.

Once their coffee had arrived, Robin switched on her tape recorder, checked it was working and fussed a little about it being near enough to Tim.

'Would you mind just speaking a little, so I'm sure I'm getting this? Give me a bit of a monologue or something.'

Tim launched at once into Iago's soliloquy:

> *Thus do I ever make my fool my purse.*
> *For I mine own gained knowledge should profane*
> *If I would time expend with such a snipe*
> *But for my sport and profit. I hate the Moor . . .*

'Wonderful!' said Robin, and played it back. 'OK, that's working perfectly . . . Yes, actually, I won't rewind, that was marvellous, I'll keep it on there . . .'

And so the fake interview began, Robin asking the series of questions she'd worked out beforehand about the uses and applications of dramatic techniques in education. Tim spoke with enthusiasm about the pleasure of bringing theatre to young people, often in underprivileged areas, and Robin asked many follow-up questions and made notes.

'. . . and I actually realised how much I enjoy it when a friend of mine – actually, it was Edie, um, Ledwell, who created *The Ink Black Heart*?'

'Oh, *so* dreadful, what happened,' said Robin sympathetically. 'I'm terribly sorry.'

'Thanks . . . yeah . . . well, it was Edie who's sort of responsible for me liking to work with kids. She used to help run art classes for special-needs children at an art collective. I wasn't working at the time, so she roped me in to help and I loved it. There's such a freshness to the way kids look at the world.'

'You draw, do you?' asked Robin, smiling.

'A bit,' said Tim. 'I'm not very good.'

'Must be a challenge, getting young people interested in theatre. They spend their whole lives online these days, don't they?'

'Oh, we explore internet use during our drama workshops – online bullying, trolls and so on, you know.'

'D'you have any children yourself?'

'Not yet,' said Tim, smiling. 'Need to find someone happy to have them with me first.'

Robin smiled, agreed that would help, then kept asking her questions. She didn't want to capitalise on his mention of Edie Ledwell yet, nor to discuss *The Ink Black Heart* before Tim had been thoroughly convinced that he and his career were the real reason she was here. She therefore mentioned his recent starring role at his local theatre, which pleased him.

'I actually had to wear a wig for the part because my character was seen both in his teenage years and in middle age and – well –'

He pointed, smiling somewhat ruefully, at his head.

'The funny thing is, the local critic thought the bald head was the fake.'

Robin laughed and said,

'Well, he gave you a very nice review.'

'Yeah, I was chuffed . . . I actually based some of the character on one of the kids who used to hang around North Grove.'

'Around where, sorry?' said Robin, still carefully ignorant of most things pertaining to *The Ink Black Heart*.

'Oh, that was the art collective where I helped out with the kids' classes. You know that kind of hunched-up "don't look at me" thing teenagers get when they're growing into their bodies?' As he spoke, Tim unconsciously took on the posture he was describing, and whatever Allan Yeoman had said about his limitations as the comic voice of The Worm, Robin was impressed by the ease with which he conveyed shyness and self-consciousness by small alterations in his own posture. 'He had really bad acne, this kid, and he always looked like he was trying to make himself as small as possible, and my character, Lionel, he's – well, he's pure evil, really, but in the play you go back and see him bullied and denigrated and . . . that's something drama can do so well in schools, actually: explore issues from life like bullying or abuse . . .'

'This is absolutely fantastic,' said Robin a few minutes later. 'God, I wish Ben could hear this – my husband, I mean. He's actually putting together a proposal for Channel 4 right now. He wants to take actors into a really deprived London school to work intensively with the kids. It's a constant fight to keep funding for the arts, especially under the Tories, so, potentially, he'd be making a really strong argument against cuts.'

'Wow, that sounds great,' said Tim, raising his now-cold coffee to his lips and taking a sip in an attempt to hide (or so Robin suspected) the sudden eagerness of his expression.

'Yeah. The project's still at a very early stage, but I'm not going to lie,' said Robin, smiling, 'that's part of the reason I'm here. Ben thought, with your background working in schools – plus the fact that you were in *The Ink Black Heart* – would be a selling point with the production company. It's instant connection with kids who live on YouTube, isn't it, who've never been in theatres in their lives?'

'Yeah, I s'pose,' said Tim, 'although, of course' – he gave an awkward little laugh – 'some of them might despise me for ever having been in it.'

'What d'you mean by that?' asked Robin, carefully surprised.

Tim glanced at the tape recorder, so Robin shut it off at once. There was no need for him to know that a second recording device was still running in her open bag.

'Well,' said Tim, 'given my time again . . . Actually, I feel disloyal saying it.'

Robin continued to look politely receptive.

'I – well, I loved Edie, I really did. She was fantastic. But, to be honest, I might not have taken the part if she hadn't been a friend. It's pretty problematic, that cartoon, you know.'

'I must admit,' said Robin, faux-sheepishly, 'I don't really know much about it. I just knew it was a huge success. Actually, one of the people at Ben's production company, Damian, is trying to make a programme about it – it's really down to Damian that I've even heard of it. I suppose I'm a bit older than the target demographic.'

'So was I,' said Tim, and Robin laughed again. 'I guess as time went on I got more and more uncomfortable with certain aspects of the characters and storylines. I don't know whether you've heard of Wally Cardew? He was playing a character called Drek, which is – God, I feel such a shit for saying this, but he was clearly a Jewish caricature.'

'Really?' said Robin.

'Yeah, you know: big nose, lived in the biggest mausoleum and kind of manipulated all the other characters. I tried to raise it with Edie. Fans were talking about it. We had a row about it, actually. She claimed Drek had nothing to do with Jewish people, that he was a kind of chaotic demon and she'd been inspired by a plague doctor's mask, but I mean, we all need to examine our unconscious biases, right?'

'Absolutely,' said Robin, nodding.

'And then Wally, who was the voice of Drek, did a YouTube video laughing about the Holocaust, so, you know – point proven.'

'Oh, wow,' said Robin, shaking her head.

'Yeah. Josh and Edie sacked him, but the damage was done,' sighed Tim. 'And it wasn't only Drek. Josh and Edie's sense of humour was – it could be problematic. Kind of dark and sometimes a bit . . . I told her I didn't want to read any more lines about The Worm being confused about being a boy or a girl, because we'd had complaints from non-binary kids. That caused another row. "A worm *is* a hermaphrodite, though."' Tim shook his head sadly. 'Edie had had a difficult childhood. You couldn't blame her for being – not ignorant, but . . .'

Tim seemed unable to think of an alternative word and simply shrugged.

'This is *exactly* the kind of discussion we should be having on the reality show, if it's made,' said Robin earnestly. 'It could be *so powerful*, listening to you deconstructing biases and so on. Actually – this is a bit off-topic, but Damian's trying to track down people who knew Edie Ledwell. He wants to make a sympathetic, balanced programme. I don't suppose *you'd* be interested in talking to him?'

'Er . . . I don't know,' said Tim uncertainly. 'You know, given that she's only recently . . . and with all the controversy around the cartoon . . . I don't know whether I'd want—'

'Totally understand,' said Robin, holding up a hand. 'No, I'll tell Damian it's a no-go. You wouldn't know anyone who'd like to talk? Anyone who was close to her?'

'Well, Edie was kind of solitary, to tell you the truth. She didn't have that many friends. There was a foster sister, though. She might be able to help. And Edie was in a new relationship when she died. Guy called Phil Ormond?'

'Yes, I think Damian knows about him.'

'I didn't much like Ormond,' mumbled Tim. 'He . . . Well, I'd better not say too much.'

'No, of course not,' said Robin, but her expression remained encouraging.

'She . . . I don't think it was a very healthy relationship, let's put it that way. I told her to get out. I wish she had.'

'You aren't suggesting—?'

'Oh, Christ no!' said Tim, with what looked like panic. 'No, I don't think he – God, no. No, I'm sure that far-right group's responsible. That's where all the trouble in the fandom was coming from, because of Drek. All these alt-right guys loved him. They started using his catchphrases and everything, and then, after Wally was sacked, they all went ballistic and started to attack Edie.

'Personally, if I'd been her, I'd have written the character out of the cartoon. Made a stand. I mean, if the alt-right find your jokes funny, should you be making them at all? Not that – I'm obviously not saying it was her fault or – because, obviously, what happened was bloody terrible. But art should be moral, right?' said Tim.

'Oh, absolutely,' said Robin.

'Right,' said Tim, looking reassured. 'I genuinely examine every new project from that standpoint. I ask myself, "What's this saying?" and also, "How could it be interpreted?" "Are there groups that might be harmed by this play?" – or production or whatever. "Does it deal in stereotypes or harmful tropes?" I don't think Edie ever thought things through like that and ... well ...'

'How did you two first meet?' asked Robin.

'Bar work,' said Tim with a rueful smile. 'We both got jobs in a bar in the West End, not far from Shaftesbury Avenue. I was between acting jobs and she was taking art classes and living in some dive of a flat. That was before she moved into North Grove and met Josh Blay.'

'That's her co-creator? Yes, Damian asked to speak to him but apparently he's still not well enough.'

'No, I —I heard he's in pretty bad shape.'

There was a slight pause, and then a torrent of words burst from Ashcroft.

'It's been bloody terrible for all of us – I mean, obviously it has – our friend's been murdered – and we've all been interviewed by the police, all of us who had any connection with the cartoon. I had to give a bloody alibi, if you can believe it,' said Tim with a half-laugh of disbelief. 'To tell you the truth, lately I've just been kind of worried I'll be tarred by *The Ink Black Heart* for ever, so you asking to talk to me about the Roving School Players – I was, I know this sounds stupid, but I was really pleased, I felt like I was getting a chance to kind of be appreciated – not appreciated, but you know what I mean – for my other work. I just want to move forwards and make a positive difference in the world if I can.'

'That's obvious,' said Robin warmly. 'I can only imagine how stressful and upsetting all this has been for all of you. Having to give an alibi—!'

'I mean, I had a cast-iron one,' said Tim, watching Robin anxiously, 'it isn't as if – I was with someone all afternoon and evening, and they confirmed it, and the police are happy, so that's that. But social media can be a kind of scary place. I mean, people can say *anything* about you on there. Twist stuff, make things up . . .'

'So true,' sighed Robin.

'The whole situation's already had real-life consequences for me. I had to leave – well, I didn't *have* to leave, but I was living in London, sharing a flat with a friend, and he pretty much asked me to move out because the police came round and I assume he thinks the alt-right'll start targeting him next or something. This is a guy I've known for years. He broke his leg six months ago and I was ferrying him around everywhere and – sorry, I don't know why I'm – I don't want to bother my parents with all this. Christ, you come here to talk about education and I'm banging on about – sorry.'

'Please,' said Robin, 'don't apologise. Of *course* you're shaken up. Who wouldn't be?'

'Right,' said Tim, looking slightly reassured, 'and if there's a chance – I mean, if you really think I'd be a good fit for your drama in schools programme, I'd rather you heard the truth from me than, you know, go looking me up on Twitter or whatever and find out the police questioned me. But as I say, I wasn't the only one they questioned. I know they went to Wally Cardew and this guy Pez as well, who only voiced one of the characters for two episodes . . . But you didn't come here to talk about all this, so, yeah – sorry. It's been a difficult time.'

'Really,' said Robin, 'it's fine. I totally understand.'

'Thanks . . . I seriously didn't mean to lay all this on you.'

Robin took a sip of coffee before saying,

'Damian told me the fandom's kind of crazy.'

'Some of them are a bit obsessive, yeah,' said Tim, with another half-laugh.

'He was telling me about some troll who's quite a bully online,' said Robin.

'Anomie?'

'Yes, I think so,' said Robin, feigning surprise that Tim had the name on the tip of his tongue.

'Oh, everyone who was connected to *The Ink Black Heart* knows who Anomie is,' said Tim. 'I mean, not *who* they are, but knows about them . . . Although I actually *do* think I know who it is,' Tim added.

'You do?' said Robin, trying to sound only mildly interested.

'Yeah. If I'm right, she's very young and kind of disturbed. I think most of these trolls need to feel important, you know? I find most of the really difficult kids, at our workshops . . .'

Five minutes and several anecdotes about the beneficial effect of drama on troubled teenagers later, Tim paused for breath.

'That's all *fabulous*,' said Robin, who'd had the presence of mind to turn the recording device back on. 'Pity you couldn't get that Ano-thingy on one of your courses.'

'Yes, I think it would help her, I really do,' said Tim seriously.

'You couldn't tell me, confidentially, who you think it is?' asked Robin, with a coaxing smile. 'Off the record. Damian would be so thrilled to interview her – you know, a warts-and-all picture of the fandom.'

'No, I – I couldn't do that,' said Tim. 'I might be wrong, mightn't I? Anyway, if it *is* her, it could tip her over the edge completely.'

'Oh,' said Robin, now looking concerned, 'if it's a case of mental illness—'

'I'm not sure she's actually mentally ill, but I know she's been in trouble with the police already and . . . No, I wouldn't want to be throwing accusations around.'

Enormously frustrated, Robin glanced down at her notes and said,

'Well, I think I've got everything I need here. This has been *such* a pleasure. I know Ben's going to be fascinated by everything you've . . . Oh,' said Robin, pretending to notice something left unanswered. 'Who's Pez, by the way? Is that someone else Damian should talk to? Is that their real name?'

'No,' said Tim.

The silence went on a little longer than Robin had expected. She'd only asked about Pez to try to lead the conversation back to *The Ink Black Heart* and Anomie one last time. Looking up, she saw that Ashcroft's mouth was hanging open, as though he'd been paused onscreen. He unfroze a split-second later and smiled.

'His real name's just passed clean out of my head,' he said. 'God. I mean, we barely knew each other, but I should be able to . . . Pez . . . Pez. *What* was his bloody name? . . . no, sorry, it's gone. But he didn't actually know Edie, not properly, to be honest, so – or not, you know, very well at all.'

435

'Not to worry,' said Robin with a shrug and a smile. 'Damian can always get the name from the credits if he needs it.'

'Yeah ... but as I say, Pez didn't – he's actually quite a ... what's the word? I'm not saying a fantasist exactly, but ... No, I'm just saying I wouldn't put much credence on stuff Pez says. He's the kind of guy who says stuff for shock value. You know the type.'

'Oh yes,' said Robin, still smiling, but very interested in this assertion.

'Only I wouldn't want anyone to get the wrong idea about Edie. Pez isn't ... What *was* his bloody name?' said Tim with an unconvincing laugh.

They took their leave of each other outside the bar, both smiling as they shook hands. When Robin glanced back thirty seconds later she saw Tim was still standing where she'd left him, typing fast on his phone.

46

I dreamed, and saw a modern Hell, more dread
Than Dante's pageant; not with gloom and glare,
But all new forms of madness and despair
Filled it with complex tortures, some Earth-bred . . .
From thine own Earth and from its happiest lot
Thy lust for pain may draw full nourishment.

Constance Naden
The Pessimist's Vision

'How'd it go?' said Strike, answering Robin's call on the second ring.

'He thinks he knows who Anomie is.'

'Seriously?'

'Yes, but he wouldn't tell me who. I pressed him as hard as I could without blowing my cover, but all he'd say is that it's a young woman, or possibly a teenage girl, who's troubled and is already known to the police. Kea Niven hasn't been caught doing anything criminal, has she?'

'Not that I've found so far,' said Strike, who currently had Kea's Twitter feed, tumblr page and Instagram account open on his laptop. However, these items had remained unexamined for the last hour and a half, because Strike had been playing *Drek's Game* on his phone.

'I take it Anomie hasn't made an appearance?' Robin asked.

'No,' said Strike, 'but I've gained a new appreciation of how tedious this must've been for you, spending hours in here.'

'All part of the job,' said Robin, who was sitting in the parked Land Rover, her glasses now off but the ash-blonde wig still on, in case Tim Ashcroft reappeared. 'I got another couple of interesting things out of Ashcroft.

'For one, the police have questioned him since you saw him at that pub in Highgate. He had to give an alibi for the afternoon of the stabbings. Somebody vouched for him being with them all afternoon and evening.'

'Did he tell you who gave him this convenient alibi?'

'No,' said Robin, 'but it would've looked *so* fishy if I'd pressed him on it.'

'Yeah, that's the problem with being undercover.'

'The other odd thing was that Ashcroft *really* doesn't want anyone talking to Preston Pierce. He claimed Preston barely knew Edie, but we know that's a lie. I had the impression Pierce knows something incriminating about Tim himself.'

'Interesting. How much d'you fancy Ashcroft as Anomie, now you've met him?'

'Not much,' admitted Robin. 'I quite fancy him as the Pen of Justice, though.'

'Really?'

'Yes. I've just gone to look at the Pen's blog again. The first post the Pen ever wrote was about Drek being a Jewish caricature that's almost word for word what Tim just said to me, including something about unconscious biases.'

'How soon after Ashcroft was sacked as The Worm did the Pen of Justice start up?'

Robin checked.

'Actually,' she said, 'the Pen of Justice started *before* Tim was dropped. It first appeared in January 2012. Tim stopped voicing The Worm in March 2013.'

'So if he's the Pen, he was calling Ledwell and Blay racists and all the rest of it for over a year, anonymously, while still working with them?'

'And why would he do that?' said Robin, thinking out loud. 'If it got out that he was the Pen, surely even the people who agreed with his criticisms of the cartoon would've thought he was a real hypocrite? No, I must've been wrong . . . I think he must just be a reader, rather than the originator . . . I'd better get back down the road. Will you keep playing the game until I can take over?'

'Yeah, all right,' said Strike heavily. 'Although I'm starting to think we should've been paying you whatever the opposite of danger money is, all the hours you've put in on this shit.'

Shortly after Robin had hung up, Strike received a text from his nephew Jack, who'd heard from his mother that Strike was temporarily housebound and, touchingly, had taken to texting enquiries.

How is your leg is it better?

Hasn't grown back yet but everything crossed, Strike responded, which elicited three laughing emoji.

In fact, Strike's stump was taking its time about returning to a state that would comfortably bear his weight. He knew perfectly well that he needed to lose about four stone, do the exercises recommended by the physiotherapist and give up smoking, because if he ended up with arteriosclerosis there might come a point where the skin at the end of his stump refused to heal at all. As he had no immediate desire to take any of these sensible measures, he was choosing to channel his self-recrimination into rage at Thurisaz, who'd forced him, or so the detective saw it, to throw the punches that had landed his leg in this state.

Strike's systematic review of all Kea Niven's online activity concluded the following day. He sent Robin a summary of everything he'd found out, then asked Pat to print out screenshots of relevant material so he could show them to Kea when he met her on Thursday. He'd found a couple of intriguing items in among her various social media accounts, which he was looking forward to asking her to explain.

Being incapable of doing much else, Strike then decided to sift through the mass of hard-right Twitter accounts surrounding *The Ink Black Heart*, in the possibly unrealistic hope of identifying his would-be assailant at the Ship & Shovell.

As Robin had already noticed, Brotherhood of Ultima Thule members usually incorporated the initials BOUT, or variations on Ultima Thule, into their usernames. They never attached their own photographs to their accounts, nor did they give their full names, which Strike assumed was a rule enforced by the Brotherhood. Most used pictures of the Icelandic vegvísir, a complex symbol resembling a compass which, as Strike discovered when he checked on the Brotherhood's website, was once believed to have been a magical symbol that would help the bearer navigate rough weather. A young Icelandic woman had tweeted at a member of the Brotherhood, pleading with him not to appropriate a symbol that had nothing whatsoever to do with white supremacy. His response had been to call her a n★★★★★-loving cunt.

Although the Brotherhood seemed to require its members not to reveal their true identities online, it seemed to be happy for them to be as aggressive and abusive as they pleased. Two members of the Brotherhood had responded in characteristic fashion to Edie's celebratory tweet about gay marriage.

Edie Ledwell @EdLedDraws

Same sex marriage legal in UK! 🌈 ✩ ♥

4.30 pm   17 July 2013

Algernon Gizzard Esq @Gizzard_Al
replying to @EdLedDraws
fuck off dyke

Lepine's Disciple @LepinesD1sciple
replying to @EdLedDraws
I can smell your stale pussy from here

Will A @will_of_BOUT
replying to @Gizzard_Al @EdLedDraws
suck a bag of dicks

True Briton @jkett_BOUT
replying to @EdLedDraws
you flap your fishy hands together for this but none of you SJW
bitches opened their cock-sucking mouths about Lee Rigby

Strike made a note of the handles @will_of_BOUT and @jkett_BOUT and kept scrolling.

An hour and one ham sandwich later, he had made his way back a further year on Edie's timeline.

Edie Ledwell
@EdLedDraws
What the hell's happening to this country that UKIP is
polling so high?

Harv @HN_Ultima_Thule
replying to @EdLedDraws
what's happening is that people can see we are
being invaded, u stupid bitch

Strike noted down the new Brotherhood handle, looked at the man's account, found no identifying details and resumed his perusal of Edie's timeline.

He'd already known, of course, that the catalyst for the far right becoming angry with Ledwell had been the sacking of Wally Cardew, but now Strike learned that from the Brotherhood's point of view there'd been an aggravating offence: the actor who'd replaced Wally was black.

Anomie
@AnomieGamemaster

So Fedwell's chosen a new Drek and if you close your eyes and listen, he's ... shit.
Wonder why she chose him? 💀

#tokenism #pandering

19.27 am 21 April 2012

A familiar name appeared directly beneath this tweet.

Yasmin Weatherhead @YazzyWeathers
replying to @AnomieGamemaster
Unfair, we should give @MichaelDavidActs a chance.

Yasmin's account, Strike noted, didn't carry a photograph, but a very flattering line drawing of herself.

Down Strike scrolled through further replies.

Lepine's Disciple @LepinesD1sciple
replying to @YazzyWeathers @MichaelDavidActs
@AnomieGamemaster
You like black c*** as much as Fedwell?

Jules @i_am_evola
replying to @LepinesD1sciple @YazzyWeathers
@MichaelDavidActs @AnomieGamemaster
Ledwell likes all sorts. I heard she sucked off her Dutch
landlord instead of paying rent

Algernon Gizzard Esq @Gizzard_Al
replying to @i_am-evola @LepinesD1sciple @YazzyWeathers
@MichaelDavidActs @AnomieGamemaster
'what is the secret of your success miz ledwell'
'strong jaw muscles and no gag reflex'

Pen of Justice @penjustwrites
replying to @AnomieGamemaster @MichaelDavidActs
Disagree MD's bad but agree casting him clumsy way of trying
to atone for previous racism in TIBH. My take on right thing
done for wrong reasons:

www.thePenOfJustice/WhyCastingMichaelDavidAsDrek . . .

SQ @#B_O_U_T_Quince
replying to @penjustwrites @MichaelDavidActs
u prick drek is not a n*****

Strike noted down the handle @#B_O_U_T_Quince, then continued reading the conversation about Michael David's casting, which
Edie – perhaps ill-advisedly – had joined.

Edie Ledwell
@EdLedDraws
replying to @penjustwrites
Were you in the room when we cast him? He was the best for
the job, nothing to do with being black

> **Pen of Justice** @penjustwrites
> replying to @AnomieGamemaster
> Disagree MD's bad but casting him clumsy way of trying to
> atone for previous racism in TIBH. My take on right thing
> done for wrong reasons:
> www.thePenOfJustice/
> WhyCastingMichaelDavidAsDrek . . .

Anomie @AnomieGamemaster
replying to @EdLedDraws @penjustwrites
If you're so thin-skinned and angry you're attacking fans on
Twitter, maybe you should fuck off and leave @theJoshBlay
in charge?

Edie Ledwell @EdLedDraws
replying to @AnomieGamemaster @penjustwrites
Believe me, there are days this sounds like a great idea.

Ruby Nooby @rubynooby*_*
replying to @EdLedDraws @AnomieGamemaster
don't say that, we love you!

Zozo @inkyheart28
replying to @EdLedDraws @AnomieGamemaster
Nooooo don ' t go !!!

Penny Peacock @rachledbadly
replying to @EdLedDraws @AnomieGamemaster
everyone talks trash on here, you've got loads of fans, we
don't want you to go

Anomie @AnomieGamemaster
replying to @rachledbadly @rubynooby*_* @inkyheart28
@EdLedDraws
#Sympathy Troll complete 👏 👏 👏

Somebody knocked on the attic door.

'Got your printouts,' said Pat's gruff voice from the landing. 'And
some cake.'

'Door's open,' called Strike, tugging his dressing gown to make
sure it covered his boxers. 'Did you say cake?'

'Yeah,' said Pat, entering backwards with her e-cigarette clamped
between her teeth as usual, a cardboard folder in one hand and a large
slice of fruitcake on a plate. 'Made it last night. Thought you might
want a bit.'

'Thanks very much,' said Strike. 'You *made* it?'

'Not for you,' said Pat unsentimentally, taking a deep pull on her
e-cigarette before removing it to say, 'Well, not *just* for you. Team
morale could be better. Good thing about fruitcake is it keeps. Got
everything you need?'

'Yeah, all good,' said Strike.

She headed for the door. Strike called after her:

'There's been grumbling, has there?'

'Nothing serious,' said Pat, pausing in the doorway. 'Robin's
handling it.'

She left. Strike ate the fruitcake, which was very good, feeling a mixture of renewed guilt, irritation at whoever it was who was bloody bitching and a totally unexpected new appreciation for Pat, who, during his incapacitation, had provided a brand of matter-of-fact assistance he found strangely soothing. The idea of baking a cake for the team was one that would never have occurred to Strike, though admittedly, right now, it was doubtful whether he'd be able to balance long enough to mix one.

Cake finished, he lit a fresh cigarette and returned to Twitter.

He was starting to feel like a truffle pig trying to do its job in a room full of incense, dead fish and strong cheese. As tedious hour succeeded tedious hour he found himself increasingly prone to becoming sidetracked by rambling arguments and threads that had nothing to do with the Brotherhood of Ultima Thule. For instance, he'd started to become interested in two of the most prolific tweeters to Edie and Anomie: Lepine's Disciple and Algernon Gizzard, both of whom seemed to have derived inordinate pleasure from attacking Edie Ledwell over the past few years.

Finally, with the aim of getting rid of an annoying itch, he went to take a proper look at Lepine's Disciple's account.

The avatar showed a blurred black-and-white picture of a young man with bushy hair and beard. Looking at the old picture, Strike thought he recognised it and turned to Google to check. Sure enough, the picture on the account was that of Marc Lépine, the Canadian mass murderer who in 1989 shot dead fourteen women before killing himself, leaving behind him a suicide note that blamed feminists for ruining his life.

As far as Strike could see, the @LepinesD1sciple account seemed to exist mainly to harass and threaten young women. Edie had been a regular target, but Kea Niven had also come in for her share of abuse, on the basis that she'd 'used' Anomie to amplify her claims of plagiarism until Anomie had 'seen through' her. Otherwise, Lepine's Disciple targeted franchises the anonymous writer believed were being ruined by female actors and writers, including *Star Wars*, *Dr Who* and a wide variety of video games. Unrelated female accounts were targeted on the basis that their owners were too ugly, too opinionated and (a particular obsession) too overweight. Lepine's Disciple frequently made common cause with alt-right accounts, including the Brotherhood of Ultima Thule, and often backed up Anomie, whose attacks on Ledwell seemed to delight him.

The account was littered with memes and stock phrases Strike had already encountered among the various Dreks and the Brothers of Ultima Thule: cartoons of 'Stacy and Chad', the shallow and narcissistic mainstream cartoon 'normies' who were getting plenty of sex, and regular mention of being 'red-pilled', or awoken to the fact that men were being subjugated and that women were, in fact, the oppressors. Lepine's Disciple was also prone to suggesting unpleasant and sometimes violent solutions to other young men's problems. To an American teenager complaining about his stepmother's strict curfew, he suggested bugging her bedroom, then playing audio of her having sex on loudspeaker out of the window. A man who'd been dumped by his teacher girlfriend was advised by Lepine's Disciple to put child porn in her handbag, then call the police. In amongst all the rage, spite and talk of a 'beta male' revolution were frank and furious admissions that the owner of the account was still a virgin.

The cumulative effect of Lepine's Disciple's output wasn't merely unpleasant to Strike but concerning. His investigative career had taught him that dangerous people very rarely exploded into violence from, as Strike put it to himself, a standing start. However, as Lepine's Disciple was anonymous and their location hidden, there wasn't much he could do about them. A small consolation was that they had only seventy-two followers, most of which, as far as Strike could judge, were bots.

Strike next turned his attention to Algernon Gizzard's account, which had just over three thousand followers. The banner picture showed Chelsea celebrating their recent Premier League win: Drogba, Ramires and Rémy lay on the grass beside the crowned trophy while the rest of the squad cheered and fist-pumped behind them. Given that Strike was an Arsenal supporter, this image didn't make him any more sympathetic to @Gizzard_Al.

The avatar showed the back of a close-cropped dark head, with a pair of aviator sunglasses worn backwards. Strike enlarged the picture, looking more closely at the sunglasses: the bridge was of leather and while the tiny silver writing on the lens was blurry, Strike thought it read 'Cartier'.

The life depicted by the account holder, always assuming it was genuinely his own, could hardly have provided a greater contrast to that of Lepine's Disciple. There was no self-hatred here; on the contrary, a tone of braggadocio and gleeful consumerism pervaded

445

almost every tweet. Gizzard often posted pictures of the red Mercedes E-Class coupé he claimed to own, though always with the number plate carefully cropped out. A picture of Chelsea playing Manchester City had been taken from a private box, champagne on ice in the foreground. The back view of a long-haired blonde in a miniskirt, walking along Bond Street, was captioned 'feeling horny so called the thot I dumped a month ago'. Gizzard regularly used the words 'thot' and 'foid' for women, words the forty-year-old Strike had to look up, learning that the former was an acronym for 'that ho over there' and the latter an abbreviation of 'femoid'.

There were two selfies, neither of which showed much of Gizzard's face. In one, a heavy eyebrow was revealed in the corner of a picture of a long white beach that looked as though it might be in the Seychelles. Half a brown eye had also been captured in a shot taken over Gizzard's shoulder, showing several models and a well-known actress clearly the worse for drink in what Strike recognised as the VIP section of a nightclub to which he'd once tracked an errant husband. Gizzard had captioned the photograph 'A snatch of thots'. The tweet had earned him over five thousand likes.

The more Strike looked at Gizzard's account, the more his subconscious made futile attempts to tell him something. What was it? He scrolled back up to the top of the page and looked at the bio.

Algernon Gizzard Esq
@Gizzard_Al
"I have no sympathy any more for the dregs of society. I don't care if they live or die" – weev

Suddenly, though nobody was there to hear him, Strike said loudly,

'Algiz. Fucking *Algiz.*'

He typed the word into Google. Sure enough, Algiz, like Thurisaz, was a rune from the Elder Futhark. The meanings assigned to Algiz were given variously as protection, defence and higher self.

'Can't be a fucking coincidence,' muttered Strike, now looking back over Gizzard's content with even more care, scrolling slowly backwards through the years, paying particular attention to those with whom Algiz had interacted. At last, back in early 2013, he found an interaction with a Brotherhood of Ultima Thule account.

Ryder T @Ultima_T_14
Gonna get seriously fucked up tonight.

Algernon Gizzard Esq @Gizzard_Al
replying to @Ultima_T_14
Auf die alten Götte!

Strike suspected the Germanic toast might just be a favourite at Odinist retreats. Still he kept scrolling and finally, in July 2011, he found something to justify the two hours he'd spent on @Gizzard_Al, who'd tweeted his approval after a far-right terrorist had slaughtered seventy-seven young people at a Labour Party camp in Norway.

Algernon Gizzard Esq @Gizzard_Al
Been reading shooter's manifesto
👍👍👍

Jamie Kettle @BlackPill28
replying to @Gizzard_Al
Fkn hero

'*Got you, you fucker!*' said Strike loudly.

Thurisaz was grinning out of the photograph attached to the Jamie Kettle account, whose location was listed as London. The only difference between his appearance of 2011 and that of the present day was that four years previously he hadn't had a rune tattooed on his Adam's apple. However, his banner photograph was the skull Strike had seen tattooed on the back of Thurisaz's head.

The account bore all the stigmata of a member of the far right Strike had come to know well: a preoccupation with immigrants overbreeding, white men being marginalised, the policing of thought and speech, and the narcissism, greed and vapidity of women. However, the account had undergone a marked change in 2012, after which nearly all political content had disappeared, leaving only infrequent posts about Kettle's two main hobbies: carpentry, of which he posted examples of his completed work, and his 1968 Norton Commando motorbike.

Strike shuffled aside the papers on his kitchen table to find the list of Ultima Thule accounts he'd been compiling, and swiftly found @jkett_BOUT, also known as True Briton, whose account had been started in April 2012: exactly the moment at which Jamie Kettle's account had been purged of political content.

'Caught because you wanted to show off your end tables,' said Strike with a grim smile as he reached for his mobile to call DCI Murphy.

47

. . . these blotched souls are eager to infect,
And blow their bad breath in a sister's face
As if they got some ease by it.

Elizabeth Barrett Browning
Aurora Leigh

In-game chats between five of the eight moderators of *Drek's Game*

```
<Moderator Channel>

<13 May 2015 23.47>

<Vilepechora, Hartella,
Worm28, Paperwhite>

Hartella: I'm so
psyched for Comic Con

Worm28: me too

Vilepechora: everyone
got their masks ready?

Worm28: lol yeah

Hartella: u going then,
Vile?

Vilepechora: don't call
me Vile

Hartella: lol

Worm28: lol
```

Vilepechora: I'll go if Paperwhite's going.

Paperwhite: why?

Vilepechora: I fkn love a redhead. Proper Viking blood

Hartella: how do u know what she looks like?

Vilepechora: lol that'd be telling

>

Hartella: is LordDrek going to Comic Con, anyone know?

Worm28: don 't know , he hasn 't been in here for ages

Worm28: I think Anomie shoud appoint another mod

Hartella: no he shouldn't

Worm28: but he 's never here any more

Worm28: Vile , has LordDrk left ?

Hartella: I'm sure he hasn't

Hartella: he's just really busy

>

>

>

>

>

<A new private channel has opened>

<13 May 2015 23.50>

<Paperwhite invites Vilepechora>

Paperwhite: How do you know I'm a redhead?

<Vilepechora has joined the channel>

Vilepechora: I'm honoured. Thought it was only Morehouse who got private channel action off you

Vilepechora: you two had a lovers tiff? Noticed he's not in much any more

Vilepechora: and you're in here all hours

Paperwhite: answer the fkn question

Vilepechora: should have said a *natural* redhead

Vilepechora: collar and cuffs match and everything

Paperwhite: how do you know?

Vilepechora: lol

Vilepechora: I'll tell u if you answer a question

>

<LordDrek has entered
the channel>

Hartella: OMG we were
just talking about you!

LordDrek: only good
things I hope?

Hartella: yeah of course!

Hartella: how are you?

LordDrek: pretty good

LordDrek: Morehouse
not around?

Hartella: no

LordDrek: good, because
getting called a Nazi every
10 minutes gets old

Hartella: I'm so sorry

LordDrek: not your fault x

Hartella: Morehouse was
so out of order

LordDrek: Anomie not in?

Hartella: no he left
half an hour ago, had
something to do

LordDrek: what is he, a
vampire? It's gone midnight

Hartella: lol

LordDrek: maybe now he's
got a taste for killing
he's gone hunting

Hartella: lol don't say
that

LordDrek: I'm not the

of mine

Paperwhite: what question?

Vilepechora: how much
would you want to tell
me who Anomie is?

Paperwhite: I don't know
who he is

Vilepechora: piss off, I know
Morehouse will have told you

Paperwhite: he hasn't

Vilepechora: but
Morehouse knows, right?

Paperwhite: yeah
Morehouse knows but he'd
never fkn tell you

Vilepechora: I know,
that's why I'm asking you

Paperwhite: why the
sudden interest?

Vilepechora: it's not sudden

Vilepechora: everyone in
the fandom wants to know
who Anomie is

Vilepechora: plus, he
killed Ledwell

Paperwhite: fuck off

Vilepechora: who did, then?

Paperwhite: maybe you

Vilepechora: cast-iron
alibi, gorgeous

Paperwhite: that shit

Paperwhite: that total
fkn bastard

one saying it, he is

LordDrek: all the fkn
time, out in the game

LordDrek: one of these
days someone'll take
him seriously

LordDrek: I know he
thinks he's kept all
the police out of here,
but it only takes one
and he's fucked

LordDrek: oy, Vilepechora

>

Vilepechora: I'm busy,
give me 5

>

>

Hartella: it's so
unfair if they really
are spying on fans

Hartella: no fan would
ever have done that

Hartella: especially
not to Josh

Worm28: why r u saying
thatt ?

Worm28: espcielly not
to Josh

Hartella: you know what
I mean

Worm28: no I don 't ,
explin

Hartella: well because
she was the one ruining
everything for cash
wasn't she?

Paperwhite: how dare he?

Paperwhite: he bangs on
aoubt rule 14 then goes
and and does that?

Vilepechora: don't worry,
I deleted it

Paperwhite: sure you did

Vilepechora: I did. My
gf's the jealous type

Vilepechora: bet u want
me to find out who Anomie
is now, don't you?

>

>

Paperwhite: are you
going to Comic Con?

Vilepechora: dunno, why?

Paperwhite: Anomie's
going to be there
dressed as Drek

Vilepechora: for real?

Paperwhite: Morehouse
told me ages ago

Paperwhite: Anomie
always goes as Drek

Vilepechora: so do tons
of people

Paperwhite: well that's
why he does it, moron

Paperwhite: what do you
think, he'd walk in with a
fkn arrow pointing to his
head saying 'I am Anomie'?

Vilepechora: lol ok

Worm28: why was she ?

Hartella: come on, Worm, everyone knows she was the one who was in it for money

Worm28: how do u know ? u wern 't there for all the meetings and everything

Worm28: how do u know j*** ddn't want more money?

Worm28: E*** came up with all the good ideas and the best carracters

Worm28: i 'm tired of evryone shitting on her

Worm28: she was a good person, I know she was

Worm28: so fuck you Hartella

<Worm28 has left the channel>

>

Hartella: er - what the hell was that?

LordDrek: lol

LordDrek: the worm turned

Hartella: I mean, it's not like I *knew* L****** or anything

Hartella: Josh would have left the cartoon free on YouTube forever. She was the one who wanted paying.

LordDrek: yeah, she sounded a right mercenary bitch

Paperwhite: I hope you do find out who the bastard is now

Paperwhite: I might have a good look for him myself

Vilepechora: great, we should team up

Paperwhite: I'm not teaming up with you

Vilepechora: why, would Morehouse be jealous?

Paperwhite: Vilepechora, if my pic turns online or anything

Vilepechora: it won't

Vilepechora: I could have tried to blackmail u with it

Vilepechora: but I didn't, because I'm a nice guy

Paperwhite: sure u are

Vilepechora: what's that supposed to mean?

Paperwhite: Halvening?

Vilepechora: fuck off, we spent ages on that research, we genuinely thought Anomie was Ledwell

Paperwhite: ok if you say so

Paperwhite: but I'm serious about my pic

Vilepechora: I swear to Odin and the Old Gods I won't use it

Hartella: well she kind of was

>

>

Hartella: u going to Comic Con?

LordDrek: wish I was but I can't ☹

LordDrek: you?

Hartella: yes. And in 3 weeks time I'm going to see a play

LordDrek: yeah? What play?

Hartella: Chekhov

LordDrek: wow, I hope you enjoy that

Hartella: kind of hoping the star will give me his autograph afterwards

LordDrek: well, you never know

Hartella: you think he might?

LordDrek: I'd say there's a very high chance of that happening

Hartella: lol

Hartella: what do you think I should do, hang around the stage door?

>

LordDrek: hang on, babe, someone's at my front door

Hartella: no problem x

Paperwhite: you said you deleted it

Vilepechora: I did. That's why I can't use it.

Paperwhite: ok well that better be true

<Paperwhite has left the channel>

<Vilepechora has left the channel>

<Private channel has closed>

<A private channel has opened>

<14 May 2015 00.04>

<Vilepechora invites LordDrek>

Vilepechora: News

>

>

<LordDrek has joined the channel>

>

>

Paperwhite: Morehouse
been in?

Hartella: no

Hartella: have you two
fallen out?

Paperwhite: no, I just
want to talk to him

>

>

>

Paperwhite: will you tell
Morehouse I need to speak
to him, if he shows up?

Hartella: yeah ok

Paperwhite: thanks

**<Paperwhite has left
the channel>**

Hartella: are you still
in here, Lord Drek?

>

>

>

>

>

>

>

>

LordDrek: get anywhere?

Vilepechora: ahe claims
not to know who he is

Vilepechora: but she
says he's going to
Comic Con, dressed as
Drek

LordDrek: that's no
fkn use, there'll be
hundreds of Dreks there

Vilepechora: That's what
I said, but she said
that's why he does it.

Vilepechora: Paperwhite's
interested in finding out
who he is, now she knows
he's been flashing her
nudes round inside the
game.

Vilepechora: I could
team up with her to try
and find him

LordDrek: fuck off, we
don't involve SJWs in
our stuff.

LordDrek: I know you've
got a hard on for
Paperwhite but you need
to lose it. Keep your
mind on your fucking job.

LordDrek: because I've got
news too, and it aint good

LordDrek: and we're safer
talking in here than the
usual because I think
the pigs might still be
watching us there

LordDrek: Thurisaz was
taken in for questioning
an hour ago

LordDrek: gimme a mo babe

Hartella: sorry, I wasn't meaning to hassle!

>

>

>

>

>

>

>

>

>

>

>

>

>

LordDrek: sorry about that, neighbour's locked himself out

Hartella: do you keep a spare key for him?

LordDrek: yeah

Hartella: lol I don't ever imagine people like you doing stuff like that for their neighbours

LordDrek: 'people like me'?

Hartella: you know what I mean

Vilepechora: fuck

LordDrek: there must've been a camera in that gents

LordDrek: anyway, the silly cunt kept his old Twitter account with his pic on it and his real name. That's how they IDed him

Vilepechora: how d'you know?

LordDrek: Uruz was at Thurisaz's place when the pigs turned up

LordDrek: They asked Thurisaz if the old account was his

LordDrek: he could hardly fkn deny it, the bike was in his drive

Vilepechora: shit

LordDrek: so I want you to go and delete that fucking Algiz account IMMEDIATELY

Vilepechora: ok, ok, I'm doing it now

>

>

>

Vilepechora: ok, it's done. Deleted

Vilepechora: but I never put my real name on it, or pics of my face

LordDrek: no, just your car, your football team and your favourite nightclub

Hartella: f***** people

LordDrek: we're still people

Hartella: lol yes I suppose so

Hartella: just hard to picture it

LordDrek: better not talk any more about stuff like that. Rule 14.

Hartella: lol, yes, sorry.

Hartella: I sometimes get a bit careless when Anomie isn't in here

Hartella: I suppose after a play's over, the actors have to go home and get an early night

LordDrek: yeah, they do

Hartella: shame

LordDrek: I think the directors would be strict about that

Hartella: I thought they would be

Hartella: but they presumably let people visit the actors dressing rooms before the play?

>

LordDrek: sorry, hun, that's my neighbour back again. Key broke in the bloody lock

Hartella: oh no

LordDrek: I'm gonna have to log out, he's going to wait at my place for the locksmith.

Vilepechora: look, someone should definitely go to comic con and try and ID Anomie

Vilepechora: he keeps saying he was the one who attacked them. If we find out who he really is, we can tip off the police. It'll take the heat off us if he's done for stabbing those two.

>

LordDrek: what are u gonna do, go round pulling masks off people?

Vilepechora: ffs it's worth a shot

Vilepechora: He'll be in a Drek mask and a Keep the Game T-shirt. I'll just get him talking

>

>

LordDrek: ok, go to Comic Con but ffs don't do anything dumb

LordDrek: don't do a Thurisaz

LordDrek: if he hadn't gone for that copper he wouldn't be in custody

Vilepechora: Thurisaz won't talk

LordDrek: that's not the point

Vilepechora: you still holding the meeting Saturday?

LordDrek: yeah, we need

Hartella: ah ok

Hartella: night xxx

>

>

LordDrek: night xxx

<Lord Drek has left the channel>

>

>

>

>

>

>

>

Hartella: you still awake, Vile?

>

>

>

>

<Vilepechora has left the channel>

to keep discipline tight right now

LordDrek: I'm still having to chat up that fat cow Hartella so. she doesn't get suspicious

>

LordDrek: she's coming to see my play. She wants an autograph outside the stage door

Vilepechora: rofl, you cuck. what are you gonna say after Michael David ignores her, pretend you didn't see her?

Vilepechora: because she won't believe that, not when she's built like a brick shithouse.

LordDrek: I know. should've pretended to be Stevie Wonder

Vilepechora: lol

<LordDrek has left the channel>

<Vilepechora has left the channel>

<Private channel has closed>

48

Sometimes, as young things will, she vexes me,
Wayward, or too unheeding, or too blind.
Like aimless birds that, flying on a wind,
Strike slant against their own familiar tree . . .

Augusta Webster
Mother and Daughter

Strike's alarm woke him early the following morning, because he was due to drive to King's Lynn to interview Kea Niven. Though mildly apprehensive about how his stump was going to bear the twin challenges of the prosthesis and operating the accelerator, his mood was lifted by the text from Ryan Murphy that had come in overnight. Thurisaz, also known as Jamie Kettle, had been found at home in Hemel Hempstead and been taken in for questioning. The police were currently examining his computer for evidence of dark-web activity and searching his house for any evidence of bomb-making equipment. While it would have been going too far to say that Strike felt falling over the Finnish woman's bag had been a stroke of luck, especially given the strain it had put on his own business, he at least had the satisfaction of knowing that his long hours immersed in Twitter had borne fruit, so he breakfasted in better spirits than he'd had for many days.

However, when he emerged from the shower Strike noticed that he had a missed call. With a strong suspicion of what he was about to hear, he accessed voicemail.

'Er – yes, hello, Mr Strike? This is Sara Niven. Kea's very poorly today, I'm afraid, so, um, we're going to have to call the interview off . . . sorry.'

Strike stood balanced on one leg, his free hand gripping the back of a kitchen chair, a bath-towel wrapped around his waist. Finally he decided the only thing to do was to proceed as though he'd never heard the message. The call had been diverted through the office number: he'd claim there'd been some technical hitch.

To his relief, the end of his stump accepted meekly the sock, the gel pad and the pressure of his weight on his false leg. His hamstring was still complaining, but as the alternative to wearing the prosthesis was making the journey to King's Lynn by train and taxi on crutches, followed by going to meet Madeline that evening with one trouser leg pinned up and half empty, his hamstring was going to have to put up with it. He did, however, decide to take the collapsible walking stick Robin had bought him, before making his way carefully downstairs, wearing a suit because he didn't want to have to return to Denmark Street and change before meeting Madeline later.

Strike was on the A14 and skirting Cambridge when Robin called him.

'Good news. Seb Montgomery definitely isn't Anomie.'

'Thank fuck,' said Strike fervently. 'About time we ruled someone out. How d'you know?'

'Anomie came into the game five minutes ago, badgering more players to go to Comic Con. Seb was out on a coffee run for the office at the time. I had eyes on him: no mobile, no iPad, no means of typing.'

'Excellent work, Ellacott,' said Strike. 'In other news, Kea Niven's mother says she's too poorly to be interviewed today.'

'Oh *bugger*,' said Robin. 'What're you—?'

'Going anyway,' said Strike. 'Fuck it. Going to pretend I didn't get the message.'

There was a slight pause, in which Strike overtook a dawdling Vauxhall Mokka.

'D'you think that's—?' began Robin.

'She's *your* favourite for Anomie,' said Strike.

Given the events of the previous week, he was feeling slightly sensitive about any suggestion he might be acting recklessly.

'No, I suppose you're right,' said Robin. 'She could keep putting us off for ever.'

'Did you read my email about Jamie Kettle?' asked Strike. He'd let Robin know he'd identified Thurisaz immediately after calling Murphy.

'Yes,' said Robin, 'fantastic. Must've taken you ages.'

'Twenty-three hours of trawling through Twitter,' said Strike. 'Murphy was pleased, though. Where are you?'

'Walking towards Harley Street. Gus Upcott's travelling by Tube in this direction, according to Midge. I'm going to take over on Gus and she can go and relieve Barclay on Preston Pierce. I think we should—'

'Mix it up a bit, yeah,' said Strike, hoping Robin wasn't implicitly criticising the decision he'd taken to stay on Wally Cardew for so many hours, thereby making himself recognisable to Thurisaz. 'Well, I'll text you once I've got Kea in my sights.'

The news about Montgomery was so cheering that Strike didn't much mind his first glimpse of a windmill, or the change in landscape to wide flat fens and marshland. He never went voluntarily into Norfolk and in fact had a slight prejudice against the whole county, because the worst of all the many places to which Strike's novelty-chasing, peripatetic mother had taken her son and daughter to live had been a Norfolk commune, a place Strike sincerely hoped no longer existed.

He entered King's Lynn shortly after eleven o'clock. His satnav led him through a series of nondescript side streets until he emerged on a concrete quay bordering the Great Ouse, a muddy-looking river that ran right past the Nivens' house. Strike parked, texted Robin that he was about to knock on Kea's front door and got out of the car, carrying his folder of screenshots. On the point of closing the car door, he reached back inside for his walking stick, though he wasn't currently feeling the need for it, then walked along South Quay to the Nivens' house and pressed the doorbell.

A high-pitched female voice shouted out from inside, although the words weren't distinguishable. After a pause of almost a minute, the door opened.

A middle-aged, vaguely bohemian-looking woman with untidy grey hair, whom Strike took to be Kea's mother, stood before him. On seeing the detective, her face registered dismay.

'Oh – are you—?'

'Cormoran Strike,' said the detective. 'Here to see Kea?'

At the announcement of his name, the high-pitched voice he'd heard previously literally screamed, from somewhere out of sight.

'No! You told me you stopped him!'

461

'Kea,' said her mother, wheeling around, but next came the sounds of running footsteps and the slamming of a door. 'Oh *no*,' said Sara Niven, and turning back to Strike she said angrily, 'I told you not to come! I rang you this morning and left a message!'

'Did you?' said Strike, leaning heavily on his stick and feigning confusion tinged with disbelief. 'You sure you used the right number? Our office answering service is usually reliable.'

'I'm sure I—'

A second, heavier door slammed. Strike deduced that Kea had just dashed out of the back door. A disconcertingly metallic voice inside the house set up a repeated cry of '*Please*, Kea! *Please*, Kea! *Please*—'

'I've just driven all the way from London,' said Strike, frowning as he leaned on his stick. 'Could I at least use your bathroom?'

'I – well—'

She hesitated, before saying reluctantly,

'All right, then.'

Sara backed away to admit Strike, pointed him towards a closed door a short way down the hall, then disappeared around a corner at the end of the hall, where Strike surmised the back door was situated, calling 'Kea? *Kea!*'

Strike paused on the doormat and looked around. Through an open door to his right lay a sitting room decorated in a busy mix of Liberty prints. A pair of lovebirds were blinking at him from a large cage. He also saw a laptop sitting open on the sagging sofa.

Strike moved quickly into the sitting room and hit the touchpad of the laptop. It was warm. Kea had been browsing dresses on the website prettylittlething.com. Strike clicked on her internet history, took a hasty picture on his mobile of the list of websites she'd recently visited, then moved as quickly as possible back out of the room and through the door Sara had indicated.

The small room contained only a toilet and sink. Neither were particularly clean. A pile of copies of the *New Statesman* and a local paper lay heaped beside the toilet. Several age-spotted prints of exotic birds hung unevenly on the walls. The strange metallic voice continued to chant '*Please*, Kea! *Please*, Kea!' from deeper inside the house.

Strike emerged from the bathroom to hear Sara shout:

'Stop it!'

The metallic voice changed its chant.

'*Stop it! Stop it! Stop it!*'

462

He followed the sound of the voices. Sara Niven was standing in the kitchen looking both anxious and angry, her back to a sink piled with dirty crockery. The baggy dress she wore was made of a sludge-green Liberty print that matched the cushions in the sitting room. There was a hole in the left foot of her thick black tights, through which her big toe was attempting to poke.

'*Stop it!*'

On a perch in the corner of the kitchen stood a large white umbrella cockatoo, which was now looking at Strike with unnervingly intelligent eyes. Having spoken the last two words, it fell to nibbling at its own foot.

'Stay well away from him,' said Sara. 'He doesn't like men.'

Strike paused obediently. Through the window over the sink he could see that half the outside courtyard had been converted into aviaries. A wide variety of coloured birds was sitting or fluttering around inside them. The kitchen smelled stale, with an overtone of vegetables.

'Kea's gone,' Sara informed Strike in an accusing voice. 'She went out the back gate.'

'Ah,' said Strike, leaning on his stick. 'That's a shame . . . I take it you know what all this is about, Mrs Niven?'

'Yes, you said on the phone: that person Anomaly, or whatever they're called,' said Sara. 'Kea said Josh thinks it's *her*, which is *totally* ridiculous.'

'Kea must have misunderstood me,' said Strike. 'I told her there's a theory going around that she's Anomie, but I never said Josh believes it. Josh only wants Kea to talk to me because he knows she's communicated privately with Anomie.'

'Look,' said Sara heatedly. 'Kea's already spoken to the police. Somebody contacted them – *totally* ridiculous – and told them Kea had been *persecuting* that girl, that Ellie Led-thing for years, and so they interviewed her – about things she said on social media, for God's sake! It's hardly *persecution*, saying you were stolen from, is it? And incidentally, Josh Blay treated Kea *abysmally*, it had an *atrocious* effect on her mental health and she ended up having to leave college—'

'Yes, I knew Kea had been unwell,' said Strike. 'Sorry, but would you mind very much if I sat down?'

He tweaked up his right trouser leg to reveal the metal rod of his prosthesis. As he'd hoped, the sight seemed to shock and fluster Sara.

'Oh, I'm sorry, I – I didn't know—'

Strike, whose sole aim was to make it more difficult for Sara to dis-lodge him from her house, settled himself on a wooden kitchen chair. The table was covered in toast crumbs. Sara now sat down automatically in the chair opposite him and absent-mindedly swept a few of them onto the floor. This wasn't the way the fastidious Strike liked to live.

'She was doing better until *this* happened,' Sara said, and Strike understood 'this' to mean the stabbings. 'But then, obviously the stress of it – I've lodged a complaint with the police. She should've had someone with her for that interview. *I* should have been there. She's chronically ill, for God's sake. It's not *her* fault he called her! And then, *what* they put her through, tracing her movements—'

'Sorry, who called Kea?' said Strike.

'Josh,' said Sara, looking at Strike with a mixture of disbelief and dismay. 'I thought you'd've known – he called her the night before he got stabbed.'

'Ah, I see.'

'But he didn't tell her he was going to the cemetery next day. She never knew *that*. Why would he tell her where – he'd hardly men-tion that Ellie Led-whatever to *Kea*, would he? But the police had her going over all her movements and, well, obviously she's had a massive relapse.'

'Yes, Kea mentioned on the phone that she's been bedbound,' said Strike.

There followed another short pause in which the fact that Kea had just run out of the house seemed to reverberate like an echo through the room.

'She has good days and bad, that's the nature of her condition,' Sara said defensively. 'The NHS is absolutely useless. "Her bloods are normal." "We recommend psychotherapy." Oh, really, *do* you?' said Sara furiously. 'And how exactly can it be a psychiatric issue, Kea being *literally* unable to get out of bed she's in so much pain, so fatigued? So you end up having to do all your own research over the internet, having to do the medical profession's job for them. I've paid for all kinds of private tests, and of course the *stress* of all *this*' – Sara made a wild gesture – 'has been atrocious, she's been in an *appalling—*'

The cockatoo took off suddenly from its perch in a whirl of white feathers, making Strike jump, and swooped off up the hall.

'You let him fly all over the house?'

'Only the ground floor,' said Sara. 'There's a door blocking the top of the stairs.'

The now-out-of-sight cockatoo set up its cry of '*Please*, Kea! *Please*, Kea!' again and the two caged lovebirds set up a series of squeaking chirrups in return.

'Josh Blay's paralysed,' Strike began again. 'The knife went through his neck. He's only recently regained the ability to talk.'

Sara seemed to shrink inside the shapeless dress.

'All he wants is to stop this internet troll continuing to whip up trouble and to stop them attacking Edie's family. Since Edie died, Anomie's started on her uncle and—'

'Kea would *never*—'

'Josh doesn't think Kea's Anomie,' Strike said. 'He only wants her to talk to me because, as I say, he knows she's been in direct contact with Anomie. Anything, the smallest detail she might know about them, could help us find who's behind the account and put Josh's mind at rest.'

'*Please*, Kea! *Please*, Kea!' said the cockatoo in the distant room.

'Oh God,' said Sara Niven, her eyes filling with tears, and Strike was reminded of another middle-aged mother who'd cried at the mention of Josh Blay, though, he was sure, for very different reasons. Sara got up, blundered to the side and grabbed both a piece of kitchen roll and an inhaler lying beside the kettle.

'Asthmatic,' she told Strike huskily, before using it, then blowing her nose as she sat down again.

'This theory Kea's behind the Anomaly account – who's saying that?'

'Online rumours take on a life of their own,' said Strike, truthfully enough. 'It isn't always easy to find out where they originated.'

'She'd never, *ever*—' Sara began again, but the out-of-sight cockatoo, which had briefly stopped shrieking '*Please*, Kea!' began imitating a ringtone so convincingly that Strike's hand went automatically to his pocket.

'Oh,' Strike said, realising where the noise was coming from. 'Sorry, what were you—?'

'Look, you don't understand,' said Sara breathlessly. 'Kea's really been through it. Her dad died when she was eighteen and she was a real daddy's girl, absolutely *w-worshipped* him. He had a stroke at work, just collapsed in the office canteen.'

'She went off to art college six months later and met Josh. Then he cheated on her and dumped her. Then that *bloody* cartoon came out and Kea realised Josh had told that Led-Thing girl all Kea's ideas . . . Josh Blay ruined my daughter's life, that's the truth, and now he sends you here asking for favours from her—'

'All right, Mrs Niven,' said Strike, making deliberately heavy weather of attempting to get to his feet again, 'you've made your position clear, but you have to understand, we're attempting to help Kea clear her name. Internet accusations, however ill-founded, have a way of spilling out into real life and affecting people's lives, sometimes for years. But if she's not comfortable helping the investigation, there's nothing more to be said and I'll leave. Thank you for letting me use your bathroom.'

Strike was almost at the kitchen door when Sara called,

'No – wait!'

He turned back. Sara seemed torn between tears and anger.

'All right, I'll – I'll call her. I'll see if she'll come back. Please *don't* open any doors or windows while I'm outside.'

Strike assumed this unusual request related to the uncaged cockatoo. Sara snatched a mobile off the kitchen side and slid out of the kitchen door into the yard, closing the door behind her.

Strike watched out of the corner of his eye as Sara pressed in her daughter's number. After a few seconds, she began to talk. Perhaps she imagined her voice wouldn't carry into the house, but the window frame was warped and Strike could hear every word.

'Darling?' she said tentatively. 'No, he's still here . . . Well, I had to, he needed the bathroom . . .'

A long pause followed, in which Kea was evidently pouring words into her mother's ear. Sara began pacing up and down in front of her aviaries, her expression fearful.

'I know that . . . Yes, of course I know that . . .'

There were bird droppings on the floor in front of the fridge, Strike noticed.

'No, but . . . No, he says Josh doesn't . . . Well, because they want to know what you . . . No, but . . . *Please*, Kea, just listen for a . . .'

Sara seemed to be listening to another long speech. At last she said,

'I know that, darling, obviously, but don't you think, if you refuse it might look as though . . . That's not fair, Kea . . . Well, but mightn't it be better to get it over with? . . . Yes . . . He's brought a folder . . . I don't know ... *Please*, Kea, don't ... Kea, how can you say that? Of course I do! ... But if that rumour's going round ...'

Strike heard the sound of wings. The large white cockatoo had landed on top of the kitchen door, from where it peered down at him with what seemed to Strike a nasty glint in its button-bright eyes.

'All right ... Yes, I'll tell him. Yes ... No, I'll make sure he knows that. All right, darling ... *Please*, Kea, don't ... Yes ... OK ... Bye dar—'

But apparently Kea had hung up.

Sara opened the back door just enough to slide back in and closed it quickly, glancing up at her cockatoo as she did so. She was breathing a little wheezily.

'She'll meet you in the Maids Head. She won't be able to stay more than twenty minutes; she's feeling too unwell.'

Sara took another large suck on her inhaler.

'Is the Maids Head within walking distance?' Strike asked.

'You're probably better driving. It's only a few minutes by car. In the Tuesday Market Place. You can't miss it.'

'Great. Well, thanks very much, Mrs Niven.'

Strike had just picked up his folder of screenshots and turned back to the hall when the cockatoo suddenly gave a loud shriek and dived. He saw a blur of white feathers and tried to protect himself with the folder, but too late: the razor-like beak had already sliced into his temple.

'Don't hit him!' cried Sara as Strike tried to smack the bird away from him, while its claws scrabbled in the detective's thick hair. Eyes closed, fearing the attacking beak would hit his eyeball next, Strike made his way blindly towards the place where he knew the front door was.

'*Don't open it!*' screamed Sara, as the cockatoo seemed intent on pursuing Strike, but the latter, unwilling to afford the bird further target practice, had already grabbed the doorknob. Whether because his repeated attempts to scare it off with the folder had worked, or because Sara's shrieks had somehow convinced it to retreat, the whirring mass of claw, beak and feathers disappeared. Blood now trickling down the side of his face, Strike wrenched open the door and stepped outside.

49

'*Fuck!*' said Strike loudly as the front door slammed behind him. The gash made by the bird's beak was deep and felt at least an inch long. He groped in his pocket for something to mop himself up with, but found nothing.

'Yew might as well 'ave went in with a tiger, as go in there with that bird,' said an elderly male voice. Strike looked around to see Sara's neighbour, a frail-looking, white-haired old man, standing on his doorstep and watching Strike wince as he tried to staunch the blood oozing out of the stinging cut left by the cockatoo. ''Ere,' said the man. 'Oi've got an 'andkerchief.'

He shuffled forwards and handed Strike a clean, folded square out of his pocket.

'That's very kind, but—'

'Do yew keep it, boi,' said the old man as Strike hesitated. 'That'll bleed a while if Oi knows that bird . . . And Oi do know that bloody bird,' he added bitterly.

Strike thanked him, accepted the handkerchief and the old man disappeared into his house.

As Strike passed Sara Niven's front window on the way back to the car he saw her glaring out at him, the cockatoo now standing on the lovebirds' cage behind her.

'OK?' she mouthed through the glass, though she looked more cross than concerned.

'Fine,' he mouthed back, insincerely.

Once back in the car, Strike called Robin, one hand still holding the handkerchief to his head.

'Hi,' she said. 'Anomie's not in the game. What happened with Kea?'

'Nothing yet,' said Strike. 'She ran out the back door when I turned up at the front. She's deigning to give me twenty minutes in the pub. One interesting titbit from her mother, though: Josh Blay called Kea the night before he met Edie Ledwell in the cemetery.'

'You're kidding.'

'I'm not. Have to say, your theory he kept in touch with her after the so-called break-up is looking more and more plausible. In other news, I just got attacked by a fucking cockatoo.'

'By a *what?*'

'A bird,' said Strike, 'with a beak like a fucking razor.'

'Shit,' said Robin, and he appreciated the fact she hadn't laughed. 'Are you OK?'

'I'll live,' said Strike irritably, chucking the bloodstained handkerchief down on the passenger seat. 'Where's Gus Upcott?'

'Inside his dermatologist's. He's carrying a bag that looks like it's got a laptop in it. I'm lurking outside the – wait, Anomie just tweeted,' said Robin. 'Sorry, I'm just going to check if anyone's just used a phone.'

She rang off and Strike opened Twitter to see what Anomie had just written.

Anomie
@AnomieGamemaster

Wear your support for Drek's Game.

T-shirts online now at https://bit.ly/2I3tYGg

#KeepDreksGame #ComicCon2015

469

Strike snorted, closed Twitter, then brought up the picture he'd taken of Kea's internet history.

Patent pink stilettos	https://www.prettylittlething.com/patentpink . . .
Faux leather leggings	https://www.prettylittlething.com/fauxleathe . . .
Hoop earrings	https://www.prettylittlething.com/hoopearring . . .
Josh Blay recovery – Google search	
Josh Blay – Google search	
Twitter Josh Blay (@realJoshBlay)	
Fayola Johnson talks mental health	https://www.buzzfeed.com/scifiwriterFayolaJo . . .
10 Tell-tale Signs You Aren't (Entirely) Cis	https://www.thebuzz.com/10tell-talesignsyou . . .
Bumblefootandspoons	https://www.bumblefootandspoons.tumblr.com
Drek's Game	https://www.dreksgame/login
Keep Drek's Game T-shirts	https://www.spreadshirt.co.uk/KeepDreksGam . . .
Cormoran Strike Jonny Rokeby – Google search	
Cormoran Strike leg – Google search	
Cormoran Strike – Google search	
Otherkin World	https://www.otherkinworld/ghostkin/fanfic . . .
Tribulationem et Dolorum	https://www.tribulationemetdolorum/forums . . .
Comic Con 2015	https://animecons.com/events/info/15951/mcm.
Twitter Wally Cardew (@the_r3&l_Wally)	
Twitter Anomie (@AnomieGamemaster)	

Eyebrows raised, Strike put his mobile down beside the bloody handkerchief and set off for the Tuesday Market Place, the cut over his left eye still smarting.

The large square he entered a few minutes later was bordered on all sides with many fine buildings, including banks and hotels. There was no market there today, and the central space was full of parked cars. The Maids Head, a squat pub of dark brick, stood right beside the larger and grander Duke's Head.

Strike parked, then used the old man's handkerchief and his own saliva to remove from his face all traces of blood, of which there was a surprising amount. Having cleaned his face, he picked up his folder and left the car, this time leaving the walking stick behind.

There weren't many people inside the bar, and a quick glance around told Strike that Kea wasn't there.

You'd better be in the bloody bathroom.

'Oooh, that looks nasty,' said the barmaid, looking up at Strike's forehead as she came to take his order. 'What happened?'

'Accident,' said Strike gruffly.

He bought himself a non-alcoholic beer. Just as he turned to look for a free table, Kea entered the bar, walking slowly and supported by a collapsible stick of exactly the type Strike had left in the car. She was wearing a baby-pink sweatshirt, matching sweatpants and white trainers. Her hair was tied back in a ponytail. Even barefaced and without filters, she was a gorgeous young woman. When she caught sight of Strike approaching she looked apprehensive. Her gaze dropped to the folder in his hand.

'Kea?'

'Yes,' she said, in the same whispery voice with which she'd spoken to him on the phone.

'Very good of you to meet me. I appreciate it, and I know Josh will too,' said Strike. 'Can I get you something?'

'No,' said Kea weakly. 'I can't actually keep anything down right now.'

Strike judged it best to glide past this comment.

'Shall we sit down?'

He stood back to let her pass, but she said in the same breathy voice, 'You'd better go first. I'm *so* slow.'

So Strike took his folder and his pint to the nearest table for two, and Kea came slowly after him, leaning heavily on her stick. If she was exaggerating her symptoms, it was only what Strike himself had done back at her mother's house, so he settled for a neutral expression until Kea had lowered herself carefully into the seat opposite him.

By piecing together Kea's own account of the previous seven years, Strike knew she was twenty-five, that her relationship with Josh Blay had lasted eighteen months, surviving Josh being kicked out of St Martin's but ending when Josh started dating Edie. Shortly after the relationship had foundered, Kea had taken a year out of her course due to ill health. She had spent most of that year at her mother's house, but, judging by her Instagram page, had made frequent trips to London, sometimes staying on student friends' couches for weeks at a time. She'd returned to St Martin's after a year, only to drop out for good two Christmases later, again citing ill health.

She looked incredibly young to Strike, with her perfect skin, an impression enhanced, perhaps, by the baby-pink sweatshirt that might have been a pyjama top. And yet something about Kea reminded him of Charlotte. There was a shadow of a dare in her behaviour. He thought he'd have known, even if he hadn't read her Twitter output, that somewhere beneath all this marshmallow softness lay steel.

'Thanks for meeting me, Kea,' said Strike. 'I appreciate it.'

'Oh no,' she said, eyeing the gash in his temple. 'Was that Ozzy?'

'If Ozzy's a large white raptor, yes,' said Strike.

'I'm so sorry,' said Kea with a sad smile. 'My mother's stupid a.f. with that bird. She sets, like, no boundaries. See?'

She held out a soft white hand, on which a thin, raised pink scar was clearly visible at the base of the thumb.

'That was Ozzy. And I've got one here' – she showed Strike her palm, which was similarly scarred – 'and behind here' – she pointed at her left ear.

'Ah. I thought it was my fault for being a bloke.'

'Um, no, he's just a bad-tempered little scrote. Umbrella cockatoos, 'specially the males, can be tricky. You've got to know how to handle them . . .'

Her voice died away.

'What's in there?' she asked apprehensively, looking down at the cardboard folder he'd laid on the table between them. 'Are those the things you wanted me to look at?'

'That's right,' said Strike, taking a sip of beer. 'You OK if I take notes?'

'Yeah, I – I s'pose,' she said. As Strike took out his notebook, she asked tentatively:

'Have you seen Josh?'

'Not yet,' said Strike. 'He isn't well enough.'

Kea's beautiful brown eyes, which were the colour of old brandy, glittered immediately with tears.

'It isn't true, is it? That he's paralysed? That's what they're saying online. That isn't right, is it?'

'I'm afraid it is,' said Strike.

'*Oh*,' said Kea.

She caught her breath, then began to sob silently into her hands. Out of the corner of his eye, Strike saw people at the bar watching them. Possibly they thought him a wicked stepfather. Kea didn't seem to care much who saw her sobbing. Charlotte hadn't minded witnesses either. Tears, screams, threatening to jump off high buildings: he'd endured it all in front of friends and, occasionally, passers-by.

'S-sorry,' whispered Kea, wiping her eyes with the back of her hand.

'That's all right,' said Strike. 'So ...'

He opened the folder.

'. . . as you know, I've been hired to find out who Anomie is. What are your thoughts on Anomie?'

'Who cares what I think?' said Kea hopelessly.

'I do,' said Strike, not unkindly. 'That's why I asked.'

She wiped both eyes with the back of her hand and said,

'Josh wouldn't want me to say.'

'I promise you he would,' said Strike.

'People will accuse me of having an agenda.'

'Why d'you say that?'

'Everyone al-always accuses me of having an agenda.'

'If speculating on Anomie's identity's having an agenda, everyone in the fandom—'

'I'm not part of the fandom,' said Kea, her anger rearing suddenly out of nowhere like a snake. 'I'm actually one of the creators.'

Phillip Ormond had glared unblinkingly across the table as he'd made a similar claim, but Ormond had known he was lying. Strike wasn't so sure about Kea.

'She stole my ideas,' said Kea, reverting to her broken whisper. 'Her being dead doesn't change that. She took my ideas and pretended they were hers. Josh admitted it to me, pretty much.'

'Did he?' said Strike. 'When was that?'

Kea blinked at Strike, her long lashes beaded with tears.

'I don't know whether he'd want me to tell you.'

'He wants you to tell me everything,' said Strike firmly.

'OK, well – did – did he tell you we started dating again?'

'Would this be in November 2013?' said Strike, expression impassive while his mind worked rapidly. He opened the folder. He'd noticed a six-month period between November 2013 and May 2014 during which Kea's online output had become suddenly and uncharacteristically cheerful, then descended into even more fury and despair than before.

'He *did* tell you?' said Kea, and Strike saw the dawning of hope in her expression.

'No,' said Strike, extracting the evidence in the folder Robin had put together, 'but you deactivated your YouTube channel around then, didn't you? And you tweeted about how happy you were feeling . . . Yeah,' he said, looking down at a couple of pages of the tweets he'd highlighted, then turning them so that Kea could read them.

Kea Niven @realPaperwhite

Woke up feeling so weird. Then I realised I'm . . . happy?

Kea Niven @realPaperwhite

I fucking love all of you who're struggling right now. I was ready to kill myself. Omg, I'd have missed so much.

The second page showed a series of tweets from six months later, by which time the old tone of grievance and passive aggression had slid back across her posts like an oil slick.

Kea Niven @realPaperwhite

If you know somebody's fragile and you drop them anyway, then yeah, it is absolutely your fault if they break.

Kea Niven @realPaperwhite

If one day you wake up and find out I didn't, it's ok. We're both where we're meant to be.

'Do these tweets span the period you and Josh dated again?' asked Strike.

Kea nodded, her eyes brimming with tears as she shoved her tweets back towards Strike.

'How's this helping you find out who Anomie is?'

'We were simply interested in the fact that you were criticising Edie much less during that time period, whereas Anomie was keeping up their harassment of her.'

'Well, that's because I'm not Anomie,' whispered Kea. 'I'm not. I can't code, I wouldn't know where to begin, making that game.'

'You've played it, have you?' asked Strike.

'No, why would I? What d'you think it *feels* like, seeing all these people go crazy for *my* ideas? I mean – did you see the heart out there, over the window' – she gestured towards the square outside – 'on number sixteen?'

'No,' said Strike.

'OK, well, they burned a witch out there in the sixteenth century . . .'

Kea told Strike the story of Margaret Read's heart bursting out of her burning chest and he agreed insincerely that that certainly sounded like the inspiration for Harty.

'Right?' said Kea. 'I mean, Harty's even *black*, like he was burned!'

'So, going back to this six months when you and Josh got back together – did you stop saying publicly that Edie had plagiarised you because Josh asked you to?'

'Yes,' mumbled Kea. 'He didn't want her to know we'd got back together, because he knew she'd go crazy and he still had to work with her on the cartoon. She was *really* unstable and kind of a bully. She was a lot older than him. I think Josh was scared of her. So we were kind of sneaking around, so nobody would know. I didn't even tell Mum, because I knew she'd be angry. Mum blames Josh for me being ill, but it wasn't *all* down to him. I was already having symptoms before we met. I suppose the stress didn't help,' she added in a whisper.

Kea suddenly reached out and grabbed the edge of the table.

'Sorry,' she gasped. 'I get terrible vertigo. Everything's spinning.'

She closed her eyes, her long lashes grazing her cheek. Strike drank some of his beer. Kea opened her eyes again.

'Sorry,' she whispered again.

'OK to continue?' asked Strike.

'Um . . . yes. This won't take too much longer, will it?'

'No,' lied Strike. 'So, it was during the second period of dating that Josh admitted he'd passed on your ideas to Edie, was it?'

'Yes,' said Kea. 'He agreed he'd probably told her the story about Margaret Read that day in the cemetery, when she claimed she came up with it all out of nowhere. And he admitted Magspie was inspired by what I'd told him about talking birds, and the Drek figure, with the big beak, well, that was taken directly from one of my pictures.'

'Which he'd shown her, had he?'

'Um . . . no, I think he must just have described it to her,' said Kea, 'but he agreed my picture and the way she'd drawn Drek were pretty much identical. But by that time they were both making a lot of money out of it all and he didn't want to upset her. She was five years older than him,' Kea emphasised, 'and super-controlling. He kind of half-promised at one point that he'd get me some credit. Then she staged that so-called *suicide attempt*,' Kea said bitterly, still holding on to the table as though she might simply slip over sideways onto the floor if she didn't, 'and Josh told me we had to take a break, because he was so scared of what she'd do next, if she found out about us.

'She was *crazy* manipulative – you have no idea. That whole suicide thing was a joke. Tons and tons of people knew there was something up with it.'

'Why didn't you tell everyone he'd dated you again, after you broke up the second time?' asked Strike. The point puzzled him, because such an announcement would surely have achieved Kea's twin goals of punishing Edie Ledwell and enhancing her own credibility.

'Because Josh said – he said it wasn't really over, he just wanted us to take a break, because he needed to keep her happy, and he was sorting out the cartoon and work and everything, and so I, um . . . yeah, I kept quiet about it.'

'Didn't he ask you to stop criticising her?'

'No. I promised I wouldn't say we'd dated again but I wasn't going to pretend she hadn't stolen my ideas, because she *had*,' said Kea ferociously. Still holding tightly to the edge of the table, she now massaged her chest with her free hand. 'Oh God,' she said in a fainter voice. 'Sorry. Tachycardia. Um . . . we might have to continue this later . . . oh wow.'

She closed her eyes again. Strike drank some more beer. Kea took several long slow breaths, massaging her chest, and finally opened her eyes.

'All OK?' said Strike.

'Um . . . I'm not sure . . . I think so,' she whispered, hand still pressed to her chest.

'So, to recap: you've never been in the game?'

She shook her head.

'Ever tried to get in?'

'*No*,' she said.

'But you've got a theory about who Anomie is? Because if so, I know Josh would want you to tell me.'

Kea took several more long, slow breaths before saying,

'OK. Well, I think Anomie's a guy called Preston Pierce.'

'And what makes you think that?'

'Um . . . well . . . he hates Josh. When Josh first went to live at North Grove, I used to visit him there and, um, Pez – that's what everyone called him – was always putting Josh down, being snide about his art and opinions. Just constantly taking the piss out of him. I don't think Pez liked having another good-looking guy around, because Pez was, like, screwing as many of the female students as he could, and I think he saw Josh as competition. But Josh – Josh likes everyone,' said Kea. 'He liked Pez, he always said he was just having a laugh, because Josh – he doesn't *see* evil.'

'Evil's a strong word,' said Strike, watching her.

'I can't explain,' said Kea, who'd stopped massaging her heart but was still holding on to the table. 'If you'd been there, you'd know. There was something strange about that art collective place, about the people who live there. There was something off about all of them. I mean, I don't care how you live or identify or whatever – I'm not into all that, like, marry, have kids, achievement bullshit, or career ladders, or whatever, but that place: I could *feel* something wrong there. I'm an empath, I'm really sensitive to atmosphere. I'm not the only one, by the way, I was talking to someone else who totally agreed that place is strange. I didn't want Josh to stay, I got such a bad vibe from it. But Josh needed a cheap room, because St Martin's had chucked him out, and I suppose *she* just knew how to take advantage and that's how it happened.'

'Who was this other person who thought North Grove was strange?'

'I can't remember the name,' said Kea, after a slight hesitation.

'Was it someone who lived there, or who went for classes?'

'I don't know who he was – he was outside it one time and we got talking, that's all.'

'Any other reason you think Preston Pierce is Anomie?'

'Um, well, he's a digital artist, isn't he? And he can code, so he could definitely have made the game. And he was seriously envious of the cartoon, especially when it started getting attention. But, um, I really knew when Anomie sent me a direct message on Twitter.'

Kea paused to be prompted.

'Go on,' said Strike.

'Anomie began with something like, "Oh, this isn't a sleazy pick-up ploy," but he wanted to say that Josh had treated me really badly and he believed my story. So I said, "Um, thanks," or something, and then he said, "You're coming off as a bit aggressive out there, but I guess that's understandable."'

'Anomie criticised you for being too aggressive?'

'I know, right?' said Kea. 'He hated her as much as – I mean, he got how full of bullshit and how fake she was. And I said, um, "I'm only sticking up for my rights," or whatever. He didn't say anything else for a few hours. I remember that, because when he came back he apologised and said he'd been giving a friend a lift to the vet's, because their cat was ill.'

Strike made a note of this.

'Anything else?'

'Yeah, then it got weird.'

'How?'

'Um, well, I said I hoped the cat was OK, but I told him I don't really like cats, because of what they do to bird populations. And then he said, "Who gives a shit about birds?" And I said, "I do, my mum breeds them and I grew up with them." So then he said, "Actually, yeah, I really like them too. I've got a parrot."

'And I thought, you're taking the piss,' said Kea. 'And then he started coming on really strong and he said if I sent him nudes he'd publicise my story even more. And I said, "I'm not giving you nudes, I don't know who you are," and then he said, "Actually, we've met."'

'"We've met"?' repeated Strike.

'Yeah,' said Kea. 'I thought that was total bullshit, like the parrot thing. Just trying to say anything to get my interest. So, um, I kind of said that to him, and he got super-aggressive with me and called me a prick tease and I ended up blocking him.'

'Can I see this conversation?' Strike asked, rapidly jotting down all he'd just been told. 'Did you keep a record of it?'

'No,' said Kea, 'because I blocked him. You can't see it any more. After I told him to leave me alone he tweeted "sue or shut the fuck up, you're starting to bore all of us" and all his little fanboys took that as a cue to start telling me I'm an – an ugly whore and a liar.'

'When did you make the connection with Preston Pierce?'

'Right after I blocked Anomie. It just clicked. The whole thing fitted. The couple who run that art collective place had a cat. It's really old and it's only got one eye. That's the cat he must've been taking to the vet.

'And, um,' said Kea, her colour now heightened, 'there's also the fact Pez tried to get me into bed, after Josh and I split up. I went round to North Grove to pick up some stuff I'd left there and Pez told me Josh and Edie were together in Josh's room and I got upset and he took me into his room and made a full-on pass at me. So, um, I suppose I've knocked him back twice, which is why he got so vile as Anomie.'

Strike finished making notes on this, then asked:

'OK, that's all very helpful. Did you know any of the other people involved in *The Ink Black Heart*?'

'Um . . . Seb Montgomery, but we haven't kept in touch. And there were a couple of Josh's schoolfriends. That's it, really.'

'Was one of the schoolfriends Wally Cardew?'

'Yeah . . . Are we nearly finished?'

'There's not much more,' said Strike. 'Sure you don't want a soft drink? Might help with the dizziness.'

'Yeah,' said Kea. 'Yeah, actually, maybe that's a good idea. Could I have a Coke?'

Strike had once before gone to fetch a suspect food and drink only to have them bolt, but he had no such qualms about Kea, and sure enough, he returned to find her still holding on tightly to the table. She thanked him slightly tremulously for the Coke and took a sip.

'You've been really helpful, Kea,' said Strike. 'Just a couple of other things . . . What d'you know about the Pen of Justice?'

'Um . . . not much.'

'Just wondered, because you've had quite a lot of contact with them,' said Strike, extracting some more printed pages from the folder and handing them over.

In fact, Kea had retweeted every single Pen of Justice blog post. Strike watched her expression as she glanced back over what she'd written in response to the Pen of Justice's critiques of the cartoon.

The Pen of Justice @penjustwrites

Yeah, the monochrome aesthetic is cool but when black = bad and white = most desirable, what does that tell us?

My take on the problematic palette of Harty and Paperwhite

www.PenOfJustice/ThePoliticsOfColou . . .

9.38 am   28 February 2012

Kea Niven @realPaperwhite
replying to @penjustwrites
sickens me to my fkn core that bitch twisted my ideas into
this racist bs

Kea flipped over the pages, her expression rigid.

The Pen of Justice @penjustwrites

Innocent jokes about the lumbricus terrestris, or mocking
genderfluidity?

My take on the transphobic overtones of The Worm.

www.PenOfJustice/WhyTheWormIs . . .

11.02 am   18 November 2012

Kea Niven @realPaperwhite
replying to @penjustwrites
just wanna be clear, she stole nearly everything from me
but NOT the worm. The worm's all hers & shows her true
trash nature

The Pen of Justice post that had provoked the angriest response
from Kea had concerned the allegedly ableist tone of *The Ink Black
Heart*. Strike had printed out all Kea's responses to those mocking the
idea that the cartoon was attacking disabled people.

Kea Niven @realPaperwhite
replying to @SpinkyDan @penjustwrites
ableist shit like #TheInkBlackHeart heightens suicidal ideation
in the disabled

Zozo @inkyheart28
replying to @realPaperwhite @SpinkyDan @penjustwrites
laughing about depression isn 't cool I agree , but Edie has
talked abt being Siucidal in the past

Kea Niven @realPaperwhite
@inkyheart28 @SpinkyDan @penjustwrites
if she killed herself now it'd make a ton of disabled people feel
a hella lot better

Kea handed the pieces of paper back to Strike.

'What d'you want?' she said coldly. 'For me to say I'm sorry, because she's dead now? I stand by every word.'

Strike said nothing.

'It's OK not to be sad when bad people die,' said Kea, her chest suddenly heaving with what Strike was certain was genuine emotion. 'It's OK to be *glad* when terrible people die. I'm not going to pretend I'm sorry. She *literally ruined my whole fucking life*. I'm so fucking *over* guilt bullshit or whatever. And she got Josh fucking *stabbed*.'

'What d'you mean, she "got" him stabbed?'

'There's *no way* whoever did it meant to hurt Josh. Someone decided to take her out and he was just *there*, so they had to attack him too.'

'Why d'you think that?'

'Because – because nobody hated Josh. Everyone knew she was the one driving it all along, doing all the shitty stuff.'

'What shitty stuff?'

'Well – I mean – all *that*, obviously,' said Kea, jabbing a finger at her responses to the Pen of Justice's many blog posts, looking incredulous at Strike's obtuseness. 'She was just a really *shit* human being.'

'You think Edie was killed by someone who didn't like the cartoon?'

'It isn't the cartoon. It's what it *means*,' said Kea.

'And who decides what it means?'

Kea laughed breathlessly.

'Oh my God – I mean – *everyone*?'

'D'you know who writes the Pen of Justice blog?'

'I thought you were trying to find out who Anomie is?'

'I am, but there's a chance the same person's behind both accounts.'

'No, I don't know who they are.'

'Has the Pen of Justice ever contacted you privately?'

'No. Why would they?'

'OK,' said Strike, placing the last batch of tweets back in the file and taking out the last two pages instead. 'Just to be clear, you've believed for the past year that you and Josh were on a break, rather than definitely broken up?'

'I – maybe, I don't know,' said Kea shakily. 'I need to go. I really need to go.'

'Did you meet as friends during that time?'

'We ran into each other a couple of—'

'How often have you talked to each other?'

'I don't know ... um ... occasionally? What's this got to do with Anomie?'

'Josh called you the night before he and Edie met at the cemetery, right?'

'Who told you that, the police?'

'No, your mum.'

Kea stared at Strike.

'Great,' she said, in a high-pitched voice. 'Thanks, Mother. Wow. That's just fucking great.'

'It's not a big deal that he called you, is it?' asked Strike, watching her closely.

'No,' she said fiercely, 'but if you want to know whether he told me he was meeting her at the cemetery, he was drunk and I couldn't hear what he was saying. OK? And as I'm sure my *fucking* mother has told you, I was in London the day it happened but I was on the Tube when they were stabbed and that's been confirmed, it's on camera. OK?'

'OK,' said Strike. 'Well, I've got one last—'

'I've had enough,' said Kea, looking around for her stick. 'I've got to go.'

'You're going to want to explain this last bit, Kea,' said Strike, 'before I hand it over to the police.'

She froze at that. Strike slid the last but one sheet of paper across the table to her.

This tweet has been deleted

This tweet has been deleted

This tweet has been deleted

Wally Cardew @The_Wally_Cardew
replying to @realPaperwhite

delete that ffs

12.39 am   12 February 2015

This tweet has been deleted

Wally Cardew @The_Wally_Cardew
replying to @realPaperwhite

because there are better ways

12.42 am   12 February 2015

Julius @i_am_evola
replying to @realPaperwhite

that psycho-bitch is gearing up to kill them
😂😂😂

12.45 am   12 February 2015

Kea pushed the paper back towards Strike as though it might bite her.
'What did all those deleted tweets say?'

'I can't remember. I was pissed.'

'These were all sent in the early hours of the day Josh and Edie were stabbed, weren't they?'

Kea said nothing. For the first time in the interview, she looked as though she might genuinely faint. She was pale and her breathing had become shallow.

'This Julius person clearly interpreted your tweets as threatening.'

'Um, well, as he's one of the blokes who constantly crops up in my timeline to call me a whore and tell me to kill myself, um, yeah, I don't really care what he thinks.'

'Wally Cardew seems to be giving you advice here, as though he knows you.'

'People tell each other what to do on Twitter all the time.'

Strike now passed the last page wordlessly across the table to Kea.

Back in 2010, an account called Spoonie Kea, whose handle was @notaparrottho, had posted an uncaptioned black-and-white selfie featuring a younger-looking Kea, who was smiling into the camera from her bed, a sheet wrapped around her apparently naked body. Beside her was a man lying on his front with his face turned away from the camera, possibly sleeping, his long blond hair spread on the pillow.

Immediately beneath this image was a response.

Wally C @walCard3w
replying to @notaparrottho
u lookin fine

Spoonie Kea @notaparrottho
replying to @WalCard3w
u too ♥

The very last thing on the page was a tumblr post of Kea's, also dating from 2010.

all my friends telling me 'rebound sex with his best mate ain't the answer' and I'm like 'well that depends on the question'.

'Those are your and Wally Cardew's old Twitter accounts, predating *The Ink Black Heart*, right?' said Strike. 'And you're not denying that's your tumblr account?'

Now very white, Kea said nothing.

'I don't know whether you and Cardew are still in a sexual relationship or just friends,' said Strike, now putting the last couple of pages back into the folder and closing it, 'but if you're thinking of getting in touch with him after this interview, there are three very good reasons you shouldn't.

'Firstly, that little Twitter chat hours before Edie's murder will look even more incriminating if you two seem to be colluding with each other.'

'I couldn't have – I'm on film, on the Tube. I never—'

'Secondly, Josh Blay's lying paralysed in hospital. If you care about him at all—'

Kea burst into noisy tears. More people stared. Strike ignored them.

'If, as I say, you care about Josh at all, you'll make sure I get to carry out this investigation, which he wants, without interference.

'And thirdly,' said Strike, 'Wally Cardew is already a person of interest to people far scarier than I am. If you've got any sense, you'll break that connection right now.'

Still sobbing, Kea struggled to her feet and walked out, far more quickly than she'd entered, though still using her stick. Well aware he was now the subject of accusatory glares from both bar staff and customers, Strike drained his beer glass, stood up and headed for the bathroom. By scowling at particularly persistent gawkers, he ensured that by the time he re-emerged nobody seemed disposed to make eye contact with him.

50

Love, Love, that art more strong than Hate,
More lasting and more full of art; —
O blessèd Love, return, return,
Brighten the flame that needs must burn.

Christina Rossetti
What Sappho Would Have Said Had
Her Leap Cured Instead of Killing Her

Robin, who was currently wearing a dark wig and non-prescription glasses, had been waiting in Harley Street for the best part of an hour for Gus Upcott to emerge from his doubtless exorbitantly priced dermatologist. Finally, at one o'clock, he appeared and headed off along the street. Robin had expected him to head back towards the Tube, but instead he shambled off looking vaguely around for what she guessed was somewhere to eat lunch.

Gus was tall, round-shouldered and skinny. A bag she thought might contain a laptop was slung over his right shoulder, which was slightly lower than the left due to the bag's weight. Anomie hadn't been in the game all morning; Fiendy1 and Vilepechora were on moderator duty.

Five minutes later, and having passed a few places Robin would have thought a young man might find more congenial, Gus turned into Fischer's, a Viennese restaurant that looked traditional and upmarket. Robin suspected the still hive-plagued young man had chosen it for its dimly lit exterior.

Having given Gus time to be seated, Robin entered to find a crowded restaurant with nicotine-brown walls, mirrored panels and 1930s paintings. Gus had been seated on a leather bench in a distant corner where it would be physically impossible to walk casually behind him and glance at the screen of his laptop, which he'd already opened. As she watched, he put on headphones and started typing, an expression of complete absorption on his face, the uneven surface of which was thrown into high relief by the glass-shaded wall lamp beside him. If Seb Montgomery had never looked much like the popular image of the internet troll, Gus, for whom Robin couldn't help feeling rather sorry, perhaps conformed better to the stereotype, with his hopefully temporary disfigurement and general air of self-consciousness.

The waiter showed Robin to a table on the other side of the room, but by carefully shifting the angle of her chair she was able to keep Gus under surveillance. Having ordered a coffee, Robin examined her iPad and saw that both Fiendy1 and Vilepechora had logged out while she'd been walking from Harley Street, and had been replaced by Hartella and Paperwhite.

Robin had been playing the game for barely a minute when Strike called her.

'You all right to talk?'

'Fine. I'm in a restaurant, watching Gus Upcott. Where are you?'

'Sitting in the car. Just left Kea. Any sign of Anomie?'

'No. How was Kea?'

'Very interesting. She thinks Anomie's Pez Pierce.'

'Really? Why?'

Strike recounted Kea's reasons.

'Well, I suppose that's plausible, as far as it goes,' said Robin. 'What did she say about Wally Cardew?'

'Virtually nothing. I saved that for last, because I thought it might make her walk out. It did.'

'Hm,' said Robin unsympathetically, glancing from the game to Gus, who was still typing, headphones blocking out the chat and clatter all around him. 'Well, if she didn't want people knowing she'd slept with an alt-right poster boy, she should have deleted her old account, shouldn't she? Or maybe she's got a few accounts and doesn't keep track of them all?'

'Common error,' said Strike. 'Look at our friend Thurisaz. What's Gus up to?'

'Typing on his laptop,' said Robin, glancing into the corner again. 'He's in a corner, unfortunately. I can't see what's on the screen.'

As she watched, Gus extended his long-fingered left hand onto the tabletop and appeared absent-mindedly to play an invisible chord before resuming his contemplation of the screen.

'He *might* be composing,' said Robin, watching Gus covertly through her clear lenses.

'How're his hives?'

'Not much better. Go on about Kea. Did she show you this alleged conversation with Anomie she had by direct message?'

'No,' said Strike. 'She said it's no longer viewable, because she blocked him.'

'Hm,' said Robin again. 'D'you think she was telling the truth?'

'Not sure. The story came out very fluently and no obvious signs of lying, although I'd say she's quite the little actress in general . . . She claims Josh admitted they'd stolen her ideas during their second period of dating, but I'm not convinced. She also claims she's never played *Drek's Game* or tried to get inside it, which is bollocks. I managed to take a picture of her internet history while I was in her house.'

'How the hell?'

'The laptop was sitting open on the sofa where she'd left it. Her mother had just run out the back door after her, so I took a chance.'

'Good going,' said Robin, impressed.

'She either entered the game, or tried to, this morning.'

'Wow,' said Robin. 'She couldn't be Paperwhite, the moderator, could she? Kea's Twitter handle's realPaperwhite.'

'You tell me,' said Strike. 'You're the one who's talked to Paperwhite.'

'We've never had much direct contact,' said Robin, 'but Worm28 told me something interesting the other night. Apparently, Anomie can veto usernames when people sign up. Nobody in *Drek's Game* is allowed to be the pure character – I mean, your name can't just be Harty or Lord Wyrdy-Grob or whatever.'

'I'd imagine pure usernames would confer status,' said Strike, 'which I think is a very precious commodity to Anomie.'

'Right – but Paperwhite was allowed to use the name without any additions.'

Both fell silent, each following their own train of thought, until Strike said:

'If Kea's Anomie, then obviously everything she's just told me about Anomie flirting with her, then getting aggressive, is bollocks. But if she's *not* Anomie, we know something else about them: they're not quite as sexless as you thought.'

'No,' said Robin. 'I suppose not ... Let's say she's Paperwhite, though ... d'you think Anomie knows who she really is, and that's why he let her have the name? You have to give your email address when you sign up, so there's got to be a chance Anomie and maybe Morehouse know people's real identities.'

Robin heard Strike yawn.

'Sorry, it was an early start. Think I'll get something to eat then head back up the road.'

'Before you go,' said Robin quickly, 'we really do need to think about costumes, you know.'

'Costumes?'

'For Comic Con. If we're going to go.'

'Oh, yeah. All right, I'll get onto that when I'm back in the office.'

For five minutes after Strike had hung up, Robin played the game, intermittently glancing up at Gus Upcott, who did nothing more interesting than consume a plate of chips one-handed and, occasionally, type, seemingly absorbed in his screen, or in whatever was playing on his headphones.

Then a private channel opened on the screen in front of Robin.

<Paperwhite MOD invites Buffypaws>

Paperwhite: hi

<Buffypaws has joined the channel>

Buffypaws: hi, what's up?

Paperwhite: Anomie wants to know whether you're going to Comic Con

Buffypaws: he already asked me that

Buffypaws: and Hartella asked me this morning

Buffypaws: are you guys on commission?

Paperwhite: lol no

Paperwhite: mods are just doing what the boss orders, as usual

Buffypaws: well-yeah I'm hoping to come

Buffypaws: haven't got my Tshirt yet

Paperwhite: great

Paperwhite: that you're coming I mean

Paperwhite: and you'll wear a mask?

Buffypaws: he's serious about that?

Paperwhite: deadly

Paperwhite: like, I think he wouldn't let anyone back in the game if they didn't hide their faces

Buffypaws: wow ok

Out in the main game, Robin saw the familiar flurry of excitement that always accompanied the arrival of Anomie. She watched the fluttering cloak appear at the game's entry point, then glanced up at Gus Upcott. He was typing as before, expression unchanged. Robin texted Nutley, Midge and Shah to inform them that Anomie had just entered the game, then turned back to the private channel, where Paperwhite had typed again.

Paperwhite: can I ask u something?

Buffypaws: yes of course

Paperwhite: did you talk to Anomie on election night?

Paperwhite: on a private channel?

Buffypaws: um yes I think I did

Paperwhite: how was he?

Robin hesitated, thinking.

Buffypaws: what d'you mean?

Paperwhite: was he weird with
you? I thought he seemed drunk or
something

Robin paused, debating what to say. Telling the truth might lead to confidences from Paperwhite. On the other hand, Paperwhite might be doing Anomie's bidding in checking whether Robin had registered the message he'd mistakenly sent her.

Buffypaws: I can't really remember.
He asked me to go to Comic Con

Buffypaws: he might've been drunk,
but if he was, he wasn't really
showing it.

Paperwhite: is that all he said to
you? About Comic Con?

Buffypaws: yeah, just wanted me to
go to Comic Con

Buffypaws: but I had to go deal
with some stuff in the middle of
the chat and when I got back the
private channel had closed

Buffypaws: so he might've said
other stuff but if he did, I
missed it

Paperwhite: ah ok

Buffypaws: why, did he say weird
stuff to you?

Paperwhite: not really weird I just
thought he was drunk and I'd never
seen him like that

Paperwhite: he's such a control
freak I wouldn't expect him to be
a drinker, you know?

Buffypaws: lol yeah

Buffypaws: well I suppose geniuses
are allowed to cut loose a bit, too

Paperwhite: lol he'd love to hear
you call him a genius

Paperwhite: hey, have you seen
Morehouse in here lately?

Buffypaws: no, haven't seen him at
all

In the pause that followed, Robin glanced up at Gus Upcott. He was still typing. She looked back at her iPad. Anomie had moved away from the entry point of the game but wasn't speaking, at least in the open game.

Paperwhite: I've fucked up

Buffypaws: what d'you mean?

Paperwhite: I did something so fkn
stupid

Buffypaws: ?

Paperwhite: to Morehouse

Buffypaws: what happened?

Paperwhite: I mentioned something
Fiendy1 once hinted

Paperwhite: I really didn't mean to
hurt him

Paperwhite: I was trying to tell
him it didn't matter to me at all

Paperwhite: but he checked out of
the game when I said it and I haven't
been able to talk to him since

Paperwhite: I keep hoping he's
going to turn up at Comic Con so
we can make up

Buffypaws: you know who Morehouse
really is?

>

>

Paperwhite: yeah

Paperwhite: but ffs don't tell him that

Paperwhite: he doesn't know I know

Buffypaws: of course I wont tell him

Paperwhite: he internet stalked me first

Paperwhite: so he shouldn't blame me, but he's touchy af

Paperwhite: I can trust u, right?

Buffypaws: yes of course

Paperwhite: listen if I'm not here and he shows up, will u please tell him I'm so fkn sorry. That I really, really want to talk to him.

Buffypaws: I will

Paperwhite: ha why I am I telling u all this?

Buffypaws: because I was here and u needed to tell someone ☺

Paperwhite: lol yeah

>

>

Paperwhite: do you think u can fall in love with someone u've never met?

Robin stared at the question. She could imagine feeling an attraction, a connection or a powerful desire to know someone better from an online meeting, but love? Love, here in *Drek's Game*, where all that was possible was typing these messages to each other, without even a photograph to feed the fantasy?

Buffypaws: maybe

```
Paperwhite: u never met anyone
online?

Buffypaws: yes

Buffypaws: but it didn't work out.
We split up

Paperwhite: im sorry

Buffypaws: no its ok
```

Robin glanced up again. Gus Upcott was gesturing for the bill. She turned back to Paperwhite.

```
Buffypaws: I'm going to have to
go, sorry

Buffypaws: but I'll definitely tell
Morehouse, if I see him

Paperwhite: thanks xxx

<Paperwhite has left the channel>

<Buffypaws has left the channel>

<Private channel has closed>
```

Anomie continued to hover in the game, probably speaking on one or more private channels but otherwise inactive. Gus had removed his headphones, leaving them hanging around his neck, and was now packing away his laptop. Robin raised her hand to request the bill for her own coffee, one eye on the game, because if Anomie said anything while Gus's laptop was in his bag she might be able to rule out another suspect. However, Anomie remained silent while Gus, avoiding eye contact with the young and pretty waitress, paid his bill. A couple of minutes later, he left the restaurant, Robin in pursuit.

51

A wondrous thing
to be so separate having been so near –
near by hate last and once by so strong love.

Augustus Webster
Medea in Athens

The prospect of picking up Madeline from her jewellery launch, taking her for a few stiff drinks and then bedding her wasn't without its attractions, but Strike's leg was sore after the long drive to and from King's Lynn and, failing going straight to Madeline's bedroom, he'd have much preferred to go home alone. Nevertheless, he'd agreed to the arrangement too far in advance to cry off now, so he returned his BMW to its garage, took himself for a kebab and chips and killed the hours until nine o'clock, trying to ignore a sense of faint foreboding that refused to lift.

It was raining by the time he entered Bond Street and, limping slightly, headed towards Madeline's flagship store. As he passed the darkened, rain-speckled shopfronts, his large reflection shambling alongside him, he noticed a gaggle of people ahead who were standing outside a dazzlingly bright window. Photographers were taking pictures of two women standing beneath a large umbrella. Judging by the length of their silhouetted legs, they were models, doubtless wearing some of Madeline's jewellery, with the dark street as backdrop. Evidently the launch was not only still in progress; the press hadn't left.

Strike took a quick sidestep out of the rain into a double doorway and texted Madeline.

**Slightly delayed. Shall I find a bar
and meet you there instead?**

Whatever Madeline answered, Strike intended to remain in the doorway for as long as it took for the press to disperse and the distant shrieks of laughter emanating from the people still hanging around in the street to die away.

A powerful whiff of cannabis met his nostrils. Turning, he realised he wasn't alone in this dark recess: Madeline's son Henry and a friend were standing there in silence, both wearing suits and sharing a joint.

On seeing Strike's face, Henry dropped the joint with a whispered 'fuck'. The friend, not having any idea who Strike was, looked blearily at him, clearly trying to work out whether it was better to pretend not to know where the smell was coming from or to retrieve the spliff now smouldering at his feet.

''S all right,' Strike told Henry. 'I won't tell.'

Henry gave a nervous laugh.

Strike had half a mind to ask Henry to return the favour and not inform his mother that, far from being delayed, he was skulking in a doorway less than a hundred yards from her party. On balance, Strike decided this would be an unfair burden to lay on the teenager, so he continued to smoke while ignoring the two boys.

'Want some?' Henry's friend enquired. He'd picked up the joint and was now holding it out to Strike, clearly feeling this was the least he could do.

'No thanks,' said Strike. 'Trying to give up.'

The friend laughed and took a long toke.

'Aren't you supposed to be in there?' Henry asked Strike, pointing in the direction of the jewellery store, outside which the models still stood laughing and joking with the photographer.

'Your mother's still pretty busy, by the look of it,' said Strike. 'I'll let her finish before I go butting in.'

'*Oh*,' said the friend, round-eyed, to Henry. 'Wait ... is he the *detective*?'

Out of the corner of his eye, Strike saw Henry nod.

'Fuck,' said the friend, sounding alarmed.

''S'all right,' said Strike. 'I left the drug squad years ago. You carry on.'

A chauffeured car had drawn up outside Madeline's store. One of the laughing girls who'd been having her picture taken ducked back into the shop, presumably to take off the jewellery. The other was still chatting to the photographer beneath the umbrella. As Strike and the two teenagers watched, the photographer touched the girl's arm.

'Kino escalation,' said Henry's friend, who'd edged forwards to watch what was going on. Henry laughed.

'It is,' said the friend. 'That's how you do it.'

'Says who?' asked Henry.

'Kosh.'

'That's all bullshit.'

'It's science,' said the friend, taking another long toke on the joint and holding it out to Henry. 'It is. Kino escalation and negging. He'll tell her she's got big feet in a minute, or something.'

'Will he fuck,' said Henry, laughing.

'He will. Day game.'

'It's night.'

'But they're on the street, not in a club or whatever.'

'You're full of shit.'

'You should read Kosh. Watch now . . .'

The photographer and the model were still talking. Another burst of laughter floated back to them in the dark street as she cuffed the photographer playfully on the arm. Her voice carried to the doorway.

'You cheeky bastard!'

'Negging,' said Henry's friend triumphantly. 'Fucking told you.'

He squinted at Strike.

'Isn't it right,' he said, his voice slightly slurred, 'if you insult a girl – like, not insult, but criticise a bit – she'll work to get your approval back?'

'I wouldn't count on it,' said Strike. 'Who gave you this advice?'

'Kosh,' said Henry.

'Mate of yours?'

'He's a pick-up artist,' said Henry. 'American.'

The model and photographer were still talking and laughing. The man touched her arm again.

Strike's mobile rang. Fully expecting it to be Madeline, he tugged it out of his coat pocket, but the number was withheld. He answered.

'Strike.'

There was a short pause. Then a deep, rasping, distorted voice said: 'Look at the letter in her coffin.'

For a second or two, Strike was too surprised to say anything.

'Who is this?'

He could hear deep breathing.

'Read the letter,' said the voice.

The line went dead.

'See? Kino escalation,' Henry's friend said, still watching the photographer and the model. 'You, like, build up how much you're touching them. It's working – look.'

'You're full of shit,' sniggered Henry, now back in possession of the joint.

Strike looked down at his mobile. The call hadn't been redirected from the office. The anonymous caller had his direct number. He now texted Robin.

Just had a second call from the person who said to dig Ledwell up. This time it was 'look at the letter in her coffin'

He replaced the phone in his pocket.

'I'm trying the digital game right now and it works,' Henry's friend was saying.

'How d'you do kino ... whatever ... online?'

'You do different stuff online.'

Another woman had just walked out of Madeline's shop, holding what looked like a goody bag. She paused and looked up and down the street. As she turned in Strike's direction he recognised her by the light still pouring out of the shop window: Charlotte. He backed into the shadows.

'... you say stuff like "if that's your real picture you're probably sick to death of blokes pestering you so I'll go now" ...'

The tapping of high heels on concrete was audible even over the sound of Henry's laughter. The imminent encounter had been almost inevitable; Strike felt as though he'd known it all along.

'I *thought* that was you.'

Charlotte sounded amused. She stood before him in a tight black dress and stilettos, her dark hair loose, a grey silk coat hanging open.

'I saw Mads's face just now when she checked her phone, and I thought, he's cancelled. She'll be pleased you're only hiding. Have you been in a fight?'

She was looking at the cut on Strike's forehead, made by the white cockatoo.

'No,' he said, and ground out the stub of his cigarette beneath his heel. Henry and his friend were now staring at Charlotte in awed silence. Strike couldn't blame them.

'Could I cadge one?' Charlotte asked Strike, looking down at the cigarette end.

'Sorry, all out,' lied Strike.

'It's nearly over,' said Charlotte, glancing back at the launch. 'Huge success. She's really talented, your girlfriend. I bought this – fabulous, isn't it?'

She held out a slender hand. Strike saw something that looked like a lump of uncut quartz on her middle finger. He said nothing.

'I wondered where you boys got to, by the way,' said Charlotte, apparently unperturbed by Strike's silence, and looking over his shoulder at the teenagers. 'I s'pose it was pretty boring in there for you.'

Henry's friend stammered something incoherent. Still smiling, Charlotte turned back to Strike.

'How's Pru's daughter?'

'Who?'

'Pru's daughter, darling,' said Charlotte. 'Your niece.'

Strike realised that his half-sister Prudence was the person under discussion.

'I've no idea.'

'You didn't know? Oh, shit,' said Charlotte, no longer smiling. 'I probably wasn't supposed to say.'

'Well, you've started now,' said Strike, remembering that Prudence had mentioned a family emergency, 'so you might as well finish.'

'Gaby told me,' said Charlotte. Gaby was another of Strike's half-sisters. He barely knew her, but she and Charlotte had moved in the same exclusive circles for years. 'Sylvie fell off a climbing wall. Harness wasn't fastened or something.'

'Ah,' said Strike. 'I didn't know.'

'I thought you and Pru were in contact these days?'

'Gaby's clearly been talking a lot.'

'Don't be pissed off,' said Charlotte. He could smell a trace of Shalimar, even through the fug of cannabis. 'I didn't mean to upset you.'

'You haven't upset me.'

The car waiting outside Madeline's store, now containing both models, pulled away from the kerb at last. The photographer disappeared into the darkness. The last few stragglers were leaving the shop, but they paused in front of the door, still talking and laughing.

'Henry?' called a voice from the middle of the group.

'Shit,' said Henry. He and his friend hurried to obey his mother's summons, leaving the last inch of their joint abandoned on the ground.

'I quite fancy that,' said Charlotte, looking down at the joint. 'Better not, though . . . Jago's probably having me watched, like I am him . . .'

She glanced up and down the street again as she said it, drawing her thin coat tightly around her.

'I went to McCabes,' she told Strike, looking him in the eye again. 'They've put someone on it, but they've got nothing so far. Jago's being really careful. I bet you'd have got results faster.'

'McCabes are good,' said Strike.

'They'd better be,' said Charlotte.

Strike wanted to walk away but didn't want to join the group still milling at the front of the shop, who were now taking selfies with Madeline.

'I wanted to go to Pru, for therapy,' said Charlotte dreamily.

'You *what*?' said Strike, goaded into a reaction, as no doubt she'd intended.

'She's supposed to be really good. She helped a friend of mine a lot. But she wouldn't take me. Said it would be a conflict of interest.'

'Of all the therapists in London, you wanted to see my sister?'

'I had no idea at the time you two were even in touch.'

'She'd still have been my sister at the time, unless this all happened in some parallel universe.'

'I just heard she was really good,' said Charlotte, unruffled. 'I quite fancied talking to somebody whose family was as fucked-up as mine. I'm bored of middle-class therapists and their tedious middle-class ideas of what's normal.'

Madeline was now ushering Henry and his friend into a black cab. The group of guests was dispersing at last. Now Madeline stood alone, staring towards Strike and Charlotte. The latter glanced at Madeline, then turned, smiling, back to Strike.

'Well, I'd better let you congratulate Mads.'

She walked away in the rain, her stilettos clicking on the pavement, her dark hair fanning out behind her.

52

Madeline, who was wearing a fitted dress of purple silk, with a heavy
amethyst necklace and vertiginous heels, stood stock still on the pavement, arms folded, half her face in shadow, half brightly illuminated by
the light still shining out of the shop window. As Strike moved out of
the dark doorway towards her, he could tell they were about to reach
that important landmark in every relationship: the first blazing row.

'Hi,' he said. 'You look great. How'd it go?'

She turned wordlessly and walked back into her shop, passing a
security guard as large as Strike himself, who was standing just inside
the door.

Two pretty young women Strike assumed were shop assistants,
both wearing black dresses, were pulling on their coats and looked
curiously at Strike as he entered. Three male caterers in white jackets
were removing empty champagne glasses from low tables and glass
cabinets. The shop, which Strike had never visited before, was like the
plush interior of a jewellery box, walls and tented ceiling covered in
midnight blue velvet, gold rope looped overhead with hanging tassels,
the floor covered in a Persian rug.

'This looks—' he began, but Madeline was bidding goodbye to
the sales assistants, then pursued one of the waiters into a back room,
where he heard her giving instructions to take the glasses and leave,

never mind wiping down the cabinets – she'd get the girls to do that the following morning.

Four enormous pictures of the models used in the advertising campaign stood on golden easels. A long-haired black woman was wearing diamond earrings so long they grazed her naked shoulders; a redhead stared through interlaced fingers, each bearing a sapphire ring; a blonde held a ruby brooch over one eye like a patch; and Charlotte stared at him with a *Mona Lisa* smile on her scarlet lips, in a heavy gold collar studded with uncut emeralds.

Madeline reappeared, following the caterers, each of whom was carrying a large box full of used glasses.

'You can go, Al,' she said to the security guard. 'I'll lock up and set the alarm.'

'You sure?' he asked.

'Yes. Go,' said Madeline in a clipped voice, slamming a hand onto a button beside a heavy wooden desk in the corner. Steel security blinds began to lower automatically over the windows.

Strike could tell Madeline had had a lot to drink. She was flushed and her voice was slightly thickened. Her determined avoidance of Strike's gaze persisted until the waiters, caterers and the security man had departed. When at last they were alone, the windows blanked out, Madeline turned to look at him.

'I knew you'd do this.'

'Do what?'

'You couldn't even come in for a couple of minutes at the end.'

'There was still a photographer outside.'

'Listen to yourself!' said Madeline with a shrill laugh. 'Who d'you think you are? *Your father?*'

'What's that supposed to mean?'

'If *Jonny Rokeby* turned up here, yes, the press would be fighting tooth and nail to get a shot of him. For fuck's sake. You're not that famous. Get the fuck over yourself.'

'The point is that I don't *want* my picture in the press,' said Strike calmly. 'I've told you this repeatedly. I don't want to be recognisable.'

'And where's your fucking paranoia about being papped when you're chatting to Charlotte Campbell in dark doorways? She told me tonight about how Jago wants to name you in the divorce—'

'That was helpful of her,' said Strike, temper now rising in spite of himself.

'—which would've been nice to hear from *you*, rather than find out in front of twenty-odd people at my fucking launch—'

'Fuck's sake, you think I wanted her to do that?'

'—and I had to pretend I knew all about it – so when did you *actually* break up with her?'

'Exactly when I told you we did,' said Strike. 'Nigh on five years—'

'So why's Jago after your blood?'

'Because he hates my fucking guts.'

'Charlotte says he found texts between the two of you.'

'Those texts were her trying to rekindle the affair. I didn't ask for them,' said Strike.

'You actually *do* think you're Jonny Rokeby,' said Madeline with another incredulous laugh. 'Women just throw themselves at you without any invitation, do they?'

'No, you were the first.'

Madeline picked up the nearest available object, which was an empty wooden jewellery box, and threw it. Her aim was so poor it would have sailed past Strike and hit the window if he hadn't reached out and caught it. Madeline advanced on him.

'You don't want anyone to know you're with me!'

'I don't give a damn who knows I'm with you.'

'That's not what Charlotte says!'

'When are you going to get it through your head that you can't trust a single fucking word Charlotte Campbell says?'

'Did you tell your darling Robin we're together?'

'Yes,' said Strike.

'Before or after Charlotte told her? Because Charlotte said she looked pretty fucking shocked to hear it.'

'Wake up, for fuck's sake. Charlotte says whatever she thinks will cause most—'

'Charlotte said, if you actually turned up to my launch, you *must* be serious about giving us a go because—'

'She's shit-stirring, Madeline, for fuck's sake!'

'—you've hushed up all your girlfriends since—'

'I'm not fucking hushing you up!'

'Why were you hiding three doorways down, pretending to be delayed?'

'I've just told—'

'Hoping to catch Charlotte as she came out?'

'Try and make up your fucking mind which of them it is you think I'm playing away with, Charlotte or Rob—'

'Maybe both – your father never confined himself to one at a t—'

'Mention my father one more time and I'm out of here.'

They glared at each other, five feet apart, and the large picture of Charlotte in her emerald-studded collar gazed at them with a half-smile on her scarlet lips.

'I'm getting the impression it matters more to you what Charlotte thinks about us than what *I* think,' said Strike. 'Is that why I had to come and pick you up here? To prove to Charlotte you've got me wrapped round your little finger?'

'You never told me you'd slept with Ciara Porter!'

'*What?*' said Strike, thrown.

'You heard me!'

'Why the fuck *would* I have told you? It was a one-night stand!'

'Or that you dated Elin Toft!'

'Jesus Christ, have I asked you for a list of all your previous—?'

'They're both people I *know*!'

Strike felt his mobile buzz in his coat pocket and reached for it.

'You'd better not bloody answer that!' shouted Madeline as he looked down at the text from Robin.

What did the voice sound like?

Strike began typing a response.

'Did you *hear* me?'

'Yeah, I heard you,' he said coldly, still typing.

Same as last time. Darth Vader. Think it's a voice change app

He put the mobile back in his pocket and looked up to see Madeline breathing hard, a rictus grin of fury on her face.

'You were saying?' asked Strike.

'I was *saying*, I thought Charlotte was an anom –' drunk, she tripped on the word. ' – malaly. Valentine said you met her at uni – I thought you weren't interested in money or fame or whatever, then I find you're carving your way through half the female celebs in London!'

'And how do you square me being some kind of starfucker with your complaint that I don't want to be photographed with you?'

'Maybe that just makes it easier for you to con the next rich woman into thinking you like her for herself!'

Strike turned and headed for the door.

'Cormoran!'

But he'd already wrenched the heavy door open and set off into the rain.

'*Cormoran!*' she screamed.

His phone buzzed in his pocket again. He pulled it out and examined Robin's new text. Raindrops speckled the phone screen. He could hear Madeline running after him on her stilettos, and what sounded like a heavy bunch of keys jangling.

Can that really be some random troll?
Because how many people knew there
were letters in the coffin?

Strike typed back, still walking:

Exactly

Another text from Robin came seconds later.

I've just heard something interesting in
the game, if it's convenient to talk
right now. If not, it'll keep

He'd just typed **now's good** when he heard a shriek, a thump and the clinking of metal behind him. He turned: Madeline had slipped and fallen, the shop keys had flown out of her hand and she was lying face-down on the wet pavement.

'Fuck's *sake*,' he muttered, limping back towards her. Madeline was trying to get up, but was hampered by the fact that one of her heels had broken. Sobbing, she clutched his hand and let him pull her upright. One of her knees was bleeding.

'Get in here,' said Strike, helping her into another covered doorway before going to retrieve the keys. 'Have you left the door unlocked?'

She nodded, still sobbing.

'Corm, I'm sorry . . . I'm sorry . . . I didn't mean any of it . . .'

'Let's just go and lock the bloody door before you lose your whole stock.'

'Wait –'

Steadying herself on his arm, she wrenched off both shoes. Still crying, barefoot and now considerably shorter, she let him steer her back towards the shop, pausing only to ram her purple stilettos into a bin.

'Corm, I'm sorry . . . it's just been so fucking stressful and . . . I didn't mean it, I honestly didn't . . .'

Back inside the plush midnight blue shop she collapsed into an armchair, put her face in her hands and cried. Strike sighed heavily and put the keys down on a glass cabinet full of glittering pendants.

'When have I ever taken a penny off you?' he asked, looking down at her. 'When have I ever failed to pay my way?'

'Never . . . never . . . I don't know why I said that . . . it was everything Charlotte said . . . I found out Jim was cheating because of texts . . . he'd been buying her presents out of my money and . . . I'm sorry, I really am . . .'

She looked up at him. She looked good even with her hair beginning to frizz and her mascara running.

'You're going to want to clean that knee,' he told her.

Madeline pushed herself out of the armchair and flung her arms around him. After a moment or two he reciprocated, kissing the top of her damp head.

'I'm sorry,' she repeated into his chest.

'I'm not Jim.'

'I kn-know,' she sobbed. 'I *do* know that. I shouldn't have had so much champagne.'

'You shouldn't listen to Charlotte fucking Campbell is what you shouldn't do,' said Strike forcefully.

'I won't . . . I know I shouldn't have . . .'

He disengaged himself gently and looked down at her.

'Go and wash your knee. I've got to make a work call, to Robin. That doesn't mean I'm shagging her.'

'I – I know,' repeated Madeline, half laughing, half crying.

'OK then. I'll stand here by the door and try and look like your security bloke.'

Still sniffing, Madeline departed for the bathroom at the back of the shop. Strike walked over to the door, positioned himself squarely in front of it, where he'd be visible to passers-by, then called Robin.

'Hi,' she said. 'It could've kept.'

'It's fine. Go on.'

'Worm28 – Zoe, I mean – just told me she had a row with Yasmin Weatherhead – you know, Hartella – last night, on the moderators' channel. Yasmin said something along the lines of "a fan couldn't have done the stabbings because they wouldn't have attacked Josh". Zoe got angry and asked whether Yasmin was saying Edie deserved what she got.

'Anyway, Zoe's just been ranting away about Yasmin to me and she let slip that she thinks Yasmin and Anomie have got some kind of sideline together. A money-making sideline.'

'Really?'

'Apparently he said something to Yasmin on the moderator channel this morning about waiting to hear what his percentage was going to be. Yasmin didn't respond in front of the other moderators, but Zoe thinks they probably went to talk on a private channel instead.'

Madeline emerged from the back room, her face cleaned up. She gave Strike a watery smile, then began moving between the cabinets, checking that all were locked.

'Very interesting,' said Strike. 'Suggests Morehouse might not be the only one who knows who Anomie is after all.'

'I know,' said Robin. 'I wonder whether there's any way we could approach Yasmin the same way we did Tim Ashcroft.'

'As a journalist?'

'Exactly. Pretend to be doing an article on *The Ink Black Heart*. "You knew them in the early days" etcetera.'

'Definitely an idea,' said Strike. 'I'm going to have to go, but let's talk that through tomorrow.'

'Great,' said Robin. 'Speak then.'

She hung up. Strike turned to Madeline, who'd now put on her coat.

'We're going to need a cab,' he said, looking at her bare feet.

'I'm sorry,' she whispered again.

'You're forgiven,' said Strike, forcing a smile.

While Madeline took out her mobile to call a taxi, Strike slipped outside to have a cigarette. This evening had brought back a tide of memories of life with Charlotte; of screams and thrown objects, outbursts of irrational jealousy and accusations of every vice she'd met in her birth family. The difference had been that he'd loved Charlotte, in spite of it all. Without love, such behaviour held no appeal whatsoever for Strike. The rain continued to fall and he smoked, leg aching, wishing himself a hundred miles away from Bond Street.

53

Sweet is the swamp with its secrets,
Until we meet a snake . . .

Emily Dickinson
XIX: A Snake

In-game chats between four of the moderators of *Drek's Game*

<A new private channel
has opened>

<20 May 2015 17.38>

<Anomie invites
Morehouse>

Anomie: we've been   <A new private channel
missing you, bwah   has opened>

>   <20 May 2015 17.40>

<Morehouse has joined   <Paperwhite invites
the channel>   Morehouse>

Morehouse: is that   Paperwhite: omg you're
right   here

Anomie: yeah   >

Anomie: Paperwhite's   >
been on here 24/7
asking people if   >
they've seen you
                                >
Morehouse: I came back
to see whether   Paperwhite: Mouse,

509

LordDrek and
Vilepechora have gone
but they haven't, I
see

Anomie: no

Anomie: but they'll
be gone by the end of
Comic Con

Morehouse: just fucking
ban them now

Anomie: iv'e got a plan
ok?

Morehouse: like the
plan to 'look into'
them?

Anomie: I swear
they'll be gone soon.
Working on it right
now

Morehouse: I think
you're just
kicking the can
down the fucking
road

Morehouse: because
they're 'good mods' and
'just did it for the
lolz'

Anomie: I'm not

>

Anomie: u were right,
ok?

Anomie: they're fkn
Nazis

Morehouse: and this
flash of insight came
to you how, exactly?

>

please talk to me

>

Paperwhite: please

>

>

>

>

>

>

>

<Morehouse has joined
the channel>

Morehouse: hi

>

Paperwhite: Mouse, I
want to apologise.
I haven't been
sleeping, it's all
I can think about.
I'm so, so sorry, i
shouldn't have said
it

Morehouse: it's ok

Paperwhite: it isn't

Morehouse: I was just
fucked off at Fiendy1
for opening her big
mouth

>

Paperwhite: wait,
what?

Paperwhite: Fiendy1's
a girl?

<A new private channel
has opened>

<14 May 2015 17.42>

510

Anomie: I changed my mind, that's all

Morehouse: An about-turn that, amazingly, coincided with me asking you to choose between me or them

Anomie: so what if it fkn did? you're getting what you want, aren't you?

>

Morehouse: you still don't fkn get it, do you?

>

Morehouse: you seem to be totally fucking indifferent to them being fascists

Anomie: call yourself a fkn scientist? Where's your proof?

>

>

>

>

>

>

Anomie: let me guess, u're talkin to Paperwhite on another chan

Morehouse: yeah. She likes to pretend to be a bloke online

>

>

>

>

Morehouse: how's your mum?

Paperwhite: not great

Paperwhite: her hair's started to fall out

Morehouse: shit

Paperwhite: yeah

>

Paperwhite: but as long as it works

Morehouse: yeah

>

Paperwhite: it's so good to talk to u again

Paperwhite: I've really missed u

Morehouse: I've missed u too

Paperwhite: so we're ok?

>

>

Morehouse: yeah, we're

<Fiendy1 invites Morehouse>

Fiendy1: I want to talk to you

>

<Morehouse has joined the channel>

Fiendy1: I did NOT tell Paperwhite you're disabled ok

Fiendy1: if she heard it from anyone it was Anomie not me

Fiendy1: so get yr facts straight before sending me an email like that again

>

Morehouse: ok whatever

Fiendy1: "whatever?"

Morehouse: u sure you always remember what you've said to people?

Fiendy1: screw you

Fiendy1: I know what your implying

>

Morehouse: I just know what you're like with half a bottle of vodka in you

Fiendy1: fuck off

511

Morehouse: so what if I am? What's your problem with me and Paperwhite?

Anomie: no problem, bwah

Morehouse: I think you fancy her yourself

Anomie: how's that work, bwah?

Morehouse: u know who she is. From sign up.

Anomie: you think I get horny over email addresses?

Morehouse: Maybe her real name's in her email and you went looking

Anomie: well you're wrong, I don't give a shit who she is

Anomie: You want to get into something with her, feel free

>

Morehouse: and rule 14?

Anomie: fuck it, you're co-creator, do what you want

Morehouse: yeah, well, I can't do what I want

Morehouse: not with her, anyway

ok x

Paperwhite: so, listen, you gonna go to Comic Con?

>

>

Paperwhite: hello?

>

Morehouse: I can't go to Comic Con

>

Morehouse: but you can go with your boyfriend.

>

Paperwhite: what?

>

>

Morehouse: your boyfriend

>

>

>

>

Morehouse: cut off T-shirt, muscles, blond

>

Paperwhite: so you've stopped pretending you don't know who

Fiendy1: I never told her you're disabled

>

Morehouse: maybe not explicitly

Fiendy1: ok, what did I say then?

>

>

>

>

>

>

>

>

>

Morehouse: probably made one of your funny wheelchair jokes

Fiendy1: that was over a fkn year ago and I told you I was sorry like a million times

>

>

>

>

512

I am

>

>

>

>

>

Anomie: why not?

Anomie: she's
obviously hot for
you

>

Morehouse: you know
why not

>

>

>

>

>

>

Anomie: bwah?

>

>

>

>

>

>

>

>

>

Morehouse: what?

Anomie: if I kick
LordDrek & Vile
out, you'll stay,
right?

Paperwhite: that
would never have
started if you'd
agreed to meet me
or even send a pic

Paperwhite: I was
pissed one night and
he was there

Paperwhite: that's
not a nice thing
to say, but it's
true

Morehouse: you look
pretty fkn happy about
it on your Instagram
page

Paperwhite: well
maybe I was hoping
you'd see it and get
jealous

Paperwhite: this
whole thing's been
so one- sided. I send
pics, you don't. I
want to meet, you
don't.

Paperwhite: what you
and I have is better

Paperwhite: but how
do I know you're not
stringing 100 other
girls along?

>

>

>

Morehouse: you did
the only thing I
ever asked you not
to do

Morehouse: fuck, I
was trying to help
you

Fiendy1: don't be so
fkn patronising

Morehouse: I'm not
patronising you,
I'm treating you
like an adult for
a change

Fiendy1: what does
that mean,'for a
change'?

Fiendy1: look you
were really nice to
me when I was going
through all my shit
and I never meant
to hurt you or offend
you

Fiendy1: I know I
upset you and iv'e
tried everything
to say sorry but
when somebody
ignores all your
emails and won't talk
in here it's hard to
make up

Fiendy1: but I
never told
anyone about
you being disabled,
nobody

Fiendy1: why woud i?

>

Morehouse: fuck's sake, you're not listening. What bothers me is you don't seem to give a shit what they are or what they might have done

Anomie: I've already told you they can't have killed Ledwell

>

Morehouse: how can you be sure?

Anomie: because I did it, obvs

Morehouse: fucking hell, what's wrong with you?

Morehouse: I'm this close to believing you, you know that?

Morehouse: You keep saying it in the game

Morehouse: What happens if someone takes you seriously and calls the police?

Anomie: ffs I'm joking

Anomie: we used to have a laugh

Morehouse: yeah we did

Morehouse: but I

>

>

>

>

>

>

>

Morehouse: I'm not

Morehouse: look, I've done a lot of thinking while I've been out of the game

>

>

>

Paperwhite: Mouse, please don't say you're leaving

Paperwhite: please

>

Paperwhite: ok well if you're leaving I've got nothing to lose have I?

>

>

Morehouse: ?

>

>

Paperwhite: I know exactly who you are, V****.

>

>

>

>

>

>

>

>

>

>

>

>

Morehouse: maybe to shit stir between me and Paperwhite?

Fiendy1: that's a total fkn lie

Fiendy1: I never wanted u as a boyfriend if that's what you're implying.

Fiendy1: I just thought u were my friend

>

>

>

>

>

>

>

514

said to Paperwhite
the other day I
feel like I don't
know u any more,
srsly

Morehouse: Ledwell's
dead, Blay's still
in hospital and u
don't seem to give a
fuck

Morehouse: it's a joke
to you

>

>

Anomie: so I like
dark humour, fucking
sue me

>

>

>

>

Anomie: you want me
to say it's a tragedy,
of course it fucking
is

Anomie: but seeing
as the world knows I
fkn hated Ledwell, I'm
not going to play the
hypocrite

>

Morehouse: just show
some commong decency
ffs

>

>

Paperwhite: and
don't you dare
complain, seeing as
you went and found
out who I am

Paperwhite: You're
even following me
on Twitter as
yourself

Paperwhite: and for
the record, now I
know who you are, I
think you're even more
incredible than I did
before

>

>

Paperwhite: today I
told Buffypaws I'm in
love with u

Paperwhite: you
can check with her
if you don't believe
me

>

>

>

Morehouse: are you
serious?

>

Paperwhite: about
which bit?

Paperwhite: shit,
no bloke's ever
made me cry as much
as you have, Snot
everywhere.

Morehouse: you think

>

>

>

>

>

>

>

>

Morehouse: I was your
friend

Morehouse: but you
broke my trust

Morehouse: I had
bloody good reasons
for not wanting
anyone to know I
co-created this
game

Morehouse: so
having a drunk
sixteen year old
dropping hints all
over the place,
thinking she's
being funny/clever
wasn't what I was
after

Fiendy1: I said I was
sorry, what else can
I do

Morehouse: nothing

**<Fiendy1 has left the
channel>**

**<Morehouse has left
the channel>**

**<Private channel has
closed>**

515

>

>

>

>

>

Anomie: fine, I'll show some common decency, kick out LordDrek and Vile, you shag Paperwhite to your heart's content and the game goes on, right?

>

>

>

>

>

>

Anomie: Morehouse?

>

Morehouse: what?

Anomie: if I do all that, you'll stay?

>

>

>

>

>

>

you know who I am?

Paperwhite: middle of the pic, green shirt, glasses, wheelchair, awesome smile, excellent teeth

>

>

>

>

Morehouse: and you told Buffypaws you love me?

Paperwhite: I asked her if she thought you could fall in love with someone you've never met

Paperwhite: becos I think I have with you

>

Paperwhite: don't feel like u have to say it back or anything

Morehouse: lol

Morehouse: well

Morehouse: I do

Paperwhite: really?

Morehouse: yeah

Paperwhite: <3 <3 <3 <3 <3 <3 <3 <3

Paperwhite: so, if we

Morehouse: I'll think about it

>

Anomie: fuck, don't do me any favours

>

>

>

>

Anomie: are you still there?

>

>

>

Morehouse: tell me something

Morehouse: when do you see the game ending?

>

Anomie: what do you mean?

>

>

Morehouse: well it can't go on forever, can it?

>

Anomie: why not?

>

take this convo to Twitter I can DM you my phone no

Morehouse: no, I don't want to talk on the phone

Morehouse: not the first time we talk

>

>

>

Paperwhite: do u have speech probs or something?

Morehouse: yeah

Paperwhite: it can't be that bad

Paperwhite: you spoke on the phone to Anomie the other week

Morehouse: that was an emergency

Morehouse: but he can understand me because we Facetimed a lot when we first created the game

Paperwhite: so let's Facetime

Morehouse: look this is hard for me

Paperwhite: I understand

>

>

>

>

>

>

Morehouse: because ffs people grow up. They get bored.

Anomie: that's why we've got to keep improving the game

>

>

>

Morehouse: this can't last forever

Anomie: it'll last as long as I want it to last

>

>

Anomie: we're in charge now, we make the rules

Morehouse: what rules?

Anomie: we hold the power. We can make sure the IBH stays the way we want it

Morehouse: you realise you sound like a

Morehouse: you don't, you couldn't, looking the way you do

Morehouse: that pic you've seen doesn't tell the full story

Paperwhite: what, he's your body double?

Morehouse: lol

Morehouse: no

Morehouse: but it doesn't show how I speak or move

Paperwhite: ffs I don't care

>

Morehouse: easy to say

Paperwhite: so we can't ever meet or talk irl?

>

>

>

>

Morehouse: you're going to Comic Con on the 24th?

>

Paperwhite: I will if you will

megalomaniac

Anomie: the will to power makes the world go round

Morehouse: thought that was love?

Anomie: love's for pussies

Morehouse: I'll try

>

Paperwhite: <3 <3 <3 <3 <3 <3 <3 <3

Paperwhite: I love you

Morehouse: love you too

54

. . . masks in flocks and shoals;
Flesh-and-bloodless hazy masks surround there,
Ever wavering orbs and poles . . .

Christina Rossetti
A Castle Builder's World

The morning after Madeline's launch, Strike and Robin met at the office where they agreed that, having gone to the trouble of creating a website and a Twitter account for journalist Venetia Hall, they'd be wasting an opportunity not to call her into service again when approaching Yasmin Weatherhead. Robin therefore tweaked the bio on Venetia's Twitter account to emphasise her journalistic credentials, and spent three hours writing a couple of articles on *The Ink Black Heart* for Medium.com in Venetia's name.

'They're terrible,' she told Strike on the phone later. He'd had to leave for Sloane Square, where he was watching Fingers lunch at The Botanist again. 'I've cobbled them together from a load of other articles.'

'Can't anyone write stuff on Medium?'

'Yes, but Venetia's supposed to be an actual journalist.'

'Well, with luck, Yasmin's literary standards aren't that high.'

Whether that was the case or not, Yasmin Weatherhead proved just as eager as Tim Ashcroft to speak to Venetia Hall. Robin received a promising response to her email a mere twenty-four hours later.

Hi Venetia,

It was a bit of a shock to get your email! Yes, I'm "the" Yasmin Weatherhead who used to work for Josh and Edie. Still in shock about what happened, as you can imagine. I think the whole fandom's kind of shaken. It was so dreadful. We're all praying Josh makes a full recovery.

Yes, I'm still a huge *Ink Black Heart* fan and in fact I'm currently writing a book all about the cartoon and the fandom! I don't know whether you know about *Drek's Game*, which is the place many fans congregate to discuss the show and the whole franchise? My book also covers the game and how central it's become to keep enthusiasm for *The Ink Black Heart* alive.

So, yes, I'd be glad to talk to you! When were you thinking? As you clearly know, I'm currently working for Lola June Cosmetics but could do evenings or any weekend except this coming one, because I'll be at Comic Con, geeking out!

With best wishes,
Yasmin

'Why don't I ask her to meet me *at* Comic Con?' Robin asked Strike by phone after she'd forwarded him Yasmin's email.

'Two birds with one stone,' said Strike, who was now tailing Preston Pierce down Swain's Lane in Highgate. 'Good idea.'

'Your costume's arrived, by the way,' Robin told him. 'When I said you'd make a lovely Darth Vader, I didn't think you'd actually—'

'Couldn't think of anything else,' said Strike. 'Just hope it's long enough.'

'I like that you bought a lightsaber as well,' said Robin. 'Right colour and everything.'

'Comic Con is *exactly* the place they'd rumble I was fishy because my lightsaber's green,' said Strike, and Robin laughed.

She emailed Yasmin back, saying that she was very excited to hear about her book and fascinated by *Drek's Game*, and asking whether she'd like to meet up at Comic Con, which would make a wonderful backdrop for Venetia's article about *The Ink Black Heart*. She also provided the number of the temporary mobile she'd used when approaching Tim.

Several hours passed without word from Yasmin, but in the interim there was an interesting development on the moderators' thread, which was reported to Buffypaws by the ever helpful Worm28.

> **Worm28:** Hartella ' s just told Anomie she can 't go to comiccon after all
>
> **Buffypaws:** omg after she's been badgering everyone to go!
>
> **Worm28:** yeah I know . Anomie 's really pssed off with her.

Robin's hunch was that Yasmin had backed out of joining the masked 'Keep the Game' group so she could meet Venetia Hall and promote her book, unmasked. Sure enough, a second email from Yasmin arrived half an hour later.

> Hi Venetia,
>
> Yes, that would be great! I was planning to be there on Saturday if that suits you?

Robin replied that it suited her perfectly and they arranged to meet just inside the ExCeL main doors at eleven.

'Which might mean she and Anomie have never met, so they won't recognise her,' Robin told Strike by phone later that evening, 'or she's counting on avoiding him in such a massive space.'

'Or,' said Strike, 'Yasmin knows Anomie isn't going to be there.'

'They *must* be going: they've been trying to get everyone else to go for weeks.'

'Sounds like the business venture they're in together is this book, doesn't it?'

'It must be,' said Robin. 'Anomie might be giving insider details in exchange for a cut.'

'Well, this is all going to make for a very interesting interview.'

'Before you go,' said Robin quickly, because his tone told her he was about to hang up, 'I've been thinking: we ought to take the Tube to Comic Con, rather than driving.'

The ensuing pause wasn't really a surprise to Robin.

'You want me to get on the Tube dressed as Darth Vader?'

'I know how you feel, but from what Worm28's said, the group from *Drek's Game* are all going to be travelling by public transport. They're young – I doubt they've got cars. I know Fiendy1's getting a coach there. If you and I take changes of disguise – well, you don't need one, you'd just have to take off the costume – we can be really flexible if we need to tail one or more Anomie suspects.'

She heard Strike sigh.

'Yeah, all right. But you'll have to help me on and off escalators because I've just tried on the bloody mask and I can't see my feet in it.'

So on the morning of Comic Con, Strike and Robin met early at the office. She transformed herself into Venetia Hall, once again donning the ash-blonde wig, pale grey contact lenses and square-framed glasses, while Strike pulled on his Darth Vader costume, which was indeed too short.

'You should've sewn on another bit of fabric,' Robin said, looking at his feet, above which several inches of trouser were visible.

'It'll do,' he said, while fitting batteries in the handle of his lightsaber. 'It's not like I'm bloody auditioning.'

Strike's appearance caused both interest and amusement out on the street and, warm and sweaty though the mask was, he was grateful his face was hidden. However, once they joined the Docklands Light Railway, they found a smattering of costumed people in their carriage, including a pair of teenage girls who were both dressed as Harley Quinn, a woman in a Poison Ivy costume with her Batman partner, and a cluster of young men, one of whom was bare-chested beneath his cloak and wore a Spartan helmet. No longer the most eccentric-looking person on the train, Strike felt somewhat more at ease.

At the next stop, they saw their first dark grey Drek mask, with its enormous plague doctor's nose and bald head. Both fantastic and sinister, the mask was made of latex which had had an unnervingly realistic skin-like texture, complete with warts and pores. It covered the whole head and neck of the wearer, whose eyes blinked through the eyeholes. The rest of the costume consisted of a black cloak that covered everything the wearer had on underneath.

Robin was sitting opposite Strike in silence, looking at something on her phone. Strike assumed she was logging into the game now that they had reception again. However, shortly after the person dressed as Drek had entered the compartment, Robin got up and sat down beside him.

'Can you hear me?' she asked in a low voice.

'Yeah, just about.'

'OK, well, I don't know whether this is going to lead anywhere or not,' Robin said quietly, 'but Midge was telling me Jago Ross still hasn't done anything incriminating.'

'Correct,' said Strike. He'd been avoiding any discussion of the Ross case with Robin, partly out of guilt that he'd added it to the agency's workload and partly because he didn't want any conversation that might lead to discussion of his unsatisfactory love life.

'OK, well, I've been hanging fire on showing you any of this, because it might not have led anywhere, but look.'

She passed Strike her phone, which he had to raise to align with the eyeholes in his mask to look at. Robin had brought up Reddit; specifically a subreddit called r/narcissisticparents, to which had been posted screenshots of a text conversation.

Posted by u/ChrisWossyWoss 11 days ago
Just a Nice Convo with My Narcissistic Father

> Hey Dad woud it be ok if I go to Milly's this exeat w/end? It's her birthday. Mum says it's ok.

You'll come to Kent as planned. Your grandmother's coming down especially to see you

Something only a spoiled, selfish little bitch would have forgotten

> I didn't forget but I thought as Ari and Tatty are going and the twins too she wouldn't mind if I didn't

You'll come to Kent and if I catch you looking less than fucking delighted to be there, you know what you'll get. The answer's no.

Looks as though another talk with your
mother is in order

> No please don't blame mum

You should have thought about that
before disturbing me at work to deal with
your social life.

> Please don't blame mum, blame me. She
> only said I could go if you said it was ok.

I'll be talking to her later.

Strike raised his eyebrows, realised that Robin couldn't see him
doing so and said,

'I take it Chris is—?'

'Christabel, Ross's eldest daughter, yes. She's fourteen and at
Benenden. I've been keeping an eye on her social media for a fort-
night, because she kept posting comments about a narcissistic parent,
though without any details it obviously wasn't much use. Anyway,
I did a lot of cross-referencing across all her media and found her
Reddit posts last night.'

'Bloody well done,' said Strike, who felt annoyed he hadn't thought
of this himself. 'Parenting in the age of the internet, eh? Kids can
all go online and share everything you think you're hiding behind
closed doors.'

'Well, exactly,' said Robin, taking back the phone, bringing up a
new page and handing it to Strike again. 'Now look at that. She posted
it while we were still on the Tube.'

Posted by u/ChrisWossyWoss 20 minutes ago
Need advice on violent father

I can't go on like this any more but I can't see any way out and
I feel so fucking helpless. I'm 14 so please don't tell me to go
non-contact or move out or leave the area or whatever because I
can't do that yet.

So my father's always been violent to me and my sisters and my
mum, pushing, slapping and he once banged my sister's head
so hard off the floor she showed signs of concussion afterwards.
when I was little I once saw him drag my mum downstairs by the
neck. He and my mum got divorced thank god but we still have
to see him. Mum never told anyone he was violent, I think she
was scared of it being made public and she probably got a better
financial settlement without fighting him. he's paying for my
schooling and although I like my school i would honestly leave
and go anywhere else if it meant I didn't have to see him again.

This weekend i'm staying with him and my grandmother and all
his kids are here (he's had two more with his second wife and the
only one of us he actually cares about is my brother, all the rest of
us are girls). He'd already given me shit because I wanted to go
to one of my friend's birthday parties instead of coming here.

So there was just a massive row because my younger sister
accidentally left one of the stable doors open this morning and
my father's hunter got out. When he found out the horse was on
the road he went ballistic. he hit my sis so hard one of her eyes
is swollen shut and when I told him to stop because I honestly
thought he was going to seriously hurt her he hit me too and now
I've got a fat lip but I don't even care about that.

my grandmother just came in my room where I am with my
sisters and said if we all go and apologise to him (what the fuck
I'm apologising for I don't know, nor my youngest sister, who
wasn't even fucking there when it all happened) she's sure it will
all be ok.

if you could see my father's house you'd think nobody could ever
be unhappy there in this beautiful big place in the middle of the
country with animals and everything whch shows people havn't
got a fucking clue. I hate this worse than any pklace on earth.

how do people like me and my sisters ever get out of this
situation. I hate him so much. Do I have to keep seeing hiM? I
hust know if I tell anyone like a teacher it'll be ten times worse
even if they believe me and people like us don't have social
workers. I just tried to call my mum abd she's not picking up.

please any advice, anything, I am honestly scared of whats going
to happen when we got downstairs.

There were four responses beneath this post.

u/evelynmae31 15 minutes ago
your father's behaviour constitutes child abuse. I'm amazed your
grandmother isn't protecting you. What about your stepmother,
could she intervene for you?

u/ChrisWossyWoss 11 minutes ago
my stepmother isn't here, my father's split up with her, too. She's
as bad as him. I just want to know what we can do to stop seeing
him. It feels like there isn't any way of not making it worse. I know
he'll punish my mum somehow.

u/evelynmae31 9 minutes ago
You shouldn't be worried about protecting your mother. She
should be protecting you.

u/ChrisWossyWoss 7 minutes ago
that isn't how it works in this family but thank you for
being so nice.

Strike looked at the screen for so long Robin leaned forwards to
check that he was still awake, but his eyes were indeed open. Realising
that she was peering at him, he handed back her mobile.

'Sorry,' he said. 'Christ. I should've – *of course* he's knocking his
daughters around. I knew he beat up at least one old girlfriend.
Charlotte told me ages back. Laughed about it.'

'She *laughed*?'

'Oh yeah,' said Strike. 'Charlotte's take on it was that the other girl
had only been with Ross for the money and the title, and got a bit more
than she bargained for. There was a strong subtext of "served her right".'

Robin said nothing.

'So when she got engaged to Ross in turn, that was the whole
bloody point,' continued Strike, eyes fixed on the person in the Drek
mask again.

'What d'you mean?'

'She thought I'd go galloping off to church on my white charger to save her . . . The question is,' said Strike, looking away from Drek to point a gauntleted finger at Robin's phone, 'how we use the knowledge he's beating his kids against Ross without making things a hundred times worse for the kids. I can just imagine what he'd do if he knew she's spilling the beans online, even under a pseudonym.'

'There must be a way,' said Robin. 'Could we tip off social services?'

'Possibly,' said Strike. 'Although as she's blocking out all proper names, I don't know how seriously they'd take it . . . This is us, isn't it?'

They got off the train amid a crowd of excited Comic Con visitors. ExCeL rose in front of them, a gigantic edifice of steel, concrete and glass, dwarfing the hordes swarming towards the entrance, which included people dressed as cartoon, film, comic strip and gaming characters.

'Oh, please,' squealed an excited mother, running to catch up with Strike as he and Robin walked towards the entrance. '*Could* he have a picture with you?'

A tiny boy dressed as Boba Fett was ushered forwards to stand grinning beside Strike while Robin moved out of the shot, trying to suppress a smile as she imagined what Strike's expression would have looked like, had he been unmasked. As the grateful family hurried off after someone dressed as Chewbacca, Strike said,

'All right, I think we should split up here. Yasmin's got to think you've only come here for her, not because you're a full-time carer to some nutcase dressed as Darth Vader.'

'It's ableist to say "nutcase",' Robin reminded him, straight-faced.

'Didn't realise you'd come as the Pen of Justice. Text me when you're done with Yasmin. I'm going Anomie-hunting.'

Leaving Robin to wait beside the main doors, Strike proceeded into the hall.

He'd never seen anything quite like it. As the only things of which Strike would have called himself a fan were Tom Waits and Arsenal Football Club, the phenomenon he was now observing was entirely alien to him. Adding to his sense of having entered a strange new dimension was the fact that he didn't recognise many of the franchises that appeared to have given birth to such mass enthusiasm. Yes, he knew who Batman and Spiderman were, and he recognised Cinderella because he'd grown up with a Disney princess-loving sister, but he had only the haziest idea what the small yellow capsule-shaped, one-eyed creature was that had just grazed his knee, and as for the multitudes of anime-influenced young women walking around with pink or purple hair, he couldn't have explained their costumes any better than he could the man ahead of him encased in what appeared to be a white and blue exoskeleton made of metal.

He was no longer conspicuous for being dressed as Darth Vader, but he was unusual in being alone. Most people had come in groups. As Strike began to walk slowly along the orange-carpeted aisles between stalls and stands, the sheer scale of the place became apparent. He'd just decided to try to find a map when two people dressed as characters from *The Ink Black Heart* brushed past him: a Paperwhite, whose face and hair were both white and who wore a long white cotton nightdress, and a partner whose face was jet black and whose head protruded out of a giant, realistically veined black human heart which, Strike assumed, had Harty's smile on the front. The couple was walking with a sense of purpose, so Strike followed, lightsaber in hand.

They passed Mad Max's car, a man in a purple suit who was riding a child's electric cart, a number of helmeted Stormtroopers who Strike felt honour-bound to salute back as they passed each other, and finally turned a corner to see a stand dedicated to *The Ink Black Heart*.

Strike slowed down, watching the small crowd milling around the stand. He recognised Zoe at once. Tiny and fragile-looking, her long black hair loose, she was wearing a cheap white cardboard mask that had been skilfully painted, Strike guessed by herself, to resemble Paperwhite. Close by Zoe was a taller and far healthier-looking girl in jeans, whose brown hair was tied up in a ponytail. Like Zoe, she was wearing a 'Keep *Drek's Game*' T-shirt and wearing a mask, which in her case was a pre-bought one of the skeletal Lady Wyrdy-Grob. Both young women were handing out leaflets that he guessed related to the message on their T-shirts.

Strike shifted position, still watching the *Ink Black Heart* fans through the eyeholes in his mask. The stand around which they'd congregated had evidently been put together by Netflix. There were cardboard cut-outs of characters, beside which people were posing for photographs and selfies, and an array of merchandise. On balance, Strike thought the company had done a pretty good job of balancing the need to serve fans with showing some respect for the fact that one of the co-creators had just been murdered. Indeed, when he shifted position to get a different angle on the group, he saw what he thought might be a book of condolence, behind which stood a woman in an official *Ink Black Heart* T-shirt, and over which three tearful teenage girls were poring.

A young man brushed past the detective. Like Strike, he appeared to be unaccompanied. He wore a black jacket, jeans and high-top designer trainers, which were very clean, appeared to be made partly of suede and had distinctive red soles. Strike watched the man with the red soles walk slowly towards the *Ink Black Heart* fans and take a leaflet from Zoe. He then penetrated the crowd around the stall and was temporarily lost to Strike's view behind a Captain America and a bare-chested Thor in a long blond wig.

Strike moved another few feet to get a better look at the constantly shifting clusters of fans. He could see at least half a dozen Dreks there, all wearing the same full-head-and-neck latex masks, but all with very different body types. Some had chosen the long black hooded cape Drek wore, others wore official T-shirts and, in two cases, 'Keep *Drek's Game*' T-shirts.

The realisation came to Strike suddenly, while he was watching one of the Dreks handing out leaflets. He knew, at last, what Drek was. The sinister, scythe-like nose, the long black cape and hood, the cheerful insistence on playing games that ended in disaster: Drek, of course, was Death.

55

. . . no, dull heart, you were too small,
Thinking to hide the ugly doubt behind that hurried
*   puzzled little smile:*
Only the shade, was it, you saw? but still the shade of
*   something vile . . .*

                                        Charlotte Mew
                                        Ne Me Tangito

'Venetia?'

Yasmin Weatherhead was prompt to the minute. She'd obviously taken a lot of trouble with her hair, which was her best feature and now fell in Veronica Lake style over one eye, partly obscuring the pale, flat face. Her wide smile revealed small white teeth, like a cat's. As tall as Robin, though much broader, she was dressed all in black: black T-shirt, leggings, flat shoes, and the same long woollen cardigan Robin had seen while watching the Weatherheads' house in Croydon.

'Yasmin! How wonderful to meet you,' said Robin, shaking hands.

Yasmin seemed to be looking around for a second person who wasn't there. Robin wondered for a second whether her cover was blown, then realised her mistake.

'Oh, I wasn't able to bring a photographer,' she told Yasmin in an apologetic tone, addressing the woman's one visible eye. 'We're quite small budget, I'm afraid, but if you could provide us with a head shot . . .'

'Oh, of course,' said Yasmin, showing her feline teeth again.

'Shall we find somewhere to sit down?' Robin suggested. 'I think there are cafés over that way . . .'

It took them more than ten minutes to make their way through the crowds, which had now swollen to the point that they were buffeted this way and that between bags, plastic guns and padded costumes. Robin and Yasmin exchanged occasional comments in raised voices, barely able to catch what the other was saying. At last they reached a Costa Coffee that had been set up in the middle of the hall and managed to slide into two seats that had just been vacated.

'I hope my tape recorder is going to be able to pick you up over all this noise,' said Robin loudly. 'What would you like to drink?'

'A latte would be lovely,' said Yasmin.

Waiting in the long line for the counter, Robin watched Yasmin, who was repeatedly combing her dark-blonde hair with her fingers as she looked out over the hordes of visitors and smiling, it seemed to Robin, rather complacently. She remembered Katya Upcott saying that she'd found Yasmin sweet and sincere upon meeting her, and wondered which of their first impressions was wrong, or whether Yasmin's air of self-importance had been adopted since she'd become a moderator in the game.

'There we are,' said Robin, smiling as she set down Yasmin's latte and taking the seat opposite her. 'Right, let's get set up.'

Robin took out the tape recorder she'd used with Tim Ashcroft, turned it on and pushed it across the table towards Yasmin.

'Could you say something into it, so I can just check I'm hearing you?'

'Oh … I don't know what to say?' said Yasmin with a little laugh. She flicked back her hair, bent down a little and said, 'Um … I'm Yasmin Weatherhead, author of *Inkhearts: A Journey Through the Fandom of the Ink Black Heart*?'

Both Yasmin's sentences had ended on a rising inflection. Robin wondered whether the upspeak was habitual, or a product of nerves.

'Perfect,' said Robin, playing it back, and indeed Yasmin's brightly girlish voice carried very well. 'All right then … press record and … off we go! Oh, you don't mind if I take notes?'

'No, please,' said Yasmin.

The handbag Yasmin was cradling on her lap was of patent leather and looked brand new. Her fingernails were immaculately painted. Robin was fleetingly reminded of a far more expensive bag, ruined by ink stains, held by grubby fingers on which there was a smudged tattoo.

'Well, we're thrilled you've agreed to talk to us,' said Robin. 'I'm going to be writing a long piece for our website, and a condensed version which I'm hoping to place with a mainstream paper. Can I ask, have you found a publisher yet?'

'We've had a lot of interest,' said Yasmin, beaming. Robin wondered whether she was using 'we' in imitation of Venetia, or whether she was referring to other people involved in the book.

'Could you give me a brief overview of what it's about?'

'Well, the fandom?' said Yasmin, and this time the upspeak made her sound incredulous that Robin had even asked. At that juncture, a girl with bright red hair, who was wearing a 'Keep *Drek's Game*' T-shirt, walked past.

'Yeah, there you are!' said Yasmin, with a little laugh, pointing. 'So, like, *The Ink Black Heart*'s attracted this incredible, passionate fandom? And I suppose as someone who's been a fan, but also an insider, I've got kind of a unique perspective?'

'Right,' said Robin, nodding before adding, 'Of course, what just happened to Josh and Edie—'

'Awful,' said Yasmin, her smile vanishing instantly, as though unplugged. 'Awful and – and shocking and – I actually had to take two days off work, I was so devastated. But – well, I know I'll have to talk about it, when the book's published, and that's just something I'll have to accept and, er, deal with?'

'Right,' said Robin, who was doing her best not to be distracted by the upspeak, which sounded particularly incongruous when murder was being discussed.

'Because I'd been to Josh, to warn him? Just a couple of weeks before it happened?'

'To *warn* him?'

'Not that something like *that* was going to happen!' said Yasmin hastily. 'No, to warn him and Edie that there were some really nasty rumours going round, in the fandom? About Edie?'

Robin noticed the slight adjustment of fact. There had, after all, been only one rumour about Edie in Yasmin's folder. Nevertheless, she took at face value Yasmin's representation of herself as a sad but conscientious bearer of a multitude of unpleasant falsehoods. She suspected that Yasmin, like Tim Ashcroft, wanted Venetia Hall to hear her version of having to meet the police from her, rather than from talking to other people.

'So I put together, like, a file? So Edie and Josh could, um, they could put PR people onto it, or whatever? And I took it to Josh and he was really grateful, because he hadn't realised what was being said? So, after I – I heard what happened, I offered to be interviewed? By the police? I thought I should? And I said to one of the officers how awful I felt, even though I was only trying to *help* Josh and Edie, because they were meeting in the cemetery to discuss the rumours I'd shown Josh? And one of the officers was really nice, he said to me, "*This isn't your fault*" and not to blame myself? He said people like me often feel, like, needlessly guilty?'

Wondering whether this sensitive officer had any existence outside Yasmin's imagination, Robin said with as much sincerity as she could muster,

'It must have been awful for you.'

'It was,' said Yasmin, shaking her head carefully so as not to disarrange her hair. 'The police wanted to know whether I'd, like, told anyone else they were going to meet at the cemetery? And I hadn't told anyone, because Josh trusted me not to? I actually thought I was the only one who knew where they were meeting? But Edie must have told someone, or told someone who told someone, I suppose? Unless it was just a random attack? Which, obviously, it could have been?'

Robin, who'd already decided that all questions relating to The Halvening would have to wait until the end of the interview, said,

'You weren't asked to give an alibi or anything awful? I mean, because you knew where they were meeting?'

'Er – yes, I was,' said Yasmin, with the first sign of constraint. 'I was at my sister's. For my niece's birthday? So obviously . . .'

'Oh, please,' said Robin hurriedly, 'you mustn't think I'm—!'

'No, no, of course not,' said Yasmin with a little laugh. Then, lowering her voice a little, she said,

'The police actually told me to be very careful, going forwards. I mean, of my own security? I'm – well,' said Yasmin, with a self-deprecating little shrug, 'I'm quite a well-known figure in the fandom? And I was known to be a friend of Josh's and the police were like "be very careful and cautious". Just in case, you know, it was, like, a vendetta against anyone who'd been involved?'

'Wow,' said Robin. 'Scary.'

'Yeah,' said Yasmin, sweeping her hair back off her shoulder. 'I genuinely wondered whether I should keep going with the book? Like, whether it was wise to raise my profile any higher, you know? But it's actually been good to have a project to, like, channel all the negative emotions into something positive? I know Phil feels the same way – that's Edie's fiancé?' she added. 'He's given the project his blessing and has actually worked with me on it, a bit? He's going to get thirty per cent of the royalties. And we're thinking of giving some money to charity? Maybe something to do with knife crime?'

'How wonderful,' said Robin. 'Poor man, *what* her fiancé must have been through.'

'Oh, Phil's devastated ... but he wants to help with the book, for, like, Edie's legacy?'

'Marvellous, yes,' said Robin, nodding.

'He's actually shared how she saw the story going forwards? I think fans are going to be really excited, knowing what she was planning? It's been absolutely amazing, listening to him talk.'

'I'm sure,' said Robin, still nodding enthusiastically. 'Wow. What a resource to have!'

'Yeah. I mean, he's really the next best thing to Edie herself, the things he knows? I, um, don't want to do spoilers or anything, but she was developing two entirely new characters for the film and they're *incredible*. Phil remembers so much detail. Obviously, I don't know whether Maverick will use them or not, but I know fans would *love* to read in Edie's own words how she saw these characters and what her idea was for the movie plot? Because she'd sketched that out too?'

'Is this all in her own handwriting or—?'

'No, there weren't actual notes, but Phil's got an amazing memory.'

'Fantastic,' repeated Robin, who was running out of superlatives. 'So, take me through the structure of your book. How are you—?'

'Well, I cover the cartoon from the very earliest days, obviously, when it first appeared on YouTube? But the book's really centred on us, the fans? And what we brought to it ourselves, and how we shaped the whole thing and I suppose it's really kind of, like, a unique phenomenon?'

She said it with no apparent irony, as devotees of a hundred other franchises tramped past the barrier separating their small table from the thoroughfare beyond.

'What would you say is *particularly* appealing about *The Ink Black Heart*?' asked Robin. 'What made *you* fall in love with it?'

'Well, the humour, obviously?' said Yasmin, smiling, 'but it's also just this crazy, perfect little romantic, spooky world? It looks so beautiful and all these characters just, you know, kind of soldiering on through everything? You know the iconic line at the end of the first episode?'

Robin shook her head. She'd never watched to the end of the first episode.

Yasmin opened her heavy cardigan and displayed the words emblazoned in white across a tight black T-shirt: WE'RE DEAD. THINGS CAN ONLY GET BETTER.

Robin laughed obligingly.

'I suppose, if you've ever felt a bit of an outsider or, you know, as if you're *wrong* or you've hit rock bottom, there's something in the cartoon for you?'

'And have you felt like that?' asked Robin, feeling rather like a therapist.

'Well, yes, a bit,' said Yasmin, nodding. 'I was, like, quite badly bullied at school?'

'Oh, I'm so sorry,' said Robin.

'No, it's fine, I mean, I'm an adult now, that's all behind me? But I suppose I've always compared myself a lot to my older sister? She was always the pretty one, and you know how Paperwhite in the cartoon talks about her sister a lot? Who's still alive and going to parties and things?'

'Yes, of course,' said Robin, nodding.

'And, obviously, there's Harty?' said Yasmin, with her widest smile yet. 'We all love Harty. Josh did such an amazing job voicing him? We all hope, when he's better, he'll come back and voice Harty again?'

The casualness with which Yasmin spoke told Robin how little she really knew about the damage inflicted upon Josh Blay's neck with the machete that had pierced it. In spite of Yasmin's easy talk of horror and fear, she seemed to Robin to be still strangely insulated from what had happened in the cemetery.

'So, yeah, in the book I go all through the early days? The fans' reactions to the different voice actors, who I knew ...'

'Yes,' said Robin, 'of course, you knew everyone! Can we back up to when you first met Josh and Edie?'

'Well, I was, like, a *massive* fan from, like, really early on? And I'd never been to Highgate Cemetery? So I went to look at it one day. And then, I must have got lost or something? Because I ended up by

North Grove. I didn't even realise the building was North Grove, where they were living – I just thought the shop looked kind of interesting? And honestly, I couldn't *believe* it when I, like, walked right into Josh! He was helping out on the till and his agent, Katya, was in there talking to him?'

Robin, who knew perfectly well that the shop at the front of North Grove wasn't visible from the exterior of the building, nodded, smiled and made a note.

'So I just sort of, like, *froze*?' said Yasmin, laughing as she combed her hair with her fingers again, 'And then I said something like "oh my God, I love you" – I meant, I loved the cartoon – I was *mortified*! But Josh was really sweet and chatty? And then he had to go and do something and I was left with Katya? She was lovely, I *love* Katya. I asked her how Josh and Edie were finding all the attention and everything? And she took my number, because I said if there was *anything* I could do to help, like a bit of typing or whatever, I wouldn't even want paying? And that's how it happened?'

'Incredible . . . Now, this game,' said Robin, pretending to consult her notes, '*Drek's Game* – was that already online at this point?'

'Yes,' said Yasmin, without any sign of embarrassment. 'It was an amazing way for fans to, like, connect? Like a big chatroom, and we were all talking about the characters and plotlines and it really kept all the enthusiasm going? It really benefited the series, you know, right from the start?'

'And *Drek's Game*'s going to be featured in your book too?'

'Yeah, I've got permission from the main creator to devote a section to it and he's given me some background? I think fans will be thrilled to hear a little bit more about the game.'

'Would this main creator be the famous Anomie?' asked Robin and Yasmin gave a little giggle.

'*Don't* ask me who it is.'

'You know, then?'

'I shouldn't say.'

'I'll take that as a "yes",' said Robin, smiling. 'If you've got permission from them to give background on the game in your book, you're obviously in direct contact?'

'Um . . .' Yasmin giggled again. 'It's all, like, very Watergate?'

'But it's a "he"?'

'Oh, yeah, everyone knows *that*,' said Yasmin.

'Anomie was sometimes a bit – er – well, I suppose "abusive" might be the word – online, towards Edie, wasn't he?'

Yasmin's smile faltered.

'Er – well – I mean, he can be kind of blunt, but he's kind of – I mean – I hate saying this now? But fans felt really disrespected? By Edie?'

'In what way?' asked Robin.

'Well, like, when she dissed the game? Like, we're all loving it, you know? So are you saying, like, we don't get the cartoon or whatever? So yeah, people were really upset by that?'

'Right,' said Robin, nodding.

'And after she did that, Anomie became . . . like, kind of a figure-head? In the fandom? He's, like, a really clever and . . . he's a cultured person? And I think the fans feel like Anomie deserved recognition from Edie for all the hard work he put in for us? And maybe some financial reward for what he's created? Because – I mean, he's someone who's overcome a lot of, like, personal stuff, you know?'

For somebody who'd so recently believed that Ledwell herself had been Anomie, Robin thought, Yasmin now seemed to be surprisingly wedded to her new theory.

'You clearly *do* know who Anomie is,' Robin told Yasmin, and by keeping an expectant, mock-inquisitorial expression on her face, Robin finally persuaded Yasmin into another giggle.

'OK, well, I just put a few little bits and pieces together and, yeah, if you sort of add it all up it's kind of obvious? And it's really inspirational to me that he did it, because of his personal circumstances? And just, maybe, it would've made all the difference to Anomie's life, and his family's lives, if Edie could have been a bit more supportive of the game? And let Anomie share in her good fortune, you know? Because she hadn't paid his—'

Yasmin stopped herself with almost comical abruptness. Robin asked herself how the sentence could have ended: *Salary? Invoice? Rent?*

'She'd let Anomie down in some way, had she?' Robin asked.

Yasmin hesitated.

'I don't want to say anything else about Anomie, if that's OK.'

'Oh, of course,' said Robin, thinking they could circle back to Edie failing to meet her financial obligations in due course.

'I suppose things got quite corporate once the cartoon left YouTube?'

'*Yes,*' said Yasmin fervently. 'That was, like, totally it. *Corporate.*

And all the people who'd been there at the start were kind of . . . I mean, in *my* case, it was a bit of a relief when Edie said they didn't need me any more? Like, I was getting really busy at Lola June? And trekking all the way up to Highgate to do their mail, I couldn't keep doing it and they weren't – I mean, what they were paying me barely covered the Tube fare? That wasn't Josh, he's kind of detached from money,' said Yasmin, with a fond smile. 'It was more – well, I say all this in the book? Because I think you've got to be *completely* honest if you're going to do something like this—'

'Oh, definitely,' said Robin.

'Edie changed? She got – well, quite grand and uptight? Like, she started thinking everyone wanted to take advantage of her? And I was seeing that up close, how she was getting? And she didn't want to work with Katya any more? She was getting quite kind of snappy with Katya, even before I left? And Katya's lovely. I *really* love Katya, and she had her own personal troubles too, so you'd think – but Edie changed, you know?'

'Now, going back a bit, just to get the timeline straight,' said Robin, 'how long did you work for Josh and Edie?'

'Just over a year?' said Yasmin. 'August 2011 to November 2012.'

'So you must have met the whole original cast?'

'Yeah,' said Yasmin, beaming again. 'Josh, Tim, Bong, Lucy, Catriona, Wally and Pez – although Pez – Preston Pierce – wasn't in the cartoon any more by the time I started working for Josh and Edie? He never thought *The Ink Black Heart* would be successful. He could be quite sarky about—'

Yasmin broke off, looking nervous.

'Please don't put that in. I don't want Pez angry at me.'

'Of course not, I won't put it in,' Robin assured her. 'In fact – '

She turned off the tape recorder.

' – let's go off the record.'

Yasmin looked as though she didn't know whether to be more excited or alarmed.

'You know it's rumoured that Preston Pierce is Anomie?' Robin said, watching Yasmin for her reaction.

'*Pez?*' said Yasmin with an incredulous little laugh. 'Oh no, it definitely isn't Pez.'

'Anomie doesn't sound Liverpudlian on the phone?' asked Robin, smiling.

'No, not at all,' said Yasmin. Robin wondered whether Yasmin had ever heard Anomie's voice. Her tone was uncertain.

'Why d'you say you wouldn't want Preston angry at you?' she asked.

'Oh, he's just one of those —' said Yasmin. 'He's ... he's like the kind of boy who used to bully me at school?'

Remembering how aggressive Pez had been to the girl with the blue hair at the evening class, Robin thought she knew what Yasmin meant.

'All right to continue?' she asked Yasmin, her finger on the record button.

'Yes, great,' said Yasmin, sipping her latte.

'Well, I'm assuming your book's going to deal with some of the *Ink Black Heart* controversies?' Robin said, the tape running once again.

'Yeah, of course,' said Yasmin, nodding. 'It's important to remain critical, even of the things you love?'

'Of course,' said Robin.

'So ... yeah, I do cover fans', like, disappointment in Edie? About some of the content, some of the jokes?'

'I've been reading a blog called the Pen of Justice, for background,' said Robin, watching Yasmin closely, but she showed no sign of embarrassment.

'Yeah, I've read that too,' said Yasmin. 'It's quite good, but I don't agree with, like, *everything*. There was this one article complaining about the way the black heart's chasing the white ghost? And I thought that was a bit of stretch, you know? Saying that was racist or whatever ... Actually, would you mind not putting that in either?' said Yasmin, suddenly anxious again. 'I mean, I'm *completely* anti-racist. I was *disgusted* when I found out Edie based Paperwhite on a black woman.'

'You knew about that?' said Robin sharply.

As soon as the words had escaped her, she regretted them. The tone wasn't Venetia Hall's: it had been accusatory. Yasmin looked taken aback.

'I think that was, um, pretty well known?' she said uncertainly.

'Sorry,' said Robin, with an apologetic smile. 'I think the first time that was made public was by Anomie, so I was wondering if he had told you.'

'Oh,' said Yasmin. 'No, I was at North Grove one day? And I was, like, updating the website for them? And Josh asked me if I wanted to have a drink, afterwards? In their room, upstairs, because they'd just finished recording an episode?'

She blushed as she said it. The memory was clearly an important one.

'Fun,' said Robin, trying to recover her lighter previous tone.

'Yeah,' said Yasmin. 'It was me, Josh, Edie, Seb – he used to help with the animation? – and Pez and Wally. And they were all smoking, um, like – you know, cannabis?' said Yasmin with a slightly nervous laugh. 'I mean, they were kind of open about doing that, so it's not, like, any big secret. I never did it, I don't really . . .'

Robin had a sudden, vivid mental picture of Yasmin perched on a hard-backed chair in a cramped, smoky bedroom, with the creators and cast members sprawled around, stoned, and the part-time assistant thrilled to be there yet uncomfortable, laughing along but listening for all she was worth.

'And, yeah, I overheard Edie telling Seb that, like, she'd based the character on this girl she used to share a flat with, or whatever? Like, the girl had a lot of guys chasing after her, and Edie said this girl kind of, like, had this technique of treating them mean? Which, like, if you've seen the cartoon, Paperwhite's always kind of nasty to Harty, who's so in love with her? But there are sometimes these, like, tiny slivers of hope, or whatever, that keep him coming back?'

'Right,' said Robin, nodding. 'That's fascinating. Fans are going to love these kinds of insights.'

'Yeah, but I didn't realise, till Anomie said later, on Twitter, that the flatmate was black? So that felt like – well, like Anomie said, it felt like punching down? Like, why would you portray a friend like that? Like, depict her as a kind of – you know, a prick tease, or whatever?'

'Although, in fairness,' said Robin, 'Edie didn't make the inspiration public. Anomie did.'

'I think Anomie just got tired of her, like, hypocrisy? She was representing herself as, like, this really woke person and behind the scenes she wasn't really like that?'

'Yes,' said Robin, 'I see what you mean. As you've mentioned politics – I'd imagine you cover the whole Wally Cardew/Drek business in your book?'

'Yeah, I've got a whole chapter on it,' said Yasmin, her expression becoming sombre. 'That was just crazy? Who'd have thought the alt-right would like anything in *The Ink Black Heart*? We were all, like, *furious* when they started flooding in and, you know, *appropriating* the character, because everyone loved Drek, he was so funny, and then Drek became this whole, like, other thing?'

'You knew Wally, obviously?'

'Yeah,' said Yasmin, now looking conflicted. 'Obviously, that "Cookies" video he did, was – I mean, they kind of had no choice but to sack him? But a lot of fans were really upset he left? Like, if he'd just put out an apology? That caused a lot of fights in the fandom. But Michael David, who took over, was amazing.'

A rosy flush, which was very obvious given her pallor, spread over Yasmin's face as she spoke Michael David's name.

'Yes,' said Robin. 'He left as well, though, didn't he?'

'Um . . . yeah, he got a part on *Casualty*,' said Yasmin. 'And he's in a new play in the West End, opening next month.'

The flush was spreading blotchily down her neck.

'But he's always kind of stayed connected to the fandom?' she continued. 'He's still part of the Inkheart community, which is just, like, so nice? I think he really loved the support he got from fans? Because when he was first cast as Drek, there was a lot of abuse, because some people still wanted Wally? And he was just so sweet and appreciative of the people who were saying we should give him a chance and everything?'

'How lovely,' said Robin warmly, but she was interested in this assertion. In all her hours spent poring over the Twitter accounts of Anomie and the other *Ink Black Heart* fans, she'd seen no sign of this engagement between Michael David and fans, nor any indication that he continued to see himself as connected to the cartoon since he'd left.

'Yeah,' said Yasmin, still blushing. 'I've, ah, actually got to know him a little bit? Because he reached out to me to say thanks for all the support when he left the cartoon? I've got tickets for his play and he's promised me an autograph afterwards?'

'Wow,' said Robin.

'Actually,' said Yasmin, looking worried again, 'please could you not put that in, either? It's, like, my friendship with Michael's private?'

'Of course,' said Robin. 'I won't mention it . . . Now, this business of The Halvening.'

She'd expected Yasmin to look worried at that, and so she did.

'You mean – like, that neo-Nazi group, or whatever?'

'Exactly,' said Robin. 'Presumably you address the possibility they were manipulating fans? In the book?'

'I . . . well, not really. I . . . I don't think any of the fans would have fallen for it, if The Halvening had tried to, like, plant fake stories or whatever?'

But the blotches on Yasmin's neck now resembled Gus Upcott's hives. When Robin remained silent and unsmiling, merely watching Yasmin through her glasses, the latter seemed to become more nervous.

'Yeah, and I told the police that? Like, yeah, some of the fans, after that article appeared in the paper, were like, "Oh, if you ever said a bad thing about Edie Ledwell you must be a Nazi trying to get her to kill herself," which was, like, so ridiculous?'

'But you'd noticed an increase in nasty rumours about Edie? You were so concerned you took a file full of them to Josh, right?'

'I – what I took to Josh was definitely, *no way* put out there by The Halvening,' said Yasmin. 'I know that for a fact, because I – well, the people saying that stuff definitely aren't Halvening.'

There was a short pause. Yasmin ran her hand nervously through her hair.

'I mean, what they were saying, it could have been true? But it wasn't. They'd just made a mistake. And anyway, one of the people saying it was black, so obviously *they* can't be Halvening.'

And now a ludicrous idea came to Robin, one she'd have instantly dismissed had the woman opposite her not blushed an even deeper red.

Yasmin couldn't, surely, believe that Michael David was anonymously playing *Drek's Game*? Was she deluded enough to think a successful actor would be devoting hours of his life to proving that Edie Ledwell was Anomie, rather than getting on with what appeared to be a flourishing career on television and stage? And if Yasmin *did* indeed believe such a fantastic lie, who exactly had expertly groomed her into believing that she was in conversation with Michael David?

'They're black? You know that for a fact?'

In the pause that followed, Robin was certain Yasmin was pinned to her chair by burgeoning fear. Perhaps the doubt she'd successfully suppressed for so long had at last crawled, scorpion-like, out of her subconscious. Perhaps, too, she was starting to suspect that Venetia Hall, who asked certain questions so sharply, wasn't what Yasmin had thought her either. Yasmin's face had blanched to an unhealthy yellow, but with those blotches still disfiguring her neck. The longer the silence between them continued, the more terrified Yasmin looked.

'Yes,' said Yasmin at last, 'I know it for fact.'

'Oh, well, if it's someone you've met face to face,' said Robin, smiling. 'So you don't think The Halvening had anything to do with Edie's death?'

'N-no,' stammered Yasmin. 'I don't.'

'Or that Anomie did it?'

Robin threw it out because there was nothing left to lose. Yasmin might be worried by now that Venetia Hall wasn't really a journalist, but the ash-blonde wig, contact lenses and glasses still meant she wasn't recognisable as Robin Ellacott.

'What d'you mean?'

'Well, you've been very eloquent on the subject of how much justifiable grievance Anomie had against Edie Ledwell,' said Robin, smiling.

'Anomie couldn't have done it,' said Yasmin. 'He couldn't have.'

'Well, I think that's everything,' said Robin, turning off the tape recorder. 'Thanks *so* much for meeting me, it's been fascinating. And best of luck with the book!'

Yasmin appeared shell-shocked. She even forgot to upspeak as they exchanged a last few empty pleasantries. Robin watched the woman walk away from the café, head bowed, and wasn't at all surprised to see her reach for her mobile and start typing. Robin, meanwhile, took out her phone and texted Strike.

Got some interesting stuff. Where are you?

56

'Well, you've done a damn sight better than I have,' said Strike twenty minutes later, from behind his Darth Vader mask.

He'd been making repeated circuits of the stands near the *Ink Black Heart* exhibit for the last hour, watching the milling throng, but the exercise had proved largely pointless. Now he was leaning up against the edge of a stall selling cushions with anime-style animals printed on them, to take the weight off his stump.

'I know it wasn't likely Anomie was going to do anything to reveal themselves,' Strike continued, his eyes still fixed on the crowd clustered around the *Ink Black Heart* stand, 'but I thought there was a slim chance I might recognise the back view of a known suspect. Nothing, except for Zoe.'

'Where is she?' asked Robin.

Prior to re-joining Strike, she'd slipped into the Ladies', taken off her wig and glasses and changed her T-shirt. While Robin thought it highly unlikely that Yasmin would want to linger in ExCeL after the interview she'd just endured, she didn't want to risk running into her again. She'd also logged back into the game, from which, for the first time, all moderators appeared to be absent.

'Went to have a coffee with another girl in a "Keep *Drek's Game*" T-shirt. Both still in their masks. I didn't follow, because there was someone hanging around who was interesting me at the time.'

'Who?'

'He's gone,' said Strike. 'He was wandering about on his own and he seemed to be keeping an eye on the same lot I am. He approached a couple of Dreks and talked to them ... Go over what Yasmin said about Anomie again?'

'Well, she says he's definitely male and hinted that Edie owed him money. She said it would have made a difference to the guy's family if she'd let him monetise the game. And there was that thing about him being clever and cultivated.'

'Cultivated,' repeated Strike. 'Would you have called Anomie cultivated, from what you've seen of his chat?'

'No,' said Robin. 'Like I said, he's kind of brash inside the game. Maybe he's different on the moderator channel.'

'But you said you think he's putting on a bit of an act in the game?'

'Well, sometimes he strikes me as trying to be a bit too much like one of the boys, you know? Sort of pointlessly crude.'

'Can't say I've seen much evidence of culture on his Twitter feed,' said Strike.

'I suppose he does know that one Latin tag,' said Robin. 'That "oderint dum" thing.'

'Did Yasmin seem that easily impressed?'

'Well,' said Robin, 'I'd have to say yes. She struck me as a bit—'

'Thick?'

'Well – definitely credulous. I mean, the Michael David stuff ...'

'Yeah,' said Strike, 'but whoever managed to persuade her they were Michael David must've been pretty slick. She's not a child. She's holding down a job. I can't imagine anyone's immediate reaction on being told they were talking to a TV star in an anonymous game would be to believe it right off the bat.'

'No, you're right,' said Robin. 'It must have been skilfully done.'

'And she says Anomie wouldn't be capable of killing anyone. Is that because of a strict moral code, physical weakness or squeamishness, would you say?'

'No idea.'

'You don't think she was saying "he" to put you off the scent?'

'Honestly, no. My impression is that she's got a new theory she's quite pleased about and she said as much to me as she dared . . . But I think she's fastened onto this new person for a reason.'

'They've given themselves away to her somehow?'

'Maybe,' said Robin, 'but I had the impression Yasmin would really *like* it to be this person with a justified grudge who's down on their luck, and cultivated, and incapable of killing anyone. She's invested in believing Anomie's a good guy? Oh no – now I'm doing it,' said Robin in exasperation.

'Doing what?'

'Uptalking. She was at it all through the interview.'

'That's him,' said Strike suddenly. 'He's back.'

Robin turned to look in the same direction as Strike.

The young man in a leather jacket, jeans and expensive red-soled trainers had reappeared. His thick dark hair grew low on his forehead. As Strike and Robin watched, Red Soles navigated around a young man in a wheelchair, who was talking to a cheerful-looking girl in a miniskirt, then approached yet another person in a Drek mask and engaged them in conversation.

'He's only interested in Dreks,' said Strike.

'Odd,' said Robin, also watching.

Red Soles was now laughing at something the Drek had said.

'Excuse me,' said the stallholder irritably to Strike. 'Would you mind moving? You're blocking people who want to look.'

Strike and Robin moved along to the next stall, which sold comic books.

'You were moving,' Strike said suddenly to Robin.

'What?'

'Moving. House. What happened to that?'

'Oh,' said Robin. 'It got postponed. I'm doing it tomorrow – that's why I'm taking a day off.'

'Shit,' said Strike. 'I should've remembered. Should have asked. Sorry.'

'That's all right,' said Robin.

Better late than never.

'Got anyone helping you?'

'Mum and Dad are driving down tonight.'

Red Soles and Drek had moved apart. Red Soles now took out his phone, appeared to send a text, then he set off, walking away from the *Ink Black Heart* stand.

'Can you hold my lightsaber?'

Strike pulled off his Darth Vader mask and struggled out of his robes.

'What're you—?'

'We're following that guy. There's something up with him.'

Strike bundled up the costume, took the lightsaber from Robin and chucked the lot down on top of the comic books.

'Give it away as a freebie,' Strike suggested to the startled stall-holder, and with Robin hurrying after him he walked as fast as his sore leg would permit after Red Soles. Fortunately, the crowds were so dense that the man hadn't got far.

'He doesn't look like the average *Ink Black Heart* fan,' said Strike to Robin as they made their way with difficulty through the slowly moving crowd. 'He was trying to find something out ... maybe the same thing as us.'

It took twenty minutes for Red Soles to gain the exit. With an appearance of relief at having got out of the crush, he took out his phone and called someone, still walking. There was no chance of getting close enough to hear what he was saying, because of the surrounding crowds still moving in and out of ExCeL.

Strike felt his own mobile vibrate and pulled it out, hoping to see news from a subcontractor.

'Midge?' said Robin as she cast a hasty glance at the game, but Anomie wasn't present.

'No,' said Strike, putting his phone back into his pocket. 'Pru.'

'Who?'

'Prudence. My sister.'

'Oh,' said Robin. 'Have you met her yet?'

'No,' said Strike, who was trying to ignore his aching hamstring. 'We were going to, but her daughter fell off a climbing wall.'

'God, is she OK?'

'Yeah. Fractured femur ... He didn't come by car, then,' said Strike, because Red Soles was clearly heading for the station, in and out of which huge numbers of people were still moving.

A burly Batman elbowed his way past Robin. A chattering group dressed in steampunk passed in the opposite direction. Red Soles was still talking on his phone.

They arrived on the platform to see Red Soles waiting for the train, at the front of the crowd. There were some grumbles as Strike used his bulk to move people aside. He wanted to get close enough to Red Soles to make sure they entered the same compartment.

Strike and Robin came to a halt within a couple of feet of their target just as he finished his conversation and put his hands in his pockets, bouncing on the heels of his expensive trainers with what seemed impatience.

They heard the approaching growl of the train.

Strike felt someone stumble into him from behind. He looked around in time to see a black figure forcing its way to the front of the platform. It hit Red Soles.

And everything seemed to slow, as happens when watching the almost inevitable extinction of life.

Red Soles fell off the platform, twisting slightly in mid-air, freeing his hands from his pockets too late. The side of his head hit the track and the crowd heard the splitting of bone and flesh on wood even over the roar of the oncoming train.

And Robin took three strides and jumped.

She heard screams behind her. A huge brown-skinned man dressed as Superman had jumped onto the tracks at the same time as Robin. As they heaved Red Soles' unconscious body upwards, others in the crowd held out their arms to assist them.

Two hands found Robin, one under her arm, one hauling on her T-shirt, and she kept tugging on the inert body with ten others, and then the train was upon them. With half an inch to spare, Strike had pulled Robin to safety, but there was another loud crack and more screams, because the unconscious man's head had slipped back and hit the side of the train.

'Fuck's sake!' yelled Strike, but nobody heard him except Robin, because everyone was shouting and screaming, and the word 'deliberate' was repeated, and an argument had broken out about exactly who had run into whom, and a man who seemed drunk took umbrage at the accusation that he'd been the one to knock the unconscious man off the platform. Red Soles lay where he'd been deposited on the platform, blood trickling from his inner ear. An official was trying to get through the crowd to him. The train remained stationary.

'Fuck's *sake*!' Strike shouted at Robin again. 'How the fuck did you think you were going to lift him?'

'I didn't know he'd been knocked out,' she said, shaking with the amount of adrenalin still coursing through her. 'Thought I could—'

'He was pushed! Someone knocked into him on purpose!' a woman was shrieking.

People were getting onto the train as though nothing had happened. The railway official was on his radio, and his colleagues came hurrying along the platform and forced a space around the motionless figure on the ground. Strike, who'd grabbed the backpack Robin had dropped, pulled her backwards out of the crush. He could feel her shaking. She realised the cold wasn't only shock: Strike had torn her T-shirt. A gaping hole beneath her arm was revealing her bra. Taking her backpack from her partner, she tugged out the top she'd worn as Venetia, and pulled it over the torn T-shirt.

'Who saw what happened?'

Two police officers had arrived.

'I did,' said Strike loudly, his voice carrying over the clamour.

One of the police officers drew Strike and Robin aside, while her colleague and the railway officials attempted to impose order on the agitated crowd. The train hadn't left. People were staring out of the windows at the injured man.

'Go on,' said the female officer to Strike, notebook at the ready.

'Guy in a Batman mask,' said Strike. 'He pushed himself into the middle of the crowd, faked being shoved to cause a diversion, then shouldered the guy onto the track. It was intentional.'

'Where's this guy? Can you see him?'

'No,' said Strike, casting an eye over the mass on the platform.

'Did you see where he went after the guy fell?'

'No,' repeated Strike. 'I was busy pulling my friend back off the track.'

'OK, well you'll need to hang around, we'll need a statement.'

They heard a siren. An ambulance had arrived. The police officer turned away.

'All *right*,' said Robin as Strike opened his mouth again. 'It was instinctive. I know it wasn't smart.'

She could feel the place where her armpit was going to bruise, from where Strike had hauled her upwards out of the path of the train. He pulled cigarettes and lighter out of his pocket as he stared at the inert figure on the ground. Red Soles' top had been pulled up to expose a small tattoo beneath his heart. It resembled a Y with a middle vertical stroke.

The train still hadn't moved out of the station. Now people were trying to get out, but the police were insisting they remained inside, presumably for questioning.

'You can't smoke here,' Robin pointed out.

'What I don't understand is why *you're* not fucking smoking,' said Strike as he exhaled. Robin, who was trying not to shake too obviously, forced a smile.

57

An in-game chat between Anomie and moderator LordDrek

<A new private channel has opened>

<25 May 2015 22.57>

<LordDrek invites Anomie>

LordDrek: come here before I hnmake you, you cnut

>

<Anomie has joined the channel>

Anomie: something I can help you with?

LordDrek: your triedd to kill my brother I know it was youj

Anomie: pretty sure I'd remember something like that

LordDrek: do nhot play games witgh me you fuck you tried to push mhy brother under a fuckibng train

Anomie: type slower, you won't make so many mistakes

LordDrek: you don't kniow who
you've messed with, you
cunt, we'll cone for you

Anomie: I know exactly who I've
messed with, Charlie boy

Anomie: your little brother isn't
as careful as you are

Anomie: 'Vilepechora' was a
mistake

LordDrek: you fcukng cunt I will
hunt you dokwn

Anomie: no you won't

Anomie: unlike you, I leave no
traces

Anomie: just been sitting here
rewinding the news footage

Anomie: fkn hysterical watching
his head smack off the side of
the train

LordDrek: I will sfauking hunt you
dowbn and ksill you

Anomie: give my love to the other
lads in the Halvening

Anomie: big sloppy kiss to your
vegetable brother

Anomie: if you're lucky he'll be
able to hold his own sippy cup
come next Christmas

LordDrek: you wait you sicjk fuck
im going to

<LordDrek has been banned>

PART FOUR

Fibres of the Ventricles. –
These are arranged in an exceedingly complex manner,
and the accounts given by various anatomists differ
     considerably.

Henry Gray FRS
Gray's Anatomy

58

O shame!
To utter the thought into flame
Which burns at your heart.

Elizabeth Barrett Browning
A Curse for a Nation

An in-game chat between two moderators of *Drek's Game*

<A new private channel has opened>

<23 May 2015 11.18>

<Morehouse invites Paperwhite>

Morehouse: Paperwhite, we've got to talk

>

>

>

<Paperwhite has joined the channel>

Paperwhite: so what's the excuse? Car crash? Alien abduction? Your Mum needed emergency surgery?

Paperwhite: no you wouldn't do that one, that'd be kind of tasteless with my mum being ill

Morehouse: i'm sorry

557

Morehouse: I'm really sorry

Morehouse: I bottled it

Paperwhite: you bottled it

Paperwhite: you know how many
hours I spent on the fkn coach?

Paperwhite: what more do you want
from me?

Paperwhite: you've had pics, sympathy,
endless chats and I'm messing up a
real life relationship just to spend
hours in the game with you

Morehouse: I deserve everything
you're saying

Morehouse: but please listen to me
because I'm fkn worried, for you
and for all of us

Paperwhite: what d'you mean?

Morehouse: did you see that guy
who got pushed in front of a train
after Comic Con?

Paperwhite: no I got the coach, I
just told you

Paperwhite: why?

Morehouse: it was Vilepechora

Paperwhite: what?

Morehouse: It was Vilepechora who
got pushed in front of the train

>

Paperwhite: wait, what

Paperwhite: he's dead?

Morehouse: maybe, by now. They're
saying on the news he got a
serious head injury

Morehouse: this is what Anomie meant by having a plan to make them leave on the weekend of Comic Con

Paperwhite: I literally don't know what you're talking about

Morehouse: he knew he was going to kill Vilepechora

Paperwhite: you're honestly scaring me. wtf?

Morehouse: weeks ago, Vilepechora said something like 'Anomie knows all about Bitcoin, we think that's how he bought the taser' or something, on the mod channel

Morehouse: I thinkt hat's what happened. Vilepechora knows Bitcoin and he told Anomie how to use it. That's how Anomie got hold of an illegal taser and a huge fucking knife without any of it being traced, Vilepechora gave him the idea

Morehouse: he didn't want to piss Vilepechora off by banning him because Vile could testify he told Anomie how to buy weapons on the dark net with crypto

Morehouse: he told me Vile and LordDrek would be gone on the day of Comic Con

Morehouse: he meant Vilepechora would be dead & LD banned

>

Paperwhite: you're nuts

Paperwhite: how would Anomie have known who to push under a train?

Morehouse: we knew what Vilepechora's real name was and what he looked like

Paperwhite: how?

Morehouse: we got interested in
the name 'Vilepechora'

Morehouse: it's an anagram

Morehouse: we worked it out then
we googled the name we got

Morehouse: and found place of
work, the lot. He looked kind of an
arsehole posing with his car. Anomie
liked it though. He liked knowing a
guy likt that was in our game

Morehouse: I always thought it was
fkn weird a guy like that was in
here.

>

Paperwhite: how could you know
that guy you googled was really
Vilepechora? What if there was
more than one person with that
name?

Morehouse: I didn't know for sure
until I saw the footage of the guy
falling in front of the train

Paperwhite: I'm googling the news
footage now

>

>

>

Paperwhite: It's really grainy, are
you sure that's him?

Morehouse: we'll know when they
give out a name won't we

Paperwhite: what's his real name?

Morehouse: the less you know the
better. And same goes for knowing
who Anomie is, before you ask

Morehouse: I'm going to leave the game tonight. I want out and you should get out too. Then I need to think out what's best. The police might think I'm fkn crazy but I think I need to talk to them

Paperwhite: you can't leave

Paperwhite: if all this is true

Paperwhite: and Anomie thinks you walked out because you're suspicious, you'llbe next. He knows everything about you. he knows where you live

Morehouse: I don't care

Paperwhite: well, do you care about ME at all?

Morehouse: of course i do, why are you saying that?

Paperwhite: because Anomie knows who I am too

Morehouse: what? how?

Paperwhite: I did a stupid thing

Morehouse: you mean sending him that picture?

Paperwhite: that was the second stupid thing

Paperwhite: the first stupid thing was, my real name was in my sign up email

Morehouse: I fkn knew it

Morehouse: I fkn knew he knew who you were

Morehouse: shit

>

Paperwhite: ok, let's look at this sensibly

Paperwhite: think aobut what you're saying for a moment

Paperwhite: this person you've known for ages, who loves the Ink Black Heart

Paperwhite: you genuinely think he could have stabbed Ledwell and Blay?

Paperwhite: you seriously think he could have pushed somebody in front of a train?

>

Morehouse: this is the conversation I keep having inside my head

Morehouse: and mostly I've still been answering 'no' but it's been getting harder and when I saw the news and then saw Vilepechora and LordDrek had been banned I thought 'fuck, it's him. He's done all of it.'

>

Paperwhite: You can't leave the game in any way that makes him think you might be going to the police.

Morehouse: Yeah, you're right. If I leave, he'll definitely suspect that.

Paperwhite: You need to act really, really happy that he's got rid of Vilepechora and LordDrek and keep him sweet while we figure out what to do.

Morehouse: And what happens when Vilepechora's real name's released and he knows I know who it is?

>

Paperwhite: pretend to think it was an accident. someone jostled him on the platform

Paperwhite: or say the guy must've pissed someone else off

>

Paperwhite: Look, I know you think I'm a coward

Paperwhite: you wanted to tell the police about that dossier LordDrek and Vilepechora planted on us and I said not to

Paperwhite: I was scared to death

Paperwhite: but this is so much worse

Paperwhite: we've let all this happen and not gone to the police

>

Morehouse: here's the joke

Morehouse: I'd phone and tip off the police anonymously but they'd think I'm pissed or fucking around because of the way I talk

Paperwhite: don't make jokes like htat

Morehouse: I spose I could write a letter

Morehouse: but how seriously would they take it?

>

Paperwhite: I could call anonymously, if you tell me his real name

Morehouse: I'm scared to. If
Anomie finds out it was a woman
who blabbed he'll know it must be
you. And if he knows who you are
he can find out where you live
as well

>

Morehouse: this is all my fault

Paperwhite: how is it?

Morehouse: I'm the one who helped
him build his fkn empire, aren't I?

Paperwhite: Vikas, please, please
don't leave me here alone

Paperwhite: let's wait and see
whether it really was Vilepechora

Morehouse: and if it is?

Paperwhite: then we'll work out a
plan.

Paperwhite: but you'd better not
fkn bottle out of meeting me face
to face if we have to.

Morehouse: ok

Paperwhite: promise?

>

Morehouse: promise

59

Presentiment is that long shadow on the lawn
Indicative that suns go down;
The notice to the startled grass
That darkness is about to pass.

Emily Dickinson
XVI

Strike, who'd been one of a dozen people to give a statement about what had happened at Custom House station, was slightly delayed for dinner with Madeline on Saturday night. She'd booked an Ottoman restaurant called Kazan, a choice Strike approved, given that he was ready for a hearty meal after no lunch, and fond of Turkish cuisine. However, the meal was overshadowed from the start by the day's events.

Knowing that the incident at the station was bound to be on the news, and suspecting that Robin's name would be released at some point, he felt obliged to tell Madeline what had happened, though giving her no information about the case. She was both fascinated and alarmed by the fact that he'd been mere feet from what he believed to have been attempted murder, and returned to the subject incessantly through two courses. This didn't help Strike's gnawing sense of unease, not only about what he'd witnessed but about the possible consequences of Robin's presence at the scene being advertised to the television-watching public.

When Madeline finally made a trip to the Ladies', he took out his phone, looked up the three-pronged Y symbol he'd seen tattooed beneath the rib cage of the young man in the expensive trainers and saw, with an increase of foreboding, that it represented the rune Algiz.

He then opened Twitter to look at the account of @Gizzard_Al, only to find that it no longer existed. He checked BBC News, which had already broken the story of the attempt on Red Soles' life, though with no names attached. In the absence of any announcement to the contrary, Strike had to assume Red Soles was still alive, but the bleeding from the ear had struck him as an ominous sign, likely to indicate a brain injury.

'Checking on Robin?' said Madeline brightly as she sat back down opposite him.

'No,' said Strike. 'Trying to find out how the guy who fell's doing.'

'She was *so* brave,' said Madeline. She was drinking only fizzy water tonight and seemed determined to be generous to his partner.

'That's one word for it,' said Strike darkly, slipping his phone back into his pocket.

By the time they got back to Madeline's house, three pictures of the individual who'd shoulder-charged Algiz had been released to the news, and a uniformed Chief Superintendent had made a televised appeal for information. Given that the pictures of the assailant been taken from frozen black-and-white CCTV footage, Strike hadn't expected them to be particularly clear, but he still paused Madeline's TV on every picture, scrutinising each one carefully.

The first showed the moment of impact, Red Soles falling forwards, hands in his pockets, Batman's full-head mask clearly visible, their body concealed by the crowd. The second picture showed a partial view of someone wearing a Batman mask getting onto the train. Again, their physique was impossible to judge because of the number of people who'd swarmed onto the train with them. Most of them, Strike knew, would have missed the attempt to kill Red Soles, their view blocked by the mass of people.

The third picture showed the back view of what appeared to be a bald-headed, heavily muscled man running up the stairs away from the scene. The assailant, as the Chief Superintendent explained, was believed to have got onto the train where they'd ducked out of sight among the other standing passengers and pulled off the Batman mask, beneath which they were wearing a full-head-and-neck latex mask. They'd then left the train and run up the stairs out of the station, mingling with the people now departing to find other means of getting home. This picture was the only full-length picture of the assailant, and the heavy musculature looked as though it was a padded costume.

What had become of the disguised assailant after leaving the station was either unknown or being withheld from the public.

'Jesus,' said Madeline, 'that poor guy. He took the full impact on his head, didn't he? Amazing he didn't break his neck.'

Strike's multiple rewindings of the bit of CCTV footage of Red Soles hitting the tracks, and of Robin and Mo (which was the name of the man in the Superman costume, with whom the credit for Red Soles' survival really lay, and to whom Strike and Robin had got talking while waiting to give full statements) jumping after him, did nothing to assuage his feeling of foreboding. Assuming Red Soles' rune tattoo had the connotation Strike had attributed to it, he thought the odds of The Halvening failing to connect Robin Ellacott with the man who'd punched one of their members in the Ship & Shovell were slim to non-existent.

'Well, Robin definitely deserves an award. I mean, they both do,' said Madeline.

They went to bed and had, at least on Madeline's part, particularly enthusiastic sex. Strike was again reminded of Charlotte, whose libido had generally been stimulated by drama and conflict, although he suspected Madeline's added demonstrativeness lay more in a desire to obliterate the memory of the row at her launch. As she was sober, she didn't fall asleep immediately afterwards, but continued to discuss what had happened at the station, apparently in the belief that this would please Strike by showing an interest in his working day. Finally, he told her he was exhausted, and they fell asleep.

She woke him the following morning with a mug of freshly brewed coffee then slipped back into bed and initiated sex again. While Strike couldn't pretend he gained no pleasure from a naked woman sliding slowly down his body to take his penis in her mouth, it was only at the point of orgasm that he was temporarily freed from his sense of foreboding, and the ominous feeling settled even more heavily over him after he'd climaxed. Even as he mumbled standard words of appreciation and affection, he was wondering how soon he'd be able to leave.

It was Sunday: Madeline was evidently expecting to spend the entire day with him, which he didn't think he could stand. While knowing perfectly well that there was nothing he could do to head off the potential threat from The Halvening, having to meet an implicit demand for reassurance that he'd entirely forgiven Madeline was forcing his stress levels higher than he thought reasonable on what was supposed to be a day off. He told himself what he craved was the quiet and peace of his attic flat, but in fact he was feeling a strong desire to contact Robin, without having any particular reason to do so. She was moving today, busy with her parents, and as Strike hadn't drawn her attention to the tattoo on the fallen man's torso there was a chance she didn't yet appreciate how precarious their position might have become.

Strike emerged from Madeline's shower an hour later to find he'd missed a call from Dev Shah. As almost anything was preferable to joining Madeline for a discussion of how they were going to spend the fine spring morning, he made an insincere show of regret, told her he'd need to ring Dev back and retreated into the bedroom to do so.

'Hi,' said Dev. 'Development on Jago Ross.'

'Go on,' said Strike.

'I was hanging around in the road outside their country pad, pretending to mend a puncture on my push bike.

'Ross drove the older three girls out through the gates, then stopped. The middle girl got out of the car. She'd forgotten something. He was yelling at her. "Stupid little shit", stuff like that. Didn't seem to give a monkey's that I could hear him.'

'Did you get a recording?'

'Started recording immediately, but the audio's pretty indistinct. He told her she had to go back on foot to fetch whatever it was. It's about a quarter of a mile up that drive. The kid had bruising round her eye.'

'Think I might know something about that,' said Strike. 'Her big sister's been sharing details of her weekend on social media.'

'OK, well, while they were waiting for the middle kid to reappear, he's yelling at the eldest. From what I could hear, she was sticking up for the middle one. I think he slapped her, but you can't see in the recording because of the shine off the car windows.

'Finally the middle kid reappears, dragging a bag. I pretended to get my bike moving, to get in a better position.

'When the girl reappeared, he got out of the car, yelling at her for taking so long. He opens the boot, chucks the bag in. Then, as she's about to get in the back seat, he kicks her in the small of the back to speed her up. Got that recorded, clear as day.'

'Excellent,' said Strike. 'I mean—'

'No, I get it,' said Dev, who sounded pensive. 'Total fucking bastard. If that was happening on some normal street—'

'The oldest girl said online, "People like us don't have social workers." Where are you now?'

'Driving in the direction of London, following them. He usually hands the younger two to the mother then drives the eldest back to Benenden.'

'Where are the twins?'

'Still at the house with the nanny.'

'OK, well that's bloody good work, Dev … 'course, his lawyer'll probably argue temporary lapse of judgement and get him on an anger management course to pre-empt the judge. But if we can get another incident or two like that, establish a pattern of behaviour—'

'Yeah,' said Shah. 'Well, I'll let you know if anything happens at the other end.'

'Cheers. Speak later.'

Strike, who'd conducted this conversation in a T-shirt and boxer shorts, now pulled on his trousers, all the while thinking about Robin and The Halvening. Finally reaching a decision, he arranged his features into a suitable mixture of regret and annoyance, and left the bedroom for the sitting room, where Madeline sat waiting.

'Problem?' she said, seeing his expression.

'Yeah,' said Strike. 'One of the subcontractors' wives has just fallen off a bloody ladder. Broken her wrist.'

The lie had sprung easily to mind, because this had once genuinely happened to Andy's wife.

'Oh. Does that mean—?'

Strike's mobile rang again. Glancing down, he saw Katya Upcott's number.

'Sorry, I'm going to have to take that as well. Trying to sort this out.'

He pressed answer once he was back in the bedroom again.

'Strike.'

'Oh, yes, hello,' said Katya's slightly breathless voice. 'I hope you don't mind me calling on a Sunday?'

'Not at all,' said Strike.

'Well, I was in to see Josh yesterday, and his doctors think he'd be well enough to see you in a week or so, if you'd still like to interview

569

him. They're limiting visitors, and his father and sister often go during the week, but if you could make next Saturday—'

'Saturday sounds great,' said Strike. 'Let me just grab a pen.'

He found one on Madeline's bedside table.

'If you like, we could meet at the hospital at two o'clock? He's in the London Spinal Cord Injury Centre. I should be there, because – well, I should be there too. He's still in an awful state.'

After scribbling the details of Blay's ward and visiting times in his notebook, Strike put the pen absent-mindedly into his pocket, bade Katya goodbye and headed back to Madeline.

'I'm really sorry. I need to sort this out. Looks like I'm going to have to take over surveillance on this bastard.'

'Shit,' said Madeline, looking disappointed, but Strike knew she wasn't going to kick up a fuss, not with the memory of their Bond Street argument still fresh in their minds. 'Poor you. Poor her, too.'

'Poor who?' said Strike, his thoughts still with Robin.

'The woman who fell off the ladder.'

'Oh,' said Strike. 'Yeah, I s'pose. Well, she's buggered up my Sunday, anyway.'

He maintained a decent show of regret as he picked up his coat and rucksack. Madeline wound her arms around his neck and gave him a lingering farewell kiss, and then, at last, he was free to leave.

He walked the length of her street and round the corner before lighting up a cigarette. Katya Upcott's call had given him a pretext to ring Robin, so he pressed her number, and she answered almost immediately.

'Hi – give me a second,' she said, and he knew immediately from the high, tearful tone of her voice that there was something wrong, more wrong than could be accounted for by moving, stressful though that undoubtedly was. Various possibilities – that she'd realised Red Soles was almost certainly a member of the far-right terrorist group, or, worst of all, that some retaliatory action had already taken place without Strike's knowledge – made him await her return with some trepidation, especially as he could hear an angry male voice in the background.

'Back,' she said, still a voice that proclaimed her on the edge of tears. 'What's up?'

'Nothing. What's up with you?'

'What d'you mean?'

'You sound like you've been crying.'

'I – well—'

'*What's happened?*' said Strike, far more forcefully than he'd intended.

'My dad – you know they were supposed to come down last night? – well, apparently he passed out in the drive right before they were about to get in the car. Mum drove him to hospital and they said he'd had a heart episode, whatever that means, and it sounded as though it wasn't a big deal, but she's just called back five minutes ago to say they're taking' – he could tell she was fighting the urge to sob – 'taking him into surgery – sorry – I'm sure it will be fine – shit, Strike, I'm going to have to go, I need to move the Land Rover—'

She hung up.

60

Oh, give me the friend from whose warm faithful breast
The sigh breathes responsive to mine . . .

Mary Tighe
A Faithful Friend Is the Medicine of Life

Robin's father hadn't thought it worth her while to hire removal men for the move. Most of the contents of the house she and her ex-husband had once shared had been sold or, in the case of the heavy mahogany bed in which he'd cheated with his now-wife Sarah, taken by Matthew. Robin hadn't had space in her rented room for the pieces she'd retained, so they were in storage. She'd bought the previous owner of her new flat's sofa, armchairs and double bed, for which she'd ordered a new mattress. Otherwise, she only needed to transport a few bits of flat-pack furniture. Michael Ellacott had assured his daughter that he was more than capable of helping load up the back of the Land Rover with the odds and ends at the storage facility and help her carry them upstairs. An academic raised on a farm, he still craved the satisfaction of manual labour, and Robin, conscious of having missed the family Christmas, had decided to humour him.

This meant that she was now left to single-handedly haul and lift everything in the storage facility into the back of the Land Rover. She'd been too busy to mope or cry for the first couple of hours, but that had changed when the unpleasant and aggressive renter of the adjoining unit had yelled and sworn when demanding that she move the Land Rover to enable him to bring his own van closer. This, coupled with Strike's voice on the phone, had finally made Robin break down. After ending the call with Strike and moving the Land Rover to accommodate the angry man's large blue van, she retreated into her storage unit to cry quietly while sitting on a cardboard box full of books. Half of her wanted to abandon the move, get in the Land Rover and head north to Yorkshire to see her father. Linda had assured Robin the procedure he was about to undergo was routine, but Robin had heard the fear in her mother's voice.

Eventually, Robin pulled herself together again and, sweating and straining, continued to unload the storage unit until at last almost every square inch of the back of the Land Rover was full, and she was able to set off for Walthamstow, a full three hours after she'd expected to be under way.

Linda finally called Robin back at half-past four, by which time she was sitting at a red light. As the ancient Land Rover had no Bluetooth, Robin snatched up her mobile and pressed it to her ear.

'He's fine,' came Linda's voice. 'Stent fitted. They say, if all goes OK he'll be home tomorrow.'

'Oh, thank God,' said Robin. The lights changed. For the first time since she'd owned it, Robin managed to stall the Land Rover, earning herself many angry blasts on the horn from the driver behind her. 'Mum, sorry – I'm going to have to go, I'm in the car. I'll call you in a bit.'

While her rational self now knew her father was out of danger, Robin's emotions hadn't caught up and she was still struggling not to cry when she turned at long last into Blackhorse Road.

Only when she turned into the parking area beside the block containing her new flat did she spot Strike standing beside the main door, a potted plant in one hand and a full bag of Tesco's shopping in the other. The sight was so incongruous, yet so welcome, that Robin gave a little gasp of laughter, which turned immediately into a sob.

'What's happened?' said Strike, walking towards her. 'How's your dad?'

'He'll be fine,' said Robin, trying to hold back tears. 'Mum just called. They fitted a stent.'

She felt like flinging her arms around Strike's neck, but the thought of Madeline, her resolve to fight any feelings for her partner stronger than friendship and an awareness that she was very sweaty dissuaded her. Instead, she leaned back against the Land Rover, wiping her eyes with her sleeve.

'Well, that's good news, isn't it?' Strike said.

'Yes, ob–obviously it is . . . it's just been a shit morning . . .'

'Want to eat before we unload the Land Rover? Because I do, I had no lunch. Don't suppose the kettle's handy?'

'It is,' said Robin, now half-laughing. 'It's in the footwell of the passenger seat with some mugs. Strike, you really didn't have to do this.'

'Take these,' said Strike, handing her the pot plant and Tesco's bag before opening the Land Rover door and retrieving the box with the kettle.

'How did you even know this address?'

'You showed me the spec weeks ago.'

This evidence that Strike wasn't as oblivious or inconsiderate as he might at times appear threatened to tip Robin into floods of tears, but she managed to hold herself together and, trying to sniff quietly, led him through the main door into a utilitarian brick hallway and, in consideration for Strike's leg, up in the lift to the second floor.

'Very nice,' said Strike, when Robin had opened the door onto a pleasant, bright and airy flat, which was slightly larger than Strike's attic and in far better repair. 'You buy this sofa off the previous owner?'

'Yes,' said Robin. 'It folds out – I thought it'd be useful.'

She carried the plant, which had large green heart-shaped leaves, into the kitchen.

'I love it,' she told Strike, who'd followed with the box of essentials, which included kettle, mugs, teabags, milk and toilet roll. 'Thank you.'

'I was worried it might count as flowers,' he said with a sideways glance. They'd once had a row in which his propensity to give Robin flowers rather than anything more imaginative had come up. Robin laughed, eyes welling again.

'No. A plant isn't flowers.'

Strike filled the kettle, then turned to see Robin extracting her iPad from her bag.

'You aren't logging into the bloody game?' said Strike as he plugged in the kettle. 'Take a day off, for Christ's sake.'

'No, I'm just looking to see whether they've caught Bat – Wait,' she said, looking at the BBC News website. 'They've released the name of the guy who was pushed onto the tracks.'

'And?' said Strike, freezing with teabags in his hand.

'He's called Oliver Peach. He's ... wow. He's the son of Ian Peach ... you know, that oddball who ran for Mayor of London? The billionaire?'

'Tech guy, yeah,' said Strike. 'Does it say how his son's doing?'

'No, just that he's still hospitalised ... his father's offered a hundred thousand pound reward for any information relating to the attacker ...'

'Your name come out yet?' asked Strike, trying to sound casual.

'No,' said Robin. She glanced at him. 'Look, I *am* sorry. I know it was—'

'Brave, it was bloody brave,' said Strike, cutting her off. Now wasn't the time to mention the apprehensions that had been dogging him for the past twenty-four hours. 'Let's have a sandwich and a cuppa and we can unpack the car.'

'Are you sure you're up to—?'

'Don't worry, I'll let you carry the heavy stuff.'

They ate the supermarket sandwiches standing in the kitchen, then, while Strike took his mug of tea back down to the doorstep to enjoy a cigarette, Robin called her mother back for a few more details on her father's procedure.

'But what about you moving?' Linda asked, sounding worried, after they'd thoroughly discussed Michael Ellacott's condition, and Robin had been satisfied that her mother wasn't minimising its seriousness. 'Have you managed to put it off?'

'I'm doing it now,' said Robin. 'Strike's helping me.'

'Oh,' said Linda, managing to load the monosyllable with an impressive amount of surprise, curiosity and disapproval. Her mistrust of Strike had tangled roots, but the injuries Robin had sustained while working for the agency, coupled with the fact that she'd run out on the first dance at her wedding to pursue her work partner, probably went deepest. Robin decided not to mention the fact that she'd nearly been hit by a train the previous day, which would doubtless be laid at Strike's door too. Hopefully her mother's preoccupation with her father's health would keep her away from the television news a bit longer.

Call ended, Robin went downstairs and began the job of bringing her things upstairs, aided by Strike, whose determination to help overrode his qualms about what this might do to his hamstring.

'I swear, there didn't seem to be this much when I was taking it out of storage,' Robin panted, passing Strike on the landing with the box of books in her arms.

Strike, who was likewise out of breath and sweating, merely grunted.

Finally, at nearly eight o'clock, the Land Rover was empty and most of the flat-pack furniture assembled.

'What d'you say to some chips?' asked Strike, sitting down heavily on the sofa. Robin could tell his leg was hurting him. 'You can't call a place home until you know where the nearest chippie is.'

'I'll go,' said Robin at once, getting to her feet and leaving a small bookshelf unfinished. 'It's the least I can do. Strike, I can't thank you enough for—'

'We're quits. You worked round the clock while I was laid up.'

He pulled a tenner out of his pocket.

'Couldn't get some lager as well, could you?'

'Of course, but I'm paying,' said Robin, waving away the money.

So she set out for Bonner's Fish Bar where, after ordering two lots of cod and chips, she absent-mindedly logged into *Drek's Game* on her phone. Anomie wasn't there. Having exchanged greetings with a couple of regular players she walked back to the new flat, stopping to pick up a bottle of wine and six cans of lager on the way. By the time she got back home, Strike had finished assembling the bookcase.

'You didn't need to do that,' she told him, propping up her phone against a table lamp so she could watch the game. 'Seriously, take a break. You've earned it ... What's the matter?' she added, because Strike was looking unhappy about something.

He hesitated before answering, then said:

'Your name's been released. Just seen it.'

'Oh,' said Robin. 'Shit.'

She gave him the lager and headed into the kitchen for a corkscrew. When she returned with a glass of wine, she said,

'Look, I really am sorry, I know I screwed up.'

'You were trying to save a life,' said Strike, already tucking into his chips with the assistance of the wooden fork provided, a can of Tennent's open beside him. 'It's hardly a fucking crime. Back in the game?' he added, gesturing towards the screen of her mobile.

'Yes,' said Robin, settling down into the armchair and trying to keep her tone normal, even though she now felt very anxious. 'Might as well keep an eye out for Anomie. Midge's on Cardew and Nutley's on Pierce. It'd be so great to rule out another – what were you calling about earlier, by the way?'

'Oh yeah – Katya Upcott says Blay's well enough for us to talk to him in hospital. I've said we'll go Saturday.'

'Great, I'll – hang on,' said Robin, whose eyes had flicked towards the game. 'Anomie's here.'

Putting down her chips, she picked up her mobile.

> **Anomie:** evening, children
>
> **Buffypaws:** hi Anomie!

'Just doing a bit of sucking up,' Robin informed Strike. 'When I'm friendly, Anomie doesn't get on my case so much or send minions after me if I'm stationary . . .'

She then texted Midge and Nutley: **Anomie in game, have u got eyes on target?** before looking back at the screen of her phone, where Anomie was still speaking.

> **Anomie:** Morehouse not been in?
>
> **BorkledDrek:** no
>
> **BorkledDrek:** sack the lazy bastard
>
> **Anomie:** lol
>
> **BorkledDrek:** I can code I can take over
>
> **Anomie:** u gotta pass the mod test first
>
> **Anomie:** recruiting now actually
>
> **Anomie:** need replacements for LordDrek and Vilepechora

'What the hell?' said Robin aloud. Before she could pose the question, many other players had done it for her.

> **Magspy7:** what, are they gone?
>
> **WyrdyGemma:** whaaaaaaat?
>
> **HartyHartHart:** omg what happened?
>
> **Anomie:** they've been fired

'Strike, look at this,' said Robin, moving to sit next to him on the sofa. 'Anomie's got rid of LordDrek and Vilepechora.'

> **Inky4Ever:** omfg why did u fire them?
>
> **Paperwhat:** shit what did they do/?
>
> **BorkledDrek:** why tf did you fire them bwah?
>
> **Anomie:** they were a pair of mukfluks
>
> **Anomie:** so let that be a warning to all of you

Two texts appeared simultaneously over the game screen.

Cardew in pub typing on his phone
Can't see Pierce he's at home

Robin swiped the texts away so they could keep watching Anomie talking to other players.

> **Dr3kBoy:** they were a laugh tho
>
> **Anomie:** they thought they could fool the Gamemaster
>
> **Anomie:** but the Gamemaster knows all
>
> **LonelikGrl:** lol how do u know everything?
>
> **Anomie:** got u all bugged

'"Got you all bugged",' said Strike. 'Who mentioned bugging recently?'

'You,' said Robin. 'You said if Gus Upcott was Anomie, he'd be bugging the upper floor of his house.'

'No,' said Strike, who'd just remembered. 'It was a bloke on Twitter. Lepine's Disciple.'

'Oh, *him*,' said Robin darkly. 'He's vile. Pops up all the time.

There's another one, I am Evola, who's as bad, if not worse ... I'll leave this running. If Worm28 comes in, I can ask her what happened to LordDrek and Vilepechora.'

She returned to her armchair, propped the phone against the lamp again and picked up her half-eaten fish and chips. As she did so, the sound of bass began thumping from the flat above. Robin glanced up.

'Your place must be noisy as well, is it?'

'Yeah,' said Strike, cracking open another can of Tennent's, 'but I'm used to it. S'pose you could try earplugs.'

Robin didn't answer. She never blocked her ears at night, whether with headphones or plugs, because she feared the inability to hear anyone moving in the dark.

'Anomie hasn't seemed to have as much insider information on *The Ink Black Heart* lately, have you noticed that?' said Strike.

'There might not be a lot to know,' said Robin. 'I doubt Maverick are doing much about the film right now, or not that they'd be pre-pared to share widely. Not with Josh still in hospital.'

'There's that,' agreed Strike. 'Another possibility is that with Edie being dead, their source of information has closed down.'

'Anomie's still being pretty foul about Grant and Heather Ledwell,' said Robin.

'"Grunt" and "Heavy", yeah,' said Strike. 'But everything he knows about them could've come straight off Heather's Facebook page. I've checked; the only detail he couldn't have got there is Grant's ex-wife having lupus—'

'There's Worm28,' said Robin suddenly, eyes on the game again. 'Hang on, I'm going to ask her what's happened ...'

While Robin typed, Strike stretched out his stump, trying not to wince.

'She thinks Anomie got rid of them to keep Morehouse happy,' said Robin, reading Worm28's response.

'Think Morehouse suspected they were alt-right?' asked Strike, who was craving a cigarette outside, but didn't really fancy navigating the stairs again.

'Maybe ... I don't mind you smoking in here,' Robin added; she'd seen Strike's hand move unconsciously towards his pocket, 'but d'you mind opening a window?'

'Cheers,' said Strike. He pushed himself to his feet and did as she asked, holding an empty can to use as an ashtray. Blackhorse Road, he noted as he looked down into the street, was busy and well-lit, but communal doorways were always a security risk. On the other hand, Robin had only moved that day: anyone wishing to retaliate against the agency for suspected surveillance would find it that much harder to find her.

'Got a burglar alarm?' he asked Robin after lighting up.

'Yes,' she said, eyes still on the game.

'And the front door double-locks, right?'

'Yes,' she said absently, still reading off her phone. 'Worm's saying Morehouse thought LordDrek and Vilepechora were "bad news". Trying to get more details . . .'

'Vilepechora,' repeated Strike. 'Bizarre name. Isn't Pechora a place?'

'No idea,' said Robin.

'Yeah,' said Strike, who'd just Googled the name on his phone. 'It's a town and a river in Russia . . . and the Pechora 2M is a surface-to-air anti-aircraft short-range missile system.'

He was having a familiar sensation: once again, his subconscious was trying to tell him something.

'Vilepechora,' he repeated.

He stuck his cigarette in his mouth, fumbled in his pocket for the pen he'd taken from Madeline's and wrote 'Vilepechora' on the back of his left hand. After staring at the word inscribed on his skin for the best part of a minute, he suddenly said 'shit'.

Robin looked up.

'What?'

'Vilepechora's an anagram of Oliver Peach.'

Robin gasped. Strike was already Googling the Peach family. The father, who'd had made millions through his tech company, had gained a lot of publicity through his unsuccessful run for Mayor of London. He was a distinctive-looking individual, with a low hairline and a penchant for suits with broad pinstripes.

'*Shit*,' exclaimed Strike again. 'They're brothers!'

'Who are?'

Robin joined Strike at the window. Flanking Ian Peach in the picture on Strike's phone were his two adult sons, Oliver and Charlie, both dark-haired, both with their father's low hairline. The younger man was clearly the wearer of the red-soled trainers who'd fallen in front of the train. The elder was wearing the corduroy jacket Strike had glimpsed in the Ship & Shovell, worn by the man trying to recruit Wally Cardew.

61

Thus drive thou hence the phantoms; cleanse my soul!
Thou sweet enchantress, with the magic spells!

Mathilde Blind
To Hope

In-game chats between four of the eight moderators of *Drek's Game*

<A new private channel
has opened>

<26 May 2015 22.02>

<Hartella invites Anomie>

Hartella: Anomie

>

<Anomie has joined the
channel>

Anomie: what's up?

Hartella: have you seen
the news?

Anomie: Have Maverick said
something about the movie?

Hartella: no

Hartella: I mean that
woman who went onto the
train tracks to rescue
the guy who fell on them

<A new private channel
has opened>

<26 May 2015 22.07>

<Paperwhite invites
Morehouse>

Paperwhite: Mouse?

>

>

<Morehouse has joined
the channel>

Morehouse: hey

582

Hartella: right by Comic Con?

Hartella: it's been on the news, you must've seen it

Anomie: haven't been watching the news, I've been busy

Hartella: well her name's been released. She's called Robin Elcott

Hartella: and she's a private detective

>

Hartella: please don't be angry. I haven't said anything that could reveal who you are.

Hartella: I definitely haven't, ok?

Anomie: that doesn't seem like something an innocent person would say, Hartella

Hartella: I swear I haven't.

Anomie: then why did you just tellme not to be angry at you?

Hartella: well I was at Comic Con because I got contacted by this woman who said she was a journalist and wanted to do a thing about the Ink Black Heart and my book and everything

Hartella: she was

Paperwhite: have you seen the news today?

Morehouse: no I've been in the lab

Morehouse: why, what's happened?

>

Paperwhite: you know that woman who jumped down onto the tracks to save Vilepechora?

Morehouse: yeah

Paperwhite: her name's Robin Ellacott and she's a private detective

Morehouse: seriously?

Paperwhite: yes

Morehouse: whoa

>

>

Morehouse: that's odd

Paperwhite: d'you think she was following someone?

Morehouse: surely not Vilepechora

Morehouse: it'd be police tracking the Halvening, I'd have thought, not a private detective

Paperwhite: Mouse, this might sound crazy, but do you think there's any chance Maverick are

wearing a wig when I
spoke to her but it was
her, I recognised her
from the news. it was
Robin Elcott

Hartella: I'm really
sorry, Anomie, it all
looked legit, she had a
website and had written
articles and everything

Hartella: but I didn't
tell her anything about
you

Hartella: I couldn't
have, I don't know
anything, do I?

>

Anomie: that's a lie

Hartella: it isn't a
lie!

Hartella: if you could
have heard me talking
about you, I was
basically telling her
what a genius you are.

Hartella: All I said
was that you're really
talented and cultured

Hartella: I didn't say
anything atall private
or that could identify
you, I swear! I don't
even know anything that
could!

Hartella: I just thought
it would be really good
for our book if I got
some coverage!

Hartella: And if the
book sells well, loads
more people will want

trying to find out who
Anomie is, to stop him
shitting all over the
film?

Paperwhite: could she
have been following
Anomie?

Morehouse: bloody hell,
that's a thought

Paperwhite: well
this could be our
opportunity!

Morehouse: what d'you
mean?

Paperwhite: we could go
to the agency and talk
to her

Morehouse: where is it?

Paperwhite: Denmark
Street in London, I
looked it up

Paperwhite: we woldn't
have to say we think he
killed anyone

Paperwhite: we could
say we're upset about
how much negativity he's
spreading in the fandom

Paperwhite: If she's
trying to find out who
Anomie is she'd probably
be really happy to
meet us. And I've just
been reading about her
agency. They work with
the police, they've
solved murder cases.

Paperwhite: This would
be as good as going to
the police, without any
of the drawbacks.

to come into the game, won't they?

Hartella: I wasn't only doing it for me!

>

Hartella: Anomie, u still there?

Anomie: so you were being a fucking benefactor to me, were you?

Anomie: and what d'you mean, I'm 'cultured'?

Hartella: I mean, you're clever and you know Latin and everything

>

>

>

Anomie: you think you know who I am

Hartella: no I don't, how could I?

Anomie: yeah, you do. 'Cultured.' You think you fkn know

Anomie: well, shall I tell you something?

Anomie: you're in deep shit

Anomie: you might've fooled the pigs into thinking uyou've had no contact with fkn terrorists, but I know different. I know who

Paperwhite: don't you think?

Morehouse: we'd end up being interviewed by the police, I bet

Morehouse: I'd have thought they'd be interested in any fan who's behaving oddly right now

>

>

>

Paperwhite: we wouldn't be accusing him of killing anyone though

Paperwhite: we'd just be two concerned people who don't like what he's doing online

>

Morehouse: you know what

Morehouse: that's actually a fkn genius idea

>

>

>

>

Morehouse: the only drawback I can see is that if she's never heard of Anomie, we're two randos who walked in off the street – or

gave you that folder
and I know you've been
creaming your panties
over one of them for
months.I could have all
3 of u locked up if I
wanted to.

Anomie: I've only kept
my mouth shut because
I didn't want the game
shut down. But if you've
blown my fkn cover, I
will see you in jail for
terrorism

Hartella: Anomie, for
god's sake, I definitely
haven't revealed who
you are, I swear I
haven't.

Anomie: you're going to
put this right

Hartella: I want to, but
how?

Anomie: I'll let you
know

Anomie: and when I tell
you what to do, you'll
fkn do it, unless you
want to end up inside

<Anomie has left the
channel>

<Hartella has left the
channel>

<Private channel has
closed>

rolled, in my case –
ranting about an online
game

>

>

>

>

Morehouse: although,
thinking about it, even
if she doesn't know wtf
we're talking about,
we'd still have put
down a marker, shown
we were worried about
him.

Morehouse: and given
that there have been
three attacks around
the Ink Black Heart
now, she might pass
his name to the police
anyway, so job done.

Morehouse: Nicole, you
are, you're a genius

>

>

Paperwhite: you're
coming with me, tho,
right? You aren't
going to bottle it
again?

Morehouse: no

Morehouse: I'd need you
to help me get there
anyway

Morehouse: fuck, though

Morehouse: when?

Morehouse: I've got
this research thing

Morehouse: I'll be in
deep shit if I don't
meet the deadline

Paperwhite: and I've
got exams but we can do
it right after.

Paperwhite: after all,
if we're right, he's
got rid of everyone he
needed to

Paperwhite: I mean, all
the people he saw as
a danger to him or the
game

Paperwhite: who else
would he want out of
the way?

Morehouse: me, probably

Morehouse: I've been
giving him a ton of
grief about LordDrek
and Vile

>

>

Morehouse: fuck, that's
him PCing me

Paperwhite: shit

Paperwhite: tell me
what he's saying

>

>

>

>

<A private channel has opened>

<26 May 2015 22.20>

<Anomie invites Morehouse>

Anomie: got a mo, bwah?

>

>

<Morehouse has joined
the channel>

Morehouse: hey, what's
up?

Anomie: we need
to talk new mods
now LordDrek and
Vilepechora are out

Morehouse: yeah

Anomie: any ideas?

Morehouse: BorkledDrek's
ok

Anomie: yeah, I was
thinking of him

Morehouse:
HartyHartHart's been in
a lot lately as well

>

Anomie: she irritates
the shit out of me

Anomie: it'd be like
having another Worm28

Morehouse: lol yeah I
see your point

Anomie: what d'you think
of Buffypaws?

Morehouse: never really
spoken to her

Morehouse: want me to
approach them or will
you do it?

Morehouse: it'd
mean more coming from
you

Anomie: why are you
blowing smoke up my
arse all of a sudden?

Morehouse: lol just
happy Vilepechora and
LordDrek are gone,
bwah

Morehouse: did you tell
them why or did you
just slice their legs
out from under them
when they were least

Morehouse: says we need
new mods

Paperwhite: act
cheerful!

Morehouse: lol

>

>

Paperwhite: has he
mentioned Vilepechora
and the train?

Morehouse: no, he's
acting like he knows
nothing about it

>

>

>

>

>

>

>

>

>

>

>

>

>

>

588

expecting it?

Anomie: lol bit of
both

Morehouse: excellent

Anomie: I'm glad
you're happy. For real.
I just want to get
back to how it used to
be.

Morehouse: with you
100%

Anomie: ok I'll sound
those two out

Anomie: catch you
later

Morehouse: cya, bwah

<**Anomie has left the
channel**>

<**Morehouse has left the
channel**>

<**Private channel has
closed**>

>

>

>

>

Morehouse: when he's
like this I start
wondering if I've
imagined the whole
thing.

>

>

>

>

Paperwhite: I've been
trying to believe you're
wrong for ages

>

>

Paperwhite: but I don't
think u are

589

62

He left her, but she followed him—
She thought he could not bear,
When she had left her home for him,
To look on her despair.

Letitia Elizabeth Landon
She Sat Alone Beside Her Hearth

When Strike called Ryan Murphy to identify Oliver Peach as a player of *Drek's Game*, and Charlie Peach as a contender for the man who'd tried to recruit Wally Cardew, he received a loud '*fuck!*' for his trouble.

'Friends of yours?'

'We interviewed both of them three months ago,' said Murphy. Strike heard the banging of a door and surmised that Murphy was taking the call somewhere private. 'They're both in the Brotherhood of Ultima Thule – I assume you know about the Brotherhood?'

'Odinist retreats and repatriating Jews?'

'Exactly, but we've found no evidence they're linked to bombings or online harassment. So they were in that bloody game, were they?'

'Oliver was,' said Strike. 'Can't be sure about Charlie, but I'd say it's odds on, given that two moderators left immediately after Oliver hit the railway track, and those two moderators seemed very matey, from what Robin's found out.'

'We've had a player in that game for weeks, but they haven't come up with anything. That rule of anonymity's bloody convenient.'

'Could've been tailor-made for terrorists,' Strike agreed.

Two days later, Murphy called Strike back with a courtesy update. The elder Peach brother, Charlie, had been interviewed again, under caution.

'He's denying everything,' said Murphy. 'Handed over his laptop and phone and there's nothing on there. He'll have others, better hidden. The guy's smart, whatever else he is.'

'Anyone interviewed Oliver? He strikes me as the weak link. Using an anagram of his name was bloody stupid.'

'He's still in hospital, and the doctors don't want us talking to him. He had to have emergency surgery to stop the bleeding from his brain. Their old man's kicking off. There's been a lot of talk of friends in high places, and legal action.'

'I'll bet there has,' said Strike.

'He's a weird bastard, the father. The wife looks mummified. Anyway, I'll keep in touch – have to say, your help's been invaluable on this. She all right, by the way?' Murphy added. 'That was a narrow escape she had.'

'Robin? Yeah, she's fine. Hiding out at home on my instructions.'

'Probably wise just now,' said Murphy. 'Well, give her my best.'

'Will do,' said Strike, but he forgot the request as soon as he'd hung up the phone.

Following the release of Robin's name to the media, the office phone had rung with requests for her to be interviewed about her actions at Custom House station. On Strike's instructions, Pat responded to all enquiries with the same statement: 'Ms Ellacott is glad to have assisted in the rescue of Mr Peach, but won't be giving further comment.' The depth of Pat's voice led a few journalists to assume they were talking to Strike and to press for her opinion on giving Robin, as well as Mohammed 'Mo' Nazar, civilian awards for bravery. Strike was unsurprised, though displeased, that it was the pretty young white woman's picture that led most of the tabloid coverage of the incident. He could only hope the interrogation of Charlie Peach would put a temporary moratorium on the terrorist group's activities, and attempted to forget, or at least shelve, his concerns about possible retaliation. This was made somewhat easier by the fact that on Wednesday the agency, which seemed to have been waiting a very long time for any breaks in their current cases, suddenly had two.

Firstly, the housekeeper at South Audley Street performed another thorough sweep for surveillance equipment and, this time, removed the black camera with its fisheye lens. Having failed to find the mechanism that turned it off, she put it into her handbag and took it with her to a restaurant where Fingers sat waiting for her, covertly observed by Nutley. As if taking the housekeeper out for a meal wasn't suspicious enough, given that Fingers usually associated with nobody but fellow children of the super-rich, he took possession of the woman's handbag and by dint of groping in its dark interior managed to turn off the camera without revealing his own face.

'So obviously she's in on it,' said Nutley, when calling to apprise Strike of what had just happened. He sounded immensely smug as usual. Strike tried not to feel aggravated by this statement of the bloody obvious, a challenge made no easier by the fact that the next words out of Nutley's mouth were: 'We should put someone on her too.'

'Good idea,' said Strike, trying not to sound sarcastic. 'Well, great work, Nutley, it's about time we had something to tell the client.'

An hour later, Barclay called from Hampstead.

'The Upcott boy's in the clear.'

'How d'you know?'

'Jus' followed him tae the pharmacy and back. No phone, no iPad, hands in his pockets all the way there an' back, an' Robin says Anomie's been active in the game fer the last hour.'

'Couldn't be better timing,' said Strike, and he proceeded to explain the results of that morning's surveillance on Fingers.

'... so I'll get the housekeeper's home address from the client and you can switch to her.'

These developments put Strike in a slightly more optimistic frame of mind, which carried him through a Thursday-night date with Madeline. It didn't escape his notice that he was now thinking in terms of getting through hours spent with her, when just a few short weeks ago their dates had been a welcome distraction in a life dominated by work. He was still enjoying the sex, but otherwise found it difficult to give her more than a fraction of his attention, because most of it was focused on concerns he couldn't, or didn't want to share with her. If she sensed this slight withdrawal, she gave no sign. She was still abstaining from alcohol in his presence.

On Saturday, and not having seen each other for a week, Strike and Robin were to meet at the garage where Strike kept his BMW, prior to driving to the London Spinal Cord Injury Centre to interview Josh Blay. As Strike was walking through the spring sunshine towards

the meeting point, his mobile rang with a number that had been put
through from the office phone.

'Strike.'

'Hello,' said a deep, resonant voice, and for a second or two Strike
thought he was about to hear another voice-changed anonymous call
advising him to dig up Edie Ledwell. 'Grant Ledwell here.'

'Ah,' said Strike, slightly surprised. 'What can I do for you?'

'I wondered whether it'd be possible to get an update.'

He spoke almost angrily, as though Strike had promised one but
never followed through. As Grant wasn't paying for the agency's services, Strike considered the resentful tone, and the fact that Grant had
called Strike at a weekend, to indicate a level of entitlement unjustified
by their relative status.

'I imagined Allan Yeoman and Richard Elgar would be keeping
you posted,' said Strike.

'Infrequently,' said Grant. 'As far as I've heard, there's been very
little progress.'

'I wouldn't say that,' replied Strike, more politely than he felt
Grant's tone deserved.

'Well, I wondered whether we could talk face to face. A couple of
things have happened this end that I'd like to talk over. Anyway, as
Edie's next of kin, I'd like to hear what's been going on.'

Reminding Grant that he wasn't the client would satisfy an immediate urge to put the man in his place, but Strike was intrigued to
know what the 'couple of things' were. He therefore agreed to meet
Grant at The Gun restaurant in Docklands, which was close to the
oil executive's place of work, on Wednesday evening.

'Bit cheeky,' was Robin's response when Strike – having accepted
with gratitude her offer to drive, as his hamstring remained painful – filled her in on Grant's request for a meeting. 'I bet he's
pissed off about Anomie's tweet last night. That's why he's calling
you today.'

'Could well be that,' Strike agreed.

After a period of relative inactivity, Anomie had revealed to fans
on Twitter that Maverick intended to make a very significant change
to Harty, the hero, in the forthcoming film.

Anomie
@AnomieGamemaster

Bad news, IBH fans. Maverick wants to change Harty from
heart to human and Grunt and Heavy gonna let them.
#takethemoneyandrun @gledwell101

8.40 pm   29 May 2015

The tweet had triggered a predictable explosion of abuse from
the Inkhearts, who'd accused the Ledwells of greed and betrayal,
then threatened boycotts and physical violence. Grant's place of
work had been revealed, pictures from Heather's Facebook page
copied and defaced, and Lepine's Disciple expressed the hope that
their baby would be stillborn. Robin, who'd watched the outburst
of rage in real time, had already checked Grant's Twitter and
Heather's Facebook accounts that morning. Both had now been
set to private.

'D'you think it's true Maverick's planning to make Harty human?'
Robin asked Strike.

'Anomie's generally been reliable about developments on *The Ink
Black Heart*,' said Strike. 'This means their source of inside information
hasn't dried up, anyway.'

They drove in silence for a while, until Strike said,

'Did you read Dev's report on Ross and his daughters?'

'Yes,' said Robin. 'Those poor kids.'

'Yeah. Obviously, from a humane point of view, I don't want Ross
to do it again, but if he does, I want it on film. A couple of incidents
like that would give me some serious leverage.'

Robin wondered, though didn't ask, how Strike intended to use
said footage, if he managed to get it. Would he take it straight to Ross,
or hand it to Charlotte to help her win her custody case?

The hour's journey ended with a long stretch of tree-lined road.
Finally, Robin turned into the hospital car park and saw, just outside
the entrance, a group of four people, who appeared to be having an
altercation. Sure enough, when Robin had parked and turned off the
engine, the sound of shrill voices could be heard, even through the
closed windows of the car.

'Is that Katya and Flavia?' said Robin, peering through the

windscreen at the woman with mouse-coloured hair, who was wearing a baggy grey coat.

'Yeah,' said Strike, taking off his seatbelt, his eyes on the group. 'And the other two are Sara and Kea Niven.'

'You're kidding?'

'I'm not. Looks like there's a fight on for the right to visit Blay.'

'Why's Katya brought Flavia, though?' asked Robin. The twelve-year-old looked thoroughly miserable.

'Maybe Inigo thinks she's infectious again.'

As they got out of the car, the three women's voices became louder, but as they were shouting over each other it was still difficult to hear exactly what was being said.

'Shall we?' said Strike, and without waiting for an answer he strode off towards the arguing group, keen to hear what was going on.

As he and Robin came within earshot, Katya, whose thin face was suffused with colour, shouted:

'He doesn't want to see her!'

'Says who?' screamed Kea, who was leaning on her stick. 'You're not his fucking *mother* or his *wife* – go and ask Josh what he wants!'

'We've driven from Norfolk!' added Sara, who today was wearing a magenta dress as shapeless as Katya's coat. 'They told us he's ready for visitors—'

'Well, you should have called me first!' said the furious Katya. 'He's already got visitors arranged today, people he *wants* to see – and here they are!' she shouted triumphantly, turning as Strike's and Robin's footsteps alerted her to their arrival.

'Oh God, *no!*' blurted Kea, her eyes on Strike. 'Not *him!*'

Robin, who'd never seen Kea in the flesh, looked at her with interest. The girl was wearing a light blue sweater with jeans. Her black hair gleamed in the spring sunshine and her porcelain skin and red lips didn't owe much to make-up. In the hand not gripping her walking stick, Kea held an envelope.

'Morning,' said Strike, looking from Kea to Sara.

'Oh God – oh God,' said Kea, dissolving into tears. 'I can't *believe* this—'

As Katya and Sara began shouting at each other again, a short, scowling, grey-haired man in blue scrubs emerged from the building.

'Could I ask you ladies to keep it down, please?'

Katya and Sara fell silent, cowed. Having glared at each of the women in turn, then shot a hard stare at Strike, as though he'd have expected the only male in the group to keep better order, he disappeared back inside.

'Josh is expecting Mr Strike,' said Katya in an angry whisper. 'So you'd better leave.'

Still sobbing, Kea held out the envelope.

'Then can you p-please at least give—'

'I'm not giving him that,' said Katya, backing away as though the letter were a gun.

'For God's *sake*, you can't refuse to take him a note!' said Sara heatedly.

'*Please*,' sobbed Kea, advancing on Katya while leaning on her stick. '*Please* just give him my letter.'

'Fine,' said Katya shortly, snatching it out of Kea's hand. 'Shall we go in?' she added to Strike and Robin.

As they followed Katya and Flavia through the glass doors, Robin glanced back. Sara and Kea had turned and were heading slowly back to their car. As she watched, Sara put her arm around her daughter's shoulders, but Kea shrugged it off.

'The nerve,' said Katya ferociously as she headed off along a corridor, leading the way to Josh's room. 'The *nerve* of them. Thank *God* I was here—'

'Have you got another cold?' Robin asked Flavia quietly, because the girl had just blown her nose.

'No,' said Flavia. 'I—'

'She did a very silly thing,' said Katya, before Flavia could answer, 'which she'd been told *not to do.*'

'It wasn't—'

'*Flavia, you were told not to bring that puppy into the house,*' snapped Katya. 'I don't want to hear *another word* about Daddy, or Gus, or dogs, or things being unfair, do you hear me?'

'You *always* side with—'

'*Flavia!*' snarled Katya, turning briefly to glare at her daughter, before saying to Strike, 'I *had* to bring her. Inigo's livid.'

As Katya led the way onwards, clearly familiar with every twist and turn of the route to Blay's room, Flavia said resentfully, though quietly,

'I'm *always* going to hospitals.'

'Are you?' said Robin, to whom the remark had been addressed. She and Flavia had fallen behind the other two.

'Yes. One time, when Gus's skin was really bad, he had to go into hospital, and then Daddy got ill the next day and he got admitted too. But to different hospitals. Daddy goes to a far nicer one than Gus. It's private. Gus usually goes NHS.'

Flavia added quietly,

'I *really* liked them both being gone.'

Robin could think of no appropriate response to this, so made none.

'I could watch what I liked on TV. I saw a thing on the news about a man in America who did a mass shooting because he couldn't get any girls to have sex with him.'

'... as if it isn't enough that she *bombards* him with letters that *completely* stress him,' Katya was saying to Strike, 'she has to turn up in person ...'

'I wanted to do my school project on that man who shot girls, but Mummy said I couldn't. Daddy thinks it's disgusting Mummy let me find out about him, but' – Flavia cast a narrow-eyed look at her mother's back – 'she was on the phone to Josh all that evening, so she didn't care what I was watching.'

Robin, who had the impression that Flavia was well aware of the picture she was painting of her home life, maintained a diplomatic silence. Ahead, Katya was saying,

'... just worried one of these afternoons I'm not going to be here and she's going to force her way in ...'

'Mummy and Daddy had a row this morning,' said Flavia very quietly, keeping a wary eye on her mother's back, 'because Daddy thinks it's obvious who Anomie is and Mummy says he can't be right and he's just saying it to be horrible.'

'Really?' said Robin, trying to keep her tone casual. 'Who—?'

But she broke off. Katya had come to a sudden halt alongside a large bin standing in a recess in the corridor. Her expression savage, Katya tore Kea's letter in half and thrust it inside.

'*There*,' she said, and set off again, Strike alongside her, Robin and Flavia bringing up the rear.

'I thought it was illegal to tamper with the mail,' said Flavia.

'Um ... I think that's only with things that go through the post office,' said Robin, whose mind was working rapidly. After a few more steps, she came to a halt herself.

'Oh damn,' she called after Strike and Katya. 'Sorry, I've left my notes in the car.'

'Well, you'd better go back for them,' said Strike, turning to look at her.

'Yes. What's Josh's room number?' Robin asked Katya.

'Fifty-one,' said Katya, looking anxious. 'But actually, they only want two people in with him at a time – I didn't realise both of you were going to come. I thought they wouldn't mind Flavia coming in with me, as she's so young.'

'I could sit outside with Flavia if you'd rather go in with Cormoran?' Robin offered, genuinely hopeful that Katya would agree: she was very interested in Inigo's thoughts on Anomie. Katya looked as though she approved of this idea too, but after glancing from her daughter to Robin and back again, and perhaps considering the likely consequences of letting her daughter talk outside her sphere of control, she said,

'No, I can't ask you to do that – bit of an imposition. No, I'll stay with Flavia, but I'll go in with Cormoran just at first, so Josh knows I'm around if he needs anything.'

'OK, I'll just get my notes from the car, then, and catch you up,' said Robin.

'Can I come with you?' said Flavia eagerly, but Katya said sharply, 'No, you stay with me.'

So Robin doubled back to the bin where Katya had thrust Kea's letter. It had a letterbox-style slit large enough for her to insert her hand, but unfortunately, the corridor was far from deserted: medical staff were walking up and down it as well as visitors. Robin skulked around until she was unobserved, then took her phone out of her pocket and slid it into the bin.

'Oh *damn*,' she said aloud, feigning exasperation.

'You all right?' said a passing nurse, who was pushing a man in a wheelchair.

'I've gone and accidentally dropped my phone in there with my rubbish,' said Robin, laughing as she inserted a hand.

'My brother-in-law did that once, with a letterbox,' said the nurse.

'Can't – quite feel it,' Robin lied, groping in the bin. 'Oh, there it is . . .'

She waited for the nurse to walk out of sight, then pulled out her phone and the two halves of Kea's letter, still in their bisected envelope, which she pocketed. Robin retraced her steps until she passed a women's bathroom, which she entered. Having locked herself in a cubicle, she pieced the torn halves of the letter together and read it.

Joshlings,

I really hope I get to see you today and give you this in person, because I don't know whether I've got the strength to say it all face to face. If I see you, I'll probably just break down. I know that's pathetic.

I don't know whether you've got my other letters. I feel like you'd have sent a message back if you'd read them. Maybe Katya ripped them up, and you don't even know I've been trying to get in touch. I know she thinks I'm the antichrist, or is that just my self-hatred talking?

Since this thing happened I've barely been able to eat or sleep. I'd kill myself right now this minute if it would make you better. Sometimes I think I should do that anyway. I'm not saying that to make you feel bad. I just don't know how much longer I can live in this kind of pain.

I've been interviewed by a private detective. He claimed you wanted me to talk to him, so I did. He was so aggressive I actually went home and vomited afterwards, but I did it because you wanted me to.

I honestly feel like if we could go back in time and you could understand a bit better where I was coming from, none of this would ever have happened. Everything went bad when you moved into North Grove. Anomie <u>has</u> to be someone there, with the quote on the window and the stolen drawing and everything. But you never wanted to believe me, that that place was bad news, because of her.

There are tons of rumours circulating about how you're doing. The detective was basically trying to terrify me all the way through the interview, so he might have been lying about you being paralysed to make me talk. I hope he was, even though it was horrendous to hear and has honestly been making me so anxious and sick I've started self-harming again.

I don't know what else to say except that you haven't seen the real me for a long time because I've been so hurt and angry. If you poke a caged animal long enough it'll attack back and that isn't the animal's fault, it simply isn't.

I didn't mean any of what I said on the phone that night. I was just so happy to see your number come up and then when

599

you said you were meeting her next day I honestly felt like my heart had been ripped open. It seemed like such a cruel thing to do, to call me up to say you were meeting her <u>there</u>. Anyone would have felt like I did but I never wanted her or you dead, that was just my hurt bursting out.

I really, really hope you're doing ok. Whatever happens and whether I'm alive or dead when you come out of hospital, remember how much I loved you and try and remember the real me.

Kiki

Robin read the letter through twice, replaced it in her pocket and set off again.

Flavia was leaning up against the wall opposite Blay's room, playing on her mobile when Robin arrived. She looked morose, though she brightened up when she spotted Robin.

'Did you go back to get Kea's letter out of the bin?' she asked.

'No,' lied Robin, smiling. 'Just to get my notes.'

'You're supposed to wait until Mummy comes out, because he's only supposed to have two visitors at a time,' said Flavia.

'Right,' said Robin. 'So, tell me. Who does your dad think—?'

The door opened and Katya emerged.

'You can go in,' she told Robin in a hushed voice. 'I'll take Flavia to the café for half an hour, but if Josh needs me you'll call, won't you?'

'Yes, of course,' said Robin. As she pushed open the door of Josh Blay's room, she heard Flavia say to her mother,

'Why couldn't I have stayed with Robin?'

'*Shut up*, Flavia . . .'

63

Behold the agony
In that most hidden chamber of the heart,
Where darkly sits remorse . . .

Felicia Hemans
Arabella Stuart

The small room, which faced south, was overwarm as all hospitals tend to be. A few 'Get Well Soon' cards stood on the bedside cabinet, along with a gold helium balloon that was slightly deflated.

In the few minutes Strike had been in Josh's room, he'd felt as though he'd been transported back to Selly Oak, the military hospital where he'd been treated after his leg had been blown off in Afghanistan. Josh Blay was sitting up in a wheelchair, dressed in pyjamas, his feet in very new-looking navy slippers, his forearms lying motionless on the armrests. Somebody had placed his phone in front of him, on a tray attached to the wheelchair. Blay's blank, withdrawn expression was familiar to Strike; he'd seen that look before on the faces of men whose attention was concentrated within themselves, where they were struggling to reach an accommodation with the strange new realities of their lives. Perhaps Strike had worn that expression himself, as he lay at night beset by phantom pain from the lower leg that had gone for ever and contemplated the end of his military career.

Josh's high cheekbones, square jaw, large blue eyes, straight dark brows and finely drawn nose and mouth were even more striking now that his hair, which had once hung beneath his shoulders, had been cut very short. The unforgiving glare of the sun pouring into the room, which was barely diffused by the lowered cream blinds, revealed the newly healed tracheostomy scar at the base of Blay's throat. There

601

were purple-grey hollows under his eyes, which had the dullness that Strike associated with fever.

'This is my partner Robin,' Strike said as she took the second plastic chair opposite Josh.

'Hello,' said Robin.

'Awright,' mumbled Josh.

'Get the notes OK?' Strike asked Robin, knowing full well what she'd gone back for.

'Yes,' said Robin, 'but I don't think we'll need them.'

'Fair enough,' said Strike, and turning back to Josh he said, 'Sorry, you were saying?'

'Yeah . . . I can feel stuff on the side tha's paralysed,' said Josh slowly, speaking as though the words were heavy and dragged up from a great depth. 'Bu' the side I can move is numb. Can' feel nuthin'. The doctors say it migh' improve a bit, but I'll never . . . never go back to normal . . .'

'Well, nerve damage is strange,' said Strike. 'It takes a long time for all the swelling to go down. It was two years before my leg was stabilised. Probably be a good while before you know what function you're going to have.'

Josh made no response.

'So,' said Strike, drawing out his notebook, 'let's talk about Anomie.'

'E's the one 'oo stabbed us.'

Josh spoke flatly, brooking no contradiction.

'What makes you say so?'

'Wha' 'e whispered, after 'e done it,' said Josh.

'"Don't worry, I'll take care of things from here",' quoted Strike.

'Yeah. Plus,' Josh took a deep breath, ''e warned me 'e was gonna do somefing, an' I ignored it.'

'What d'you mean, he warned you?'

'S'all on there,' said Josh, looking down at the mobile on the tray, his arms and hands motionless. 'Passcode's double six, double seven, five, two. If you go to photos, there's a folder titled "Anomie".'

Robin picked up the mobile, opened it and went looking for the folder.

''E's been direct messagin' me on Twitter for years,' Josh continued. 'Ed told me to block 'im, an' Yeoman said so as well, but I didn' like being told what to do, so I didn't.'

His fever-glazed blue eyes bore into Strike's.

'So tha's the kind of arsehole *I* am.'

'Can't see that was such a crime,' said Strike.

'I believed all the shit Yasmin gave me, in tha' folder, as well,' said Josh, still staring at the detective as though willing Strike to condemn him. 'All that bull about Ed being Anomie.'

'Plenty of intelligent people manage to believe far stranger things every day,' said Strike. 'The people who put together that dossier have had a lot of practice. They're good at what they do.'

'Found it,' said Robin, who'd just located the folder full of screenshots.

With a scraping of rubber-tipped chair legs on the floor tiles, Strike drew nearer to Robin so that both could read the messages Anomie had sent Josh privately over Twitter.

Idea: Harty should start murdering again
15 August 2012

He should start stabbing tourists in the cemetery. Funny and unpredictable twist.
15 August 2012

Idea: have Paperwhite trapped back in her coffin unless she agrees to a date with Harty.
12 September 2012

Drek could trick her back inside. Trickster-god aspect of character. Paperwhite reaps just reward of hubris.
12 September 2012

Wyrdy-Grobs are getting really one note. Idea: Lord WG should bury Lady for good. Wall her up in the mausoleum and go looking for fresh bones to jump (<- good, funny line)
4 January 2013

Idea: new character. Harty's owner's brain escapes the grave. Machiavellian character, nice contrast to Harty. Ongoing battle between rational and emotional sides of killer.
26 August 2013

You're losing everything that made this good. Stop selling out. Need for fresh storylines and new characters becoming ever more evident. See previous messages.
20 January 2014

You need me. I know what fans want.
18 March 2014

You need me if you want to get fans back onside, Josh.
22 May 2014

Idea: old tramp dies of heart attack in cemetery, becomes
gross ghost who competes with Harty for Paperwhite. Harty
now looking a lot better to her, but he rejects her.
29 July 2014

I thought you were less obtuse than Ledwell but starting to
fear you aren't.
19 September 2014

It's becoming ever clearer that you don't actually understand
The Ink Black Heart, Josh. I'm offering you assistance to
correct and improve, an offer you'd be unwise to pass up.
1 October 2014

Idea: you announce Ledwell's departure within an episode of
the cartoon. Have Anomie enter in last seconds of episode.
Fans would go crazy for this.
29 October 2014

Anomie: a being whom even Drek fears. Visual: see my
appearance in game. Essentially a void-like creature into
which all unsatisfactory characters disappear.
29 October 2014

Your pretensions to being hero-creator are now utterly
destroyed. I was prepared to give you credit for the germs of
what could have been interesting ideas in the right hands. You
have now betrayed the fandom and I realise I was wrong to
offer myself as collaborator. There can be only one Ἀρχηγέτης.
12 November 2014

Understand this: a film deal will be the end. You've
been warned.
10 February 2015

'What does that Greek word mean?' Robin asked Strike.

'Think it relates to the Archegetes heroes,' said Strike, who was still scanning the line of messages. 'Ancient Greeks who founded settlements or colonies.'

'The tone of these is interesting,' said Robin.

'The narcissism, you mean?' asked Strike, while Josh's feverish eyes darted back and forth between the two detectives. 'Suggesting they become a character in the game . . .'

'There's that, yes, but the language is more intellectual and grown-up, isn't it? There's no swearing, no laddishness – using that Greek word – '

'Yeah, these messages correlate a bit better with Yasmin's "cultured" comment, don't they?' Strike looked up at Josh. 'Is this everything Anomie sent you?'

'No,' said Blay. 'There was more I didn' bovver takin' pictures of. But it was the same: shit ideas for the cartoon.'

'Have you shown these messages to the police?'

'Yeah,' said Josh.

'And?' said Strike.

'Don't fink they took it seriously. They're fixated on that right-wing group.'

'Are you OK with us taking copies of these?' Strike asked.

Josh nodded, and Robin sent the folder of Anomie's messages to her own phone.

'Katya says you're tryna work out 'oo might've known all the insider stuff,' Josh said in a hollow voice. 'I'm not gonna be any 'elp. I can' remember 'oo knew what, when. I've spent most of the las' five years pissed or stoned ... We were both doing a lot of dope. Ed sometimes forgot 'oo she told stuff as well ... She got it in 'er 'ead Anomie was Seb, because she told 'im Paperwhite was based on an old flatmate ... but she told me that, back when we made the character, and she prob'ly told ovver people ... She forgot stuff too,' said Josh pathetically, and Robin felt an almost painful twist of pity in her stomach.

'Katya says you thought Anomie was Bram de Jong for a long time,' said Strike.

'S'pose you fink I'm a moron, after reading those messages,' said Josh dully, 'but Bram's got an IQ of 140. 'E was tested at school. He sometimes acts like 'e's free years old, but ovver times, if 'is voice 'ad broken, you'd fink 'e was forty ... 'Ave you 'eard about 'is mum?'

'We know she died,' said Robin.

'She was murdered,' said Josh, 'in Amsterdam.'

'Shit,' said Strike and Robin simultaneously.

'Yeah ... she was an addict, doin' sex work to buy drugs. Bram was six or somefing when she died ... She used to lock 'im in 'is room when she 'ad men in. A punter strangled 'er and left the apartment. Bram was stuck in 'is bedroom for two days or somefing ... 'Is aunt went round, because 'is mum wasn't answering the phone, and she found the body and Bram still locked in.'

'God,' said Robin quietly. 'How awful.'

'Yeah,' said Josh heavily. 'Not surprisin' 'e's disturbed. I fort 'e was funny when I firs' moved into North Grove, but after a bit ... I fink he set fire to my room while I was asleep, the day before – before this all 'appened. Mariam blamed me. Fort I'd dropped my spliff. I woke up wiv people yellin' and throwin' water about. The curtains were on fire ... Mariam was screamin' – I'd drunk a lot of beer and 'ad a lot of dope,' said Josh, 'so I was, you know, confused about what was goin' on. I let Mariam kick me out and it was on'y once I was outside in the dark I kind of put two and two together and fort: *Bram*. That's the kind of fing 'e does.'

'Tries to kill people?' said Strike, watching Josh closely.

'I dunno if 'e genuinely wants to kill anyone,' said Josh in a flat, detached voice. ''E jus' seems interested in seeing how far 'e can go. Nils could probably stop him if 'e tried, but he's not bovvered ... I don't fink he really wanted to 'ave to take responsibility for Bram ... Katya told you Bram was spying on me an' Ed through an 'ole in our bedroom wall for weeks?'

'She did, yes,' said Strike.

'Tha's what put it in me 'ead that 'e was Anomie. 'E ... 'e saw fings, when 'e was livin' with his mum, you know? Fings a little kid shouldn't've seen ... 'E's kind of fucked up an' 'e's got a genius-level IQ, so ... yeah, I fort it was Bram for ages ... but I s'pose tha' was because it was the easy answer.'

Robin could hear how dry Josh's mouth was. She wanted to offer him a drink but felt diffident about doing so: he wouldn't be able to hold the glass and she wondered whether he'd find it intrusive if she offered.

'Why d'you say it was an "easy answer"?' asked Strike.

'Well, I s'pose ... if it was some fucked-up kid 'oo didn' really understand what 'arm he was doin', it wasn't any of our mates. But it wasn't Bram 'oo stabbed us. That fing they said about "taking care of fings from 'ere" was too ... it wasn' somefing Bram would say.'

'Why not?' Strike pressed him.

Josh stared at the detective again, his eyes unfocused, apparently thinking. Finally he said,

'If Bram stuck a knife in someone, it'd be to see what 'appened next. 'Ow they looked, or 'ow it felt to kill someone ... 'E'd be doing it for *that,* in itself, not because 'e wanted to take anyfing over. Bram isn' creative. Nils bangs on abou' that a lot. Always tellin' Bram to sit down and make somefing, or paint somefing . . . Nils thinks art's everyfing.'

'But you thought Bram might've been abusing Edie online, over a period of years?'

'Yeah, but that . . . it'd be . . . like an experiment. Like pulling wings off a fly. Jus' to see 'ow much 'e could wreck 'er . . . But the person 'oo stabbed us . . . When you wanna take charge, you're . . . you're wanting to create, aren' you? Bram jus' wants to smash stuff up.'

'So, while it was going on, you thought the online abuse was done purely to watch Edie suffer?'

There was another pause and then, suddenly roused from his depressive torpor, Josh said,

'You needn't tell me I'm a shit. I know I should've stood up for 'er—'

'I wasn't—'

'I know I should've told Anomie to fuck off, an' blocked 'im. D'you fink I don't sit here finking about that all fuckin' day and night now?'

Before Strike could answer, the door of Josh's room opened and Katya poked her head inside, timidly smiling.

'Everything all right?' she whispered.

'Yeah,' said Josh, with an effort.

'Can I get you anything, Joshy?'

'No, I'm good, fanks.'

'You look hot,' she said. 'Shall I open—?'

'No,' repeated Josh. 'I'm good.'

'I'll just get you some iced water, then,' said Katya, and she withdrew.

Josh, whose colour was indeed higher than it had been when Strike and Robin had entered the room, looked back at Strike. The latter said,

'I assure you, I'm not blaming you for—'

'I know what I should've done,' said Josh, his breathing laboured. 'I know that now.'

Katya reappeared with a large glass of iced water, two straws protruding from it.

'Shall I—?' she offered, bending down to hold it for Josh while he drank, but he shook his head.

'I'll drink some in a minute. Fanks,' he added. Katya left again.

'Katya's great,' said Josh, after a short pause and with a trace of defensiveness, as though he sought to head off any discussion of the relationship.

Gesturing towards the water, Strike said,

'D'you want me to—?'

'No.'

A charged silence followed, broken by Robin.

'You were at Katya's, weren't you, the night before you were attacked?'

'Yeah,' said Josh. 'I wen' there because I didn't 'ave any money on me when Mariam chucked me out ... Woke up Inigo, going upstairs ... 'Ave you met Inigo?'

'Yes,' said Strike.

''Spect 'e said I'm a waste of space, did he?' said Josh. 'Inigo could've been anyfing, according to 'im: artist, musician, writer ... you name it, 'e'd've been world class at it, if he 'adn't got ill ... So now 'is son's got to do what 'e couldn't. That's why the poor bastard's got chronic 'ives. An'—'

He broke off.

'"And"?' Strike prompted him.

''S'not relevant ... I talk too much. Ed always said I'd tell anyone anyfing. She fort that's 'ow Anomie got hold of everyfing, because I never knew when to shut up. She was prob'ly right, as well. But I 'ated it when it all got so ... professional. It was a ton of fun in the beginnin' and then we 'ad to act different.'

'Different how?' asked Strike.

'Like ... we couldn't ask fans for suggestions any more, like we did at the start. This farver of a twelve-year-old wanted money. 'E said we'd used the kid's idea, when we 'adn't, we 'adn't even seen her comment ... It all got complica'ed, fast.'

'Well,' said Strike carefully, 'we're interested in people who were close to you and Edie, who could've known your ideas and details about your lives.'

'I've bin froo all of them, in me 'ead,' said Josh, now staring down at the tray in front of him. 'I can' believe any of 'em woulda done that to Ed.'

'You can't think of anyone who had a grudge against her?'

'Well—'

Whatever Josh had been about to say, he bit it back. It was, Strike reflected, a hell of a time for Josh Blay to have learned discretion.

'Did Inigo like her?' asked Strike and Josh looked up, surprised.

'I wasn' gonna say "an' Inigo's Anomie" just then,' he said, and almost, though not quite, smiled. 'I was gonna say, "an' 'e's a shit to Flavia".'

'Yeah, we witnessed a bit of that,' said Strike, satisfied merely with keeping Josh engaged. 'Why's that, d'you think?'

'I s'pose she doesn' do nuffing for 'is ego, the way Gus does.'

'How faithful is Inigo, would you say?' Strike asked.

'Wha'?'

'You heard me,' said Strike. 'If Inigo's got a lover, that person's of interest to this enquiry. They could've known details about the cartoon and Edie, through him.'

'I – fuck . . . You know abou' 'is girlfriend, do you?' said Josh.

'Tell me what *you* know, and we can see whether we already knew it.'

'I'm tryna – tryna turn over a new leaf,' said Josh. 'Keep me mouf shut. I don't wanna cause more trouble.'

'You aren't causing trouble. You're helping us rule people out,' said Strike. 'How did you find out about the affair?'

Josh hesitated, then said,

'Katya told me. She'd been doing classes at Norf Grove for a few monfs an' suddenly Inigo started makin' the two kids go to 'er lessons as well. To get 'em out of the 'ouse. 'E was 'aving it away wiv someone 'e'd met online . . . the woman was goin' over to the 'ouse ev'ry Fursday evening.'

'Poor Katya,' said Robin quietly.

'Yeah . . . Flavia copped to wha' was going on. They got back to the 'ouse one night an' Flavia noticed lipstick on a wine glass on the drainin' board, and Katya never wears make-up. It was still wet from Inigo washin' it out. I fink that's why Inigo's such a bastard to Flavia, because she dobbed him in. 'E 'asn't forgiven her. But that affair's not still goin' on, is it? This was . . . free, four years ago, mus' be. 'E told Katya he ended it.'

'What d'you know about this other woman?'

'She was married an' 'er name was . . . Mary, I fink. Katya sort of . . . she poured 'er 'eart out to me about it,' said Josh, looking faintly uncomfortable, 'an' I fink Inigo knows I know, which is part of the reason 'e doesn' like me . . . I don' really get why Katya's still wiv 'im, to be honest. Inigo's minted. She'd prob'ly get a good divorce settlement, but she's kind of ground down, I s'pose ... You won' tell Katya I've told you?'

'No,' said Strike, 'but we might need to have a quiet word with Inigo. Don't worry. He doesn't have to know where we got the information.'

'Sly bastard,' said Josh. 'And 'im a bishop's son ...'

But the mood of interest and faint amusement departed as soon as it had come.

'S'pose I'm a fucking 'ypocrite for calling him sly. I've done a bit of sneakin' around meself.'

'Kea Niven?' Strike asked matter-of-factly. 'I expect you know there's a theory out there that *she's* Anomie?' he added, once again omitting to mention that the originator of the theory was sitting beside him.

'Yeah, a few people online fort she was, once,' said Josh, without heat. 'I wondered as well, but she can' be. There was a long time, when Edie and I were togevver, when Kea couldn't've known anyfing about Ed or the cartoon, and Anomie seemed to know everyfing.'

'Kea visited North Grove, didn't she?' Robin asked.

'Yeah, when I firs' moved in, because we were still togevver. She didn' want me to stay. I fink she felt threatened by the 'ole scene, and she didn' like Ed being the resident ... sort of – well, girl every-one fancied.'

'Who fancied Edie, specifically?' said Strike, pen poised.

'Well – Pez,' said Josh. 'I used to fink Nils did a bit too. An' me ... Kea could tell I did, and it was easier to slag off the whole set-up ...'

'I fucked all that up so bad,' said Josh, now staring at the floor. 'Ed always said I never wanted to piss anyone off, but if you're gonna piss people off, they'd rather be told straight, than lied to ... I should've ditched Kea but I kept it goin' for a bit because ... because I'm a fucking coward, I s'pose ... Have you met 'er?'

'Yes,' said Strike.

'Did she tell you we started up again for a bit? After me and Ed split up?'

'She did, yeah,' said Strike.

'That was so fuckin' stupid,' said Josh quietly. '*So* fucking stupid ... I don't know wha' I was playing at. She'd kind of ... stalked me after the firs' time we split, so I knew what she was like. What the fuck was I playin' at, getting back with 'er? I walked into this bar in Camden one night, and I knew it wasn't coincidence she was there, but I was pissed, miserable about it endin' with Ed and . . . well, she's 'ot.'

'We've all been there,' said Strike, as a memory of Annabel's shimmered through his mind. Neither man noticed Robin's slight raise of the eyebrows.

'She was even worse, second time round. Jealous as fuck, and she kept tellin' me if I dumped 'er again she'd top 'erself. So there was five or six monfs of tryin' to keep it quiet, because I didn't want Ed to know. I knew Ed'd think it was, like . . . you know . . . the ultimate betrayal, or wha'ever, sleepin' with Kea again, after all the bollocks Kea had talked about Ed rippin' her off.'

'Kea claims you confirmed some of those accusations, when you started dating her again.'

'I never,' said Josh, looking Strike in the eye. 'The most I told 'er was I never knew magpies could talk before she told me. All the rest of it was, like: *"swear on your muvver's grave you never told Edie Ledwell about Margaret Read's 'eart"*. And I said, "I don't swear on me mum's grave, but I didn'." She 'ad a fuckin' mania for tryin' to make me swear fings on me mum's grave. When we met, it was somefing we 'ad in common, that we'd bofe lost a parent . . . She's written me all these letters since this 'appened,' said Josh. 'Telling me she's self-'armin' and wha'ever . . . What the fuck does she expect me to do abou' tha', now?

'When Ed found out I was seein' Kea again, everyfing turned to shit between us. We couldn' talk wivvout tellin' each other 'ow much of a fuckin' bastard we fort the ovver one was . . .

'Then, while I was trying to work out 'ow to end it wiv Kea wivvout 'er killin' 'erself, Ed overdosed,' said Josh, his eyes unfocused, staring at the floor. 'She rang me, while she was still downin' paracetamol and whisky. Said she was gonna go away for a bit an' . . . an' she wanted me to 'ave the pin number on her phone, because she'd left some ideas on there . . . 'Er voice was really slurred . . . I knew she must've taken somefing.'

'She wanted to tell you there were ideas on her phone, even while she was overdosing?' said Strike.

'Oh yeah,' said Josh. He didn't seem to find anything odd in the behaviour. 'You didn't know Ed. *The Ink Black 'Eart* . . . it meant everyfing to her – back then, anyway. I fink, by the end, she was sick of it . . . but back then, she wouldn't've been able to *stand* the idea of us fuckin' it up after she'd gone. She probably fort, if she didn't tell me where to find 'er ideas, I'd team up wiv Kea to keep writing it . . .'

He fell silent, staring at the floor again, then continued,

'I went to try an' see 'er in the 'ospital after she overdosed and Ormond was there, standing guard over the room. 'Ave you met him?'

'We have, yeah.'

''E told me Ed didn't want to see me and fings got a bit – you know – physical. A male nurse separated us and asked me to leave.

'That night, I got the idea in me 'ead that *Ormond* was Anomie. I was stoned,' said Josh heavily. 'It made sense at the time. I fort, maybe Ormond was persecutin' Ed to make 'er feel like she needed someone like 'im, you know, some ex-policeman with a Ford Fiesta, and once 'e'd got her softened up, 'e'd turn up at Norf Grove to get 'is hooks into 'er . . . but next day, when I was straight again, I knew it was bollocks . . . Where would Ormond 'ave been gettin' 'is information, all those monfs before 'e ever met us?

'We used to call 'im the geographer,' Josh went on, 'because 'e's the sort of wanker 'oo finks being able to read a map is some – some massive 'uman achievement. We on'y found out 'e taught computing when he asked us to go and talk to his class. I never understood what 'e was doing at Norf Grove . . . he's the DIY sort, you know? Jus' wanted to do fuckin' welding . . .'

'Tell me about your flat in Millfield Lane,' said Strike. 'Did Kea ever have a key to it?'

'No,' said Josh. 'Why?'

'Have the police told you that Edie's phone moved out of the cemetery after you were both stabbed and ended up on Hampstead Heath, very near your flat?'

'No,' said Josh, looking vaguely surprised.

'Did anyone other than you have a key to the place?'

'The builders 'ad my only spare.'

'Did you have your key on you when you were attacked?'

'No. Like I said, I got chucked out wiv only me phone on me. The key'll still be in my room at Norf Grove, probably.'

'OK, that's helpful,' said Strike, making a note. 'Now, when exactly did you break up with Kea the second time?'

'After Ed overdosed. I told Kea I needed a break to clear me 'ead. I fuckin' *begged* 'er not to put it online that we'd dated again . . . I knew all the fans would say me goin' back to 'er proved 'er story . . .

I'm such an arsehole,' said Blay bitterly. 'Aren't I? What the fuck did I do all that for? Why did I date Kea again? Why did I believe that shit Yasmin showed me?'

'We've all got stuff we wonder that about,' said Strike. 'All of us.'

'Your stuff didn't kill anyone,' said Josh.

'Nor did yours,' said Strike.

'Yeah, it did,' said Josh, the colour rising in his gaunt face. 'I never blocked Anomie, never stood up for Ed – I let it 'appen, because I'm fuckin' weak. I'm *weak*,' he said, his teeth gritted. 'I didn't wanna get shit off fans. I didn't wanna listen to anyone's advice except Katya's, because she tells me what I wanna 'ear. I'm like fuckin' Bram, except I don't set fire to people or chuck rocks at them. I cause worse fuckin' 'arm by tryna 'ave an easy fuckin' life . . .

'I shouldn' be alive right now. I was the one 'oo deserved to fuckin' die and I was the one 'oo was wearing a jacket that stopped the knife goin' as deep in my neck as 'e meant it to. An' I've got a fing called *situs inversus*. All my organs are reversed, like, mirror image. My 'eart's on the right-hand side. Anomie fort 'e was stabbin' me frew the 'eart, but he punctured my lung instead. I never knew I was the wrong way round inside, never needed an X-ray before all this 'appened. *Situs inversus* . . . it's the kind of freaky fing Ed would've really lik—'

Robin felt she should have known it was coming. Josh burst into tears. His nose streamed, his head slumped, but he was unable to cover his face with his hands or double over: his body remained as still as a waxwork model.

Strike got to his feet, walked over to the bedside cabinet and took a box of tissues from it. Returning to his seat, he pulled a handful of tissues out of the box.

'No,' gasped Josh.

'You can drown in snot if you like,' said Strike, 'but if you want to help us catch this bastard—'

'Shall I?' said Robin, unable to help herself.

'No,' choked Josh. 'Fine,' he sobbed, and Strike wiped Josh's face and nose as pragmatically as if he'd been cleaning a windscreen, threw the damp tissues into the bin, then sat down again, placing the tissues on the tray in front of Josh.

'It's my fault Ed's dead,' sobbed Josh. 'It's all my fuckin' fault.'

'It's the fault of the fucker who stabbed you both,' said Strike firmly. 'Don't do that to yourself. You didn't make this happen.'

'All – all I wanna do now is live long enough to see fuckin' Anomie caught and fucking jailed. After that . . . I'll be checking out.'

'No, you won't,' said Strike calmly.

'Don't tell me what I will or won't be fuckin' doing,' spat Josh. 'You can still fuckin' walk!'

'And you can still think and talk. Six months' time, you might have more function back. A year after that, they might've found a way to mend your spine. They're making progress on this stuff all the time. Stem cells. Implanted chips.'

'And in the meantime—'

'Yeah, well, that's the hard bit, isn't it? Acceptance of the present. You've got to stop thinking long-term for a bit.'

'If you're gonna lecture me about fuckin' *mindfulness*,' said Josh savagely, 'I get plenty of tha' from the psychiatrist. *Fuck* livin' in the moment. I don't wanna live like this. I don't wanna live at all. I don't fucking *deserve* to.'

'You didn't cause these stabbings,' said Strike forcefully. 'Another human being bought a taser, a machete and, I strongly suspect, a disguise, with the intention of ending two lives. If you need a reason to keep going right now, you should hold onto the fact that you're going to be the star witness at this fucker's trial, and if you need a reason to live beyond that, you ought to remember that you were the one Edie called when she believed she was facing death, because she still trusted you with the thing that mattered to her more than anything else.'

'I don't give a *fuck* about that *fuckin'* cartoon,' said Josh, starting to sob again.

'Well, you should,' said Robin quietly. 'I recently met a fan whose life was saved by *The Ink Black Heart* – literally. She told me she decided to keep living, just to keep watching it. What you and Edie did was extraordinary. Cormoran's right: you're the only one, now, who can do what Edie would want done. She wouldn't want you to check out. She'd want you to do what only you can do.'

'The fucker took 'er phone,' said Josh, tears falling faster than ever. 'That's where all her ideas are.'

'Let us worry about finding that phone,' said Strike, taking more tissues out of the box as he spoke and again wiping Blay's face. 'Blow your nose and have some water.'

Josh let Strike wipe his face and allowed Robin to angle the straw from the water to his mouth. When Josh had drunk his fill, and Strike had thrown away the second lot of damp tissues, the detective said,

'I want to know who knew you and Edie were meeting in the cemetery that day.'

'Only Mariam,' said Josh hoarsely. 'I was talkin' to 'er while she was cookin', when Edie called me. Mariam fort it was a good idea we were gonna meet, talk it all over. But there's *no way* Mariam—'

'Could anyone have been eavesdropping?'

'I dunno . . . maybe. There's a big larder off the kitchen. But I didn' 'ear anyone in there.'

'Who else was living at North Grove at the time?'

'Nils and Bram.'

'Would you have expected Mariam to tell Nils you were meeting Edie?'

'Yeah.'

'Tell me about Nils.'

''E's . . . a bit mad,' said Josh. 'Eccentric. You never know what 'e's going to think about stuff. 'E's loaded. His father was a multimillion-aire industrialist and Nils in'erited everyfing. 'E's always wanted to live the way 'e does – do art, live in a commune, polyamorous . . . 'e an' Mariam 'ave got an open relationship. Nils sleeps with Freyja, anuvver woman at Norf Grove, sometimes. 'Er partner seems OK with it . . .'

'You said earlier Nils fancied Edie.'

'Yeah, I fink 'e did, but 'e never got anywhere with 'er.'

'Did she like him?'

'Not much, by the end,' said Josh. ''E's kind of libertarian . . . voted for that weird fucker, Ian Peach, for Mayor of London.'

Strike and Robin avoided looking at each other.

'How're Nils's computer skills?' asked Strike.

'Good,' said Josh. 'Funny fing is, 'e'd probably be really good in tech, but all 'e wants to do is be an ar'ist – but Nils can' be Anomie. Why the fuck would 'e do that to us? To Edie?'

'We're just talking about people who could've known you were meeting at the cemetery,' said Strike. 'So: Mariam, Nils and Bram. Who else was around?'

'Freyja, Al an' Star were out, they'd gone to visit friends . . . I s'pose there was Pez,' said Josh, and his expression clouded. ''E came to see me last week. I was pleased to see 'im, I always liked Pez. But I kind of got the impression he wasn't 'ere to . . . Well, 'e said straight out what 'e wants: me to get 'im a job on the movie. So ... yeah,' said Josh, swallowing. 'That was weird. 'E was talking about being able to imitate my art style and stuff ...'

'Could Pez have been in the larder when you were talking to Mariam?' Strike said. 'Outside the kitchen door? Outside the window?'

'I s'pose so,' said Josh. 'But Pez can't be Anomie, no way ...'

'We're still just talking about people who could've known you were meeting in the cemetery,' said Strike. 'Who else?'

'Well,' said Josh slowly, 'the fing is, about North Grove ... people just walk in an' out all the time. Students, people visiting the shop ... Oh,' he said suddenly, 'there's a girl who 'elps out there, these days. Zoe. Tiny little fing with tattoos all up 'er arm. I s'pose she could've been 'iding round the corner ...'

While Strike was writing down the name as though it was new to him, Robin said,

'Josh, on the subject of North Grove, and people coming in and out – would you know anything about a drawing that was stolen?'

'*My* drawin', you mean?' said Josh, looking surprised. 'Of the vampire? Did Kea tell you?'

'Yes,' said Robin. It wasn't really a lie: she'd just read about the theft in Kea's letter.

'Yeah ... that was when Maverick wanted us to come up wiv more characters for the movie. I wanted to put the vampire in. They fort there was a vampire in the real cemetery, in the seventies. Edie fort it was corny, 'avin' a vampire, but I drew 'im so she could see what I was finking. I wanted 'im to be inept, like, tryna kill tourists but never gettin' enough blood to live on, so 'e was, like, weak an' feeble ...'

'Did you write notes on the drawing, of how you saw the character?'

'Yeah,' said Josh, 'I did. On the back. Bu' I left the sketch downstairs, in one of the art rooms, an' it disappeared.'

'When was this?' said Robin.

'Can' remember exac'ly. Las' year some time. It was when Kea and I were datin', the second time. I told 'er, because I was really pissed off someone 'ad taken it. It disappeared one evening when there were classes on, so it could've been anyone ... a student, someone picking them up ... it's kind of a free-for-all when there are loads of classes going on, people goin' in an' out. I should've put the drawin' upstairs.'

'OK, thanks,' said Robin, making a note. 'While we're on the subject of new characters, did Edie tell you about two she was planning, for the movie? Phillip Ormond says she told him all about them, in detail.'

'She told me she'd 'ad a couple of ideas, but she never said what they were. She never liked talkin' about stuff until she'd worked it all froo in 'er own head. But maybe she was diff'rent with Ormond ... You'd think 'e'd wanna tell *me*, if 'e wants to see 'er stuff onscreen ... except 'e fuckin' 'ates me, so 'e wouldn't.'

And he can't monetise them himself, if he gives them to you, Robin thought.

'So you left North Grove in the dark the night before the stabbings,' Strike resumed, 'without money, but with your mobile and the dossier Yasmin had brought you?'

'Yeah.'

'And once outside, you called—?'

'Kea,' said Josh miserably. 'Yeah. By acciden'. I was pissed, and 'er name's right underneaf Katya's on me phone. I told 'er I was meeting Edie next day in the cemetery, an' that I needed a bed for the night, and then Kea started screamin' in my ear, and I realised I was talking to 'er, not Katya ...'

'You're sure you told Kea where you were meeting?' asked Robin.

'Yeah, because that's what she went apeshit about,' said Josh. 'Me callin' 'er up and tellin' 'er details of my "date" with Edie. See, when we were dating the firs' time, Kea an' I went on one of those walking tours in the old part of the cemetery? Tha' was a sore point, me goin' there wiv Edie afterwards, and talkin' about it in interviews ...'

'Could anyone have overheard your accidental call to Kea?' asked Strike. 'Can you remember anyone standing around in the street? Did anyone follow you, pass you?'

'Not that I can remember,' said Blay. 'I didn't notice anyone ... but I was pretty out of it.'

'Did you speak to anyone else on your way to Katya's, either on the phone or in person?'

'No,' said Josh.

'You said you woke Inigo up, going inside the Upcotts' house. Did you tell him what you were going to do next day?'

'No, 'e was properly fucked off I was there. I wen' straight to bed in the spare room.'

'And the following morning?'

'I discussed it all with Katya. I showed 'er the dossier.'

'Was Inigo in a position to overhear what you were saying?'

'No. 'E was upstairs,' said Josh. 'Katya and I were downstairs, in the kitchen.'

'Who else was in the house?'

'Flavia was at school and Gus was in 'is room.'

'Could Gus have heard what you were talking about?'

'No. 'Is door was closed. We could 'ear him practisin'.'

'Did you talk to anyone else before you left the Upcotts' house?'

'No,' said Josh. 'I didn' talk to anyone else ...' He turned rather white, so that even his lips were drained of colour and the purple shadows around his eyes seemed darker.

'... until I woke up at the 'ospital wiv me 'ead shaved.'

'Are you able to tell us what you remember of the attack?' said Strike.

Josh swallowed again.

'I was late. I was 'urrying, because I fort Ed might've left. She always got pissed off wiv me for bein' late for everyfing.'

He tried to say something else but produced no sound. After clearing his throat he went on,

'I was 'eading for the place where we were going to meet. It's where we were getting stoned the day she 'ad the idea for the cartoon.'

'Where exactly is that?'

'In a patch of graves where you're not s'posed to go. It's off the path and some of the tombs are unstable. Near a grave Edie always liked. It's got a pelican on it. Be'ind there. You couldn' see us from the paths on either side. There's a bit of an 'ollow.'

'Did you pass anyone on the way?'

'A big guy, bendin' over a grave. He must've worked there. I was late an' 'urrying. Then I heard runnin' footsteps be'ind me.'

'What kind of footsteps?'

'Fast. Not really light, but too light for it to be the bloke I'd just passed, bendin' over the grave. The police asked me that. The guy I saw was big. 'Eavy.

'And then I felt somefing like – it was like an 'orse kickin' me in the back. I wen' right over, face forwards, on the ground. And then 'e – 'e stuck the knife in me back and me neck. It was agony like – you can't – and then 'e took the phone ou' of me pocket and the folder wiv – the folder I'd taken with me – and said the fing about "I'll take care of fings from 'ere" and ran off.

'I can' remember anyfing after that until wakin' up in hospital. Can' remember the guy finding me in the cemetery or the ambulance or anyfing. I woke up wiv all my hair shaved off an' – an' like this.'

The door opened again, revealing Katya, Flavia and a small blonde nurse.

'I'm sorry,' said the nurse, 'but that's visiting time up.'

'OK,' said Strike, 'could I have one more question, and then we're done?'

'Just one,' she said, and retreated, taking Katya and Flavia with her. Strike waited until the door had closed before turning back to Blay.

'The big guy you passed, bending over the grave, as you were heading towards the sleeping angel. Was he bald?'

Josh opened his mouth, his eyes unfocused, thinking back to the last time he'd been able to move freely in his healthy young body.

'I ... I fink he was. Yeah ... yeah, he was.'

'You've been a lot of help, Josh,' said Strike, closing his notebook and getting to his feet. 'We'll keep you posted on developments.'

''Ow did you know he was bald?' asked Josh.

'I didn't,' said Strike. 'But I think there's a fair chance the bald head was a latex mask and the body you thought was big and muscular was a padded suit. That explains why the footsteps didn't sound heavy enough to match their weight.'

'That was Anomie?' said Josh, staring up at the detective.

'Yeah,' said Strike. 'I think it was.'

64

. . . he was glad to have an ear
That he could grumble to, and half in jest
Rail at entails, deplore the fate of heirs,
And the misfortune of a good estate . . .

Jean Ingelow
Brothers, and a Sermon

Robin found it very hard to forget the image of the paralysed Josh Blay weeping in his overheated hospital room, in front of a glass of iced water he couldn't lift. Her thoughts travelled repeatedly back to the young man in the wheelchair over the next couple of days, wondering how he was, what was the likelihood of him recovering even a small amount of feeling and movement, and when, or whether, it was reasonable to expect him to be able to reconcile himself to a life into which he'd been so traumatically thrust.

She thought about Strike too, because she'd seen a previously unknown side of her partner at the hospital. He'd often let her take the lead when sympathy was required in dealing with suspects and employees. His tendency to foist what she'd sometimes heard him call 'touchy-feely' stuff onto Robin had been the trigger for their biggest row to date, in which, among other things, the subject of afterthought-flowers had been raised. Before the interview with Blay, she'd have assumed that if a nose needed blowing or a face wiping, Strike would have expected her to do it: indeed, when tears had finally burst from Josh, Robin had somehow felt it was her proper job, as the only woman in the room, an idea perhaps implanted by the sight of the overwhelmingly female nursing staff they'd passed on their way through the hospital. Yet Strike had done it, and done it with precisely the undemonstrative male efficiency Blay had felt able to accept.

Robin soon became angry with herself for dwelling on that unexpected display of empathy: this wasn't the way you fell out of love, and she once again employed the reliable counter-irritants of reminding herself about Strike's new girlfriend and his ill-defined involvement in his ex-fiancée's divorce case.

Strike's memories of their trip to the hospital were intermingled with thoughts of Robin too, though they took a less sentimental turn. Not for the first time, he had cause to marvel at the fact that the woman who'd come to him as a temporary secretary had proven to be the agency's biggest asset. Retrieving Kea's letter from the bin, digesting the contents at speed, recognising that there was one point in there that needed to be clarified with Josh and doing so without fuss or display might not have been the showiest piece of detective work Robin had performed to date, but the incident stuck with Strike as a perfect example of the kind of initiative he'd come to count on from his partner. If anything were needed to make him value this rare and valuable quality still more highly, it was the continuing irksome presence of Nutley, whose self-congratulation at his own lacklustre performance stood in such stark contrast to Robin's unassuming industry.

Josh Blay was far from the first young man the ex-SIB officer had met who'd been maimed by the violent act of another human being. In truth, he suspected that had he met Blay whole and healthy, he might well have found him unlikeable. Strike knew himself to be prejudiced against certain lifestyles and mindsets, because of early and unhappy exposure to exactly the kind of boundary-free, convention-defying living so enthusiastically embraced at North Grove. His own habits of self-discipline, and his preference for cleanliness and order over squalor and chaos, had been forged largely in reaction to his mother's lifestyle. Strike had spent too many hours of his youth enduring the tedium of the perennially stoned to find either pleasure or excitement in the haze of drink, drugs and rock music that had been Leda's natural habitat. The drugged, drunk, long-haired and beautiful Josh Blay would have been precisely the kind of young man Leda found most attractive; another reason for Strike's usual antipathy for the type.

Yet, to his own surprise, Strike had found matter to admire in the young man he'd met in the spinal unit. Blay's self-reproach had been founded upon a dispassionate assessment of his own past behaviour that had impressed the detective. Nobody could be blamed for self-pity in a situation like Blay's, but Strike had been impressed by the fact that he'd expressed most distress about the death of his ex-girlfriend and collaborator. The detective, who was still sometimes visited in his dreams by the severed torso of Sergeant Gary Topley, who'd been ripped in two by the blast that took Strike's leg, understood survivor's guilt, and the shame that infused the darkest thoughts of the still-living, however damaged their own bodies. Perhaps most surprisingly, because their investigation to date had tended to suggest that Blay had been a mere makeweight in the partnership that had spawned *The Ink Black Heart*, Strike had found Blay shrewd and insightful in some of his comments to the detectives. He felt that no previous interview had advanced him so much in an understanding of Anomie's psychology, and the animator's own thoughts had been as valuable as the sight of those private messages.

It was in this frame of mind, with the smell of hospital disinfectant still metaphorically in his nostrils, that Strike set out for his early dinner with Grant Ledwell on Wednesday evening, choosing to take public transport to Docklands rather than drive, given the still-vulnerable state of his hamstring.

The restaurant Ledwell had chosen, The Gun, lay on the banks of the Thames. The sign outside had a fake bullet hole the size of a grapefruit punched in it, and the decor inside was traditional. Strike, who appeared to be the first diner of the night, was shown past a wall of sporting firearms into an otherwise empty wood-panelled room, and sat down at a table for two which gave a clear view of the Millennium Dome, the curved white tent-like structure visible on the opposite bank.

Just as Robin had done in Colchester, Strike had time to ponder what it said about the man he was about to meet that he'd chosen this particular venue. Setting aside the fact that Grant had wanted the detective to come to Docklands, where his workplace, the Shell headquarters, lay, rather than meeting Strike in central London, which would have been far more convenient for Strike, the smart gastropub exuded, from leather-bound menus to shotguns, a kind of idealised masculine Englishness.

Feeling that he wasn't, strictly speaking, on duty, Strike ordered himself a pint, which had just arrived when his mobile rang. He half-expected it to be Grant, announcing that he was going to be late, thus consolidating his power play, but saw that the call had come through from the office, from which Pat would now have departed.

'Strike.'

'Oh,' said an unfamiliar male voice, sounding surprised. 'I, er, didn't expect anyone to pick up. Just wanted to leave a message for Robin.'

'I can take one,' said Strike, reaching into his breast pocket for a pen.

'Er – OK. Well, if you could ask her to call Hugh Jacks back, that'd be great. I'm not sure my previous messages have been passed on.'

'Has she got your number?' asked Strike.

'Er, yeah, she has,' said Jacks. 'So – yeah. If you could ask her to call me back. Er – thanks, then. Bye.'

He rang off.

Strike lowered his mobile, frowning slightly. He'd assumed Hugh 'Axeman' Jacks had passed in and out of Robin's life without leaving any impression on it. So she had the man's phone number, but wasn't returning his messages? What did that mean? Was Jacks hassling her for a date? Or was Robin refusing to answer calls to her mobile because they'd argued, reducing the man to leaving voicemail messages at her place of work?

'I'm not late, am I?'

Strike looked up. Grant Ledwell had arrived, wearing a grey suit and a mauve tie, and looking, as he had last time they'd met, like a bulldog in a too-tight collar, with his bristle-cut hair, low brows and heavy underbite.

'No, bang on time,' said Strike, putting his mobile back in his pocket.

Whether because he'd forgotten that Strike was bigger than he was, or for some other reason, the aggression Grant had displayed during their phone call wasn't quite as evident in person. After shaking hands and settling himself in the chair across the table, Grant said gruffly,

'Good of you to meet me. Appreciate it.'

'No problem,' said Strike.

'I – ah – apologise if I was – er – offhand when I called you. We, er, we've been through it a bit since I last saw you.'

'I'm sorry to hear that,' said Strike, and with an effort he put Hugh Jacks out of his mind.

'Yeah … it's been getting to Heather. All the online … I tell her not to look at what the bastards are saying, but she keeps doing it, then has hysterics. You married?'

'No,' said Strike.

'Kids?'

'No,' said Strike again.

'Well, pregnant women . . .' Grant cleared his throat. 'She's getting all these ideas about people coming to hurt her and the girls. I've told her, they're just a bunch of cowards, hiding behind their keyboards, but . . .' – Grant drummed his thick fingers impatiently on the table-top – 'I could use a bloody drink.'

He hailed a waiter and ordered himself a glass of red wine. When the waiter had retreated again, Grant said,

'Did you see what Anomie tweeted, Saturday night? About Maverick wanting to change Harty into a human? I'm starting to think Elgar and Yeoman should have another look at the people in their offices.'

'It was true, then, was it?' asked Strike.

'Yeah, it's true,' said Grant. 'Come on. Who's going to watch a film with a bloody heart bouncing around, chasing a ghost?'

'People liked it in the cartoon,' said Strike.

'That's different, though, isn't it?' said the oil executive impatiently. 'We're talking big-screen now, a more mainstream audience. The, er – what do they call it? The treatment – looks good to me. To be honest, I can't see what all these people saw in the – it's funny, of course,' said Grant, catching himself. 'Very, er . . . creative. But is it going to translate to a movie the way it is?'

'I wouldn't really—'

'Well, Maverick don't think so, and they're the professionals.'

Grant's wine arrived. He took a large slug, which seemed to calm him slightly.

'After Anomie tweeted, all hell broke loose. I was up half the night with Heather. She wants to pack up and go somewhere they can't find us. Some sick bastard said he hopes our baby will be born dead, if you can believe it. I'd have invited you over to the house, rather than meeting here, but she's got her mother over to keep her company,' said Grant, and he took another slug of wine before continuing. 'I've told her, "There are plenty who'd like to have our problems." I said, "With the money we're looking at, if this thing does well, we could move to a bloody gated community if you want." I asked to see figures on merchandise as soon as we took over Edie's share and, well' – he gave a little laugh – 'I work in oil, I'm not exactly a stranger to healthy balance sheets, but I was surprised to see how much revenue's there already.

''Course, it'll all need managing,' Grant added quickly, lest Strike think him too fortunate. 'It's a damn sight more complicated than people would imagine, stuff like this. I'm finding that out. I'm thinking of auditing Netflix to make sure they're passing everything on. Hasn't been done yet. I don't know what Allan Yeoman's been doing for his fifteen per cent, frankly . . .

'But we've *got* to find out who Anomie is. We can't keep having this kind of crap, every time there's a decision to be made about the property. So, yeah. That's why I called you. To find out what's going on.'

'Well, we've ruled out a couple of people,' said Strike, 'and we were able to speak to Josh Blay on Sat—'

'*He's* only interested in making things worse for us,' said Grant coldly. 'Shall we order?'

He flipped open his menu and before Strike could ask how Josh Blay was making things worse for the Ledwells, Grant said,

'I didn't want to say this over the phone, but there's something else. We've had a couple of strange – and this is one of the main things that's got Heather worried, to tell you the truth – a couple of strange phone calls. Anonymous.'

Strike took out his notebook.

'Go on.'

'They were made to my mobile. Heather picked up the first time, because I was in the bathroom. The voice on the end of the line told her to dig up Edie.'

'Is that all?'

'Well, it's enough, isn't it?' said Grant hotly. 'What kind of sick—?'

'I meant, is that all they said?'

'Oh, I see – well, I don't know.'

The waiter returned. Both men ordered steak and chips. Once the waiter had moved beyond earshot, Grant said,

'They might've said more, but Heather screamed when she heard that and – well, she dropped my bloody phone. Cracked the screen,' said Grant irritably. 'By the time I arrived to see what had scared her, whoever it was had hung up.'

'When did this happen?'

'Not long after that lunch where you were hired.'

'What time of day?'

'Evening.'

Strike made a note.

'And the second call?'

'That was about ten days ago. Evening, again. Caller number was withheld, but I answered.'

Grant drank more wine.

'I'm pretty sure it was someone using one of those voice-change things – apps – the voice was quite deep and robotic – and,' Grant glanced around and dropped his voice, 'they said, "Dig up Edie and look at the letter," then hung up. Heather thinks it's Anomie. Maybe it is, but if so, Christ knows how he got my number.'

'How difficult would it be for someone to get it through your office?'

'Well . . . possible, I suppose,' said Grant. As with his wife and her Facebook page, Ledwell seemed not to have considered the most pro- saic explanation. 'But my assistant wouldn't have given my number to anyone who sounded like *that*, like some deep-breathing cyborg. They'd've had to have come up with a pretty good story.'

'Did you check with your assistant, to see if she'd given out your number to anyone?'

'No,' said Grant tetchily, 'I'm hardly – I don't want to discuss this kind of stuff with people at the office. There's been enough nosiness about the – about what happened. Well, Edie was using the family name, so people have unavoidably made the connection . . .'

Scowling slightly, he finished his wine, giving Strike time to reflect that Ledwell had been Edie's surname quite as much as Grant's.

'. . . hardly the kind of thing I want people gossiping about. No, until I know how much – I mean, I don't know what the future holds for me, career-wise. So I don't want to bring this stuff to work.'

Grant raised his hand for the waiter and ordered a second glass of wine, and Strike wondered how much of Grant's discomfort with people at his workplace knowing about Edie was rooted in them knowing she'd spent a life in poverty, in foster care, while her uncle had been enjoying a healthy income in Oman.

'Who exactly knew there were letters in the coffin, do you know?' asked Strike.

'No idea. Heather and I didn't broadcast it. It was a pain in the – I mean, we had enough to organise, between the funeral and press calling at the house, without having to tell the undertaker to hold off closing the bloody coffin because those two wanted to shove letters in there.

'Obviously the undertaker knew, because I asked him to put it in there, but he's bound by confidentiality, or so you'd think, and the Upcott woman knew, because Blay dictated his letter to her. Ormond knew, obviously. *He* probably told everyone at the funeral. I said to Heather, we should've checked his pockets for bloody onions, the way he was carrying on.

'So, yeah, any number of people could know there's a letter in there by now, but what I want to know is, who'd be bloody sick enough to call Edie's relatives and advise them to dig her up, and who's trying to imply Ormond killed her? Because unless they're just doing it for kicks, to upset us, that's the idea they're trying to plant, isn't it? They can't be saying Blay did it, because – well, he didn't stab himself in the neck, did he?'

Strike thought he detected in Grant's voice a trace of disappointment that he had to give Blay this much credit.

Grant's second glass of wine arrived and he drank a third of it before shrugging off his suit jacket and hanging it over the back of his chair.

'You said just now that Blay's making things worse for you,' said Strike.

'Damn right he is. He contacted Maverick on Monday to say he doesn't want Harty changed. He said *Edie* wouldn't have wanted that. Perfectly obvious what he's up to.'

'Is it?'

'Course it is. Bargaining tactic, isn't it? He wants more money before he'll agree to any alterations.'

Strike wondered whether what he and Robin had said to Blay during their visit had roused the animator from his indifference to what happened to *The Ink Black Heart*.

'Bloody Katya Upcott'll be encouraging him. Revolting woman.'

'"Revolting"?' repeated Strike.

'You don't have to do business with them. Ethics of alley cats, the pair of them. They know the studio won't want to be seen to go against Blay's wishes while he's hospitalised, so they think they've got Maverick – and us – over a barrel. One tweet from Mr Josh Blay about how Maverick are wrecking his precious bloody story and all hell'll break loose, and Heather and I will be in the firing line again. But I can guarantee you this: he'll get more revenue than us over my dead body. If you knew what I know, you'd agree it's bloody disgusting that Blay's trying to use Edie as a bargaining tool.'

Grant gulped down more wine.

'What exactly *do* you know?' asked Strike.

'What?'

'What d'you know,' repeated Strike, 'that makes you think it's "disgusting" for Josh to say Edie wouldn't have wanted these changes?'

'Well – I don't think he actually gives a toss she's gone. Things have worked out bloody well for Mr Blay.'

'Yeah, you said that when we last met,' said Strike. Grant wasn't his client; he wasn't obliged to treat the man's opinions with respect. 'But I can't see how things can have worked out "bloody well" for a man who's paralysed from the neck down.'

'Well, that part's – obviously, that's very unfortunate, but, look – Blay could've called Anomie off any time he wanted. Seems to me everybody's been happy to let this situation fester, and now my family's paying the price. Nobody's attacking Josh Blay, you'll notice. Nobody's telling Blay they're coming for him and his kids. Well, I say, "If it walks like a duck and quacks like a duck, it's a duck." When are people going to wake up and start asking why Blay gets away scot-free all the time?'

'You're not suggesting,' said Strike, 'that *Blay's* Anomie?'

'Well ... no,' said Grant reluctantly. 'I understand Anomie's been in the game since Blay got stabbed and he can't be doing that in his present condition, can he?'

'No,' said Strike, 'he can't.'

'But you've got to admit, it's pretty bloody fishy, the way Anomie's interests and Blay's coincide. Neither of them want Harty changed to human, they both wanted Edie gone from the cartoon—'

Two plates of steak and chips now arrived. Even though he hadn't finished his second glass of wine, Grant ordered a third, before undoing his top button and loosening his tie.

'What makes you think Blay wanted Edie gone?' Strike asked.

Grant cut off a bit of steak and ate it before answering.

'Well, if you must know,' he said, 'Edie told me he did.'

'Really?'

'Yeah. She – rang me last year. Said Blay wanted her out. Wanted advice. Well, it's family, isn't it? I s'pose she thought she could trust me.'

He finished his glass of wine, still maintaining eye contact, then said,

'This might not be the way Blay wanted to take over, but ... well, careful what you wish for, eh? Thank you,' he added, as the waiter delivered the third glass.

Strike's mobile now vibrated in his pocket and he took it out. Robin had texted him.

Wally Cardew isn't Anomie. Currently in back of ambulance. Call when you can

Strike let his knife and fork fall.

'Excuse me, got to take a call,' he said to Grant, getting up from the table and walking as quickly as he could towards the door of the pub, pressing Robin's number as he went.

'Hi,' she said, answering on the second ring. 'It could've waited.'

'Why the hell are you in an ambulance?' said Strike, nearly knocking a woman over as he emerged onto the street.

'What? Oh, sorry – *I'm* not in the ambulance, Cardew is.'

'Jesus Christ, Robin,' said Strike, relief and temper vying with each other. 'I thought – what's happened?'

'Quite a lot, actually,' said Robin.

Strike could hear her walking along a street. He lit a cigarette while listening.

'I arrived to take over from Dev at four. He told me there'd been shouting from inside Wally's flat mid-afternoon. MJ came out looking furious and, Dev says, as though he'd been roughed up. His nose was bleeding. Then Wally's sister came out of the flat and went running after MJ and they disappeared together across the estate. Dev says he saw the grandmother and Wally close to the windows, shouting at each other.

'Everything was quiet for a couple of hours after I arrived, but I noticed a group of about five or six men sort of congregating on a corner not far away. A couple of them looked as though they were in their teens. I wouldn't be surprised if they were relatives of MJ's. They were watching Wally's door.

'Then Anomie entered the game and about five minutes later Wally came out of the flat talking on his mobile. He wasn't paying attention and—'

'They jumped him.'

'Yes, and he didn't stand a chance. They had him on the ground and were kicking him in the face, the balls – basically anywhere they could reach. People were looking out of windows and someone must've called the police, because they were there quickly. The attackers ran for it when they heard the siren, and I think the police must have called the ambulance. Wally looked quite badly hurt. I got out of there,' Robin said, forestalling Strike's next question. 'They don't need me, there were loads of witnesses. But Anomie was talking in the game while Wally was lying on the ground with the police standing over him, so as far as we're concerned—'

'Yeah, that's the end of Wally Cardew,' said Strike, standing aside to let more people enter The Gun. 'Well, I never thought it was him. If he's not smart enough to check out of the window for relatives bent on revenge, he's not clever enough to be Anomie.'

'How's Grant?'

'Reasonably interesting. He's been having the same anonymous calls I have. "Dig her up and read the letters."'

'Seriously?'

'Yeah. I'd better get back to him – oh,' said Strike, on the verge of stubbing out his cigarette, 'Hugh Jacks called the office. He wants you to ring him back.'

'Oh, for God's sake,' said Robin, who sounded irritated. Strike waited for elaboration, but none was forthcoming. 'OK, I'll let you get back to Grant. Speak tomorrow.'

She hung up and Strike, after one last drag on his Benson & Hedges, returned to Grant Ledwell.

'Any news?' asked Grant, as the detective sat down again.

'Another suspect ruled out,' said Strike, picking up his knife and fork again. 'So, aside from these two anonymous phone calls and the online harassment, have you had any other communications you're worried about? Has anything else happened that was out of the ordinary?'

'Only at the bloody funeral,' said Grant thickly, through a mouthful of steak. As Strike had noticed at the Arts Club lunch, the man was a noisy chewer: he could hear Grant's jaw clicking. The executive swallowed, then said succinctly:

'Freakshow.'

'Really?'

'Oh yeah. We had a whole crowd of oddballs outside the church, weeping and wailing. Wearing T-shirts with bloody black hearts on them and holding black candles. Tattoos all over them. One idiot came as a ghost. When the coffin arrived, they were all trying to throw bloody black flowers at it. Cloth, obviously – but what a *total* bloody lack of respect – one of them hit a pallbearer in the eye.

'Then, inside the church, there was this *child*, this enormous *boy* – somebody told me afterwards he lives at that art collective – who *would not shut up*. Loud comments, asking what the vicar was up to – at one point, the little bastard gets up and walks up to the front, bold as brass. Heading right for the coffin. His mother – I assume she's his mother – went running up the aisle after him and dragged him back to the pew.

'Then, when I stood up to give the eulogy, some bastard booed. Couldn't see who it was.'

Strike, though silently amused, maintained an impassive expression.

'So, yeah, then we set off for the cemetery and the crowd of circus rejects outside bloody follow us. I wanted her cremated, but Blay and Ormond both insisted she'd wanted to be buried in Highgate Cemetery, which costs an arm and – anyway, I thought it was bloody distasteful, given that that was where she'd – but we gave in, because ... well, we gave in.

'So we're standing there around the grave and a hundred-odd people who look like Hallowe'en extras are watching from a distance and crying as though they knew her personally. Mind you, at least they were in black. Some of the so-called mourners were in bloody yellow. "It was her favourite colour." Christ's sake. I was just glad we hadn't taken the kids – although Rachel insisted on coming. My eldest. She never even met Edie, but any reason to take a day off bloody school.'

Attacking his steak anew, Grant said,

'So then, at the wake – I have to say, these artists manage to get through plenty of food and booze – two of them nearly got into a fight. Rachel told me about this bit, because by this point, Heather and I were sitting in a side room – you know she's pregnant, and there'd been a lot of standing. And by this time I was thinking, if anyone wants to come and give us their condolences, they can bloody well come and find us.'

Strike suspected that the boo in the church might also have accounted for this unwillingness to mix.

'Rachel was out in the main room, talking to the Upcott children. Boy and a girl. The boy's got some horrible skin condition,' said Grant, as though this were something Gus had consciously adopted, 'but at least Katya had made them wear bloody mourning – and Rachel said some tall bald bloke who was called – I can't remember – maybe Jim—'

'Tim? Tim Ashcroft?'

'Did he do the voice of one of the characters?'

'Yeah. The Worm.'

'Then it's him,' said Grant, drinking more wine. 'So Jim – Tim – whatever – approaches Rachel and the Upcott kids, and he's making small talk, and then this Liverpudlian comes over.'

'Pez Pierce?'

'What?'

'Think that might've been the Liverpudlian bloke's name.'

'Well, I don't know his name,' said Grant impatiently, 'but I heard his accent when he was standing behind me in the graveyard. I've never liked the Scouse accent. Always sound like they're taking the piss, don't they? And he was one of the ones wearing yellow. Yellow shirt and a bloody yellow kipper tie.

'Anyway, Rachel says he'd had a bit to drink. Well, they all had, we could hear them all talking and laughing. You'd've thought it was a bloody party. And Rachel told us this Fez, or whatever his name is, staggered up to Jim and said, "I know what you're up to and you can fucking well stop it right now." And Jim said he didn't know what Fez was talking about, and according to Rachel, Fez pushed Jim in the chest and said words to the effect, "doing it at her fucking funeral", and then Ormond noticed what was going on and intervened.

'If I'd been there, I'd've slung them both out on their ear. And then Fez told Ormond to fuck off – this is at a *funeral*, mark you – and walked out and Jim left not long afterwards. I will say, *he* had the decency to stop by our room and say how sorry he was. Pretty much the only one who did.

'No, I tell a lie . . .'

Grant's eyes were bloodshot now, and large patches of sweat had spread from under each arm of his shirt.

'Right at the end, that gigantic Dutchman who runs the commune or whatever it is . . . long hair . . . wearing some kind of yellow *smock,* with his jeans,' said Grant contemptuously. 'Came lurching up to us as everyone was leaving and gave me a package. He stank of weed. He'd obviously been outside to have a joint.

'And he said, "It was a triumphal death."'

'"Triumphal"?' repeated Strike.

'Yeah. Then he shoves this package into my hands and says, "Open it later. Thought you should have a copy." Then he walks away again. No "sorry for your loss", nothing.

'I opened the package in the car. You've never seen anything like it. He'd done this . . . this . . . I don't know how to describe it. If that's his idea of bloody art . . . Bits of it were painted, but other bits were photographs. Words pasted over it. Greek stuff. Lines of poetry and tombstones in the background and Edie in the middle, kneeling, looking like she was . . .'

For the first time, Strike thought he saw some flicker of distress in the man sitting opposite him. Grant took another slug of wine, but some missed his mouth and fell in dark droplets on the table.

'. . . weird figures in the background and a gigantic . . . well, it doesn't matter. But the thing was an abomination.'

'Have you still got—?'

'No, I bloody haven't,' snarled Grant Ledwell. 'Binmen took it the next day.'

65

The email Strike sent Robin following his dinner with Grant Ledwell, which she read while sitting on a bench in Sloane Square the following morning, concluded:

We're running low on original suspects: only Tim Ashcroft, Kea Niven and Pez Pierce left. I keep asking myself who we might have overlooked. A few ideas for new lines of inquiry:

Who knew about the Harty-to-human change?
I called Allan Yeoman this morning. He's adamant only ten people knew Maverick were considering changing Harty from heart to human: half a dozen people at the film company, all of whom have signed non-disclosure agreements, so risk losing lucrative jobs if they talk about the script outside the studio; Yeoman himself, but he hasn't even told his own wife and says he's kept it from everyone at his agency for fear of leaks; Josh Blay; Grant Ledwell; and Katya Upcott.

1) **Josh**
I texted Katya for a list of people who've visited Josh in hospital. Answer: other than herself and Blay's father, brother and sister,

only two: Mariam Torosyan (who's visited three times) and Pez Pierce. I'm going to call Josh later and find out whether he discussed the proposed change with either of them. If he did, the news could have travelled back to North Grove and presumably to a fairly wide group of people.

Of our known suspects, Pez Pierce is still looking like the most plausible Anomie to me. He's got the artistic/digital skills, had access to all the personal stuff about Edie from living with her at the collective, and there's a decent chance Josh told him about the Harty/human proposal. If Pierce renews his offer of a drink tonight, I think you should accept and I'll take over Buffypaws duties while you're with him.

I'd also like to take a closer look at Nils de Jong. 'Triumphal death' is a bloody odd way to describe murder, even if you're stoned. We haven't got the manpower to put surveillance on Nils until we've ruled someone else out, but anything you can find out about him while at North Grove would be helpful. NB: apparently the painting he gave Grant was a copy. I'd be interested to see the original.

2) **Grant**

Very hard to imagine Grant letting this information slip. Heather strikes me as generally gossipy, but is currently paranoid and scared, so she's probably being more discreet than usual.

However, it struck me as odd that Grant's eldest daughter, Rachel, insisted on going to Edie's funeral. She's sixteen and had never met Edie. Grant's take is that Rachel just wanted a day off school, but as she lives outside London with his ex-wife (he wasn't specific about their location, I'll do some digging online) I'd have thought faking a stomach ache would've achieved the same result with far less effort. At this point, any teenager with connections to the Ledwells/the Upcotts/North Grove who's acting strangely needs checking out.

3) **Katya**

I can't imagine Katya discussing something this sensitive outside her own household, but if she mentioned it at home, any of the other family members could have passed on the information, whether deliberately or innocently. Flavia's friends are too young to fit the Anomie profile, but we should check out Gus's mates. I also think we should try and find out who Inigo's 'darling child' is.

4) **Tim Ashcroft and Kea Niven**

These two now look less likely as Anomie to me. Neither have any (ongoing) connection with North Grove/the Ledwells/the Upcotts that we know about, so it's hard to see how they'd have known about the Harty/human development.

I'd like to find out why there's bad blood between Pez and Ashcroft, just to exclude the possibility it's Anomie-related. Otherwise, I propose putting proper surveillance on Kea with a view to ruling her out and keeping surveillance on Ashcroft for the same reason.

Having finished reading this email, Robin replaced her mobile in her bag and checked her iPad, where the game was running as usual. Anomie wasn't present, so she raised her gaze instead to the windows of Fingers' third-floor flat. As she stared up at the squares of glass, which had turned to quicksilver in the spring sunshine, she pondered the possibility that Anomie was somebody they hadn't even considered. If you didn't focus on the details, she thought, Anomie could be one of millions, just another anonymous person on the internet, but when you looked closer – at the skill set needed to produce the game, the intimate knowledge of Edie's past and of developments within the cartoon, not to mention the deep-rooted animosity that must surely have driven these years of harassment – it seemed astounding that the culprit had remained hidden this long.

Robin didn't feel very excited about any of her partner's suggestions for possible new suspects and suspected that Strike, too, considered it more of a box-ticking exercise than the pursuit of meaningful leads.

After Robin had spent a further half hour's fruitless surveillance of Fingers' flat, Nutley arrived to take over, approaching with the slight swagger that was habitual to him. Nutley seemed to have an irresistible urge to proclaim himself a man who knew more than he was letting on, to the extent that Robin always had the feeling on handovers that he might nudge her in the ribs and wink, and she resented having to take onto herself the burden of making the swap look natural.

'Just past one o'clock,' she told Nutley, checking her watch as she spoke.

'What?' said Nutley.

'You just asked me the time. *Don't* sit where I was sitting,' she implored him, as Nutley made to do just that.

As she headed for the Tube, Robin consoled herself with the thought that if Fingers was looking out of the window, he'd probably assume she was removing herself from the vicinity of an annoying man, who'd changed his mind about sitting down once she'd left. Even so, she couldn't help wishing they could find someone better than Nutley, or that the agency's workload would become manageable enough to let him go.

While in theory she had the afternoon off, Robin had decided to transform herself into Jessica Robins early, because she wanted to visit Highgate Cemetery before heading for her evening class at North Grove, and it felt unsafe to wander around so close to the art collective without her disguise. Her reasons for visiting the cemetery were mixed. She felt curious about the place whose digital representation she'd been virtually living in for weeks, and wanted to see the place where Edie and Josh had been stabbed. She also felt an only partly acknowledged desire to visit Edie Ledwell's grave. A fear of being told she was being ghoulish or over-emotional had prevented her from telling anyone, least of all Strike, what she was intending to do. On the other hand, she thought as she adjusted Jessica's wig in the bathroom on the office landing, it wasn't as though she was wasting the agency's time: she could have spent her few free hours doing something pleasurable, like ... but Robin couldn't really think of anything she'd rather do than visit Highgate Cemetery. Peering into the cracked mirror to check her hazel contact lenses, she remembered Ilsa's words at dinner: *Honestly, you're just like him ... The job comes first.* But as dwelling on her compatibility with Cormoran Strike was something she was making a conscious effort not to do, Robin pushed that thought firmly out of her mind, and headed back into the office.

'Looks quite good on you,' said Pat, casting a critical eye over Robin's brunette wig, winged eyeliner, scarlet lipstick and black suede jacket.

'Thanks,' said Robin as she moved back to the inner office, where she'd left her iPad and bag. 'I'm hoping to be asked out for a drink.'

'Really? Who by?' Pat called after her, but Robin didn't answer immediately. She'd just caught sight of her iPad. While she'd been in the bathroom, Anomie had not only logged onto the game, but had opened a private channel to Buffypaws.

'Hang on, Pat, got to deal with something here.'

```
<A new private channel has
opened>

<4 June 2015 14.13>

<Anomie invites Buffypaws>

Anomie: afternoon

    >

    >

    >

    >

    >

    >

Anomie: hello?

    >

    >

    >

    >

Anomie: I haven't got all fucking
day you know

    >

    >

<Buffypaws has joined the
channel>
```

Buffypaws: hi, really sorry, I was talking to my boss

Anomie: is that right?

Anomie: well, that could be a problem

Buffypaws: sorry?

Anomie: you should be

Anomie: I was thinking of making you an offer

Anomie: but if your job means you have to keep taking half hours off, it's not going to work

Buffypaws: what kind of offer?

Anomie: moderator

Anomie: replacing LordDrek

Robin let out such a loud gasp that Pat called through from the outer office,

'You all right?'

'Fine!' Robin called back.

Buffypaws: omg I'd love that

Anomie: lol yeah I thought you would

Anomie: got to work for it, though

Buffypaws: how?

Anomie: test

Anomie: I do it on a private channel

Anomie: all answers within 15 seconds so I know you haven't got time to go & look stuff up

Buffypaws: this sounds hard

Anomie: it is

Anomie: keeps out the normies

Anomie: you can have a week to revise

Anomie: Ink Black Heart, episodes 1-42

Anomie: plus the game

Anomie: plus, bonus question: you guess who I am

Buffypaws: lol

Buffypaws: has anyone ever got that one right?

Anomie: no

Buffypaws: if I guessed right, would you tell me?

Anomie: you won't guess right

Anomie: but it amuses me to see how wrong people are.

Anomie: so, Thursday next week, yeah?

Anomie: 2pm

Buffypaws: ok

Buffypaws: thanks so much!

<Anomie has left the channel>

<Buffypaws has left the channel>

<Private channel has closed>

Elated, Robin texted the news to Strike, who was currently watching the housekeeper of South Audley Street, then placed the iPad in her bag and returned to the outer office.

'Been asked out for that drink?' asked the office manager, observing Robin's cheerful expression.

'Something far better.'

'Dinner?'

'No, I've been invited somewhere I've been hoping to go for weeks.'

'With Hugh Jacks?' persisted Pat, who took a healthy interest in Robin's love life, or lack thereof.

'Oh shit,' said Robin, coming to a halt and clapping a hand to her forehead. 'Hugh Jacks.'

After Jacks's last message, she'd decided that she ought to call him back and make her lack of interest in him clear, but on waking the resolution had gone clean out of her head. Robin was naturally disinclined to hurt people's feelings, and as she headed down the metal staircase, iPad in bag, she felt a mixture of dread and resentment at having to tell Jacks what ought, surely, to be patently obvious after such a prolonged lack of response to his many advances.

Half an hour later, just as Robin was emerging from Highgate station, her mobile rang.

'Moderator channel, eh?' said Strike without preamble. 'Bloody good going.'

'I'm not in yet,' said Robin, now walking towards the cemetery. 'I've got to pass a test on the cartoon and the game, administered by Anomie, a week today. The final question is guessing who Anomie is, so I'd better try and think up the most flattering answer.'

'Anyone ever guessed right?'

'I asked that. Apparently not, but it amuses Anomie to hear the answers.'

'Egotistical prick,' grunted Strike.

'How's our housekeeper?'

'Currently doing her shopping in Aldi. No Fabergé boxes concealed about her person that I can see. Nutley take over Fingers all right?'

'Well, he arrived on time,' said Robin, 'but I wish he'd be less—'

'—of an arsehole? Me too. Trust me, I want him gone as soon as it's practical. All set for North Grove tonight?'

'Yes,' said Robin.

'Let's hope Pierce has still got the hots for Jessica. In other news: Midge lost Tim Ashcroft.'

'Shit, really?'

'Kind of thing that could happen to anyone. She was tailing him out of Colchester by car and got stuck behind a stalled lorry at a roundabout, so he's currently unwatched. She thinks he was heading for London, but – did you read my email?'

'I did, yes, and I agree: he's not our strongest contender for Anomie. Still be good to rule him out for sure, though.'

'Exactly. Well, I'll let you get back to your afternoon off. Good luck at North Grove tonight. Let me know how it goes.'

Strike rang off, Robin replaced her mobile in her bag and continued towards the cemetery.

As she turned into Swain's Lane, the long walled road that ran, steeply sloping, between the two halves of the graveyard, she saw a group of young people up ahead: four women and a man, two of them wearing *Ink Black Heart* T-shirts. On the back of the man's was written one of Drek's catchphrases: *I is lonelik and borkled*, and on one of the girl's, one of Paperwhite's: *sad, so very sad.* The group paused between the entrances to the East and West sections, talking animatedly and looking from one entrance to the other. Robin was certain they were trying to discover which way lay the older, West part, where Edie was buried and where the murder had happened, but which necessitated joining a guided walking tour. Hanging back, Robin watched them turn right.

When she drew level with the entrance she saw them purchasing tickets and regrouping on the other side of the ticket box, in a courtyard bordered by arches where a small knot of people were already waiting for a guide. Apparently she had a little time before the next tour started so, with a hard knot of anxiety in her stomach, but telling herself that it was best to get it over with, she moved out of sight and earshot of the assembling tour group, blocked her caller ID and called Hugh Jacks.

He answered after a few rings, sounding impatient.

'Hello?'

'Oh – hi, Hugh,' said Robin. 'Er – it's Robin Ellacott here.'

'Robin!' he said, sounding surprised and pleased. 'Hang on, let me get somewhere I can talk . . .'

She heard him walking, presumably away from colleagues.

'How are you?' he asked.

'Fine,' said Robin. 'How are you?'

'Not bad. Better for hearing from you. I was starting to think I'd been ghosted.'

Robin, who didn't think it qualified as being ghosted if there'd been no previous relationship, said nothing. She could tell Jacks had been expecting reassurance, because he sounded a little more certain when he went on,

'Yeah, so – I was wondering if you fancied dinner sometime.'

'Um,' said Robin, 'I – I don't think so, Hugh. Thanks, though.'

When he didn't respond, Robin added, inwardly cringing,

'It's – I'm just not really – you know – ready to date right now.'

Silence.

'So – well, I hope you're doing OK,' Robin said in a rushed voice, 'and, er—'

'Well, no, actually,' said Hugh, and his sudden shift to what sounded like cold fury shocked her. 'I'm *not* doing OK, *actually*. I've only come back to work this week after being signed off for depression.'

'Oh,' said Robin, 'I'm sorry to hear—'

'I've been discussing you with my therapist, as a matter of fact. Yeah. Wasted a lot of time talking about you, and what it feels like to call someone repeatedly, and for them not to even deign to return your calls.'

'I – don't know what to say to that.'

'You *knew* I'm in a pretty fragile place—'

'Hugh,' said Robin again, now caught between guilt and rising irritation, 'if I gave you the impression I was interested—'

'My therapist has been saying I should let it go, but I kept telling her what a nice person you were, but now it turns out you're just another—'

'Goodbye, Hugh—'

But she wasn't quick enough to cut off his last word,

'—*bitch*.'

Robin's heart was pumping as though she'd just sprinted a hundred yards. She glanced instinctively over her shoulder, but Hugh wasn't running towards her along the lane, and she felt angry at herself for being so irrational.

He's an arsehole, Robin told herself, but she still needed a few seconds to compose herself before heading back to the gothic gatehouse to buy a ticket for the tour.

The group in the courtyard had now grown to a dozen people. Apart from the *Ink Black Heart* fans, there were a couple of American tourists and an elderly couple in matching horn-rimmed glasses.

Robin joined the periphery of the group, trying not to think about Hugh Jacks, or about the last word he'd spat in her ear. *Bitch*. She suddenly remembered the polite and almost equally embarrassed way DI Murphy of the CID had received her botched refusal of a drink and felt an increased liking for the man, even though she barely knew him.

The tour guide who arrived a few minutes after Robin had joined the group was a middle-aged, bespectacled man wearing a cagoule, whose eyes travelled automatically to the two young people wearing *Ink Black Heart* T-shirts with, Robin thought, a slight air of bracing himself.

'Good afternoon! I'm Toby and I'll be your guide today. Our tour lasts around seventy minutes. A couple of bits of housekeeping before we set off: if you're interested in seeing Karl Marx's tomb, you should know that it's in the East section. Entrance is free with the ticket you've just bought.'

Robin already knew this. Josh and Edie, and subsequently Anomie and Morehouse, had taken some liberties with the layout of the cemetery, compressing the two halves into one and jumbling together graves that in reality were separated by Swain's Lane.

'If you're interested in seeing any particular grave—'

The young woman in the Paperwhite T-shirt, and an elderly woman in glasses, spoke up simultaneously.

'We really want to see Edie Ledwell's—'

'Is Christina Rossetti included on the tour?'

The guide answered the elderly woman first.

'Yes, we can certainly visit Rossetti's grave. She's down a bit of a cul-de-sac. We'll visit her towards the end, so we don't have to double back.

'But I'm afraid,' he added, addressing the young woman in the Paperwhite T-shirt, 'we don't visit Miss Ledwell's grave. It's in a private plot, you see. This is still a working cemetery, and families—'

'*Her* family didn't give a shit about her,' said the young man in the Drek T-shirt in an audible whisper, which the tour guide pretended not to hear.

'—have the right to privacy, so we ask visitors to be respectful. Cameras are permitted, but pictures are for personal use only – and please, no eating, drinking or smoking while we're in the cemetery, and keep to the paths. Some of the tombs are unsafe.'

'We *will* see de Munck's grave, though?' said a stout young woman with purple hair, who was part of the *Ink Black Heart* group.

Robin had no idea who de Munck was, or why their grave should be of particular interest to the fans.

'We pass de Munck, yes,' said the guide.

'Well, that's something,' the girl said to her friends.

The tour group set off, not up the main steps to the cemetery but past a large memorial to the dead of the First World War, and up a narrow path. From the low grumblings of the *Ink Black Heart* fans immediately ahead of her, Robin gathered that the guide wasn't taking them along their preferred route. Keeping to the rear of the party by design, Robin glanced into her bag at her iPad, where the game was still running. The only moderator present was Hartella, and nobody, thankfully, was waiting to talk to Buffypaws on a private channel.

The tour guide led them up a narrow, earthy path bordered on both sides by graves and, on the right, by a high brick wall. All was in shadow, because of the dense canopy of trees overhead, and the air was laden with the scent of damp greenery, of musty bonemeal and fungal earthiness. The guide was talking, but Robin couldn't hear much of what he was saying because the *Ink Black Heart* fans were conversing in whispers right ahead of her.

'They can't have got in *here*,' said the young woman in the Paperwhite T-shirt, looking up at the twelve-foot-high wall.

'It's all on the other side, I think,' said the man in the Drek T-shirt, peering left through trees and creeper-draped graves. 'I don't recognise any of this.'

But when the party reached the top of the pathway, the girl in the Paperwhite T-shirt let out a little gasp, and the purple-haired girl made to clutch her heart. Robin understood the reaction: her own sense of déjà vu was uncanny.

Here was the winding path that wound upwards through the ivy-tangled trees, along which little Harty bounced in perpetual tragi-comic pursuit of the beautiful Paperwhite; here was the forest of broken classical columns, crosses, stone urns, marble caskets and obelisks among which the sinister shadow of Drek lurked, ready to jump out at other players and urge them to play his game.

The tour guide paused beside a chest tomb topped by a statue of a horse, explaining to the elderly couple and the American tourists that it belonged to Queen Victoria's horse slaughterer. However, Robin's attention had been caught by a square stone obelisk surmounted by a huge knot of thick, fibrous creeper, whose thick tendrils had descended around the monument, giving the appearance of a parasitic, spider-like alien attempting to swallow the grave whole. This was the grave on which Magspie, the character first voiced by Pez Pierce, habitually roosted. The *Ink Black Heart* fans were excitedly taking pictures.

The tour group moved off again, Robin wondering whether she found the cemetery more beautiful or creepy. On every side, ivy, grass, ferns, brambles and tree roots had run amok, mocking the formal grandeur of the monuments. Creepers had shifted the heavy stone lids of tombs; ferns had sprouted on graves where no flowers had been laid for a century; tree roots had lifted headstones that now sat crookedly, bowing to the earth.

Another frisson of excitement ran through the *Ink Black Heart* fans when they reached the tomb of Mary Nichols, which featured a life-sized sleeping angel. This, as Robin knew, was Paperwhite's tomb in the cartoon. The ghost was usually found draped over it, mourning her deceased state, and the *Ink Black Heart* fans begged one of the tourists to take a picture of all of them grouped in front of the grave.

They then passed between huge stone Egyptian pillars and entered the Circle of Lebanon, a sunken stone amphitheatre where double rows of mausoleums lined the walls. The girl in the Paperwhite T-shirt squealed as she spotted the grand gothic tomb that most closely resembled that of Lord and Lady Wyrdy-Grob in the cartoon. While the guide talked of the Victorian fondness for Egyptian iconography, the *Ink Black Heart* fans took selfies and pictures of each other in front of the mausoleum.

They left the Circle of Lebanon and passed the grave of William Wombwell, who the tour guide explained was a Victorian menagerie-owner, which explained the large stone lion topping his tomb, then led them back onto a long concrete path bordered by still more graves and trees, which marched into the distance in every direction.

Quite suddenly, the young man in the Drek T-shirt in front of Robin came to a halt, pointing at a tombstone that stood on a steep rise above the path, surrounded by thick undergrowth. To Robin's slight surprise, she saw again the image she'd heard Groomer explaining to Legs back in the William Morris Gallery: the mother pelican plucking at her own breast, with a nest full of hungry chicks, beaks upturned, ready to be fed with her blood.

The girls surrounding the young man in the Drek T-shirt were now clutching each other.

'That's it, that must be it!'

'Oh my God,' breathed the girl in the Paperwhite T-shirt, speaking through the fingers she pressed to her mouth. 'I'm going to cry.'

The guide had stopped too. Turning to face the group, and ignoring the agitation displayed by the *Ink Black Heart* fans, he said:

'This unusual headstone is that of Elizabeth, Baroness de Munck. The device of the pelican represents sacrifice. This tomb was erected by Elizabeth's daughter, Rosalbina ...'

But Robin wasn't listening. She'd just remembered what Josh Blay had said about the place where they'd had the first ideas for the cartoon – the place where Edie had been murdered. *'Near a grave Edie always liked. It's got a pelican on it.'*

'Take my picture,' said one of the *Ink Black Heart* fans to another, handing over her phone with trembling hands. The young man in the Drek T-shirt glanced towards the guide; Robin was certain he was wondering whether he might get a chance to climb the slope and peer into the hollow where Edie's body had been found. The *Ink Black Heart* fans hung back when the group moved on, but a backwards glance from the tour guide made them walk on reluctantly, looking over their shoulders as they went.

Robin, bringing up the rear, took herself slightly to task for a feeling of revulsion towards the *Ink Black Heart* fans, for wanting photographs of the place where Edie had been stabbed. But was she any better? Now she'd seen the place where it had happened, she understood just how skilful – or lucky – the killer had been. They'd clearly known the route to that sequestered patch of graves off the paths, supposedly unvisitable by visitors. They'd also avoided tour groups and managed to make their way out of the cemetery undetected. Robin glanced around: there were no CCTV cameras anywhere. She thought of the two masks the would-be killer of Oliver Peach had worn. It would have been child's play, here, among these densely packed trees and monuments, to strip off one disguise and reveal another. Perhaps the killer had waited for a tour group and assimilated him or herself quietly into it, or perhaps they'd left the way they'd come in.

Lost in thought, Robin had dropped slightly behind the group, which was now proceeding towards Christina Rossetti's grave. She was just wondering where Josh had been found, when she heard a loud '*psst*'.

Robin gave a start and looked around. A pair of doleful eyes and a mop of curly hair were visible through an overgrown patch of vegetation. Pez Pierce was standing, half-concealed in greenery, sketchbook in hand, and grinning at her.

'What—?'

Pez pressed a finger to his lips, then beckoned. Robin glanced at the tour group, which was rounding a bend in the path. Nobody looked back, so she picked her way carefully through the undergrowth. As thorns tore at her clothes, Robin rapidly debated whether or not she should continue the London accent she'd faked when talking to Pez last time, given that Zoe might have told Pez that Jessica was from Yorkshire. As she stepped into the small clearing where Pez was standing, she decided to split the difference.

'I thought you could only get in here with a tour guide,' she whispered in her own accent.

'Not if you know the secret way in,' said Pez, also smiling. He was holding a sketchbook in his hand. 'What's a workaholic like you doing touring graveyards?'

'I had a dental appointment, so I took the afternoon off,' said Robin. 'Never been here before. It's incredible, isn't it?'

'Oh, yeah, I can hear it now,' said Pez.

'Hear what?'

'That you're from Yorkshire. Zoe told me. She told me you'd just split up from your boyfriend too.'

'Well – yeah,' said Robin, with a stab at a brave smile. 'Also true.'

The wet, waist-high vegetation surrounding them meant they were necessarily standing very close together, on a mossy patch of uneven ground between tombs and trees. Robin could smell Pez through the thin creased T-shirt he was wearing: a strong animal smell, almost, but not quite, BO, and she had a sudden, intrusive memory of Pez's penis.

'Do I get a prize if I tell you a third true thing about yourself?'

'Go on,' said Robin.

'You haven't checked your emails this afternoon.'

'What are you, psychic?'

'No, but your drawing class has been cancelled.'

'Oh, *bugger*,' said Robin, feigning disappointment. 'Is Mariam OK?'

'Yeah, she's fine, just overcommitted. Some political thing she forgot she had on. Kinda thing that happens all the time at North Grove. You won't be the only one who didn't realise. People'll turn up as usual and just have a drink in the kitchen or do a drawing on their own. That's how we roll, like. Or are you the kind of person who'll write and complain?'

'No, of course I'm not!' said Robin, mock-offended, as Jessica would surely be, at being considered so hidebound and uptight.

'Glad to hear it. Where're they off to?' Pez asked, looking after the tour group.

'Christina Rossetti,' said Robin.

'Don't you want to see it?'

'I don't know,' said Robin. 'Is it interesting?'

'I can tell you the only interesting story about that grave,' said Pez. 'Then we could go for that drink.'

'Oh,' said Robin, with what she hoped was a decent show of bashfulness, 'um – yeah, OK. Why not?'

'Great. C'mon then,' said Pierce. 'We'll have to go round the long way, stay out of the way of the tours. And I'll need to drop this back home first,' he added, holding up his sketchbook.

They set off through the trees and graves, eschewing the paths where the tour groups roamed. Several times, Pez reached out to help Robin over tree roots and over rocky ground strewn with fragments of stone and she let him take her hand. After the third time, he kept holding it for a few steps before dropping it.

'So what's the story about Rossetti's grave?' asked Robin.

She felt a possibly paranoid desire to keep Pez talking as they moved through dark trees, hidden from the sight of any other human.

'Ah,' said Pez, 'well, Rossetti's not the only one in there.'

'No?'

'No, there's also a woman called Lizzie Siddal. She was Christina's brother's wife. She overdosed and when they buried her, Dante put the only manuscript of his poems in the coffin with her. Grand gesture, like.'

'Romantic,' commented Robin, tugging her ankle free of some ivy.

649

'Seven years later,' said Pez, 'Dante changed his mind, had her dug up and took them out again. Wormholes through the pages and everything . . . but art before tarts, eh?'

Robin Ellacott didn't think it a particularly funny line, but Jessica Robins giggled obligingly.

66

One of the children hanging about
Pointed at the whole dreadful heap and smiled . . .
There is something terrible about a child.

Charlotte Mew
In Nunhead Cemetery

'What've you been drawing?' Robin asked Pez, once they'd emerged from the cemetery and were heading for North Grove.

'Got an idea for a cyberpunk thing,' said Pez. 'There's a time-travelling Victorian undertaker in it.'

'Oh wow, that sounds great,' said Robin. Pez spent most of the short walk to the art collective talking her through the story, which, to her slight surprise, did indeed sound both elaborate and engaging.

'So you write as well as draw?'

'Yeah, a bit,' said Pez.

The colourful hall of the art collective seemed dazzling after the melancholy shade of the cemetery.

'Won't be a minute, I'll just put this upstairs,' said Pez, indicating the sketchbook, but before he could set foot on the spiral staircase Nils de Jong appeared from the direction of the kitchen. Enormous, blond and scruffy, he was wearing his old cargo shorts with a smock-like cream top spattered here and there with paint.

'You've got a visitor,' he informed Pez in a low voice. It was hard to tell whether Nils was smiling or not, because of the naturally upwards curl of his wide, thin-lipped mouth. 'He's just gone to the bathroom.'

'Who?' said Pez, his hand on the banisters.

'Phillip Ormond,' said Nils.

'The fuck does he want with *me*?' asked Pez.

651

'Thinks you've got something of his,' said Nils.

'Like what?'

'Here he is,' said Nils in a louder voice, as Ormond appeared around the corner.

Robin, who'd never set eyes on Ormond before, noted his neat, well-groomed appearance, so out of place here at North Grove. He was wearing a suit and tie and carrying a briefcase, as though he'd come straight from school.

'Hi,' he said to Pez, unsmiling. 'Wondered if I could have a word.'

'Wharrabout?'

Ormond glanced at Robin and Nils, then said:

'Kind of delicate. It's about Edie.'

'All right,' said Pez, though he didn't sound happy. 'Wanna come to the kitchen?'

'Mariam's in there with her lot,' said Nils.

'Fine,' said Pez, slightly irritably. 'Come upstairs.'

He turned to Robin.

'You all right to—?'

'Yes, of course, I'll wait here,' said Robin.

So the two men headed up the spiral staircase together in silence and disappeared from view, leaving Robin alone with Nils.

'You haven't seen a cat, have you?' asked the Dutchman, peering down at her through his tangled blond fringe.

'No, sorry,' said Robin.

'He's disappeared.'

Nils looked around vaguely, then back at Robin.

'Zoe tells me you're from Yorkshire.'

'I am, yes,' said Robin.

'She's sick today.'

'Oh, I'm sorry. I hope it's nothing serious?'

'No, no, I don't think so.'

There was a pause in which Nils peered around the otherwise empty hall as though his cat might suddenly materialise out of thin air.

'I love this staircase,' Robin said, to break the silence.

'Yeah,' said Nils, turning his huge head to look at it. 'An old friend did that for us ... You know the drawing class is cancelled tonight?'

'I do, yes,' said Robin. 'Pez told me.'

'You can still do a drawing, if you like. Mariam arranged some ferns and things. I think Brendan's in there.'

'That would've been great, but I've said I'll have a drink with Pez.'

'Ah,' said Nils. 'D'you want to sit down while you're waiting for him?'

'Oh, thanks very much,' said Robin.

'Come,' said Nils, indicating that she should follow him in the opposite direction from the kitchen. His enormous sandalled feet made a slapping sound on the floorboards as he shuffled along. As they passed the studio where the drawing class was usually held, Robin spotted the elderly Brendan, working diligently on his sketch of ferns.

'The kitchen is full of Armenian revolutionaries,' said Nils, coming to a halt at a closed door and pulling a jumble of keys out of his pocket. 'No peace in there. Politics . . . you interested in politics?'

'Quite interested,' said Robin cautiously.

'Me too,' said Nils, 'but I always disagree with everyone, and Mariam gets pissed off. My private studio,' he added, leading the way into a large room that smelled powerfully of turps and cannabis.

The word 'mess' was barely adequate. The floor was covered in rags, discarded paint tubes, crumpled paper and rubbish like chocolate wrappers and empty cans. The walls were lined with flimsy wooden shelves which were crammed not only with pots of brushes, tubes of paint and various artists' palettes, but tattered paperbacks, bottles, rusted bits of machinery, lumpy clay sculptures, masks ranging from wood to fabric, a dusty tricorn hat, various anatomical models, a wax hand, assorted feathers and an ancient typewriter. Stacks of canvases were propped everywhere, their backs facing the room.

Rising up out of the ankle-deep litter like weird fungal growths were a few examples of Nils de Jong's art. They were all so aggressively ugly that Robin, wading through the detritus on the floor as she approached one of two low armchairs, decided that they were either works of genius or simply dreadful. A clay bust of a man with rusty cogs for eyes and bits of what looked like car tyre for hair stared blindly at her as she passed.

As Robin sat down in the rather smelly cloth-covered armchair to which Nils pointed her, she spotted a collage on an easel in front of the window. The picture, which was predominantly sludge green and yellow, featured Edie Ledwell's photographed face superimposed on a painted kneeling figure.

'I'm sorry about your cat,' she said, dragging her eyes away from the collage. 'Has he been gone long?'

'Five days now,' sighed Nils, sinking into the other armchair, which emitted a creaky groan at being asked to accept his weight. 'Poor Jort. It's the longest he's ever been away.'

After what Josh had said about Nils and Mariam's open relationship, Robin had wondered whether Nils's interest in getting her into his studio was sexual, but he seemed mostly sleepy, and certainly not inclined towards seduction. On a small pedestal table beside him was an ashtray in which lay a half-smoked carrot-sized joint, extinguished but still filling the air with its pungent smell.

'I love that,' lied Robin, pointing at the collage with Edie's face on it. Edie was surrounded by an odd assortment of beings: two human figures wearing long robes, a giant spider and a red parrot, which was carrying a marijuana leaf in its beak and appeared to be landing in her lap. Two phrases, one in Greek, the other in Latin, had been printed onto thick cream paper and pasted across the canvas: *Thule ultima a sole nomen habens* and ὅ μιν ἑκάεργος ἀνήρπασε Φοῖβος Ἀπόλλων.

'Yes,' said Nils, surveying his picture with drowsy complacency. 'I was pleased with it, it came off well . . . I got interested in the possibilities of collage last year. There was a Hannah Höch retrospective at the Whitechapel Gallery. You like Höch?'

'I don't know her work, I'm afraid,' said Robin truthfully.

'Part of the Berlin Dadaist movement,' said Nils. 'You know the cartoon, *The Ink Black Heart*? Do you recognise my model?'

'Oh,' said Robin, feigning surprise, 'that isn't the animator, is it? Edie whatever-she-was-called?'

'Ledwell, yes, exactly. You spot the inspiration for the composition?'

'Er . . .' said Robin.

'Rossetti. *Beata Beatrix*. Picture of his dead mistress.'

'Oh,' said Robin. 'I must go and look at that.'

'In the original,' said Nils, gazing at his canvas, 'there is a sundial, not a spider. That,' he said, pointing at the creature, 'is an orb weaver spider. They hate the light. Even night is too bright for them. They've been found in a crypt in Highgate Cemetery. The only place in Britain they've been discovered.'

'Oh,' said Robin again.

'You spot the symbolism? Spider, representing industry and artistry, but hates the light. Cannot survive in the light.'

Nils now noticed what looked like a strand of tobacco caught in his straggly beard, and pulled it out. Robin, who was hoping to distract his attention long enough to take a photograph of the collage featuring Edie to show Strike, pointed at the bust of the man with cogs for eyes and said,

'That's fabulous.'

'Yes,' said Nils, and again it was hard, given the strange masklike upward curve of his mouth, to tell whether he was genuinely smiling or not. 'That's my papa. I mixed his ashes into the clay.'

'You—?'

'Yes. He killed himself. Over a decade ago now,' said Nils.

'Oh, I'm – I'm so sorry,' said Robin.

'No, no, it didn't mean much to me,' said Nils with a slight shrug. 'We didn't get on. He was far too modern for me.'

'Modern?' repeated Robin.

'Yes. He was an industrialist ... petrochemicals. Big man in the Netherlands. He was full of that empty social democratic liberalism, you know ... management-workers council, a crèche ... all to keep his little cogs happy.'

Robin nodded noncommittally.

'But no grounding in anything real or important,' said Nils, staring at the grotesque bust. 'The kind of man who buys a picture to match his carpet, you know?'

He gave a little laugh and Robin smiled.

'A week after Mama died, Papa found out he had a cancer – a treatable cancer, but he decided to kill himself anyway. Have you read any Durkheim?'

'No,' said Robin.

'Borrow it,' said Nils, with a wave of his enormous hand. 'Émile Durkheim. *On Suicide.* We keep a little lending library in the bathroom ... Durkheim describes Papa's complaint perfectly. *Anomie.* You know what that is?'

'An absence,' said Robin, who hoped her tremor of surprise hadn't been visible, 'of normal ethical or social standards.'

'Ah, very good,' said Nils, smiling lazily at her. 'Did you already know, or did you look it up after seeing it on our kitchen window?'

'I looked it up after I saw your window,' lied Robin, smiling back. In her experience, men enjoyed giving women information. Nils chuckled, then said,

'Papa had no inner life. He was hollow, hollow ... profit, acquisition and ticking little social-democratic boxes ... his death grew naturally out of his life. Anomic suicide: Durkheim describes it well. Everyone's death is a fulfilment, really. Don't you think?'

Robin's honest answer would have been no, but Jessica Robins replied,

'I hadn't ever really thought of it like that.'

'It's true,' said Nils, nodding his head ponderously. 'I can't think of anybody I know whose death wasn't inevitable and entirely fitting. You understand the chakras?'

'Er – they're areas of the body, aren't they?'

'A little more than that. Hindu tantrism,' said Nils. He now picked up his dead joint and showed it to her. 'D'you mind if I—?'

'No, please,' said Robin.

Nils lit up using an old and battered Zippo. Enormous plumes of smoke issued from the joint.

'My father's cancer was in his prostate,' said Nils from inside his cloud of blue smoke. 'Second chakra: *svadhishthana*. Diseases of the second chakra stem from a lack of creativity and emotional isolation. I've got something here . . .'

He lumbered unexpectedly to his feet. In the time it took him to cross the room, Robin had whipped out her mobile, taken a picture of the collage, then hidden her mobile back in her bag.

'. . . where is it?' mumbled Nils, rooting among his cluttered shelves, moving aside objects, some of which fell to the floor without him showing much interest in their fate.

'Careful!' said Robin in sudden alarm.

An angle-bladed sword had dropped off the shelf and missed Nils's sandalled foot by inches. He merely laughed and stooped to pick it up.

'My grandfather's *klewang*. I did a little steel etching on it – see? You know what that says?'

'No,' said Robin, looking at the slightly wobbly Greek letters on the blade.

'κληρονομιά. "Legacy" . . . Where's that book?'

He pushed the sword back onto a shelf, but after a minute's further listless poking around he said, 'Not here,' and returned to Robin empty-handed. The low armchair groaned again as it accepted Nils's heft.

'So,' said Robin, 'in the case of somebody like – well,' she said, pointing at the picture of Edie, 'how was Edie Ledwell's death a fulfilment?'

'Ah,' said Nils, blinking blearily up at the painting, 'well, that was down to a lack of what I'd call the *aristocratic* outlook.' He took another huge drag of his joint and exhaled, so that Robin could only dimly see his features. 'I don't mean "aristocrat" in narrow class terms ... I mean a specific attitude of mind ... An aristocratic nature has *detachment* ... takes a broad, generous view of life ... can withstand changes of fortune, good or bad ... but Edie there had the bourgeois mindset ... possessive of her achievements ... worried about *copyright*, upset by criticism ... and success destroyed her, in the end ...'

'You think art should be free?' Robin asked.

'And why not?' said Nils. He held out the joint. 'You want?'

'No, thanks,' said Robin. She was already feeling lightheaded from inhaling the second-hand smoke. 'But' – she softened the question with a little laugh – 'you don't think worrying about copyright got her killed, surely?'

'Not copyright exactly ... no, Edie was killed because of what she'd *become*.'

'Become?'

'A hate figure. She made herself hated ... but she was an artist.'

Staring at the blurry green kneeling figure with Edie's head pasted onto it, Nils said,

'And what greater tribute is there to the power of an artist's work than that they are destroyed? So in that sense, you know, she had her triumph in death ... they recognised her power ... she was sacrificed for her art ... but if she'd known how to ... how to *inhabit* her power ... then all would have gone better for her ...'

Nils took another long pull on his joint. His voice was becoming progressively sleepier.

'People can't help what they are ... innately ... Your friend Pez ... classic Western type ...'

Robin now heard Bram's voice in the distance, singing in Dutch again before shouting 'Nils?' Nils raised a thick finger to his lips, smiling at Robin.

'*Nils?*'

They heard Bram's footsteps running down the corridor and then a fist pounded the door. Robin guessed that Nils usually locked it when he was inside the studio, because Bram didn't try the handle.

'I know you're in there, Papa, I can smell the weed!'

Robin suspected that Nils might have feigned an inability to hear his son if she hadn't been present. Instead, he laughed and said,

'All right, boy . . .'

Pulling himself upright, he set down the joint and headed to the door. Bram appeared, wide-eyed at the sight of Robin sitting there, and cackled.

'Papa, were you trying to—?'

'This is Pez's friend,' said Nils, drowning out the end of Bram's sentence. 'What d'you want?'

'Can I take *overgrootvader's* sword to school?'

'No, boy, they'd expel you for sure if you do that,' said Nils. 'Now, get out. Go play.'

'*Drek is lonelik and borkled*,' said Bram. '*Drek is lonelik and bork-led. Drek*—'

'Nils?' said a female voice. The woman with the crew cut Robin had previously seen now appeared, with her toddler in her arms. 'There's a guy at the door about the boiler.'

'I'll wait in the hall,' Robin said pleasantly to Nils, getting to her feet. 'You'll want to lock this room up again if you're not in here.'

She hoped, by mentioning locking the studio door, to remind the stoned Nils to do it. Robin didn't particularly like the idea of Bram getting his hands on his great-grandfather's *klewang* and she was relieved to hear the jangle of keys behind her as she walked away, back to the hall.

Pez was still nowhere to be seen, but a man in a blue boiler suit was staring in bemusement at the gigantic Monstera deliciosa, the spiral staircase and the hundreds of drawings and pictures hanging on the walls. Nils lumbered past Robin in a fug of cannabis fumes to greet the repairman and lead him off towards the kitchen. The woman with the crew cut smiled at Robin, then climbed the spiral stairs, whispering to the toddler in her arms, who was giggling.

Alone, Robin pulled out her mobile to text Strike the photo she'd taken of the collage. Before she could do so, however, a voice as shrill and loud as a whistle spoke almost in her ear.

'*DREK WANTS PLAY GAME, BWAH!*'

With a gasp of surprise, Robin jumped and wheeled around. Bram had sneaked up behind her, holding a small plastic device to his mouth. On seeing Robin's shock he roared with laughter. Robin stuffed the mobile back into her bag, heart racing, and forced a smile.

'You like *The Ink Black Heart*, do you?'

'I like Drek,' said Bram, still talking through the device, which distorted his voice into an ear-piercing whine.

'Does that do other voices?' Robin asked, as a sudden suspicion struck her.

'Maybe,' said Bram. He pressed a button and his voice became hoarse and rasping. '*I can do this one, too.*'

'Where did you get that? It looks fun.'

'*From the Science Museum,*' said Bram in the rasping voice. He then lowered the voice-changer and said, 'Who're you?'

'Jessica,' said Robin. 'I have art classes here.'

'I thought you were Pez's friend?' said Bram, and the suspicion in his voice, and shrewdness of his gaze, made Robin understand why Josh had said Bram sometimes seemed forty.

'I'm that as well,' said Robin. She pointed at the voice-changer. 'That'd be a really good way of making prank calls. Have you ever done that? I used to make them,' Robin lied, 'with my brother.'

Bram merely smirked.

'D'you want to see some of Pez's art?' he asked her.

'I'd love to,' said Robin, assuming she was about to be directed to one of the pictures on the walls all around them.

'It's upstairs,' said Bram, grinning as he beckoned her to follow him up the staircase.

'I'm not sure I should go up there,' said Robin.

'Nobody'll care,' said Bram. 'Everyone's allowed everywhere here.'

'Where exactly *is* the art?' asked Robin, without moving. She had no intention of being led by Bram into Pez's bedroom. Much as she might have liked to know what he and Ormond were saying to each other, she thought she'd have a better chance of extracting that information from Pez over a drink than by bursting into his bedroom with Bram.

'It's in Edie and Josh's old room,' said Bram.

The temptation of seeing this was irresistible, so Robin followed Bram up the spiral staircase to the next floor.

Bram seemed weirdly excited as he led her down the corridor, which was narrow, carpeted and punctuated by small flights of two or three stairs. The place would have reminded Robin of a small hotel if most of the doors hadn't stood carelessly open, revealing untidy bedrooms.

'That's mine,' said Bram unnecessarily: the room was littered with what looked like mostly broken toys. 'This is theirs.'

Unlike most of the others, the door beside Bram's was closed. To Robin's surprise, the boy glanced up and down the empty corridor before drawing a key out of his pocket and unlocking it.

The room was north-facing. It smelled of charred wood and fabric, with an undertone of dank rottenness. The overhead lamp was bulb-less. Once Robin's eyes had become accustomed to the gloom, she realised the place had been left in the state Josh had left it a few months previously. Blackened curtains still hung at the window, their tattered ends swaying a little in the breeze made by the door as it opened. The double bed had been stripped to reveal a partially burned mattress. Some of the sketches on the wall had been reduced to fragments still held in place by tarnished drawing pins, but the largest piece of art – if it could be so called – remained, because it had been painted directly onto the wall. It was at this piece of graffiti that Bram was pointing, watching eagerly for Robin's reaction.

Somebody – Pez, if Bram was to be believed – had painted a six-foot-long, meticulously detailed picture of a penis entering a vagina. Above this had been painted the same words inscribed on Mariam's window in the kitchen below.

> *A state of anomie is impossible*
> *wherever organs in solidarity with one another*
> *are in sufficient contact,*
> *and in sufficiently lengthy contact.*

'What d'you think?' asked Bram through barely suppressed giggles.

'Very good,' said Robin matter-of-factly. 'Somebody certainly knows how to draw genitalia.'

Bram seemed slightly frustrated by this response.

'It was Pez. He did it when they were out. Edie didn't like it.'

'Didn't she?' said Robin indifferently.

'I know who killed her,' said Bram.

Robin looked at him. He was so tall he was almost at her eye level. Remembering what had happened to his mother, she couldn't help feeling sorry for the boy, but neither his avid expression nor his patent desire to inspire shock or fear was endearing.

'Then you should tell a grown-up,' said Robin.

'*You're* a grown-up,' said Bram. 'If I tell you, you'll have to do something about it, won't you?'

'I meant a grown-up like your dad, or Mariam.'

'How did you know she wasn't my mum?' he asked.

'Somebody told me she wasn't,' said Robin.

'D'you know what happened to my real mum?'

'No,' said Robin.

'A man strangled her to death.'

'That's terrible,' said Robin seriously. 'I'm very sorry.'

She suspected that Bram had expected her to accuse him of fibbing. For a split-second, his grin faltered. Then he said loudly,

'I don't even care. It's better living with Nils. He gives me anything.'

'Lucky you,' said Robin with a smile, turning to glance at the rest of the room.

This couldn't, she thought, be the place where Josh and Edie had recorded that early video, back when they'd been so obviously in love, because that room had had a single bed. She couldn't see Josh's wallet or any keys. A dartboard had survived the fire, because it hung at the opposite end of the room, and a drawing was pinned to it, out of which three darts stuck. Curious, Robin approached the board, and with a slight thrill of surprise saw that it was a rather bad pencil drawing of Inigo Upcott, which she identified mainly by the fact that Katya had written his name above her own signature.

'Who put this poor man's picture on the dartboard?' she asked Bram lightly.

Receiving no answer, she turned and found herself staring straight into the face of a dead rat.

Robin shrieked, stumbled back against the wall and felt the flights on the darts prick the back of her head. The rat, which was partially rotten, had no eyes: its teeth were yellow, its thick, wormlike tail was stiff. It stank of alcohol, and Bram was thrusting it at her, laughing. A large jar full of murky liquid now sat on the floor beside the bed, its lid off.

'No,' Robin shouted, pushing Bram aside and half running out of the room into the deserted corridor and hurrying back the way she'd come, trying to resist a primal urge to sprint, even though she couldn't hear Bram coming after her.

When she reached the top of the stairs she saw Pez standing alone in the hallway below looking annoyed, but his expression lightened when she began to descend the stairs.

'Thought you'd done a runner.'

'No,' said Robin, trying to compose herself. 'Bram wanted to show me something up there.'

'Oh Christ,' said Pez, looking half amused. 'What?'

'Something you painted on a wall,' said Robin, trying for a similarly amused expression.

'Shit, did he show you that?' said Pez, his face falling. 'It was a joke – and that door's supposed to be locked.'

Robin had just reached the hall when Bram came thundering down the stairs behind her.

'Where did you get a key for Josh's room?' Pez demanded of the boy.

Bram shrugged insolently, then looked Robin directly in the eye.

'Zoe did it,' he said with a wide grin, then ran off around the corner, heading towards the kitchen.

67

Now he sets me down as vexed.
I think I've draped myself in woman's pride
To a perfect purpose.

Elizabeth Barrett Browning
Aurora Leigh

'What did Zoe do?' asked Pez.

'No idea,' lied Robin. 'He's a – a funny boy, isn't he?'

'"Funny"'s one word for him,' said Pez with a snort. 'C'mon. We'll go to The Gatehouse.'

Pez's previous good humour seemed to have been dented by his conversation with Ormond, though his spirits recovered once they'd walked out into the mild early-evening air. As they walked towards the pub, he questioned Robin about her marketing career, which she'd fortunately invented in sufficient detail to supply ready answers.

'Don't you find it boring, though?' asked Pez.

'Of course I do,' said Robin, and Pez laughed.

'Sorry I was so long upstairs,' he said.

'It's fine. I was talking to Nils.'

'Yeah?' said Pez, grinning. 'What didja think of him?'

'Interesting,' said Robin, and Pez laughed again.

''S OK, you can say he's weird. It's norras if he's me dad. Wha' was he talking about, like?'

'Er ... Hindu tantrism, capitalism, suicide, anomie' – Robin watched out of the corner of her eye for any reaction, but saw none – 'the aristocratic outlook, death being a fulfilment ...'

'You gorr'all his greatest hits,' said Pez, grinning. 'He's harmless, just eccentric, like . . . he thinks he's a natural aristocrat because he survived being left millions by his dad.'

'Must've been a real challenge,' said Robin, and this time, when Pez laughed, he reached out and lightly touched her arm.

'You're funny,' he said, slightly surprised.

'He showed me some of his art too.'

'Yeah? Wha' didja think?' Before Robin could answer, Pez said, 'Fucking dreadful, innit? Don't worry, we all know it's shit. He's gone through everything: painting, sculpture, etching, printmaking, digital stuff – an' las' week he was talking about gettin' into woodcuts.'

'Has he ever sold anything? Oh no, wait – he thinks art should be free, right?'

'Yeah,' said Pez. 'Easy to say if you've already got millions in the bank, like. Sometimes he holds little one-man shows at North Grove an' all the old faithfuls, the students who've hung out there for years, come an' drink wine and tell him he's a genius. I think some of 'em even believe it. Kind of sweet really . . . Did he tell you what race you are?'

'What *race*?' repeated Robin. 'What d'you mean?'

'Might need a beer before we go there,' said Pez. The Gatehouse was now in sight: a large black-and-white timbered building with seats and tables outside.

'You wanna sit inside or out?' asked Pez.

'In,' said Robin. Now that she and Pez were no longer standing beneath the shadowy canopy of trees in the cemetery, she feared close scrutiny of the wig and the coloured contact lenses.

'What d'you want?' Pez asked as they entered a very large bar area, with brick walls and wooden floors, in which many tables stood, a third of them already occupied.

'Glass of red, please,' said Robin. 'I'll just nip to the loo.'

The wallpaper in the Ladies' featured rhododendrons and parrots. Robin locked herself into a cubicle, texted Strike the photo of Nils's collage of Edie, then called him. He answered almost immediately.

'Aren't you in art class?'

'It was cancelled, so I'm having a drink with Pierce instead. Listen, I've just sent you a photo of the painting Nils de Jong gave to Grant Ledwell – copied to give to him, I mean – and now I need you to make notes of everything that's just happened while I can still remember it all, because I haven't got time to do it myself. Pez is waiting for me in the bar.'

'Go,' said Strike.

Robin rattled through Ormond's visit to Pez, everything she could remember about Nils's ramblings on Edie's death, described Josh's room in detail and finished with a brief account of Bram's behaviour, culminating in his accusation against Zoe. Throughout, she could hear the rapid scratching of Strike's pen.

'Jesus Christ, that's enough to be going on with,' said Strike when she'd finished. 'Well done.'

'So you need to log into the game right now,' Robin continued. 'Last time I looked, Anomie wasn't in there, but that's over three hours ago.'

'Becoming Buffypaws as I speak,' said Strike, and she heard his fingers tapping the keyboard.

'OK, I'll call you once drinks are over.'

'Right you are. Good luck.'

Robin hung up, left the cubicle, checked her reflection in the mirror to make sure neither her wig nor her contact lenses had shifted, set her mobile to record, replaced it in her bag, hoping it would pick up Pez's conversation over the noise of the pub, then headed back out of the bathroom.

Pez was sitting at a circular table for two in a far corner, beside a window, a glass of red wine and a pint of lager in front of him. He'd moved his chair closer to Robin's, so that instead of sitting opposite each other they were virtually side by side.

'So,' said Robin, smiling as she sat down, shrugging off her black suede jacket as she did so – Pez's eyes travelled automatically to her breasts and back to her eyes – 'what was that about Nils telling people their races?'

Close to, Robin could smell Pez's body odour again. His bare arms were muscled, his fingernails dirty. Take away the jeans and T-shirt and he'd look like a Caravaggio saint, with his large dark mournful eyes and the tangle of black curly hair.

'He divides people he meets into races,' said Pez, then, seeing Robin's expression, added, 'only white Europeans, like. He gorrit out of an old book. Yeah, six races of white Europeans. He reads weird stuff nobody else has ever heard of and he loves an argument, even if he's stoned. Contrarian, like.'

'So when he told me you're a typical Western man, was that the race thing?'

'Ha, did he?' said Pez with a slight eye-roll. 'Yeah. I'm a Western man. Small and dark.'

Robin almost said, 'You're not small,' but bit the words back before she could speak them: she'd been thinking of height, but the words might have been interpreted in a quite different way.

'Everyone's short compared to Nils, though,' she said.

'Yeah, but Westerns are Latin-looking and emotional, and they like spectacle.'

'So what race does Nils think *he* is?'

'Nordic,' said Pez. 'Big blond warrior-creator. Best race to be, obviously.'

'So it's all a joke, but Nils comes from the master race?' said Robin. Pez laughed.

'Yeah. Mariam gets really pissed off when he starts on the race stuff, but Nils says she's just pissed off because she's a Dinaric type, and they're inferior to Nordics.'

Robin laughed along with him, though she didn't find it very funny.

'One time, Nils told this old guy in a wheelchair – it was an end of term party, we have them all the time, any excuse – he was a classic Alpine. That's a real inside joke for the North Grovers, because anyone Nils doesn't like, he says they're an Alpine, like. Alpine's basically code, like, for "boring arsehole". Petit bourgeois, narrow-minded.'

Robin, who was wondering whether the putative Alpine could possibly have been Inigo Upcott, laughed on cue.

'But the funny thing was, this old bloke knew the book where Nils had gorrit from, ha ha ha, so he knew Nils was saying he was conventional an' sluggish an' wharrever else Alpines are. Why aren't you drinking your wine?'

'I am,' said Robin, taking a sip. 'So did the man in the wheelchair say, "How dare you call me sluggish and narrow-minded"?'

'No, he said' – Pez affected a tone of pompous outrage – '"The racial theories of Mister Wharrever-the-Old-Fascist's-Called have been entirely discredited," and wheeled himself away. I gorrin a row with the same guy later about the Beatles and after that he told his wife it was time to go and he wheeled himself out of there and we never saw him again, ha ha.'

'Which of you liked the Beatles and which didn't?' said Robin.

'Oh, we both liked 'em,' said Pez. 'Beatles, innit? I can't remember how we got there now, but we ended up arguing about which album's only got songs by McCartney and Lennon on it. I was right,' said Pez. '*Hard Day's Night.* Birrof a fuckin' cliché, being from Liverpool and liking the Beatles, but—'

He pulled down the neck of his T-shirt to expose the fine circle of print running around the base of his strong throat. Robin leaned slightly closer to read it, and with a swift dip of the head Pez had kissed her.

In the whole course of her life, Robin Ellacott had had a sum total of two men's tongues in her mouth: that of her husband, whom she'd started dating at seventeen, and that of the boy she'd dated at fifteen, whose kisses had been sloppier than those of her family's Labrador. For a fraction of a second she tensed, but Jessica Robins wasn't Robin Ellacott: she'd had all the boyfriends Robin hadn't; she'd been on Tinder; she'd visited London clubs with her girlfriends, so Robin reciprocated with feigned enthusiasm, while Pez put his hand into her hair to hold her head stationary, his lips pressed hard against hers, his tongue working in her mouth so that she tasted lager she hadn't drunk and felt Pez's hot breath on her upper lip.

When she considered that Jessica – who had all the experience Robin lacked, but was no pushover – had had enough, she pulled away, and Pez released her, his hand running through the wig, which thankfully was made of human hair. Robin had had to justify the expense when she'd bought it, but she'd told Strike that, up close, the synthetic ones just weren't the same.

'You are fucking gorgeous,' said Pez in a husky voice.

'I was only trying to read your tattoo,' said Robin demurely.

'"*It's getting hard to be someone, But it all works out, It doesn't matter much to me*",' he quoted. '"Strawberry Fields Forever". It runs all the way around the back of me neck.'

'*Doesn't* it matter much to you?' asked Robin, wondering how best to work the Strokes into the conversation.

'Not much,' said Pez. 'Why? You like men who drive big cars and earn big bucks?'

'No, they bore the crap out of me,' said Robin and Pez let out a shout of laughter. If this were a genuine date, Robin thought, while her heart thumped fast with a mixture of nerves and exhilaration, she'd be doing exceptionally well. 'So, how did you end up living at North Grove?'

'I were in here one night and I met a guy who lived there, when I was struggling to make rent. He's left now, bur'ee told me they had a spare room. I went along and met Nils, he liked me and said, "Yeah, come join us," like. Been there ever since. Where d'you live?'

'Kentish Town,' said Robin, who'd prepared her answer.

'Yeah, Zoe told me you were near her,' said Pez. 'Alone?'

'No, I've got two flatmates,' said Robin, with the objective of stymying any suggestion they retire to her flat for some privacy. 'Nils says Zoe's ill today.'

'Is she?' said Pez, without much interest. 'Well, she's anorexic, like. Never eats. Typical *Ink Black Heart* fan.'

'What d'you mean?'

'They're all fucked-up, the ones who really ger'into it. Looking for something, like. Self-harm and all that. Why aren't you drinking your wine?'

'I am,' said Robin, although in truth she'd had only three sips, whereas Pez had nearly finished his pint. 'I'm not a big drinker.'

'We'll have to do something about that,' said Pez.

'Has anyone called Zoe to see whether she's OK?'

'Mariam, probably,' said Pez. He drank the rest of his pint straight off. 'Needed that,' he said, and Robin wondered whether it was the conversation with Ormond that had made him crave alcohol.

'I'll get you another one,' said Robin.

'You haven't even—'

'Not a competition, is it?' asked Robin, smiling, and Pez smiled back.

'OK, cheers.'

She stood up and headed for the bar, feeling Pez's eyes on her back as she went. She'd deliberately ignored his first reference to *The Ink Black Heart* and intended to reintroduce the subject only once he'd had a bit more to drink.

When Robin returned with his pint, Pez reached out and took her free hand as she sat down.

'You aren't what I thought you'd be,' he said, considering her with a slight smile on his face.

'Why, did you think I was an Alpine?' said Robin as she allowed him to interlace his fingers with hers.

'No,' said Pez, grinning, 'bur' I thought you'd be more uptight, like.'

'I'm very uptight,' said Robin. 'You must've brought something out in me.'

Pez laughed. His hand was hot and dry.

'So, d'you get back to Liverpool much?' she asked, thinking of Pez's Instagram page, which revealed month-long sojourns in his home city.

'Yeah,' he said. 'Me old man's got motor neurone disease. He's widowed, like. On his own.'

'Oh, that's sad,' said Robin, disconcerted.

'Me sister mostly looks after him, but she's gor two autistic kids, so I go home sometimes to do my bit. Give her a break, like.'

'That's really good of you,' said Robin. 'Wow . . . you aren't what I thought you'd be either.'

'Yeah?' said Pez, staring at her with a half-smile, his warm fingers tight in hers. 'What's *that* mean, like?'

'You're kind,' said Robin. 'Decent. I thought you were . . . I don't know . . . an artist-playboy.'

'Why? Because I got me kit off for the art class?'

'Oh, I was fine with that,' said Robin, and Pez laughed again. 'So, what other music do you like?'

'Anything good, I don't care,' said Pez with a shrug. 'So, when did you break up with your boyfriend?'

''Bout six months ago,' said Robin. 'What about you?'

'Haven't seen anyone properly for over a year. I do all right, though.'

'I'll bet you do,' said Robin, and Pez pulled her in for another kiss. As she feigned enthusiasm, his teeth clashing with hers as he pressed her face to his, his hand at the back of her head again, Robin wished he'd stop touching her wig, and couldn't help suspecting that she was being used, like the lager, to distract Pez from his worries. There was a certain recklessness about this no-holds-barred technique. Once again, she was the one who broke contact, and he emitted a small groan as she did so.

'I don't normally do this kind of thing by daylight,' she whispered, glancing around at the other drinkers. Two middle-aged men at the bar had evidently been watching the clinch and wore smiles of vicarious pleasure. Pez, who'd now shifted his chair even closer to hers, slid his arm around her, thumb caressing her shoulder blade.

'No problem,' he said. 'It'll be dark soon.'

'Drink your pint,' said Robin, 'and tell me about your work. Mariam said you're really good.'

'I am,' said Pez. 'Jus' can't get anything steady, like. Partly 'cause I gorra keep goin' home to look after me da'. He's lasted a lot longer'n they thought he would when he was diagnosed. I've gorra couple of things in the pipeline, though – maybe. Depends.'

'Show me some of your stuff,' Robin said. 'Bet you're on Instagram.'

'I am, yeah,' said Pez.

He had to take his hand from around her to take out his mobile and bring up Instagram.

'There ya go.'

He slid the phone towards her.

'*Wow*,' said Robin.

She wasn't feigning enthusiasm this time: the pictures were all extremely accomplished. As she scrolled slowly through line drawings, fantasy art, anime, short cartoon clips in different styles, Pez leaned nearer again, putting his arm over the back of her chair, and told her about each one.

'That was a comic-book commission ... That was for an advert, but the client didn't like it. Still got paid, though ... That was for an indie game developer that went bust. I'm still tryna find out if I can get me stuff back ...'

'Did you do all this at North Grove?'

'Most of it, yeah. Nils has got all the latest tech.'

'Pretty,' said Robin, pausing on a familiar face. Kea Niven's heart-shaped face was looking up out of a cartoonish portrait of a black-haired woman in long, slinky green robes, most of her breasts exposed. A huge sickle moon hung in the night sky behind her.

'Lunatic,' said Pez with another snort. 'She was dating a guy at the collective. I needed a model for a sexy witch, so I asked her to pose. She only agreed to try and make her boyfriend jealous. Gor uptight when he didn't wanna come and watch. He was copping off with another girl while she was downstairs with me in the studio.'

'Ouch,' said Robin.

'Yeah,' said Pez, smirking. 'After he ditched her, she come round North Grove to "ger some stuff back", and when she got to his room the door was locked and she heard 'em fucking, so she come running into mine in hysterics. Twenty minutes in there, she launches herself at me – bur' I don't like 'em crazy.'

Noting that this was an exact reversal of the story Kea had told Strike, in which Pez had made the pass and Kea rebuffed him, Robin kept scrolling down through the Instagram page, looking for anything she could use as a pretext for leading the conversation back to *The Ink Black Heart*.

'Is that Nils's cat? The one that's gone missing?'

'Yeah,' said Pez, looking down at the picture of the sleeping tortoiseshell cat. 'I was tryna gerra commission to illustrate a kids' book about pets. I don't like cats, I'm allergic. Maybe they could tell, and that's why I never gor the job. That thing's only gor one eye, but you can't see when it's asleep.'

'How did it lose an eye?'

'Dunno, never asked ... It's been away nearly a week. It's either been run over or Bram's strangled it.'

'What?' said Robin, pretending to be shocked.

'He's a little psycho. I'm moving out soon as he reaches six foot. Probably be next Tuesday, the way he's growing ... Yeah, that's enough of that,' he said suddenly, placing his hand over hers as an angular black-and-white figure in a long Victorian tailcoat appeared.

'I was enjoying looking at it!'

'And I was enjoying the other stuff and you stopped me,' said Pez, smiling as he slid his mobile back into the pocket of his jeans.

'So,' said Robin, as Pez began caressing her back with his thumb again, 'did you give that man back the thing he was after?'

'No,' said Pez, his smile fading at once.

'What was it?'

'Nuthing. I lost it. Burrit wasn't his.' After a brief hesitation he added, 'His girlfriend gave it me.'

'Oh,' said Robin. 'But then – why would he—?'

'His girlfriend was Edie Ledwell. The girl who did *The Ink Black Heart*. The one who was murdered.'

'*Oh*,' said Robin again. 'Poor man!'

'What?' said Pez, and then, 'Oh. Yer, I s'pose.'

Pez drank a lot more of his pint, while Robin's mind worked fast.

'Look,' she said, having taken a swift decision, 'er – since you've mentioned her – I – I didn't know whether I should tell you this, but it kind of creeped me out.'

'What did?'

'Well, I *do* know what that boy was talking about, back there.'

'Who, Bram?'

'Yeah. He just told me Zoe killed that girl. Edie.'

For a moment, Pez simply stared at Robin.

'Bram said Zoe killed Edie?'

'Yes,' said Robin. 'I mean, obviously I didn't *believe* him. It was just an odd thing for a kid to say.'

'Jesus Christ,' muttered Pez, removing his arm from around the back of Robin's chair to run his hands through his curly black hair before draining the rest of his second pint.

'I shouldn't have told you,' said Robin quietly.

'I just thought I could have one evening without thinking about it, like.'

'Oh, I – I'm sorry I mentioned it,' said Robin, now allowing the faintest note of grievance to creep into her voice. It wasn't Jessica Robins's fault she'd been taken into that burned-out bedroom by a disturbed child and been burdened with talk of murder. Jessica Robins was taken aback by this sudden change of tone, and starting to think Pez wasn't the amusing and charming man she'd taken him for.

'No,' said Pez quickly, 'don't – it's not your fault. It's just been horrible. Since it happened. Everyone wants to talk about it all the fucking time and what's the fucking point? I mean, she's fucking dead, isn't she? Talking about it all the fucking time isn't gonna bring her back . . . Bram doesn't like Zoe, that's all. She babysits him sometimes. He doesn't like anyone who tries to tell him what to do. You've seen her: she couldn't fucking lift a machete, let alone fucking use one . . . You *ever* gonna finish that wine?'

'Yes,' said Robin, careful to keep just the right amount of reserve in her voice.

'Sorry,' said Pez, now looking partly contrite, partly irritable. 'It's been – we've all been through it, since it happened. I had the police talk to me.'

'Seriously?'

'Yeah. They talked to everyone who knew Josh and Edie, like. Even Mariam.'

'You're kidding!'

'Nope. She knew Josh and Edie were meeting in the cemetery that afternoon, see. But she was taking an afternoon class when it happened. Special-needs class. Kids. I were in the studio working on me comic-book idea.'

'The time-travelling undertaker?'

'Yeah,' said Pez, although he didn't look particularly flattered that Robin had remembered. 'Anyway, people saw me, like, passing the door, so I was in the clear for murder. But then the pigs wanted to know if I was this troll who was persecuting Edie on Twitter.'

He gave a snort of derision.

'I shared a fucking building with her for three years – if I wanted to harass her, I'd hardly need to go on the fucking internet. Anyway, I know who that troll was, it's not hard to fucking work out.'

'Who was it?' said Robin, trying to keep her voice casual.

'Bloke called Wally Cardew,' said Pez without a second's pause for thought.

'Did you tell the police that?'

'Yeah. Told 'em I knew it was him all along. Anomie – that's what the troll's called—'

'Anomie?' said Robin. 'That's weird. Nils was just—'

'Yeah, the name was one of the reasons I knew it was Wally. I heard Nils explaining it to him – he'll have gorrit off the window in the kitchen.'

'Oh, you know this guy personally?'

'Yeah, we were both in *The Ink Black Heart*, like. Voiced characters. I was only in a couple of episodes, because I had to go back and look after me da' for a bit, and when I got back someone else had taken over, doing a fake fucking Scouse accent.'

From his expression, Robin deduced that Pez hadn't been happy about this.

'Wally's gorra mate who can code – I remember him telling me about the guy trying to get some game made by a developer – and this troll, Anomie, runs an online game based on the cartoon, with a mate. So, yeah – not rocket science, is it?

'Gonna get another pint,' said Pez. 'Sure you don't want another wine?'

'No, I'll finish this first,' said Robin.

Pez went to the bar, while Robin's mind raced. Several of the things Pez had just said about himself fitted the tentative profile of Anomie she and Strike had come up with, and yet she'd imagined that if she sat face to face with Anomie she'd feel it, know it instinctively, because the malevolence and sadism they'd displayed during their long persecution of Edie Ledwell would leak from them, however cunningly they might try to conceal it. Pez Pierce might not have been her ideal drinking companion, but she couldn't imagine him devoting hours of his life to the game, or to a relentless campaign of harassment conducted over Twitter. He was a gifted artist, a success with women, a lover of music: he seemed to Robin to live a mostly satisfying life in the physical world and not to need the dubious pleasures of an anonymous online persona.

When he returned to the table and sat down, Robin said:

'Why did they replace you on the cartoon? Wouldn't it have been better to use someone who's genuinely from Liverpool than someone faking the accent? I *hate* people imitating my accent,' she added. 'There's a guy at work who thinks it's really funny to start up with the "ee bah gum" stuff whenever I speak in a meeting.'

'Fucking Londoners, innit?' said Pez. He drank from his fresh pint. 'Edie said they didn't know when I'd be back from me da's, so they went on without me. Let's not talk about that fucking cartoon,' he added. 'I told you, I wanna night off.'

'OK,' said Robin, taking care to look taken aback and a little offended again.

'Ah, no – look, I'm sorry,' said Pez, unbending at once in the face of her coolness. 'I just – I still can't get me head round it, like. Wor 'appened.'

'Well, I'm not surprised,' said Robin. 'It's horrendous.'

Pez slid his arm over the back of her chair again.

'Did I mention you're fucking gorgeous?'

Robin let him press his mouth to hers again. This kiss was gentler, not a protracted affair of clashing teeth, tongue and saliva, which seemed only appropriate, mere seconds after discussion of murder. When Pez had released her, Robin said quietly,

'Maybe it would help you to talk about it.'

'Offering to be my therapist?' he asked, looking into her eyes while stroking her shoulder blade.

'Well, I'm not licensed,' said Robin, 'but on the bright side, I offer services you can't get on the NHS.'

He let out another shout of laughter, and before he could ask exactly what she was thinking of, Robin said seriously,

'Maybe you *should* speak to someone. This must have been really traumatic for you, and you've got enough stress in your life, haven't you, with your dad being ill and everything?'

He looked slightly taken aback by that.

'Why did you and your boyfriend split up?'

'He cheated,' said Robin, 'with a friend of mine. Why're you asking that?'

'Because you're gorgeous *and* sweet. He must've been a right dick.'

Oh, not again, thought Robin, as Pez moved in for yet another kiss. It was the longest so far: at least he wasn't touching her hair, but as his mouth ground against hers harder than ever and his tongue moved in her mouth, he slid both arms around her, so that he almost pulled her out of her chair.

'Control yourself,' she whispered against his mouth, half laughing as she extricated herself with some difficulty. 'God. People are staring.'

'Just wanted some of that non-NHS therapy.'

'You've forgotten the talking part,' said Robin, and mainly to stop him kissing her again she now downed the rest of her glass of wine, while Pez continued to stroke her upper back.

'That's the spirit,' he said, watching her drink.

'I wasn't kidding,' said Robin lightly. 'You've been through some-thing horrible. I can tell you're upset.'

'Ar, don't go thinking I've lost me best friend,' said Pez roughly. 'I fell out with her long before it happened.'

'Why?' asked Robin.

'You don't wanna hear about that,' said Pez. 'Trust me. You don't wanna know.'

'OK,' said Robin, and once again she allowed a little more coolness into her voice, as well as a trace of hurt. Jessica Robins didn't like being treated as though she ranked only slightly higher than a pint of lager in terms of distractions. She liked a bit of conversation before being persuaded into bed. After a few seconds' charged silence, Pez said,

'All right, bur I warned you. OK, well – one of the other guys voicing one of the characters on the cartoon was hanging round in the computer room at North Grove, waiting for his scene or wharrever. I walked in and I noticed him shut down what he was looking at pretty fast, like, and I was curious, like. Never liked this guy. Public school, rich parents, tryna tell everyone else how much privilege they had. One time Wally dug up a picture of this guy's prep school. Gorrit off the internet, like. Blew it up an' stuck it on the wall with Tim's face pasted over one of these little pricks in their little pink caps, an' he wrote over it, "Tim learning to despise white cis-het privilege".'

Robin laughed.

'Tim didn't like that,' said Pez with a certain satisfaction. 'Norrat all. I've met people like him on jobs. Middle-class arseholes who resent you for growing up working class. Like they think you're showing off. Trying to get an unfair advantage in the oppression stakes or something.'

Robin laughed again.

'Anyway . . . d'you know what lolicon is?'

'No, what is it?'

'It's cartoons of little girls. Drawings of them doing stuff. You know – sexy stuff. It's a Japanese thing, or that's where it started. It's all over the net now.'

'*Oh*,' said Robin, her mind now racing. 'I mean . . . gross.'

'Yeah . . . so that's what Timmy Superwoke was looking at when I walked in. He didn't have time to wipe the history, because Edie come in right after me and told him she needed him for the scene, like. I went straight over and checked what he'd been browsing.

'Anyway, I told Edie what he'd been looking at, once they'd all gone home, like, and we had a row. She didn't believe me. She fuckin' hero-worshipped this guy. She always wanted to be liked by clever people. She'd never done A levels or nothing. No higher education. She couldn't see this Tim guy was a prick. She thought he was clever just because he's got that kind of accent, like.

'But she went and asked him about wor I'd said. He said I was lying, and she believed him. Then we had a proper row, because I said if he was kinky for kids, she shouldn't be bringing him into North Grove to help with children's classes, like. I know it was only drawings,' said Pez, 'but some of it was proper hardcore. She told me I was bitter and all sorts of shit.'

'Why would she think you were bitter?' asked Robin, sounding suitably indignant on Pez's behalf.

'Because they'd had the big success, I s'pose,' said Pez darkly. 'So after tha', we didn't talk a lot.'

He drank some more beer, looking sullen, then went on,

'See, before she met Josh – that's the guy she did the cartoon with – we had a kind of thing going. Not serious. And we were working on a thing togeth—'

Pez cut himself off.

'And now I've gor her fucking boyfriend coming round tryna make me hand over what's mine. Well, he can fuck *right* off,' said Pez, though Robin thought she detected some unease beneath the anger and bravado. 'It's mine and I'm fucking keeping it.'

So you haven't lost it, thought Robin, but sweet, kind Jessica Robins expressed only sympathy for her date's justifiable resentment, before offering to buy him a fourth pint.

68

The jealous doubt, the burning pain,
That rack the lover's heart and brain;
The fear that will not own it fear,
The hope that cannot disappear . . .

Letitia Elizabeth Landon
The Troubadour, Canto 2

Tired of the confines of the office and his attic flat, Strike had decided to spend the evening at The Tottenham, where he could enjoy a couple of pints while continuing his online investigations. However, The Tottenham had been atypically full for a Thursday night, so he'd headed instead to The Angel, only to find a sign on the bar declaring that the use of mobiles and laptops was forbidden in the establishment.

His craving for beer increasing with each thwarted attempt to get some, he came to rest at last in The Cambridge, a large and noisy pub situated on the edge of Theatreland, where he'd no sooner sat down with his first pint of Doom Bar than Robin had called, asking him to take over as Buffypaws in *Drek's Game*. In consequence, he'd had to abandon the lines of investigation he'd planned and had spent the last two hours pretending to be Buffypaws in the company of successive pints, and a burger and chips. Other than one private-channel conversation with Fiendy1, his stint in the game had been uneventful, Anomie absent throughout.

At a quarter to ten, with Strike still in The Cambridge and becoming increasingly bored of the game, his mobile rang.

'Strike.'

'Evening,' said Nutley. 'Got a bit on Kea Niven.'

Strike had sent their newest subcontractor to King's Lynn in the hope of finally ruling Kea out of the investigation. The choice of Nutley had been largely dictated by Strike's desire to keep the man out of his own vicinity.

'Go on,' said Strike, picking up a pen and drawing his notebook closer to him.

'She's been out for a drink with some friends,' said Nutley. 'Local wine bar.'

'Walking all right, then, is she?' asked Strike.

'She's got a stick with her,' said Nutley, 'and her mates have been going up and down to the bar for her.'

He waited to be prompted. This habit was one of many of Nutley's that Strike found extremely irritating.

'Is that it?'

'No,' said Nutley, sounding amused that Strike could think so. ''Bout twenty minutes ago, her mobile rang and she went outside the bar to take the call. I went too. Pretended I wanted a fag.'

Nutley paused to be praised for his initiative. When Strike's only response was silence, Nutley continued,

'Yeah, so she was talking to someone on the phone and got kind of hysterical. Wanting to know why they hadn't called her back sooner and stuff. She was saying she's got to get a message to Josh and wanted this person to arrange it. She said people on Edit are saying terrible things about her and they aren't true and it's all been faked, or something. And,' said Nutley, with the air of a man about to produce a rabbit out of a hat, 'she said she thinks Anomie's behind it. The stuff on Edit.'

'You sure she wasn't saying "Reddit"?' asked Strike, not bothering to keep the exasperation out of his voice.

'What?'

'*Reddit*,' repeated Strike.

'Yeah, it might've been,' said Nutley, after considering the point for a few seconds, 'but like I say, she was kind of hysterical, it was hard to hear exactly what she was going on about. They're all arty types, though, aren't they, so I thought Edit might be some kind of—'

'Did you get the name of the person she was talking to?'

'Didn't hear her say a name.'

Of course you fucking didn't.

'OK, good job, Nutley,' said Strike, his tone contradicting his words. 'Write it up for the file and call me if anything else happens.'

Once Nutley had rung off, Strike turned back to *Drek's Game*, very much wishing he too had somebody he could send up and down to the bar in his stead. The surrounding tables were full of people laughing and talking: he was the only solitary drinker, a forty-year-old oddball with his laptop, gaming alone while craving a smoke. He'd just avoided being attacked by a digital vampire, then successfully steered Buffypaws past a stone lion with the help of Robin's cheat sheet ('type "You is bad stony mukfluk, bwah"') when a text arrived from his half-sister Prudence.

He still hadn't met her, of course. While he'd been laid up with his leg and overwhelmed by work, she'd been preoccupied with her injured daughter.

Hi. Sylvie's doing much better, so I wondered how you might be fixed for next Thursday for a quick drink?

Deciding he needn't answer immediately, Strike returned his attention to his laptop screen. Five minutes later, his mobile buzzed with a second text, then rang before he could look at it: it was Robin calling, so he answered immediately.

'Hi,' she said. 'I've just left Pez. Has Anomie been in the game?'

'No,' said Strike, and Robin groaned. 'But I've had a one-on-one chat with Fiendy1, who knows his football, I must say. Sanest person I've met on here so far. You should've told me Buffypaws was a Man U supporter, though.'

'Shit, wasn't that in the notes? Sorry. It was the first team I could think of.'

"S'fine, I got by,' said Strike. 'I'd've thought it was only polite to make it Arsenal, though. How was Pez?'

'I've just sent you a recording of the interview. I haven't listened back to it, so I don't know how much my mobile picked up. The pub was quite noisy.'

'Having the same problem,' said Strike, raising his voice over a gaggle of particularly raucous people who'd just arrived at the next table.

'I'll write up my notes as soon as I can, just in case it hasn't recorded. I got some interesting stuff out of him.'

'Where are you right now?' asked Strike, who thought he could hear traffic.

'Heading for Junction Road,' said Robin. 'Trying to flag down a cab.'

'The hell are you going to Junction Road for?'

'It might be nothing, but I've got a feel— Strike, that's a cab. I'll see you at the office tomorrow and we can catch up.'

Robin waved at the approaching cab, which slowed, gave the driver the address and got in.

Though she'd done her best to sound natural on the phone, she was feeling definitely flustered. The last hour of her supposed interview with Pez, which she'd edited out of the recording she'd sent Strike, had consisted largely of prolonged bouts of kissing and increasingly determined attempts to get her back to North Grove 'just for another drink, like'. Robin was prepared to do a lot for the Strike Detective Agency and had an eight-inch-long scar on her forearm to prove it, but she didn't think sleeping with Pez Pierce lay within the scope of duties Strike could reasonably expect of her, even if spending the night with him might have enabled them to rule him out as Anomie.

As the cab moved off along Highgate High Street, Robin reflected that she was collecting quite a range of male reactions to rejection lately. Pez's had fallen about midway between Hugh Jacks's cold fury and Ryan Murphy's awkward, immediate retreat. He'd tried manipulation ('Wha', you think you can't trust me, like?'), passive-aggression ('No, I jus' thought you were into me, like') and, finally, a request for her number. Robin had given him the one belonging to the burner phone she'd used with Tim Ashcroft and Yasmin Weatherhead, and, after another clinch outside The Gatehouse, during which Pez pressed her so hard against his body she could feel every muscle through his T-shirt, she'd left at last.

Half-guilty, half-pleasurable confused and confusing thoughts jostled in Robin's head as the taxi bore her on towards Zoe's flat. Pez Pierce wasn't the kind of man she generally found attractive: she wasn't a fan of filthy fingernails or a strong, unwashed smell; she didn't particularly like him, nor had she once forgotten that she was there to extract information from him. However, while his tongue had been probing the deepest recesses of her mouth and his hands caressing her back, her body, which had forgone any form of sexual contact for three years, hadn't much cared what her brain was up to. The slightly uncomfortable truth was that her physical response to Pez hadn't been entirely feigned. Robin wasn't sure whether she felt more abashed or proud, because Pez Pierce, a man with (she suspected) an extensive sexual history, didn't seem to have detected anything in her responses that gave away a lack of experience. This last reflection led her straight back to the memory of that moment outside the Ritz with Strike; fortunately for her peace of mind, the cab completed the short journey to Junction Road at this point, drawing up beside the shabby corner building where Zoe Haigh lived.

A light was shining in one of the second-floor windows, at which hung a thin pink curtain. Robin walked around the corner into Brookside Lane and examined the buzzers beside the door she'd seen Zoe enter. Zoe's name wasn't beside any of them, so, hazarding a guess, she pressed the top one.

Nobody answered. Robin pressed again. Another minute passed. Of course, the building was in such poor repair it was perfectly possible the bell didn't work. Robin pressed a third time.

'Hello?' said Zoe's voice, sounding tinny over the intercom.

'Zoe, hi,' said Robin, broadening her Yorkshire accent again. 'It's Jessica, from North Grove? I was just passing on my way home and wondered if you were OK. They told me you were ill.'

'Oh,' said Zoe. 'Yeah, I'm fine. Just – just a stomach upset.'

'Is there anything you need?'

'I – no. Thanks a lot, though,' said Zoe.

'OK, well, hope you feel better soon,' said Robin.

'Yeah. Thanks,' said Zoe.

Robin now crossed to the opposite pavement, eyes on Zoe's window. The silhouette of a person passed behind the thin pink curtain. It looked too large to be Zoe's. Glancing around to make sure she wasn't being observed, Robin carefully removed the brunette wig and put it into her bag, then took out her hazel contact lenses. Now, if anybody looked down into the dark street, they'd merely see a blonde woman, apparently waiting for a lift.

A full hour passed. Nobody entered or left the building. Still Robin waited.

At ten to midnight, a young black man approached the door and unlocked it. Robin dashed across the road.

'Sorry, d'you mind if I come in? I've left my front door keys at my friend's place and she's not answering the doorbell.'

The young man made no objection.

The hallway was dirty and the uncarpeted concrete stairs littered with cigarette butts and the odd food wrapper. The stairwell smelled as though at least one person had used it as a urinal.

Robin climbed the narrow stairs behind the tenant, who disappeared through a door on the first-floor landing, leaving Robin to proceed up to the second floor alone, turning her mobile to silent as she went.

As Robin approached the top landing, she saw, by the light of a single unshaded lightbulb hanging from the ceiling, two doors, one closed, the other ajar. The latter revealed a cupboard-sized bathroom, its walls covered in grubby, cracked tiles, a shower head dangling over the toilet beneath. Robin doubted the conversion had been legal.

The closed door looked as though it could be forced open with one good kick. Well aware of the risk she was taking, Robin crept towards it and pressed her ear to the crack where the cheap wooden door met the frame.

She could hear a male voice. The cadence sounded angry, but the speaker, perhaps aware of how far sound would travel inside this shoddily built building, hadn't raised his voice loudly enough for Robin to catch more than a few words.

'. . . play-acting . . . free choice . . . pressuring me . . .'

Robin checked her phone again. It was now past midnight. Zoe's guest might be planning to stay the night, but his tone was far from lover-like. Robin remained where she was, ear pressed against the crack in the door.

'. . . do me harm . . .'

Now Zoe's voice rose, high-pitched and tearful, far easier to hear than the man's.

'I *never* wanted to hurt you, ever!'

'Keep your bloody voice down!'

Zoe complied, but Robin could tell by the rise and fall of her voice that she was pleading, the words indistinguishable.

Then Robin heard footsteps from inside the room: they seemed to be approaching the door.

She retreated down the concrete stairs as quietly as possible and had reached the first-floor landing before she heard Zoe's door open.

'No, please,' she heard the girl saying. '*Please* don't go—'

'Get off me. *Get off.* You start threatening—'

'I wasn't, I wasn't threatening, I was only—'

'*Who started this?*'

'I did, I did, I know—'

'I told you at the time, I was the one taking the fucking risk—'

Robin kept descending, trying to make as little noise as possible, until she reached the ground floor, where she pressed herself against the wall so that she wouldn't be visible if either Zoe or her companion looked down into the stairwell.

'Please stay, please, I didn't mean it, I just—'

'It's late. I've got to go. I've got a lot of thinking to do.'

'No,' wailed Zoe, and her voice echoed off the dingy walls.

'I said, *keep your fucking voice down!*'

There was the sound of scuffling. Under cover of the noise, Robin quietly opened the door onto the street and stood, still listening, ready to escape.

'*Get off me.* You've put me in a hell of a fucking position and now you're blackmailing—'

'I'm *not*,' wailed Zoe.

Heavy footsteps were now descending the stairs. Robin slid out of the door, stripped off the jacket Jessica Robins had worn on every trip to North Grove, hurried to a position ten yards away and bowed her head, pretending to be looking at her phone.

Peering through the hair now hiding her face, Robin watched Tim Ashcroft stride out of the building and head towards a parked Fiat. Seconds later, a sobbing, barefooted Zoe followed. She tried to stop Ashcroft entering the car, but he threw her off with ease, and having slammed the door in her face drove away, but not before Robin had snatched a picture of his car.

Zoe stood shivering and crying in the road until the car had disappeared from sight, her emaciated silhouette that of a twelve-year-old girl. Robin quickly bowed her head again as Zoe re-entered the building, without having given the blonde woman a single glance.

Once the door had closed, Robin pulled out her notebook and pen, dropped into a crouch, rested the notebook on her knee and scribbled everything she could remember of the small amount of the argument she'd heard. *Blackmail . . . who started this? . . . you put me in a hell of a position . . . I was the one who took the risk . . .*

She got back to her feet again and checked the time on her phone. She'd have liked to call Strike immediately, but it was surely too late: he'd be asleep.

Little though she knew it, Robin's assumption was wrong. At that moment, her partner, who'd left The Cambridge an hour previously, was wide awake and sitting smoking at his small kitchen table. In front of him lay his mobile and notebook, the latter open to a double page he'd just filled with questions and observations about the recording of Robin's interview with Pez, which her phone had picked up reasonably well, given the background noise of the pub.

While Robin was flagging down a cab to take her back to Walthamstow, Strike was frowning slightly as he replayed the recording repeatedly, searching for the parts of the recording in which he was particularly interested.

A long silence, followed by Pez saying in a husky voice,

'*You are fucking gorgeous.*'

'*I was only trying to read your tattoo,*' said Robin, her voice slightly arch. Strike fast-forwarded.

'*You're kind. Decent. I thought you were ... I don't know ... an artist-playboy.*'

'*Why? Because I got me kit off for the art class?*'

'*Oh, I was fine with that,*' said Robin. Pez laughed. Strike fast-forwarded again.

'*Haven't seen anyone properly for over a year. I do all right, though.*'

'*I'll bet you do,*' said Robin with a laugh in her voice.

Another long silence, followed by what sounded like a moan from Pez. Then Robin whispered something Strike couldn't catch. Three times he replayed the recording, finally deciding that what Robin had said was:

'*I don't normally do this kind of thing by daylight.*'

Which made sense of Pez's rejoinder:

'*No problem. It'll be dark soon.*'

He fast-forwarded again.

'*Did I mention you're fucking gorgeous?*'

Another long pause. Then Robin said:

'*Maybe it would help you to talk about it.*'

Strike fast-forwarded again.

'*Well, I'm not licensed, but on the bright side, I offer services you can't get on the NHS.*'

He'd never heard Robin talk like that, never imagined she could flirt that well. He'd thought ... what? That she was some innocent schoolgirl?

Strike had told himself there were good reasons she might have been panicked by his ill-advised approach outside the Ritz, but now he learned that she was perfectly prepared to accept a sexual overture if it advanced a case . . . or, perhaps, if it was made by a muscular young artist whom, apparently, she'd already seen naked.

'*Because you're gorgeous* and *sweet. He must've been a right dick.*'

Another long silence. Then Robin's voice:

'*Control yourself . . . God. People are staring.*'

'*Just wanted some of that non-NHS therapy.*'

Strike sat smoking and scowling at the kitchen wall for another twenty minutes before rousing himself to go to bed. The awareness that he had no reasonable grounds for complaint – that, far from feeling aggrieved and unsettled, he ought to be congratulating his partner on a job well done – did nothing to restore his equanimity.

69

She served him meekly, anxiously,
With love—half faith—half fear.

Letitia Elizabeth Landon
She Sat Alone Beside Her Hearth

In-game chats between five original moderators and one new moderator of *Drek's Game*

\<Moderator Channel>

\<4 June 2015 23.57>

\<Worm28, Fiendy1, Hartella>

\<Anomie has entered the channel>

\<BorkledDrek has entered the channel>

Anomie: So here he is, our new moderator

Worm28: oh wow hi !!!

Fiendy1: *applauds*

Hartella: congrats, BorkledDrek

BorkledDrek: hey guys

Fiendy1: what score did he get on the test?

\<A new private channel has opened>

\<5 June 2015 00.02>

\<Anomie invites Hartella>

\<Hartella has joined the channel>

Anomie: I'm going to need you to do it again tomorrow. Same times

Hartella: Anomie, I can't. I've got a work

687

presentation

>

>

Anomie: 64%

Anomie: respectable

Worm28: much bettre than I did

Worm28: Fiendy1 got 83 %

BorkledDrek: whoa

Worm28: Anomie, when's Buffypaws going to do the test ?

>

Anomie: week today

Worm28: hey BorkledDrek who did u guess Anomie is?

BorkledDrek: Josh Blay's brother

Fiendy1: lol

Fiendy1: that's a common one, isn't it?

Fiendy1: Hartella guessed that, didn't you?

>

>

Fiendy1: Hartella, you in the bog?

BorkledDrek: lol

Anomie: have to go off sick then, won't you

Hartella: please, Anomie

Hartella: I've been working on it for weeks

Anomie: guessing you haven't been working on your fkn presentation as long as I've been working on the game

Anomie: and you were happy enough to endanger that, weren't you? Talking to fkn journos about me

Hartella: Anomie, I didn't tell her anything that could have identified you

Anomie: 'cultured'

Hartella: why do you want me to do it, anyway?

Anomie: work it out, it's not difficult

Anomie: and you'll do as you're told if you don't want to go to jail, Ms terrorist enabler

<Anomie has left the channel>

<Hartella has left the channel>

<Private channel has

closed>

<Anomie has left the channel>

BorkledDrek: this is so cool, being in here

Fiendy1: d'you like the carpet?

BorkledDrek: lol yeah it's great

BorkledDrek: so who did u guys guess Anomie is?

Fiendy1: Luciano Becchio

BorkledDrek: the footballer?

Fiendy1: yeah, I had no fkn idea

BorkledDrek: lol

BorkledDrek: so when can I start banning people?

Fiendy1: knock yourself out

Fiendy1: we usually wait til they've done something wrong tho

BorkledDrek: lol

\>

\>

\>

\>

\>

<A new private channel has opened>

<5 June 2015 00.06>

<Fiendy1 invites Worm28>

<Worm28 has joined the channel>

>

> Worm28: hey what ' s
up ?

> Fiendy1: do u think
Hartella's all
> right?

> Worm28: what do u mean
?

>

> Fiendy1: she's being
really quiet

> Worm28: I think
she's still sad
> about LordDrek
going

<Paperwhite has joined
the channel>   Fiendy1: yeah maybe

Paperwhite: evening   Fiendy1: oh big fkn
                           surprise
BorkledDrek: hi
                           Fiendy1: her lady
Paperwhite: oh wow, new   ship's arrived to
mod!   flirt with the new
                           boy
BorkledDrek: lol yeah
                           Worm28: she ' s ok
Paperwhite: Morehouse   really
been in?
                           Fiendy1: She's a shit
BorkledDrek: not since   stirrer
I have
                           Worm28: she was nice to
Paperwhite: so I hear   melast nite
you're a good coder
                           Worm28: I was feeling
BorkledDrek: am I   so shit & I came in
allowed to answer   here and she told me
that?   it'd be ok

Paperwhite: what, becos   Fiendy1: fuck's sake
of Rule 14? you said u   Worm you've got low
code in front of Anomie   standards
& he didn't ban u, so
we're ok   Worm28: what 's that
                           sppuosed to mean?
BorkledDrek: lol ok

690

BorkledDrek: yeah I'm a decent coder

BorkledDrek: not as good as them tho

BorkledDrek: Anomie and Morehouse

BorkledDrek: this game's fkn incredible

Paperwhite: make sure you tell them that, they'll love it

<Worm28 has left the channel>

BorkledDrek: I already told Anomie

Paperwhite: no wonder he likes you ;)

BorkledDrek: lol

>

Paperwhite: some prick's trying to get age/sex/location off girls again

Paperwhite: by Stoney

Paperwhite: Drekkk5, see him?

Paperwhite: Want to take him out? Your first banning?

BorkledDrek: haha fkn great

>

>

Fiendy1: anyone can say 'it'll be ok'

Worm28: wat so I ' m pathetic or something am i ?

Fiendy1: no of course not, I'm just

<Worm28 has left the channel>

Fiendy1: oh ffs

<Fiendy1 has left the channel>

<Private channel has closed>

<A new private channel has opened>

<5 June 2015 00.15>

<Fiendy1 invites Hartella>

>

<Hartella has joined the channel>

Fiendy1: U ok?

Fiendy1: you're being really quiet

Hartella: no I'm fine

Hartella: just busy at work

691

Fiendy1: ah ok

>

Hartella: thanx for asking, tho xx

>

<Hartella has left the channel>

BorkledDrek: YES!

Paperwhite: hahaha

<Fiendy1 has left the channel>

BorkledDrek: fkn amazing!

<Private channel has closed>

Fiendy1: what happened?

Fiendy1: Paperwhite send you a nude?

BorkledDrek: what?

BorkledDrek: no

Fiendy1: Give her time

<Fiendy1 has left the channel>

Paperwhite: just so u know, I don't give out nudes

Paperwhite: she's got a problem with me because I'm with the guy she likes

BorkledDrek: omg the mod chan's full of intrigue!

Paperwhite: you don't know the half of it

70

While I was fearing it, it came . . .

Emily Dickinson
XCVIII

Strike, who'd sat up until 1.30 a.m. making notes on Robin's interview with Pez, was woken at 5 a.m. by the phenomenon known as 'jumping stump'.

He'd suffered myoclonic spasms in the remaining portion of his right leg in the months following his amputation, and this unexpected recurrence was highly unwelcome. Unable to get back to sleep due to the uncontrollable twitching and jerking, he finally dragged himself out of bed and hopped to the bathroom, using the door jamb and walls for balance.

His leg continued spasming in the shower. Soaping himself, he found himself thinking more seriously than ever before about his health. He was forty and several stone overweight; his diet was poor and his hamstring had torn twice and remained vulnerable. He knew his circulation and overall fitness were being compromised by his heavy smoking and that his vague resolutions to resume the daily exercises recommended by the physiotherapist were forgotten as soon as made. At least once a week he acknowledged that he ought to give up cigarettes, but continued to get through a pack a day; he bought bags of salad then threw them out without having opened them. As his stump continued to jerk, he saw it as a mute appeal: something had to change.

Having towelled himself off, Strike put on his prosthesis, hoping the weight of it would hamper his stump's involuntary movements, then made himself a mug of tea and, notwithstanding his stern self-talk in the shower, lit a cigarette. As he sat back down at the small kitchen table, where his laptop and notebook remained from the night before, he remembered that he was supposed to be having dinner with Madeline tonight.

The prospect brought him no pleasure: on the contrary, a leaden weight of obligation and aggravation settled in the pit of his stomach. He drank his tea, staring out of the window at the pigeons on the roof opposite, silhouetted against the crystalline early-morning sky, and asked himself how he'd got himself in this mess. He'd been accused before now of subconsciously sabotaging relationships because he didn't really want commitment: he remembered being lectured by Ilsa on the need for compromise and forgiveness after splitting up with a short-term girlfriend whom he'd dated during one of his many breaks with Charlotte. Of course, Ilsa, like every single one of his friends, had had an overriding aim: to see him settled down with literally anyone but Charlotte. And he'd tried, hadn't he? He'd genuinely tried to give the relationship with Madeline a chance. The sex was good; there were things about her he found endearing, even admirable, but there was no avoiding it any more: something essential was missing.

Strike's leg was still trying to jump around, even with the prosthesis on; his false foot shifting irritably on the floor. Yawning, he flipped open his laptop to check today's rota. Robin was supposed to be tailing the housekeeper of South Audley Street this morning. Strike picked up his mobile and texted her.

> **Be good to have a catch up on Anomie today. Nutley got some stuff on Kea last night. You can leave the housekeeper unwatched. Dev's on Fingers, he'll know if they meet up**

Having sent this message, Strike made and ate some porridge, rather than frying up the bacon he really fancied, dressed and proceeded carefully downstairs to the office, partly because it would stop him smoking: he tried to keep the workplace cigarette-free.

He took the ever-expanding Anomie file out of the filing cabinet, then settled himself at his computer, intent on pursuing the online investigations he'd had to abandon the previous evening, while impersonating Buffypaws in *Drek's Game*.

An hour passed, but Strike's attempt to find friends of Gus Upcott came to nothing. He was unable to find any trace of the music student online, other than a seven-year-old clip from a school concert, in which a teenaged Gus played what seemed to Strike to be an exceptionally difficult cello solo. If Gus used Twitter, Instagram or Facebook, he was doing so under a pseudonym and his social life remained as much of a mystery as it had when Strike began looking.

He drew a similar blank on Grant Ledwell's daughter Rachel, coming up only with a year-old photo on Instagram. The picture showed a group of laughing teenagers at the back of a bus. One dark-haired girl had pulled her beanie hat down over her face, so that only her chin was visible. She was making the rock 'n' roll salute with both hands, little fingers and index fingers raised, and the tag read @RachLedwell. However, when Strike went to find @RachLedwell's Instagram account, he found it had been deleted. Returning to the page with the bus photo, he worked his way slowly through the rest of the pictures until finally, after a bit of cross-referencing of school uniforms and landmarks, he deduced that the owner of the page (@ShellyPinker) lived in Bradford, which meant that all Strike had for a further hour's work were the words 'Rachel Ledwell - Bradford?' in his notebook.

Yawning again, he headed into the outer office to make himself another mug of tea, grateful that at least his leg had stopped twitching.

Back at his desk, he found a return text from Robin on his phone.

Great, because I've got a lot to tell you. Would you mind if I came in at 10? I've been up all night, working

Strike looked at this message for a full minute, a multitude of possibilities running through his mind. Robin had said she was going to Junction Road; he'd assumed that meant she wanted, for reasons unknown, to visit Zoe or watch her flat. '*Did I mention you're fucking gorgeous?*' What exactly had kept her up all night? '*Control yourself . . . God. People are staring.*' Pez Pierce surely couldn't have accompanied Robin to Junction Road? Had she promised to go back to North Grove after Junction Road? '*I don't normally do this kind of thing by daylight.*'

Now scowling, Strike texted back **OK**, turned his attention back to his computer and typed 'Kea Niven Reddit' into Google.

There was an immediate hit. Feeling even more aggravated by Nutley, who could have done this simple bit of follow-up on his own phone, Strike opened a Reddit page headed:

r/TrackCriminalBitches

Strike scrolled slowly downwards. He was surprised that the page hadn't been shut down, because it seemed to be one long exhortation to vigilantism, its purpose to expose the personal details, addresses and employers of women who'd been convicted of crimes against men, or (in the view of those posting their profiles) had falsely claimed to be victims of male crime themselves. Photographs of all the women had been provided for easier identification. Above a picture of a tired-looking blonde in her thirties was written:

baba_yaga Melanie Jane Strong made false accusation of domestic violence against ex-husband to deprive him of contact with his kids. Female judge fell for it hook line and sinker. Currently living at 3 Parteger Avenue, Cheam, SM1 2PL. Works for local solicitor Miller, May & Bricknell, tel no: 020 8443 8686

And above a picture of a very pretty black-haired girl who looked in her mid-twenties:

john_baldwin Lying bitch Darcy Olivia Barrett made false sexual assault accusation against boyfriend. Living at 4b Lancaster Drive, Hoxteth. Instagram: @ViolaD97 Twitter: @DarkViola90 kids at 98 Raglan Road, Barnet, EN4 788 tel no: 020 8906 4359 Call and let family know what a cunt she is.

It took Strike only a couple more minutes to find Kea's name. The item had been posted ten days previously.

DrekBw88h This crazy bitch threatened to kill her ex-boyfriend and his girlfriend the night before they were actually fucking stabbed http://dailymail.co.uk/news/murder-of-animator-in-highgate-cemetery.html
She's now deleted these tweets. Spread these screenshots far and wide.
Twitter: @realPaperwhite
tumblr: *http://bumblefootandspoons.tumblr.com*
https://www.instagram.com/keaniven
http://patreon.com/KeaNivenArt

Kea Niven @realPaperwhite

when u find out by accident just how deep the betrayal goes and you've been lied to for months @realJoshBlay @EdLedDraws

12.10 am   12 February 2015

Kea Niven @realPaperwhite

You're about to find out there are fucking consequences to stabbing people thru the heart and walking away @realJoshBlay @EdLedDraws

12.25 am   12 February 2015

Kea Niven @realPaperwhite

you treat people with contempt long enough they will retaliate. Violence begets violence @realJoshBlay @EdLedDraws

12.26 am   12 February 2015

Wally Cardew @The_Wally_Cardew
replying to @realPaperwhite
delete that ffs

12.39 am   12 February 2015

Kea Niven @realPaperwhite
replying to @The_Wally_Cardew
why the fuck should I/

12.40 am   12 February 2015

Wally Cardew @The_Wally_Cardew
replying to @realPaperwhite
because there are better ways

12.42 am   12 February 2015

Kea Niven @realPaperwhite
replying to @The_Wally_Cardew
I don't give a shit

12.42 am   12 February 2015

Wally Cardew @The_Wally_Cardew
replying to @realPaperwhite
well you shd

12.44 am   12 February 2015

Strike flipped open the Anomie file and pulled out the printed list of websites visited by Kea prior to Strike's interview with her. He'd previously given this list only a cursory glance, but now he'd found out Kea made a barely veiled threat of violence against Josh and Edie less than twenty-four hours before they'd been stabbed, he felt she deserved a little more of his attention.

Scanning the list of websites, he mentally discounted the Buzzfeed quiz on being cis, the shopping sites, the Googling of his name and of Josh's, his attention finally coming to rest on a website called 'Tribulationem et Dolorum'. He brought the website up on his computer.

It proved to be a support group for people suffering from chronic illness, most commonly ME. The overall look was amateurish and in places the formatting had gone awry. However, after perusing the message boards for half an hour, Strike finally found something interesting, dating from 2013.

Arke: Hi, chronic fatigue sufferer here (EDS) really just looking to connect with others going through the same stuff. I've just turned 24, should be completing my studies at art school but had to drop out due to multiple health issues.

John: Welcome, Arke! Very pleased to have you join us. I hope you find our resources helpful. We're a friendly community and I trust you'll find the support you're looking for!

Arke: Thanks so much! This looks a great site, one of the best I've found x

John: We try our best! May I ask, is your handle in reference to the Greek goddess of that name?

Arke: Yes, can't believe you know that! For several reasons she kind of speaks to me – the shadow rainbow. Don't shine as brightly as I should! Can I ask, did you design this site?

John: I did indeed.

Arke: Oh wow, it's really great! Like I say, I'm an artist. This has a really great look. I love the colour palette and the whole vibe. I could tell when I looked at it it wasn't an amateur job!

John: High praise from an artist! I dabbled in web design before I was stricken with Myalgic Encephalomyelitis, which sadly forced me to give up work.

Arke: Oh I'm so sorry. How long have you had ME?

John: 12 years

Arke: Urgh that's awful. Have you got a supportive doctor?

John: I'm fortunate enough to be able to go privately these days and have found a doctor who suits me. Prior to that it was a struggle, which is why I created this website.

Arke: I'm being told to try Graded Exercise Therapy, but I'm hearing bad things about GET online.

John: I don't recommend it. In my own case it dramatically worsened my fatigue.

Arke: Right, that's what I heard. And being told I should try CBT felt like they were telling me this is all in my head.

John: Yes, I'm afraid too many doctors are profoundly ignorant about the realities of the condition. If you're comfortable private messaging me, I'm happy to share the medications and treatments that have been of some benefit to me.

Arke: oh totally, that's so kind!

John: Just click on speech bubble top right.

Strike now turned to the home page.

About the Founder of Tribulationem et Dolorum

John is a creative whose flourishing career in publishing (plus successful sidelines in both art and music!) were cut short when he developed Myalgic Encephalomyelitis (ME) over a decade ago. He continues to make art and music within the necessary limitations of his condition. A selection of John's compositions can be heard at www.IJU.MakesSounds and he can also be found advocating for the chronically ill (and sharing his political opinions!) on Twitter as @BillyShearsME

'Can he, now?' muttered Strike, as he navigated to @BillyShearsME's Twitter account.

This proved to be composed mostly of attacks on the medical profession, contemptuous strictures on both the Conservative and Labour parties and occasional links to www.IJU.MakesSounds.

The door to the outer office opened. Glancing up, he saw Pat entering, her arms full of post, e-cigarette already clamped between her teeth.

'You're in early,' she grunted.

'Following a lead,' said Strike.

Five minutes later, he found what he was looking for.

Kea Niven
@realPaperwhite

when youre too depressed to do anything except stare at the ceiling and youd quite like to die except that requires effort

1.50 pm   4 September 2014

Lepine's Disciple @LepinesD1sciple

replying to @realPaperwhite

whiny narcissistic bitch says what?

1.51 pm   4 September 2014

ME Rights @BillyShearsME

replying to @LepinesD1sciple @realPaperwhite

You know nothing of what this young woman has gone through, nor does she deserve to have that kind of language thrown at her.

1.57 pm   4 September 2014

Lepine's Disciple @LepinesD1sciple

replying to @BillyShearsME @realPaperwhite

Grandpa's got a semi 😂 😂 😂

1.59 pm   4 September 2014

ME Rights @BillyShearsME

replying to @LepinesD1sciple @realPaperwhite

the standard of discourse as elevated as ever here, I see

2.03 pm   4 September 2014

Before Strike could fully compute what he'd just read, he heard running footsteps. He looked up: Pat was sprinting towards him. She'd barely slammed the door on the outer office when there was a deafening boom and the door blew inwards, cracking in two. The lower hinge held but the upper portion fell, hit Pat in the back and would have sent her sprawling had Strike not caught her. Debris was flying everywhere; Strike felt something sharp slice his neck as he dragged Pat down behind the desk. From the outer office came the sound of falling glass and rubble, and the caustic smell of smoke and chemicals filled the air.

'Package,' Pat shouted into Strike's ear. 'Started to undo it – realised it was hissing—'

Metal echoed, something heavy hit the floor in the outer room and Strike felt the floor shake. The smoke was becoming thicker. His eyes were watering. From out on the street he heard shouting.

'I've dropped my bloody e-fag,' said Pat crossly, looking down at herself.

'Stay there,' Strike ordered her.

He got slowly to his feet, squinting through the smoke. Plaster dust was still raining from the ceiling beyond the door. Pat's computer monitor lay on the floor, its screen smashed. Her desk had cracked in two and was still smouldering. Chunks of wood and plaster littered the floor.

'Police, please,' said Pat, who in spite of Strike's command to stay down had also stood up, to use the phone on his desk. 'Strike Detective Agency here, Denmark Street. We've been sent an explosive device and it's exploded. No, no injuries . . . Oh, have you? . . . Right ho . . . They're already on their way,' said Pat, replacing the receiver. 'Someone must've called it in.'

'Not bloody surprised,' said Strike. An accumulation of excitable voices in the street outside was becoming audible, even over the ringing of his ears.

'I want my fag back,' said Pat, peering at the floor outside.

'Have one of mine,' said Strike, handing her his pack of Benson & Hedges and lighter. 'You're not going out there till we know it's safe.'

After five minutes' wait, during which no more of the ceiling fell in, Strike decided it was time to get out.

He picked up the Anomie file, then insisted on holding Pat's arm to guide her over the debris as they made their careful way towards the outer door, from which the glass had blown out. The walls bore scorch marks, there were deep dents in the filing cabinets and stuffing bulged through the rips in the fake leather sofa. Wires dangled from two large cavities in the ceiling, one of which looked as though it had almost blasted through to his attic flat above. Fury rose inside him.

You cowardly fucks.

'I'd just had that bloody cleaned,' grumbled Pat, surveying the dust-covered coat still hanging incongruously from its peg. Her hand-bag lay on the floor, its contents strewn everywhere. As she bent to pick them up, Strike heard an approaching siren.

'Cavalry's here. Come on.'

'Just a mo, I want to find—'

'Christ's sake, Pat, I'll buy you a new bloody e-cigarette. Let's go.'

Strike didn't like to think what state his flat was going to be in. Grateful at least for his habit of always bringing his phone, car keys and wallet down to the office, to minimise unnecessary trips back upstairs, he ushered Pat out onto the landing and together they descended into Denmark Street.

71

These monsters, set out in the open sun,
Of course throw monstrous shadows: those who think
Awry, will scarce act straightly.

Elizabeth Barrett Browning
Aurora Leigh

At ten to ten, Robin emerged, somewhat bleary-eyed, from Tottenham Court Road Tube station and headed through the ongoing roadworks towards the office. She'd only had two hours' sleep, so Strike's message that she needn't tail the housekeeper of South Audley Street today had come as a relief.

As she approached Denmark Street she saw a police car and a small crowd, among whom she recognised some of the people who worked in the various music shops around the office. With a feeling of awful foreboding, she sped up, and when she reached the knot of people staring towards the office and followed their gaze, she saw blue-and-white police tape blocking the entrance to the agency's building and a uniformed officer standing outside.

Robin fumbled for her phone with shaking hands. A text from Strike had arrived while she'd still been on the Tube.

Parcel bomb sent to office. Pat and I OK. In Starbucks

'Oh, thank God,' gasped Robin, setting off at a run across the road.

Strike and Pat were sitting at the back of the coffee shop. There was blood on Strike's collar and Pat looked paler than usual.

'Jesus,' said Robin, hurrying over to them, and finding nothing else to say she repeated, '*Jesus!*'

'He was definitely on our side an hour ago,' said Strike. 'We've been told to stay in here. They're going to have more questions. I think they're waiting for the CID.'

'What – how—?'

'Parcel,' said Pat, in her deep, gravelly voice. 'Started to open it, heard it hissing. Then – *kaboom*.'

'Place is wrecked,' said Strike. 'Bits of the ceiling have fallen in. We're lucky my bed didn't fall through the floor.'

'Are you—?'

'Paramedics have looked at us,' said Strike, with a glance at Pat. 'We're fine. I've let Barclay and co know what's happened.'

'Think I'll just nip to Boots,' said Pat, reaching for her handbag, which Robin now noticed was scorched.

'You stay there,' said Strike firmly.

Pat, in his fairly expert opinion, was in shock. Her matter-of-fact gruffness might have been complimented by the paramedic who'd given them a cursory examination, but Strike had noticed how much her hand had shaken when taking a sip of her coffee.

'What d'you need, Pat?' said Robin.

'He wouldn't let me go back for my electronic fag,' complained Pat, with a bitter look at Strike.

'I'll go and get you a new one,' said Robin at once.

'You won't know the right sort to get,' said Pat petulantly, 'and I can't remember what it's called.'

'Get one of whatever they've got,' Strike advised Robin, thrusting a couple of twenty-pound notes into her hand. 'And, failing that, gum and patches.'

As Robin left, Strike asked Pat,

'Did you have any breakfast?'

'Of course I had breakfast, what kind of stupid question is that?'

'Think you need some sugar,' said Strike, heaving himself up. He felt no ill will towards the office manager for her pettishness; indeed, he empathised. His own reaction to shock tended to take the form of irritability. He returned to the table with two Danish pastries and fresh coffee, and after glaring at the plate he'd set in front of her Pat condescended to break off a piece and eat it.

'You realise you just saved both our lives?' Strike told her, sitting down again. 'If you hadn't twigged and pulled that door shut—'

He bumped his plastic coffee cup gently against hers.

'You're a bloody marvel, Pat. Plus, you make a great fruitcake.'

Pat pressed her lips together, frowning. Her eyes had become unusually moist. Strike fleetingly considered putting an arm around her, but could almost feel her bony shoulders shrugging him off.

'S'pose it's that terrorist group you've pissed off,' she said.

'Must've been. That wasn't an amateur effort.'

'Bastards.'

'You said it.'

'My uncle died in an IRA pub bombing. Woolwich. '74.'

'Shit, I'm sorry,' said Strike, startled.

'Wrong place. Wrong time. Hard to get your head round. Well,' said Pat, with a glance towards the table top, beneath which Strike's fake leg was hidden, 'I don't need to tell *you* that.'

She ate some more Danish pastry. Strike saw a blue Toyota Avensis pass the window and thought he recognised the profile of Ryan Murphy, the CID officer who'd previously visited the office.

'They might want to take us to New Scotland Yard,' said Strike. 'To give statements.'

'I'm not bloody going anywhere. Why can't we do it here?'

'Maybe we can,' said Strike placatingly.

'Where's Robin?' said Pat in frustration. Strike could almost feel her craving for nicotine. The first police on the scene had asked them to stay put inside the café, not to hang around outside on the pavement. That suited Strike, because it was surely only a matter of time before the press turned up.

By the time Robin returned, carrying a plastic bag full of various e-cigarettes, two CID men had joined Strike and Pat: Murphy, and an older black man with greying hair. So worried was Robin about what had just happened that the sight of the back of Ryan Murphy caused her barely a tremor. She arrived at the table in time to hear Pat insisting obstreperously that she didn't want to go to New Scotland Yard, she hadn't done anything wrong, and why couldn't she just say what she had to say right here?

Strike knew Murphy had taken the measure of Pat's state of shock by his calm response.

'We'd just like to talk to you somewhere a bit more private, Mrs Chauncey. Oh, hello,' he added as Robin joined them.

'Hi,' said Robin. 'Here you are, Pat. Hopefully one of them will be OK.'

While Pat accepted the carrier bag and poked disconsolately at the contents, Strike said to the CID officers,

'There's a pub just up the road with a basement room. They'd probably let us use it for half an hour or so. We're regulars.'

So the party walked the short distance to The Tottenham, Strike and Pat both seizing the opportunity to smoke a proper cigarette as they went. Robin found herself walking behind them, sandwiched between Murphy and his colleague, whom he introduced as Neal Jameson, before saying,

'You OK?'

'I wasn't there,' said Robin. She felt irrationally guilty for not having been in the office when the bomb went off.

'Still a shock,' said Murphy.

'Yes,' said Robin.

The barman at The Tottenham was obliging. A couple of minutes after they'd arrived, the two CID officers, Strike, Robin and Pat were sitting around a table in the otherwise deserted red-carpeted basement room.

'OK, Mrs Chauncey,' said the older officer, flicking open his notebook while Pat tried to open one of the e-cigarettes. Her hands were still shaking, so Strike took the packet from her, unwrapped it and began to put the device inside together. 'If you can tell us in your own words what happened.'

'Well, the postman came up the stairs right behind me,' said Pat.

'Usual postman?'

'Yes,' said Pat. 'He knows me. I took our mail from him on the landing.'

'How big was the package?' asked the CID man.

Pat mimed a shoebox-size shape.

'Heavy?'

'Yeah,' said Pat, watching beadily as Strike filled the e-cigarette with fluid.

'What was written on it, can you remember?'

'*Their* names,' said Pat, nodding at Strike and Robin.

'Can you remember anything about the handwriting?'

'Educated,' said Pat. 'We sometimes get nutters writing. You can always tell, by the handwriting.'

'Green ink?' said Murphy with a smile.

'The worst one was in purple,' said Pat, almost smiling back. She always had a soft spot for handsome men, and Murphy was certainly good-looking, as Robin, shaken though she was, now appreciated: high cheekbones and that full upper lip, and wavy hair somewhat like Strike's, though lighter in colour. 'Some daft bugger thought the Royal Family had all been replaced with imposters.'

The two CID officers laughed obligingly.

'But this wasn't nutter handwriting?' asked Murphy's colleague.

'No,' said Pat. 'Black ink, everything spelled right. They don't always get "Ellacott" right and most people call *him* "Cameron".'

'Don't suppose you noticed the postmark?'

Pat accepted her filled and functional e-cigarette from Strike, took a long drag on it as though it were oxygen, then said,

'Kilburn. I live there,' Pat elucidated. 'You notice when it's yours, don't you?'

'True,' said the CID man. 'So you took the package . . .'

'Took it into the office, put it down on the desk. Took off my coat, opened one of the letters, then started to open the parcel. What with the nice handwriting and everything, I thought it was a thank-you present,' she said, with a hint of defensiveness. 'They sometimes get chocolates and booze from clients. I got one flap open and then I heard it hissing. And I – I just knew,' said Pat.

She turned a little whiter. Robin got silently to her feet and left the room.

'I ran into his office,' Pat continued, indicating Strike, 'and slammed the door, and it went off.'

'Well, if everyone had your powers of observation and quick reactions, Mrs Chauncey,' said the older CID officer, 'our jobs would be a hell of a lot easier.'

'Forensics are going to need at least twenty-four hours,' Murphy said to Strike. 'You live over the office, right?'

'Yeah,' said Strike. 'I'm assuming you'd advise me to clear out.'

'I would, yeah,' said Murphy. 'From what I've just heard, it might be structurally unsound. And—'

'Yeah,' said Strike again. He didn't need it spelled out in front of Pat that once The Halvening realised their attempt on his and Robin's lives had failed, they might start looking for other ways to get to them.

Robin returned, holding a glass of what looked like port, which she set down in front of Pat.

'I don't need that,' said Pat.

'Drink it,' said Robin firmly, sitting down again.

'Could've got me a pint while you were there,' said Strike. 'I was bombed too, you know.'

The two CID officers laughed again.

'OK,' said Neal Jameson, 'I'm going to write this out in full and ask you to sign it, Mrs Chauncey.'

While he was writing out Pat's statement, Murphy turned to Robin.

'I've just been telling your boss—'

'He's my partner,' said Robin, at the same time Strike said, 'She's my partner.'

'Ah, sorry. Just been telling your partner, it'd be wise to stay out of the office for a bit. What's – I don't mean to be personal – what's your home situation? D'you live—?'

'Alone,' said Robin. 'I've only just moved. Walthamstow.'

'Right by me: I'm in Wanstead. Could be helpful, you only just having moved. All the same—'

'I've got all the usual security,' said Robin, cutting him off.

Murphy's colleague had finished writing. Pat, whose colour had returned after a few sips of port, read the statement through and signed it.

'Right,' said Strike to Pat as he got to his feet, 'I'm taking you home.'

'There's no need for that,' said Pat irritably.

'Don't worry, it's not because I like you,' said Strike, looking down at her. 'Just don't think I can find another office manager with your skill set.'

Robin saw Pat's eyes fill with tears. As Strike moved towards the stairs, Pat at his side, Robin called after him,

'Cormoran, I've got that sofa-bed, if you need it.'

She wasn't sure he'd heard her, because he made no response, and a second later she wished she hadn't said it: of course, he had Madeline Courson-Miles to stay with.

The two CID officers were now talking quietly together. Robin picked up her bag, ready to leave.

'Want a lift?' said Murphy, looking round.

'What – to Walthamstow?' said Robin incredulously.

'Yeah,' said Murphy. 'This was s'posed to be my day off, but Neal called me in over this business. He's going back to the office. It's not far out of my way; I'm going in that direction anyway.'

'Oh,' said Robin, 'I – yes, all right then.'

72

You face, today ... mark me, not
A woman who wants protection. As to a man,
Show manhood, speak out plainly, be precise
With facts and dates.

Elizabeth Barrett Browning
Aurora Leigh

Why the hell had she said yes, Robin wondered. Shock? Two hours' sleep? A residual recklessness left over from last night's impersonation of the experienced Jessica Robins? As she followed Murphy and his colleague out of the pub, she wondered whether it was paranoid to question Murphy's statement that he had the day off. She considered saying 'actually, I'll take the Tube,' or 'I forgot, there's something I need to do in town,' but moment to moment she put it off, and soon they'd reached the blue Avensis and the two CID officers were agreeing their next steps. Robin heard Angela Darwish's name. The older officer crossed the road and ducked under the tape now blocking the end of Denmark Street and Murphy and Robin got into the car.

'Hell of a thing to happen,' said Murphy, pulling away from the kerb.

'Yes,' said Robin.

'Could you go and stay with friends, maybe?'

'I'll be fine at home,' said Robin. Perhaps Murphy took her peaky appearance to denote shock, but it was only because she'd been up virtually all night. Wishing to deflect any more helpful suggestions, she said,

'It's not the first time we've been sent something horrible. I got a severed leg through the post once.'

'Yeah, I remember reading about that in the press,' said Murphy.

A pause followed, in which Robin cast around for neutral topics of

711

conversation and, tired as she was, failed to find any. Murphy broke the silence.

'How's your Anomie case going?'

'Not as well as we'd like.'

Another silence. Again, Murphy ended it.

'I'm off on holiday this evening.'

'Oh, really?' said Robin politely. 'Where are you going?'

'San Sebastián,' said Murphy. 'My sister lives out there with her family. Every time I visit I wonder why I live in London. I was looking forward to it – haven't had a holiday in two years – but last night we had a major breakthrough in our murder case. I considered delaying going out to Spain, but it's my sister's fortieth the day after tomorrow. I might well be the next murder victim if I skip it.'

'Which murder case?' asked Robin, certain she knew.

'Yours. The animator.'

'You've got Edie Ledwell's killer?' said Robin, now looking directly at Murphy.

'We think so. The evidence is all pointing one way – but I can't say who it is. Not until he's arrested.'

Murphy glanced at the clock on the dashboard.

Robin's tired mind was suddenly racing with questions.

'Did he talk to someone? Admit it?'

'No,' said Murphy.

There was another short silence, during which Robin tried to think of other ways to wheedle information out of him, although she could tell from the expression Murphy was wearing that he knew exactly what was going through her head. At last he said,

'It was the phone. Ledwell's phone.'

'He's got it?'

'Not any more,' said Murphy. 'He chucked it in a duck pond in Writtle.'

'Where's that?'

'Out Chelmsford way.'

She could tell Murphy was going to tell her more, knew he wanted to explain how they'd got their man, even if the man's identity couldn't be shared. In his place, she'd have felt the same temptation. She, too, knew the satisfaction of laying out pieces of the puzzle for somebody who appreciated what it had taken to get there.

''Bout a fortnight after she was killed,' Murphy said, 'someone turned Ledwell's phone on for fifteen minutes, then shut it off again. We traced the signal to the car park of Westfield shopping centre in Stratford. Ever been there?'

'No,' said Robin.

'Biggest shopping centre in Europe. You can imagine what size the car park is. We collected the CCTV footage. A thousand-plus cars, plenty of people using their phones. We took every number plate, pictures of everyone we could see with a mobile and started sifting through it all.

'Five days after that, the phone was turned on again for ten minutes, then shut off. Signal traced to a field in Kent. No cameras nearby, but we got hold of the nearest CCTV footage – which wasn't that near. We started looking at number plates of cars entering and leaving the general area, plus pedestrians, cyclists, looking for a match with any of the cars or people we'd got from Westfield. Slow work, as you can imagine.'

'They were choosing the places they were using the phone pretty carefully,' said Robin.

'Very,' said Murphy. 'Making our lives as difficult as possible. Couldn't get any matches between the two locations. We still aren't sure why they were turning the phone on at all. You'd think it'd be smarter not to touch it. They didn't make any calls. Our presumption is that there was information on there the killer wanted.'

'You know Edie Ledwell stored ideas for the cartoon on her phone?' asked Robin.

'Yeah, Blay told us that,' said Murphy. 'Anyway, three weeks ago, a man gets out of a car at the duck pond in Writtle in the early hours of the morning, face concealed in a scarf, and chucks something into the water. He was seen by a teenage kid having a cheeky smoke out of his bedroom window while his parents were asleep. This kid was quite interested, so next morning he wades into the pond, pulls out an iPhone and takes it home. After an hour or so, it occurs to the kid that there's something fishy about what just happened, so he goes downstairs and tells his parents. The mother takes the phone to the local police station. We get contacted, get our forensic and tech guys onto it – obviously, it had been under water all night, so it was a specialised job – but once they'd done their stuff, sure enough it was Ledwell's.

'CCTV footage showed a Ford Fiesta entering and leaving the area at the right times. False plates. We go back and look at the Westfield pictures and—'

'There's a Ford Fiesta there with a number plate ending CBS,' said Robin.

Murphy looked round so quickly Robin said, 'Traffic light!', fearful they were about to hit the car in front. As Murphy slowed down he said,

'How—?'

'I've seen him in it,' said Robin, whose thoughts had been thrown into a state of total disarray. She felt astonished, confused and a strange, sick sense of – what was it? Disbelief? Anticlimax? 'I noticed the letters on the number plate.'

'Because of the American news channel?' said Murphy.

'Yes,' lied Robin. 'Don't worry, I'm not about to call the press. What about Blay's phone: has he used that at all?'

'No, that one hasn't been turned on since it disappeared. We're assuming Ormond's got it at home, unless he's disposed of it somewhere else. We dragged the Writtle duck pond and it wasn't there.'

'I only saw him last night,' said Robin for the second time that morning, as waves of incredulity washed over her.

'Where?'

'North Grove Art Collective. He was trying to get something from one of the people who lives there.'

'Really? What?'

'I don't know. I think a drawing or a piece of writing Edie did . . . I – I can't believe this. I don't know why – although, I suppose . . .'

She didn't finish the sentence, but Murphy had followed her train of thought.

'First person you look at is the partner. You were the one who spotted the bruising on her neck.'

'I thought he was taking a detention when she was killed?'

'He left early and told the girl not to tell anyone, unless she wanted a week's worth.'

'God . . . so he knew where they were meeting?'

'Yeah. Confidentially, we've got reason to believe he put a tracker on her phone, which she didn't know about. We're still trying to unlock it. Apple won't help. Civil liberties. But he clearly knew the passcode, to open it twice.'

'They're going to arrest him today?'

'Yeah. He's gone to work as usual. We're going to nab him once he leaves school. Arresting a guy in front of a load of kids isn't smart.

We'd rather not have the press onto this until we've got him in an interview room.'

So it had been Phillip Ormond all along, the ex-policeman and teacher whom Edie had thought would keep her safe from all the threats and harassment. A jealous partner, stalking her as she went to meet her ex-boyfriend, stabbing both of them then leaving with their phones ... Of course, it made sense of certain things. The ability of the murderer to know exactly where Edie was, the phone being used only where it would be most difficult to pinpoint who'd used it, which implied knowledge of police methods, and the extraordinarily detailed knowledge about the two new characters for the film that Yasmin had said Ormond had.

Murphy was now asking her about her own holiday plans. Robin pulled herself together enough to describe learning to ski, back at New Year. The conversation was only lightly personal, but it was pleasant and easy. Murphy made Robin laugh with a description of a friend's accident on a dry ski slope, where he'd taken a date he was keen to impress. At no time did he mention his previous invitation for a drink, nor did he make her feel uncomfortable in this small space, and she was grateful for both these things.

They were approaching Blackhorse Road when Robin suddenly said, astounded by her own bravery,

'Listen – that time you called me about a drink – the reason I was so – I'm not used to people asking me out.'

'How's that possible?' said Murphy, keeping his eyes on the road.

'I've just got divorced – well, a year ago now – from someone I was with since we were seventeen,' said Robin. 'So – anyway, I was in work mode when you called, and that's why I was a bit – you know – clueless.'

'Ah,' said Murphy. 'I got divorced three years ago.'

Robin wondered how old he was. She'd have guessed a couple of years older than her.

'Have you got kids?' she asked.

'No. My ex didn't want them.'

'Oh,' said Robin.

'You?'

'No.'

They'd pulled up outside her flat before either spoke again. As she picked up her bag and put her hand on the door handle, Murphy said,

'So . . . if, after I get back from holiday, I called you again and asked you out . . .?'

It's only a drink, said Ilsa's voice in Robin's head. *Nobody's saying you've got to jump into bed with him.* An image of Madeline Courson-Miles flickered before Robin's eyes.

'Er –' said Robin, whose heart was hammering. 'Yes, OK. That'd be great.'

She thought he'd look pleased at that, but instead he seemed tense.

'OK.' He rubbed his nose, then said, 'There's something I should tell you first, though. It's what you say, isn't it, "come out for a drink"? But, ah – I'm an alcoholic.'

'Oh,' said Robin again.

'Been sober two years, nine months,' said Murphy. 'I've got no problem with people drinking around me. Just need to put that out there. It's what you're supposed to do. AA rules.'

'Well, that doesn't make any – I mean, thanks for saying,' said Robin. 'I'd still like to go out some time. And thanks for the lift, I really appreciate it.'

He looked cheerful now.

'Pleasure. Better get back to my packing.'

'Yes – have fun in Spain!'

Robin got out of the car. As the blue Avensis pulled away, Murphy raised a hand in farewell, and Robin reciprocated, still amazed at herself. It had been quite some morning.

She'd just unlocked her front door when her mobile rang.

'Hi,' said Strike. 'Is that offer of the sofa-bed still open?'

'Yes, of course,' said Robin, both confused and pleased, entering her flat and pushing the door shut with her foot. 'How's Pat?'

'Bloody grumpy. I got her home all right. Told her to get an emergency appointment with her doctor. Half the door flew off and hit her in the back. I can tell she's sore: she could've cracked something. She told me to piss off, though not in those exact words. Probably thinks I'm accusing her of being too old to survive a door hitting her.'

'Strike,' said Robin, 'I've just found something out. They're about to arrest Phillip Ormond for murder.'

Silence followed these words. Robin walked into her kitchen and set her handbag down on the counter.

'Ormond?' repeated Strike.

'Yes,' said Robin, moving towards the kettle. She explained about

716

Edie's phone being turned on and off, and the sighting of Ormond throwing it into the pond in Writtle.

Another long silence followed.

'Well,' said Strike at last, 'I can see why they think they've got their man, but I've still got questions.'

Robin felt strangely relieved. After telling her he'd be there by six because he needed to buy himself some essentials, Strike rang off.

73

My rival his mischief devises –
What matter? his treachery's void.
I scorn him: I know whose the prize is.

May Kendall
The Last Performance

In-game chats between four moderators of *Drek's Game*

<Moderator Channel>

<5 June 2015 15.58>

<BorkledDrek, Anomie>

<Morehouse has entered the channel>

BorkledDrek: Hey Morehouse!

Morehouse: hi

BorkledDrek: you're not often here in the afternoon

Anomie: he's a busy man

Morehouse: exactly

>

<A new private channel has opened>

<5 June 2015 16.00>

<Anomie invites

718

>

>

>

>

BorkledDrek: numbers are down

Anomie: not for long

BorkledDrek: ?

>

>

Anomie: when Maverick make their next announcement, this place is gonna explode

BorkledDrek: you know what they're gonna say???

Anomie: the Gamemaster knows all

BorkledDrek: dude, how do u know all this stuff??

BorkledDrek: you're an insider, right? At Maverick?

>

>

>

BorkledDrek: sorry have I offended u?

Morehouse>

Anomie: you finished your exams, bwah?

Morehouse: it's not an exam, it's a research thing

Anomie: oh yeah, I knew that

Morehouse: Paperwhite been in?

Anomie: doubt it'll be long now you're here

>

>

>

Anomie: and here she is. Telepathy or coincidence?

Morehouse: telepathy, obviously

Anomie: you're a fkn physicist, you don't believe in that shit

Morehouse: then it was coincidence

Anomie: fine, go and private channel her

Morehouse: you know you're my number 1

Anomie: lol

<A new private channel has opened>

<5 June 2015 16.03>

<Paperwhite invites Morehouse>

Paperwhite: Mouse?

>

>

>

>

>

>

>

>

>

719

Anomie: you fag

>

>

>

>

>

>

Anomie: lol no, u
haven't offended me

Anomie: I get info
injected directly
into my veins, my
friend

BorkledDrek: so tell
me

BorkledDrek: what are
they gonna do?

BorkledDrek: go on,
tell me, I won't tell
anyone

Anomie: I'll tell
you once you
take over from
Morehouse

BorkledDrek: ?

Anomie: if Morehouse
has an accident I
mean

BorkledDrek: lol

BorkledDrek: you want
my theory?

Morehouse: go talk to
BorkledDrek, he thinks
you're a god

Anomie: true. But then,
I am

<Anomie has left the
channel>

<Morehouse has left
the channel>

<Private channel has
closed>

>

Paperwhite: hello?

>

>

Paperwhite: are you
chatting up a hot
fellow scientist?

>

>

>

<Morehouse has joined
the channel>

Morehouse: sorry, I
was keeping Anomie
sweet

Morehouse: you've seen?
The bombing?

Paperwhite: Yes!!!
wtf?

Morehouse: they're
saying it was The
Halvening

Paperwhite: I know, I
saw

Morehouse: well this
fits, it all fits,
doesn't it?

Morehouse: that
Ellacott woman
jumped down to help
Vilepechora

BorkledDrek: I think you're a mate of Josh Blay's

>

>

>

>

->

Anomie: you might be right

BorkledDrek: did you know Ledwell as well?

>

Anomie: yeah

Anomie: but she fucked me over

BorkledDrek: seriously?

>

>

>

Anomie: yeah she was a fkn bitch

Morehouse: so they probably thought she was following him, not Anomie

Paperwhite: that makes sense.

Paperwhite: but if Ellacott's not at the office, how do we find her?

Morehouse: we'll call the number, we'll find a way

Morehouse: how many more exams u got?

Paperwhite: 2

Morehouse: not long til we meet then

Morehouse: unless you've got cold feet and don't want to

Paperwhite: fuck off, Morehouse

Paperwhite: I've been begging u to meet me for how long?

Morehouse: lol

74

Yet—sayst thou, spies around us roam . . .
That there is risk our mutual blood
May redden in some lonely wood
The knife of treachery?

Charlotte Brontë
The Wood

If there was one upside to getting bombed out of his home and office thought Strike, as he walked down Kilburn High Road buying himself underwear, socks, toiletries including cream for his stump, a couple of shirts and a pair of pyjamas (the first he'd owned since his teens, but which he thought he ought to wear at Robin's), it was that it gave him a cast-iron excuse not to have dinner with Madeline that night, especially as the bomb was now being reported on the BBC News website.

'*What?*' she said, when he called her from the doorway of Superdrug to tell her what had happened. 'Oh my God – who – why—?' He heard her gasp. 'I've just seen it online! It's Corm!' he heard her call to some unknown person, presumably one of her sales girls. 'He's been sent a parcel bomb and it bloody went off!'

For reasons he couldn't quite put his finger on, Strike didn't like the fact that Madeline was telling one of her sales staff this, although the bombing was hardly private information, given that the BBC had it.

'Come and stay with us!' said Madeline, turning her attention back to Strike.

'I can't,' said Strike, reaching for a cigarette. 'The Met say it's best for me to lie low for a while. I don't want to bring this stuff down on you and Henry.'

'Oh,' said Madeline. 'D'you think——? I mean, nobody really knows about us, do they?'

Not for want of trying from you, was Strike's immediate, ungracious thought.

'They're terrorists,' he said. 'They watch people.'

'*Terrorists?*' repeated Madeline, now sounding truly scared. 'I thought it was some random nutcase?'

'No, it's the same group that sent pipe bombs to those MPs. The ones that went after your friend Gigi.'

'Oh my *God*,' said Madeline again. 'I didn't realise you were investigating——'

'We're not. We just ran afoul of them because of another case. I can't tell you any details. It's better you don't know.'

Given that you'll just pass it straight on to your sales girl.

'No, I s'pose . . . but where are you going to go, then?'

'Travelodge or somewhere, I expect,' lied Strike. 'I'll call you when I know what's going on.'

'Call me anyway,' said Madeline, 'whether you know what's going on or not. I want to know you're all right.'

After Strike had hung up, he noticed how much lighter of heart he felt, knowing he didn't have to go to Pimlico that night. He reached automatically into his pocket for a celebratory cigarette, but after taking out the familiar gold packet he stood for a few seconds looking at it, then replaced it in his pocket and re-entered Superdrug.

Having bought all immediate necessities, plus a cheap rucksack to carry them in, he headed into McDonald's where, remembering the condition his stump had been in that morning, he reluctantly eschewed a burger and bought an unsatisfactory salad. After this, still being hungry, he bought an apple pie and a coffee, consuming the former while trying not to resent three skinny teenagers at the nearest table, who were all tucking into Big Macs.

Though tired, Strike felt agitated. Adrenalin tingled in his veins, urging him to take some kind of retaliatory action, but instead he ate his pie, staring into space while people laughed and clattered all around him. The consequences of the bombing were sinking in, now that he had no Pat to look after and no practical tasks to distract him. He had no access to his laptop, no computer and no printer. All the work materials he had were his notebook, the Anomie file and his phone.

He picked up the last, intending to open Twitter to check what

Anomie was up to, then noticed that he had two new texts, one from his half-sister Prudence and one from Shanker, a friend dating back to his teens with whom he remained in touch, in spite of the fact of Shanker's incurable criminality. He opened Prudence's first.

I've just seen your office has been bombed. Really hope you're ok

Strike texted back:

I'm fine. Might have to take a rain check on our drink, though. Police are advising me to lie low. Hope all OK with Sylvie

He then opened Shanker's offering.

Who the fuck have you pissed off this time you silly cunt

Before he could answer this, his phone rang. Seeing that it was his sister Lucy he hesitated, but then decided it was best to get it over with.

'*Why didn't you call me?*' were her first, heated words.

'I was just about to,' said Strike, wondering how many more women he was going to have lied to before the day was through. 'I've been with the police.'

'Well, you could have sent a text! I nearly had *heart failure* when Greg rang and told me!'

'I'm fine, Luce. Literally got away with a scratch.'

'Where are you? The BBC say the building's been seriously damaged! Come to us!'

Strike repeated the story he'd told Madeline, emphasising the dangers to anybody he was currently associating with, and, by impressing upon her the risk to her sons, managed to convince her that it was best he retired to some anonymous, cheap hotel. Nevertheless, she talked for twenty minutes, begging for reassurances that he'd be careful, until Strike told her mendaciously that the police expected to arrest those responsible within days. Only slightly reassured, she finally rang off, leaving Strike irritable and still more tired.

He now opened Twitter. There had been no recent tweets from Anomie, but his eye was caught by one of the hashtags currently trending on the site: #FuckWallyCardew.

Prior to this morning's discovery that Wally had been in touch with Kea on the night before the stabbings, Strike mightn't have been much interested in whatever Wally had done to earn Twitter's disapprobation. Now, however, he clicked on the hashtag to find out what was going on.

Aoife @aoifeoconz

lol about fkn time #FuckWallyCardew

www.tubenewz.com/youtube-drops-Wally-Cardew-over-racism-allegations/html

---

Sammi @Sammitch97
replying to @aoifeoconz
omg he beat up MJ??? #FuckWallyCardew #IStandWithMJ

Drew C @_drewc^rtis
replying to @Sammitch97 @aoifeoconz
why'd he beat up MJ?

SQ @#B_O_U_TQuince
replying to @ydderidna @_drewc^rtis @Sammitch97 @aoifeoconz
because the sandn***** was fucking his sister

SQ @#B_O_U_T_Quince
replying to @ydderidna @_drewc^rtis @Sammitch97 @aoifeoconz
then a bunch of P***s put Wal in hospital

SQ @#B_O_U_T_Quince
replying to @ydderidna @_drewc^rtis @Sammitch97 @aoifeoconz
and some brothers gonna have something to say about that @Heimd&ll88

Strike slid his phone back into his pocket, wondering when he'd next be able to get into his attic. He didn't feel he could stay at Robin's for more than a couple of nights, but equally he didn't like the idea of leaving her alone in that neat little flat, not until the threat presented by The Halvening was eliminated. Evidently the white supremacists felt no gratitude whatsoever towards her for attempting to save one of their number's lives: all that mattered was that both she and Strike appeared to be tailing their members. That bomb had been no empty threat: but for Pat's quick reactions, he might now be lying in hospital with another body part sliced off him, consumed by guilt about their office manager's death.

Mentally running over immediate practical concerns, Strike's thoughts turned to his BMW, sitting in its expensive garage. As far as he remembered, there was plenty of parking on Robin's street. In spite of his aching hamstring, he thought he might return to the garage, pick up the BMW and then drive out to Walthamstow, so that he had the car available should he need it. After drinking the rest of his coffee, he heaved himself up off his plastic chair, shouldered the rucksack now holding what, for the time being, were almost all his worldly possessions, and limped off again.

75

It gave your curses strength, it warmed
Your bones the coldest night,
To feel you were not all alone
Again the world to fight.

Emily Pfeiffer
The Witch's Last Ride

While Strike was heading back into central London, the equally tired and worried Robin was walking around her local supermarket. She knew how hearty an appetite Strike had, and the contents of her fridge weren't going to be equal to the job of feeding him without substantial reinforcement. As she dropped a whole chicken into her trolley, she wondered why Strike had chosen to stay with her instead of with Madeline. She wouldn't put it past him to have concerns about her safety: he'd sometimes displayed protective instincts that, while occasionally exasperating, had their endearing aspect. If she were entirely honest with herself, she was very shaken by what had happened that morning, and glad he was coming to stay. After all, both their names had been written on the bomb and she felt a need to be with the only person who understood how that felt.

As she queued at the checkout, Robin's mobile rang. It was her mother. Just as Strike had with Lucy, Robin took the call only because she knew ignoring it would make matters worse.

'Robin? We've just seen the news! Why on earth—?'

'I wasn't there when it went off, Mum,' Robin said, shuffling forwards in the queue.

'*And how were we supposed to know that?*'

'I'm sorry, I should have called you,' said Robin wearily. 'We had to give police statements and everything, and I've only just—'

'Why did you have to give a statement, if you weren't there?'

'Well, because it was an attack on the agency,' said Robin, 'so—'

'They're saying on the news it was a far-right terrorist group!'

'Yes,' said Robin, 'they think so.'

'Robin, *why's a far-right terrorist group targeting your agency?*'

'Because they think we're interested in them,' said Robin, 'which we aren't ... Are you going to ask who *was* in the office when it went off, or—?'

'You can hardly blame me for worrying about my daughter first!'

'I'm not blaming you,' said Robin, moving forwards again and starting to load her shopping onto the conveyor belt one-handed. 'Just thought you might be interested.'

'So who—?'

'Pat and Strike. They're OK, though, thanks to Pat's quick reactions.'

'Well, I'm glad,' said Linda stiffly. 'Obviously I'm glad. So now what? D'you want to come home?'

'Mum,' said Robin patiently, 'I *am* home.'

'Robin,' said Linda, clearly on the verge of tears, 'nobody wants to stop you doing what you love—'

'You do,' said Robin, unable to help herself. 'You *do* want me to stop me doing it. I know this is a shock, it was a shock to me too, but—'

'Why not apply for the police? With the experience you've got now, I'm sure they'd be *glad* to—'

'I'm happy where I am, Mum.'

'Robin,' said Linda, now audibly crying, 'how long before one of these near misses—?'

Robin felt tears start in her eyes too. She was exhausted, stressed and scared. She understood her mother's panic and pain, but she was a grown woman of thirty and she was going to make her own decisions now, no matter who it upset, after long years of doing what other people – her parents, Matthew – wanted her to do: the safe, dull and expected thing.

'Mum,' she said again, as the cashier began scanning her purchases and she tried to open a plastic bag one-handed, '*please* don't worry, I—'

'*How d'you expect me not to worry?* Your dad's just out of hospital and we turn on the news—'

Fifteen more minutes passed before Robin was able to terminate the call, by which time she felt still more exhausted and miserable. The prospect of Strike arriving was the only thing that cheered her up as she made her way back up the road, laden with heavy bags of food and drink.

Once back at her flat she busied herself putting away her shopping, sorting out clean bedclothes for the sofa-bed and, in a spirit of defiance against her mother, logging onto *Drek's Game* on her iPad, which she left running while she did her various household tasks, checking periodically to see whether Anomie had appeared. She also put the printouts she'd made in the early hours of the morning onto the small table behind the sofa, which had room for three chairs at a pinch.

Atypically for Strike, he arrived exactly when he'd said he would. Robin had barely put the chicken in the oven when the doorbell rang. Robin buzzed him in through the main entrance, and waited for him at the open door of her flat.

'Evening,' he said, panting slightly as he reached the top of the stairs.

He handed her a bottle of red wine as he entered the flat.

'Thanks for letting me stay. Appreciate it.'

'No trouble at all,' said Robin, closing the door behind him. Strike took off his coat and hung it on a set of hooks that hadn't been there on moving day. He had the characteristic drawn expression that meant he was in pain, and as she followed him upstairs, Robin saw that he was using the banister to haul himself upwards.

Strike, who hadn't seen the flat since Robin had fully finished unpacking, glanced around the sitting room. There were framed photographs on the mantelpiece that hadn't been there on moving day, and a Raoul Dufy print hanging above them, showing a seascape viewed through two open windows.

'So,' said Strike, turning to look at Robin. 'Ormond.'

'I know . . . I bought lager, d'you want some?'

'Hang on,' said Strike as Robin turned automatically towards the kitchen, taking his 'yes' for granted, 'which has got more calories, beer or wine?'

She froze in the doorway, astonished.

'Calories? *You?*'

'I've got to get some of this weight off,' said Strike. 'My leg's not coping.'

He so rarely mentioned his stump that Robin decided not to exploit the opportunity for humour.

'Wine,' she said. 'Wine's got fewer calories.'

'I was afraid you were going to say that,' said Strike gloomily. 'D'you mind giving me a glass of that, then?' he said, nodding at the bottle in her hands, and then, 'Can I do anything?'

'No, sit down,' said Robin. 'There isn't anything to do. I've just bunged a chicken and some baked potatoes on.'

'You didn't need to cook,' said Strike. 'We could've got a takeaway.'

'What about the calories?'

'There is that,' conceded Strike, lowering himself onto the sofa.

When Robin returned, she handed him a glass of wine, then sat down in an armchair opposite him, positioned her iPad where she could watch the game, from which Anomie was still absent, and said,

'So, yes. Ormond.'

'Well,' said Strike, who'd taken a welcome sip of wine, 'I can see why they've arrested him. He had the phone.'

'But you don't think it's him,' said Robin.

'It *could* be him,' said Strike, 'but I've got a few queries. I'm sure they've occurred to the Met too.'

'Murphy said the phone might've had a tracker on it. Put there by Ormond.'

'If he's saying that, I'll lay you odds he knows it's on there. Well, if Ormond put a tracker on her phone without her knowing about it, it looks pretty bloody bad for him, doesn't it? He had the means of locating her and a strong motive for stealing the mobile after killing her, to remove the tracking app.'

Strike set down his wine on the table beside the sofa, opened his rucksack and, to Robin's surprise, took out a pack she recognised, after combing Boots for them that morning, as an e-cigarette.

'You're not trying to give up smoking?' she asked incredulously. She'd assumed Strike would die with a Benson & Hedges clamped between his teeth.

'Thinking about it,' he said, ripping off the cellophane as he spoke. 'Never had one of these . . .

'So,' said Strike returning to the main point as he began to put the e-cigarette together, 'let's say, for the sake of argument, Ormond's taking his detention at school, checks the tracking app and sees Edie's heading for the cemetery. He's suspicious. He's sure she's meeting Blay. He tells the kid who's in detention that he's got to go, and he threatens the kid with a week's worth of detentions to stop her telling anyone he left early ... Well, that's a hell of a shaky alibi, for a start. I wouldn't want to pin my hopes of getting away with murder on a schoolgirl I'd put in detention.'

'Maybe he wasn't planning to kill Edie when he set out.'

'But he slipped a machete into his briefcase, just in case?'

'OK, good point,' said Robin, suppressing a yawn. 'Where's Ormond's school, in relation to the cemetery?'

'Close to The Flask, where I interviewed him. Very short walk. If he took the Fiesta, he could've got to the cemetery within minutes.'

Both sat in silence, thinking, while Strike filled the e-cigarette with nicotine fluid and Robin checked the game: still no Anomie. At last, she said:

'Is it possible the man Blay passed in the cemetery – the big bald guy we think was in disguise – was Ormond?'

'Theoretically possible,' said Strike, as he screwed the top onto his e-cigarette, 'but there are logistical issues. Did he take the disguise to work, on the off chance he was going to commit murder? And where did he put it on? Be bloody risky to do it at school. If he was taking a detention, there were probably other staff members around.'

'Does he live in Highgate?'

'No. Finchley.'

'So the phone moving onto Hampstead Heath needs explaining too,' said Robin. 'Surely, if he'd just stabbed Edie and Josh he'd get back in his car and get out of there as fast as possible, not take a detour to Number One Pond?

'It's funny, though, isn't it?' she went on, 'because the police initially thought whoever had the phone went to Number One Pond to throw it away, and Ormond *did* end up throwing the phone in a pond – just a different one.'

'Which is interesting, I agree,' said Strike. 'What made him decide to dispose of the phone in a pond? Maybe it was finding it beside a pond in the first place. Maybe that planted a subliminal idea.'

'You think he tracked the phone onto the Heath and found it lying in the grass?'

'That's one possibility. The other is that he found himself face to face with whoever had taken it.'

'Why wouldn't he tell the police that?'

'Panic?' suggested Strike. 'He doesn't want to admit he was in the vicinity of the cemetery when it happened, doesn't want to admit he was tracking her?'

He now turned on the e-cigarette in his mouth and inhaled, frowning.

'But if he came face to face with the killer,' said Strike, exhaling vapour, 'how did he get the phone off them? Was there a fight?'

'Maybe the killer pretended they'd found the phone – you know, just lying on the ground – and Ormond said it was his and they handed it over?'

'Think that's more plausible than Ormond wrestling them for it,' said Strike, nodding. 'Assuming our big bald guy bending over the grave was the killer, they might've stripped off their disguise by then, so he could've taken them for a normal passer-by . . .

'However,' said Strike, 'if Ormond met the killer when they were still masked up, it explains quite a lot of what he said to me when I interviewed him. Can't remember whether I told you this, but when he talked about Anomie hiding behind a keyboard he made a gesture suggesting a mask. What if he thinks the masked person he met was Anomie? If it was, Anomie saw *him* in the vicinity of the murder scene, and saw *him* holding Edie's phone, which leads us neatly back to "Anomie would cast suspicion on anyone else to save their own neck". It might also explain "I've got no reason to say it was him". Freud would have a field day with that one. If my hypothesis is right, Ormond *has* got a bloody good reason for thinking the killer was Anomie, because he came face to face with them, and so he defended himself against a charge I hadn't made: that he had eyewitness evidence he was concealing.'

'That hangs together,' said Robin. 'So Ormond's got Edie's phone—'

'—but he hasn't found *her*. He gets in his car and drives home.

Waits. She doesn't come back. He calls the police and fairly quickly realises she's been murdered. He makes a snap decision to lie about his movements, scared that the tracker, and the fact he's got her mobile, will see him accused.'

Robin checked the game again, saw that Anomie was still absent, then pointed at the e-cigarette.

'How is it?'

'Not as good as a real one,' said Strike, looking down at it. 'But I s'pose I could get used to it. Least I won't stink your flat out.'

'Want more wine?'

'Thanks,' said Strike, holding out his glass. 'So, Nils de Jong sounds quite a character.'

'He's very odd,' said Robin. 'Like I told you, he's kind of a – well, a hippy with fascist overtones. All that "aristocratic outlook" and the race stuff: I wasn't expecting that at all. And I told you what he said about Edie's death being a "fulfilment", didn't I?'

'It will have been a fulfilment, for the killer,' said Strike. 'So what else were you doing all last night? You said you were working.'

'I was,' said Robin. 'I was at Junction Road till past midnight and then I spent most of the early hours on social media. In a nutshell, Zoe's mysterious boyfriend is Tim Ashcroft. I saw him leaving her flat last night.'

'Ashcroft?' said Strike, taken aback. 'I wouldn't have put those two together in a million years.'

'Well, Zoe's got – or she *had* – something Ashcroft likes a lot,' said Robin, unsmiling. She now got up to retrieve the printouts she'd made before Strike arrived and handed them to him. 'That's what I was doing most of the night. Have a look, while I start some gravy.'

Robin left for the kitchen. The pages she'd handed Strike comprised Twitter threads, some dating back several years. He began to read.

Timothy J Ashcroft

@TheWormTurning

Happy New Year InkHearts!
Love from The Worm

11.10 am   1 January 2011

Zozo @inkyheart28
replying to @TheWormTurning
Thanks Timothy ! And to you , I love
The Worm !!!!
💔💔💔

Timothy J Ashcroft

@TheWormTurning
replying to @inkyheart28
Thanks, but is this cartoon not a bit
old for you?!

Zozo @inkyheart28
replying to @TheWormTurning
😊 I'm nearly 14!!!!!!

Timothy J Ashcroft @
TheWormTurning
replying to @inkyheart28
ah ok I was worried we were
corrupting u!

Zozo @inkyheart28
replying to @TheWormTurning
😂 no I 'm not that innocent 😂

Timothy J Ashcroft

@TheWormTurning
replying to @inkyheart28
tell me more . . . .

Zozo @inkyheart28
replying to @TheWormTurning
😂😂😂😂😂😂😂😂😂😂

Timothy J Ashcroft

@TheWormTurning
replying to @inkyheart28
Well I've followed you back, so you can
tell me privately if you feel too shy in here!

Timothy J Ashcroft

@TheWormTurning
It's The Worm's Birthday (well, mine)
#TheInkBlackHeart

9.14 am   1 November 2011

MrsHarty @carlywhistler_*
replying to @TheWormTurning
Happy birthday, I love The Worm so
much, he's so cute!

Timothy J Ashcroft

@TheWormTurning
replying to @carlywhistler_*
You're pretty cute yourself, but how
come you're tweeting at this time in the
morning? Shouldn't you be in school?!

MrsHarty @carlywhistler_*
replying to @TheWormTurning
Day off, I'm ill

Timothy J Ashcroft

@TheWormTurning
replying to @carlywhistler_*
Well, I'm following you back because
you were nice enough to wish me
happy birthday x

Laura H @InkHeart<3
I would die in battle for The Worm 💔
#TheInkBlackHeart

7.13 pm   30 November 2011

Timothy J Ashcroft

@TheWormTurning
replying to @InkHeart<3
The worm would die in battle
for you too!
How old are you?

Laura H @InkHeart<3
replying to @TheWormTurning
omg I can't believe you saw that!!!!!! 13

Timothy J Ashcroft

@TheWormTurning

Just finished recording next episode, big character moment for The Worm!

9.32 pm   23 December 2011

Orla Moran @BlackHeartOrla
replying to @TheWormTurning
tell us now!!!!!!!!!

Timothy J Ashcroft

@TheWormTurning
replying to @BlackHeartOrla
Bossy! How old are you?

Orla Moran @BlackHeartOrla
replying to @TheWormTurning
😂 😂 😂 14 why?

Timothy J Ashcroft

@TheWormTurning
replying to @BlackHeartOrla
Give me a follow and I might DM you some details!

Orla Moran @BlackHeartOrla
replying to @TheWormTurning
omg 😊

Timothy J Ashcroft

@TheWormTurning
replying to @InkHeart<3
Well, that's a follow from The Worm!

The Pen of Justice

@penjustwrites

When black = evil and white = most desirable, what does that tell us? My take on the problematic palette of #TheInkBlackHeart

www.PenOfJustice/
ThePoliticsOfColou . . .

9.38 am   9 February 2013

Zozo @inkyheart28
replying to @penjustwrites
this is really good , I hadn't though of it like that

Pen of Justice @penjustwrites
replying to @inkyheart28
thanks hot stuff

Expressionless, Strike flipped over the page.

The Pen of Justice

@penjustwrites

Harmless fan fave or antisemitic stereotype?

My take on the problematic character of Drek

www.PenOfJustice/
AntisemiticCartoon . . .

11.02 am   28 February 2012

Netflix UK & Ireland

@N£tflix

We are delighted to announce that smash YouTube success #TheInkBlackHeart will be premiering on Netflix in June 2013, with new content and a second series already in development. Read full story here: www.NetflixUK/TheInkBlackHeart...

9.12 pm   5 February 2013

Penny Peacock @rachledbadly
replying to @penjustwrites
Edie Ledwell said Drek was inspired by
a plague mask though

Pen of Justice @penjustwrites
replying to @rachledbadly
This isn't just about the nose! How
old are you?

Penny Peacock @rachledbadly
replying to @penjustwrites
14, why?

Pen of Justice @penjustwrites
replying to @rachledbadly
wow, you look older. if you read
the whole piece you'll see Drek
manipulates everyone and lives in the
largest mausoleum, ie, is richest

Penny Peacock @rachledbadly
replying to @penjustwrites
He doesn't live in the biggest
mausoleum tho, Lord and Lady WG do.

Penny Peacock @rachledbadly
replying to @penjustwrites
And he doesn't manipulate people, they
just humour him because he's bored

Pen of Justice @penjustwrites
replying to @rachledbadly
hey, I'm always up for an intelligent
debate! That's a follow from me!

MrsHarty @carlywhistler_*
so, I'm coming to London, what are the
best things to see?

7.45pm . 14 March 2012 .

Pen of Justice @penjustwrites
replying to @carlywhistler_*
Me

Esther Cohen @happ£_bunn££
replying to @N£tflix
Wonderful news, happy for these two
very gifted creators!

Pen of Justice @penjustwrites
replying to @N£tflix
Very much hope @N£tflix will listen
to fans' concerns about problematic
material before TIBH reaches a
wider audience

Caitlin Adams @CaitAdumsss
replying to @penjustwrites
@N£tflix
only one way to fix that #FireFedwell

Penny Peacock @rachledbadly
replying to @CaitAdumsss
@penjustwrites @N£tflix
idon't want her fired, all the decent
ideas are hers

Pen of Justice @penjustwrites
replying to @rachledbadly
@CaitAdumsss @N£tflix
agree she's v talented, just think
certain changes wd improve cartoon

Penny Peacock @rachledbadly
replying to @penjustwrites
@CaitAdumsss @N£tflix
but I don't want to get rid of Drek, turn
Harty pink or stop Paperwhite being a
ghost like you do

Pen of Justice @penjustwrites
replying to @rachledbadly
@CaitAdumsss @N£tflix
lol, u're obviously a regular reader of
mine! how old r u?

Penny Peacock @rachledbadly
replying to @penjustwrites
@CaitAdumsss @N£tflix
you already asked me that. why do you
always want to know how old girls are?

MrsHarty @carlywhistler_*
replying to @penjustwrites
😂 🖤

MrsHarty @carlywhistler_*

so, my dad won't let me go to
london 🙄 😡

8.02pm . 20 March 2012 .

Zozo @inkyheart28

IT 'S MY BITHDAY AND I 'M IN
LONDON !!!!!!
🎆 🎆 🎆 🎆 🎆 🎈 🎈 🎈 🎈

10.02 am   28 March 2012

Timothy J Ashcroft
@TheWormTurning

Not gonna lie, I was gutted to be
ousted from #TheInkBlackHeart, but
new projects coming!

"We're dead. Things can only get better."

11.14 am   25 March 2013

Ruby Nooby @rubynooby*_*
replying to @TheWormTurning
I'm so sad I luved you as the worm

Timothy J Ashcroft
@TheWormTurning
replying to @rubynooby*_*
your beautiful face just made my
day better 🖤

Ruby Nooby @rubynooby*_*
replying to @TheWormTurning
oh wow I never thought you'd
reply!!!!!!! 🖤 🖤 🖤

DrekBwah14 @DrekBwah14
replying to @rachledbadly
@penjustwrites @CaitAdumsss
@N£tflix
because he's a nonce

Pen of Justice @penjustwrites
replying to @DrekBwah14
@rachledbadly
@penjustwrites @CaitAdumsss
@N£tflix
Why is the go-to insult for fascists
always 'paedo'? Blocked.

DrekBwah14 @DrekBwah14
replying to @penjustwrites
@rachledbadly
you're still a fkn nonce 😂

Zozo @inkyheart28

when u think somebody cares u and
ur mum died
and they don 't answer ur DMs or texts
and u wonder why u keep bein loyal

9.05 am   14 May 2012

Pen of Justice @penjustwrites
replying to @inkyheart28
check ur phone I've texted u

The Pen of Justice
@penjustwrites

God I hate wrapping presents.

9.32 pm   23 December 2014

Darcy Barrett @DarkViola90
replying to @penjustwrites
me too it's shit.

Lepine's Disciple @LepinesD1sciple
replying to @DarkViola90
@penjustwrites
takes shit to know shit

Timothy J Ashcroft
@TheWormTurning
replying to @rubynooby*_*
lol how old are you?

Ruby Nooby @rubynooby*_*
replying to @TheWormTurning
12

Timothy J Ashcroft
@TheWormTurning
replying to @rubynooby*_*
naughty girl, you shouldn't be
on Twitter!

Ruby Nooby @rubynooby*_*
replying to @TheWormTurning
I mean 13!

Timothy J Ashcroft
@TheWormTurning
replying to @rubynooby*_*
lol well you've got a follow from me

Andrew Whistler @andywhistler8
replying to @TheWormTurning
@rubynooby*_*
still at it, are you?

Andrew Whistler @andywhistler8
replying to @TheWormTurning
@rubynooby*_*
ah, you've blocked me. no fucking
surprise.

Timothy J Ashcroft
@TheWormTurning
replying to @juiceeluce
Love your little dog! How old are you?

The Pen of Justice
@penjustwrites
replying to @carla_mappin5
You really get these issues! How
old are you?

The Pen of Justice
@penjustwrites
replying to @LepinsD1sciple
@DarkViola90
go have another wank, incel

Lepine's Disciple @LepinesD1sciple
replying to @penjustwrites
@darkling_b
she's too old for you, paedo

The Pen of Justice @penjustwrites
replying to @LepinsD1sciple
@DarkViola90
blocked, arsehole

Ellen Richardson @e_r_inkheart
replying to @penjustwrites
I really love how you interpret
everything for us 💔

The Pen of Justice @penjustwrites
replying to @e_r_inkheart
Thank you! 💔 How old are you?

Ellen Richardson @e_r_inkheart
replying to @penjustwrites
13

The Pen of Justice @penjustwrites
replying to @e_r_inkheart
Followed for being so nice!

Ellen Richardson @e_r_inkheart
replying to @penjustwrites
Oh wow 💔

Timothy J Ashcroft
@TheWormTurning
replying to @mollydeverill1
Good point! How old are you?

Timothy J Ashcroft
@TheWormTurning
replying to @annaff0rbes
Cute picture! How old are you?

Timothy J Ashcroft
@TheWormTurning
replying to @tash&&&rgh
You're funny! How old are you?

Robin re-entered the room just as Strike finished reading. His expression was forbidding.

'Have you read it all?'

'Yeah.'

'I think he created the Pen of Justice account as a fallback. He wanted to keep his connection to the *Ink Black Heart* fandom, even if he lost The Worm. Meanwhile, he could snare straightforward fangirls as Tim, and critics as the Pen.'

'And he started grooming Zoe when she was what – fourteen?'

'Thirteen,' said Robin. 'She lied to him, claimed to be a year older than she is. She first came to London on her fourteenth birthday. I've checked online records. She's only seventeen now. Did you see the father who got wise to him? "Still at it, are you?"'

'The guy who stopped his daughter going to London? Yeah. Smart man . . . and now Ashcroft's going into schools with his theatre group. Jesus Christ.'

Robin picked her notebook off the table and opened it at the scribbled results of her eavesdropping in Junction Road.

'Zoe and Ashcroft were arguing last night. I got inside the building and had a listen outside her door. Ashcroft seemed to be accusing Zoe of blackmail, which she denied. He said to her "who started this?" and "you put me in a hell of a position", and said he was the one who took the risk – no elaboration on what the risk was, but obviously he might've meant their relationship. Other than that, it was all Zoe begging him not to leave and him saying he had "thinking to do". Of course,' said Robin, closing the notebook, 'she's aged out of his sexual preference now, hasn't she? He seems to like them best around thirteen or fourteen. I wondered whether that's why she's starving herself, to keep looking as young as possible.'

'Fucking *hate* paedophiles,' muttered Strike, as Robin's upstairs neighbour began playing rap loudly.

'Does anyone like them?' asked Robin.

'Yeah, other paedophiles. They're very much birds of a feather, in my experience. Well, this explains your friend Pez having a go at Ashcroft at the funeral, doesn't it? Wasn't Ashcroft talking to a couple of underage girls?'

'I don't know whether Rachel Ledwell's underage,' said Robin, 'but Flavia Upcott definitely is. And what d'you mean "my friend" Pez?' she added, because there'd been an undertone in Strike's voice she hadn't much appreciated. He raised his eyebrows, a slight smirk on his face, and Robin, to her own irritation, felt herself turning pink.

'I did what I had to do to get information out of him,' she said coldly, and left the room again, ostensibly to stir the gravy, but in fact to give herself time to stop blushing.

Regretting his attempt at archness, which in truth had been a clumsy attempt to find out how much Robin had enjoyed those parts of the interview that had involved kissing and, perhaps, being groped by Pez Pierce, Strike considered calling an apology after her. Before he could do so, however, his mobile rang. It was Madeline.

Strike hesitated, staring at the screen. Madeline had wanted him to call her back, which of course he hadn't done. He was supposed to be sitting alone in some anonymous Travelodge and suspected that if he ignored Madeline's call she'd ring back every ten minutes until he answered.

'Hi,' he said, taking the call.

'How are you? Did you get a hotel room?'

'Yeah, just checked in,' said Strike, keeping his voice low. 'Can't talk for long, I'm expecting an update from a subcontractor.'

'I'm worried about you,' said Madeline. 'Bloody hell, Corm. A *bomb*. It's terrifying.'

Robin re-entered the room, her colour still high. Failing to notice that Strike was on the phone, she said,

'Look, I don't much appreciate—'

She broke off, seeing the mobile held to his ear.

'Who was that?' asked Madeline.

'Room service,' said Strike.

'No, it wasn't,' said Madeline, while Robin stared down at him with accusatory eyes. He had a strong feeling both women knew exactly what was going on: yielding ill-advisedly to the impulse of the cornered male, he attempted to brazen it out.

'It was.'

'Corm,' said Madeline, 'I'm not stupid.'

Robin left the room again.

'I don't think you're stupid,' said Strike, now closing his eyes, as if he were a child on an out-of-control bike, careering towards a wall.

'So who was that woman, and what doesn't she appreciate?'

Fuck, fuck, fuck. He ought to have left the flat before taking the call, but he was so tired, and his leg so sore, he hadn't wanted to get up. He opened his eyes again and fixed them on the Raoul Dufy print on the wall. What wouldn't he give to be sitting alone by a window overlooking the Mediterranean right now?

'I'm having a quick drink with Robin,' he said. 'To talk over agency stuff. How we're going to carry on without access to the office.'

There was a long silence, then Madeline said,

'You're staying with her.'

'No I'm not,' said Strike.

'But it's OK to meet Robin this evening and risk terrorists finding *her*—'

'They're already onto her,' said Strike. 'The bomb was addressed to both of us.'

'Sweet,' said Madeline coldly. 'It's like you're married, isn't it? Well, I'll let you get on with your drink.'

The line went dead.

A swarm of angry, anxious thoughts buzzed rapidly through Strike's brain: *It's got to end. You fuckwit. I don't need this tonight. It was never going to work. No point calling back. Got to end it. Apologise.*

Strike pushed himself off the sofa and limped to the kitchen where Robin stood with his back to her, stirring gravy.

'Sorry,' said Strike. 'I was being a dick.'

'Yes,' said Robin coldly. 'You were. You wouldn't take that tone with Barclay, if he had to chat up some woman to get information.'

'I'd say far worse than that if Barclay had had to snog some woman to get stuff out of her, believe me,' said Strike, and when Robin turned to look at him, half annoyed, half grudgingly amused, he shrugged and said, 'Banter, innit? It's what we do.'

'Hmm,' said Robin, turning away to give the gravy another stir. 'Well, I'd have thought you'd be pleased I got so much out of Pierce.'

'I *was* pleased,' said Strike. 'You did bloody well. That chicken smells great.'

'It'll need another half an hour,' said Robin. She hesitated, then said, 'Who were you claiming I was room service to?'

'Madeline,' said Strike. He had no energy left for lying. 'She wanted me to stay with her. I said I was going to a hotel. Just easier.'

Robin, who was very interested in this information, kept stirring the gravy, hoping to hear more but not wanting to ask for it. However, as Strike didn't enlarge on the subject, Robin turned down the heat under the saucepan and both returned to the sitting room.

While Robin checked the game and greeted various players to

make sure Buffypaws wasn't completely inactive, Strike took out his notebook and turned to the pages in which he'd written observations on Robin's interview with Pez.

'You really did do great with Pierce,' he said.

'All right,' said Robin with a slight eye-roll as she refilled both their glasses, 'there's no need to overdo it.'

'I imagine you've noticed how many boxes on our Anomie profile he ticks? Knows a lot about the Beatles, doesn't like cats—'

'That was only ever a guess—'

'—part-time carer for his father – he also knows a way into that cemetery without getting caught—'

'I know that, but—'

'—and by the sounds of it, he and Edie were working on something together and she left him in the lurch, going off with Josh and writing a smash hit with him. That's grounds for serious resentment.'

'She didn't necessarily leave him in the lurch,' said Robin. 'She might not have thought whatever she and Pez were doing was any good. Changed her mind. They'd argued about Tim as well. Maybe it wasn't fun working with him after that.'

'Might not be how Pierce sees it. You don't think he's Anomie, do you?' said Strike, watching for her reaction.

'Well . . .' Robin hesitated, 'he's got the ability to create the game, but we knew that all along. I don't know . . . When I was with him, I just didn't *feel* it.'

By exercising heroic self-restraint, Strike refrained from making the most obvious of the ribald comments that occurred to him.

'I mean,' said Robin, who thankfully hadn't noticed any sense of strain in Strike's expression, 'Anomie's vicious – sadistic. I just didn't get that from Pez. He can definitely be crass – I told you about that thing he painted on Josh and Edie's wall – and he was quite aggressive to the *Ink Black Heart* fan who turned up at our first drawing class and said she was there to "soak up the magic" or something. She *was* a bit annoying,' Robin added, taking a sip of wine, 'but there was no call for him to be that cruel. Yasmin Weatherhead seemed scared of him. I could imagine him making fat jokes. He's that type.

'But barring his dad being ill, which must be a big strain, he's not doing badly in life, as far as I can see. He's popular with women. He's found a place to live that suits him. And he's getting work, even if it's not as steady as he'd like. I s'pose it's the same objection I had to Gus

Upcott. To be as good as they are in their respective fields would take hours and hours out of every day, and if there's one thing we know for sure about Anomie, it's that they've a lot of time on their hands.'

'True,' said Strike. 'Well, speaking of people with a lot of time on their hands, I turned up something new myself this morning. Didn't have time to print it out before the bomb went off, but the bottom line is: Kea Niven made some very threatening comments on Twitter on the night before the attacks, which she deleted, but which have since turned up on Reddit. She was talking about stabbing people through the heart.'

'*Oh* – that's what Cardew was trying to get her to delete?'

'Exactly. Their little rebound fling doesn't seem to have been the end of their acquaintance, which is interesting, as is his comment "there are better ways". Pity we've ruled out Cardew, in a way, because personality-wise he seems to fit Anomie better than almost anyone, and I note Pierce thinks so too.

'Anyway, Kea's been up to more than making threats on Twitter,' Strike went on, now reaching for his phone and bringing up the Tribulationem et Dolorum website. 'Have a look at that. It's from a couple of years ago.'

Robin took the phone and read the conversation between Arke and John that Strike had found that morning.

'Now go and have a look at the "About the Founder" page,' said Strike.

Robin did so, and then, with a look of dawning enlightenment, read aloud:

'"A selection of John's compositions can be heard at www.IJU. MakesSounds . . ." IJU? Not . . .'

'Inigo John Upcott,' said Strike. 'Precisely.'

Robin stared at Strike.

'But then—'

'Remember Inigo's spirited defence of Kea, when we were round at their house? Words to the effect of "Blay treated that young lady extremely badly"? I've got a strong suspicion that he and Kea have had a lot more contact than one online discussion about chronic fatigue.'

'You don't think—?'

'She's his "darling child"? I do, yeah.'

'Wow,' said Robin slowly, looking back down at the Tribulationem et Dolorum site. 'Well, there's no way this is coincidence. She didn't turn up on that website without knowing who ran it.'

'I agree. She was looking for a sneaky way to keep tabs on Josh and Edie. I don't doubt there came a point, once she'd convinced Inigo she was there for the fascination of his personality, that they "discovered" their mutual connection to Josh and Edie and I'm sure Kea was suitably amazed at the bizarre twist of fate. On short acquaintance, I'd say Inigo's a man with an outsize ego. I don't think Kea would have had too hard a job convincing him she was maintaining contact because he was such a wise, talented man, rather than because she wanted to wheedle information out of him. And all of this shunts Kea right back up the Anomie suspect list, doesn't it? We thought she had no means of knowing about the proposed Harty-to-human change, but if we're right, she's had a direct route into the Upcott household since 2013.'

'D'you think she and Inigo have met in real life?' asked Robin.

'That's something we'll need to ask Upcott. They've clearly got each other's phone numbers, if she's the "darling child" he's been reassuring and promising to help.'

'She surely wouldn't have—?' began Robin, before breaking off.

'Who knows?' said Strike, who'd correctly guessed how the sentence would have ended. 'Some people'll go to any lengths to further their interests.'

Both thought immediately of Robin letting Pez Pierce thrust his tongue into her mouth.

'I'm supposed to be taking over on Ashcroft tomorrow,' said Robin.

'We'll rejig the rota,' said Strike, picking up his phone again. 'And we'll do Upcott together, first thing.'

Robin suspected the suggestion they stick together was motivated by Strike's apprehensions about The Halvening, but as she had no real complaints about spending the morning with Strike, she merely said as she got up,

'The chicken'll be nearly done. Keep an eye on the game. I'll just steam some veg.'

'"Steam",' repeated Strike, as though he'd never heard the word before.

'Something wrong with steaming?'

'No. Just never done it. I normally fry everything.'

'Ah,' said Robin. 'Well, you might want to change that, if you're worried about calories.'

She retreated to the kitchen, leaving Strike to email Pat about the rota and send texts to Midge, Dev, Barclay and Nutley. Having done this, Strike replaced his phone in his pocket, checked *Drek's Game* to make sure that Anomie was still absent, then looked around the sitting room.

What would he have guessed about the occupant, if he hadn't known who lived here? She liked reading: the books had partially overflowed the small bookcase he himself had helped put together, and he noted how many works on criminology were crammed along-side the novels. Apparently she had a fondness for Fauvist art, given that there was a second print hanging over the dining room table: Matisse's *Still Life with Geraniums*. He'd have known the occupant of this flat didn't earn the kind of money, or have the same kind of family, as Charlotte, whose flat, which Strike had briefly shared, had been full of bits of antique furniture left to her by various relatives. The blue and cream curtains Robin had hung since he'd last been here weren't expensive, nor did they have heavy rope tiebacks or beaded fringing, while the lampshade overhead was a cheap white Chinese lantern. He'd have guessed she was habitually neat and clean, because this room bore no air of having been hastily organised for his arrival: no Hoover tracks on the carpet, no smell of Pledge in the air. He saw with some pleasure that Robin had put the philodendron he'd bought her in a blue china pot. The plant was now sitting on a corner table, looking healthy: apparently she watered plants too. After taking another pull on his e-cigarette, he heaved himself to his feet to look at the framed photographs on the mantelpiece.

He recognised Robin's parents, beaming at what appeared to be, judging by the silver balloons behind them, a twenty-fifth anniversary celebration. Her mother Linda hadn't often worn that smile when face to face with Strike; but then, she'd become less enamoured of him with every dangerous episode in which her daughter had been involved, working for the agency. A second picture showed a gig-gling toddler in a pink spotted swimsuit, standing beneath a garden sprinkler: Strike assumed this was Robin's niece. The third picture showed the adult Robin arm in arm with her three brothers, all of whom Strike had met; the fourth, a chocolate Labrador; and the fifth a group of people sitting at a dinner table, with a spectacular view of the Matterhorn at sunset visible through the large window beside them.

Glancing behind him to make sure that Robin wasn't going to

reappear, he picked up this picture and examined it. A different toddler was sitting in a high chair at the end of the table, a plastic spoon
clutched in his chubby hand. Robin was smiling at the camera from
a seat about halfway down the table, and a sturdy-looking man with
a neat sandy beard and eyes that Strike found fishy was sitting beside
her, also beaming, with his arm along the back of Robin's chair. Strike
was still holding this picture when Robin returned, holding cutlery.

'Matterhorn,' he said, replacing the picture where it had stood.

'Yes,' said Robin. 'It was so beautiful. Has Anomie been in?' she
asked, pointing at the iPad.

'No,' said Strike. 'Let me help carry stuff through.'

Both were so tired that talk was desultory over dinner, during
which Robin paused regularly to move Buffypaws in the game.
Anomie didn't appear and the only moderators present were
Paperwhite and Morehouse, neither of whom chided Buffypaws for
spending long periods inactive.

'If I'm going to pass the moderator test I'll have to find some time
to revise the cartoon next week,' Robin said as they cleared away their
plates at the end of dinner.

'I know,' said Strike. 'We'll have to prioritise that.'

Strike checked whether Ormond's arrest had been reported after
washing up, but none of the news sites they visited were yet carrying
the story. They retired to their respective beds shortly afterwards,
and if both were aware of the intimacy of Robin handing Strike his
own clean bath towel and a pile of clean bedding, and of using the
same bathroom, each hid it beneath a matter-of-factness bordering
on brusqueness.

Lying in his brand-new pyjamas, with the end of his stump creamed
and his prosthetic leg propped up against the wall, Strike barely had
time to reflect that Robin's sofa-bed was surprisingly comfortable
before falling into a deep sleep.

Getting ready for bed barely twelve feet away, Robin could hear
Strike snoring even over the rap being played upstairs, which amused
and slightly reassured her. She'd been savouring the pleasures of living
alone since moving into Blackhorse Road, enjoying the independence
and the peace, but tonight, after the bombing of the office, it was
consoling to have Strike there, even if he was already fast asleep and
rumbling like a tractor. Her last conscious thought before drifting off
to sleep herself was of Ryan Murphy. Even though a date with him

hadn't yet happened, and might never happen, the possibility had somehow redressed an imbalance between her and Strike. She was no longer a lovesick fool committed to celibacy in the hope that Strike might one day want what he so clearly didn't want. Soon she'd sunk into a dreamworld where she was once again on the verge of marrying Matthew, who was explaining to her in the vestibule of the church, as to a child, that if she'd only asked him he could have told her who Anomie was, and that her failure to see what was so patently obvious to everyone else proved she wasn't fit for the job that had so nearly separated them for ever.

76

What inn is this
Where for the night
Peculiar traveller comes?

Emily Dickinson
XXXIV

When she entered the sitting room the following morning at seven, Robin found Strike already dressed, the sofa-bed returned to its usual state and Strike's bedding neatly folded. She made both of them tea and toast, and as they consumed it at the table where they'd eaten dinner Strike said,

'Let's head straight for the Upcotts' and find out what Inigo's been sharing with Kea. Then, depending on what he tells us, we'll go to King's Lynn.'

'OK,' said Robin, though she looked unhappy.

'What's the matter?'

'Just wondering what's Katya going to say when she realises Inigo's been in communication with Kea all this time.'

'I'd imagine she'll be seriously pissed off,' said Strike, with a slight shrug. 'Not our problem.'

'I know, but I can't help feeling sorry for her. I think their kids might be happier if they split up, though ...'

Strike's phone buzzed. He picked it up, read the text that had just arrived and his expression became immediately furious.

'What's happened?' asked Robin.

'Fucking Nutley!'

'What's he done?'

'He's fucking resigned, is what he's done!'

'*What?*' said Robin. 'Why?'

'Because,' said Strike, who was rapidly scrolling down through the paragraph of self-exculpation Nutley had sent, 'his wife doesn't want him working for us now we've been bombed. "I know this leaves you shorthanded and once this terrorist situation's cleared up, I'd be happy—" Oh, *would* you be fucking happy, you useless piece of shit?'

'Listen,' said Robin, as the consequences of one fewer subcontractor passed rapidly through her mind. 'You should do Inigo alone. I'll take over on Ashcroft as planned and—'

'We're sticking together,' said Strike. 'It was both our names on the fucking bomb, both our pictures on the fucking news story and I'm taking these Halvening fuckers seriously, even if you aren't.'

'Of course I'm taking them seriously, what are you—?'

'Then don't suggest wandering off on your own,' said Strike angrily, getting up from the table and, forgetting all his resolutions of the previous day, heading downstairs for a proper smoke on the street.

He knew perfectly well he'd just been unwarrantedly aggressive to Robin, but the thought merely increased his bad temper as he smoked two cigarettes back to back while texting the news of Nutley's resignation to Barclay, Midge and Dev. He found himself completely in sympathy with Barclay, who texted back: **Cowardly fucking cunt**.

Having returned to Robin's sitting room, Strike found the breakfast things cleared away and Robin ready to leave. As he'd expected, her manner was frosty again.

'Sorry I snapped,' said Strike before she could say anything. 'I'm just worried.'

'So am I, funnily enough,' said Robin coolly, 'but when you say "wandering off", as though I'm some airhead who—'

'I didn't mean that. I don't think you're an airhead, but – fuck's sake, Robin, that bomb was the real fucking deal, not just something to put the frighteners on us. Plus, we know they've got a particular thing about women getting above themselves.'

'So, what – you're going to tail me until they've rounded up The Halvening?'

'No – I don't know. Let's just go and talk to Inigo. Proving Kea's Anomie would solve our manpower problems, at least.'

They took Strike's BMW, Robin at the wheel, and spent most of the twenty-minute drive in silence. Robin couldn't help but remember that the last time they'd visited the Upcotts' she'd been angry at

Strike, too: that had been right after she'd found out he was dating Madeline. She wondered what the aftermath of Strike's lie about room service had been. He didn't appear to have spoken to Madeline since, unless the loud snores she'd heard last night had been faked and he'd been texting from beneath the bed covers. Nor had she forgotten Charlotte. Investigating Jago Ross had been the thing that brought the agency to breaking point, a fact Strike seemed curiously averse to acknowledging.

But, unbeknownst to Robin, Strike's thoughts were running parallel with hers. Unless he could find a replacement for Nutley immediately, they didn't have the capacity to cover all current cases and there was no doubt that Ross would be the easiest to drop. Even if his own future as an investigator were for ever scuppered by being associated with such a high-profile divorce, everyone else would still have jobs. Perhaps, he thought, it was his duty to withdraw surveillance from Ross, whatever the consequences.

He was at this depressing point in his ruminations when his phone buzzed again. Looking down, he saw a text from Madeline.

Please call me when you can. I think we need a proper talk

Strike put the phone back in his pocket without responding. He knew exactly where this was heading: the same way all his relationships went, to the place where expectation met resistance and imploded.

All right, he thought as he scowled out of the window, *I shouldn't have lied about where I was spending the night, but if I'd told you the truth there'd have been a scene anyway.* Was it a crime to have tried to avoid conflict, to have striven to save both of them grief?

He'd tried, hadn't he? He'd turned up when he was supposed to, given her flowers when it was appropriate, listened to her work worries and had what he believed to have been mutually exciting sex: what else did she want? *Honesty,* he heard Madeline say, as women always said, but honesty would have meant admitting that he'd started the relationship because he'd wanted a distraction from complicated feelings for another woman, and Madeline's response would surely be that he'd used her. *So what? People use each other all the time,* Strike told an imaginary Madeline, taking deep pulls on the e-cigarette he'd refilled for use in the car. *Ward off loneliness.*

Try and find what they're lacking. Show the world they've snagged a prize. And he remembered Madeline trying to take a picture of the two of them for her Instagram page, and the row on the night of her launch, and could already hear himself saying, *I think we want different things.* He ought to get it printed on cards, ready to hand out at the start of relationships, so nobody could say they hadn't been warned . . .

'Shit,' said Robin.

Strike looked round to see a Range Rover pulling out from the line of parked cars in front of the Upcott house.

'I think Inigo's in there,' said Robin, peering through the windscreen. 'Yes . . . he is. Gus is driving. What do we do?'

'Follow,' said Strike. 'Probably a medical appointment. Be easier to talk to him away from Katya anyway.'

'He's going to be furious we've tailed him,' said Robin.

'Probably,' said Strike, 'but it'll be a damn sight harder for him to get rid of us face to face. Anyway, he's got it coming, the sneaky bastard.'

However, Inigo and Gus didn't stop at either a doctor's surgery or a hospital, but continued east. Robin could see Inigo's profile, turned towards his son. He appeared to be telling Gus off. Occasionally, she saw a wagging finger.

'The hell are they going?' Strike wondered aloud, a full hour after they'd started following the Range Rover, as they reached the Dartford Crossing, the long, cable-stayed bridge crossing the Thames.

'Inigo can't be attending a hospital this far away, can he?' said Robin. 'He's *really* having a go at Gus.'

'Yeah,' said Strike, who was also watching the aggressive finger-jabbing. 'Not much wrong with Inigo's stamina, is there?'

'I thought Gus was supposed to be his favourite child.'

'The fact he's covered in hives might indicate that's a pretty stressful position to maintain,' said Strike. 'Maybe he's just told Inigo he wants to jack in the cello.'

The Range Rover continued along the M2 for another hour.

'I think they're going to Whitstable,' said Robin at last, as the Range Rover turned into a road called Borstal Hill. 'Could they be visiting someone?'

'Or,' said Strike, who'd had a sudden idea, 'they've got a second home. It's the kind of place where well-off Londoners would buy a little seaside residence . . . convenient for weekends . . .'

He took out his phone again, brought up the website 192.com and searched 'I J Upcott' and 'Whitstable'.

'Yeah, I'm right,' he said, 'they own another house here. Aquarelle Cottage, Island Wall.'

Robin followed the Range Rover into the heart of the pretty little town, past timbered houses and terraces of cottages in ice-cream colours, then along Harbour Street, which was lined with art galleries and curio shops. At last, the Range Rover made a couple of right turns, which took them into Keam's Yard car park. Robin parked the BMW at a distance from the Range Rover and together she and Strike watched in the wing and rear-view mirrors as Gus got out of the car, unloaded his father's wheelchair from the boot, helped Inigo descend, then pushed Inigo in his wheelchair around the corner and out of sight.

'Think we should give them ten minutes,' Strike said, checking the clock on the dashboard. 'Bet Gus'll be coming back to the car for bags. I don't want to give them a heads up we're here until they've put the kettle on and taken off their shoes. One good thing,' he added callously, 'it's very hard to do a runner in a wheelchair.'

77

You weep: 'I had such lofty aims.
My soul had yearnings truly great.
Than broken altars, dying flames,
I had deserved a better fate . . .'

May Kendall
Failures

Having watched Gus unload a pair of suitcases from the back of the
Range Rover and given him sufficient time to carry them into the
house, Strike and Robin got out of the BMW. A pebble beach lay
on the other side of the car park's stone wall, and the Cornish-born
Strike experienced that slight lift of the spirits the smell of the sea and
the sound of lapping waves always gave him.

Island Wall, which lay right around the corner from the car park,
was a narrow street that sloped downwards. The terrace of painted
houses on the right-hand side would have an unimpeded rear view
of the sea. Aquarelle Cottage, which lay several houses down, was
painted eau-de-nil, and the stained-glass fan window over the door
depicted a galleon in full sail.

There didn't appear to be a bell, so Strike lifted the anchor-shaped
knocker and rapped twice. Barely ten seconds passed before Gus
opened the door.

Recognising Strike and Robin, his expression changed to one
of horror. Robin had time to note that his hives, though no longer
encroaching on his bloodshot eyes, remained as inflamed as ever.

'Who is it?' called Inigo from inside the house.

Gus turned to see his father wheeling himself into sight. Inigo, too, seemed temporarily stunned by the appearance of the two detectives, but his habitual manner reasserted itself almost at once.

'What the—?'

'Morning,' said Strike, with what Robin felt was remarkable sang-froid given the look of rage on Inigo's face. 'Wondered whether we could have a word, Mr Upcott?'

Inigo wheeled himself closer. Gus pressed himself against the wall in a manner that suggested he'd have liked to disappear into it.

'Have you—? How did you even know I was—? *Have you been following me?*'

Slightly regretting that it would've been impolitic to say, *Obviously we have, you pompous prick*, Strike said, 'We were hoping to catch you at home in Hampstead, but as you were pulling away when we turned up, we came after you.'

'Why?' demanded Inigo. 'What – why—? This is outrageous!'

'We think you might have information that's important to our investigation,' said Strike, slightly raising his voice, because a couple of young women were passing and he suspected that Inigo would fear the neighbours knowing his business even more than the possible consequences of letting Strike and Robin inside. Sure enough, though he looked, if anything, angrier, Inigo said,

'Don't stand on the doorstep shouting! My God, this is a complete – absolute—'

Robin's years with the agency had taught her that, however unwelcome a visit from a private detective might be, nearly everyone wanted to know why they'd come, so she was unsurprised when Inigo snarled,

'I'll give you five minutes. *Five.*'

He attempted to reverse away from them as they entered, but in his agitation collided with the wall.

'Bloody help me!' he barked at his son, who hurried to do so.

The house, as they saw once they'd stepped inside and closed the door, had been adapted to the high standard of their Hampstead home. The ground floor had been converted into an open-plan area incorporating kitchen, dining and sitting areas, all with smooth floorboards. To the rear of the house were French windows which opened onto a garden that had also been adapted for Inigo's wheelchair, with a sloping stretch of decking that led up to a platform, on which stood a large sunshade, table and chairs, that overlooked the sea. A palm tree stood in the middle of a small patch of lawn, rustling gently in the warm breeze.

'Go and unpack,' Inigo snarled at his son, who seemed only too happy to leave his father's vicinity. As the sound of Gus's footsteps receded upstairs, Inigo manoeuvred his wheelchair into position beside a low coffee table and gesticulated rudely at Strike and Robin to sit down in two armchairs covered in striped blue and white canvas.

Watercolours dotted the walls of the room, which were painted white. Remembering the Tribulationem et Dolorum website ('He continues to make art and music within the necessary limits of his condition') Robin wondered whether they were Inigo's or Katya's, and what Mariam or Pez would make of them: to her, they seemed insipid and amateurish. The largest, which had been given a whimsical driftwood frame, showed Island Wall as they'd entered it, with Aquarelle Cottage on the right; the perspective had gone a little awry, so that while the street looked of immense length, vanishing to a point on the horizon, the houses appeared far too big for their setting. An electric keyboard stood in one corner and on a music stand sat a book of print music, *30 kleine Choralvorspiele* by Max Reger, on the front of which was a line drawing of the German composer who, being cross-looking, paunchy and bespectacled, bore a remarkable resemblance to their unwilling host.

'So,' said Inigo, glaring at Strike, 'to what do I owe this intrusion into my privacy?'

'To Kea Niven,' said Strike.

Though he attempted to maintain his obstreperous expression, Inigo was betrayed by the slight, convulsive closing of his hands on the arms of his wheelchair and the twitch of his silent mouth.

'What in the world do you imagine I can tell you that my wife hasn't?' he said after too long a pause.

'Quite a lot. We believe you've forged a private relationship with Kea Niven, without your wife's knowledge, dating back at least a couple of years.'

Strike allowed silence to spread between them like ice: dangerous to break, impossible to glide past. At last the older man said,

'I don't see that my private relationships – and I'm far from admitting that this particular relationship exists – can have the remotest relevance to your enquiry. That's assuming,' said Inigo, now turning red where he'd previously been pale, 'that you're still trying to find out who this Anomie person is. Or has Katya engaged you to investigate me instead?'

'Currently, we're only investigating Anomie.'

'And your proof of this alleged relationship is . . .?'

'Mr Upcott,' said Strike patiently, 'a man of your intelligence knows I'm not going to lay out everything we know so you can tailor your story accordingly.'

'How bloody *dare* you suggest I have any reason to "tailor" anything,' exploded Inigo, and Robin could tell he found it a relief to become openly angry. 'I'm in contact with any number of chronically ill people through a website I run. Yes, Kea visited the website for advice. I gave her exactly what I'd give any person suffering from this lousy condition of ours, which doctors barely believe exists.'

'But you didn't tell your wife Kea Niven had contacted you?'

'I didn't know who Kea was at the time. She visited the website under a pseudonym, as many users do. There's shame and stigma attached to having conditions the bloody medical profession think are psychosomatic, I'll have you know!'

'But there came a point when you found out who Arke was?'

In the slight pause that followed, they heard a creak on the stairs. Inigo's head turned so quickly Robin wouldn't have been surprised if he'd given himself whiplash.

'What are you doing?' he roared as Gus hastily descended the stairs again.

'I've unpacked,' said Gus, appearing in the doorway looking apprehensive. 'I really need to leave now if I'm going to—'

'And I'm supposed to get essentials in for myself, am I?' shouted Inigo.

'Sorry, I forgot,' said Gus. 'I'll get them now. What d'you—?'

'Use your bloody initiative,' said Inigo, turning back to face Strike and Robin. He waited, breathing heavily, until they'd heard the front door close, then said in a more controlled voice, 'as far as I can remember – and I talk to a lot of different people online – after a couple of weeks Kea happened to mention something that led me to understand she'd been involved in some way with that damned cartoon, and – yes, we, ah, mutually discovered our rather *remote* offline connection.'

'It didn't strike you as an odd coincidence that she'd shown up on your website?'

'Why should it?' said Inigo, now growing red in the face. 'A huge number of people visit my site. It's considered one of the best online resources for people suffering from chronic fatigue and fibromyalgia.'

'But you didn't tell your wife?' Strike asked again.

'There's such a thing as patient confidentiality, you know!'

'I didn't realise you're a doctor.'

'Of course I'm not a bloody *doctor*, you don't need to be a *doctor* to have certain *ethics* around sharing personal details of people who come to you for medical advice and psychological support!'

'I see,' said Strike. 'So it was regard for Kea's privacy that stopped you telling Katya you were talking to her?'

'What else would it be?' asked Inigo, but his attempt at a counter-attack was undermined by the increasing redness of his face. 'If you're implying – utterly ridiculous. She's young enough to be my daughter!'

Remembering Katya's claim to have felt maternal towards Josh Blay, Robin couldn't decide whether she felt more distaste or compassion for the miserable Upcotts, who'd each, it seemed, sought solace and, perhaps, the hope of a recovered youth through their relationships with twenty-somethings.

'And you've since met Kea face to face, of course,' said Strike, taking a shot in the dark.

At this, Inigo turned crimson. Robin wondered in a slight panic what they'd do if he had a heart attack. Raising a shaking hand and pointing it at Strike, he said hoarsely,

'You've been following me. This is a despicable infringement – *outrageous* invasion of my – my—'

He began to cough; indeed, he sounded as though he was choking. Robin jumped up and hurried to the kitchen area, grabbed a glass off the shelf and filled it with tap water. Inigo was still coughing when she returned, but he accepted the water and, though spilling a good deal of it down his front, managed to take a few mouthfuls. At last he regained some semblance of control over his breathing.

'I haven't witnessed you meeting Kea,' said Strike, adding, less truthfully, 'I was asking a question.'

Inigo glared at him, watery-eyed, mouth trembling.

'How many times have you and Kea met?'

Inigo was now visibly shaking with resentment and rage. The water in his glass slopped onto his thigh.

'Once,' he said. '*Once*. She happened to be in London and we met for coffee. She was feeling particularly ill and wanted my advice and support, which I'm happy to say I was able to give her.'

He attempted to put the glass of water down on the coffee table; it slipped through his shaking hand and smashed on the hard-wood floor.

'For fuck's SAKE,' bellowed Inigo.

'I'll do it,' said Robin hastily, jumping up once again and heading for kitchen roll.

'Outrageous – *outrageous*,' repeated Inigo, his breathing laboured. 'This whole – to follow me *here* – you invade my space – and all because I've attempted to help a girl—'

'—who had a sizeable grudge against Edie Ledwell,' said Strike, while Robin returned and sank into a crouch beside Inigo to mop up the water, 'who claimed Ledwell had stolen all her ideas, who harassed Ledwell online, who stalked Blay after they split up and made violent threats against both of them on the night before the stabbings.'

'Who says she made threats?' asked Inigo furiously, while Robin carefully picked up the shattered glass.

'I do,' retorted Strike. 'I've seen the tweets she deleted after she'd sobered up. Wally Cardew advised her to do it. Probably the only sensible thing he's done since we've started investigating this case. Did you know they're still in contact? Were you aware she slept with Wally after splitting up with Blay?'

It was hard to tell what effect these questions had on Inigo, because his face was already mottled and empurpled, but Strike rather thought he saw a flicker of shock. Strike's hunch was that Inigo had been captivated by a girl he saw as vulnerable and innocent, and indeed he could imagine Kea playing that part very well.

'I don't know what you're talking about,' said Inigo. 'I have no idea who this Cardew person is.'

'Really? He played Drek until he was sacked for an antisemitic video he put on YouTube.'

'I didn't keep up with all the shenanigans around that damn cartoon. All I know is that Kea's a vulnerable young person who got caught up in a bad situation, and I'll tell you this, right now: she most *definitely* isn't Anomie. Absolutely not.'

'So you never discussed *The Ink Black Heart* with her?'

After a slight pause Inigo said,

'Only in the broadest terms. Naturally, after I realised who she was, we *mentioned* it. She felt she'd been plagiarised. I offered her my advice. As an ex-publisher, I have some expertise in that area.'

'So you were supporting her in her plagiarism claims?'

'I wasn't *supporting* her claims, I was merely giving her an intelligent sounding board,' said Inigo as Robin carried the broken glass back to the kitchen and put it in the bin. 'Her mental health was suffering from the feeling that she'd been taken advantage of – used, then tossed aside. She was in need of a friendly ear: I supplied it. Kea and I have a great deal in common,' he added, turning still redder.

Strike remembered the bare-faced beauty of Kea, sitting opposite him in the Maids Head, as he looked into the puffy, middle-aged face, with its enlarged pores and its purplish bags beneath the pale grey bespectacled eyes.

'I happen to know *exactly* how it feels to be cut off in one's prime,' Inigo continued, 'to know that one could have excelled, only to watch others succeed while one's own world shrinks around one and all one's hopes for the future are dashed. I was pushed out of my bloody job when this bastard illness hit me. I had my music, but the band, my so-called friends, made it clear they weren't prepared to accommodate my physical limitations, in spite of the fact that I was the best bloody musician of the lot of them. I could have done what Gus has done, gone the scholarship route, oh yes. And I had a lot of artistic talent too, but this bloody illness means I've been unable to dedicate the necessary time to pursue it in any meaningful—'

Robin's mobile rang. She'd been about to retake her seat, but now, having pulled her phone out of her pocket with apologies, glanced at the caller's number, then said,

'I think I'd better take this, sorry.'

As there was no private place to talk in the open-plan area where they were sitting, Robin headed back outside onto the street. As she left, Inigo took off his glasses and mopped his eyes, which Strike now realised had filled with tears during his recitation of his various losses. After replacing his spectacles shakily on his nose, he gave a loud sniff.

But if Inigo Upcott was expecting sympathy from Strike, he was disappointed. He who'd once lain on a dusty road in Afghanistan, his own leg blasted off, with the severed torso of a man who'd minutes previously been bantering about a drunken stag night in Newcastle lying beside him, had no pity to spare for Inigo Upcott's crushed dreams. If Upcott's work colleagues and bandmates hadn't been inclined to generosity, Strike was ready to bet it had been due to the bullying, self-aggrandising nature of the man sitting opposite him, rather than any lack of compassion. The older Strike got, the more he'd come to believe that in a prosperous country, in peacetime – notwithstanding those heavy blows of fate to which nobody was immune, and those strokes of unearned luck of which Inigo, the inheritor of wealth, had clearly benefited – character was the most powerful determinant of life's course.

'Did you pass on to Kea anything your wife told you, about nego-tiations with Maverick and so forth?'

'I – may have mentioned it,' said Inigo, his resentment at Strike's matter-of-fact tone very evident, and he repeated, 'but only in the broadest terms.'

'Has Kea asked you to pass messages to Josh?'

'Occasionally,' said Inigo, after a slight hesitation.

'But you haven't passed those messages on?'

'I have no contact with Blay.'

'And I suppose you can hardly ask your wife to take him messages from Kea.'

Inigo's only response was to tighten his lips.

'Have you promised Kea any assistance, aside from advising her on her plagiarism claims?'

'I've given her some reassurance.'

'Reassurance about what?'

'She's well aware my wife dislikes her,' said Inigo. 'It's certainly crossed Kea's mind that she might be accused of being Anomie, or of having something to do with Ledwell's death. I merely promised her I'd talk sense into Katya. I repeat,' said Inigo forcefully, 'Kea *cannot* be Anomie.'

'What makes you so sure?'

'Well, firstly, she's *too unwell*,' said Inigo loudly. 'Any sustained work – building and maintaining an online game of the type in question – would be impossible for her, due to her medical problems. She requires a good deal of rest and sleep – not that sleep comes easily with this bloody illness.

'Moreover, Anomie's attacked Kea online. She was very unpleasant indeed to Kea. Kea was very upset by it.'

'"She"?' repeated Strike.

'What?'

'You just referred to Anomie as "she".'

Inigo scowled at Strike, then said,

'My wife didn't want me telling you this on your first visit. I agreed not to, because I didn't want Katya whining and complaining afterwards. There's a limit to how much I can cope with; I'm not supposed to be stressed. But after all,' said Inigo, temper flaring again, 'she can hardly complain, when I'm followed and *harassed* in a place that's supposed to be a *sanctuary* for me . . .

'Yasmin Weatherhead's Anomie,' said Inigo. 'She works in IT, she's nosy, manipulative and was always in it for all she could get. *I* could see what that bloody girl was up to as soon as she crossed our threshold. Katya doesn't want to admit it, because, of course, *she* was the one who brought the damn woman into their circle. Just one more bloody stupid thing Katya's done, but she's always surprised when it all blows up in her face.'

'Yasmin Weatherhead works in PR, not IT,' said Strike.

'You're mistaken,' said Inigo, with all the arrogance of a man unused to contradiction. 'She's very adept with computers, very knowledgeable. I was having a problem with mine one day and she fixed it.'

'D'you have any reason to think she's Anomie, other than her working in IT?'

'Certainly. I heard her admit to it,' said Inigo, now with an air of malicious triumph. 'I accompanied Katya to a Christmas party at that damned art collective. I needed the bathroom. Took a wrong turning, and there was Yasmin in a clinch with that revolting man who runs the place.'

'Nils de Jong?' said Strike, now taking out his notebook for the first time and opening it.

'I don't know what his bloody name is. Gigantic haystack of a man. Stank of pot. He'd just been spouting Evola at me.'

'Evola?' repeated Strike, now writing. He had an idea he'd heard the name recently, though couldn't think where.

'Julius Evola. Far-right philosopher. Ludicrous racial theories. A rather determinedly eccentric classmate of mine at Radley was partial to him. Used to carry *The Myth of the Blood* around and read it ostentatiously at meal times.

'The two of them didn't realise I was there. It was dark where they were standing and I made no footsteps, obviously,' said Inigo, indicating his wheelchair again. 'Anyway, I heard her say it. "I'm Anomie."'

'You're certain of that?' asked Strike.

'I know what I heard,' said Inigo, his jaw clenched. 'Go and question the two of *them*. For all I know, they're in it together. He might be Morehouse, mightn't he?'

'Ah, you know the name of Anomie's partner?'

'I've had no choice but to know,' snarled Inigo. 'Between Katya and Blay talking endlessly about Anomie and that damn game, and Kea worrying she'll be accused, I'm as well-informed as anyone can be who's got virtually no interest in the matter.'

'Have you told Kea your theory about Anomie?' Strike asked Inigo.

'Yes.' His tone softened. 'She doesn't believe it. She's naive in some ways. Unworldly. She's convinced Anomie's an unsavoury Scouse artist who lives at that bloody North Grove as well. Something Presley, I think he's called. He was at that party too. He's a cocky little bastard, and apparently he sexually assaulted Kea once, when he got her into his bedroom. Disgusting,' spat Inigo. 'Naturally it left its mark. Kea says this Anomie made a play for her, sexually, online, which led her to think it was this Presley.

'Kea's an innocent,' said Inigo, the colour rising in his face again. 'She doesn't realise the games people play. It wouldn't occur to her that a *woman* would try to lure her into a sexually compromising conversation.'

'What do you imagine Yasmin would achieve, by doing such a thing?'

'A hold over her. Something to use against her, to threaten her with. Yasmin's highly manipulative, not to mention a snoop.'

'What makes you say that?'

'Her behaviour, in our house,' said Inigo. 'She'd make excuses to drop by, if Blay and Ledwell weren't available, or had forgotten to pass on emails or what have you. Eyes everywhere. Little questions. Scavenging for information. Oh, I can see how Katya was taken in at first. Yasmin pretended to be concerned and sympathetic, nothing too much trouble. Then, gradually, one realised she was a parasite, pure and simple. *She's Anomie.*'

They heard the front door open and Gus reappeared, laden with bags of food from Sainsburys, followed by Robin, who looked tense.

'Dad,' said Gus, 'I'm going to have to go if I'm going to make it to—'

'And I'm supposed to put all that away, am I?' his father demanded.

'I'll do the milk and stuff,' said Gus, who seemed torn between fear and a desperate desire to leave that had made him, perhaps atypically, assertive, 'but if I don't go now—'

He hurried towards the kitchen and began taking bottles of milk and other perishables out of the bags and placing them hurriedly into the fridge.

'Whose fault is it,' his father called savagely over his shoulder, 'that you need extra tuition because you've fallen behind? *Whose fault*, you bloody malingerer?'

Gus, whose expression was hidden by the fridge door, didn't answer. Inigo turned back to Strike and said peremptorily,

'There's nothing else I can tell you. That's everything I know. This is all going to cause me endless stress and disruption,' he added, on a fresh surge of anger.

'But whose fault is it,' said Strike, getting to his feet – he was tired of this petulant, arrogant, embittered man, and disliked the contrast between the way he treated his children and the solicitude he displayed towards a pretty young woman who'd groomed him so expertly – 'that you hid from your wife that you've been chatting up Kea Niven on the sly?'

Robin saw Gus look round, wide-eyed, as he closed the fridge. For a brief moment, Inigo appeared winded. Then he said in a low growl,

'Get the hell out of my house.'

78

Why should I praise thee, blissful Aphrodite?
Thou dost not guide,
Rather with conflict dire my mind divide . . .

Katherine Bradley and Edith Cooper
Ψάπφοι, τί τὰν πολύολβον' Αφρόδιταν

'Who was that on the phone?' Strike asked Robin, once both were back on the pavement. He had a feeling her strained expression related to the call she'd just taken. Robin moved a few feet away from the Upcotts' front door before turning to face him.

'Police. They've been tailing a guy they know is Halvening. He went to Blackhorse Road an hour ago and took pictures of the block where my flat is.'

'Fuck,' said Strike. 'OK, let's—'

He broke off. Gus Upcott had just emerged from Aquarelle Cottage and he looked alarmed to find the two detectives still hanging around.

'Were you waiting for me?'

'No,' said Strike and Robin simultaneously.

'Oh,' said Gus. 'Well, I'm – I'm going that way.'

He pointed back towards the car park.

'So are we,' said Strike, so the threesome walked in silence back up the street. As they rounded the corner, Gus suddenly blurted,

'She's not the only one he talks to.'

'Sorry?' said Strike, whose thoughts were still with The Halvening, and Robin's flat.

'My father talks to another woman.'

Gus had the air of one determined on some reckless course of action. The daylight was cruel to his disfigured complexion, but somewhere under the hives was a good-looking boy. He smelled as young men who aren't especially dedicated to hygiene often smell; a little dank and oily, and his crumpled black T-shirt looked as though it had been worn for days.

'Off the same website. I've seen her messaging him. She's called Rachel.'

When neither detective spoke, Gus said,

'He's been unfaithful to my mother before. She thinks it all stopped.'

'Rachel,' repeated Robin.

'Yeah,' said Gus. '*I* can't tell Mum. He'd kill me. Anyway, I've got to go.'

He walked away, unlocked the Range Rover and got into it, leaving Strike and Robin to proceed to the BMW, which they entered before either said another word.

'What else did the police say?' Strike asked, once both car doors were closed. He was currently far more concerned about terrorists than Inigo Upcott's love life.

'Well, they've got a plainclothes officer watching my flat now,' said Robin, who was staring straight ahead at the car park wall, rather than at Strike. 'And they're still tailing the guy who took the pictures. They haven't arrested him, because they think he's quite low-level and they're hoping he's going to lead them to the higher-ups ... or to the bomb-makers.' She now dropped her gaze to the mobile she was still holding. 'The policeman said he'd text me a – he has,' she added.

She opened the photo that had just been sent to her and held out her phone so that Strike could look at it too.

'Yeah, he looks the part,' said Strike. 'Eighty-eight on his bicep, Hitler Youth hair ... slight overkill, in fact. What's the police's advice?'

'Clear out,' said Robin. 'In case anything arrives by post.'

'Good,' said Strike. 'If he hadn't said it, I would've.'

'Bugger,' said Robin, bowing her head so that her forehead rested on the steering wheel and closing her eyes. 'Sorry. It's just ...'

Strike reached out and patted her on the shoulder.

'How would you feel about staying overnight in Whitstable? Nice enough place. Nobody knows we're here. We'll take stock, work out a plan of action. You missed the meatiest parts of Inigo too. Plenty to discuss.'

'Really?' said Robin, lifting her head again, wanting distraction from the thought of her new home, so briefly a haven, now a target for the far-right.

'Yeah. He thinks Anomie's Yasmin Weatherhead.'

'Is she hell,' said Robin, and Strike was vaguely amused to see Robin's scorn at Inigo's theory, even in the face of her new and formidable worries. 'Yasmin's not that good an actress, and nobody gullible enough to think they were having an online affair with a successful TV actor could have kept themselves hidden this long.'

'I agree. But Inigo claims he overheard her confessing to being Anomie while snogging Nils de Jong at a North Grove Christmas party.'

'*What?*'

'I know. Not as unpleasant an image as Ashcroft and Zoe, but—'

'I don't believe Inigo heard that,' said Robin. 'Sorry, but I don't. If the clinch happened, I'll bet they were drunk—'

'Nils must've been, anyway.'

'*He's* not exactly a catch,' retorted Robin. 'A stoner fascist, who comes with a kid who might slit your throat in the night?'

Strike laughed.

'Although,' Robin added, unsmiling, 'he *is* a multimillionaire. And a potential source of gossip on Josh and Edie. And Mariam obviously sees something in him ... and the other woman who lives there sleeps with him too ... am I a prude? I couldn't live like that. I don't get it ...

'What was I saying?' she asked absently. Her thought processes had been disrupted: eighty-eight on his bicep, photographs of her flat, *clear out, you don't know what might be coming through the post.* 'Drunk, yes,' said Robin, forcing herself to focus. 'I bet Nils was just rambling on about anomie, Alpines and chakras, all his usual stuff – Pez said they're his greatest hits – and Inigo misheard something she said back.'

'Think you could well be right,' said Strike. 'Inigo didn't say how much he'd drunk either. He could've been pissed as well. I got the impression he's so angry at Katya he wants Anomie to be her fault somehow.'

'D'you think he's jealous, because she's in love with Blay?' asked Robin.

'Not sure it's even that,' said Strike. 'That probably hurts Inigo's ego, but it's not as though he hasn't played away himself, is it? No, I think he's just raging at the world for not granting him the appreciation he deserves and he takes it out on his wife. You were there for the spiel about him being a multi-talented genius who was cut off in his prime, weren't you?'

'Yes,' said Robin, though she added, 'In fairness, he *is* ill.'

'He owns two very nice houses and he's well enough to have affairs, paint, play the keyboard and run a website,' said Strike. 'Daddy the bishop left him a lot of cash, by the looks of it. I can think of plenty of people more deserving of pity than Inigo Upcott. You missed another interesting point, though. He's just told me where Nils got all that Alpine racial crap. It comes from a writer called Julius Evola. Far-right philosopher.'

'Evola?' repeated Robin. 'I feel like I've seen that name somewhere . . .'

'Yeah, I thought I'd heard it recently, too, but I couldn't remember where.'

Robin sat ransacking her memory for a brief spell, then said,

'Oh, of course. *I* said it to you. *I am Evola.*'

'What?' said Strike, confused.

'It's the username of one of the trolls who hang around the *Ink Black Heart* fans on Twitter. I am Evola. He's basically a second Lepine's Disciple, who's there to tell girls to kill themselves, or that they're ugly whores.'

'Ah,' said Strike. 'Yeah, I remember . . . I assume you'll need to buy some stuff, if we're going to check into a B&B? Because I will. No, sod it,' he said, reaching into his pocket for his own phone. 'I'm not in the mood for slumming it. It's a business expense; let's go somewhere decent.'

When he looked down at his mobile's screen he found a new text from Madeline waiting for him. From the couple of visible sentences, it looked as though it might be lengthy. He swiped it away without reading it and Googled places to stay in Whitstable.

'Marine Hotel looks good. Three stars, seafront, just up the road . . . I'll ring them now—'

But before he could do so, the phone in his hand rang. It was Madeline.

'I'll take this outside,' said Strike.

In fact, he didn't want Robin to watch him letting the call go to voicemail. He got out of the car. Gus and the Range Rover had departed: in their place stood an old Peugeot, from which a family with two tiny boys was disembarking. Strike walked away from the BMW, his phone still ringing, and climbed the short flight of concrete steps that led up out of the car park, pausing at the top looking at the wide expanse of sea beyond the pebble beach. He'd have liked to descend the steps on the other side, but his prosthetic leg definitely wouldn't be equal to the unstable surface, so instead he breathed deeply of the familiar, comforting briny smell, watching the sea curl into lacy ruffles around a long wooden breakwater, while his mobile rang in his hand. When at last it had stopped ringing, he opened the text Madeline would have undoubtedly expected him to have read before they next spoke.

If you're angry at me, I'd rather you told me so, rather than give me the silent treatment. What I can't take is being lied to and taken for a fool. When a man pretends the woman he's working with is room service, he shouldn't be surprised when his girlfriend is suspicious and pissed off. I'm too old to play stupid games, I've been through this kind of shit too many times and I'm not OK with being told transparent lies about where you are and who you're with. I'm sure you'll take the view that I'm being possessive and unreasonable, but for me this is a matter of basic self-respect. I was warned this is what you're like, I didn't listen and now I feel like I'm a bloody fool for ever going near you. After last night, I think I'm owed an actual conversation rather than having to chase you by text, so please call me.

Expressionless, Strike dialled voicemail and listened to the message Madeline had just left, which comprised three words delivered in a cold voice: 'Please call me.'

Instead of doing so, Strike rang the Marine Hotel. Having secured two rooms for the night, he returned to the BMW and a blank-faced Robin.

'We're in at the Marine Hotel. You all right?'

'Fine,' she said, with an air of pulling herself together.

'Good,' said Strike. 'Let's go and get something to eat, buy toothpaste and socks, and we can log back into that bloody game once we're at the hotel.'

79

Love never comes but at love's call,
And pity asks for him in vain;
Because I cannot give you all,
You give me nothing back again.

Mary Elizabeth Coleridge
An Insincere Wish Addressed to a Beggar

Having bought various necessities for an overnight stay and consumed sandwiches in a local café, Strike and Robin arrived at the Marine Hotel at two o'clock. The long red-brick building, which had many gables and doors onto the street, had white timber balconies running along its length. Separated from the pavement by a low, neat hedge, it faced the beach across the road and looked smart and well-maintained.

Strike had been told on the phone that he'd been lucky to secure the last two vacant rooms for this Saturday night, and on setting eyes on the hotel's front as they drove around to the rear car park, conceived an optimistic hope that he'd at least be able to conduct his forthcoming talk with Madeline from one of those sea-view balconies, preferably with a whisky from the minibar in his hand.

This bittersweet vision was shattered at reception, where a large suited man repeated cheerfully that they were very fortunate to have got the only two vacant rooms, which were on the top, balcony-free floor.

'Numbers thirty and thirty-two. Up the stairs, double back, up the next flight, then another flight to your rooms.'

'Is there a lift?' asked Strike, taking the keys and handing one to Robin.

'There is,' said the man, 'but not up to those particular rooms.'

With a brief smile he turned to greet a couple right behind Strike.

'Great,' growled Strike as they climbed the first narrow staircase, which was covered in a seventies-style carpet patterned with orange and brown leaves. 'No offer to help with luggage either.'

'We haven't got any luggage,' said Robin reasonably: each was carrying a small, not particularly heavy rucksack.

'Not the point,' panted Strike as they approached the second flight. His hamstring had had enough of stairs and the end of his stump was starting to smart again.

'Three stars doesn't mean Ritz-type service,' said Robin, forgetting that there'd been a tacit taboo over the mention of the Ritz since their evening there. 'Anyway, I think this is the best the accountant'll let us get away with.'

Strike made no reply: his stump was starting to shake with the effort of climbing and he was afraid the spasms of the previous morning might be about to recur. The third flight of stairs took them past a small alcove behind the banisters, in which stood a display of model yachts and earthenware pots. The now-sweating Strike found this irritating rather than charming: if they had spare space, why not put in another fucking lift?

At last they reached a small landing where two doors stood side by side, evidently occupying two halves of a single eave.

'Swap,' said Robin, taking the key to number 32 out of Strike's hand and handing him that of number 30.

'Why?'

'You can have the sea view. I know you've got that Cornish thing going on.'

He was touched, but too out of breath and worried about his leg to become effusive.

'Thanks. Listen, I've got a couple of things to deal with. I'll knock on your door when I'm done and we can discuss plans.'

'Fine,' said Robin. 'I'll go and log into the game.'

She opened her door and entered a pleasant attic room which had a sloping white timber ceiling and a view over the car park to the rear of the building. It contained both a double and a single bed, both with spotless white counterpanes. Robin imagined their accountant, who was a singularly humourless man, asking why they couldn't have cut costs by sharing. Barclay's comment after his sole encounter with the man had been 'Looks like he shits staples.'

The unpacking of Robin's new rucksack – she'd felt uncomfortable turning up at a hotel with shopping bags – took only a few minutes. Having hung up the shirt she'd bought, she placed her toiletries in the en-suite bathroom, then sat down on the double bed, where three electronic devices – her own phone, the burner phone of which Pez Pierce had the number and her iPad – now lay.

A text from her mother had arrived while she and Strike had been checking in.

How are you? Have you had any updates from the police?

Fully alive to the irony of her mother's text sitting on top of the picture of the young terrorist who'd been surveying her new flat, Robin typed back:

I'm fine! Police are updating us regularly, they say they're making progress. Please don't worry, I promise you I'm taking all precautions and completely OK. Love to Dad xxx

She then picked up the temporary phone and, with a slight sinking of the heart, saw that Pez Pierce had sent her a photo.

Please don't be a dick pic, she thought, opening it, but Pez had sent what she supposed might be considered the opposite: a drawing of a naked brunette, one arm placed coyly across her breasts, the other hand hiding her pubis. It took Robin a few seconds to realise that the drawing was supposed to be her, or rather Jessica. Underneath, Pez had written a single word:

Accurate?

Both picture and message had been sent over two hours previously. Jessica Robins surely had a busy social life, so Robin decided a two-hour lapse was perfectly reasonable, and texted back:

Spot on. You draw shoulders MUCH better than I do

She tossed the burner phone aside and picked up her iPad to log into the game. Anomie was absent: the only moderators present were

Hartella and Fiendy1. To Robin's surprise, Fiendy1 immediately opened a private channel to her.

> **Fiendy1:** I went and looked at
> that Ferdinand header on YouTube
>
> **Fiendy1:** fkn incredible

Robin stared at this message, totally at a loss. Who was Ferdinand? Was this message even meant for her?

> **Fiendy1:** £18m transfer fee seems
> like nothing now lol

Football, thought Robin, remembering how Strike had told her that he and Fiendy1 had enjoyed a private-channel chat the night before last, while he was impersonating Buffypaws. She had half a mind to bang on the wall and ask Strike what they'd said to each other, but as he'd said he had things to take care of, she grabbed her phone and Googled 'Ferdinand £18m transfer fee' instead.

While Robin was deducing that Fiendy1 was talking about Rio Ferdinand, who'd scored a famous header for Leeds United against Deportivo in 2001, Strike was sitting a few feet away on his own double bed, in a room that was a mirror image of Robin's. He'd done no unpacking, because his priority had been removing his prosthesis. Instead of enjoying his sea view, he was now watching his stump twitch uncontrollably inside his trouser leg.

A cursory glance around the room had revealed the absence of a minibar, which he now supposed was only to be expected – this wasn't, as Robin had pointed out, the Ritz – but which made him feel no more kindly towards the hotel. Perhaps whisky mid-afternoon was a bad habit to slip into, but between the bombing, the arrival of a young Halvening member on Robin's street, the recurrence of spasms in his stump and the imminent prospect of a 'proper talk' with Madeline, a calming shot of alcohol would have been highly welcome.

Little though he wanted to speak to her, he had to get Madeline out of the way, as he put it to himself, because he had quite enough on his plate without being harassed by an angry girlfriend. Well aware he'd behaved in a less than exemplary fashion, he was prepared to issue an apology, but then what? Lying back on the pillows, he seemed to see only an ever more constricting tunnel of mutually increasing resentment if he continued the relationship. While his stump jumped around as though electric pulses were running through it, he thought he should have seen from the first that his and Madeline's lives were fundamentally incompatible. She needed a man happy to stand beside her and beam while the camera flashes exploded; she deserved someone who cared about her enough to look past a scene born of stress and too much alcohol, and he qualified on neither count. He took a deep breath, picked up his mobile and pressed her number.

Madeline answered after a few rings, her voice as cold as it had been in her voicemail message.

'Hi.'

When it became clear that she was waiting for him to say something, he asked,

'How are you?'

'Fairly shit. How're you?'

'Been better. Listen, I want to apologise for last night. I shouldn't have lied, it was shitty behaviour. I thought there'd be a row, so—'

'—you made sure there'd be one.'

'Not intentionally,' said Strike, wishing his leg would stop its uncontrollable jerking.

'Did you stay at Robin's last night, Corm? Tell me the truth.'

He turned his head to look out at the horizon, where the azure of the sky met the teal of the sea.

'I did, yeah.'

There was a lengthy silence. Strike said nothing, hoping that Madeline would end things now, without any further effort on his part. However, the next sound he heard was quiet but unmistakeable sobs.

'Look,' he began, with no real idea what he was going to tell her to look at, but Madeline said,

'*How could I have been so stupid as to fall for you?* People *told* me, they *warned* me—'

He wasn't going to fall into the trap of asking who these people were, because he was certain there was only one: she whose disintegrating marriage was currently threatening his livelihood.

'—but you didn't seem like that at all—'

'If you mean by "that", that I'm sleeping with Robin, I'm not,' he said, reaching for his e-cigarette only to discover that the damn thing was out of charge. 'You've been the only person I've slept with all the time we've been together.'

'Past tense,' she sobbed. 'I've *been* the only person.'

'We're talking about the past, aren't we?'

'Do you want this, Corm?' she demanded, her voice higher than usual, choking back tears. 'Do you actually *want* to be with me?'

'You're great,' he said, inwardly cringing at the necessity for these empty, formulaic words, which spared nobody any hurt but offered the speaker a comforting conviction of their own kindness, 'and it's been great, but I think we want different things.'

He expected her to argue, perhaps to shout at him, because the scene at her launch had revealed a perfect willingness to wound when hurt. Instead, after a couple more sobs, she hung up.

80

Pulled abruptly out of a deep sleep by a couple of knocks on the bedroom door, Strike blinked dazedly at the sloping timber ceiling for a couple of seconds, wondering where he was, and upon remembering that this was a hotel in Whitstable, he glanced at the sky out of the window and guessed that it was early evening.

'Strike?' said Robin's voice from outside the door. 'Are you OK?'

'Yeah,' he called back in a hoarse voice. 'Give me a minute.'

The spasms in his leg had subsided. He hopped to the door, which wasn't quite as difficult as it might have been, because there was a handily placed chest of drawers and a brass end to the bedstead.

'Sorry,' was his first word upon opening the door. 'Fell asleep. Come in.'

Robin knew he wouldn't have taken off his prosthesis if he hadn't been in a lot of pain, because he always hated the comment and enquiry it engendered. He hopped awkwardly back to the bed and dropped back down onto it.

'What's going on with your leg?'

'Keeps moving of its own bloody accord.'

'What?' said Robin, glancing at the prosthesis propped against the wall, which made Strike give a grunt of laughter.

'Not that. My stump. Spasms. I had them after they first amputated it and they came back a couple of days ago.'

'Shit,' said Robin. 'D'you want to see a doctor?'

'No point,' said Strike. 'Sit down,' he added, gesturing to a wicker chair. 'You look like you've got news.'

'I have,' said Robin, taking the seat. 'Ormond's arrest was just on TV. Apparently the police have applied to hold him for another twenty-four hours.'

'So he hasn't coughed to murder yet.'

'Can't have done. But there's something else—'

'D'you mind,' said the still sleep-befuddled Strike, 'if I have a smoke before we get into the rest?' He ran a hand through his dense, curly hair, leaving it looking unchanged. 'I'll have to put my leg back on. And I'm bloody starving ... there wasn't much to those sandwiches at lunch, was there?'

'D'you want help getting downst—?'

'No, no,' said Strike, waving her away. 'I'll be fine.'

'Shall I go and get us a table in the dining room, then?'

'Yeah, that'd be great. Meet you downstairs.'

Robin headed for the ground floor, concerned about Strike but also full of barely suppressed excitement. She'd been so consumed by the line of investigation that had suddenly opened before her after her chat with Fiendy1 that she'd hardly noticed the afternoon slipping by, and only at ten past six had it occurred to her Strike hadn't returned.

A helpful young female member of staff pointed Robin into a dining room, which had walls painted the colour of slate, with bow windows facing the sea and pieces of corrugated white coral displayed on the mantelpieces. A waiter showed her to a table for two and Robin, having ordered herself a glass of Rioja, chose the seat facing the sea, which she thought only fair, given that she'd given Strike the sea-view room. She then propped up her iPad on the table, on which the game was still playing.

Anomie was still absent, which was starting to intrigue Robin. Unless she'd missed an appearance during their journey into Whitstable, this was the longest they'd failed to appear in the game since she'd joined it, and she couldn't help reflecting that Phillip Ormond was currently in custody and undoubtedly unable to use any electronic device.

Meanwhile, Pez Pierce had texted Jessica Robins several more times since Robin had responded to his drawing. Robin had invented an evening with her parents to quell Pez's expectation of regular texts, but that hadn't stopped him sending messages, the latest of which was, **So when am I gonna see u again?** – to which Jessica had coyly replied, **I'll check my availability. Gtg, my dad's complaining I'm on my phone too much.**

The waiter brought her wine, and as Robin sipped it she found her thoughts drifting towards her ex-husband, Matthew. She'd never have been sitting here if she'd still been married. The mere idea of her texting Matthew to say 'the office has been bombed, Strike's coming to stay on the sofa' was a bad joke: Matthew had taken against Strike from the start, and she could just imagine what he would have said if Robin had phoned home to say, 'Cormoran and I are going to spend the night in a hotel in Whitstable together.' For a few seconds she luxuriated in the feeling of freedom this gave her, but then her thoughts jumped immediately to Madeline, and Strike's lie about room service: she suspected that one of the things he'd wanted to do upstairs was soothe his girlfriend's feelings. She wondered what Strike sounded like when he was trying to sweet-talk somebody. She'd never heard him do it.

It doesn't matter, she told herself sternly. *You've got this* – by which she meant the investigation, not the Marine Hotel and the Rioja – *which is better. Friends and work partners is better.* And before her feelings could mount any counter-arguments, she picked up her phone, opened Twitter and checked to see whether there'd been any response to the long direct message she'd sent an hour earlier to a young *Ink Black Heart* fan. If Robin's theory was correct – and she was certain it was – the girl's response might be extremely important to the Anomie case, but none had yet arrived.

It took Strike half an hour to reach the restaurant, because he'd taken a quick shower in the hope that it might ease his aching muscles before descending carefully to the street for a cigarette. He noticed as he walked across the room that Robin had changed into her new blue shirt. The dark walls threw her distinctive, vivid colouring into high relief and it crossed his mind that he might compliment her on the fact that the colour of the shirt suited her, but before he could do so, she said:

'How's your leg?'

'Not bad,' he said, sitting down. 'Tell me what your other news is.'

'Well,' said Robin, 'firstly, I had a private-channel talk with Fiendy1 this afternoon. You two got in a bit deep on the football the other night: I had to do a lot of Googling to catch up. Rio Ferdinand, header against Deportivo, legendary win for Leeds, etcetera ...'

'Sorry,' said Strike with a grin, 'should've put it in the notes. What are you drinking?'

'Rioja. It's good.'

'Great – I'll have the same as she's having,' he told the waiter, who'd appeared promptly at their table. When he'd left, Strike said,

'I'm taking it you're not looking this excited because you went and watched Ferdinand's header?'

'Correct,' said Robin. 'I'm looking excited because I found out Leeds United are also known as the Peacocks.'

'And that makes you excited because ...?'

'Because I think I've made a breakthrough, a major one. I feel like an idiot for not seeing it before, but there are so many millions of people on Twitter I just ... Take a look at these.'

Robin closed Twitter on her phone, opened photos instead and brought up the first of the screenshots she'd taken that afternoon, which showed the last portion of the long private-channel conversation she'd had with Fiendy1.

> **Fiendy1:** this is my last day in here
>
> **Fiendy1:** I only came in to say goodbye to Worm but she's not here
>
> **Fiendy1:** talking to you these past couple of days has been the most fun I've had in here for ages
>
> **Buffypaws:** you're not really leaving?!
>
> **Fiendy1:** I've got to
>
> **Fiendy1:** This place has been making me ill, I'm not kidding
>
> **Fiendy1:** I know you want to be a mod but seriously, don't do it. This place is fkn toxic.

Strike swiped right and read on.

> **Buffypaws:** have you told Anomie you're going?

Fiendy1: no

Fiendy1: I'm just going to disappear

Fiendy1: there's a lot about this place you don't know

Fiendy1: I'm so anxious my mum wanted to take me to the doctor

Fiendy1: but it's not a doctor I need

Buffypaws: what do you need?

>

>

>

Fiendy1: to find someone who can stop Anomie

Strike's wine arrived, but he was so absorbed he didn't notice; it was Robin who thanked the waiter.

Buffypaws: what do you mean, 'stop Anomie'?

Fiendy1: Never mind. Just don't become a mod, seriously. I'm so ashamed I took part in any of this I can't think about anything else. I've gtg

<Fiendy1 has left the channel>

Strike looked up at Robin and opened his mouth to speak, but she said,

'Keep swiping. There's a lot more.'

He did as he was told and found himself looking at a series of screenshotted tweets, the first of which dated back more than three years. The profile picture showed a teenage girl with dark brown hair, heavy eyebrows and a wry smile. She'd used no filters on her picture and didn't appear to be wearing make-up, which made her highly unusual in Strike's recently acquired experience of young female Twitter users.

Penny Peacock @rachledbadly

had a row with my father on the phone & he called me a fiend from hell #HappyNewYear

1.58 pm   1 January 2012

Penny Peacock @rachledbadly

I freaking LOVE this. Play the game, bwahs!

www.TIBH/TheGame.com

7.55 pm   9 February 2012

Penny Peacock @rachledbadly

so I wuz suspended for smoking in school bathroom 😂 😂 😂

0.49 am   27 February 2012

Penny Peacock @rachledbadly

so fkn durnk rn

0.49 am   14 April 2012

ME Rights @MEBillyShears

Promising research into mitochondrial dysfunction and pathophysiology of ME here: bitly.sd987m

3.49 pm   14 May 2012

Penny Peacock @rachledbadly
replying to @MEBillyShears

Do you know anything about lupus?

6.02 pm   14 May 2012

ME Rights @BillyShearsME

check out the 'auto-immune' section of my website
www.TribulationemEtDolorum.com

6.26 pm   14 May 2012

'Penny's been in touch with Inigo?' said Strike.
'Keep reading,' said Robin.

Penny Peacock @rachledbadly

@TheMorehou©e ALPHA CENTAURI Bb BABY!

8.51 pm   16 October 2012

Morehouse @theMorehou©e
replying to @rachledbadly
Yeah I know! Wouldn't pack your bags just yet, though.

Penny Peacock @rachledbadly
replying to @theMorehou©e
don't be a killjoy

Morehouse @theMorehou©e
replying to @rachledbadly
just saying... it might not actually be there.

Penny Peacock @rachledbadly
replying to @theMorehou©e
wtf????

Morehouse @theMorehou©e
replying to @rachledbadly
it's a working hypothesis, that's all. There's some scepticism.

'Have you got to the Morehouse astronomy stuff yet?' asked Robin.
'Just reached it.'
'I've been kicking myself, because I noticed some of their interac-
tions – I told you, remember? The schoolgirl Morehouse talked to?
But I never joined the dots.'

Seeing that Strike didn't appear to have connected them yet either, she said, 'Keep going.'

Penny Peacock @rachledbadly

Really looking forward to the game tomorrow, my father supports the Blues and I support the Whites and I genuinely want to see us SMASH them.

5.45 pm   18 December 2012

Ron Briars @ronbriars_1962
replying to @rachledbadly
How did you and your dad end up on opposite sides of that hundred years war?!

Penny Peacock @rachledbadly
replying to @ronbriars_1962
He left when I was 12 and me and my mum moved to Leeds to be with her family.

5.57 pm   18 December 2012

Ron Briars @ronbriars_1962
replying to @rachledbadly
Ah ok. It's a bit personal, then?

Penny Peacock @rachledbadly
replying to @ronbriars_1962
Just a bit.

'Wait,' said Strike, looking up at Robin, who was now smiling at him. 'Leeds United? Her dad called her a fiend from hell?'

'And her mother's got lupus,' said Robin, 'and Gus just told us his father talks to a woman called Rachel.'

'How's that relevant?'

'Strike, ignore "Penny Peacock" and look at her handle.'

Strike looked down at the next two tweets.

Penny Peacock @rachledbadly

Shit. SHIT.
SHIIIIIIIIIIITTTTTTTT   #LeedsvChelsea

9.32 pm   18 December 2012

Penny Peacock @rachledbadly

Great and there's my father texting me. He can't remember my birthday but he'll text to gloat that fucking Chelsea won.

'Rachled—' he began. 'Wait. "Rach led badly" – as opposed to—?'
'Rach led *well*,' said Robin, beaming. 'Keep reading.'

Penny Peacock @rachledbadly

If you had a famous relative u never met would you get in touch with them

9.13 pm   28 January 2013

Julius @i_am_evola
replying to @rachledbadly
not if I looked like you. They'd wonder why Ringo Starr had turned up on their doorstep dressed in a skirt

---

'Ready to order?' asked the waiter brightly, appearing once again at their table.

'No, sorry,' said Robin, hastily pulling the printed sheet towards her and choosing spaghetti with pesto at random.

'Order me something filling but not fattening,' said Strike without looking up, because he was now absorbed in a lengthy Twitter thread that Robin had screenshotted in segments. His request wasn't an easy one to fulfil: the menu, which included items Strike would undoubtedly have loved, like pork belly and battered cod, wasn't very diet-friendly. Robin asked for a steak with salad instead of chips, and the waiter departed.

'Where are you?' she asked Strike.

'On the long one about Ledwell lying about being broke,' he said.

Anomie
@AnomieGamemaster

Those buying Fedwell's sob stories of poverty
should know her well-off uncle gave her 2 big lots
of cash in early noughties. #EdieLiesWell

10.30 pm   26 April 2013

Moonyspoons @m<>nyspoons
replying to @AnomieGamemaster
Always thought there was something fishy about that
homeless shit. #IStandWithJosh #EdieLiesWell

10.32 pm   26 April 2013

Yasmin Weatherhead @YazzyWeathers
replying to @AnomieGamemaster
I think she was skint but nowhere near what she pretends. Eg,
I don't buy the homeless bit.

Penny Peacock @rachledbadly
replying to @YazzyWeathers @AnomieGamemaster
she's not lying. She really was down and out

Lepine's Disciple @LepinesD1sciple
replying to @rachledbadly @YazzyWeathers
@AnomieGamemaster
she went down for £££ we heard

> **Max R** @mreger#5
> Not proud of it, but I paid @EdLedDraws for a blow job
> back in 2002.

Julius @i_am_evola
replying to @LepinesD1sciple @rachledbadly
@YazzyWeathers @AnomieGamemaster
#OnTheGame 😂😂😂😂😂😂😂😂😂😂😂

Johnny B @jbaldw1n1>>
replying to @LepinesD1sciple @rachledbadly
@YazzyWeathers @AnomieGamemaster
#GreedieSucksWell 😂😂😂😂😂😂😂😂😂

Max R @mreger#5
replying to @LepinesD1sciple @rachledbadly
@YazzyWeathers @AnomieGamemaster
I'm not the only one, apparently she sucks off her Dutch
landlord instead of paying rent #OnTheGame

Penny Peacock @rachledbadly
replying to @mreger#5 @LepinesD1sciple @YazzyWeathers
@AnomieGamemaster
seriously fuck off the lot of you

Moonyspoons @m<>nyspoons
replying to @rachledbadly @mreger#5 @YazzyWeathers
@AnomieGamemaster
I'm so over Ledwell and her defenders. She is a disgusting
bigot and a proven liar

Penny Peacock @rachledbadly
replying to @m<>nyspoons @mreger#5 @LepinesD1sciple
@YazzyWeathers @AnomieGamemaster
Well I know her family and I know she's telling the truth so piss off

---

Just as Strike looked up to say something, Robin, who'd closed the screen on her iPad showing the game, and opened Twitter instead, gave a small gasp.

'Hang on,' she said, 'keep reading. I need to answer something.'

Strike did as he was told, and Robin read Rachel Ledwell's three-word response to her direct message, which Robin had sent from a Twitter account she'd created that afternoon for the purpose, called @StopAnomie.

Who are you?
Penny Peacock

A woman who thinks Anomie's
done enough damage to
this fandom and should
be stopped.
Stop Anomie

She waited with bated breath, but no further message from Rachel appeared. She looked up at Strike.

'Where are you now?'

'I'm reading more of these talks she's having with Morehouse about astronomy,' said Strike.

Penny Peacock @rachledbadly
@theMorehou©e

26 black holes in Andromeda.

Or are you going to tell me they don't exist, either?

10.02 pm   12 June 2013

Morehouse @theMorehou©e
replying to @rachledbadly
Lol, no, they're there. This is genuinely exciting.

Penny Peacock @rachledbadly
@theMorehou©e

Kepler-78b?

8.25 pm   5 November 2013

Morehouse @theMorehou©e
replying to @rachledbadly
opposite of Alpha Centauri Bb: does exist, but shouldn't

'This definitely reads as though they know each other,' said Strike. 'What is he, an astrophysicist?'

'Paperwhite told me she worked out who Morehouse was, because Fiendy1 gave her a hint on the moderator thread. Morehouse got angry with Paperwhite for finding out whatever it was, but I doubt it was that he's an astrophysicist. I'd have thought that'd be something you'd be quite proud of.'

'You know, I'm interested in Morehouse's tone,' said Strike.

'In what way?'

'I don't think he's as young as she is. In fact, from the way he writes, he could be any age. A professor, even.'

'I agree,' said Robin, who was still keeping half an eye on @StopAnomie's direct messages. 'And in all the public tweets of his that I've seen, he hardly ever swears.'

'And in this constant variable one —'

He angled Robin's phone so that she could see what he was talking about.

Penny Peacock @rachledbadly

"Give an example of when you would use a Constant variable."
Paging @theMorehou©e

10.33 pm   11 November 2013

Morehouse @theMorehou©e
replying to @rachledbadly
c'mon, you know this

Penny Peacock @rachledbadly
replying to @theMorehou©e
I'm so f*n knackered can't u just do it for me?

Morehouse @theMorehou©e
replying to @rachledbadly
lol no got my own work to do

' — he's talking like an older brother or . . . I dunno, an uncle.'

'A pretty cool uncle, seeing as she feels free to swear to him.'

'On the other hand, there's nothing creepy here. He's no Ashcroft.'

'Funny you should mention Ashcroft. He's coming up.'

Strike swiped left, but Robin was no longer paying attention, because Rachel had just responded to her last direct message.

Why are you coming to
me for help?
Penny Peacock

Heart now racing, Robin typed her reply.

Because I think you're a
decent person who feels the
same way I do and I think you
could give me information that
would help me stop Anomie.
Stop Anomie

While Robin was waiting in some trepidation for Rachel's response, Strike started on the next Twitter thread.

Anomie @AnomieGamemaster

Greedie Fedwell's lastest piece of #sympathytrolling. 'I prefer small places, it's how I grew up.'

Does this place look small to you?

1.53 pm   15 August 2013

Attached to the tweet was a picture of a terraced house, the door number clearly visible.

The Pen of Justice @penjustwrites

@AnomieGamemaster @rachledbadly

Whatever Ledwell's faults, it isn't ok to reveal her address. Reported.

1.56 pm   15 August 2013

Anomie @AnomieGamemaster
replying to @penjustwrites @rachledbadly
Where did I reveal the address, please?

1.57 pm   15 August 2013

Penny Peacock @rachledbadly
replying to @AnomieGamemaster @penjustwrites
He's right, take it down

1.58 pm   15 August 2013

The Pen of Justice @penjustwrites
replying to @rachledbadly @AnomieGamemaster
Don't play games, Penny

1.58 pm   15 August 2013

Penny Peacock @rachledbadly
replying to @penjustwrites @AnomieGamemaster
I'M NOT ANOMIE

1.58 pm   15 August 2013

Lepine's Disciple @LepinesD1sciple
replying to @EdLedDraws
If anyone wants the full address of that flat, DM me, I've got it
😂😂😂😂😂😂

'Wait – so Ashcroft thought Rachel was Anomie?'

'He still thinks so. If you read the next bit, you'll see why he told me Anomie's a disturbed young girl who's been in trouble with the police.'

Penny Peacock @rachledbadly

Caught doing graffiti in Hyde Park. Just left police station been charged. My mother says it's the wrost day of her life.

7.19 pm   7 February 2014

Penny Peacock @rachledbadly
replying to @rachledbadly
bit of a slap in the face for my father. Turns out him leaving her while she was critically ill was less painful

---

Penny Peacock @rachledbadly
replying to @rachledbadly
than me writing LUCY WRIGHT IS A BITCH on a wall.

Penny Peacock @rachledbadly
Anyone else been done for graffiti? Trying to reassure my mum they're not going to hang me.

Lilian Asquith @LilAsquith345
replying to @rachledbadly
maybe drop the bravado. Graffiti is criminal damage. I frankly
don't understand what makes people do it.

Penny Peacock @rachledbadly
replying to @LilAsquith345
we is lonelik and borkled

7.42 pm   7 February 2014

In spite of himself, Strike gave a small snort of laughter, but
Robin wasn't paying attention; Rachel had just answered her last
direct message.

> What makes you think I've got
> information?
> Penny Peacock

Robin downed the last of her glass of Rioja and typed:

> I think you know who
> Morehouse really is - and
> Morehouse knows who
> Anomie is.
> Stop Anomie

After a few seconds, Rachel answered.

> Morehouse would never tell you
> Penny Peacock

As this was neither a denial of knowing who Morehouse was, nor
a refusal to talk, Robin's excitement quickened.

> I might be able to persuade
> him. I've got some experience
> at this kind of thing.
> Stop Anomie

While Robin waited on tenterhooks, Strike was reading the final
screenshot on her phone.

Penny Peacock @rachledbadly

So I got a referral order for my grafitting & I'll probably have to go & clean it off or something.

4.27 pm   8 July 2014

Penny Peacock @rachledbadly
replying to @rachledbadly
My mum says it serves me right and I texted my dad and he'd forgotten I was in court today. #TopParenting

---

Penny Peacock @rachledbadly
replying to @rachledbadly
so now I'm going to have some vodka to celebrate haha. #notgoingtojail

---

Lepine's Disciple @LepinesD1sciple
replying to @rachledbadly
They should lock femoids like you up just for bein so ugly

Penny Peacock @rachledbadly
replying to @LepinesD1sciple
Will you just FUCK OFF

'I've been waiting for someone to tell Lepine's Disciple to fuck off,' said Strike, pushing Robin's phone back across the table towards her. 'He's the kind of bloke who should be told to fuck off, loudly and often ... Everything all right?' he asked, because Robin was wearing a very tense expression while watching the iPad in her hands.

'Fine,' said Robin. 'I could use another glass of wine, though.'

As Strike hailed the waiter, Rachel's response appeared on the screen in front of her.

Are you a journalist?
Penny Peacock

Or police?
Penny Peacock

As Robin began to type very fast, Strike wondered what on earth she was up to. Her silence suggested something private, and he suddenly remembered that call to the office from Hugh Jacks which had been put through to his phone the night he'd had dinner with Grant Ledwell. He'd never found out what was going on between them. Now he remembered the photograph of that fishy-eyed bloke with his arm around her in Switzerland on her mantelpiece. When the two fresh glasses of wine arrived, he drank while covertly watching Robin, trying to decide whether she looked more like a woman arranging another holiday with her boyfriend, or breaking up with him.

In fact, Robin was typing:

> Neither. I'll tell you everything
> if you meet me. I can
> guarantee you total anonymity
> and we can meet face to
> face in a crowded place by
> daylight anywhere you like. If
> you don't like the look of me,
> you can leave immediately.
> If you decide when you get
> there you don't want to talk
> to me after all, you can just
> leave. Nobody ever needs to
> know you met me or that you
> helped me, if that's what you
> decide to do.
> Stop Anomie

Why won't you tell me who
you are now?
Penny Peacock

> Because if you tell anyone,
> you could hamper me trying to
> stop Anomie
> Stop Anomie

Their waiter now returned to their table with their food. Robin shifted slightly to allow him to place her bowl of pasta in front of her, her gaze fixed on her iPad. Strike looked down at his own plate: where there should have been chips, there was only salad. He supposed he had only himself to blame for this, so picked up his knife and fork and began to eat in silence while Robin continued to type.

I want to help but I'm scared
Penny Peacock

I understand, but you've got nothing
at all to fear from me, I swear
Stop Anomie

My mum's ill. She can't take me
getting in trouble again
Penny Peacock

You won't be in trouble.
Nobody even needs to know
you're meeting me
Stop Anomie

Could you come to Leeds?
Penny Peacock

Of course
Stop Anomie

Tomorrow afternoon?
Penny Peacock

'Strike,' said Robin, looking up with an expression of excitement that made him fear the worst: possibly a proposal of marriage made by text. 'Could we go to Leeds tomorrow?'

'Leeds?'

'Rachel Ledwell's agreed to talk to me.'

'*What?*'

'I'll explain in a minute – can we go?'

'Of course we can fucking go!'

So Robin typed:

Yes
Stop Anomiie

You can't come to my house
because of my mum
Penny Peacock

That's OK
Stop Anomie

There's a place called
Meanwood Park

Penny Peacock

Go in through the entrance by the
cafe and take the right-hand path

Penny Peacock

There's a stone bridge over
the stream on the left, like
broken slabs

Penny Peacock

On the other side of the stream
there's a tree with two big
boulders on either side of it

Penny Peacock

Near the tree there's a bench with
the name Janet Martin on it

Penny Peacock

I'll meet you at Janet Martin's
bench at 3 o'clock

Penny Peacock

Wonderful. I'll see you there x

Stop Anomie

Robin put down her iPad, drank most of her second glass of Rioja straight off, then told Strike everything. He listened in mounting astonishment, and when she'd finished her recital he said,

'Fucking *hell*, Ellacott – I fall asleep for three hours and you crack the fucking case!'

'Not yet,' she said, flushed with excitement, wine and the pleasure these words had given her. 'But if we get Morehouse, we get Anomie!'

Strike picked up his wine glass and clinked it against hers.

'Want another one?'

'Better not. It must be three-hundred-odd miles to Leeds. I don't want to fail a breathalyser test.'

She picked up her fork at last and began eating her pasta.

'How's your steak?'

'Bloody good, actually,' said Strike, wondering whether to say what he wanted to say, and finally deciding to do so. 'I thought you might be emailing Hugh Jacks.'

'*Hugh Jacks?*' said Robin incredulously, her next forkful of spaghetti suspended halfway to her mouth. 'Why on earth would I be doing that?'

'Dunno. He's calling you at work, I thought something might be going—'

'*God*, no,' said Robin. 'Nothing's going on between me and Hugh Jacks.'

A combination of Rioja and elation at securing a rendezvous with Rachel Ledwell had loosened the guard Robin had kept over herself over these last few months. Right now, she felt more kindly towards her partner than she had in weeks.

'Tell me something,' she said. 'If a woman ignored you knocking on her bedroom door, a Valentine's card and sundry phone calls, would *you* think she was interested?'

Strike laughed.

'I'd have to say, on balance, no.'

'Thank God,' said Robin, 'because you wouldn't be much of a detective if you couldn't read clues like that.'

Strike laughed again. The relief he was currently feeling was telling him something, he knew that, but now was hardly the moment to sink into an introspective reverie, so instead he drank more wine and said,

'Nice hotel, this.'

'I thought you were pissed off it hasn't got a lift to the attic and nobody helped you with your imaginary luggage?'

'But they do a good steak.'

Robin laughed in turn. As he'd asked about Hugh Jacks, she briefly considered asking him how things were going with Madeline, but decided against posing a question that might ruin her current good mood. The rest of dinner passed pleasantly, with inconsequential talk, jokes and laughter that might have seemed extraordinary to their fellow diners, had they known how recently Strike and Robin had been sent a bomb.

81

. . . golden gates between us stretch,
Truth opens her forbidding eyes . . .

Mary Elizabeth Coleridge
An Insincere Wish Addressed to a Beggar

An in-game chat between two moderators of *Drek's Game*

<A new private channel has
opened>

<6 June 2015 23.29>

<Morehouse invites Paperwhite>

<Paperwhite joins the channel>

Paperwhite: you've seen? Aobut
Ledwell's boyfriend?

Morehouse: literally 2 mins ago

Morehouse: been in the lab all
afternoon

Morehouse: jesus. I can't get my
head round it

Paperwhite: now what?

Morehouse: I don't know

Paperwhite: the police won't have
arrested him for nothing

Morehouse: no

Morehouse: but they haven't
charged him yet

Paperwhite: Mouse, do you WANT
Anomie to have killed her?

Morehouse: bloody hell, of course
I don't

Morehouse: but explain Vilepechora

Paperwhite: maybe that was
completely unconnected

Paperwhite: maybe NONE of it's
been Anomie!

Morehouse: if they charge Ormond,
all we'll know is that A didn't
stab Ledwell and Blay

Paperwhite: but babe, if he didn't
stab them, where was his motive
for attacking Vilepechora?

>

Morehouse: I don't know

Morehouse: maybe I've just spent
so many hours worrying myself
sick he's done it all I'm finding
it hard to adjust

>

Morehouse: have you noticed
anything funny about him on the
mod channel recently?

Paperwhite: more than usual, you
mean?

Morehouse: twice, instead of
typing 'oderint dum metuant' he's
typed 'oderum dum mentum'

Paperwhite: so?

Morehouse: so that's not like him

Paperwhite: maybe he was drunk?

798

Morehouse: and a couple of nights ago, when you weren't on, he agreed with BorkledDrek that All-Star Batman and Robin was actually very good.

Paperwhite: so?

Morehouse: so that's like Nigel Farage saying what England really needs is a hundred thousand Turkish immigrants

Paperwhite: lol

Morehouse: it's odd

Paperwhite: maybe he was trying to schmooze BorkledDrek?

Morehouse: Anomie doesn't schmooze anyone

Morehouse: He thinks we're there to schmooze him, not the other way round

Paperwhite: lol true

Morehouse: well if Ormond's charged, it'll be a massive fuckign relief

Morehouse: but even the fact I thought Anomie might've done it has been a wake up call for me

Morehouse: I've been thinking a lot lately about what he was doing to Ledwell

Morehouse: harassing her and posting her address and the rest of it

Morehouse: I don't like myself very much when I think about it all

Morehouse: I should've stopped him. I made excuses for him in my head

Morehouse: Nicole, even if Ormond killed her, I'm leaving and I think you should too. Anomie and this game are bad news

Paperwhite: yeah

Paperwhite: I've been thinking the same thing

Paperwhite: God it'll be weird without the game in my life though

Paperwhite: I'll probaby just text you all day and night instead

Morehouse: suits me

Paperwhite: <3

Morehouse: so . . .

Paperwhite: ???

Morehouse: I think we should Facetime

Paperwhite: OMFG!!!!!

Morehouse: now?

Paperwhite: I can't believe this

Paperwhite: will you tell me who Anomie is as well?

Morehouse: why the fuck not

Morehouse: no hang on

Paperwhite: MOUSE YOU CAN'T SAY THAT THEN CALL IT OFF

Morehouse: no, someone's at my door

Morehouse: give me a mo

>

>

>

>

>

>

>

>

>

>

>

>

>

>

>

>

>

>

>

>

>

>

>

>

>

82

Girls blush sometimes because they are alive,
Half wishing they were dead to save the shame . . .
They have drawn too near the fire of life, like gnats,
And flare up bodily, wings and all.

Elizabeth Barrett Browning
Aurora Leigh

Robin was so anxious not to miss the opportunity to speak to Rachel Ledwell that she and Strike were on the road again by eight o'clock the following morning. The sky was cloudless, and both were soon squinting in the dazzling sunlight, Robin now regretting that she hadn't bought sunglasses back in Whitstable.

Strike, who'd recharged his e-cigarette overnight, took occasional unenthusiastic drags on it as they drove up the M11. When he wasn't vaping, he watched *Drek's Game*, into which he'd logged before they got into the car. He was having some difficulty moving Buffypaws around, because he had to use his left hand. His right was needed to press down hard on his thigh, because his stump had again woken him by spasming, and was still trying to jerk around of its own accord. In consequence, he'd reluctantly eschewed the full English offered by the Marine Hotel, instead opting for porridge and fruit salad.

'Is Anomie in?' Robin asked.

'Nope,' said Strike.

'Any moderators?'

'Paperwhite and BorkledDrek. Mind you, we've got nobody watching Kea Niven or Tim Ashcroft at the moment, so even if Anomie turns up we're not going to be able to rule either of them

802

in or out. *Fucking* Nutley,' said Strike. 'I hope he asks for a reference, because I'll give him one he won't forget in a fucking hurry.'

A twenty-minute silence followed, until Strike, profoundly bored with the game, logged out of it and picked up his e-cigarette again.

'How d'you manage to not gain weight, doing this job?' he asked Robin.

'What?' asked Robin, whose attention was mostly concentrated on the questions she was intending to ask Rachel Ledwell, assuming she turned up. 'Oh ... well, I plan a bit. Try and take healthy stuff with me when I'm doing surveillance, so I don't end up grabbing chocolate to keep myself going.'

'Healthy stuff, like—?'

'I don't know – nuts? Sometimes I make sandwiches ... Is your leg bad?' she asked. She'd noticed, but not mentioned, him pressing his stump to the seat.

'Not bad enough to eat like a squirrel.'

'I don't eat like a *squirrel*,' said Robin, 'but I don't fry everything and I don't eat chips with every meal – since you ask.'

Strike sighed deeply.

'I was hoping to hear there's a magic pill.'

'Sorry,' said Robin, overtaking a dawdling Volvo, 'no magic pill ... I take it you're hungry?'

'Only fairly.'

'We could stop at Cambridge Services, but not for long. I really don't want to be late for Rachel, assuming she turns up.'

They drove on for a few minutes, until Strike said:

'It's all a bit *The Spy Who Came in From the Cold*, this meet-by-the-bench business.'

'I bet it's a teenage thing,' said Robin. 'It's probably where she goes to meet mates ... listen, I hope this is OK –'

She felt awkward about saying the next bit, because she'd never done it before.

'– but I think I should meet her alone. She doesn't know anything about you, and you might be a bit scary for a teenager. Also, she's only expecting one person.'

'Makes sense,' said Strike, dragging on his pale imitation of a proper cigarette. 'I'll wait in that café she mentioned ... maybe they'll have chips.'

They made a brief stop at Cambridge Services, where Strike

consumed a coffee and a tasteless oat bar while checking work emails. Robin, who'd noticed his expression change, said apprehensively,

'What is it?'

'Dev,' said Strike.

'He hasn't resigned as well?'

'No . . . the reverse . . . bloody hell, he's managed to chat up one of Charlotte and Jago's nannies. Last night, in a pub in Kensington . . . she was pissed . . . told him neither of the people she works for are fit to be parents . . . "has witnessed the father being violent to his girls on multiple occasions". Shit, this could be good.'

'Glad you're happy,' said Robin drily.

'You know what I mean. Obviously I'd rather he wasn't kicking the shit out of his kids, but if he is, I'll be bloody delighted to be the one to expose him.'

But you won't expose him, will you? thought Robin, as she drank her own coffee. *If you expose him, you've lost your hold over him.* She wondered, too, at the ease with which Strike had glided over the part saying neither parent was fit to have charge of their children, but perhaps, deep down, he found it impossible to believe Charlotte was a bad mother. Aloud, she merely said,

'I'd have thought a couple like that would have non-disclosure agreements in place for employees.'

'Yeah, probably,' said Strike, who was still reading Dev's report. 'All the kids are at Ross's place in the country again today . . . Midge is there . . . Christ, if we could just get Ross off our backs it would help a lot.'

After half an hour at the services, they drove on, finally arriving in Leeds an hour before the scheduled appointment with Rachel, and wending their way, with the help of the BMW's satnav, towards Meanwood Park.

'I don't think that's the entrance she meant,' said Robin as they passed a miniature temple-like gate, with a slated roof and stone pillars. 'It must be the next one . . . yes, I can see the café.'

'You've still got fifty-five minutes,' said Strike, checking his watch.

'I know,' said Robin as she turned into a small car park and drove the BMW into a parking space, 'but I want to get into position early and keep an eye out for her. You wait in the café and I'll come and meet you after I've interviewed her – or after it's clear she's not coming.'

So Strike entered the Three Cottages Café alone. He hadn't been offended by Robin suggesting that it was best that he – a bulky six-foot-three male, whose resting expression he knew to be stern, bordering on threatening – didn't attend the interview with a frightened teenage girl, but as he ordered a coffee and resisted the temptation to ask for a scone, his thoughts lingered on the way Robin had taken charge of this particular line of inquiry. If he was absolutely honest with himself, this was the first time he'd seen her as a true partner, an equal. She'd secured the interview through her own ingenuity, then taken charge of how the interview was to unfold, telling him, effectively, that he was surplus to requirements. He wasn't annoyed; on the contrary, he was almost amused by his relegation to a waiting role at a circular table in the airy café overlooking the sweeping lawns of Meanwood Park.

Meanwhile, Robin was heading out into the park, which was already crowded on this sunny Sunday afternoon. Following Rachel's instructions, she turned right when the path split and walked on, with a wide stretch of parkland punctuated with trees to her right and a stream to her left, which was bordered on both sides by more trees.

After a couple more minutes she reached the bridge Rachel had mentioned: it comprised uneven, broken slabs lying across the stream, and she quickly spotted the tree with large standing stones on either side of it, and the bench with its small metal plaque:

Janet Martin

(28.02.67 – 04.12.09)

Loved Yorkshire

Loved Life. Was Loved.

Yorkshire born and bred, Robin sat down on the bench feeling kindly towards Janet Martin and scanned her surroundings. Her suspicion that this was a place Rachel came regularly to meet friends was strengthened by what she saw. The bench lay on a path partially screened from the main park by the trees that grew on either side of the stream that ran in front of it. She could imagine teenagers enjoying alcohol here, away from the prying eyes of people playing frisbee or sunbathing on blankets.

Forty minutes passed, during which time three dog-walkers passed her. Shortly after the last had gone by, Robin spotted somebody on the other side of the stream, walking slowly towards the bridge.

In spite of the heat of the day, the girl was wearing baggy jeans, a thick, oversized, checked shirt and bulky trainers. Dark hair fell just to just below her shoulders. Robin sat very still, as though the girl was a wild animal she might scare away with a sudden movement. Twice the girl paused, staring towards Robin, perhaps taking the measure of her, or checking that she was indeed alone. At last she crossed the bridge.

Two things struck Robin immediately as the girl moved into plain view. Firstly, she bore a marked resemblance to her aunt, Edie Ledwell: she had the same square face and generous mouth, though Rachel's eyes were dark and her nose was aquiline. Secondly, she was at that stage of self-consciousness that Robin remembered vividly, when a girl's body stopped being a mere vehicle for sensory pain and pleasure, and became something that attracted lascivious scrutiny and judgement. As she walked towards the bench she folded her arms self-protectively, staring at Robin and clearly uncertain whether Robin was indeed the person she was meeting.

'Rachel?' said Robin, standing up with what she hoped was a reassuring smile. 'I'm Robin, otherwise known as Stop Anomie.'

She held out her hand. Rachel unfolded her arms to shake it, and Robin felt the dampness of the girl's palm.

'Your directions were great,' said Robin, sitting back down on Janet Martin's bench. 'I love this park. D'you know the names on all the benches?'

'No,' said Rachel, 'only this one.'

She stood playing with the hem of her too-heavy shirt, then sat down next to Robin on the bench. Robin judged her to be sixteen at most.

'I used to meet my cousin on this bench, before she moved away. We used to live on opposite sides of the park.'

'Where did your cousin move to?'

'Bradford,' said Rachel.

'Not too far away,' said Robin.

'No,' said Rachel.

The stream chattered on past them, and a Labrador barked merrily as he dashed after a ball thrown by his owner on the opposite bank. Rachel took a deep breath, then said,

'You're Buffypaws, aren't you?'

'Yes,' said Robin.

'I knew you must be,' said Rachel. 'It was too much of a coincidence, me saying I wanted to find someone to stop Anomie and you direct messaging me right after. So what are you, if you're not police or a journalist?'

Reaching into her pocket, Robin pulled out her purse and handed Rachel a business card.

'That's me. I'm a private detective. My partner and I have been hired to try and find out who Anomie is.'

She could tell the name of the agency on the card didn't mean anything to Rachel, and deduced that Grant hadn't told his daughter about their hiring. Sure enough, Rachel's next question was,

'Who's paying you?'

'I can't tell you that, I'm afraid,' said Robin. 'But they're good people. They want to stop Anomie, and they care about *The Ink Black Heart.*'

When Rachel continued to look apprehensive, Robin added,

'As I told you last night, Rachel, nobody ever needs know you've spoken to me. This is completely off the record. I'm not even going to take notes.'

'D'you know my surname too?' said Rachel in barely more than a whisper.

'Yes,' said Robin.

Rachel's eyes filled with tears.

'Do you think I'm disgusting?'

'Of course not,' said Robin, no longer smiling. 'Why would I?'

'Because she was my aunt and . . .'

Tears spilled down Rachel's face, her shoulders slumped and she began to sob. Robin rummaged in her bag for a tissue and slid it into Rachel's hand.

'Thanks,' sobbed Rachel.

'Why are you crying?' asked Robin quietly.

'Because I was one of them,' sobbed Rachel. 'I was in *Drek's Game* and she probably thought we all hated her, but we didn't, not all of us . . . I just wish I hadn't ever got involved with Anomie . . . I wish I'd written to her or something and told her how much I loved the cartoon, so she knew *one* p-person in her family was . . .'

Rachel's voice now became incomprehensible, because she'd pressed both hands and the tissue over her face.

'. . . and I went to her funeral,' sobbed Rachel, lowering her hands, 'and I logged into Twitter on the train coming home, and people were joking about digging her up, and when I got home I drank, like, half a bottle of vodka and I wish . . . I wish I'd never . . . and I haven't got anyone to talk to about all this, because if my mum knew I was in that game – she thinks the fans are to blame, and she says my dad's benefiting from murder and . . .'

Her voice disintegrated into hiccups and sobs.

'Rachel,' said Robin gently, 'I never saw you being mean inside the game, or bullying anyone, least of all Edie. It's not a crime to be a fan.'

'I should've spoken up more,' sobbed Rachel. 'On the n-night we heard she was dead, all Anomie cared about was how many p-people were coming into the bloody game. Why did I stay?'

'Because they were your friends,' Robin said. 'Because you had fun with them.'

'You're being nice,' said Rachel, mopping her eyes, 'but you don't know everything that's gone on. Anomie kept joking about the stabbings and we all just kind of let it go, and then there were some other people in the game and I *knew* they were bad news, and so did Morehouse, but he wasn't talking to me any more, so I couldn't ever discuss it with him. You don't know everything that's gone on,' repeated Rachel. 'If you knew, you *would* be disgusted with me.'

'Let me tell you what I think went on,' said Robin. 'I think LordDrek and Vilepechora claimed that Edie herself was Anomie, and they gave some of the moderators a dossier of evidence that supposedly proved it.'

Rachel's start was almost comic, but Robin pretended not to have noticed it.

'I think Hartella said she'd take the dossier to Josh, which she did, and I think she told you Josh was going to meet Edie and confront her about being Anomie – but the day after they were supposed to meet, you heard they'd both been stabbed.'

'How d'you know all that?' said Rachel, looking terrified.

'I pieced it together,' said Robin, worried by the fear on Rachel's face; she didn't want the girl running for it. 'But Rachel, you were at best a bystander. You didn't cause any of it. None of it was your fault.'

'I could've told Edie what was going on, I could've warned her where that dossier came from—'

'How?' said Robin reasonably. 'You'd never met each other. I doubt her agent would have passed on your call. He might not even have believed you were her niece. Well-known people get all kinds of strange messages from people who've never met them.'

'I should've *tried*,' said Rachel passionately, tears leaking out of her eyes again.

'You didn't know what that dossier was going to lead to, and you'd have been putting yourself in a lot of danger if LordDrek and Vilepechora found out you'd tried to interfere with their plans. You need to cut yourself some slack, Rachel. None of this is your fault.'

Rachel sniffed, the stream chattered on and children shrieked out in the main park, running around and playing with balls. Robin suspected that pressing Rachel for Morehouse's name would be unwise until she'd built more trust, so she asked,

'How did you come across *The Ink Black Heart*? Did you just find it on YouTube and start following it, or—?'

'No,' said Rachel, looking down at the tissue she was twisting between her hands. 'I heard about it from this guy I used to talk to on Club Penguin – the social media site for kids? It was kind of sweet. We were all cartoon penguins, talking to each other.'

She gave a shaky little laugh.

'Yeah, so, there was this boy called Zoltan in there, and we became Club Penguin friends. He used to tell me about his dad, who was really abusive, and *my* dad had just dumped my mum when she was really ill and run off with a woman at work, and Mum and I had moved up to Leeds from London and I didn't know anyone yet, so I used to go on Club Penguin all the time to talk to Zoltan and we'd kind of try and support each other.

'And Zoltan found the first episode of *The Ink Black Heart* on YouTube and he told me I *had* to go and watch it, that it was the funniest thing he'd ever seen, so I did and I absolutely loved it. We were both *obsessed* with it.

'And then I found out it was my aunt who'd made it,' said Edie quietly, 'and I was so psyched, I couldn't believe it. I told Zoltan I was Edie Ledwell's niece and . . . he got weird. He started claiming to actually know her and then he said she'd flirted with him. I don't think he was much older than me. It was all just crap, total crap. I told him I knew he was lying and we had a row, but I kind of backed down because he was my friend and I thought he was so unhappy at home maybe he needed to make things up, you know, to feel better about himself, or impress me back, or whatever.

'But then,' said Rachel with a sigh, 'he changed. He started to, you know, try and get together with me. He'd never come on to me before, we were never like that, we were just really good mates who used to talk about the cartoon and our problems ...

'I knew he was only trying to make me his girlfriend because I was Edie's niece,' said Rachel miserably. 'We'd both joined Twitter by then and I put up my real picture and he started using all these stupid lines on me that didn't sound like him at all: "If that's your real photo you're probably sick to death of men coming on to you," and stuff. "Sorry I haven't been in touch, had to drive a sick dog to the vet" – he was too young to drive, it was all so sad and stupid.'

Robin's fingers were currently itching for a notebook, because she found what Rachel was telling her very interesting, but she settled for concentrating hard, so she could relay it all accurately to Strike later.

'When I told him to stop with the bullshit and the smarmy lines he got really, really angry and horrible. He – he threatened to rape me and kill my mum.'

'*What?*' said Robin.

'Yeah ... and then he deleted his Club Penguin and Twitter accounts and I never heard from him again. But that's the reason I decided to be a boy when I joined *Drek's Game*, because things got so weird and nasty with Zoltan. It's just easier to be a bloke. You don't get all that crap.'

'Are you sure Zoltan disappeared?' Robin asked her. 'He sounds like some of the men who still hang around in the *Ink Black Heart* fandom.'

'Yeah, I know,' said Rachel. 'There was a guy called Scaramouche who was on Twitter for a bit, hanging round all the Inkheart threads, and I thought he might be Zoltan under another name, because he tried the same kind of lines on Worm28. She told me about it. He said to her, "I've reported Lepine's Disciple for hassling you," and then, when she didn't thank him enough, or offer him a hand-job – sorry,' said Rachel, turning red.

'That's OK,' said Robin, amused to think that she'd reached an age where a teenager might think she was shocked to hear about hand-jobs.

'So, yeah, when Worm wasn't all over him with, like, gratitude, and offering to sleep with him, or whatever, he kind of did the same thing Zoltan did to me: called her a bitch and a slag and stuff. There's a *ton* of that stuff in the *Ink Black Heart* fandom. Like, you're not a proper *Ink Black Heart* fan till the Pen of Justice has tried to get in your pants.'

'Does he do that a lot?'

'All the fucking – sorry,' said Rachel again.

'That's OK,' Robin said. 'Swear as much as you like. You should hear my partner when he's annoyed about something.'

'Yeah, well, the Pen pervs on young girls all the time,' said Rachel. 'He's such a creep. "Oh, I really like your theory on Magspie – how old are you?" "Wow, that's such an intelligent point – how old are you?" He does it so often he loses track of who he's done it to. I've had it about three times.

'The last time he tried it on me I told him I was Anomie by direct message, just to mess with him. I wanted to scare him off, because if Anomie decides you're the enemy you're in real trouble. And the Pen believed me, ha ha ... but after a bit I had to tell him I'd been joking, because he started saying it on open Twitter and people kind of believed him ... I was sort of famous for about three days ... well, in the fandom ... but then they all got another theory about who Anomie was and they left me alone.

'I've been a *proper* Inkheart,' said Rachel, staring at the rushing water. 'Hardcore. I did everything, all of it ... like, you're not a proper Inkheart until you've had a crazy row with someone about whether Paperwhite's a bitch or not, or debated whether the stone lion's hiding a clue about Harty's owner in its tomb.

'And I did all the things real hardcore Inkhearts do, to try and get inside information and stuff.'

'Like what?' said Robin, careful to sound casual.

'Well, like, we all knew Josh's agent's husband ran this website about ME, so we all used to go on there under fake names and try and get stuff out of him. Actually, he's quite nice. I still talk to him sometimes about my mum. He keeps up with all kinds of medical research and one of the articles he told me about, I printed out so Mum could take it to her specialist ... he's been really nice about Mum's lupus.

'I loved it all in the beginning, it was like we were all detectives or something, mining for clues about what was coming next, and whenever a new episode came out we'd all analyse it and it was just a load of fun ... and Anomie was cool in the beginning, she honestly was. I liked her.'

'"She"?' repeated Robin. '"Her"?'

'Yeah,' said Rachel quietly. 'I *know* it's a girl. I had this talk with her, really early on, when the game had just started, just the two of us. This was before Edie upset her. Yeah, so, when we were talking, Anomie said to me, "Edie and I are basically the same person." Like, that's not something a boy would say, is it? She was going *on and on* about how alike they were. Anomie really kind of *worshipped* Edie in the beginning . . . yeah, I could tell it was a girl. I *did* think she was a bit . . . I don't know . . . like, I was obsessed with the cartoon, I really was. But she was on another level.

'Then Edie said she didn't really like Anomie's game, and Anomie – her reaction – I know what girls are like when you get on the wrong side of them,' said Rachel bitterly. 'If you say *one* wrong thing, if you don't toe their stupid line, that's it, you're, like, the *devil* or something. The girls at my school are real bitches,' said Rachel, turning red again. 'If you don't get up at, like, five a.m. to put on your false eyelashes and so much make-up you have to chisel it off at night, and if you like football and gaming and astronomy instead of lip-synching to Ariana Grande on Instagram and posing with your tits out, you're, like, a subhuman *freak* and a big *lesbian*. There's this one girl, Lucy Wright – my mum wanted to go into school and complain about Lucy bullying me, but there was no point. It'd only make it worse . . .'

Rachel was now ripping the damp tissue into shreds. A young couple with a cockapoo came walking along the path. The man was carrying a baby in a papoose on his back, and Robin waited until they'd passed out of earshot, the baby's head nodding in its sunhat, before saying,

'Tell me about Morehouse.'

Rachel swallowed, and tears sprang into her eyes again.

'He was . . . he was, like, my best friend in the game. He thought I was a guy for ages. We've got loads in common, we like the same kind of stuff – well, he doesn't follow football really, but he was crazy about science and space, and we both loved gaming. He was kind of like my new Zoltan, only Morehouse was actually a nice guy. Even after he found out I was a girl he didn't change the way he spoke to me, and he kind of –'

She took a deep, shuddering breath.

'– kind of helped me, because I'd started bunking off school because of the bullying,' said Rachel, wiping her eyes again, 'and I got into trouble with the police for graffitiing, and he just kept telling me I had to get my act together, because I was too clever not to try and get to uni, and I needed to stop drinking and study, and once I got into uni I wouldn't have to deal with all the bitches at school any more.'

'Did you tell Morehouse you thought Anomie was a girl?'

'Yes,' said Rachel, 'and he denied it, but I could tell he was just protecting her. I thought they were together at first – you know, boyfriend and girlfriend, like Josh and Edie. He said, "She's my sister, not my girlfriend" – like, as a joke, or he *said* he was joking. But even the way Anomie was, knowing that Morehouse and I were having private-channel chats – she was jealous, I could tell. She was the same when Paperwhite came along as well. She's possessive of Morehouse.

'Morehouse always said to me, "He's a guy, don't go saying he's a girl in front of him, you'll be banned," but I knew she was pretending to be a boy, probably for the same kind of reasons I was. After Morehouse made that sister comment, I went to find out whether he had one, because I thought, well, why not, maybe they *are* brother and sister.'

'And has Morehouse got a sister?' asked Robin, keeping her tone neutral.

'Yes, but I knew she couldn't be Anomie. She's a lawyer. She just can't be.'

'So,' said Robin, 'you'd found out who Morehouse really was by that time?'

A long pause followed. Finally, Rachel nodded.

'And,' she said miserably, 'that's what ended our friendship. He'd warned me to never, ever try and find out who he really was. I didn't think he was serious, but he was, because when I told him I'd identified him he went ballistic. I was really upset and . . . I tried to apologise, but he wouldn't private-channel me . . .

'Then I got really pissed off, because it wasn't as though I was going to expose him on Twitter or anything, he was my *friend*. And then, one night, I got drunk in my bedroom, and I was on the moderator channel and – and I made a kind of joke about something I knew about him . . . and that was it. He went *apeshit*. He's only spoken to me privately once since, and that was when he attacked me for telling Paperwhite he's disabled, but I never told her. She probably just remembered the stupid joke I made about him doing wheelies . . . like, in his wheelchair . . .'

'He's in a wheelchair?' said Robin, her thoughts flying irresistibly to Inigo Upcott. Rachel nodded, then burst into tears again.

'I'm sorry,' she said through her sobs. 'If Paperwhite hadn't arrived we might've made it up, but the two of them became, like, best friends really fast, and he didn't have any time for me any more ...'

Robin passed Rachel another tissue and waited for the worst of her sobs to subside before saying quietly,

'How did you find out who Morehouse really was?'

'He made a mistake on Twitter,' said Rachel in a broken voice, as she frantically mopped her eyes. 'He accidentally posted a link on the Morehouse account instead of his personal one. He realised what he'd done after about ten seconds and deleted it, but I'd spotted it, so I went and found the link.

'It went to some crazy astrophysics research project at Cambridge University. He'd told me a few things about himself, when we were private-channelling in the game, so I kind of had clues. He said he was older than me, but he wouldn't tell me his real age, and he said he'd made the game with Anomie for fun, because it was, like, a nice break from his work, because it was so high pressure. I guessed he was brown-skinned, because he once called himself perma-tanned when I said I had sunburn, and one of the surnames on the research project was Indian.

'So then I went onto the Cambridge website and looked up the astrophysics department and different colleges and stuff and finally I found a photo of him, in his wheelchair, posing with all the other researchers.

Rachel flushed again.

'He's really good-looking. I can see why Paperwhite's so into him ... Anyway, then I had his real name, so I went back onto Twitter and found his personal account, where he tweets about space and posts pictures of Cambridge and stuff.

'He's got cerebral palsy. I think it must be quite bad, because he talked about having to adapt his computer and stuff. I think,' said Rachel naively, 'he must be a kind of genius, because he doesn't look *that* old ... Anyway ...'

She turned to look directly at Robin again. As the dappled light fell onto her tear-stained face, Robin was struck anew by her strong resemblance to Edie.

'You *won't* tell him it was me who helped you find him?'

'Of course not,' said Robin.

Rachel took a deep breath, then said,

'OK. His name's Vikas Bhardwaj, and he's a doctor in astrophysics at Gonville and Caius College.'

83

They are all of them so faithless,
Their torment is your gain;
Would you keep your own heart scathless,
Be the one to give the pain.

Letitia Elizabeth Landon
Cottage Courtship

'The only entry I can find for a Dr Vikas Bhardwaj under thirty is in Birmingham,' said Strike, three-quarters of an hour later in the Three Cottages Café, after he'd heartily congratulated Robin on her successful interview, then opened 192.com on his phone. 'Might it be his parents' house?'

'Could be where he's registered to vote,' said Robin, 'but let's call them first, rather than drive to Cambridge and back up again.'

'I'll do it,' said Strike, getting up. 'I can have a quick smoke outside.'

He returned five minutes later.

'Yeah, he's in Cambridge. I think I've just talked to his mum. She said he's "at his college".'

'Bloody typical. We passed him on the way up here,' said Strike once he and Robin were back in the BMW and heading back south on the M11. 'Could've paid him a visit after I'd had that coffee and bar of sawdust at the services.'

The sun dazzled them again as they drove south.

'Maybe it's best we beard him in his den by night,' said Strike. 'Probably in the lab all day.'

'It's Sunday. Maybe he'll be out at the pub.'

'Then we'll wait for him. I'll sleep outside his room if I have to. Thanks to you, we're bloody close to cracking this case.'

'There was something else Rachel said, that I haven't told you yet,' Robin told him. 'It's not relevant to Vikas or Anomie, but it's still odd.

'She said she first found *The Ink Black Heart* through a boy she used to talk to, online, on a site for kids called Club Penguin. He called himself Zoltan . . .'

Robin related the story of Zoltan, his attempts to turn Rachel into a girlfriend once he'd found out she was Edie's niece, his sudden, violent threats when she'd told him to stop pestering her and then the deletion of his accounts.

'. . . but the funny thing is,' said Robin, 'the chat-up lines Zoltan started trying to use on Rachel, I've had used on me by random blokes hanging round the fandom. *Exactly* the same. It's like they're working off a blueprint.'

'Lines, like what?' said Strike, preparing to be amused.

'Well, one of them was "if that's your real picture you're probably sick to death of blokes direct messaging you so I'll go now". I set up my Twitter account so anyone could message me, because I wanted to talk to as many *Ink Black Heart* fans as I could. Obviously, it wasn't my real picture, I used a stock photo of a teenage girl. Anyway, it was all very self-deprecating and unthreatening, you know, but when I didn't respond he got aggressive, fast. I was a stuck-up bitch who thought I was too good for him.'

'Say his opening line again?' said Strike, now frowning.

'"If that's your real picture, you're probably sick to death of blokes messaging you." And Rachel told me about another guy, who she suspected was Zoltan under a different name, who came on to Zoe Haigh on Twitter, saying he'd defended her against another man who was harassing her and then expecting Zoe to sleep with him out of gratitude, or something.

'Well, a guy called Max did *exactly* the same thing to me on Twitter. He said, "This isn't a sleazy pick-up ploy, just wanted to tell you that guy was out of order and I've reported him." But I came across Max again yesterday when I was looking through all those tweets, researching Rachel, and he's definitely no Sir Galahad. He was one of the people harassing Edie – in fact, he was the originator of the rumour she'd been a sex worker.

'*And*,' Robin continued, 'Rachel told me Zoltan once told her he'd had to drive a sick dog to the vet. Didn't you tell me Anomie told Kea Niven he had to drive a—'

'—sick cat to the vet, yeah,' said Strike, now thoroughly intrigued. 'You know, I'm sure I've heard that "if that's your real picture" line somewhere else, as w— Wait,' he said suddenly, pulling out his phone.

Robin drove in silence while Strike looked up something on his phone. Five minutes passed. Then Strike said,

'I was right. I'm on the website of a guy called Kosh with a K, who describes himself as "the internationally famous Pick-Up Artist who has taught millions of men how to get sex from women within hours of meeting them! Bestselling author of *Bang!* and *Game*." I've just downloaded his *Digital Game* ebook. You ready?'

'Go on,' said Robin, so Strike read aloud:

Digital Game

Repeat after me: you will not find a wife on the internet.

Women online can get as much dick as they want. Even 4s or 5s get hit on regularly, which means they've gotten—

'He's American,' Strike interjected.
'And I'm warming to him already,' said Robin.

—gotten used to considering men as disposable chew toys. By playing the numbers game, women online might even get the occasional shot at an alpha.

If a woman has a proven pattern of internet hook-ups, you'll never be safe from the implicit threat that you can be replaced as long as her lazy little fingers can operate the mouse. No man wants to leave a wife at home knowing she'll be hunting fresh dick at the click of a few buttons.

That's the bad news.

The good news is that this frees you from the usual constraints of in-person Game. Digital Game is the most ruthless and in some ways the most enjoyable of all Game: minimum effort, maximum pay off – as long as you're prepared to accept lower grade pussy.

'Lovely,' said Robin.

But if it's pussy in quantity rather than quality you're after, get yourself online. By internalizing the following ground rules and putting in a small amount of effort, you'll be certain of achieving hook-ups regularly and with ease.

'Then we've got the infallible steps to securing said hook-ups,' said Strike.

1. Carpet-bombing

You may have to hit on anywhere between 50–100 girls to ensure one or two hook-ups, in addition to nudes/camcorder action.

If you follow these steps consistently, your digital game will become effortless. One great advantage of Digital Game is that you can target large numbers of women simultaneously. I seriously advise keeping a chart so you know where in the process you are with each target.

'That was Tim Ashcroft's mistake,' said Robin. 'Not keeping a chart. Rachel told me he's hit on her three times, by mistake.'

2. Know your prey

Most available pussy on general apps such as Twitter, tumblr, etc trend liberal/SJW – another reason you won't find a future life partner here. SJW women are spoiled, self-centered, entitled and often aggressive. They're also astonishingly easy to Game if you know the rules.

SJWs have an added layer of falsity compared to most women. They want alphas, but are ashamed of it. They love a white knight, but pretend they don't. They want equality, but to be treated like the little princesses they secretly believe themselves to be.

Sensitivity, apparent respect for boundaries and faking interest in their opinions are key to hooking an SJW.

'How do you even know about this guy Kosh?' Robin asked.
'A sixteen–year–old boy told me about him . . . But listen to this . . .'

3. Opening lines

The following are guaranteed openers I have used over and over again to secure hook-ups. One of the advantages of Digital Game is that you aren't reliant on looks/in-person charm/tone of voice/body language. Simply cut, paste, and wait.

- If that's your real picture you're probably sick to death of men in your DMs so I'll go now.
- Given what women get on this lousy platform, I feel the need to state upfront this isn't a cheesy come-on, but the point you just made about [politics/social justice/lousy behaviour of men] is spot on.
- This isn't a sleazy pick up ploy, just wanted to say that [guy who has disagreed with her/harassed/insulted her] was seriously out of order/ I've reported him.

'I can't believe this,' said Robin, glancing sideways. 'So all these idiots are using Kosh lines?'
'There's more,' said Strike. 'This bit's interesting.'

4. Negging

Negging works online just as it works off. Once you've caught her attention with your fake interest in her opinions/concern about her welfare/appreciation for her looks, find something to criticize or disagree with. Keep it small and safe.

Destabilized, she will then work to regain your approval.

- [about her picture] but I guess you've used a load of filters, right? Everyone does.
- Guessing you haven't read [insert SJW fave such as Noam Chomsky/Ta-Nehisi Coates/Anand Giridharadas and be ready with a single quote from the author]
- You came off as a little aggressive but I guess that's understandable.

'Kea said Anomie told her she was coming off as aggressive, but that he supposed it was understandable,' said Strike, 'which I thought at the time was a bit fucking rich, coming from Anomie . . .'

5. Promote fear of abandonment

She thinks you're a good guy and she's started working to regain your approval: now fall silent for anything from an hour to a full 24 hours, depending on your target. 8s and 9s shouldn't be kept waiting long, because they have other options. For a 4 or 5, 24 hours will seal the deal. She needs to know you have a life/other demands on you, aside from an online interaction with a stranger.

6. The alpha in cuck's clothing

Return without apology — you owe her nothing as yet, because she's given you nothing. Reason for absence reveals you as an alpha without needing to be explicit: you are physically/emotionally strong, popular, financially solvent, and competent. You're framing yourself as a reliable good guy without explicitly declaring yourself one.

- Guy across the hall needed me to lift his fridge so he could get some damn baby toy from out under it.
- My sister's ex has been making himself a nuisance. Said I'd stay the night.
- Had to drive a friend to pick up his dog from the vet's.

'So that's where all these sick dogs and cats come in?' said Robin.
'Looks like it.'

7. Broaden scope of convo

She's glad to be the focus of your attention again and the reason
for your temporary absence has increased your worth in her eyes.
Now ask her questions about herself, the better to tailor your own
background story to her specific agenda. If she's a single mother,
you were raised by a single mother, who did an awesome job. If
she's worried about poverty, you volunteer at a local food bank.
If she's concerned with racial injustice, you were just talking that
issue over with your black best friend . . .

'Kea,' said Strike, 'told me that after Anomie mentioned the cat
she said that she doesn't like them, because of what they do to bird
populations. When she said her mother breeds parrots, he immediately
claimed to own a parrot too.'

Robin said nothing for a few seconds, then asked,

'So you think Kea was telling you the truth about this interaction?
She didn't show it to you, right?'

'No,' said Strike. 'She told me she'd blocked Anomie after he got
nasty, so you couldn't see it any more. What's bothering you?'

'Well – a bunch of men or teenage boys are clearly hanging around
the *Ink Black Heart* fandom, trying to pick up liberal, left-wing women
and girls, right? All using Kosh lines?'

'Agreed.'

'Well, Kea's bound to have been hit on by one of them, surely? She's
very pretty and she's been all over Twitter for the last couple of years.'

'You think she made up the story about Anomie hitting on her? Just
quoted an interaction she had with one of these other guys?'

'Yes – without realising it's all a blueprint and could be traced back
to Kosh. Also, I don't understand why she didn't save that conversation
with Anomie if it happened, because it makes Anomie look a bit of
an idiot, doesn't it? Especially the parrot bit. And it also supports her
claim not to be Anomie. "Look, he's harassed me too."'

'Fair points,' said Strike. 'So you're inclining to Rachel's theory
that Anomie's female?'

Robin thought for a while. Finally she said,

'I just don't know. Until I spoke to Rachel, I thought the closest we've got to the real Anomie are those direct messages they sent Josh – very arrogant, apparently educated and clearly feeling they should take over Edie's creative role. But the conversation Rachel's just described to me, which happened back when it all began, is odd, isn't it? *"Edie and I are basically the same person."* Rachel said that isn't how the average boy or man speaks, and I agree. I'm certain Rachel was telling me the truth about that conversation: she's clearly torturing herself with regret about ever having joined the game. I can't see why she'd lie.

'I told you, right back at the start of the investigation, I thought there was something up with Anomie and sex. No flirting, no trying to meet or date any of these girls trying to get their attention. In the game, yes, they're different, they can be crude and aggressive, but as I said to you, it sometimes feels a bit contrived – what's expected of them as a man online.'

'Well, I always liked your Kea-as-Anomie theory,' said Strike. 'But for the sake of argument, let's say Anomie *did* try and hit on Kea, using Kosh lines. There's no reason Anomie couldn't also be masquerading as one of these Maxes and Zoltans who're out there trying to pick up girls, is there?'

'No, I suppose not,' said Robin, 'but why bother with other accounts to try and pick up girls, when all the *Ink Black Heart* girls are fascinated by Anomie?'

'To keep Anomie clean and anonymous?'

'That's possible,' said Robin doubtfully, 'but my God, if Anomie's running the game, tweeting all the time *and* trying to pick up as many girls as possible using Kosh's system, when would they ever sleep?'

'Certainly wouldn't leave much time for anything else,' agreed Strike. 'And we've got another mystery now, haven't we? What the hell is Vikas Bhardwaj, astrophysicist at one of the world's most prestigious universities, doing chumming around with Anomie?'

'"She's my sister",' quoted Robin. 'You know, I wondered—'

Strike's mobile rang and went immediately to Bluetooth. He answered the call and Midge's voice came out of the speaker.

'Strike?'

'Yeah, I'm here, and so's Robin.'

'I've got news . . . on Ross . . .'

Midge sounded out of breath. Strike and Robin glanced at each other.

'Everything all right?' said Strike.

'Yeah ... fine ... I just had to run ... about half a mile ... just getting my breath back ...'

'You've been at Ross's place in the country, right?'

'Yeah ... I've been trespassing ... Don't go apeshit, I had to ... it was the only way I could get what we needed ...

'OK,' said Midge, after drawing a deep breath. 'So I've been sitting up on a hill overlooking the place, watching the grounds through binoculars.'

'This is a hill belonging to Ross, I take it?'

'Yeah, but it was the only vantage point where I could see properly. I was behind trees. Anyway, about an hour ago two of the older girls appeared, leading ponies out into a – what d'you call a place where you ride that's not a field?'

'Outdoor school?' suggested Robin.

'OK, that, if that's what it is,' said Midge. 'Strike, I think you're going to be pissed off about some of this, but I'd fookin' do it again.'

'Unless you took the kids out with a sniper rifle, I can't afford to sack you when we're this shorthanded,' said Strike. 'Get on with it.'

'All right, well, they were jumping little jumps and stuff, and then Ross came out to watch them, so I started filming.'

'OK, filming on private property's illegal, but letting that go ...'

'And the younger girl went to pieces with her dad watching. The pony kept refusing. So the fooker went into the school and put the bar on the jump up higher and told her to do it again. She got the pony over, but it knocked the top bar off. So he put the bar up higher.

'I knew what were going to happen,' said Midge. 'I could feel it coming. Knew he was going to get violent. So I went down the hill, still filming—'

'He saw you?' said Strike, glaring at the speaker from which Midge's voice was issuing.

'Not then, he didn't,' said Midge. 'I got down behind one of those bushes with all the flowers on, whatever they're—'

'Forget the fucking horticulture, *what happened?*'

'She was telling him she couldn't do it. Crying and shaking – so then the eldest girl starts telling her father to leave her sister alone. Ross walks right over to the elder girl, drags her off her pony, slaps her round the face and sends her inside. She tried to stay and he hit her again, so she went.

'I should've gone for him then,' said Midge, 'because the other bit wouldn't have happened, but I stayed hidden, filming, and then he turned to the littler kid and told her to jump the fucking jump, and whack the pony with the whip until it managed it. The top bar was taller than the pony. It was fookin' ridiculous.

'The kid was terrified, but Ross was yelling at her, so she just charged straight at the jump, whacking the pony with the whip like he was telling her to, and the pony just smashed through the poles and went down. It rolled over and I heard her scream. The pony couldn't get up because it had got a leg caught and she was trapped beneath the pony.

'And that's when I went running out of the bush,' said Midge. 'I know first aid. I couldn't leave the kid there like that—'

'And I'm sure Ross was delighted to let you have a look at her, and had no questions about why you were hiding in a fucking bush—'

'*What was she supposed to do?*' said Robin heatedly, who was entirely on Midge's side. 'Keep filming while the girl got crushed to death?'

'I was climbing over the fence when Ross managed to drag the pony off her, but I think the girl had a broken leg at the very least. White as a fookin' sheet.

'So then Ross sees me,' said Midge, 'and shouts "who the fook are you?" or something and – you won't like this bit either, Strike—'

'You told him you'd got the lot on film?'

'I did, yeah,' said Midge. 'And then he came after me with the horse whip. Thought that was the kind of thing that went out with the Victorians.'

'He left his daughter lying on the ground with a broken leg to chase you?' said Robin in disbelief.

'"Course he fucking did,' said Strike. 'He's the whole reason she's got a bloody broken leg, he's hardly going to start worrying about her now, is he? I take it you outran him?' Strike asked Midge.

'"Course,' said Midge. 'He's not very fit. Well, he gets driven everywhere, doesn't he, lazy arsehole? So, yeah. I've got a film for you with a good bit of child and animal cruelty on it. Thought you'd be pleased about that bit, at least.'

'I am,' said Strike. 'Hopefully Ross'll think you're some horse-welfare crank . . . Well, I wouldn't have advised those tactics, but you got excellent results. Well done.'

When Midge had hung up, Strike heaved a long sigh of relief.

'Well, with that, the film Dev got and the pissed nanny, I think that's Ross well and truly fucked. Once Bhardwaj has told us who Anomie is, we're down two cases and can focus on Fingers and a fat payday all round.'

Robin didn't answer. Strike glanced sideways at her, registered her stony expression and guessed immediately what lay behind it.

'I'm not happy the kid got hurt.'

'I never thought you were,' said Robin coolly.

'So why the Medusa stare?'

'Just thinking: those girls aren't going to be helped by knowing their father's been filmed hurting them. All that's likely to happen is that he'll be a bit more careful about who's watching.'

Strike took his e-cigarette out of his pocket as he turned his gaze back to the M11 and said,

'I haven't forgotten trying to get them some help. If I can do both, I will.'

84

It was almost seven o'clock when Strike and Robin finally entered the outskirts of Cambridge. The clear spring sky now had an opaline gleam, and Robin, though tired, noticed the increasing frequency of beautiful classical buildings as they made their way towards Vikas Bhardwaj's college.

'This is ironic,' said Strike, who was reading from the college's website on his phone. '"*Caius*" – one of the blokes the place was named after, obviously – "*was renowned for his unusual entry rules, barring the sick and infirm, as well as the Welsh, from studying here*" ... Well, obviously all sensible people will be with him on the Welsh, but I doubt Caius would have wanted to miss out on Vikas Bhardwaj ... Christ, and Stephen Hawking was here, too ... fourth-oldest college ... one of the richest ...'

'It's not easy to get to, I know that,' said Robin, who could see the college clearly on the satnav but was being directed down a series of streets that seemed to be taking her further away from it. 'Are you up to walking? I don't think we'll be able to park next to it, what with all these bus lanes and pedestrianised areas.'

'Yeah, no problem,' said Strike, flicking across to another window on his phone, which showed a photograph of Vikas, who was in his wheelchair, dressed in a light green shirt and jeans, surrounded by a group of fellow researchers. Vikas was indeed very handsome, having thick black hair, a square jaw and a singularly charming smile, and looked to Strike as though he was in his mid-twenties. He could tell the younger man had dysfunction in his hands, which were curled in on themselves, and clearly in his legs, because like Inigo Upcott's they showed signs of muscle wastage. According to the caption beneath the picture, Vikas and his colleagues were studying neutron stars, a subject about which Strike knew precisely nothing, and were posing in Tree Court, which gave a backdrop of viridian lawn and buildings of golden stone.

'Doesn't look like an ideal place for a wheelchair-user to live,' commented Strike, eyeing the narrow doorways behind Vikas, which undoubtedly gave on to stairs even narrower and steeper than those at the Marine Hotel.

A few minutes later, Robin parked and they got out, Robin now consulting her own phone for directions.

They passed many young people also taking the soft evening air. The sun imparted a golden glow to the old brick buildings. Robin, whose own student life had ended so grotesquely, found herself remembering those brief months of happiness and freedom she usually avoided thinking about because of what had happened to her in the stairwell of her halls of residence. She'd come to believe over the intervening years that had the rapist in the gorilla mask never reached out of that dark space and seized her, she and Matthew would have split up before they were twenty, drawn apart by competing interests and lives. Instead, Robin had dropped out, gone home to her parents in the small Yorkshire town where she'd been raised, and clung to the only man in the world who seemed safe. As these memories remained painful, she determinedly refocused her attention on her surroundings.

'It'd be a wonderful place to study, wouldn't it?' she said to Strike as they crossed a bridge over the River Cam and looked down upon the willow-fringed water, on which two young students were punting.

'Yeah, if you like statues and toffs.'

'Wow,' said Robin, smiling up at him. 'I never knew you were this chippy. You're Oxbridge yourself, why the attitude?'

'I'm failed Oxbridge,' he corrected her as they entered Garret Hostel Lane, a narrow alleyway between old brick buildings.

'It isn't failing if you choose to leave of your own accord,' said Robin, who knew Strike had dropped out of Oxford University after the suspicious death of his mother.

'Yeah, I'm sure that's what Joan told the neighbours,' said Strike, who well remembered his aunt's bitter disappointment at him leaving Oxford.

'What did you study?' asked Robin, who'd never asked. 'Classics?'

'No. History.'

'Really? I thought, because you know Latin . . .'

'I don't know Latin,' said Strike. 'Not properly. I've just got a good memory and a GCSE.'

They turned into Trinity Lane.

'In one of the squats my mother took us to live in,' said Strike, to Robin's surprise, because he rarely talked about his childhood, 'there was a guy who'd been a classics teacher at some major public school. I can't remember which one now, but I know it was famous. The guy was an alcoholic who claimed to have had a nervous breakdown. Well, he was pretty unstable, so maybe he had, but he was a real shit as well.

'I was about thirteen and he told me I'd never make anything of myself, because, among other things, I lacked all the basics of a gentleman's education.'

'Like what?'

'Well, like classics,' said Strike. 'And he quoted some long Latin tag at me with a sneer on his face. I didn't know what it meant, so obviously I couldn't really make a comeback – but I *really* didn't like being fucking patronised when I was a kid.'

They continued along Trinity Lane, between more ancient brick buildings.

'Anyway,' said Strike, 'when we left the squat, which I remember as being about a day later, I nicked all the bloke's Latin books.'

Robin let out a shout of laughter: she hadn't seen that coming.

'There was a copy of Catullus in there,' said Strike. 'You ever read any Catullus?'

'No,' said Robin.

'It's filthy – I knew, because there was English on one side and Latin on the other. It's basically sex, buggery, blow jobs, poems about people Catullus didn't like being arseholes, and his infatuation with a woman he called Lesbia, because she was from the island of Lesbos.'

'She presumably wasn't . . .?'

'No, she liked men, a lot, according to Catullus. Anyway, I didn't ever want to be patronised by any fucker spouting Latin at me again, so I used the bastard's books to learn enough to get a GCSE two years later, and memorised a ton of quotes.'

Robin started to laugh so uncontrollably that Strike began to laugh too.

'What's so funny?'

'You learned Latin to prove a point to a man you were never going to meet again?'

'He patronised me,' said Strike, who was still grinning, but couldn't really see why she thought his behaviour unusual. 'And I'll tell you this: there's nothing like Latin for slapping the fuck out of people who think they're better than you. I've used it several times to good effect.'

'This is a whole new side of you,' said Robin, trying with difficulty to suppress her laughter. 'I should've told you no gentleman can hold his head up until he thoroughly understands sheep reproduction. You'd probably have run off to get a degree in it.'

'No offence to your father,' said Strike, grinning, 'but if you need a degree to understand how sheep reproduce, you've got bigger worries than whether you're a gentleman . . .

'I used Latin on Charlotte, the night I met her,' he added unexpectedly, and Robin stopped laughing to listen. 'She thought I was just some oik, obviously, but she was humouring me because she wanted to piss off Ross when he came looking for her at the party. They were dating and they'd rowed – she was trying to make him jealous.

'Anyway, she *was* studying classics,' said Strike as they entered Senate House Passage. 'She told me she loved Catullus, expecting me not to have heard of him, so I reeled off Catullus Five, his first love poem to Lesbia, in its entirety. The rest is history: sixteen years of fucking pain. Appropriate, really, because Lesbia led Catullus a right fucking dance . . . Is this it?'

Gonville & Caius College towered above them, its arched entrance barred by a black iron gate and its ornate face of dun-coloured stone defying the modern world represented by the surrounding shops. Three statues of unsmiling fourteenth- and sixteenth-century men stared down at Strike from their niches. A stretch of brilliant green lawn was visible through the bars of the gate, and more golden buildings surrounding it. What appeared to be a porters' lodge was unoccupied: there was no sign of any human.

'Locked,' said Strike, trying the gate. 'Obviously. Shit.'

But then, while they were still staring through the bars, an Asian woman in her thirties came into view, dressed in white linen trousers and a T-shirt, and carrying a laptop bag. Before she could pass out of sight, Strike called through the locked gate,

'Excuse me? Hello? You know Vikas Bhardwaj, don't you?'

He was certain she was one of the people he'd just seen in the picture of Vikas's research group, and sure enough she paused, frowning slightly.

'Yes,' she said, approaching the gate.

'We're friends of his, we were passing through and thought we'd surprise him,' said Strike, 'but he's not answering his phone. You wouldn't happen to know—?'

He saw her gaze move from him to Robin and back again. As Strike would have guessed, the presence of Robin seemed to convince her he was harmless.

'Have you been to his rooms?' she asked.

'We thought his rooms were here,' said Robin.

'No, no, he's over in the Stephen Hawking Building.'

'Ah, of course,' said Strike, feigning exasperation with himself. 'He told me that. Thanks very much.'

She smiled briefly and turned back into the college. Robin was already looking up the Stephen Hawking Building on her phone.

'It's a long walk. It'd make sense to go back to the car and drive there.'

So they retraced their steps, and after a short journey in the BMW arrived at a modern S-shaped building in pale grey stone, surrounded by a garden in which heavy-headed roses bloomed amid a mass of greenery. A sign asked visitors to visit the porters' lodge, but a dreamy-eyed, long-haired man had just opened the main door, so Robin called,

'Excuse me, we're friends of Vikas Bhardwaj — could we come in with you?'

The long-haired man held the door open in silence. Robin had the impression of somebody so deep in their own abstractions that they barely registered what they were doing.

'Which way is Vikas's room, would you happen to know?' Robin asked. 'We're friends of—'

The long-haired man merely pointed left in silence, then passed out of view.

'He shouldn't have done that,' said Strike as they passed a portrait of Stephen Hawking. 'You don't just let people into a building like this.'

'I know,' said Robin. They'd tightened security around her old halls of residence after the attack on her, but still people left the main door propped open for friends.

'OK, *this* is wheelchair-friendly,' said Strike. The floors were smooth and the slightly curved passage into which they turned wide, with white doors appearing at intervals.

At the far end of the corridor a tall, thin white man and a short black woman appeared to be examining something on a wall.

'No names on doors,' said Strike. 'Let's ask them. If they don't know, we'll start knocking.'

When they heard Strike and Robin's footsteps, the man and woman looked around quickly. Both their expressions were anxious, even scared.

'Would you happen to know which is Vikas Bhardwaj's room?' asked Strike.

'It's this one,' said the woman, pointing at the door beside which she was standing, to which was fixed a brief, typed note in large letters that enabled both Strike and Robin to read it quickly.

Gone to Birmingham. Back Monday.

'Who are you?' asked the man.

'I'm a private detective,' said Strike.

Robin knew exactly why he'd said it. Something was wrong, she could feel it: the fear in the faces of the pair facing them, the note claiming Vikas was where they knew he wasn't and the faint, unpleasant smell in the air, which reminded her of Josh and Edie's old room in North Grove, where a dead rat had been quietly decomposing in a jar. Her heart had begun to race: it knew what her mind didn't want to accept.

'You were supposed to be meeting him?' Strike asked the frightened-looking pair.

'Yes,' said the woman.

'Has someone gone to get the porter?'

'Yes,' said the man.

Neither of them seemed to doubt Strike's right to pose these questions, and that in itself was confirmation that both knew something was badly wrong.

'Does he normally type his notes?' asked Strike.

832

'Yes,' said the woman again, 'but that's not his font. He always uses Comic Sans. For a joke.'

'He's not answering his phone,' said the man.

'He hasn't answered it all day,' said the woman.

Hurried footsteps sounded behind them and all four turned to see another woman, blonde and bespectacled, jogging towards them.

'The porter's not there,' she panted. 'I can't find him.'

'Car,' Strike told Robin. 'Glove compartment. Skeleton keys. Could you go with her?' he asked the blonde woman. 'So she can get back in?'

The woman seemed glad to be told what to do. The two women hurried away.

'You haven't called the police?' Strike asked the man.

'We only got here ten minutes ago,' he replied, looking thoroughly frightened. 'We thought the porter—'

'Call them now,' said Strike. 'When I open the door, nobody's to go in, unless he's still alive.'

'Oh God,' said the woman, and she covered her mouth with her hand.

The man had taken out his mobile and called 999.

'Police, please,' he said in a shaking voice.

Strike was now examining the note on the door without touching it. In the top corner he spotted a mark so faint it was barely visible: the faintest pink oval, as though of a latex-covered thumb.

Running footsteps and jangling keys announced the reappearance of Robin and the blonde.

'We're concerned about a disabled friend of ours,' the tall thin man was telling the police. 'He's not answering his phone or opening his door ... Yes ... Stephen Hawking Building ...'

Strike took the keys from Robin and after trying a couple of different ones succeeded in turning the lock. He pushed the door open.

The black woman's scream was ear-splitting. Vikas Bhardwaj was sitting in his wheelchair facing the door, with his back to his desk and computer. His white shirt was stiff with dried brown blood, his eyes and mouth were open, his head was hanging askew, and his throat was slit.

PART FIVE

At the apex the fibres turn suddenly inwards,
into the interior of the ventricle,
forming what is called the vortex.

Henry Gray FRS
Gray's Anatomy

85

While forensics were still busy at the crime scene, and the ambulance waited to take away Vikas Bhardwaj's body, Strike and Robin were separated from Vikas's friends by the police and shown into a small box of a room with one high window. It seemed a strange mix of office and cupboard, having shelves of files along one wall, a couple of chairs and a bucket and mop in the corner. Here, they gave statements to a uniformed local officer with bright red hair, who was at no pains to conceal his suspicion of the pair of them, and whose questions about Strike's skeleton keys were aggressive.

Strike gave a lucid account of Vikas's participation in the online game, and made deliberate mention of the fact that The Halvening had infiltrated it, in the hopes that this would expedite the arrival of people competent to deal with the case, but these details appeared only to irritate the red-headed officer further. A second officer entered the room, holding a mobile phone. The red-headed constable left the room to take the call, and after ten minutes returned to tell Strike and Robin to stay put.

They remained in their box-like room for another hour, undisturbed by anyone but the devastated porter, who brought them tepid coffee in plastic cups.

'He was a lovely man, Dr Bhardwaj,' said the porter. 'One of the nicest we—'

His voice broke. After depositing the coffee on the table, he left with his hand to his eyes.

'Poor sod,' said Strike quietly as the door closed. 'It's not his fault.'

Robin, who didn't think she'd ever forget the image of Vikas Bhardwaj's gaping throat wound, the tendons and severed arteries clearly exposed, said,

'What d'you think they're keeping us for?'

'For higher-ups to get here,' said Strike. 'I'm hoping we'll see some familiar faces. That's why I mentioned The Halvening to that ginger prick.'

The high window was showing a patch of star-strewn black sky before the door opened again and Strike saw with relief the small, neat figure of Angela Darwish.

'We meet again,' she said. Strike made to get up, to offer Darwish one of the two chairs, but she shook her head.

'Thank you, no. I've just read your statements. So Bhardwaj was in your online game? The one The Halvening infiltrated?'

'He wasn't just in it, he co-created it,' said Strike.

'Do they know how long he's been dead?' Robin asked Darwish.

'At a rough guess, twenty-four hours,' said Darwish.

So, thought Robin, it had already been too late when she and Strike had stopped for coffee at Cambridge Services.

'Plenty of CCTV cameras round here,' said Strike, who'd noticed them on his way in. 'I'd have said it's extremely secure, unless the idiot who let us in is in the habit of holding the door open for strangers.'

'The idiot who let you in is a doctor of theoretical physics,' said Angela Darwish. 'They're interviewing him now. That's the problem with communal buildings. They're only as secure as the least security-conscious person living there. That said, I don't think we're going to have too much trouble identifying the killer. As you say, there are cameras everywhere – somebody must've been desperate to get rid of this poor man, to risk getting their face on that amount of film.'

'I've got a feeling it's going to be a latex mask that's on camera,' said Strike.

He found Darwish's lack of reaction to this comment interesting.

'We'll try and keep your names out of the press,' she said. 'You don't need more media exposure, not after that bomb.'

'Appreciate it,' said Strike.

'Where are you staying?'

'No idea,' said Strike.

'Well, let us know when you do,' said Angela Darwish. 'We'll probably need to talk to you again. I'll walk you out,' she added. 'Don't worry: I've vouched for you to the police.'

'Thanks,' said Strike, flinching as he got to his feet. His right knee was throbbing again. 'I don't think that ginger bloke took to us much.'

'Skeleton keys have that effect on some people,' said Darwish with a dry smile.

As they headed towards the street through the dark garden, Robin saw parked police cars. Clusters of students stood together outside the building, horrified, no doubt, at what had happened to one of their own.

'Well, safe travels, and don't forget to let us know where we can find you,' said Darwish as they reached the BMW. Raising her hand in farewell, she walked away.

'You all right?' said Strike once he and Robin were back in the car.

'Fine,' she said, which wasn't entirely true. 'Now what?'

'We could stay at Nick and Ilsa's?' Strike suggested, without much conviction.

'We can't. She's pregnant. They don't need houseguests who've got The Halvening after them.'

'Well, if you feel up to driving back to London, we could find another hotel – maybe somewhere near the office so we can access our stuff once we're allowed back in? But if you'd rather stay here overn—'

'No,' said Robin, who'd had enough of Cambridge to last her a very long time, 'I'd rather go back.'

86

Oh weary impatient patience of my lot! —
Thus with myself: how fares it, Friends, with you?

Christina Rossetti
Later Life: A Double Sonnet of Sonnets

The brutal murder of Vikas Bhardwaj, who'd entered Cambridge University at the age of sixteen, whose precocious genius had seen him become a doctor of astrophysics at the age of twenty-three and who'd already won an international prize for research, made a justifiable noise in the media. Robin, who read every news story, found herself filled with what she felt to be barely justified grief for the young man she'd never met. Was it wrong, she wondered, to feel that his murder was particularly dreadful because he'd been so brilliant?

'No,' said Strike, at lunchtime two days later, when she put the question to him in the café of the hotel on Poland Street where both were now staying. They were waiting for the rest of the team to arrive for a long overdue face-to-face catch-up. Strike had decided that as the office had so recently been bombed, team morale had to be prioritised over a few hours' lack of surveillance. 'I'd happily take Oliver Peach getting run over by a train if we could have Bhardwaj back. What use is bloody Peach to anyone?'

'You don't think that's a bit . . . eugenics-y?' said Robin.

'Only if I personally start shoving tossers in front of trains,' said Strike. 'But as I'm not going around killing people I don't like, I don't think there's much wrong with admitting some people contribute more to the world than others.'

'So you don't subscribe to "any man's death diminishes me"?' said Robin.

'I wouldn't feel remotely diminished by the deaths of some of the bastards I've met,' said Strike. 'Did you see what Bhardwaj's family said in *The Times* this morning?'

'Yes,' said Robin, without mentioning that the statement had reduced her to tears. In addition to pleading for help in finding his killer, Vikas's family had spoken of their immense and lasting pride in the genius who'd never let his disability stand in his way, and for whom astrophysics had been his entire life.

'That filled in a lot of gaps for me,' said Strike.

'In what way?'

'A doctor in astrophysics seemed a very unlikely candidate for spending so much time on an online game. But then we find out he was at Cambridge at sixteen, severely disabled – I'll bet he was lonely as hell. That game was his social life. Inside the game, he didn't have to deal with speech and mobility issues. It must've been a relief to stop being the child prodigy and just be another fan, meeting other fans.'

'And having a best friend in Anomie.'

'Yeah,' said Strike, 'which is an interesting point, isn't it? Who would Vikas Bhardwaj be most likely to buddy up with, of our remaining suspects?'

'I've been wondering that myself,' said Robin.

'Kea's good-looking,' said Strike. 'I can imagine a lonely young bloke being pretty excited about being her best mate.'

'True,' said Robin. 'But then, if you didn't know about Ashcroft's paedophiliac inclinations, you might think he was a nice guy.'

'And from what I heard on your recording, Pierce can be charming when he wants to be. Plus he knew Ledwell and Blay. Lived with them. That'd be a thrill for a fan.'

They sat in silence for a few seconds, both thinking, before Strike said,

'Well, the press still haven't cottoned on to the fact that we were there, thank Christ . . . Everything go all right at your flat yesterday?'

'Yes, all good,' said Robin.

After checking with the police that it was safe to do so, she'd returned home briefly to pick up a holdall full of clean clothes to take back to the hotel. During her hour at her flat, she watered the slightly wilted philodendron and, for one mad moment, considered taking it back to the hotel with her.

Robin suspected that the state in which she'd first entered the Z

Hotel, tired after hundreds of miles of driving, and fresh from finding the corpse of Vikas Bhardwaj, might have prejudiced her against the place, but she found her room, which was decorated in shades of grey, both cramped and unpleasantly soulless. Unlike Strike, she was almost constantly holed up there because she had to revise for the moderator test Anomie would be giving her in under a week's time.

Her partner, on the other hand, was perfectly happy. His years in the army had inured him to regular changes of residence; he preferred his spaces clean, uncluttered and utilitarian; and the cramped conditions were useful for times when he wasn't wearing his prosthetic leg. The hotel was also ideally situated for keeping an eye on the repairs to the office and accessing all the amenities of the area he knew best.

Midge and Barclay were the first of the subcontractors to arrive for the team meeting, Midge wearing black jeans and a vest top that made Robin acutely conscious of the lack of tone in her own upper arms.

'Everything went as planned this morning,' were Midge's first words to Strike.

'What happened this morning?' asked Robin, who'd spent every hour since 7 a.m. watching episodes of *The Ink Black Heart* and trying to memorise plots and important lines.

'Paid a visit to Jago Ross's first wife,' said Midge. 'Showed her those videos we've taken, of him knocking their kids around and forcing that little girl over that fence on her pony.'

'And?' said Strike.

'She's going to apply for sole custody,' said Midge. 'She promised not to call Ross or her lawyer before tonight, though.'

'Good,' said Strike.

'Are you going to—?' Robin began, but Barclay said at the same time,

'Found anyone to replace Nutsack yet?'

'I'm working on it,' Strike told Barclay, although in truth he hadn't had time to address their manpower problem since returning from Cambridge. Most of that morning had been devoted to a meeting with the office landlord who'd become understandably twitchy about renewing their lease since the bombing, and had required a good deal of placating.

'Well, Midge and I've go' news on Fingers,' said Barclay.

'Excellent,' said Strike. 'Tell us when Dev and Pat get here: they're only a minute away.'

Robin was pleased to see that Pat looked entirely as usual when she arrived with Dev, her spry walk indicating that the door that exploded inwards on her hadn't caused any lasting injury. Nor had Pat's manner undergone any change: when she cast a look of disfavour at the triangular stool she was supposed to sit on, Strike got up to offer Pat the sofa, at which she growled,

'I can manage a stool, I'm not decrepit yet,' and sat down, pulling furiously on her e-cigarette.

When everyone had ordered food and drink, Strike said,

'I thought we should have a face-to-face. I know it's been tough on all of you, Robin and me taking off for a few days. Just want you to know we appreciate how much work you've been covering in our absence and you sticking with the agency, after what happened.'

'Police any nearer catching the bomber?' asked Dev.

'We haven't had an update yet, but it can't be long, not with MI5 involved,' said Strike, hoping he wasn't being over-optimistic. 'So, what's the latest on Fingers?'

'The hoosekeeper's resigned,' said Barclay.

'Interesting,' said Strike.

'Aye. I stood next tae her at a bus stop last night while she was telling Fingers she definitely didn't want tae come back tae work, ever, because she was scared.'

'Scared? Scared of what?' asked Strike.

'Of the KGB,' said Barclay.

'There isn't any KGB any more,' said Robin. 'And also: what the hell?'

'From what I could hear,' said Barclay, 'Fingers has been tellin' her his stepfather's under surveillance by the Russian government, so he's had her ferretin' all the hidden cameras oot and givin' them to him, because he says his mam mustn't be worried, because she's ill. But,' said Barclay, 'Midge knows a bit more aboot that.'

'Yeah. Ill, my arse,' said Midge succinctly. 'The mother's here in London. Arrived two days ago. I tailed her and Fingers yesterday and by a bloody good stroke of luck I got a seat beside the pair of them at the champagne and caviar bar in Harrods.'

'I'll look out for that in your monthly expenses,' said Strike.

'If it's any consolation, it were horrible,' said Midge. 'I've never had caviar before.'

'There wasn't a cheaper option?'

'Fooking hell, Strike, I was sitting at a caviar bar – what were I going to do, ask if they could do me a pork pie?'

Robin laughed.

'Anyway,' said Midge, 'I heard their whole conversation. She's planning a divorce. If you ask me, Fingers has been nicking stuff because he wants to get as much out of that house as he can before the locks change.'

'Or,' said Strike, 'she's had him nicking stuff she fancies keeping rather than fighting for in court – presumably in the hope that the housekeeper would be blamed.'

'Wouldn't surprise me,' said Midge. 'Fingers and his mum seem very cosy.'

'OK, well, that's excellent work from both of you. We stay on Fingers and maybe his mother too while she's here. How old is she?'

'Dunno ... mid- to late forties?' said Midge. 'Might look younger if it were dark. She's gorra face full of fillers. Under a bright light she looks like she's had anaphylactic shock.'

'I'm just wondering,' said Strike, 'whether, as she's planning a divorce ... Has she been pretty social since she hit London?'

'She eats every meal out,' said Midge. 'Night before last she went to a bar in Knightsbridge with a couple of women who look just like her.'

Strike's gaze moved speculatively to Dev, who said,

'What?'

'Might be worth a good-looking art dealer chatting her up. See whether she asks him to value or sell the stuff Fingers nicked.'

'I know fuck-all about art,' said Dev.

'You only need to specialise in whatever it is we know is gone from the house,' said Strike.

'Why'm I no' being picked for this job?' said Barclay, deadpan.

'Know a lot about art, do you?' asked Strike.

'Did a City an' Guilds in Fabergé an' welding.'

Even Pat laughed.

Once their sandwiches had arrived, Strike said,

'So: Anomie.'

The blank faces of the subcontractors told him that they weren't particularly enthused about the new subject.

'We've got three strong candidates left,' said Strike. 'It's really going to be legwork until we've ruled someone else out.'

'It could take years at this rate,' said Midge.

'Robin's close to getting into the moderator channel in the game,' said Strike. 'I think her getting in there's going to be key to breaking the case.'

Strike couldn't blame the subcontractors for looking sceptical. The agency had five investigators, one of whom was currently out of commission because she was trying to pass Anomie's test, and they were supposed to be running surveillance on six people.

'Look,' said Strike, 'I know we're stretched, but Ross should be off our books tonight.'

'You're going to see him?' asked Robin.

'Yep,' said Strike without elaboration. As he didn't want a whole-team discussion about Ross, his long entanglement with Charlotte or his guilt about having added the case to their workload in the first place, he turned the conversation back to Anomie, allocating each subcontractor a suspect on whom they'd resume surveillance that afternoon.

87

Great loves, to the last, have pulses red;
All great loves that have ever died dropped dead.

Helen Hunt Jackson
Dropped Dead

At half-past eight that evening, by which time Jago Ross had usually returned from work, Strike arrived in Kensington and walked to the huge, solid-looking red-brick block with white stone facings inside which Jago had an apartment. Sure enough, all the second-floor lights were on, so Strike rang the bell beside the front door, which was partly made of glass and through which could be glimpsed a luxurious lobby. A porter wearing black livery answered when Strike rang, but didn't admit him.

'Here to see Jago Ross,' said Strike. 'Cormoran Strike.'

'I'll ring upstairs, sir,' said the porter, who spoke in the hushed tones of an undertaker, and closed the front door gently in Strike's face. The detective, who was confident that Ross would see him, if only to have a chance to be offensive and threatening in person, waited without undue concern, and sure enough the porter returned after a couple of minutes, opened the door and admitted the detective.

'Second floor, flat 2B,' said the porter, still in the hushed, unctuous voice of one offering condolences to an important dignitary. 'Lift straight ahead.'

As Strike could plainly see this, he didn't consider the information worth a tip, so he walked across the lobby, which was carpeted in royal blue, and pressed the brass button beside the lift doors, which slid open to reveal a mahogany-panelled interior complete with a bevelled mirror in a gilt frame.

When the doors reopened, Strike found himself on the second-floor landing, which was furnished with more royal blue carpet, fresh lilies standing on a table, and three mahogany doors to separate apartments. The name ROSS was engraved on a small metal plaque on the middle door, so Strike rang another brass doorbell and waited.

It took Ross nearly a minute to answer. He was as tall as Strike, though much thinner, and looked, as he'd always looked, like an Arctic fox, with his white hair, narrow face and bright blue eyes. Still in his business suit, he'd loosened his dark blue tie, and held a crystal tumbler of what looked like whisky. He stood back, his expression impassive, to allow Strike to enter the hall, then closed the apartment door and walked silently past his visitor into what appeared to be a drawing room. Strike followed.

Strike knew the flat was owned by Ross's parents and the decor was almost parodically 'old money', from the slightly faded but still lustrous brocade curtains to the antique chandelier and Aubusson carpet. Dark oil paintings of dogs, horses and what Strike assumed were ancestors covered the walls. Prominent among the silver-framed photographs on the table behind the sofa was a picture of the young Ross wearing the white tie and black tailcoat of Eton.

Ross seemed bent on making Strike speak first, to which the latter had no particular objection – indeed, he was keen to get this over with as quickly as possible – but before he could start, he heard footsteps.

Charlotte walked out of a side room, wearing black stilettos and a clinging black dress. She looked as though she'd been crying, but her expression on seeing Strike was simply astonished.

'Corm,' she said. 'What—?'

'And the Oscar for best actress . . .' said Jago from one of the sofas, his arm stretched along its back, ostentatiously at ease.

'I didn't know he was coming!' Charlotte fired at her husband.

'Of course you didn't,' drawled Jago.

But Charlotte was looking at Strike, who saw, with profound mis-givings, that she'd flushed with what looked like pleasure and hope.

'Have I walked into a marital reunion?' he asked, with the dual aim of dampening Charlotte's expectations and getting them all to the point as quickly as possible.

'No,' said Charlotte, and in spite of her reddened eyes she gave a little laugh. 'Jago called me round here to offer to buy my children from me. If I want to avoid being painted as a psychotic tart in court,

I can walk away now with a hundred and fifty thousand, tax-free. I suppose he thinks it'll be cheaper than taking this to trial. A hundred and forty-five for James, and five for Mary, I imagine. Or is she even worth that?' she flung at Ross.

'Well, not if she takes after her mother,' said Jago, looking up at her.

'You see how he treats me?' Charlotte said to Strike, searching his face for some sign of pity.

'It's my final offer,' Jago told his wife, 'and I'm only making it so your kids don't have to read the truth about their mother, once they're old enough to read the press. Otherwise, I'm more than happy to go to trial. "They gave the kids to the father, because the mother was a real Charlotte Ross," they'll say, once I've got through with you. Apologies,' Jago added, turning lazily to Strike. 'I know how much this must pain you to hear.'

'I don't give a toss which one of you gets custody,' said Strike. 'I'm here to make sure my agency and I are kept out of your shitshow.'

'That won't be possible, sadly,' said Ross, though he looked far from miserable. 'Nude photos. "I'll always love you, Corm." Saving her life, when it would have saved me a lot of time, trouble and money if she'd just died in the loony bin—'

Charlotte seized a polished malachite sphere the size of a grapefruit from the nearest table top and threw it, aiming it at the mirror over the mantelpiece. As Strike could have predicted, it fell far short, landing with a dull thud on a pile of books heaped on the coffee table, then rolling harmlessly onto the carpet. Jago laughed. As Strike could also have predicted, Charlotte then snatched up the next-nearest object, an inlaid tortoiseshell box, and threw it at Jago, who warded it off with a swipe of the hand that deflected the box into the grate, where, with a loud crack, it broke apart.

'That,' he said, no longer smiling, 'was eighteenth-century and you're going to fucking pay for it.'

'Oh, am I? *Am* I?' shouted Charlotte.

'Yes, you crazy bitch, you are,' said Jago. 'That's ten grand off my offer. A hundred and forty, and you get to see the twins, supervised, six times a year.'

He turned back to Strike.

'I hope you don't think you're the only one she's been playing around with, though, because—'

'*You lying fucking bastard!*' screamed Charlotte. 'I did *nothing* with

Landon and you know it, you're just trying to shit-stir between Corm and me!'

'There is no "Corm and me", Charlotte,' Strike said. 'There hasn't been for five years. If you two could control yourselves for a couple of minutes, I think you'll both want to hear what I've got to say, because it's highly relevant to this conversation.'

Both seemed a little surprised at that, and before either of them could interrupt Strike went on, addressing Jago,

'One of my subcontractors went to visit your ex-wife today. She showed her video evidence of you kicking and slapping your daughters outside your house in Kent, and in the grounds. Your ex has also seen footage of you forcing one of them to take a jump on her pony, which resulted in her serious injury. My subcontractor tells me your ex is now thinking of filing for sole custody, using the evidence my agency's collected.'

It was impossible to know whether Ross had turned pale, because the man had always looked as though antifreeze ran in his veins rather than blood, but he'd certainly become unnaturally still.

'I posted copies of the same films to *your* house this afternoon,' he told Charlotte, who unlike Ross had now flushed pinker than ever, and looked exhilarated. 'Needless to say, I've kept my own copies.

'If my name gets mentioned in court during your divorce case,' Strike continued, looking Ross straight in the eye, 'I'll send that footage straight to the tabloids and we'll see which story they're more interested in: a baseless claim that I had an affair with a married woman, or the aristocratic millionaire with connections to the royals who kicks the shit out of his little girls and forces accidents that break their legs because he thinks he's untouchable.'

Strike now headed for the door before pausing.

'Oh, and incidentally: one of your many nannies is on the verge of quitting. Obviously my agency wouldn't covertly record a private conversation, but one of my detectives made extensive notes after chatting her up in a pub. In her opinion, you're both unfit to be anywhere near kids. No doubt you've got non-disclosure agreements with her, but I'm sure the papers would bear her legal costs in return for all the gruesome details.

'So don't forget: I've got the nanny's name and address, and the notes of her conversation. And I've got those videos. One call to a news desk and we'll see whose name gets dragged through the mud.

So you both think long and hard about involving me in any of your shit ever again.'

No sound followed him up the hall. The Rosses appeared to have been struck dumb. He closed the door of the flat firmly behind him.

The porter in the lobby looked surprised to see Strike again so soon and stood up to open the door for him. As Strike could have opened the door easily himself, he didn't consider that worth a tip either, so left with a 'goodnight' and headed out into the darkness towards Kensington High Street, where he hoped to find a cab.

But as he approached the street a couple of minutes later, he heard the click of high heels on stone behind him, and knew exactly whose voice he was about to hear.

'Corm – *Corm!*'

He turned. Charlotte walked the last few feet on her thin heels, breathless, beautiful and flushed.

'*Thank you*,' she said, reaching out to touch his arm.

'I didn't do it for you,' said Strike.

'Don't kid a kidder, Bluey.'

She was smiling now, scanning his face for confirmation.

'It's the truth. I did it for myself and the older kids.'

He turned again, pulling out his cigarettes as he walked, but she ran to catch him up, grabbing his arm.

'Corm—'

'No,' he said bluntly, shaking her off. 'This wasn't about us.'

'You bloody liar,' she said, half laughing.

'I don't lie,' he lied.

'Corm, slow down, I'm in heels.'

'Charlotte,' he said, turning to face her, 'get this through your head. My agency was under threat. Everything I've worked for over the last five years would've gone to shit if I'd been dragged into your divorce case. I don't want to be in the gossip columns.'

'Yeah, I heard about you and Madeline splitting up,' she said, half smiling, and he knew that nothing he'd just said had made any impression on her. 'Corm, let's go for a drink and celebrate. Your agency's safe, I'm free of Jago—'

'No,' repeated Strike, turning to walk away again, but this time she grabbed his arm so tightly that dislodging her would have meant risking knocking her over as she teetered in her stilettos.

'Please,' she said softly, and he knew she still believed the old power she'd exerted over him for so long lingered, that beneath his anger and impatience lay the love that had survived so many ugly scenes. '*Please.* One drink. Corm, I told you when I was dying – when I was *dying* – they could have been my last words. *I love you.*'

But at that his patience ran out. Prising her grip free with his fingers he said,

'Love's one long fucking chemistry experiment to you. You're in it for the danger and the explosions, and even if I wasn't done with *you*,' he added brutally, 'nothing on earth would make me want to help raise Jago Ross's kids.'

'Well ... it'll be joint custody now, I expect. They won't be with me all the time.'

With those words, the busy night seemed to slow again around Cormoran Strike, and the constant growl of traffic seemed suddenly muted. This time he wasn't staring down into Robin's face, full of alcohol and desire: the seismic change had happened inside him because he felt something break and he knew, at last, that there was no putting it back together.

It wasn't that he saw the truth of Charlotte in that instant, because he'd come to believe that there was no single, static truth about any human being, but he understood, once and for all, that something he'd taken to be true wasn't.

He'd always believed – had *had* to believe, because if he couldn't believe that, what on earth was he doing, going back to the relationship over and over again? – that however damaged and destructive she was, however prone to generating mayhem and inflicting pain, they shared a similar core, where certain inalienable principles lived. In spite of all evidence to the contrary – her malice and destructiveness, her craving for chaos and conflict – he'd cleaved romantically to the idea that her childhood, which had been every bit as disrupted, chaotic and, at times, frightening as his own, had left her with a desire to refashion her corner of the world into a saner, safer, kinder place.

And now he saw that he'd been entirely wrong. He'd imagined her own vulnerability meant an instinctive rapport with other vulnerable people. Even if you didn't want children, as indeed he didn't, because he didn't want to make the sacrifices necessary to raise them, surely you'd do anything in your power to prevent them having to spend half their time with Jago Ross? Whatever else he might have thought of Charlotte, never once had he doubted that she'd now do what Ross's ex-wife was preparing to do: to fight to keep the children safe from their father.

'Why are you looking at me like that?' said Charlotte, now impatient.

In fact, it had just registered upon Strike, as he took in the skin-tight black dress that had been the least of his concerns in Jago's flat, that Charlotte had gone to her estranged husband's dressed for seduction. Possibly her plan had been to re-bewitch Ross, although perhaps the unknown Landon was waiting hopefully in some Mayfair bar, while Charlotte tried to rekindle the affair with the man she'd never quite given up.

'Goodnight, Charlotte,' said Strike, turning around and walking away, but she ran after him, catching his arm.

'You can't go like that. Corm, come on,' she said, half laughing again, 'one drink!'

But a vacant taxi was speeding towards them. Strike raised his arm, the taxi slowed, and barely a minute later he was drawing away from the kerb, leaving one of the most beautiful women in London staring blankly after him.

88

Behold, how quickly melted from your sight
The promised objects you esteemed so bright . . .

Mary Tighe
Sonnet

Little though he'd wanted to share a drink with Charlotte, Strike now very much wanted one, so he stopped at an off-licence on the way back to the hotel where, disregarding his diet, he bought both whisky and beer.

The plastic bag full of alcohol clanked a little against his false leg as he walked back along the hotel corridor, past Robin's room, which lay five away from his own. He'd just taken his key card out of his pocket when he heard a door open behind him and, glancing around, saw Robin's head sticking out into the corridor.

'Why aren't you answering your texts?' she asked.

From her expression, Strike could tell something was wrong.

'Sorry, didn't hear it buzz – what's up?' he said, walking back towards her.

'Could you come in here?'

Only when he reached her did he see that she was wearing a pair of pyjamas that comprised grey shorts and a matching T-shirt. Possibly an awareness of the fact she was conspicuously bra-less hit Robin at the same time as Strike, because when he reached the door she went to grab a towelling robe off her bed and pulled it on. The warm room smelled of shampoo and Robin had clearly been using a hairdryer.

'I've got good news,' she said, turning to face him as he closed the door, 'and bad.'

'Bad first,' said Strike.

'I've screwed up,' she said, picking up her iPad and handing it to him. 'I took the last picture in the nick of time. I'm so, so sorry, Strike.'

Strike put down his bag of alcohol, sat on the bed, because there was no chair, and examined the pictures of what had been happening in the game in the last hour.

<A new private channel
has opened>

<9 June 2015 21.45>

<Anomie invites
Buffypaws>

Anomie: What are you
doing in here? You
should be revising for
the mod test

<Buffypaws has joined
the channel>

Buffypaws: I've been
revising for hours

Buffypaws: needed a
break!

Anomie: have you seen
Fiendy1?

Buffypaws: no, sorry

>

>

Anomie: well if you're
going to be a mod,
you should know there
are going to be some
changes

Anomie: Morehouse has
left

<A new private channel
has opened>

<9 June 2015 21.47>

<Hartella invites
Buffypaws and Worm28>

Hartella: hi

<Worm28 has joined the
channel>

<Buffypaws has joined
the channel>

Buffypaws: hi, what's
up?

Worm28: Hartella has
Morehouse really left
???

Buffypaws: what?
Morehouse has gone?!

Hartella: Anomie says

Buffypaws: omg really?

Anomie: no loss

Anomie: BorkledDrek's going to assist me if the game needs updating

Anomie: and going forwards, no private channels, I'm shutting them down

Anomie: moderator channel and main game, that's all there's gonna be

Anomie: no more talking behind my back

>

>

>

Anomie: are you talking on any other private channels right now?

>

>

>

Buffypaws: yes

Buffypaws: talking to Hartella and Worm28

Anomie: good, you didn't lie

Anomie: that's good

he wasn't pulling his weight

Worm28: I can 't believe it

Worm28: I thought they were like best friends ?

Worm28: why couldn ' t we just get more mods and let morehouse do less ?

Hartella: Anomie's happier without him

Hartella: have either of you seen Fiendy1?

Buffypaws: no

Worm28: no, why?

Hartella: he's disappeared

Hartella: missed two modding sessions already

Hartella: Anomie's going crazy

Hartella: he's emailed him and everything

Buffypaws: oh wow, that's weird

Worm28: maybe he 's ill ?

Hartella: he can't be ill, we all have to let Anomie know if we can't mod

Worm28: what if he 's had an

Anomie: I need to know I can trust my mods

Anomie: are they asking if you know where Fiendy1's gone?

Buffypaws: yes

Buffypaws: but I don't

>

>

>

>

>

>

>

>

>

>

>

>

>

>

>

>

>

>

accident or something

Hartella: he can't have done

Hartella: I think Anomie would know. Pretty sure he knows who all the mods are in real life.

Worm28: but Fiendy1 wouldn 't leave the game

Worm28: he 'd have told me

Worm28: no way he 'd just go

Hartella: have you got contact details for him?

Worm28: no of course not . rule 14

Worm28: have u heard if the police have charged P***** O***** yet?

Hartella: they haven't and they won't

Hartella: it wasn't him

Hartella: people need to stop shooting their mouth off about stuff they don't know about

Worm28: when have i shot my mout off ?

Hartella: not you i

<A new private channel has opened>

<9 June 2015 21.56>

<Paperwhite invites Buffypaws>

Paperwhite: is Anomie talking to you?

>

>

>

<Buffypaws has joined the channel>

Buffypaws: hi

Paperwhite: just tell me, is Anomie talking to you

>

>

>

Buffypaws: not at the moment but we've got a private channel open

Paperwhite: what's he been saying?

Buffypaws: asking me whether I know where

Anomie: are you talking to anyone else on a private channel at the moment?

>

>

>

>

>

>

>

Buffypaws: sorry, needed the loo

Anomie: answer the question

>

Buffypaws: no

Buffypaws: I'm only talking to Worm28 and Hartella

Anomie: are you sure about that?

Anomie: your little trip to the bathroom happened as soon as Paperwhite arrived

Buffypaws: I hardly know Paperwhite

Anomie: and you're definitely not talking to her now?

Buffypaws: I just told you, I'm not

mean all the Inkhearts on Twitter saying he did it

>

Hartella: he definitely didn't

Worm28: how do you know ?

Hartella: i just know

>

Hartella: urgh look. Paperwhite's back

>

Hartella: I thought she'd leave if Morehouse did

Hartella: she's such a sneaky bitch

Worm28: why is she ?

Hartella: sending nudes to all the men

Hartella: she'll probably do it to you next, Buffy

Hartella: got to keep her fan club numbers up

Hartella: Fiendy1 was right about her

>

Buffypaws: she sends nudes?

Hartella: to all the blokes yeah

Fiendy1 is

Buffypaws: and he told me Morehouse has gone

Paperwhite: don't tell Anomie I'm talking to you

Paperwhite: I'm begging you

Paperwhite: please don't

Buffypaws: ok I won't

Paperwhite: thanks xx

>

>

Buffypaws: I can't believe Morehouse left the game

Paperwhite: he had no choice

Paperwhite: I'm leaving too

Buffypaws: why???

>

>

>

Paperwhite: bc Morehouse was my whole reason for being here

>

Paperwhite: you're nice, so take this seriously

Anomie: the thing about BorkledDrek is, he's smart enough not to get too smart

Buffypaws: I don't know what you mean

Buffypaws: I'm not trying to be smart

>

Anomie: you're just friendly, eh?

Buffypaws: well i have talked to her but not tonight

Buffypaws: it's why i love the game, talking to other fans.

Anomie: hinc cum hostibus clandestina colloquia nasci

Buffypaws: what does that mean?

Anomie: this

<Buffypaws has been banned>

Worm28: you don 't know thatt

Hartella: I know for a fact she sent them to Anomie and Morehouse

Hartella: I saw one. Vile showed me

Worm28: seriusly ?

Hartella: yeah when I asked Vile to swap mod shifts with me one time

Hartella: he said 'if you can prove you look better than this naked I'll swap'

Hartella: and I said 'who's that girl?'

Hartella: and he said Paperwhite

Hartella: she sent it to Anomie 'by mistake' and then Anomie showed it to Vile, and I think he passed it round all the guys, like she

<Buffypaws has been banned>

Buffypaws: take what seriously?

>

>

>

Paperwhite: don't ever get on Anomie's wrong side

Buffypaws: that sounds ominous

Paperwhite: EVER

>

>

>

Buffypaws: Paperwhite?

<Paperwhite has left the channel>

>

>

<Buffypaws has been banned>

'Anomie knew,' said Robin, as Strike finished reading and looked up. She was now sitting beside him on the bed. 'They *knew* I was talking to Paperwhite. I shouldn't have lied, but I was worried about her and—'

'They might not have known for sure,' said Strike, 'although I s'pose they could've found a way to watch private channels.'

'*Shit*,' said Robin, putting her face in her hands. 'All that work, for nothing.'

'It wasn't for nothing,' said Strike reflexively, because she looked so wretched. He drew the bottle of whisky out of its plastic bag, trying to think of something to say that wasn't *but we really didn't need this.*

'Paperwhite's the one who was in a relationship with Morehouse, right?' he said, looking around for a glass or even a mug.

'Yes, and she claimed she knew his real identity.'

'So she knows he's been murdered. Hardly surprising she's clearing out,' said Strike. 'The question is whether leaving the game will put her in more danger, because if Morehouse told her who Anomie is, and Anomie knows who *she* is – and we know he's seen her picture, at the very least – she might be lucky not to end up with a knife in her back.'

'What do we do?'

'I'll tell Murphy what's happened tomorrow,' said Strike, 'although as he and Darwish seem convinced The Halvening's behind everything, I'm not sure how interested he's going to be. At least I'll have a pretext for asking what they got off the CCTV cameras in Cambridge.'

'What does that bit of Latin mean?' asked Robin. 'The thing Anomie said before banning me?'

Strike looked back down at the iPad.

'You said "It's why I love the game, talking to other fans" and the response, roughly translated, is "from which secret meetings with enemies are born". So, yeah, he now considers Paperwhite an enemy ... Pity Vilepechora didn't show *you* that picture of Paperwhite.'

'Yasmin saw it. She doesn't like Paperwhite. She might've kept the picture as proof she was breaking Rule 14.'

'That's an idea,' said Strike, now tugging his pen and notebook out of his pocket and writing a reminder to himself. 'Might pay Yasmin a visit. Desperate times and all that. Want some whisky while you tell me the good news?'

'Oh,' said Robin, who'd almost forgotten there was good news. 'Kea Niven's definitely not Anomie.'

'What?' said Strike, taken aback. Kea had recently moved right up to the top of his personal suspect list.

'Midge called half an hour ago. It's Sara Niven's birthday and she and Kea have been out for dinner at an oyster bar with friends. Kea hasn't been typing on her phone at all, and as you've just seen, Anomie's been very active on private channels tonight.'

'Shit,' said Strike, frowning as he uncorked the whisky. 'No,

I don't mean that – it's good she's been ruled out, but that only leaves us with—'

'Tim Ashcroft and Pez Pierce,' said Robin. 'I know. I've had to field calls from Pez all evening too. He's after a date. Maybe I should accept.'

Strike gave a noncommittal grunt. 'Got a glass?'

'Only one. It's in the bathroom, holding my toothbrush.'

'OK, I'll get mine and come back.'

It was only after Strike had left the room that Robin remembered he'd just come back from confronting Jago Ross: her despair over being banned from the game had driven everything else from her mind. She went to get the glass from her bathroom and when Strike reappeared with his own tooth glass in hand, she said,

'How did—?'

But Strike cut across her.

'It's just bloody happened again! Just then, when I was getting my glass! One of those voice-change calls! The Darth Vader voice!'

'You're kidding?' said Robin.

'"If you dig up Edie you'll know who Anomie is. It's all in the letter." I said, "Who are you?" And there was a weird growl and they hung up.'

They stared at each other.

'That's new, mentioning Anomie, isn't it?' said Robin.

'It is, yeah,' said Strike. 'Previously it was "if you want to know the truth" and "if you want to know who killed her".'

He picked up the whisky and poured a double measure into the glass in Robin's hand. As she sat back down on the bed, drawing her robe around her, she said,

'I told you Bram's got that voice-change device, didn't I? He used it on me at North Grove.'

'Did it make him sound like Darth Vader?'

'It did, a bit.'

Strike, who'd also poured himself a large whisky, took a sizeable gulp, sat down beside Robin on the bed, took out his e-cigarette and said,

'You think Bram's making the calls?'

'Trying to get Edie dug up feels *very* Bram.'

'Would he have known there were letters in the coffin?'

'Probably,' said Robin, after a slight hesitation. 'Mariam and Pez have both been in contact with Josh, haven't they?'

'Would Bram be *interested* in the letters?'

'I don't know . . . he's a very strange kid. Far cleverer than you might think when he's just shouting Drek catchphrases. You heard what Pez said: he's got a genius-level IQ.'

Strike took a deep drag on his e-cigarette, then said,

'Grant Ledwell thinks whoever's making these calls is trying to cast suspicion on Ormond, and it's hard to fault his logic. Nobody in their right mind's going to think Josh killed Edie, nearly sliced his own head off, then dictated a confession to Katya to put in the coffin. But Ormond's been arrested, so why keep harping on the letters?'

'Bram might not have thought that far ahead. It's like Josh said: he might just be trying to see what will happen next.'

'You'd have thought a kid with a genius-level IQ would know full well that nothing will happen. You don't start digging up bodies on the say-so of an anonymous Darth Vader sound-a-like. Anyway, from what we know of him, I'd have thought Bram's more the type to break into the cemetery at night and try and dig her up himself.'

'Don't,' said Robin with an involuntary shudder.

'There's also the fact that nobody at North Grove should know we're investigating Anomie. Whoever keeps calling me clearly *does* know, which ought to make them one of a very small group of people . . . always assuming we haven't been rumbled, of course. Our pictures have been in the papers a lot recently and Tim Ashcroft, Pez Pierce and Yasmin Weatherhead could have connected you with Jessica Robins or Venetia Hall.'

'But the anonymous calls started before that,' said Robin.

'True,' said Strike.

Both drank some whisky, then stared blankly into thin air for a while, contemplating this new problem, the vapour from Strike's e-cigarette drifting between them.

'If the caller genuinely wants Edie dug up,' said Robin finally, 'why aren't they saying explicitly what they know, or think they know, about the letters?'

'Well,' said Strike slowly, 'the obvious answer would be because they're scared of being identified. I might ask Murphy whether the police have had any of these calls.' Strike picked up his pen again and wrote another reminder to himself in his notebook.

'There has to be something we're not seeing,' said Robin, who was still staring into space. 'Or *someone* we're not seeing . . . Did you have any luck with friends of Gus Upcott's?'

'Couldn't find any trace of him online, except for an old YouTube clip of him playing the cello. We could put surveillance back on him, see who he's meeting,' said Strike, though he didn't sound enthusiastic. 'But you said it right at the start: Anomie surely can't be a friend-of-a-friend-of-a-friend of Josh's or Edie's. The speed with which insider information's shared doesn't suggest a long chain of communication.'

'Is there any point trying to ferret out Inigo Upcott's ex-mistress?'

'We can give it a go, but I can't see a middle-aged woman as Anomie either.'

'Then we go back to Pez and Ashcroft, don't we?' said Robin. 'They're the only two we haven't ruled out. I bet Ashcroft knows Latin. He had that kind of schooling.'

'True, but what would he get out of creating the game that he couldn't get far better from being the Pen of Justice? The game's a lousy vehicle for grooming little girls – Rule 14. If you can't give personal details, how's he going to find out whether they're in the right age group?

'That rule's so strange . . . what did Anomie and Morehouse want to achieve with it?'

'Christ knows, but I note Hartella thinks Anomie knows the real identity of all the moderators. It's one rule, literally, for Anomie, and another for everyone else. Anomie's got all the power.'

There was another silence, in which Strike, who'd already finished his whisky, poured himself another.

'I keep going back to North Grove,' said Robin. 'I still think North Grove's the . . . the *hub* of all this. I'm *certain* Anomie's at North Grove, or *has* been there. The quotation on the window. That stolen drawing of Josh's—'

'That could've been nicked by anyone.'

'But the vampire's in the game,' said Robin, turning to look at Strike. 'It's not in the cartoon, but it's in the game. Anomie and Morehouse thought they were getting out in front of Josh and Edie, putting the vampire in, but it never ended up in the cartoon.'

'That,' said Strike, to whom this hadn't occurred, 'is an

excellent bit of reasoning, and it takes us straight back to Pez Pierce, doesn't it?'

'And on paper he looks good, I know he does,' said Robin. 'He's definitely got the skill set, he had a grudge against Edie ... but Anomie just doesn't *sound* like him. The Latin. The ... the *obses-siveness*, the vitriol ... I'm not saying Pez didn't have complicated feelings for Edie, he definitely did, but ... He wore yellow to her funeral because it was her favourite colour ... If he's acting, it's a better act than I've ever seen ... D'you mind?' she added, her eyes on the whisky.

'Have as much as you want,' said Strike, handing her the bottle.

He smelled her shampoo again as her hair swung forwards and though trying to keep his eyes on her face, he noticed her breasts move beneath the thin T-shirt material of her pyjama top.

There was another pause, during which Robin poured herself a large measure of whisky, set the bottle down on the floor and said,

'Evola ... I am Evola ... you don't think that's a weird coinci-dence too?'

'What?' said Strike, who was mainly trying not to think about Robin's breasts.

'That there's a troll hanging around the *Ink Black Heart* fandom, using the name Evola, when he's one of Nils's favourite—?'

Robin gave a sudden gasp.

'*He's in the North Grove bathroom.*'

'Who is?' said Strike, confused.

'*Evola!* I'm *sure* I saw one of his books in the bookcase! Nils told me it was a little lending library, to borrow whatever I wanted – it had a yellow spine – wait ...'

She snatched up her iPad again and for a minute or so was silent. Then she said,

'*Ride the Tiger* by Julius Evola. That book's in the North Grove bathroom.'

'Are you suggesting I am Evola and Anomie are the same person?'

'I ... no ...' said Robin uncertainly. 'It's just strange ...'

'Because I think this one really could be a coincidence. We know *The Ink Black Heart* attracted a load of neo-Nazis and alt-right types. Evola's their kind of writer.'

'True,' sighed Robin. '*God*, I wish all the misogynists and fascists would clear out of the way.'

'Me too, but I don't think that's going to happen any time soon. They're having too much fun.'

'So what happened with Jago Ross?'

'Oh,' said Strike, who'd forgotten that he hadn't yet told her. 'Well, it was pretty short and sweet . . .'

He told the story of what had happened in Kensington while drinking his third large whisky.

'. . . so his first wife is going to apply for sole custody.'

'I'm glad,' said Robin fervently. 'Oh, I'm really glad, I thought you were just going to hold the threat of the videos over him . . . those poor kids . . . but their mother must've *known*? The girls surely told her what was going on?'

'Probably likes the alimony,' said Strike cynically. 'Easier not to rock the boat, isn't it? Maybe she told herself the girls were exaggerating. Mind you, her kid coming home with a broken leg must've been a shock, and then seeing how it actually happened, on camera . . . Bottom line, I'd imagine a nice quiet accommodation will be reached, because Ross isn't going to want that footage shown in court. It's not like he gives a shit about his daughters. He seems fixated on the son and heir.'

'But if you've sent Charlotte the videos as well—'

Strike drained his third glass of whisky.

'She doesn't seem interested in sole custody. It'd hamper her social life.'

Robin had never heard him talk in that tone about Charlotte before.

'I'd better let you get to bed,' said Strike unexpectedly. He heaved himself to his feet, then picked up his whisky and his bag of beer. 'Night.'

Robin was left staring at the door, wondering why Strike had left so suddenly. Had memories of Charlotte overwhelmed him? *Sixteen years of pain*, he'd said in Cambridge, but there must have been pleasure too, to keep drawing him back over and over again.

Well, that's Madeline's problem, not yours, Robin told herself. She finished her whisky and headed back into the bathroom to clean her teeth.

In fact, the reason Strike had left so precipitately was because, after nearly half a bottle of Macallan on an empty stomach, he'd thought it best to remove himself from Robin's vicinity. Bare-faced, sweet-smelling and conspicuously clean in her pyjamas and robe, talking intelligently about the case and expressing compassion for children she'd never met, she couldn't have presented a greater contrast to Charlotte. Strike feared loss of control – not some clumsy physical overture, although much more Macallan and even that might have been a risk – but a caving-in to the temptation of talking too personally, of saying too much, while the two of them were sitting on the same bed, in an invitingly anonymous hotel room.

It was quite enough that their office was currently in ruins and the Anomie case virtually impenetrable: he didn't need to screw up the only relationship that was currently keeping him sane.

89

The mighty are brought low by many a thing
Too small to name . . .

Helen Murphy Hunt
Danger

Strike took it upon himself to call each of the subcontractors next morning, to tell them the agency had lost its access to *Drek's Game*. As he'd expected, each responded with a single expletive, which he was glad Robin hadn't heard. Strike then told Barclay and Dev that they should continue to watch Pierce and Ashcroft respectively.

'What's the fuckin' point?' asked Barclay.

'Anomie might tweet,' said Strike. 'That's all we've got right now.'

The detective then called Ryan Murphy, only to be told he was in a meeting and would call back, so Strike walked up to Denmark Street for the first time since the bombing to check on the progress of the builders and see what could be salvaged from the wreckage.

Robin was in Sloane Square again, watching Fingers' windows, when Strike called her an hour later. He'd agreed to her undertaking daytime surveillance in the light of their current lack of manpower, but hadn't been happy about it.

'How's the office looking?' she asked.

'Better than I expected. The walls and ceiling have been replastered and they've fitted a new door on the inside office. We'll need some new furniture, and a new PC and desk for Pat. There's still no glass in the outer door, it's boarded over. My flat's OK now they've fixed the office ceiling.

'But that's not why I'm calling. I've just spoken to Murphy. They've released Ormond without charge.'

'*Oh*,' said Robin. 'Did you tell him about Paperwhite?'

'Yeah,' said Strike. 'Can't say he seemed overly excited, but he still wants to see us both at New Scotland Yard as soon as possible.'

'What?' said Robin. 'Why?'

'He's being quite cryptic. Says there's something we can help them with, and something they might be able to help *us* with. I've called Midge, she'll take over from you.'

'Strike, she hasn't had a day off in weeks.'

'I've promised her a long weekend. Meet you at the front of the building,' said Strike, and rang off.

So, having handed over to Midge, Robin took a taxi to New Scotland Yard, an enormous pale grey building facing the Thames. She found Strike smoking a short distance from the main doors.

'This is all a bit odd, isn't it?' Robin said as she reached him.

'It is,' agreed Strike, grinding out his stub beneath his false foot. 'Murphy didn't sound like a man who's lost his main suspect. He actually sounded pretty happy about something. I said I'd call him when we arrived.'

Murphy came to collect them in person, and a short lift ride later they found themselves in a small room furnished with a round table and several metal-legged chairs. Already present was Angela Darwish, who shook hands with both Strike and Robin on arrival. A sleek black box sat on the table, which Strike recognised as a surveillance recorder.

The room's single window looked out on the river, which today was a blinding mass of white sparkles, and admitted so much unfiltered sunshine that the plastic seats drawn up around the table were almost uncomfortably hot. Having closed the door and joined them at the table, Murphy said, smiling,

'You're here because of a cat.'

'A cat?' repeated Robin.

'Yep. I'm about to play you something we recorded a week ago, courtesy of a couple of listening devices in an old lady's flat.'

'What are you, the council?' Strike asked Angela Darwish. 'Rentokil?'

Angela smiled, but didn't answer. Murphy pressed a button on the black box.

They heard soft thuds that sounded to Strike like footsteps on carpet, as though someone was pacing. Then a voice spoke, and within a few words Strike recognised it as that of Wally Cardew.

'Uruz?'

A short pause, then,

'Yeah, I got in, but it weren't no good ... It took me about five fuckin' goes to remember me password ... Yeah ... but it's all changed, I couldn't see none of the people I used to talk to ... Well, I weren't in there that long, because, like, I only joined it after I got sacked, like, to try and whip up a bit of support ... Ha ha, yeah ... No, it's shit, anyway ... yeah, they've got a new mod, so I asked 'im a couple of questions, but nuffing. Then Anomie fuckin' turned up and asked me what I was doin' back in there, suspicious, like, and 'e started asking a ton of fuckin' questions, and I couldn't remember what I'd told 'im about meself back then, because obviously I was pretending to be some random shit-muncher, didn't want anyone knowing I was in the game bigging meself up ... Ha ha, yeah, exactly ... But I got one of me answers wrong, and the fucker fuckin' banned me ... Yeah ... No, man, I know that ... I wanna 'elp, I'll do whatever ... Yeah, OK ... Yeah ... Tell 'im I still wanna 'elp, though ... Tell 'im I'm ready to take the meeting wiv 'is old man any time ... Yeah, I know ... Will do ... OK, laters.'

Murphy pressed pause.

'Cardew's been trying to find out who Anomie is, inside *Drek's Game*,' said Strike.

'Bang on,' said Murphy. 'You'll notice they use their code-names whenever they speak to each other by phone, but we identified Uruz a while back. Uruz was round at Thurisaz's house when we picked him up.'

'Thurisaz is Jamie Kettle,' Darwish told Strike, 'the man you—'

'Punched,' said Strike. 'Yeah, I remember. I don't do it often. I mean, I can keep track of them.'

Darwish actually laughed.

'We didn't have anything on Uruz at the time,' said Murphy, 'but his tattoos gave us a good steer on what his politics might be.'

'You'd think men trying to operate in the shadows might think twice about tattooing swastikas all over themselves,' commented Strike.

'We think,' said Darwish, 'Uruz and Thurisaz were picked for their brawn, not their brains.'

'Anyway, we ID-ed Uruz pretty quickly,' said Murphy. 'He's the one who was casing your flat,' he told Robin, 'and he gets careless when he's had a pint or seven. We had a plainclothes guy with him while he was telling his mates about a well-funded far-right web channel that's about to start up. Very pleased with himself about having this insider information, little Uruz. He said a multi-millionaire was behind the project, and there'd be a celebrity on it who couldn't speak freely on YouTube . . .'

'The multi-millionaire wouldn't happen to be Ian Peach, would it?'

'I couldn't comment,' said Murphy, with the ghost of a wink. 'So: this is a second recording, which we got yesterday afternoon.'

He pressed the button again. This time, Wally's excited voice echoed slightly, as though he'd shut himself in a bathroom.

'Uruz? I've got somefing big . . . Yeah. I've found out 'oo Anomie is . . . Yeah! I was finking of goin' to see Heimdall and tell 'im in p— . . . Oh, right . . . No, I get it . . . Shit, are they?'

Murphy hit pause.

'Heimdall, who's the brains of the operation, is smart enough to know people are watching him and his father,' said Murphy. 'That's why he's using minions as runners, obviously.'

He hit play again and Wally said,

'Well, my place is safe . . .'

Murphy gave a snort of amusement.

'. . . Yeah, defs . . . No, any time tonight . . .'

Indistinctly, in the background of the tape, an elderly woman's voice could be heard making an enquiry.

'Gimme a minute, Gran,' called Wally, who then spoke in a lower voice, 'No, she should be out later . . . Yeah, OK . . . Yeah . . . See ya then.'

Strike presumed Wally had hung up before starting to sing in a low voice:

There is a road an' it leads to Valhalla
where on'y the chosen are allowed . . .

Murphy pressed pause again.

'Tune and lyrics by Skrewdriver,' said the policeman. 'Popular at Odinist retreats, I hear . . . So, this next recording was made yesterday evening. Watch out for the cat.'

Murphy pressed the play button for the third time.

Apparently none of the listening devices installed in Mrs Cardew's flat were in the hall, because the noise of a door opening sounded distant, as did the first exchange between the two men.

'Dagaz, my man.'

'Wally's got a rune name now?' said Robin quietly, and Murphy nodded.

The sound of laughter was followed by the door closing. More muffled footsteps, as though on carpet, followed, then an elderly female voice spoke loud and clear.

'D'you want a cup of tea, either of you?'

'No, thanks.'

'No fanks, Gran, I got beer. Give us 'alf an hour, OK? . . . No, 'e's in 'ere, 'e'll be fine . . . Just lookin' out the window . . .'

'That'd be the cat, who's looking out of the window?' asked Strike.

'Exactly.'

Another door closed.

'Fort she was going out,' said Wally apologetically. 'Good to see you, bro. 'Ow's Algiz?'

'Still not right, poor bastard. Jumpy. Bad headaches . . .'

A faint creak, a soft shifting of material, as though seats had been taken.

'. . . he might be, like, brain-damaged for ever, so if you know who this fucker is—'

'OK, so I'm, like, nine'y-nine per cent sure. 'Elp yourself.'

The unmistakeable sound of ring pulls being torn off cans of beer followed.

'So,' said Wally, 'there's this guy on Twitter called Lepine's Disciple –'

Robin glanced at Strike.

'– 'e's always liking me tweets, and 'e sometimes comes – used to come and post comments on mine and MJ's show.

'So, last night, 'e tags me in on an argument 'e's 'aving wiv some arsehole called the Pen of Justice and 'e says 'e knows Anomie.'

'Who does, the Pen—?'

'No, Lepine's Disciple. So I followed 'im back and direct messaged him, an' I said, "You know Anomie?" An' 'e says, "Yeah, 'e's a mate of mine." Load of shit abou' Anomie being a fuckin' genius

an' stuff an' then I says, "So what did 'e 'ave against Ledwell?" and
'e tells me she fucked 'im over big time – sounded like they were
screwing – then the slag swanned off with all the money to shack
up wiv Josh Blay.'

'Did 'e give you a name?'

'Didn't need to. I know exactly 'oo that is. Guy called Pe—'

A loud clunk was heard and the voices became suddenly distant.

'—ierce – fucking cat – and 'e lives at the 'ippy—'

Another loud clunk.

'—to record at. Like I said, I'm nine'y-nine per—'

Still more clunks: Robin could visualise Wally repositioning
the object in which the listening device was hidden, which had
evidently been knocked to the floor by the cat. The voices became
clear again.

'—'ard on for 'er, 'cause I remember saying to Josh, that fucker
don't like you, watch your fuckin' back. 'E's after your bitch. 'E fort
'e was a better artist than Josh an' 'e does animation – I'm nine'y-nine
per cent, it's 'im. One of 'is nicknames round the commune was
Horse, 'cause 'e 'ad a fuckin' massive c—'

Uruz laughed. Murphy stopped the recording.

'We're hoping,' he said, 'you might be able to tell us—'

'Pez Pierce,' said Robin. 'Full name: Preston Pierce. He's from
Liverpool and he lives at the North Grove art commune place in
Highgate.'

'Excellent,' said Darwish crisply, as she and Murphy both got to
their feet. The latter said to Strike and Robin,

'Will you two wait here?'

'No problem,' said Strike.

'It's been a pleasure,' said Darwish, holding out a cool hand,
which Strike and Robin shook in turn. 'I hope your office wasn't
too badly damaged.'

'Could've been a lot worse,' said Strike.

Darwish left. Strike and Robin looked at each other.

'Lepine's Disciple is a real-life friend of Anomie's?' said Robin.

'I wouldn't bet on it.'

'He *does* stick up for Anomie a lot.'

'So do a load of far-right trolls.'

'That story fits Pez, though.'

'Yeah . . . I s'pose,' said Strike who looked unconvinced.

'*You're* the one who's always thought Pierce was a frontrunner for Anomie.'

'Don't you think Ledwell being a slag who cheated on Anomie is *exactly* the kind of story a woman-hating virgin would come up with?'

'I suppose so,' said Robin, 'but—'

Murphy now returned, holding a manila envelope which he placed on the table without comment.

'Given that your office was bombed, and you've given us significant leads in this case, I think you deserve to hear how they tripped themselves up. It's later on the recording you've just heard.'

He fast-forwarded, then pressed play.

'—on't stroke the fucker, it'll just scratch you . . .'

He fast forwarded.

'—fuckin' bricked up so I 'ad an 'ate wank over Kea Niven's Insta—'

'That goes on a while,' said Murphy, cutting off Uruz's laughter as he advanced the tape again. 'Some left-wing ex-girlfriend Cardew hasn't managed to get back into bed.'

He pressed play yet again.

Uruz's voice now sounded distant, as though the two men were talking in the hall once more.

'This is it,' said Murphy, turning up the volume as Uruz's voice issued from the speaker again.

'Nah, Eihwaz . . . new lock up . . . fucking pigs . . . nah, not Ben . . .'

More indistinct conversation, some laughter, then Uruz said,

'. . . getting better at . . . haha . . . don't tell him that . . . Anyway, Charlie's gonna be fuckin' stoked.'

'Glad to 'elp. Give 'im my best, and to Ollie.'

'Will do.'

'Bingo,' said Murphy, pressing stop. 'Real names. The tossers had too much beer. Heimdall, head of the whole thing: Charlie Peach. We looked into him a couple of months back, but he came up clean. Very savvy, very smart, never makes a slip.'

'Pity he can't say the same about his brother,' said Strike.

'Yeah, he's a cocky little shit, or he was. That brain injury's not healing any time soon. And the third guy they mentioned, Ben – we already knew Eihwaz was the bomb-maker, and them calling him "Ben" was confirmation that our prime suspect *is* the

872

guy. Engineering graduate: respectable-looking, decent job. You wouldn't pin him as a neo-fascist on first meeting him.'

'Benefit of a university education, isn't it?' said Strike. 'Teaches you to tattoo your Nazi rune name on your arse, not your forehead.'

Murphy laughed.

'He's clever, but he's still a wrong'un. Cautioned for stalking an ex-girlfriend and got a suspended sentence for attempted GBH as a teen. I'd be surprised if the defence doesn't order a psychiatric assessment. The longer you talk to him, the weirder he is.

'Anyway, at six this morning we made a series of simultaneous arrests. We believe we've got the whole top tier of The Halvening—'

'Congratulations,' said Strike and Robin together.

'—which means you two should be safe to go home.'

'Fantastic,' said Robin, relieved, but Strike said,

'And what about Anomie?'

'Well,' said Murphy, 'as you've just heard, Charlie's convinced Anomie tried to push his brother under the train. I've just sent a couple of people out to this North Grove place to warn Pierce he might be a target. It's possible Charlie Peach has given an order to take him out, and we can't guarantee we've got all the small fry yet.

'I'd strongly advise you to stay well away from Pierce until you get the all-clear from us. You don't want to be seen to get in The Halvening's way again, not until we're sure we've got all of them. Mind you, even if we've missed a couple of low-level guys, they're going to be crapping themselves once they see the news.'

'You don't think Anomie pushed Oliver Peach in front of the train, do you?' Strike asked, watching Murphy carefully.

'No,' said Murphy. 'We don't.'

'So who did?'

Murphy leaned back in his chair.

'Ben, the bomb-maker, got his suspended sentence for pushing a kid in front of a car. The kid survived, but it was a close thing.

'Three months ago, Ben and Oliver Peach had a proper bust-up online, before they realised we were watching them. At the time, we only had suspicions about their real identities. Charlie would rather believe your Anomie pushed his brother off the platform than one of the men he recruited into The Halvening – human nature, isn't it? – but we think it's going to turn out to be Ben-the-bombmaker.'

'Is using latex masks a Halvening staple?'

Murphy picked up the manila envelope as he said,

'Since you mention it, it is.'

'It is?' said Robin, who hadn't expected this answer.

Murphy now tipped a series of photographs out of the manila envelope and slid two of them across the table. Both pictures had been taken on the street by night, and showed a male figure in a hoodie, his face jowly and expressionless. He was examining the letterbox of a small office that faced a street.

'Those were taken eighteen months ago. The guy's wearing a latex mask that covers the whole head and neck. There's a very shady bloke in Germany who'll make them to any specifications, and The Halvening have bought several. Those masks are getting far too realistic for our liking. The Halvening aren't the only crims using them. There was a big bank job in Munich recently where the whole gang were wearing them.'

Murphy pointed at the pictures Strike and Robin were examining.

'That's the constituency office of Amy Wittstock. Two days after Mask came sneaking around at night, checking that letterbox, a pipe bomb arrived with the morning post.

'These,' Murphy went on, pushing another couple of pictures across the table, 'were taken the night Vikas Bhardwaj was murdered in Cambridge.'

The picture showed a dark man in a wheelchair wheeling himself towards the door of the Stephen Hawking Building.

'This is Vikas?' said Robin.

'Look again,' said Murphy. 'That wheelchair isn't motorised. It's one of the fold-up lightweight ones.'

'Wait,' said Robin. 'This is—?'

'—the killer,' said Murphy. 'They wore a brown-skinned latex mask, it was evening, and the same idiot who let you in let this guy in, thinking they were Vikas.'

Sure enough, there in the second picture was the same long-haired man helpfully holding the door open for the man in the wheelchair, while staring abstractedly at his phone. The third picture showed the dark man in the wheelchair leaving the grounds, head bowed beneath his hoodie. Strike handed the pictures back to Murphy.

'What happened after the killer got off the grounds?'

'The wheelchair was found folded up in bushes down a lane – but not the hard drive.'

'What hard drive?'

'Oh – I didn't tell you. The hard drive on Bhardwaj's computer was gone, which figures. If he'd been talking to anyone online about his suspicions, they wouldn't want to leave that behind.

'It looks as though the killer took a line across some gardens, so no CCTV footage. We're still examining pictures from the cameras positioned nearest the gardens. It won't be long till we've identified the individual, but I'm ninety per cent certain we've already got whoever it was in custody. We think this Vikas guy got suspicious and twigged who the Peach brothers were, so had to be taken out.'

'Very similar m.o. to the stabbings in Highgate Cemetery,' said Strike. 'Kill, then head for parkland or bushes, still disguised.'

'Yeah. Whoever perpetrated these attacks has got strong nerves and did a lot of planning. Charlie Peach trained his people well – even if one of them went rogue and tried to kill his brother.'

'And Ormond's off the hook,' said Strike.

'Yeah,' said Murphy. 'He didn't make it easy for himself, not telling us the truth right off, but we got there in the end ... Confidentially, he eventually 'fessed up to having put a tracking app on Edie's phone, so he could keep tabs on her. He was taking his detention and saw the phone moving towards Highgate Cemetery when she was supposed to be at home in the flat in Finchley. He immediately guessed she was going to meet Blay, so he chucked the detention and went after her, raging.'

'She hadn't told him she was going to meet Josh, then?' said Robin.

'No,' said Murphy. 'His story is that by the time he got in his car the phone was leaving Highgate Cemetery and heading out onto Hampstead Heath. He drove there, followed the signal and found the phone lying in the grass. He picked it up and he claims that while he was standing there a "strange figure" emerged out of the trees and came running towards him.'

'Strange how?' said Strike.

'He says it looked like a troll. Lumpy body, bald ugly head with big ears. Latex mask, obviously,' said Murphy. 'The person took one look at Ormond standing there with her phone – which had a bright yellow cover on it, so was distinctive – then took off into the trees and vanished.'

'So he thinks this masked person dropped the phone, realised they didn't have it and ran back for it?' asked Robin.

'Yeah,' said Murphy. 'And Ormond panicked once he heard she'd been murdered, because he knew he'd been a minute away from it. "I knew you'd think I was sus, everyone always thinks it's the partner, don't they, I panicked, wouldn't have hurt a hair on her head—"'

'He probably didn't hurt a *hair*,' said Robin. 'Her throat, on the other hand . . .'

'I don't think there's any doubt he was abusive, but we pretty much tore his flat apart. No sign of Blay's phone, or the murder weapon, or the dossier the killer took. We didn't have grounds to hold him any longer, but I'm as certain as I can be that he's in the clear for murder.'

'You think the masked person was Halvening,' said Strike.

'Yeah,' said Murphy, gesturing towards the photographs of masked individuals, 'I do. Now we've got them in custody we can search all their hangouts and I think there's a good chance we'll find Blay's phone and the murder weapon.

'Anyway,' said Murphy, collecting up the photographs, 'you tipping us off about that game was extremely helpful.'

'Can I ask one more question?' said Strike.

'Go on. Can't promise I'll answer.'

'Have the Met been getting anonymous phone calls telling them to dig up Edie Ledwell's body?'

Murphy looked taken aback.

'No. Why – have you?'

'Yeah,' said Strike.

'Trolls,' said Murphy.

'Maybe,' said Strike.

Murphy accompanied them back downstairs.

'Been kind of busy with this case since I got back from Spain,' Murphy told Robin in a low voice while the oblivious Strike walked ahead of them, checking Twitter on his phone. 'But now things have calmed down . . .'

'Great,' said Robin self-consciously.

'I'll call you,' said Murphy.

As he bade them farewell, he repeated,

'And keep away from Pez Pierce. Like I say, we don't know that we've got them all.'

90

We lack, yet cannot fix upon the lack:
Not this, nor that; yet somewhat, certainly.
We see the things we do not yearn to see
Around us: and what see we glancing back?

Christina Rossetti
Later Life: A Double Sonnet of Sonnets

'Let's get a drink and something to eat,' said Strike, 'but well away from here. I don't want any stray policemen hearing what I've got to say.'

They headed away from the Thames into the heart of Westminster and finally entered St Stephen's Tavern, a small, dark Victorian pub which lay directly opposite Big Ben and the Houses of Parliament. Robin found a corner table at the back of the pub and five minutes later Strike set down a pint of Badger and a glass of wine, eased himself with some difficulty around the small, iron-footed table and lowered himself onto the green leather bench beneath the mirrored panels.

'Is your leg all right?' Robin asked, because Strike had grimaced again.

'It's been better,' he admitted. Having taken a welcome sip of beer, he said,

'So, according to Lepine's Disciple, Edie screwed Anomie over, possibly after actually screwing him.'

'But you're sceptical.'

'I believe that's what Lepine's Disciple told Wally,' said Strike, opening the menu and looking in vain for something he wanted to eat that might also plausibly support weight loss. 'I'm just not sure I believe Lepine's Disciple. He's talking to a YouTuber he clearly admires. Wouldn't be the first time some prick on the internet made up a story to try and big himself up. Claiming to be a mate of Anomie's and in on all their secrets wouldn't cost him anything ... How many calories would you say are in a cheeseburger and chips?'

'A lot,' said Robin, now perusing the menu herself. 'But they've got a veggie burger. You could have that, without the chips.'

'Fine,' said Strike gloomily.

'I'll order,' said Robin, getting up, to spare Strike more walking.

Once she'd returned, she asked,

'What is it you didn't want any stray policemen hearing?'

'Well,' said Strike, dropping his voice because a family party of four had just sat down at the next table, 'I can see why the Met think all the attacks have been Halvening. Halvening-style masks used each time – Edie on the Direct Action list – Vikas *could* have found out something about the Peach brothers inside the game and become a danger to them.

'If all we had were the murders of Edie and Vikas, I'd tend to agree with Murphy that The Halvening are the likely culprits, but I'm still not buying that Josh was attacked by a terrorist, and I think it's a hell of a stretch to suggest Ben-the-bombmaker decided to murder Oliver Peach by such a risky method, in such a crowded place. To me, that attack is far better explained if Anomie's the assailant. That was a desperate move, the kind of attack that happens because the perp knows they've got one chance and can't afford to miss it. It was a bloody huge risk to take, and however weird Ben-the-bombmaker might be, if he's clever enough to make bombs he's smart enough to know his life's worth less than nothing if Charlie believes he tried to kill Oliver.

'From all we know about him, Charlie's smart. He's already slid out of the Met's clutches once. He's not a man who's going to jump to conclusions out of nowhere. So what makes him so certain Anomie attacked his brother? Did he know Anomie had arranged to meet Oliver at Comic Con? Or suspect that Anomie had lured him there?'

'Possibly,' said Robin.

'I'm certain Oliver went to Comic Con to try and ID Anomie. He kept approaching Dreks and trying to talk to them. I know that's not proof,' he added, as Robin opened her mouth to speak, 'but I watched the guy for an hour. He was definitely trying to find someone. So either he *did* find Anomie, who now knew exactly who to attack, or Anomie already knew what Oliver looked like, because he did what

I did and Googled the idiot. So while Oliver's trying to find Anomie, Anomie's watching Oliver and waiting for his opportunity.'

'But why attack Oliver at all?'

Strike drank more beer, then said,

'I'm starting from the premise that, unlike his big brother, Oliver is a fucking idiot. Anagram of his real name in the game, rune-name on a Twitter account full of identifying photos, then he puts on his best designer gear to go to Comic Con, where I assume he was supposed to be discreet. Would you agree he's a guy with a big mouth, a big ego and a dangerous sense of invulnerability?'

'I would, yes,' said Robin.

'OK, then. I think there's a strong chance that Oliver showed off his knowledge of Bitcoin, the dark web and criminally connected latex mask-makers on a private channel to impress Anomie. The Peach brothers must've done a lot of sucking-up to Anomie, to get made moderators.'

'What – so you think Anomie learned some of The Halvening's tricks directly from Oliver?'

'I do, yeah – and if that's what happened, he was dangerous to Anomie. Oliver could testify that Anomie had that knowledge, because he was the one who gave it to them.'

Again, Robin opened her mouth to speak, and again Strike correctly read her mind.

'Look, I know it's speculation, but there's one thing we know for sure: once Anomie and members of The Halvening were in direct contact, there was a sudden change in the way people were attacked.

'The Halvening m.o. was well established before they got inside that game: masks for surveillance work, bombs for the Direct Action list and online harassment for the indirect list – which was how Edie was supposed to die. She was meant to get bullied into a state where she'd take her own life. The Halvening aren't a hands-on organisation. All their killing's been done at a remove: sending bombs through the post, whipping up online mobs.

'Then, out of the blue, we get two murders and two attempted murders which don't follow the pattern: three stabbings and a push from a train platform, all committed by someone wearing a mask, which I assume, from the Met's conviction that it's all terrorism, they've identified as the handiwork of the dodgy Halvening-affiliated guy in Germany.

'Then we get the banning of LordDrek right after Oliver hit the

train tracks. Why did that happen so fast after the attempted killing?
I think it was so Charlie couldn't start mouthing off about Anomie's
attempted murder inside *Drek's Game*.'

'It fits,' admitted Robin cautiously, 'but—'

'I keep going back to the question of why The Halvening would've
stabbed Blay,' said Strike. 'Blay wasn't on either of their lists and we
know he wasn't mere collateral damage: he didn't get killed because
he was defending Edie from the attacker, but because he was late and
never reached her. What did the attacker's "I'll take care of things
from here" mean, if it wasn't about the cartoon?'

'I don't know,' admitted Robin.

'Why would The Halvening take Josh and Edie's phones? They'd
have done better to leave them exactly where they were. There was
nothing that could've incriminated them. They were just burdening
themselves with objects that tied them to the murder scene. Taking
the dossier would make sense, because that's easily burned – but why
the mobiles?'

'I don't know,' said Robin again. 'But the taking of the dossier
surely makes more sense if it *was* The Halvening who killed them.'

'Not necessarily,' said Strike. 'Maybe Anomie didn't know what
was in there, and thought they were nicking a folder of pictures or
new plot lines. *Or,*' said Strike, 'Anomie had got wind of the contents
somehow, and didn't want anyone to know the game had been infiltrated by terrorists.

'And why would The Halvening want the hard drive of Bhardwaj's
computer? Again, they're just saddling themselves with an incriminating bit of evidence. It would've been too late to repair the damage,
if they thought he'd been sending out emails saying he thinks he's
identified them as terrorists. But if the killer was Anomie, the disap-
pearance of the hard drive makes sense. They were trying to make
sure nobody linked Morehouse to Bhardwaj. At a bare minimum,
that hard drive would have shown that Bhardwaj was the one coding
the game. Let's not forget, the police haven't got a shred of hard evidence Vikas had found out the Peach brothers' true identities, but we
know he knew Anomie's.'

'But—'

'Let's say, for the sake of argument, Vikas became convinced
Anomie was behind the attacks on Edie, Josh and Oliver Peach. What
if Anomie suspected Vikas was about to contact the authorities?'

'But we've got no proof that happened either.'

'Can you explain the ice-cold way Anomie told you that Morehouse had left last night? Anomie knows Vikas has been murdered, it's been all over the news. Where's the shock and grief? They were supposedly friends. D'you think the way Anomie spoke about Morehouse was natural, if they'd had nothing to do with his murder?'

'No,' said Robin. 'I don't.'

They both drank, thinking. Beside them, the two teenagers in the family group were both typing onto their phones, ignoring their parents. Finally, Robin said,

'D'you think it's worth doing some research on Lepine's Disciple?'

'I had a look at his account a while back. I doubt it'll give us much. He's just an anonymous little scrote who doesn't like women.'

'But in the interests of thoroughness—'

'Yeah,' said Strike with a sigh, 'if you want to have a look, carry on. Personally, I think we're far more likely to get what we need from Paperwhite than Lepine's Disciple. There's got to be a chance Morehouse told her who Anomie is. I'm going to tackle Yasmin tonight. Visit her at home, take her by surprise. If she's still got a photo of Paperwhite it'll give us a head start on finding her.'

A barman now brought them two veggie burgers.

'Why haven't you got chips?' Strike asked, looking at Robin's plate.

'Solidarity,' she said, smiling.

'But I could've nicked some,' sighed Strike, picking up his knife and fork.

91

Strike's leg was giving him far more trouble than he wanted to admit to Robin. Another bout of spasms had woken him that morning, and hot pain shot through his hamstring every time he stepped on his prosthesis, reminding him that it would prefer to carry less weight and, ideally, none at all.

If he'd had a choice, he'd have stayed at the Z Hotel for another night and rested up, but as Murphy had said they were safe to go home, and mindful of the accountant's jaundiced view of what constituted business expenses, Strike returned to the hotel with Robin only to pack his things and carry them back to his attic flat on Denmark Street.

The climb up the three flights of stairs added substantially to the pain in his stump. An afternoon nap prior to visiting Yasmin Weatherhead in Croydon was rendered impossible by the loud noises of the builders in the office below. Strike therefore sat at his small kitchen table, leg elevated on a second chair, and ordered a new desk, filing cabinet, PC, computer chair and sofa online, to be delivered in a few days' time.

The news of The Halvening arrests had hit the news a couple

of hours after he'd arrived home. Strike whiled away the rest of the afternoon vaping and drinking coffee while refreshing various news sites. Unsurprisingly, most news reports led with the news that the two sons of Ian Peach, tech multimillionaire and once aspiring Mayor of London, had been led in handcuffs out of his Bishop's Avenue house, which had Grecian columns and a brand-new Maserati parked in the drive. Pictures of Uruz, with his 88 tattoo and slick blond hair; skinheaded Thurisaz, his rune prominent on his Adam's apple; Ben-the-bombmaker, whose unsmiling photograph revealed a wall-eyed glare; and Wally Cardew, described in the caption of his picture as a 'well-known YouTuber', were among those relegated to the foot of the story. Nineteen young men were now in custody, most of them from London, although arrests had also been made in Manchester, Newcastle and Dundee. Strike well understood the satisfaction Ryan Murphy and Angela Darwish must be experiencing; he'd known it himself, at the conclusion of cases, and he envied them the sense of resolution.

At five o'clock, Strike set out for Croydon, and a little over an hour later was to be seen limping along Lower Addiscombe Road, the sleepy residential street where Robin had sat in the Saucy Sausage café, watching the front of the Weatherheads' house.

Strike decided to observe the Weatherhead home for a while before knocking on the door. While his stump didn't much appreciate being asked to support him while loitering outside the row of closed shops opposite for forty minutes, he felt justified in his decision when he at last spotted blonde Yasmin walking up the street, typing on her phone as she went, a large messenger bag slung over her shoulder and wearing the same long black cardigan she'd sported in the photographs Robin had sent him weeks before. Barely raising her eyes from her phone, she turned automatically towards the front door of the family house and disappeared inside.

Strike waited five minutes, then crossed the road and rang the doorbell. After a short wait, the door opened and Yasmin stood there, still holding her mobile and looking mildly surprised to see a stranger on the doormat.

'Evening,' said Strike. 'Yasmin Weatherhead?'

'Yes,' she said, looking puzzled.

'My name's Cormoran Strike. I'm a private detective. I was hoping to ask you a couple of questions.'

The look of mild confusion on Yasmin's round, flat face turned instantly to fear.

'Shouldn't take long,' said Strike. 'Just a couple of questions. Phillip Ormond knows me and can vouch for me.'

An older woman now appeared in the hallway behind Yasmin. She had thick dark grey hair and the same flat face as her daughter.

'Who's this?'

'He's just – just someone who wants to ask me some questions,' said Yasmin.

'What about?' said Mrs Weatherhead, blinking up at Strike with sheep-like eyes.

'About my book,' Yasmin lied. 'I – all right, come in,' she added, to Strike. 'It won't take long,' she assured her mother.

Strike suspected that, like Inigo Upcott, Yasmin's need to know why he wanted to talk to her outweighed her very obvious fear. She led him into a front room overlooking the street and closed the door firmly on her mother.

The space had an air of having been recently redecorated: the pristine light blue carpet was giving off a rubbery smell of newness and the cream leather sofa and chairs looked as though they'd barely been sat on. The large flatscreen television dominated the room. A cluster of photographs displayed on a side table mostly featured the same two little dark-haired girls, who Strike guessed, given the lack of resemblance to Yasmin, were her nieces.

'You can sit down,' said Yasmin, so Strike took the sofa while she placed herself in an armchair and set her mobile down on the arm.

'When did you talk to Phillip?' she asked.

'A few weeks ago,' said Strike. 'My agency's been hired to find out who Anomie is. I'd have thought he'd have told you that.'

Yasmin blinked rapidly a few times, then said,

'It was your partner, who talked to me at Comic Con, wasn't it?'

'That's right.'

'Well, I've already told the police everything I know, which is nothing?' she added, and he noticed the uptalking Robin had mentioned.

'That's not what you told my partner. You told her you'd put clues together to find out Anomie's identity.'

Yasmin's right hand was playing with the perfectly manicured nails of her left. Since getting home, she'd changed her shoes for a pair of Ugg boots, which had made large, flat imprints on the new carpet.

'You're Hartella in *Drek's Game*, of course,' said Strike.

The colour now drained out of Yasmin's lips. If it occurred to her to return an incredulous 'I'm *what*?', she was plainly incapable of delivering the words with any conviction, so merely stared at him, mute.

'I don't know whether you've seen the news this afternoon,' said Strike. 'Nineteen members of a far-right terrorist group—'

Yasmin burst into tears. The heavy fall of dark blonde hair concealed her face as she sobbed into her hands, while her thick legs, planted in their Uggs on the carpet, trembled. Strike, whose instinct was that he'd get more out of Yasmin by being businesslike rather than sympathetic, waited in silence for her to regain control.

After nearly a minute, Yasmin raised her head again. Her face was as blotchy as her neck now, and she'd wept away her mascara, which made pale grey smears beneath her swollen eyes.

'I don't know anything,' she said in a pleading voice. 'I *don't*!'

Having no tissue on her, Yasmin wiped both eyes and nose on the arm of her black cardigan.

'We both know that's not true,' said Strike, unsmiling. 'Where did you get that dossier of supposed proof that Edie Ledwell was Anomie?'

'I put it together myself?' she said, in barely more than a whisper.

'You didn't,' said Strike calmly. 'Someone else put that dossier together, and passed it to you inside *Drek's Game*.'

Given the puffiness of Yasmin's eyes, Strike guessed this wasn't the first time she'd cried today. Perhaps seeing the news of The Halvening arrests had sent her scurrying into the bathroom at work, where she'd wept in terror of what was to come, before carefully reapplying her make-up.

'We know two members of The Halvening infiltrated the moderator channel,' he said. 'The police will soon find the devices used by LordDrek and Vilepechora –'

She gasped at the names, as though he'd thrown freezing water at her.

'– to play *Drek's Game*. MI5 are on the case, too. It's not going to be long before they track you down and –'

Yasmin began to cry again, one hand over her mouth as she rocked backwards and forwards in the chair.

'– ask why you didn't tell them—'

'I didn't know!' she said, through her fingers, 'I didn't! I *didn't!*'

'—where that dossier came from.'

There was a soft knock on the sitting-room door, and it began to open.

'Would you like a cup—?' Mrs Weatherhead began.

'No!' said Yasmin in a strangled voice.

Mrs Weatherhead edged further in through the door, looking concerned. Like her daughter, she was wearing Uggs.

'What's going—?'

'I'll tell you afterwards, Mum!' whispered Yasmin. 'Just *go away!*'

Yasmin's mother withdrew, looking worried. Once the door had closed, Yasmin put her face back in her hands and began to sob again. Muffled words escaped her, which to Strike were indistinguishable until he caught 'so ... *humiliating* ...'

'What's humiliating?'

Yasmin looked up, her nose and eyes still streaming.

'I thought ... I thought LordDrek w-was ... an actor? He *told* me he was, he was really convincing ... s-so I went to his p-play ... and told the woman on the stage door Hartella w-was there ... he'd p-promised me an autograph ... backstage? ... And ... he looked straight p-past me and I was saying "It's me! It's me!" and ...'

A storm of sobs ensued.

'If you keep pretending they were never in the game, you'll look like you're one of them,' said Strike remorselessly. 'People will think you helped them willingly.'

'They can't,' said Yasmin, looking up with a kind of desperate defiance. 'I mean, like, everyone who knows me knows I'm super left-wing? And all my social media proves it?'

'People tell lies about themselves online all the time. A prosecutor would argue you were pretending to be a left-winger to cover up your real beliefs.'

She stared at him for a second or two, eyes swimming with tears, and then, not altogether to the detective's surprise, she lashed out.

'I thought you were s'posed to be finding out who *Anomie* is? It's the police's job to find out about The Halvening, not yours! Or are you just trying to make yourself more *famous* or something?'

'If you'd rather talk about Anomie, let's do that,' said Strike. 'Ever wondered whether they're the one who killed Ledwell?'

'Of course not!' said Yasmin, with a hint of a gasp.

'Even though they've been boasting they killed her, inside the game?'

'That's just – I mean, he's joking?' said Yasmin, trying for incredulity.

'And it's never occurred to you that it's not a joke? That Anomie actually did it?'

'Of course not!' she repeated.

'How's your book going? Anomie still getting part of the proceeds?'

'It's not – it's on hold? Because––'

'Because one of your co-authors was arrested for murder, and the other might have actually done it?'

'Because – because now doesn't feel like the right time,' she said breathlessly.

'You realise all the detailed information Ormond gave you about Edie's new characters, and the plot of the film, came off the phone he picked up and hid after she'd been murdered?'

Strike knew that, somewhere behind the aghast expression and swollen eyes, Yasmin's dreams of press interviews and flattering photographs, of enhanced prestige in the fandom and status as a published author were crumbling to dust.

'If it turns out Anomie murdered Edie Ledwell and paralysed Josh Blay––'

'Josh *isn't* paralysed,' said Yasmin with desperate certainty. 'I know people have been saying that, but he isn't. I've heard he's getting much better?'

'Where did you hear that? From someone on Twitter, who knows a guy whose sister works at the hospital? Josh is paralysed down one side of his body and has lost feeling in the other – as I know, because I interviewed him in hospital.'

Yasmin turned still paler, her trembling fingers playing with her cuff.

'If Anomie was the attacker––' persisted Strike.

'If Anomie's who I think he is, he *can't* have done it,' whispered Yasmin. 'He *physically* can't have done it.'

'Who,' said Strike, 'd'you think Anomie is?'

Yasmin hesitated, then said,

'Inigo Upcott.'

Strike hadn't expected that.

'Why d'you think it's Upcott?'

'Just because ... Anomie sounds like him? Anomie knows Latin, and Inigo was always using bits of Latin? And from things Anomie's said: he has a hard life, and obviously Inigo's in a wheelchair? And Anomie was *really* angry when Edie ditched Katya, and I know Inigo was angry that Katya was never paid for anything she did for Josh and Edie, because I heard him complaining about it a couple of times when I was at their house? And once, when I was round there,' said Yasmin, 'I saw Inigo playing the game?'

'You did?' said Strike.

Yasmin nodded, dabbing at the end of her dripping nose with her cardigan sleeve.

'His PC was glitching? And I went to help him with it, and I saw what he'd been doing when it froze? He was inside the game. I thought at the time he'd just gone to have a look? Because Josh and Edie had been round at Katya's and talking about the game, and Anomie? But then, later on, I started putting two and two together—'

And you made twenty-two.

'—and it made sense, because he's housebound, and he's always on his computer? And he's an artist and he was hearing us all talk about *The Ink Black Heart* all the time? He probably did it just for fun, as a project ...'

'D'you think Anomie talks like a man of sixty-odd?'

'Well – yes?' said Yasmin, defiant again. 'Inigo's got ... he's got a temper? He swears a lot and he didn't like Josh? But he seemed to like Edie, at first, so when she was nasty about the game, it probably really upset him? After all the time and trouble he'd put into it?'

'Did you like Inigo?'

'I – yes. I – I felt sorry for him, being so ill? And when I was first going round there he was nice, but he's – he's quite – he *can* be a bit of a bully and I suppose ... Anomie can as well? But,' she added defensively, 'it was just a *theory*, that's all ...'

Strike wondered whether Yasmin had lived in a virtual world of anonymous people for so long that probability and plausibility had fled from her reasoning processes. One theory seemed to be as good as the next, as long as it satisfied her need to feel herself an insider. These qualities had made her very valuable to The Halvening, but far less useful as a witness.

'You and Inigo were both at a Christmas party at North Grove one year, weren't you?'

'Yes?' said Yasmin, who didn't seem to understand the relevance of the question.

'He told me he saw you in a clinch there, with Nils de Jong.'

Yasmin looked shocked, but Strike thought he saw a faint gratification.

'He – he asked me for a kiss under the mistletoe, that's all.'

'Would it surprise you to know that Inigo claims he heard you confessing to Nils that *you're* Anomie?'

She let out a gasp of shock.

'That's a complete lie! I mean – that's ridiculous!'

'Can you remember what you and Nils were talking about, before he kissed you?'

'I – we'd all had a lot to drink? And – I think he told me I looked unhappy and he wanted to cheer me up? And he – he kind of pulled me under the mistletoe?'

Strike strongly suspected that no man had ever done such a thing to Yasmin before.

'Nils wasn't talking about anomie in the abstract?'

'What d'you mean?'

'Anomie, as in a state of amorality?'

When Yasmin simply looked confused, Strike said,

'You never noticed that the word "anomie" is engraved into the kitchen window at North Grove?'

'Is it?' said Yasmin, with what appeared to be genuine surprise.

'Have you ever talked to Anomie – the person, that is – on the phone?'

'No. Only by email.'

'What's their email address?' asked Strike, pulling his notebook out of his pocket.

'I'm not giving you that.' Her red eyes were watering again, but she was frightened. 'Anomie would *kill* me.'

'You might not be far wrong,' said Strike. 'You realise Morehouse has been murdered?'

'What? No, he – *what?*'

Strike saw her slow thought processes struggling to catch up with what she'd just been told.

'I don't believe you,' she whispered at last.

'Look it up,' said Strike. 'Vikas Bhardwaj. Cambridge University. His throat was slit.'

Yasmin now looked as though she might throw up.

'How d'you know he was Morehouse?' she said faintly.

'If you check the news stories,' said Strike, ignoring the question, 'you'll notice the murder happened the night Morehouse disappeared from the game.'

'I don't believe you,' she said again, but she was trembling. 'You're just trying to scare me.'

Through the net curtains at the window Strike now saw a portly man with grey hair walk up the front path, carrying a briefcase. Shortly afterwards, he heard a mumbled conversation outside the sitting-room door and guessed Yasmin's anxious mother was telling her father that a large stranger was badgering their daughter.

The door opened and Yasmin's father walked in, still holding his briefcase.

'What's going on? Who's this man, Yasmin?'

'It's nothing – I'll tell you afterwards—'

'*Who is he?*' said Yasmin's father, who looked understandably alarmed at the sight of his daughter's streaked, swollen eyes.

'Cormoran Strike,' said the detective, getting unsteadily to his feet while his hamstring screamed for mercy. He held out his hand. 'I'm a private detective and your daughter's helping me with a case.'

'A priv— What is this?' blustered Mr Weatherhead, ignoring Strike's hand as Yasmin's mother sidled into the room behind him. 'Is this still about that damn cartoon?'

'Just leave it, Dad,' whispered Yasmin. '*Please.* I'll be out soon and I'll – I'll explain.'

'I—'

'*Please*, Dad, just let me finish talking to him!' said Yasmin a little hysterically.

Her parents reluctantly retreated. The door closed again. Strike sat back down.

'You understand, don't you,' said Strike, before Yasmin could speak, 'that when all this comes out – which it will, because, as I say, the Met and the security services are seizing The Halvening's computers and phones as we speak – the public, the media and a jury are going to hear that you willingly took possession of a dossier of fabricated evidence against Edie Ledwell, which had been cooked up by a terrorist organisation that wanted her dead, and carried it to Josh Blay to turn him against her? How d'you think you're going to look, Yasmin, when the world hears you kept on cheerfully playing the game after you knew terrorists had infiltrated it – continued *moderating* the game, no less – while planning a book based on information stolen from a dead woman? I'm warning you now: the head of The Halvening is going to claim it was Anomie who stabbed Ledwell and Blay, and that Anomie tried to kill one of their members by pushing him in front of a train. And whether it was The Halvening or Anomie, you're in it up to your neck.'

Yasmin slumped over with her face in her hands and started to cry again.

'Your one hope,' said Strike loudly, to make sure she heard him over her shuddering sobs, 'is to do the right thing, now, voluntarily. Get out of the game, tell the police everything you know, and help me trace Anomie.'

'I c-can't help you, how can I? If it's not Inigo . . .'

'Firstly, you can give me Anomie's email address,' said Strike. 'Secondly, you can help me find the moderator who calls herself Paperwhite.'

'What d'you want to know about *her* for?'

'Because I think she's in danger.'

'How?'

'Morehouse might've told her who Anomie is.'

'Oh . . .'

Yasmin wiped her face on her sleeve, smearing her make-up still further, then said,

'I don't know anything about her.'

'You've been in *Drek's Game* together for months, you must know something. We know you were showed her picture by Vilepechora.'

'How d'you know—?'

'Never mind how I know. Did you keep the picture?'

'No – she was—'

'Naked?'

'Not – not entirely.'

'Describe her.'

'She's . . . pretty. Slim. Red-headed.'

'What sort of age?'

'I don't know . . . early twenties? Maybe younger?'

'Did she ever drop any hints about where she lives?'

'She . . . she once said she was miles from London, when—'

'When . . .?' Strike prompted her.

Yasmin played nervously with the wet sleeve of her cardigan, then said,

'When I told the other moderators that Josh and Edie were going to meet . . . to discuss the dossier.'

'Did you tell them *where* they were meeting?' asked Strike sharply.

'No. Paperwhite asked and I said wouldn't tell her, because Josh would never have forgiven me if some autograph-hunter turned up? And she got in a huff and said she couldn't turn up even if she wanted to, because she was miles away from London? And then she said it was obvious where they were going to meet and stormed off.'

'D'you think most *Ink Black Heart* fans would guess that Josh and Edie were going to meet in the cemetery?'

'Maybe?' said Yasmin. 'I mean . . . it was their place, wasn't it? That's where . . . it all happened.'

'Can you think of anything else Paperwhite said about her life, or where she lived?'

'No. I just know all the men seemed to fancy her? But she likes – she liked Morehouse best.'

'How many people d'you think saw this partially nude photograph?'

'All the blokes, probably? Vilepechora told me she meant to send it to Morehouse, but sent it to Anomie by mistake? Vilepechora probably showed all the other men . . .'

'All right,' said Strike, making a note. 'Now give me Anomie's email address.'

After a moment's hesitation, she picked up the mobile she'd put on the arm of the chair, opened her email account and said,

'It's cagedheart14@aol.com. All lower case. The number's digits.'

'Thank you,' said Strike. 'Fourteen . . . like Rule 14?'

Yasmin, who was busy mopping her face with her sleeve again, nodded.

'Out of interest, what are the other thirteen rules?' Strike asked.

'There aren't any,' she said in a thick voice. 'There's only that rule.'

'So why's it called "fourteen"?'

'It's Anomie's favourite number.'

'Why?'

She shrugged.

'OK,' said Strike, now closing his notebook and taking out his wallet. 'You've been very helpful, Yasmin. If you'll take my advice, you'll contact this man –' he opened his wallet, pulled out Ryan

Murphy's card and handed it to her – 'and tell him everything you've just told me. All of it. And then I'd advise removing yourself from that game, permanently.'

'I can't,' said Yasmin, white-lipped.

'Why not?'

'Because Anomie said – if I did –'

She suddenly emitted a humourless, slightly hysterical laugh.

'– he said he'd tell the police I helped terrorists? But I s'pose . . . if I've told the police myself . . . and at least I won't have to keep . . .'

Her voice trailed away.

'At least you won't have to keep . . .'

Yasmin wiped her eyes again, then said plaintively,

'Anomie's been . . . kind of blackmailing me?'

'To do what?'

'To . . . he's been making me be him, in the game?'

'What d'you mean?' said Strike as a horrible suspicion assailed him.

'He's been making me pretend to be him? In the game, at certain times? He gave me his log-in details and told me when I had to do it, or he'd tell the police about the dossier?'

'How long have you been doing this?' said Strike, as his mind passed rapidly over all the suspects they'd eliminated on the basis that they'd been device-free while Anomie had been in the game.

'I don't know,' said Yasmin with another sob. 'Since . . . It was after I told Anomie I met your partner? At Comic Con?'

'Jesus Christ,' said Strike. Trying not to show the rage now consuming him, he said, 'That didn't seem an odd request to you?'

'Well, kind of . . . I asked him why he wanted me to do it, and he just told me I had to.'

'Can you remember when, exactly, you've "been" Anomie? Did you keep a record?'

'No,' said Yasmin miserably. 'It's happened loads of times, I can't remember them all . . . Why?'

'Because,' said Strike, who no longer had any scruples about scaring a woman so dangerously obtuse, 'you've been helping Anomie set up alibis. If I were you, I'd try hard to remember whether you were impersonating Anomie on the night Vikas Bhardwaj got his throat cut. I think the Met is going to be pretty interested in that bit of information.'

He heaved himself to his feet again, so angry at her that he left without another word.

Yasmin's parents came bustling down the hall towards the sitting room as Strike opened the front door, and the last thing he heard before slamming it behind him was their anxious voices questioning their daughter, and Yasmin's answering wail of distress.

92

To-night again the moon's white mat
Stretches across the dormitory floor
While outside, like an evil cat
The pion prowls down the dark corridor,
Planning, I know, to pounce on me, in spite
For getting leave to sleep in town last night.

Charlotte Mew
The Fête

At first, Robin felt glad to be home in Blackhorse Road. It was a little strange to be suddenly alone – no Strike to talk things over with, or to sit with in companionable silence in the car – but the slight sense of dislocation could be ignored while loading dirty clothes into the washing machine, putting away her toiletries, watering her philodendron and making a trip to the supermarket to restock her fridge.

However, as the day wore on, she found it harder to pretend her nerves weren't jangled, that she felt completely secure. Haunted by images she couldn't forget – Vikas Bhardwaj's severed neck, the grotesque latex masks used by the pipe bomber, the young man with the 88 tattoo taking pictures of her flat – made her draw her curtains early and double-check that she'd set the burglar alarm.

She'd just sat down to eat scrambled eggs on toast when the unfamiliar ringtone of the burner phone in her bag made her jump. When she retrieved the mobile, she saw a text from Pez Pierce.

You won't believe the day I've had

Robin considered her answer for a few seconds before texting back:

Why, what's happened?

Pez's answer came almost immediately.

I've had the fucking police round. Some arsehole's told them I'm that guy was trolling Edie. Now they're saying I need to go into hiding. Some far-right nutters are after the troll. The same guys that are all over the news

OMG, Robin texted back. **Are you serious?**

She had a strong feeling she was about to be asked to lend Pez her sofa, and sure enough:

Couldn't come and crash at yours, could I?

I'm really sorry, Robin replied, **we've got two people staying.**

Yeah a lot of my mates have got 'people staying' now I've got terrorists after me

I'm sorry, Robin texted back, **it's true. Let me know where you're staying? I could come over and cheer you up.**

She didn't have the slightest intention of going to meet Pez, but she could think of no other way of persuading him to tell her his location so that they could keep track of him. However, probably irritated that she hadn't offered him sanctuary, he didn't respond. In one way, Robin was relieved: she wasn't sure her nerves were equal to an evening of text flirtation with Pez Pierce, who might yet prove to be the person Strike believed had cut the throat of the young genius in Cambridge and left him to choke to death on his own blood.

Her upstairs neighbour was once again playing loud music, and for the first time the pounding bass bothered Robin: she wanted to be able to hear unusual noises. Having finished her dinner and washed up, she tried to settle down to examine Lepine's Disciple's Twitter account but found it hard to concentrate. When Strike called, she seized the phone with relief.

'Hi,' she said. 'How did it go with—?'

'You won't fucking believe this,' said Strike.

'What's happened?'

'Ever since Comic Con, Yasmin's been pretending to be Anomie for hours at a stretch, but she hasn't kept a note of exactly when she's been doing it. She twigged that the woman who'd interviewed her was you after she saw your picture in the paper, told Anomie she'd been interviewed by an undercover detective, and Anomie then blackmailed her into impersonating them in the game.'

'*What?*'

'So every fucking suspect we ruled out since Comic Con is back in.'

'But that's—'

'Just about every fucker we suspected in the first place, barring Seb Montgomery. I'm going to have to sit down and work it out, but *Jesus Christ*, we didn't need this. I thought we were down to two people. And as far as Paperwhite goes ...'

'Well,' said Robin, once Strike had finished telling her everything Yasmin had said about Paperwhite and struggling to find any trace of a silver lining, 'well, that's *something*. Redhead, pretty, young, lives miles away from London ...'

'Yeah, it narrows it down to a few hundred thousand women. If you've got any good ideas about how we identify which of them is Paperwhite, call me back,' said Strike.

After they'd said goodbye, Robin sat for a few moments, shocked and dismayed by the new development, until a bang out in the hallway made her jump. She turned in her chair, staring towards the landing. Her front door was secure, the alarm was on, so it was absurd – wasn't it? – to worry that anyone was trying to get in. After a few seconds, in which she felt her heart beat far more rapidly than was normal in a healthy, stationary woman, she got slowly to her feet and walked to the door, pressing her ear against it and wishing she had a spyhole. She could hear nothing. Doubtless somebody walking upstairs had dropped something, yet the image of Vikas Bhardwaj, murdered in his wheelchair, throat agape, eyes dull, suddenly re-intruded itself into her mind's eye.

For the first time since finding Vikas's body, Robin's thoughts jumped to Rachel Ledwell. The girl must have heard Vikas was dead by now.

And then an idea hit Robin with the jarring surprise of an electric shock. Hurrying back to her laptop, she clicked away from Lepine's Disciple's Twitter feed, brought up direct messages, opened the conversation she'd previously had with Rachel, and began to type.

Rachel, it's me, Robin. I
assume you've seen the
dreadful news about Vikas. I'm
so sorry.

I'm now trying to make sure
nobody else gets hurt. If you
can, please message me
back. There's something you
might be able to help me with.
Stop Anomie

Robin knew perfectly well that the girl might not be on Twitter
right now, that she might be so thoroughly and understandably
repulsed by the online world that it would be hours or even days
before she saw the message. Even so, Robin stared at the screen as
though she could will Rachel onto Twitter with the power of her
mind, and then saw three dots appear beneath her own message:
Rachel was typing.

Was Vikas already dead when you
got there?
Penny Peacock

Yes. It's awful. I'm so sorry,
Rachel. I can imagine how
you're feeling.
Stop Anomie

Robin waited on tenterhooks.

Do you know who did it? Do
the police?
Penny Peacock

Not yet.
Stop Anomie

There was a pause of around a minute. Robin was about to type
again when she saw the three dots, and after another minute a far
longer message from Rachel appeared.

I'm so scared. I've been crying
non-stop. My mum thinks I'm
depressed, she wants to take me to
the doctor, but I can't tell her what's

899

really going on. Do you think it was
someone from the Halvening?
Vikas wanted to kick LordDrek
and Vilepechora out of the game
because he was convinced they
were Halvening. Maybe they killed
him in revenge. Maybe he found
out who they really are, he could
have done, he was really clever,
and he called the police? I saw all
those arrests on the news today
and I've been sitting here reading
all the news reports and reading
what people think on Twitter.
I thought the police might say
the Halvening killed Vikas, but
they haven't.
Penny Peacock

I don't know much more
than you do right now, but I
do want to stop anyone else
getting hurt.
Stop Anomie

But the Halvening have all
been arrested.
Penny Peacock

Robin began to type, but at the same time three dots appeared, so she stopped and waited for Rachel's new message.

You think Anomie did it
Penny Peacock

Robin hesitated, wondering how best to proceed.

Not necessarily, although the
last time I was in the game,
Anomie was behaving quite
strangely for someone whose
friend's just been murdered.
Stop Anomie

Strange, how?
Penny Peacock

Very cold and matter-of-fact. It
didn't seem natural.
Stop Anomie

The longest pause yet ensued, but then the three dots reappeared, and another long message from Rachel followed shortly afterwards:

> this is like a nightmare. I keep remembering something really weird Vilepechora said ages ago. it was when Morehouse came on the mod channel to tell Vile and LordDrek to get out of the game. They denied being Halvening and then Vile said for a joke that Anomie murdered Edie and used Bitcoin to buy the knife and the taser. Vile said Anomie knew all about that kind of dark web stuff. I never saw Anomie talking about cryptocurrency but now I'm thinking maybe she and Vilepechora discussed it on a private channel. I got really angry about them all talking like that about my aunt getting killed, like it was funny, and I left the channel. But ever since I saw what happened to Vikas I've just been going round and round in my head, because Anomie was always joking that she'd stabbed Josh and Edie. And it could have been a girl who's done it all, because Josh and Edie were tasered first so they couldn't fight back, and Vikas couldn't have fought back from his wheelchair could he?
>
> Penny Peacock

'Bingo,' said Robin under her breath. She messaged back:

> I understand why this is so distressing, Rachel, I really do.
>
> Stop Anomie

> You don't. You can't.
>
> Penny Peacock

It's bad enough thinking that
Edie and Vikas were killed by the
Halvening, but if it was Anomie,
I've been friends with a murderer.
I was helping moderate a
murderer's game.
Penny Peacock

Even if Anomie's guilty, you
couldn't possibly have known
they were capable of murder.
If everybody who made a joke
about wanting to kill someone
actually did it, none of us
would be safe to walk down
the street.

My number one priority
now is to try and get hold
of Paperwhite. There's a
possibility she knows who
Anomie is. She might also
be able to shed light on
whether Vikas was planning
to go to the police with
suspicions about Anomie or
the Halvening.
Stop Anomie

I don't know who Paperwhite is, I
never did.
Penny Peacock

We know there was a picture
of her circulating on the
moderator channel. Anomie
shared it with Vilepechora
and Vilepechora showed it to
Hartella, so I was wondering
whether anyone ever showed
it to you. I know they all
thought you were a man.
Stop Anomie

A pause followed. Robin's heart was beating almost as fast as it had when she'd thought the letterbox had rattled.

Vilepechora did
Penny Peacock

He and LordDrek always thought I
was a gay man
Penny Peacock

He said 'if you don't get a hard
on at this we'll know for sure
you're queer'
Penny Peacock

Robin knew she had to phrase her next message sensitively, because she hadn't forgotten that Rachel's bullies had called her a lesbian.

Rachel, can you check and see
whether you deleted it, please?
Because if you forgot to, that
photo could help us find her.
Stop Anomie

Robin waited, hardly breathing. The pause went on and on, and it gave her hope, because if Rachel had deleted the image she'd surely have said so at once. Then the three dots appeared, and Rachel answered.

I'll check. I didn't mean to keep it,
but I'll see whether I did.
Penny Peacock

She's got it, thought Robin. She neither knew nor cared whether Rachel had kept the picture out of spite, or to try to find out the identity of the girl who'd stolen away her best friend online: all that mattered was that she'd kept it.

Three minutes passed, which felt to Robin like thirty. Then Rachel returned.

I've got it.
Penny Peacock

Sending it now.
Penny Peacock

The picture appeared before Robin had time to type her thanks. The girl in the picture wasn't merely pretty: she was beautiful.

Twenty at most, she was slim, with long red hair, cream-coloured, lightly freckled skin, high cheekbones and large hazel eyes. Wearing nothing but an unbuttoned light pink shirt, she'd posed pressing her breasts together with her arms, the shirt barely covering her nipples. A stretch of flat stomach was revealed and the picture cut off just below her belly button.

> Rachel, thank you SO MUCH. This could help us enormously.
> Stop Anomie

> Please will you let me know what happens? I can't stand not knowing what's going on. Anything would be better than this.
> Penny Peacock

> Of course. I'll keep in touch. And please go easy on yourself. You've been a massive help and none of this is your fault. None of it x
> Stop Anomie

> X
> Penny Peacock

Robin now saved the picture of Paperwhite to her laptop, opened up Google to perform a reverse image search and pasted the picture into it.

The 'similar images' found were, as Robin supposed she should have expected, of the cheesecake or soft porn variety. She found herself looking at a multitude of women baring their breasts in open shirts, none of them resembling Paperwhite. However, this told her something useful, which was that Paperwhite had never posted the picture online, which suggested it genuinely was a picture sent privately to a boyfriend, or somebody she considered a boyfriend.

Robin looked closely at the background of the picture. It showed a dimly lit bedroom, possibly a student's room, as there was a desk in the background. When she enlarged the picture, she saw a shallow box on the desk, which was labelled Faber-Castell Soft Pastels, which Robin recognised as art supplies rather than sweets.

She now cropped the picture to just the girl's face and pasted that into the app instead.

A range of far more promising images appeared: headshots of young redheads, some of which looked professionally produced, others candid. Robin moved slowly through the pictures, scrutinising each face carefully, until at around picture sixteen she stopped.

It showed the same girl: same eyes, same cheekbones, same long mane of red hair. Now very excited, she clicked on the picture. It had come from Instagram. Robin navigated to the page and let out a loud '*Yes!*'

The girl's name was Nicole Crystal. As Robin scrolled down through the pictures on her account, she saw that she was a student at the Glasgow School of Art. The page was littered with examples of her work, which even to Robin's untrained eye seemed to demonstrate huge talent. However, there were occasional selfies, and one of them caused Robin to pause, slightly disconcerted. A handsome blond young man in a cut-off black T-shirt was embracing Nicole from behind, his lips pressed to her cheek. As Robin moved further down she saw a couple more pictures of the same man, one of which had a heart drawn around it.

Did this man know his girlfriend had been spending hours in the game talking to Vikas Bhardwaj? That she'd been sending him provocative pictures?

Robin clicked on Nicole's followers, scanned them for Vikas's name, but couldn't find it.

She then opened Twitter and searched for Nicole Crystal. Several accounts appeared, but she located the right one without difficulty: Nicole had used her own picture and full name, with her location listed as Glasgow, but she seemed to use Twitter far less frequently than Instagram. Her last post, which had been a retweet of an account called Women's Art, had been made over ten days previously, before Vikas's body had been found.

Again, Robin clicked on the followers and after several minutes' searching found what she was looking for. Vikas Bhardwaj's real account was following Nicole's.

So immersed was Robin in her discoveries that the sound of her mobile ringing made her jump. It was the office number, which diverted to Strike or Robin's mobiles if it went unanswered. Assuming that Strike had got back to Denmark Street rather more quickly than she'd expected, she snatched up the phone and answered it.

A whisper spoke into her ear, each word carefully enunciated.

'*I . . . am . . . going . . . to . . . kill . . . you.*'

The line went dead.

93

Strike's leg was now hurting him so badly he stopped to rest for fifty minutes on a bench at Victoria Station. Telling himself his leg felt a lot better, and that joining the queue for a taxi would be just as onerous as continuing the journey by Tube, he limped back into the Underground, then let two trains pass, because he needed to give his stump a rest before asking it to bear his weight again. By the time he emerged from Tottenham Court Station, night was falling and he was barely restraining himself from saying 'fuck' aloud on alternate steps. He now felt as though splinters of glass were digging into his stump and he could no longer distinguish whether they were due to his cramping muscles or his white-hot hamstring. Bitterly regretting the decision not to bring a walking stick with him, and sweating with the effort of keeping himself moving forwards, he found himself mentally offering bargains to a God he wasn't at all sure he believed in. *I'll lose weight. I'll stop smoking. Just let me get home. I swear I'll take better care of myself. Just don't let me collapse in the fucking street.*

He was afraid his stump was about to give way again and that he'd have to endure the humiliation of collapsing into a heap in public. It had happened once before, and he knew perfectly well what the sequel would be, because he wasn't a frail old lady to whom instinctive aid was offered by strangers: surly-looking, bulky, forty-year-old men of six foot three didn't automatically engender trust in the breasts of the public; they were assumed to be drunk or dangerous, and even passing taxi drivers tended to turn a blind eye to large men gesturing frantically from the gutter.

To his relief, he made it out of Tottenham Court Road station, still upright. Now he leaned back against the wall, taking deep breaths of night air, and keeping all his weight on his healthy left foot while his heart rate slowed, and a procession of lucky bastards with two fully functioning legs walked glibly past him. He was tempted to hobble to The Tottenham, but that would merely provide a temporary respite: what he needed was to get back to Denmark Street, and if he managed to crawl up the three flights of stairs, there'd be ice-packs in the fridge and painkillers in the cupboard, and he'd be able to take off the prosthesis, sit comfortably in his pants and swear as loudly as he liked.

Purely to justify standing still a few minutes longer, and determined not to smoke, he pulled his mobile out of his pocket, glanced at it and saw, to his slight surprise, a text from Robin.

Got good news. Call me when you can.

He couldn't have explained why, but it seemed to him that he might be able to walk more comfortably if he were talking to Robin at the same time, so he pressed her number, then pushed himself off the friendly supporting wall and began to limp off down Charing Cross Road, phone pressed to his ear.

'Hi,' she said, answering on the second ring.

'What's the good news?' he asked, trying not to grit his teeth.

'I've identified Paperwhite.'

'*What?*' said Strike, and for a few steps the pain in his leg did indeed seem to lessen. 'How?'

Robin explained, and Strike forced himself to concentrate, and when she'd finished speaking he said, with as much enthusiasm as he could muster while in this degree of pain:

'Pure fucking brilliance, Ellacott.'

'Thanks,' she said, and he didn't notice how flat she sounded, because he was concentrating on not breathing too heavily.

'We could send Barclay up to talk to her,' said Strike. 'His neck of the woods, Glasgow.'

'Yes, I thought that too,' said Robin, who, like her partner, was trying hard to sound natural. 'Er – something else just happened.'

'Sorry?' said Strike, because a double-decker bus was thundering past.

'Something else just happened,' repeated Robin loudly. 'I just got a call, diverted from the office. It was somebody who said they're going to kill me.'

'*What?*'

Strike stumbled to the side of the pavement, away from the traffic and the passers-by, and stood still, a finger in his free ear, listening.

'They were whispering. I *think* it was a man, but I can't be a hundred per cent. They said "I am going to kill you", and hung up.'

'Right,' said Strike, and colleagues in the military would have recognised the peremptory tone that brooked no argument. 'Pack up now. You need to get back to the Z Hotel.'

'No,' said Robin, who was now pacing her small sitting room, which satisfied her need to work off her adrenalin. 'I'm better off here. The alarm's on, the door's double—'

'The Halvening know where you fucking live!' said Strike furiously. Why the *fuck* couldn't she just do as she was told?

'And if they're outside right now,' said Robin, who'd been resisting the urge to peer through the curtains, 'the stupidest thing I could do is walk out on my own.'

'Not if there's a taxi waiting for you,' Strike contradicted her. 'Tell them you want a male driver. Ask him to come upstairs to help you with bags, say you'll pay a cash tip for his help and take your rape alarm with you in case anyone rushes you.'

'Whoever it was, they were just trying to scare—'

'They're fucking terrorists – everything they do is supposed to scare the shit out of people!'

'You know what?' Robin said, her voice rising in pitch, 'I don't need you shouting at me right now, OK?'

He now heard her panic, and with an effort similar to that which had got him up the last broken escalator, repressed the deeply ingrained instinct to shout orders in the face of danger.

'Sorry. OK, well – if you don't want to come back into town, I'll come to you.'

Climbing three flights of stairs to pack a bag, then making it all the way back down and journeying out to Walthamstow was the last thing he wanted to do, but the sound of the outer office exploding was still fresh in his memory.

'You're just trying to guilt me into—'

'I'm not trying to guilt you into anything,' said Strike harshly, now setting off again, limping more heavily than ever. 'I'm taking seriously the possibility that one of those fuckers is still at large and hoping to take down one more uppity woman before the whole organisation goes up in smoke.'

'Strike—'

'Don't bloody – *shit*,' he snarled, because his trembling leg had buckled. He staggered, succeeded in remaining upright, and limped on.

'What happened?'

'Nothing.'

'It's your leg,' said Robin, who could hear his ragged breathing.

'It's fine,' said Strike, cold sweat breaking out over his face, chest and back. He was trying to ignore the waves of nausea now threatening to engulf him.

'Strike—'

'I'll see you in about—'

'You won't,' she said, sounding defeated. 'I'll – OK, I'll go back to the hotel. I'll ring for a cab now.'

'Will you?'

It came out more aggressively than he'd intended, but his stump was now shaking so badly every time he put weight on it he knew he'd be lucky to reach the door of the office on both feet.

'Yes. I'll call a cab, I'll ask for help with my bags – everything.'

'All right then,' said Strike, turning into Denmark Street, which was deserted except for a woman silhouetted at the far end. 'Call me once you're in the taxi.'

'I will. Speak in a bit.'

She rang off. Now giving into the impulse to swear under his breath every time he put down his right foot, Strike continued on his ungainly way towards the door to his flat.

Only when he was within ten yards of her did he recognise Madeline.

94

And that was when I thrust you down,
And stabbed you twice and twice again,
Because you dared take off your crown,
And be a man like other men.

Mary Elizabeth Coleridge
Mortal Combat

'Are you *drunk?*' she called as he put out a hand and used the wall of the nearest shop to stabilise himself.

'No,' he said.

As she walked unsteadily towards him, he knew at once that the same couldn't be said of her. She looked thinner than the last time he'd seen her, and her high silver heels and short metallic dress suggested that she'd come straight from a party or, perhaps, the launch of some book, album or beauty product: somewhere, at least, at which people were seen, and photographed, and reassured that they were important.

'I wanna talk to you,' she said, her voice slurred. 'I wanna fuckin' *talk* to you.'

Strike was in so much pain, and consumed by so much anxiety and anger after the call with Robin, that he felt nothing but a desire for this scene to be over as quickly as possible.

'Let's hear it, then,' he panted.

'You *fucking bastard.*'

She swayed slightly. The small bag dangling from a chain in her hand was hanging open.

'Right,' said Strike. 'Is that it?'

'Fuck you. *Fuck you.* I was gong – goinga – write you a letter, but then I thought, no, he's gonna hear it face t'face. *Direckly.* You *lying fucking bastard.*'

In spite of every resolution he'd made on the journey, Strike pulled his cigarettes out of his pocket. If God wanted to mess with him this badly, all deals were off.

'*Sucha* good guy, aren' you?' she sneered at him. '*Such* a fuckin' *hero.*'

He lit up, took a long drag on his cigarette, then exhaled.

'Don't remember claiming to be either.'

'Yeah, you did. *Yeah, you fucking did.* An' you were *using* me ... using me all alone ... all 'long. Well, you've got what you fucking wanted now, *'aven't you?*' she bellowed, her East End accent suddenly very pronounced.

'All I want,' said Strike, smoking as he looked down at her, 'is to go to bed and be left—'

'You – fucking – *bastard*!'

She punched him as hard as she could in the chest. He stepped backwards; she nearly overbalanced, and as she staggered on her heels a lipstick slid out of the open bag and rolled away.

Strike attempted to walk past her, but she grabbed his sleeve and, hanging on with both hands, said,

'You were using me, an' *I know why* – '

With a sense of déjà vu, Strike tried to prise her off his arm; his lit cigarette fell to the ground.

' – you fucking *user,* you fucking *parasite* – '

'How about you go and dry out,' he said, struggling to release himself without breaking her fingers, 'and send me that letter.'

Left hand still clutching his sleeve, she pummelled his back with her right until he twisted around and seized that too. Once again, he saw the rictus grin she'd displayed on the night of her launch in Bond Street.

'"*Don't talk about my daddy!*" – but you're just fucking like him – on'y not as fucking successful – and you pretend you don't want the fucking public – publicity – but you o'ny fuck famous – an' you think you've got her now, haven't you?'

'Stop embarrassing yourself,' Strike said, still trying to disengage without hurting her.

'*Me*, embarrass? Ev'ryone knows she's messing around with Landon Dormer! An' you ride to her fucking rescue, and you think she wants *you*?'

'She does, yeah,' said Strike, the instinct for cruelty that lies within every angry lover coming to his aid. 'She's fucking gagging for me. But I don't want either of you, so how about you try and find some fucking dignity and—'

'You bastard. You fucking bastard. You come into my life – Henry's life—'

'Henry doesn't give a shit about me, and I don't give a shit—'

'—and it was all for *her,* wasn't it? To make her jealous—'

'You keep believing Charlotte – have another drink—'

'—an' I've got an interview w'the *Mail* next week – an' I'll tell them—'

'Pure class, threatening me with the fucking—'

She twisted in his grasp and kicked out as hard as she could. Strike felt her stiletto heel stab his thigh and as he stepped backwards his real foot skidded on the lipstick she'd dropped and with a yell of pain he went down backwards, lower back smacking into concrete and the back of his head banging down seconds later.

For a few seconds, he thought he might vomit. He rolled over and pushed himself up onto all fours, hardly caring whether she was about to keep kicking. He was trapped in a vortex of pain, his stump spasming and jerking, his hamstring screaming for mercy.

Somewhere above him she was talking, pleading. He couldn't make out words: he wanted her to disappear, to leave for ever. Out of the corner of his eye he saw her kneel down beside him, now sobbing.

'Corm—'

'Fuck off,' he said hoarsely, while his prosthesis scraped the ground, stuck to the spasming stump. 'Just go. Just fucking go.'

'I didn't mean to—'

'*Go.*'

She struggled to her feet.

'Corm, please – let me—'

'GO!'

She was still crying, but after a period that might have been seconds or minutes he heard her uneven footsteps heading back towards Charing Cross Road. When they'd died away, he tried to struggle to his feet, but his stump absolutely refused to bear his weight.

As he crawled to the door of his office, he came across the cigarette he'd dropped, still burning, picked it up again and jammed it into his mouth. His stump dragging behind him, he reached the doorstep, manoeuvred himself gingerly into a sitting position on it, took a drag of his cigarette and leaned back against the black door.

The night air felt cold on his wet face, the stars over London as dim as they always were over the metropolis, and he experienced one of those moments of simultaneous confusion and clarity that belong to the drunk and the desperate, in which Yasmin Weatherhead's flat face blended with the twisted grin of Madeline, and he thought about the dossier of convincing lies that had led to murder and paralysis, and the unwritten letter of accusations he could have burned without reading.

And then, on the step of his office, while half of him was wondering whether he'd have to sleep where he was sitting, something floated up through his subconscious into his conscious mind. Every woman who'd hoped to make a life with him had complained about this: the way something hard and impenetrable in his brain lived forever in a problem-solving realm, no matter what was going on around him: in fact, only one woman had never moaned about it—

His mobile rang in his pocket and he pulled it out.

'I'm in the cab,' said Robin.

'Good,' said Strike, still smoking.

'I don't think there was anyone outside. I think I'm a bit paranoid.'

'We got bombed. You're not paranoid.'

'How's your leg, Cormoran?'

'Fucked,' said Strike. There was no point lying any more; he doubted he'd be fully ambulatory any time soon. 'But on the bright side, I've just realised we might have a lead.'

95

But this place is grey,
And much too quiet. No one here,
Why, this is awful, this is fear!
Nothing to see, no face.
Nothing to hear except your heart beating in space
As if the world was ended.

Charlotte Mew
Madeleine in Church

An in-game chat between a creator and a moderator of *Drek's Game*

```
<Moderator Channel>

<11 June 2015 00.15>

<Present: Worm28>

>


>


<Anomie has joined the channel>

Worm28: omg , at last !

Worm28: I 've been wondring where
everyone is

Worm28: Hartella 's supposed to
be modding with me tonite

Anomie: She's left. She's not
coming back
```

Anomie: she just told me

Worm28: what ? !

Worm28: why would she leave ???

Anomie: because she's a fucking traitor

Anomie: I'm about to send you 2 pictures and I want you to look at them carefully

<Anomie wants to send you a file>

<Click alt+y to accept the file>

>

>

>

Worm28: who are these people ?

Anomie: fuck's sake, are you that stupid? Read the fucking captions

Anomie: have you met either of them?

>

>

>

Worm28: no

Anomie: are you sure?

Worm28: yes

Anomie: they could've been undercover. Wearing wigs or something

Worm28: no I 've never met them

Anomie: are you lying?

Worm28: no

915

Worm28: why are yhou asking if I 've met them ?

Anomie: they've been hired to find out who I am

Anomie: because Maverick wants to shut down the game

>

Anomie: why aren't you saying anything?

Worm28: I 'm just shocked

Anomie: are you hiding something?

Worm28: no of course not

Anomie: you'd better not be

Anomie: bad things happen to people who hide things from me

Worm28: I know you 're joking but don 't say things like that

Anomie: are you telling me what to do?

Worm28: I just don 't like those knid of jokes

Anomie: you'll know I'm not joking when you see what happens to those two fucking detectives

Anomie: I've already warned that bitch what's coming

Anomie: tell me the truth: did Fiendy1 meet with them? Is that why she left?

Worm28: what do you mean she ?

Anomie: Fiendy1 was a girl, you dumbass

Anomie: those detectives have worked out who some of the mods are

Anomie: he was at Hartella's parents' house this evening

Anomie: so tell me, has Fiendy1 met them?

Worm28: no

Worm28: I mean I don 't know

Worm28: Fiendy1 just disappeared

Worm28: she never told me why

Worm28: everyone's disappearing

Worm28: we 're down to four mods

Anomie: three. Can't you count?

Worm28: you , me , BorkledDrek , Paperwhite

Anomie: Paperwhite's going to be disappearing soon, but not til it's convenient

>

Worm28: you 're scaring me

Anomie: good

Anomie: if those detectives come anywhere near you, you let me know immediately

Worm28: ok

Anomie: but I might have Ledwell and Blayed them before they get to you

Worm28: Anomie don 't

Worm28: don 't make jokes like that I hate it

Anomie: you think I wouldn't?

Anomie: because dream on if you think that

Anomie: you'll be ok though

Anomie: as long as you stay loyal

<Anomie has left the channel>

>

>

>

>

>

>

>

>

>

>

<Worm28 has left the channel>

<Moderator Channel has closed>

96

If every good idea could be realised cleanly and without delay, investigative work wouldn't be the long, hard slog Cormoran Strike knew it to be. He therefore managed to be stoic about the fact that when he called Grant Ledwell's number the following morning at nine, he heard an international ringtone that went straight to voicemail. After leaving a message saying that he'd be grateful if Grant could call him back, he hung up, then rang Ryan Murphy.

The CID man took as seriously as Strike could have wished the news that Robin had received a death threat by telephone the previous evening, approved Robin's decision to relocate rather than remaining in her flat, said he'd put a man back in Blackhorse Road to watch her flat, and promised to pass on news of any further Halvening arrests.

'As a matter of fact, I'm about to interview one of your gamers. They say they've got information for us.'

'She called you, did she?' said Strike. 'Good.'

'How did you know it's a woman?'

'Because when I interviewed her last night, I advised her to tell you everything.'

'I'm starting to think we should have you on retainer,' said Murphy.

Strike's third call was to Midge, because he needed to tell her that, as of twelve hours ago, most of the Anomie suspects they'd previously ruled out were now back in.

'Fook,' said Midge. 'So that's – what? – half a dozen people we've got to watch? And the only way we can rule them out is by Anomie being on Twitter when they aren't?'

'It isn't half a dozen,' Strike said, well aware that this was cold comfort. 'We've been warned away from Pez Pierce by the CID, so take your pick: Kea Niven in King's Lynn or Tim Ashcroft in Colchester.'

'What about Wally Cardew?'

'He's definitely out,' said Strike. 'He's been trying to help The Halvening identify Anomie. It can't be him.'

'What if he's bullshitting?'

'I don't think he is,' said Strike, who'd imagined that his imminent phone call to Robin was going to be the most stressful of the day, and wasn't enjoying this amount of pushback. He'd slept badly, partly due to the pain in his stump but also because of the tender lump on the back of his head, caused by falling over backwards into the road following Madeline's kick.

'What about the Upcott kid?' said Midge.

'I can't remember when we ruled him out,' said Strike, who hadn't yet gone back through the case file.

'It was after Comic Con, because when Barclay called to tell me not to bother taking over surveillance on him I was reading about Robin jumping on the train tracks.'

'Shit,' said Strike. 'OK, well, if you want, you can go to Hampstead. I don't care, I just want to know we're keeping tabs on one suspect today.'

'What about Phillip Ormond? We never ruled him out as Anomie. Never watched him, even.'

'He doesn't fit our profile.'

'He fits it better than the Upcott boy. He's a computing teacher.'

'Anomie was active before Ormond ever met Edie. Where would Ormond have got all the personal stuff on her?'

'I had a case up in Manchester where a husband made three fake profiles on Facebook and started really fooking with his wife, harassing her, trying to see if she were playing around . . .'

Strike chose to let Midge get the story out of her system, but he was barely listening. When at last she'd finished, he said,

'Look, we've got a manpower problem. All I care about is that we keep watching one suspect, so take your pick: Tim Ashcroft, Kea Niven or Gus Upcott.'

Midge chose Gus, a decision Strike was certain she'd taken because she preferred not to have to drive out to King's Lynn or Colchester, and rang off.

Strike drained his mug of heavily sugared mahogany-coloured tea, then phoned Barclay and asked him to fly up to Scotland to locate and interview Nicole Crystal.

'I'll get a picture to you this morning. She attends Glasgow School of Art, but term's ended, so I'd imagine she'll be back at her parents' house in Bearsden, which—'

'Aye, I know where it is,' said Barclay. 'Posh end o' Glasgow. I'm asking her if she knows who Anomie is, presumably?'

'Yeah, but tread carefully. Her online boyfriend's been murdered, she almost certainly knows it and she's probably bloody scared. Tell her we know she's Paperwhite in *Drek's Game*, give her plenty of reassurance she's done nothing wrong, and then find out as much as you can.'

To his relief, Barclay took the assignment without complaint and rang off.

Now, bracing himself, Strike called Robin.

'Hi,' she said, answering immediately and sounding cold. 'I've read your email.'

He'd sent the email in question at one o'clock that morning, after dragging himself upstairs and letting himself into his attic flat. Once there, he'd removed his shoes, trousers and prosthesis to examine his stump, which began spasming again as soon as he lifted it. There was an angry red puncture mark where Madeline's stiletto had hit him, his hamstring was in searing pain, his knee was puffy and the skin at the end of his stump inflamed, all of which had forced him to a couple of unwelcome conclusions.

Firstly, and even though he feared advice and treatment that would put him out of action, the time had come to seek medical assistance. Secondly, as he'd be unable to accompany Robin anywhere for at least the next couple of days, and as all the other subcontractors were busy – Dev still tailing Fingers' mother from restaurant to bar in the hope of striking up a conversation about Fabergé or Greek antiquities – Strike wanted Robin out of harm's way.

'All agreed, then?' said Strike, the muscles in his stump now twitching again, even though he had it elevated. 'You keep looking into Lepine's Disciple—'

'Which you think is pointless,' said Robin.

'No, I agreed we should look at him, in the interests of thoroughness.'

'I know what you're doing, Strike,' said Robin. 'I'm not stupid. We're supposed to be covering multiple suspects, but you want me shut away in a hotel room watching Twitter.'

'You had a death threat,' said Strike, who was rapidly reaching the limit of his patience. 'They know your address and what you look like, and your name was on that fucking bomb, same as mine.'

'Then why aren't *you* hiding away in some bloody—?'

'*Because I've got to go to hospital,*' he snarled.

'What?' said Robin sharply. 'Why? What's happened?'

'My fucking leg got blown off,' said Strike.

'Oh shit, is it really bad? Well, then, let me—'

'*No*, you're not fucking coming with me,' he said, so tense he was barely refraining from shouting. 'Can you *please* just stay put, so I've got one less thing to fucking worry about?'

'Fine,' snapped Robin, but after a short pause she added, 'But could you call me when you can, and let me know how you are?'

Strike agreed to do so, hung up and then, using chair backs, the door handle and his chest of drawers for balance, hopped into his bedroom to get dressed.

Having no illusions about the likelihood of getting an appointment with his specialist at such short notice, Strike had decided to present himself at UCH Accident and Emergency and wait his turn. He planned to say that he'd fallen the previous night and was now in a lot of pain, which was perfectly true, although, of course, it omitted mention of the fact that he'd been in agony even before he fell, and also of the months of neglect of his stump that had brought him to this point. He didn't doubt that a doctor would see right through the story, but he hardly cared: all he wanted was a large bottle of heavy-duty prescription painkillers, which would enable him to continue working.

Fifty minutes later, as he was travelling by taxi, his crutches propped beside him and his right trouser leg pinned up, his mobile rang.

'Strike.'

'Hi,' said a gruff male voice over a slightly crackling line, 'Grant Ledwell here.'

'Ah, Grant,' said Strike, 'thanks for getting back to me. Wondered whether we could have a face-to-face? Just to get you caught up on recent developments?' he added, untruthfully.

'Yeah, that'd be great,' said Grant, sounding enthusiastic. 'I'm in Oman currently, but I'm back Monday. It'd have to be evening again. Would nine be too late? Could you come to us?'

Strike, who was keen to interview the Ledwells in their own home, said both time and place suited him perfectly.

'Great, because Heather won't want me going out, so soon after I get back from Oman, but she'll want news of Anomie. Hasn't liked me going away and leaving her alone in the house.'

Grant gave him the address in Battledean Road, Strike thanked him and hung up.

The Accident and Emergency department at St Mary's was, as he'd expected, extremely busy. Children sat wailing in their mothers' laps; old people awaited their turn in miserable silence; representatives of every ethnicity in London were reading magazines or looking at their phones; a young woman was doubled over with her arms folded over her stomach; and a dishevelled-looking young white man, whose hair was matted into dreadlocks, sat emitting random yelps and oaths at the far end of the waiting room. Unsurprisingly, the only vacant seats lay in his vicinity.

Strike swung himself on his crutches to reception, gave his details to an exhausted-looking woman, then headed for a seat close by the yelping man, who Strike assumed was either seriously mentally ill, under the influence of drugs, or both.

'*Yeah, you fucking do that!*' the man shouted, staring into space, as Strike lowered himself into a chair two along and breathed in his pungent smell of stale urine and BO. After propping his crutches against the seat beside him, he pulled out his phone, purely to have something to look at and avoid his neighbour's gaze, and opened Twitter.

Anomie had tweeted a quotation just a few minutes previously.

Anomie @AnomieGamemaster

I have learned to hate all traitors, and there is no disease that I spit on more than treachery – Aeschylus

1.18 pm   11 June 2015

The responses to this tweet were coming in rapidly, proliferating as Strike repeatedly refreshed the page.

Andi Reddy @ydderidna
replying to @AnomieGamemaster
Grunt Ledwell's sold out to Maverick, right?
#InkBlackHeartCashIn #HartyIsAHeartNotAHuman

Lucy Ashley @juiceeluce
replying to @AnomieGamemaster
omg, has Josh agreed to change Harty?
#HartyIsAHeartNotAHuman

Moonyspoons @m<>nyspoons
replying to @AnomieGamemaster
seriously, if Josh has agreed to this . . .
#HartyIsAHeartNotAHuman

Well aware he might be displaying bias quite as much as the angry fans jumping to conclusions, Strike wondered whether Anomie's talk of treachery was in any way connected to Yasmin, who, if she'd taken Strike's advice, would now have left the game for good. But if it was Yasmin's defection that had caused Anomie's tirade about treachery, she must have gone back into the game to tell Anomie she was leaving: an idiotic thing to do, but then Strike considered Yasmin an extremely foolish woman. He wasn't even sure he'd put it past her to mention his own visit to her house.

'*Get the fuck out of it!*' shouted Strike's neighbour, who appeared to be having an argument with an imaginary antagonist.

And if Yasmin *had* gone back into the game to announce her departure, Strike thought, and *had* told Anomie about the detective that had scared her out of the game, then the call to the office phone, which had diverted to Robin's mobile, might not have had anything to do with The Halvening at all. That call might just have been made by the person Strike believed had stabbed Edie Ledwell through the heart and slit Vikas Bhardwaj's throat, who'd left Josh Blay partially paralysed and Oliver Peach with a significant brain injury.

Even as these thoughts chased each other rapidly through Strike's mind, Anomie tweeted again.

Anomie @AnomieGamemaster
One must, it is true, forgive one's enemies-- but not before they have been hanged. .
Heinrich Heine

And now a different part of Anomie's fanbase swam into view, circling the young female fans who'd responded last time like sharks.

SJW Destroyer @Br0ken729
replying to @AnomieGamemaster
🤙 🤙 🤙

Julius @i_am_evola
replying to @AnomieGamemaster
hang bitches over the bed like mobiles 😂
watch 'em rot while you're dropping off to sleep

Arlene @queenarleene
replying to @i_am_evola @AnomieGamemaster
people like you and Wally Cardew give this fandom a bad
name, Anomie's not being literal

Lepine's Disciple @LepinesD1sciple
replying to @queenarleene @i_am_evola
@AnomieGamemaster
ugly cunt who'd make a great mobile says what now?

'Mr Thomson,' called a distant voice. Strike looked up: two male orderlies had arrived to escort his dishevelled neighbour away for examination and, no doubt, to ensure that he got there without causing trouble. The young man got up without complaint, and though he was unsteady on his feet, he did nothing more than shout 'Yer all fucking lunatics!' A ripple of weak laughter spread through the waiting room, now that the young man was in the care of the men in blue overalls. Relieved to be free of the man's smell, Strike turned his attention to Twitter again and saw that Anomie had now tweeted for a third and a fourth time.

Anomie @AnomieGamemaster
The type of hero dear to crowds will always have the
semblance of a Caesar.

Anomie @AnomieGamemaster
replying to @AnomieGamemaster
His insignia attracts them, his authority overawes them and his
sword instills them with fear.

Intrigued by this sudden burst of quotation and declamation from Anomie, Strike wasn't surprised that these last tweets had caused some confusion among Anomie's followers.

MrsHarty @carlywhistler_*
replying to @AnomieGamemaster
are you still talking about Harty? What does this mean?

Baz Tyler @BzTyl95
replying to @AnomieGamemaster
You feeling all right, mate?

SJW Destroyer @Br0ken729
replying to @AnomieGamemaster
have you been hacked?

Lepine's Disciple @Lep1nesDisciple
replying to @Br0ken729 @AnomieGamemaster
No he hasn't been hacked, it's obvious what he means, dickhead

---

Lepine's Disciple @Lep1nesDisciple
replying to @Br0ken729 @AnomieGamemaster
why are you all so fucking stupid?

The mobile in Strike's pocket rang. Seeing Pat's home number, he answered.

'Hi, what's up?'

She'd called to talk about the delivery of new office furniture and a couple of rota issues. Strike did his best to answer all her queries, while keeping an ear out for a doctor calling his name.

'... and I promised Midge a long weekend,' he concluded, 'so you'd better mark that down too.'

'Right ho,' said Pat in her deep, gravelly voice. 'And I've had a couple of dropped calls this morning, from the same number. Diverted from the office.'

'Really?' said Strike, fumbling in his pocket for a pen. 'Give me the number.'

She did so. Strike jotted down the digits on the back of his hand and saw it was a mobile number he didn't recognise.

'And they hung up when you answered, both times?'

'Breathed a bit, the second time,' said Pat.

'Could you tell whether they were male or female?'

'No. It was just breathing.'

'All right, well, let me know if it happens again,' said Strike. 'And make sure you've got the door locked.'

As he inserted the mobile back into his pocket, a voice called: 'Cameron Strike?'

'That's me,' Strike shouted back at the distant woman with short grey hair, who was wearing scrubs and holding a clipboard.

Ten minutes later he was sitting on a hospital bed, screened from the rest of the ward by an encircling curtain, his trousers and crutches on a chair beside him, while the grey-haired woman carefully examined first his stump and then his healthy leg. Strike had forgotten how thorough medics were. He really did just want painkillers.

'And you fell backwards, did you?' she said, now looking through her glasses at the irritated end of his stump.

'Yeah,' said Strike.

'Can you raise it for me?'

He did so, made a muffled exclamation of pain, then let it fall again. As soon as the stump hit the bed it began to jerk around.

'Has that happened before?' she asked, observing the involuntary movements.

'A bit,' said Strike, who'd started to sweat again.

'How often?'

'It's been happening on and off for the last couple of weeks. I had spasms in it right after it was amputated, but they stopped after a few months.'

'Your amputation was when?'

'Six – no, seven years ago.'

'Fairly unusual for myoclonus to start up again, seven years on,' said the doctor. She moved around the bed.

'What's this mark on your leg?' she said, pointing at the red indentation left by the steel tip of Madeline's stiletto. 'Did that happen during the fall?'

'Must've done,' lied Strike.

His leg was still jerking, but the doctor was now looking into Strike's face.

'Are you aware your face is twitching?'

'What?'

'The right side of your face is twitching.'

'I think I'm just wincing,' said Strike.

He was starting to fear a battery of unwanted tests, or, worse, an overnight stay in hospital.

'All right, I'm going to lift your leg myself. Tell me when it's painful.'

'It's painful,' said Strike, when she'd raised the stump barely three inches off the bed.

'Your muscles are very tight. I'm just going to have a feel of your hamstring. Tell me if—'

She felt gently down the back of his thigh.

'Yeah,' said Strike through gritted teeth, 'that hurts.'

'All right,' she said, lowering the stump carefully back onto the bed, where it continued to jerk around, 'I'd like to do an ultrasound. Your knee's quite swollen, and I want to know what's going on with that hamstring.'

'My hamstring's gone before,' said Strike. 'I've just pulled it. If I can just get some painkillers—'

'I'm concerned about these spasms,' said the doctor, looking intently into his face again. 'I'd like to do some blood tests and have a colleague take a look at you. I'll be back in a bit.'

'Why blood tests?' said Strike.

'Just to exclude any underlying problem. Calcium deficiency, for instance.'

She disappeared through the curtain, pulling it shut behind her, leaving Strike to raise his fingers to his face to see whether he could feel twitching, which he couldn't. As he sat there in his boxers, hating his surroundings, loathing the feeling of vulnerability and enforced dependency hospitals always gave him, he heard his mobile buzz. He swung his legs over the edge of the bed, dragged his coat off the back of the chair and retrieved the phone, only to see a long text from Madeline which began:

Corm, I'm truly sorry, I was drunk,
I'd just run into Charlotte and

He deleted the text without reading it, then blocked her number. As he did this, he felt for the first time a muscle in the right-hand corner of his mouth twitching: a slight movement, but nevertheless perceptible.

He'd barely stretched his legs back out on the bed when a middle-aged female nurse arrived to take blood.

'You'll want to take that off,' she said, nodding at his shirt. 'We won't be able to roll that sleeve up high enough.'

Thinking resentfully that she was entirely wrong in thinking that he wanted to take off his shirt, he nevertheless did as he was told. As the nurse strapped the tourniquet around his upper arm, then inserted her needle and drew a syringe of blood from him, his mobile buzzed yet again.

'You can't answer that yet,' said the nurse unnecessarily, as Strike glanced towards it.

When she'd departed, taking two tubes of Strike's blood with her, he pulled his shirt back on, then picked up the phone and saw a text from Midge, who'd attached a video clip.

Only sighting of Gus Upcott so far. Do we know who the massive weirdo is?

Strike opened the video and saw the unmistakeable form of Nils de Jong ambling up the Upcotts' street, a cardboard box under one enormous arm, and his mobile in his other hand. Wearing his old cargo shorts, a crumpled shirt and sandals, his blond hair falling over the peculiar Greek mask of his face, he appeared engrossed in whatever he was reading on his phone. Shortly before reaching the Upcott residence, Nils paused, put down the cardboard box, typed something, then picked up his box again and headed to the front door. He knocked on the door, which opened, and Strike saw a glimpse of Gus before both retreated into the house. The video ended.

Nils de Jong, Strike texted back. **Owner of North Grove Art Collective. Possibly handing over some of Josh's possessions to Katya**

He'd just sent this message when a black male nurse pulled back the curtain. With some misgivings, Strike saw that the man had brought a wheelchair.

'Ultrasound?' said the nurse, who had a heavy Brazilian accent.

Strike wondered fleetingly what would happen if he said, 'No thanks, just had one.'

'I can walk.'

'No, sorry, the doctor wants you in here,' said the smiling nurse, patting the arm of the wheelchair. 'You can bring your blanket.'

So Strike, still holding his mobile, was wheeled off the ward with a thin blanket covering his naked legs and boxer shorts, just one more specimen of injured humanity, transported against his wishes towards an assessment he'd have preferred not to have.

The probe was icy against his leg and painful when pressed over his hamstring. The face of the male doctor who was watching the monitor beside the bed displayed no emotion until Strike's mobile buzzed again, and then he glanced irritably at the phone before looking back at the screen. After a few minutes the grey-haired female doctor reappeared to speak in a low voice with her colleague. Strike might as well not have been present.

'All very inflamed,' said the man, pressing the probe to the side of Strike's knee cap.

'Torn ligaments?'

'Possibly minor tearing . . .'

He moved the probe painfully around to the back of Strike's thigh again.

'That's a grade two . . . possibly three.'

He pressed the probe even harder into the back of Strike's stump, and Strike attempted to distract himself from the pain by imagining punching the doctor in the back of the head.

'Can't see anything here that'd necessarily explain the myoclonus. The muscles are very tight . . .'

Strike was wheeled back onto the ward by the Brazilian nurse, who helped him back onto the bed, told him a doctor would be back to see him shortly, and left Strike alone in his curtained cubicle again.

Strike now read the text that had just come in, which was from Robin.

What's happening? How's your leg?

Still waiting for them to tell me, Strike replied.

Anomie's behaving very oddly on Twitter

Yeah I've noticed

The curtain around Strike's bed opened again, to reveal a new nurse: short, plump and Hispanic-looking.

'The doctor's going to be a little while. Would you like a cup of tea?'

'I really just need painkillers,' said Strike, who was as keen not to be a burden on the NHS as any overworked doctor could wish, and found this offer of tea ominous, because it implied he wouldn't be leaving any time soon. However, when the nurse simply looked expectant, he said,

'Tea would be great, thanks.'

'Milk and sugar?'

'Everything you've got.'

Maybe chuck in some co-codamol.

Strike sat back against the pillows and looked dispiritedly around at the inside of his curtains. Footsteps clattered and scuffled past his bed. Somewhere in the distance a baby was crying. His mobile buzzed again, and on picking it up he saw another text from Robin.

If you want a display of real hypocrisy, go and have a look at Tim Ashcroft's Twitter feed right now. His own, not the Pen of Justice

So Strike opened Twitter, and went to look at Tim's account.

One hour previously, Tim Ashcroft had tweeted a link to a *Daily Mail* story, above which he'd written:

Tim Ashcroft @TheWormTurning

As a close friend of Edie Ledwell's, and as somebody who works with schoolchildren and takes safeguarding seriously, I'm frankly appalled
www.DailyMail/ParentsDisgustedAs . . .

3.10 pm   11 June 2015

Strike clicked on the link, the headline of which read:

Parents "Disgusted" as Teacher Questioned Over Murder Remains in Post

He scanned the news story, which, as he'd expected, concerned Phillip Ormond, who was currently suspended from his job pending investigation by his school board. The story managed to suggest that Ormond was an unpleasant and unpopular teacher, but stopped just short of saying he'd stabbed his girlfriend and her ex-lover. Most prominence was given to the remarks of the mother whose daughter had been instructed by Ormond to lie for him, when he'd left her detention early to track Edie's phone.

'He threatened Sophie if she told the truth. She was too scared to tell us for days. Then she came to me in tears, because she'd seen his girlfriend had been killed that afternoon, and told me the whole story. I called the police straight away. I don't care if he wasn't charged, that's not the point. The fact remains that he told a fourteen-year-old to lie for him, and as far as I'm concerned, that's a sacking offence.'

Strike returned to Twitter. Tim, he saw, hadn't been content with his first remarks, but had followed up the first tweet with a couple of others.

Tim Ashcroft @TheWormTurning

(Btw, apologies for linking to that fascist rag, but seems like the parents spoke to them directly so that's where the story is)

Tim Ashcroft @TheWormTurning

Point is, asking a 14-year-old girl to lie for you is disgusting behaviour. This man isn't fit to work with children or teenagers.

Andi Reddy @ydderidna
replying to @TheWormTurning
You're one of the good guys, Tim

Strike texted back:

Superb bit of performative nice-guying from Ashcroft there. Paedo 101

The nurse returned with his tea, which was far too milky. As he thanked her, his stump began to jump around again. Sitting up straighter, he pressed down hard on it with his right hand, forcing it to stay still, willing it to behave, not to give him away, not to make these well-intentioned medics advise that he stay here for more tests.

'You all right?' the nurse asked, watching him pin his stump to the bed.

'Fine,' he said. He could feel the flickering muscle in his right cheek now.

The nurse left. Strike's mobile buzzed yet again: another text from Robin.

And we missed a row about Kea Niven last night. Search #FuckKeaNiven

Strike did as he was told.

There had evidently been a small Twitter storm around Kea shortly before midnight. The trigger had been Wally Cardew's arrest, which had clearly been hotly discussed online. Left-wingers who'd always despised him were now gleefully anticipating his imprisonment, while his long-time defenders were equally certain there'd been a mistake and that he couldn't possibly be a member of a terrorist cell. The battle had generated the hashtags #FreeWally and #NoCookiesInJail, and in the midst of the furore someone had dug up the old tweets between Wally and Kea that indicated at best some form of acquaintance, and at worst an affair. It hadn't taken long for Kea's tumblr post from 2010 ('all my friends telling me "rebound sex with his best mate ain't the answer" and I'm like "well that depends on the question"') to be posted to Twitter, at which point the *Ink Black Heart* fandom had turned on Kea with the ferocity of a hungry alligator.

Inkheart Lizzie @inkylizy00

OMG look at this, Kea Niven and actual Nazi Wally Cardew were actually… fucking?

> **Wally C** @walCard3w
> replying to @notaparrottho
> u lookin fine
>
> **Spoonie Kea** @notaparrottho
> replying to @WalCard3w
> u too ♥

10.37 pm   10 June 2015

933

Loren @l°rygill
replying to @inkylizy00
Oh wow. I've always supported her, but if this is true…

Moonyspoons @m<>nyspoons
replying to @paperwhiteghost @inkylizy00 @l°rygill
if you screw fascists you *are* a fascist. End of. #fuckKeaNiven

---

Johnny B @jbaldw1n1>>
replying to @m<>nyspoons @paperwhiteghost @inkylizy00
@l°rygill
So you must've screwed a whale #FreeWally

Drek's Cock @drekscokkk
replying to @dickymacD @marnieb89
😂😂😂😂😂😂

At this moment, the doctor with the short grey hair returned.

Strike listened with divided attention as she told him what he already knew: that both his hamstring and his knee were damaged, and that only time and rest could heal them.

'You should make an appointment with your specialist, but at a bare minimum I'd advise you to keep weight off your leg for four weeks. You might need six.'

'*Four weeks?*' said Strike, his attention no longer drifting. He'd been banking on being told to keep his leg up for a week, which he'd been planning to interpret as three days.

'It varies according to the patient, but you're a tall man,' said the doctor. 'You're asking your stump to bear a lot of weight. I strongly advise you contacting your specialist and making an appointment for a fuller assessment. In the meantime, keep your prosthesis off, keep that leg elevated, rest, apply ice to the swollen areas and take care of the end of your stump, because you don't want that skin to break down any further.

'As for your spasms,' she went on, 'inflammation and muscle tightness might have triggered a renewal of your nerve symptoms, but we'll know more when we get your blood results back.'

'Which'll be when?' said Strike, who now wanted nothing more than to leave the hospital before they could stick any more probes or needles into him.

'Shouldn't be long,' she said. 'I'll come back when we've got them.'

The doctor left again, leaving Strike to wonder whether he was indeed deficient in calcium. He ate plenty of cheese, didn't he? And it wasn't as though he'd broken any bones lately: surely, if he was calcium deficient, he'd have fractured something in one of his recent falls?

But thinking of these brought back memories of the time he'd fallen downstairs several years previously, and of the time his hamstring had packed up while following a suspect, leaving him crumpled on the pavement. He thought of the junk food that made up most of his diet, of the smoker's cough that attacked him every morning, and remembered crawling through the gutter last night, pausing only to pick up the cigarette he'd dropped. He felt like calling the doctor back and saying, 'I know why this has all happened. It's because I take no care of myself. Write that on the chart and let me go home.'

Seeking distraction from self-recrimination, he picked up his mobile again and scrolled on down through the Twitter comments about Kea Niven.

Max R @mreger#5
replying to @drekscokkk @dickymacD @marnieb89
SJW slags pretend they want pacifists but only real men get them wet #FuckKeaNiven

---

Max R @mreger#5
replying to @drekscokkk @dickymacD @marnieb89
she fucked Wally because she knew he was a killer. That's what slags like.

The curtain opened: the doctor was back.

'All right, your bloods look normal, which is good. It's possible,' she added, 'that these spasms are psychogenic.'

'Meaning?'

'They could be caused by psychological factors. Are you under a lot of stress at the moment?'

'No more than usual,' said Strike. 'Any chance of painkillers?'

'What have you been taking?'

'Ibuprofen, but they're having about as much effect as Smarties.'

'All right, I'll give you something stronger, just to get you through the next week, but they're no substitute for rest and ice packs, all right?'

After the doctor had left, and while Strike was pulling his trousers back on, two contradictory thoughts fought for dominance inside his head. His rational side was telling him firmly that the investigation into Anomie was finished, at least as far as their agency was concerned. With the senior partner off his feet for at least a month, and a dearth of available subcontractors, there was simply no way to cover the necessary work.

But that streak of stubborn self-reliance that more than one ex-girlfriend had called arrogance insisted it wasn't over yet. Barclay hadn't reported back on Paperwhite, and there was a chance Strike's forthcoming visit to Grant Ledwell, if handled correctly, might at last lead them to Anomie.

97

Was she a wicked girl? What then?
She didn't care a pin!
She was not worse than all those men
Who looked so shocked in public, when
They made and shared her sin.

Mathilde Blind
The Message

When Strike woke at eight o'clock the following morning, it was to a realisation that the whisky he'd drunk the previous evening definitely didn't mix well with tramadol. Now he felt sick and unbalanced, sensations that hadn't entirely worn off by eleven, when he received a phone call from Barclay.

'News,' said the Scot.

'Already?' said Strike, who'd been hopping unsteadily to the bathroom when Barclay called, and now stood clutching a chair back to balance.

'Yeah, but it's no' whut you're expecting.'

'Nicole's not at her parents'?'

'She's here, aye, I'm with her now. She'd like tae talk tae you. FaceTime, preferably.'

'Great,' said Strike. 'Would she be OK if Robin joins the call?'

He heard Barclay relay the question.

'Aye, she'd be OK wi' that.'

'Give me five,' said Strike. 'I'll let Robin know.'

Strike's phone call found Robin still in her dressing gown in her claustrophobic bedroom at the Z Hotel, even though she'd been hard at work for three hours. What was the point in getting dressed if you never left your room?

937

'She wants to speak to us? Fantastic,' said Robin, jumping up and trying to throw off her dressing gown one-handed.

'I'll send you details, just give me a couple of minutes,' said Strike, who was still desperate for a pee.

Robin hurried to pull on a T-shirt and brush her hair, lest Strike imagine she'd been sleeping all morning, then hurried back to the bed, which was the only place to sit, and opened her laptop. Meanwhile Strike, whose hair looked the same brushed or unbrushed, had exchanged his own shirt for one that looked less crumpled, and sat back down at his small kitchen table.

When the call commenced, both Strike and Robin were surprised to find themselves looking not only at the pre-Raphaelite beauty that was Nicole Crystal, but two more people who could only be her parents. Though neither had red hair, her mother had the same high cheekbones and heart-shaped face, and her strong-jawed father looked precisely as tense and angry as Strike would expect a man to look on finding out that his daughter's erotic photograph had led to an entanglement with private detectives.

'Good morning,' said Strike. 'Thanks very much for talking to us.'

'No problem,' said Nicole cheerfully. Her accent was nowhere near as thick as Barclay's. The room behind the Crystal family had a stylish simplicity that Strike suspected had been achieved through the use of a very expensive interior decorator. 'Um ... I'm not Paperthing. White. Whatever. In that game.'

She spoke without a trace of constraint, unease or embarrassment. If anything, she seemed intrigued by the situation in which she found herself.

'I don't know how my picture got in that game. I seriously don't. I don't even like *The Ink Black Heart*!'

'Right,' said Strike, who couldn't see any tell-tale sign of lying in her merry face. 'You've heard of the cartoon, though?'

'Oh yeah,' said Nicole brightly. 'A friend of mine's big into it. She loves it.'

'Did this friend ever have access to your photograph?'

'No, never,' said Nicole.

'Could she have got hold of the picture without you knowing?'

'She'd have had to go into my photos on my phone. Anyway, she's Christian Union. She's really, you know ... I mean, there's no way she'd be into *that*. Sending nudes.'

Judging by the expression on the face of Nicole's father, he very much wished that the same could be said of his daughter.

'When was the photo taken, can you remember?' asked Robin.

''Bout ... two and a half years ago?' said Nicole.

'And did you send it to anyone?' asked Robin.

'Yeah,' said Nicole. 'My ex-boyfriend. We were dating during our last year in school, but then he went off to study at RADA and I stayed up here to do art.'

'He's an actor?' said Strike.

'Wants to be, yeah. I sent him pictures while we were doing the long-distance thing for a term.'

A muscle twitched in Nicole's father's jaw.

'What's your ex's name?' said Strike, reaching for a pen.

'Marcus,' said Nicole. 'Marcus Barrett.'

'Are you still in touch with him?' asked Robin. 'Have you got a phone number?'

'Yeah – but you're not going to be horrible to him, are you? Because I honestly can't imagine Marcus—'

'Give them his damn number,' said Nicole's father shortly.

'*Dad*,' said Nicole, looking sideways at her father, 'come on. Don't be like that.'

Mr Crystal looked as though he intended to be 'like that' for a very long time.

'Marcus could've been hacked,' said Nicole, looking back at Strike and Robin. 'It happened to a friend of mine: they got pictures off the cloud – mind you, her password was *so* easy to guess. I *honestly* can't see Marcus intentionally putting a picture of me online – we're still friends! He's a really nice guy.'

'Which of you ended the relationship?' asked Strike.

'I did,' said Nicole, 'but he was sweet about it. We're in different cities and we're still young. He's dating someone else now.'

'Does Marcus have flatmates?' asked Robin, who was trying to think who else, plausibly, could have accessed the photograph.

'He shares a flat with his sister. She's four years older than he is and she's *lovely*. Why would Darcy want to show everyone my tits?'

Nicole laughed. Her mother said quietly,

'Nic, this isn't funny.'

'Oh, come on, it is a bit,' said Nicole, who seemed totally unfazed by the fact that everyone on this call had seen her half-naked. When neither of her parents smiled, she said with a shrug, 'Look, I'm an artist. I'm not as uptight about nudity as you are.'

'It's not a question of being uptight,' said her father, staring fixedly at the screen rather than at his daughter. 'The point is that when you give men these kinds of pictures you've effectively given them a means of blackmailing you, or shaming you—'

'But I'm not ashamed,' said Nicole, and Robin believed her. 'I look pretty hot in that picture. It's not like it's an *open-leg*—'

'*Nicole*,' said both her parents, in exactly the same tone.

'So, to be clear,' said Strike. 'To the best of your knowledge, the only person who's ever seen this picture is Marcus Barrett, correct?'

'Yep,' said Nicole. 'Unless he showed it to a friend, I s'pose, but I don't think he would.'

'You said you sent him pictures, plural,' said Strike.

'I did, yeah,' said Nicole.

'Has this picture, or any of the others, ever turned up anywhere you weren't expecting it to?'

'No,' said Nicole.

'Were the other photographs similar to this one?'

'More or less,' said Nicole. 'I think there was one full nude.'

Nicole's mother put her face briefly in her hands.

'*What?*' said Nicole impatiently. 'He was surrounded by a bunch of sexy drama students, I had to give him something to – you know – *think about*.'

She burst into peals of laughter again.

'Sorry,' she said through her giggles. 'I just – this has all been a bit of a shock. I never expected to be talking to private detectives because someone's been catfishing with my pictures.'

'Catfishing?' repeated her father.

'*You know*, Dad,' said Nicole. 'Pretending to be me to get some action.'

'So,' said Strike, 'to be clear: you've never been inside *Drek's Game*?'

'No, never,' said Nicole.

'And you've never interacted with a man online who called himself Morehouse?'

'No, never,' repeated Nicole.

'And you've never spoken to, messaged, or had any contact with a Dr Vikas Bhardwaj?'

Nicole opened her mouth to reply, then hesitated.

'Actually . . . wait,' she said, now frowning. 'I . . . Wait there.'

She got up and walked out of view, her parents looking anxiously after her. Now Strike and Robin spotted Barclay sitting silently in a distant armchair. Someone had made him a mug of tea.

Nicole returned with her mobile in her hand.

'There's a guy following me on Twitter,' she said as she sat back down between her parents. 'He keeps liking my tweets, but I don't know him . . . he's called something like Vikas . . . hang on . . .'

For nearly a minute she searched her Twitter followers.

'Is that him?' she said at last, turning her mobile screen to face the camera.

'Yes,' said Strike, looking at Vikas's picture. 'That's him. Did you ever message him, or have any direct—?'

'No,' said Nicole, 'I just noticed him liking all my tweets and I didn't really understand why he was following me. He's a scientist, isn't he?' she said, turning the mobile back to examine Vikas's account.

'He was,' said Strike. 'He's dead.'

'What?' said Nicole and her father simultaneously. The girl no longer looked amused.

'He was murdered,' said Strike, 'in Cambridge, last—'

'Not the astrophysicist?' said Nicole's father, aghast. 'The one in the wheelchair?'

'Exactly,' said Strike.

A lengthy pause followed, the three Crystals staring into the camera, horrified.

'Oh my God,' said Nicole at last.

'We'd very much like to talk to Marcus,' said Strike. 'Could you give us his number?'

'I . . . don't think I should give you his number without asking him first,' she said, now looking as tense as her parents.

'Nicole . . .' began her father.

'I'm not just dropping all this on him without any warning. He's a friend of mine, Dad!'

'It really would be better if you *didn't* call him first,' said Strike, but Robin could have told him that nothing he said would change Nicole's mind.

'No, I'm sorry,' said the art student, staring into the camera, 'there's *no way* Marcus had anything to do with – with any of this. He just *wouldn't*. I'm not giving you his number without telling him what it's about, he'd *never* do that to me. I *won't*,' she told her father, who'd opened his mouth to speak. She turned back to Strike and Robin.

'I'll tell Marcus to call *you*, OK? Once I've spoken to him.'

They had no choice but to accept this. After thanking the Crystals for their time, Strike bade them a good morning. When they'd vanished from the screen, Strike and Robin were left staring at each other.

'Shit,' said Robin.

'Well ... yeah,' said Strike.

98

Leering at each other,
Brother with queer brother;
Signalling each other,
Brother with sly brother.

Christina Rossetti
Goblin Market

There being little else he could do while trapped in his attic with an ice pack permanently pressed to his stump, Strike allocated to himself the task of looking into Marcus Barrett online. Though still slightly groggy due to the tramadol, he succeeded in identifying Barrett's Instagram account, because the young man had used his full name, and posted many pictures of rehearsals and a smattering of selfies taken outside the RADA building. Barrett was a handsome young man, black-haired and dark-eyed, with the kind of features Strike imagined a romantic novelist might call chiselled.

Strike started from a position of cynicism about Nicole's insistence that her ex-boyfriend would never have deliberately shared her picture with others. Years spent investigating the messy aftermaths of broken relationships, not to mention the toxic fallout of his and Charlotte's many partings and the recent ugly scene with Madeline, had left Strike with few illusions about the depths to which spurned lovers might sink in their desperation to wound those who'd left them.

However, as the detective scrolled slowly down Marcus's Instagram page he found a group photograph dated the previous December and captioned '#ChristmasParty #OldSchoolGang #Fettes', which featured both Marcus and Nicole. Strike had to admit the ex-boyfriend and girlfriend looked on very good terms, arms draped around each other's shoulders, beaming along with the rest of their old schoolmates.

Moreover, as Nicole had told them, Marcus had clearly moved on to a new relationship. There were many photographs featuring Marcus in company with a slender blonde just as good-looking as Nicole, and, judging by the number of clinches and kisses featured, their mutual attraction was genuine. Barrett's sister was tagged in many photographs too: black-haired like her brother, and similarly good-looking. One of the pictures showed brother and sister singing karaoke together at a party, captioned '#Timber #Pitbull&Ke$ha #MurderYourFaveSong'.

While well aware Instagram didn't necessarily represent the truth of anybody's life, there was clear evidence that Marcus Barrett had a very active social life, and unless he was already a world-class actor seemed to be thoroughly enjoying himself in London. There were pictures of gatherings in pubs, in restaurants and at home in his flat, which Strike deduced from local landmarks lay in fashionable Shoreditch. The Barrett family, like the Crystals, seemed to have plenty of money: though both were still in their twenties, the siblings were sharing a flat that looked larger and better furnished than Strike's own.

Only one set of photographs gave him pause for thought. Back in 2013, presumably shortly after his break-up with Nicole, Marcus had visited Highgate Cemetery with some friends and had posted pictures of himself looking moody in a long black coat among the urns, broken columns and weeping angels.

''Course, it could've been a sight-seeing trip,' Strike told Robin by phone on Sunday evening. 'Got to remember the place is a tourist attraction, not just a crime scene.'

'And he still hasn't called?' asked Robin, who was back in her dressing gown, still in the hotel room she now thoroughly despised.

'Nope,' said Strike. 'I smell panicked phone call from Nicole and then equally panicked conversations between Barrett family members.'

'You think he's lawyering up?'

'Bound to be,' said Strike. 'Don't think many parents would want their son's name dragged into a murder case. But I know one thing: it can't be him who's been impersonating Nicole in the game. He's doing a full-time course, and as far as I can see he spends most of his free time partying. I thought Nicole was being naive, but I have to say, I'm now inclining to her point of view. They clearly *are* still friends. I don't see him as the revenge porn type.'

'So who on earth's Paperwhite?'

'I've been thinking about that,' said Strike, now taking a drag on his vape. He hadn't smoked since his visit to A&E, although there was still half a pack of Benson & Hedges in his coat pocket. 'Wondering which came first: Nicole, or her photos.'

'You mean, someone got hold of her photos, then went looking online for who she really is?'

'Exactly, which we know is possible, because you did it. Whoever nicked her photos would have had a ready-made persona to step into, because she's put a ton of personal information online. So everything would check out if Vikas tried to find out who he was talking to in the game: there she is, art student, Glasgow, same pictures—'

'It was still a risk, impersonating her,' said Robin. 'What if Vikas had contacted the real Nicole directly – phoned her, or asked to FaceTime?'

'I've been thinking about that. I don't know whether you noticed, but his computer seemed to be heavily adapted. What if he had speech problems? What if whoever was impersonating Paperwhite knew it, and counted on him preferring to talk to her online, rather than in person?'

'Oh God, it's horrible,' said Robin, closing her eyes.

'Yeah, it is – but it's also genius. Paperwhite would've been safe to press Vikas for offline contact, knowing he wouldn't comply. A really superb bit of manipulation.

'There's something else. A lot of people have passed through the kids' flat, judging by his Instagram. They're big party people, the Barretts. Nicole's photos could've been on multiple devices, if Marcus synced them, and any of those devices could've been stolen or opened without his knowledge. I've just been looking into how you hack someone's iCloud as well. It's possible, even without a password.'

'Anything on Marcus's sister?'

'I can't find any separate social media for her, so I don't know what she does for a living, but one thing I noticed: there aren't only kids in their party pictures – I mean, some of the people they socialise with look like they're in their thirties or forties.'

'You think they're her workmates?'

'I do, yeah, which suggests she's got a busy offline life as well.'

A yawn overtook Strike. Between the tramadol and hours online, he felt more than ready to turn in for the night.

'How're you getting on?' he asked.

'Well, I've dug as deeply as I can on Lepine's Disciple,' said Robin, whose eyes were dry and itchy from hours of staring at a computer screen, 'and I've put it all in a master document for you, but I've been looking into three other accounts as well. You know that Max person, on Twitter, who started the rumour about Edie being a sex worker? He tried to chat me up, using a Kosh line.'

'All the trolls are kind of blurring into one for me,' admitted Strike.

'Well, he tweeted something about Wally being a killer, on Wednesday.'

'Oh yeah,' mumbled Strike, 'think I saw that.'

'I got interested in him, and when I went systematically back through his tweets I realised he's one of four accounts who're always circling Anomie whenever they're on Twitter. It was hard to spot, until I started really focusing on them – but they've been coordinating with each other, and Anomie.'

'What d'you mean, "coordinating"?' asked Strike, rubbing his eyes in an effort to stay alert.

'Well, for example: in 2011, Lepine's Disciple accused Edie of lying about how her mother died. He quoted a line from an interview Edie did, where she said she remembered her mother being "drugged up". Lepine's Disciple tweeted that Edie was trying to pretend her mother had been an addict. About a minute later, Max posted Edie's mother's obituary, which said she died of cancer.'

'He had the obituary lined up and ready to post?'

'Exactly. And then Anomie retweeted both Lepine's Disciple's out-of-context quote and the obituary posted by Max to his fifty thousand followers, and right after *that* someone called Johnny B – who also tried to hit on me using Kosh, by the way – posted a photo of Edie's mother, jeering about how she looked, and then Julius "I am Evola" joined in, saying a friend had overheard Edie claiming her mother was a junkie, which Anomie also retweeted.

'The five of them planned it between them – there's just no other plausible explanation – to make her look like a liar. The whole thing happened over the space of a couple of minutes. They must have done a lot of digging to get hold of the obituary and the photo, although I checked – both are online, but in pretty obscure corners of the internet.

'They've coordinated attacks like that a few times, but there's something else: they're setting each other up to use Kosh lines on girls.'

'What d'you mean?' asked Strike, fighting to concentrate.

'Either Lepine's Disciple or Julius will say something really vile to a girl, then Max R or Johnny B will move in and claim to have reported them. But it's all staged, because they're clearly friends. Lepine's Disciple and Julius have had a few temporary suspensions for harassing girls, but they always come back.'

'They're potentially sacrificing their Twitter accounts so their mates can use Kosh on girls?'

'Yes. They're acting like . . . I don't know . . . a kind of tag team.'

'Any indications as to who any of them really are?'

'No. Locations are all hidden and none of them say much about their real lives. It's just made me wonder about Anomie,' said Robin, sitting back on her pillows and staring at the blank face of the TV on the wall. 'I've been picturing somebody pretty bitter and lonely, but clearly they're capable of inspiring sympathy and admiration, if only from a bunch of fairly horrible people.'

'Vikas Bhardwaj sounds like a decent bloke,' said Strike, 'and he knew exactly who Anomie was, and stuck with them for a long time.'

Both were silent for a while, Robin still staring at the TV on the wall, Strike vaping at his kitchen table and mostly thinking about how tired he was.

'The new office furniture's being delivered tomorrow, isn't it?' said Robin at last.

'Afternoon, yeah,' said Strike. 'And in the evening I'm meeting Grant Ledwell. I was going to ask you if you'd drive me over there.'

'Oh, thank God,' said Robin fervently. 'I'm going crazy, stuck in this room. Why don't I come over to the office in the afternoon, help set everything up, and we'll go from there?'

When Strike hesitated, she said,

'Look, if The Halvening know where I am, they've had ample opportunity to come and bang on the door and pretend to be an electrician or something. I doubt they're going to stab me on a ten-minute walk to the office, on a crowded street, in broad daylight.'

'Yeah, all right,' sighed Strike. 'Come over at two.'

On this note, they hung up. Strike remained where he was for a few more minutes, exhausted, drowsy, but dreading the effort it would require to get himself into bed. His notebook lay open beside his laptop, showing the email address Yasmin had given him for Anomie, but he'd done nothing with it as yet. Unlike Yasmin, Anomie was clever: they'd surely be suspicious of any approaches from strangers right now.

Sitting in a cloud of nicotine vapour, the sky outside his window showing the edge of the moon, Strike found himself staring at his nephew Jack's report on the Battle of Neuve Chapelle, which remained tacked up on the kitchen cupboards.

Though the village of Neuve Chapelle had been successfully captured from the Germans, it had come at the cost of staggering loss of life, not only because of a lack of munitions and poor communication, but because a thousand men had died unnecessarily, trying to make it past that uncut barbed wire surrounding the fortified German trenches.

In the slightly dreamlike state induced by the tramadol, Strike tried to visualise the Anomie case in military terms. The still-impregnable target was ringed about with wire that remained uncut: not merely the fortress-like security that Vikas Bhardwaj had built into the game, but also aided and abetted by four anonymous trolls.

So what was the lesson to be drawn from Neuve Chapelle? *Cut the wire before sending your infantry forwards.*

Strike yawned yet again, too tired to push the analogy any further and, pre-emptively wincing, pushed himself up from his chair.

Meanwhile, in the Z Hotel, Robin had already got into bed, but her brain remained stubbornly alert, continuing to throw up ideas and tentative theories as though it were shuffling a deck of cards and showing her random pictures. Having tried to sleep for twenty minutes, she turned her bedside light back on, sat up and opened her notebook to the last page she'd written, where she'd listed the usernames of the four accounts that had been so useful to Anomie, and to each other.

After a while, and unsure why she was doing it, Robin reached for the pen on her bedside table and wrote down a fifth name: *Zoltan*, Rachel's first-ever online friend, whom Rachel believed had then adopted another online persona, called … What had it been? For some reason Robin had a vague mental image of a harlequin.

She now bent over the side of her bed to pick up her charging laptop, opened it and searched 'harlequin'.

'*Scaramouche*,' she said aloud, once she'd read an article about stock characters in Italian Commedia dell'Arte. Scaramouche was a clown: cunning, boastful and fundamentally cowardly, an odd name to choose if you were trying to persuade young women into sex. Again, without really knowing why she was doing it, Robin wrote *Scaramouche* beneath *Zoltan*, stared for a moment at the six names, then reached again for her laptop.

99

We never know how high we are
Till we are called to rise . . .

Emily Dickinson
Aspiration

'If you're not going to say anything,' came Pat's deep, irritable voice from the outer office, 'stop bloody calling.'

It was half-past one on Monday afternoon and Strike, who was sitting at his desk in the inside office, crutches propped against the wall, was eating biscuits while he dealt with his overburdened email inbox. Now he called through to Pat,

'Same number? Just breathing again?'

'Couldn't hear any breathing this time,' said Pat, coming to the open door, e-cigarette in hand. Behind her, the outer office was almost empty but for the phone sitting on the floor and the piles of case files Pat was sorting, ready to go into the new filing cabinets. 'Just silence. Bloody idiot.'

'Might call that number back when I've dealt with this lot,' said Strike, returning to an email from the landlord, who seemed to feel that the bombing justified an increase in rent, a view Strike didn't share. 'You all right?'

'Why wouldn't I be?' asked Pat suspiciously.

'Being back in here,' said Strike. 'After what happened.'

'I'm fine. They've got them all now, haven't they? And I hope they throw away the bloody key,' Pat added, moving back to her files.

Strike returned to his email. A couple of minutes later, having sent a polite but firm response to the landlord, he started writing an update for Allan Yeoman. He was still trying to word his opening paragraph

in a way that suggested progress without actually mentioning any
when he heard Pat say,

'You're not supposed to be in today.'

Strike glanced up, assuming Robin had arrived early, but it was
Dev Shah who appeared in the doorway between the inner and outer
offices, wearing a broad grin.

'Nailed them,' he told Strike. 'Fingers and his old dear.'

'You serious?' said Strike, gladly abandoning his email.

'Yep. Chatted her up last night in the Connaught bar. She was
there with her sister. Or a woman who uses the same plastic surgeon.'

Dev pulled out his wallet, extracted a smartly engraved business
card and handed it to Strike, who saw the name Azam Masoumi,
followed by 'Dealer in Antiquities and Objets d'Art'.

'Mr Masoumi arranges the sale of valuables for private clients,' said
Dev, 'and he doesn't charge anything like the commission of the big
auction houses.'

'That's very good of him. I'll bet he's discreet as well.'

'Mr Masoumi prides himself on his discretion,' said Dev, deadpan.
'Some clients don't want it known that they're selling valuable objects.
Mr Masoumi completely understands their predicament.'

'And that did it?'

'Not on its own,' said Dev. 'I also had to buy her and her sister
a shit-ton of drinks and guess she was fifteen years younger than
she is. The bar closed and she invited me back to Fingers' flat for
a nightcap.'

'Was Fingers there?'

'No, which was bloody lucky, because I don't think he'd have liked
to see how his mum was behaving.'

'Frisky, was she?'

'It all started getting very Mrs Robinson. When I made noises
about leaving, she tried to keep my interest by showing me a Fabergé
box and a head of Alexander the Great, which she says were gifts from
her estranged husband.'

'He's going to be seriously fucking estranged once he hears all this.
Did you get pictures?'

'Yep,' said Dev, pulling his mobile out of his pocket and showing
Strike the images of the two objects, which together were worth over
a million pounds.

'And you got out of there without being Mrs Robinson-ed?'

'Narrowly escaped by making a dinner date for tonight.'

'You,' said Strike, struggling into a standing position on his one leg, and holding out his hand, 'have just won Employee of the Week.'

'Do I get a certificate?'

'I'll get Pat to type one up once her computer gets here.'

'Leg bad again?' asked Dev, glancing down at Strike's empty trouser leg.

'It'll be fine,' said Strike, dropping heavily back into his chair.

'Where's everyone else?'

'Barclay's flying back from Glasgow as we speak – he's been visiting his parents – Midge is on her day off and Robin's about to arrive, as is our new furniture.'

'Want me to hang around and help?'

'No, you've earned your time off. I'm planning to bung the delivery guys a hundred quid if anything needs putting together.'

Ten minutes after Dev had left, Robin arrived. She was as delighted as Strike to learn that the Fingers case was now wrapped up, but shocked by the sight of Strike in the flesh. His skin had a slightly grey tinge, his eyes were bloodshot and he was sporting forty-eight hours' worth of stubble. However, she passed no comment, merely holding up the USB stick she'd brought with her.

'When the printer arrives, I'll be able to show you everything I've got on Anomie's troll posse. What're you up to?'

'Trying to compose an email to Allan Yeoman, but there's a limit to how often you can say "promising developments" without actually reporting a development.'

'Hopefully Grant Ledwell will 'fess up this evening.'

'He'd better,' said Strike, 'or I'm going to have to find a positive spin for "this investigation is fucked".'

The first delivery of furniture arrived at three o'clock, and the next two hours were dedicated to filling up the new filing cabinets, assembling Pat's desk, setting up her new computer and printer, and stripping plastic wrap from the new sofa, which was covered in red fabric.

'You didn't want fake leather again?' said Robin as she and Pat rolled the sofa into position while Strike watched, balanced on his crutches and frustrated by his inability to help.

'I got sick of the old one farting every time I moved on it,' said Strike.

'This'll stain if anyone spills coffee on it,' said Pat, e-cigarette clamped between her teeth. She moved around her new desk and lowered her bony frame into her new computer chair.

'But this is better than the old one,' she admitted grudgingly.

'Almost worth getting bombed for, wasn't it?' said Strike, looking around the outer office, which, between the fresh paint and the new furniture, had never looked so smart.

'When are they going to replace the glass?' asked Pat, pointing at the still boarded-up half of the door onto the landing. 'I like being able to see the outline of whoever's outside. Gives you early warning.'

'Glazier's coming end of the week,' said Strike. 'I'd better finish that email to Yeoman.'

He moved on his crutches back into the inner office. Robin had just started printing off the results of her investigations into Lepine's Disciple and his friends when the office phone rang again.

'Strike Detective Agency,' said Pat.

Pat listened for a few seconds, then said,

'*What d'you want?* If you're trying to be funny—'

'Same number as before?' said Strike, reappearing at the door between the two rooms. Pat nodded. 'Give it to me,' he said, but Pat, whose surly expression had changed suddenly to one of suspicion, covered the mouthpiece with her hand and said,

'She's asking for Robin.'

Robin pressed the pause button on the printer and held out her hand for the receiver, but Pat, still looking at Strike, whispered,

'She sounds like a weirdo.'

'Pat,' said Robin firmly. 'Give it to me.'

Looking as though no good could come of it, Pat handed over the receiver.

'Hello?' said Robin. 'This is Robin Ellacott speaking.'

A voice whispered in Robin's ear.

'Were you Jessica?'

Robin locked eyes with Strike.

'Who is this?' Robin asked.

'*Were* you?' said the faint voice.

'Who am I speaking to?' Robin said.

Now she could hear the girl breathing. Those shallow breaths surely indicated terror.

'Do I know you?' Robin asked.

'Yes,' whispered the voice. 'I think so. If you were Jessica.'

Robin slipped her hand over the mouthpiece and said quietly: 'It's Zoe Haigh. She wants to know whether I was Jessica.'

Wondering whether the admission was worth the risk, Strike hesitated, then nodded. Robin removed her hand from the receiver and said,

'Zoe?'

'Yes,' said the voice. 'I – I –'

'Are you all right? Has something happened?'

'I'm so scared,' whispered the girl.

'Why are you scared?' asked Robin.

'Please . . . will you come and see me?'

'Of course,' said Robin. 'Are you at home now?'

'Yes,' said Zoe.

'All right. Stay there, I'll be there as fast as I can.'

'OK,' whispered Zoe. 'Thank you.'

The line went dead.

'She wants to see me,' said Robin, checking her watch. 'Maybe it'd be better if you got a taxi to Ledwell and I'll—'

'The hell you will. What if it's a set-up? What if she's the bait and Anomie's lying in wait?'

'Then we'll find out who they are,' said Robin, turning the printer back on.

'Right before you get your throat slit, you mean?' said Strike over the swish of pages.

Pat's head was turning between the partners, as though she was watching a tennis match.

'Zoe's flat is up two flights of stairs,' said Robin, without looking at Strike.

'And how d'you think I got back in here? Levitated?' asked Strike, omitting to mention that he'd done most of the journey on his backside.

'Strike, I honestly don't think Zoe is luring me to my doom.'

'You didn't think we'd find Vikas Bhardwaj with his jugular severed either.'

'Funny,' said Robin coolly, now turning to face her partner, 'I don't remember *you* predicting that either.'

'The difference,' said Strike impatiently, 'is that I've learned my bloody lesson. I'm coming with you. If we go to Junction Road now, we'll have plenty of time before Ledwell's at nine.'

When Strike had disappeared back into the inner office to collect his phone and wallet, Pat said, in the low growl that passed for her whisper,

'He's right, you know.'

'No he bloody isn't,' said Robin, taking the pages out of the printer and reaching up onto the shelf behind Pat for a plastic sleeve to put them in. 'If he tries punching anyone else, or if he falls downstairs again, he'll be out of action for—'

She broke off as Strike returned to the outer office, still glowering.

'Ready?'

Robin knew, by the expression on her partner's face, that he'd overheard what she'd just said.

100

But a wild courage sits triumphant there,
The stormy grandeur of a proud despair;
A daring spirit, in its woes elate,
Mightier than death, untameable by fate.

Felicia Hemans
The Wife of Asdrubal

Neither detective spoke during the first ten minutes of the drive to Junction Road. Strike was smouldering with quiet resentment about the fact that Robin currently considered him a liability rather than an asset. Ever sensitive to her partner's moods, Robin felt the prickly quality of his silence, and spent the early part of the journey trying to muster both the courage and the right words to address it.

At last, as they sat waiting for a traffic light to change, she said, eyes on the road ahead,

'You said to me once that we've got to be honest with each other or we're screwed.'

Strike kept his silence until the light turned green and they were moving forward again.

'So?'

'You said you worried more about me when I was out on my own than you'd worry about a male subcontractor, because the odds were always going to be against me if I came up against a violent—'

'Exactly,' said Strike, 'which is why—'

'Can I finish?' said Robin, her tone calm, though her pulse was racing.

'Carry on,' said Strike coldly.

'And you told me I needed to fix my panic attacks, because

956

you didn't want it on your conscience if I screwed up and got hurt again.'

Strike, who now knew exactly where the conversation was heading, set his jaw in a manner that Robin, had she seen it, would have described as mulish.

'I've never nagged you about you looking after yourself,' said Robin, her eyes still fixed on the road. 'Not once. It's your life, and your body. But the day you told me I had to get therapy, you said it wasn't only *me* who'd have to live with the consequences if I got myself killed.'

'So?' said Strike again.

A mixture of masochism and sadism made him want to force her to be explicit. Now starting to feel aggravated, Robin said,

'I know you're in pain. You look terrible.'

'Cheers. Just the shot in the arm I needed.'

'Oh, for God's—' said Robin, now barely keeping a curb on her temper. 'You'd *never* let anyone else go out on a job in your condition. How exactly do you think you're going to defend yourself, or me, if—?'

'So I'm dead weight in my own fucking agency, am I?'

'*Don't* twist my words, you know *exactly* what I'm saying—'

'Yeah, I'm a middle-aged cripple you'd rather leave in the car—'

'*Who said anything about your age?*'

'—while you walk merrily into what could be—'

'"Merrily"? Could you *be* any more patronising?'

'—a fucking *ambush*—'

'I've factored that in and—'

'Oh, you've factored that in, have you? *That'll* stop you being fucking stabbed through the neck when you walk in the door—'

'FOR CHRIST'S SAKE, STRIKE!' Robin shouted, slapping the steering wheel with both hands, the tension she'd been carrying with her since the bombing finding cathartic relief at last, 'I DON'T WANT YOU TO FUCKING KILL YOURSELF! I know you feel – I don't know – *emasculated* by being on crutches, or something—'

'No, I bloody don't—'

'You talk about honesty, but you're *not* fucking honest, not with me, not with yourself! You know why I'm saying this: *I don't want to lose you.* Happy now?'

'No, I'm not fucking happy,' said Strike automatically, which was both true and untrue: in some barely acknowledged part of his brain he'd registered her words, and they'd lightened a burden he'd barely known he was carrying. 'I think we're dealing with a fucking serial killer here—'

'So do I!' said Robin, infuriated by the lack of acknowledgement of something it had cost her a great deal to admit. 'But I know Zoe, and you don't!'

'Know her? You had one twenty-minute walk with her—'

'Sometimes, twenty minutes is enough! She was terrified on the phone just now, and I don't think it's because Anomie had a knife to her throat: it's because she's about to betray Anomie! I know you think I'm some ditsy, naive fool who "merrily" walks into dangerous situations—'

'I don't think that,' said Strike. 'I don't.'

Now there was silence in the BMW. Strike was processing what he'd just heard. *I don't want to lose you.* Was that something a woman would say about what he feared, in his darkest moments, he'd become? A crock, a fat, forty-year-old, one-legged chain-smoker, deluded about his attractiveness and competence, still imagining himself the gifted amateur boxer with a washboard stomach who'd been capable of pulling the most beautiful woman at Oxford University?

But Robin wasn't feeling comforted; on the contrary, she felt vulnerable and exposed, because she'd just said what she'd been trying not to say for a long time, and was scared that Strike had heard in that 'I don't want to lose you' more than her worry that he'd do himself some cataclysmic injury in hauling himself up the steep concrete steps in Zoe's building. She feared he'd divined her pain at the idea of Madeline, and her wish for an intimacy that she was trying to persuade herself she didn't crave.

After a few minutes she said, trying to keep her voice even and rational,

'You *are* this agency. It'd be nothing without you. I've never told you to rest up, or stop smoking, or eat better. It wasn't my business – but now you're making it my business. I've got a rape alarm in my bag and whoever's in Zoe's room when I get there, I'll make sure they know I didn't come alone. You look mean enough, even sitting in a car. Anyone looking out of the window's going to think twice about hurting me, knowing you're right outside, but you won't be able to get up those stairs without endangering yourself, and I'd be more worried about you than myself if somebody came at us.'

Strike said nothing, because he was enduring the always-humiliating experience of facing his own hypocrisy and delusion. If it came to a knife fight, he was less than useless.

'Have you really brought your rape alarm?'

'Yes,' said Robin, now turning into Junction Road, 'because I'm not some flaky—'

'I never thought you were ... All right, I'll stay in the car. But call me once you're in there. If I haven't heard from you after five minutes, I'm coming up.'

'Fine,' said Robin.

They were driving past the toy shop, and now Zoe's wedge-shaped corner building lay straight ahead. Robin turned the BMW into Brookside Lane and parked.

'You could look over the Lepine's Disciple stuff, while I'm in there,' she said, taking the plastic folder of printed material off the back seat and handing it to him. 'I spent a long time on that last night. I'd like to think somebody read it.'

As she unclipped her seatbelt, Strike said,

'Just be careful, all right?'

'*I will*,' said Robin firmly, as she left the car.

101

My men and women of disordered lives . . .
Broke up those waxen masks I made them wear,
With fierce contortions of the natural face—
And cursed me for my tyrannous constraint . . .

Elizabeth Barrett Browning
Aurora Leigh

The stairwell of Zoe's building, with its smell of grime and stale urine, felt no less depressing the second time Robin entered it. As she climbed the concrete stairs, she slipped the rape alarm she carried with her constantly out of her bag and held it primed in her hand.

On the top floor, she tapped softly on Zoe's door.

It opened at once. The emaciated girl facing Robin looked as though she was greeting Death in person, but Robin had been right, and Strike wrong: there was nobody else in the room, only Zoe, gaunt and terrified, her black-ringed eyes searching Robin's face now that she saw it without disguise.

'Can I come in?' asked Robin.

'Yeah,' said Zoe, backing away.

Her room contained a single bed, which she'd covered with a thin black cotton throw patterned with white stars, on which was an old laptop. The unlined pink curtain hung limply at the window and a two-ring electric hob sat on top of a fridge that looked as though it dated from the eighties, beside a small sink that appeared to be coming away from the wall. There were no cupboards; only shelves. A single saucepan and a couple of tins of low-calorie soup stood on the shelf over the fridge, while on the shelf over the bed were a few items of cheap make-up, a deodorant, some pencils and pens and a

pad. Zoe's meagre stock of all-black clothes was folded and piled up
in a corner. This left a square yard of floorspace covered in stained
light green carpet.

However, Robin barely noticed any of this on entering the room,
because all her attention was given to the walls and ceiling, every
single inch of which had been covered in tacked-up drawings done
in pencil and black ink. They were immensely detailed and ornate:
the extraordinary, unstoppable effusions of an incurable creative.
The talent displayed on these dilapidated walls was almost shocking to Robin.

'Wow,' she said quietly, her eyes roving over the walls. 'Zoe . . .
these are *amazing . . .*'

A small tremor of pleasure passed across the girl's frightened face.

'I've got to make a quick call,' Robin said. 'Nothing to worry
about,' she added, seeing Zoe's increased anxiety. 'Then we can talk.'

She pressed Strike's number.

'Zoe's here,' she told him.

'Alone?'

'Yes.'

'All right, good luck,' said Strike, and Robin hung up, then
switched her phone to record without telling Zoe what she was doing
and slipped it back into her bag.

'D'you wanna sit down?' whispered Zoe.

'Great, thanks,' said Robin, and both of them sat on the bed.

'Why did you want to see me, Zoe?'

'Because,' Zoe took a deep breath, 'Anomie – the guy who created
Drek's Game? He says he's going to kill you and your partner. He said
he's going to *Ledwell and Blay* you. He showed me pictures of you
out of the paper the other day, that's how I realised you were Jessica.
I know I annoyed that man who kept answering your phone at the
office – I were hanging up because I were so scared, and – and my
boyfriend said I shouldn't contact you, that I'd be in trouble, but I had
to, because *I think he killed Edie.*'

'You think your *boyfriend*—?'

'No!' squealed Zoe. 'No – Anomie! I've just been talking to this
girl who calls herself Paperwhite online, and—'

'Is she in *Drek's Game* right now?'

Zoe looked shocked that Robin knew exactly where Paperwhite
was.

'Zoe, would you let me speak to her, please? Don't worry. She doesn't have to know it isn't you.'

'But you don't know how to—'

'I know all about the game,' said Robin. 'I'm Buffypaws. Or, at least, I have been for the last couple of months.'

'*You're Buffypaws?*' said Zoe in a wondering voice. '*You're* the one I've been—?'

'That's right.'

Gaping, Zoe turned the laptop round so that Robin could see the moderator channel, and a private channel in which Worm28 and Paperwhite had been talking. Robin scrolled quickly back, to see what had already been said.

<Moderator Channel>	<Private Channel>
<15 June 2015 17.47>	<15 June 2015 17.47>
<Present: BorkledDrek, Worm28, Anomie>	<Present: Paperwhite, Worm28>
BorkledDrek: but why though?	Worm28: but what if he did ?
>	Worm28: what if he 's not joking ?
>	Paperwhite: don't be stupid,. of course he didn't
>	
Anomie: because I want all conversations to stay on the moderator channel from now on	Worm28: how do you nkow that ? because he keeps saying he did
BorkledDrek: Didn't Morehouse leave an instruction manual or anything?	Paperwhite: I know who Anomie is and there's no way he could have done it
BorkledDrek: I don't know how to get rid of them.	Worm28: you know who Anomie is ?
	>
Anomie: you told me you can fucking code	>

BorkledDrek: I can

BorkledDrek: but this
is a different level

BorkledDrek: anyway,
people like the private
channels

Anomie: people have been
abusing private channels,
so do as you're told

Paperwhite: yes

Paperwhite: you haven't
been telling people
Anomie killed Ledwell,
have you?

Worm28: no

Worm28: of course not

>

'Were you telling Paperwhite you think Anomie killed Edie?'
Robin asked Zoe, who nodded.

Robin now put her fingers on the keyboard, reminding herself to
duplicate Zoe's idiosyncratic punctuation, as Paperwhite spoke again.

>

>

>

>

Anomie: people like a ton
of shit they shouldn't.
Just do as you're told

>

>

>

BorkledDrek: gtg

<BorkledDrek has left
the channel>

>

>

>

Anomie: Worm?

Paperwhite: good,
because Anomie will be
really fkn angry with you
if he finds out you have

Worm28: I haven ' t
told anyone

Worm28: did Morehouse
tell you who Anomie is ?

Paperwhite: No, Anomie
told me himself

Worm28: seriously ??

Paperwhite: yeah. We've
become friendly.

Worm28: wow . I thought
you 'd be pissed off at
him for getting rid of
Morehouse

Paperwhite: Morehouse
was a slimy bastard

Paperwhite: good riddance

Worm28: I thought u

> were really good friends

>

Worm28: hi

Paperwhite: no, once
I got to know him I
realised he was a creep

Anomie: are you talking
to anyone on a private
channel right now?

>

Robin wasn't about to make the same mistake twice.

Worm28: yes , I 'm
talking to Paperwhite

>

>

Anomie: and would you be
comfortable if I was able
to see what you're saying?

>

Worm28: yes

Paperwhite: haha,
you're in trouble now

Anomie: really?

>

Worm28: yes , I would

Paperwhite: liar

And now Robin paused, looking between the two channels, and her heart began to race.

Worm28: it's funny

>

Worm28: the way you
and Paperwhite never
speak at the same time

>

>

>

Worm28: isn't it?

>

>

>

>

<Worm28 has been banned>

<Worm28 has been banned>

Robin slowly closed the laptop.
'What happened?' Zoe said anxiously.
'I'm afraid Worm28's just been banned.'

'*Oh, no!*' Zoe whispered, pressing her hands to her face and survey-ing Robin over her fingertips through her enormous, black-rimmed, sunken eyes. 'Oh shit – is he angry? Did you tell him what I were saying, about him killing—?'

'I didn't have to. You were talking to Anomie all along. Anomie and Paperwhite are the same person.'

'*What?* Oh my God – oh no – he'll come and get me, now – he'll come and bloody—'

Zoe stood up in a panic, looking as though she was about to scoop up her meagre possessions and flee.

'Zoe, sit down,' said Robin firmly. '*Sit down.* I can help you, I *prom-ise* I can help you, but you've got to tell me what you know.'

The girl lowered herself back onto the bed, gazing at Robin with those huge, sunken eyes. Finally, she whispered,

'Anomie's who you think he is.'

'Who *I* think he is?' said Robin.

'Yes,' said Zoe, tears leaking from her eyes. 'That's why you were talking to him, in disguise, isn't it? If I'd known I'd never, ever've gone near him—'

'Zoe, are you talking about Tim Ash—?'

'No!' squealed Zoe. 'Of course not.'

But she caught herself pressing her lips together as though fright-ened of what would fall out of them next.

'Listen, I know you and Tim are – in a relationship,' said Robin, her hesitation due to the fact that she hated to dignify Tim's exploitation of this damaged, isolated girl with the word 'relationship'.

Zoe's face crumpled again, and Robin was struck anew by her strange old-young appearance, the fragility of her bones, and the childlike way she wiped her eyes on the back of her tattooed hand.

'He'll end it now,' she sobbed. 'He'll be mad that you know. He'll think I told you.'

As she said it, she picked up her phone and checked the time.

'Are you expecting him?'

'Yeah,' said Zoe, tears still trickling down her hollow cheeks. 'He wanted to come over, because of me saying I wanted to con-tact you. He didn't want me to. He's always nervous about police and that.'

Yeah, I'll bet he is, thought Robin, but she said,

'I'd have thought he'd want Edie's death investigated. He was her friend, wasn't he?'

'He *does* want the killer caught, he just ... he thinks people won't understand about us, so he doesn't like it when I talk to strangers ... He were really angry when I started working at North Grove ... but he didn't start it – us – *I* did,' said Zoe earnestly. 'It weren't his fault. I were the one who kissed him first.'

'How old were you?'

'Thirteen, and he didn't want to, because of how old I were. It were *me* that started it. It's my fault, not Tim's.'

'You forced him, did you?'

'N-no,' said Zoe, with a half-sob. 'He told me he were in love with me, but he said we couldn't do nothing because of how old I was, and I said it didn't matter. He didn't want to do nothing physical, though. I made it happen.'

'Have you told Tim you think Anomie killed Edie?'

Zoe nodded, tears still trickling down her face.

'Have you told him who you think Anomie is?'

'Yeah, but he says I'm being silly.'

'Zoe, please tell me who—'

'But I thought you *knew*, I thought that's why you were at North Grove!'

'You think it's Pez Pierce?'

'No,' whispered Zoe. 'It's Nils.'

102

. . . and since you're proved so vile,
Ay, vile, I say—we'll show it presently . . .
you tricked poor Marian Erle,
And set her own love digging its own grave
Within her green hope's pretty garden-ground . . .

Elizabeth Barrett Browning
Aurora Leigh

Back in the BMW, Strike had just finished reading Robin's notes on the four Twitter accounts that had been so useful to Anomie in disseminating false information on Edie Ledwell. Now he wound down the window, took a deep pull on his vape and turned back to the pages he'd found particularly interesting.

All four accounts had described Anomie as 'brilliant' and 'a genius'; all four had called Edie Ledwell variations on 'slut', 'whore' and 'gold-digger'; and all four hinted that she'd dropped Anomie as a friend, or that she and Anomie had once been in a sexual relationship.

Strike turned to another page. Beneath the heading *Beatles Again*, Robin had pasted another tweet.

Julius @i_am_evola
replying to @rachledbadly

not if I looked like you. They'd wonder why Ringo Starr had turned up on their doorstep dressed in a skirt

9.15 pm   28 January 2013

Strike then reread the section titled *Duplicated Phrases*. All four accounts were fond of saying 'I can smell your stale pussy from here' to women; Julius I am Evola and Max R had both told girls that if they were raped every time they said something stupid they'd be 'permanently full of cock', and they and Lepine's Disciple had also expressed in almost identical terms the opinion that all women should be 'starved down to optimal breeding weight'.

Strike turned back to the first page, where Robin had pasted the first-ever tweets by Lepine's Disciple.

Lepine's Disciple @LepinesD1sciple

Marc Lepine was a God

Lepine's Disciple @LepinesD1sciple

14 femoids dead hahahahahaha

Lepine's Disciple @LepinesD1sciple

lined them up and shot them

Lastly, Strike turned back to Robin's final summary page.

The accounts all attack random girls, but three women have come under sustained fire for years: Edie Ledwell, Kea Niven and Rachel Ledwell.

The foursome didn't turn on Kea until Anomie did, i.e. after he tweeted 'sue or shut the fuck up, you're starting to bore all of us'. At that point, it was open season on her, and they treated her nearly as badly as they were treating Edie.

The strange thing is that Anomie's never attacked Rachel Ledwell, yet she's had nearly as much abuse from the foursome as Kea. That made me think there's a separate, non-*Ink Black Heart*-related grudge against Rachel.

One possible culprit is Zoltan, Rachel's old friend from Club Penguin. Rachel cut contact with Zoltan when he started using Kosh lines on her, and thinks he might then have become Scaramouche, because Scaramouche did the same to Zoe Haigh. Both Zoltan and Scaramouche's accounts have disappeared from Twitter, but the tone of the abuse the foursome send Rachel could suggest ongoing resentment at an ex-friend who turned them down.

Beneath this, Robin had pasted examples of tweets the foursome had sent to sixteen-year-old Rachel.

Johnny B @jbaldw1n1>>
replying to @rachledbadly
Still riding the cock carousel, hoping to get yourself an alpha?
Dream on, u saggy-titted mess

Julius @i_am_evola
replying to @rachledbadly
skanky bitch who thinks she's too good for betas says
what, now?

Max R @mreger#5
replying to @rachledbadly
Ugly dykes like you should be put in camps and
correctively raped

Lepine's Disciple @LepinesD1sciple
replying to @rachledbadly
at least when your mummy dies you'll have something in
common with #GreedieFedwell

Looking up from the pages, frowning, Strike now caught sight of somebody in the wing mirror: a tall, balding man walking determinedly towards Zoe's shabby black door.

At once, Strike threw the papers he was reading onto the driver's seat and lowered the window.

'Oi!'

Tim Ashcroft turned with a start and, correctly locating the source of the shout, stared at the man with thick dark stubble and a pugilist's bent nose.

'I want a word with you,' said Strike.

Looking wary, Ashcroft approached Strike, stopping a few feet away.

'Something I can help you with?' he asked in his polite Home Counties voice.

'Yeah, there is. My name's Cormoran Strike. I'm a private detective.'

He watched with satisfaction as Tim's polite smile evaporated.

'You're off to visit Zoe Haigh, I take it?'

Tim waited a few seconds too long before feigning puzzlement.

'Who?'

'The underage girl you've been fucking for the last four years,' said Strike.

'I ... what?' said Tim. 'Is that what Zoe's told you?'

'I thought you didn't know who she was?'

'I didn't hear you properly,' said Tim. Strike could see the faint glimmer of sweat on Ashcroft's hairless upper lip. 'I know Zoe, yes. She's quite a troubled young—'

'But that's how you like them, right? Easier to manipulate if they've got fuck-all self-esteem and no family to drag you into court.'

'I really don't—'

'Oh, I think you do,' said Strike.

He opened the car door. Tim backed away, looking very scared, but as Strike heaved himself up onto his one leg, using the roof of the car to balance, then pulled out his crutches, Ashcroft appeared to regain some courage.

'I'm afraid you've got the wrong end of the—'

'Not making an ableist joke about my amputation, are you?' said Strike, advancing on Ashcroft, who took a step backwards. 'I might have to start my own blog. "My take on why the Pen of Justice is a paedophile, and why that should fucking trouble you."'

Tim took another step back.

'I don't know what Zoe's been telling people,' he stammered, 'but she's not right in the—'

'Mental, is she? A nutter?'

'Girls sometimes get crushes on older men – read more into things than—'

'Oh, she should've realised your dick was inside her *platonically*, should she?' said Strike, swinging himself closer to Tim, who kept retreating. 'D'you know what's going to happen now?'

'What?' said Tim.

'I'm going to try and persuade her to go to the police. If she doesn't want to cooperate, I'll go back through all the other little girls you've been following on Twitter. My partner's put together quite a tidy file on you and your online behaviour. There's at least one irate father out there who I'm sure would be delighted to hear from me.'

Tim now looked as though he might fall to his knees or burst into tears.

'If you ever come near Zoe Haigh again,' said Strike, 'I'll personally perform an amputation, and it won't be your fucking leg. Understand?'

'Yes,' whispered Tim.

'Now, get the *fuck*—'

The black door behind Tim opened, revealing Robin and Zoe.

'Tim!' cried Zoe.

Ashcroft ignored her and began to walk quickly away. As Zoe stared after him, he broke into a run and disappeared around the corner. Strike and Robin's eyes met, and the latter knew at once, if not the specifics then the gist of what must just have happened.

'We're going to give Zoe a lift to the Tube,' said Robin. 'She's going to take my room at the Z Hotel tonight.'

'No,' said Zoe, who Strike now saw had grubby tear tracks on her cheeks. 'I want to see Tim—'

'But he doesn't want to see you,' said Strike.

'Why not?' wailed Zoe, fresh tears spilling down her face.

'We can talk about that in the car,' said Strike, opening a rear door. 'Get in.'

103

Much is finished known or unknown:
Lives are finished; time diminished;
Was the fallow field left unsown?
Will these buds be always unblown?

Christina Rossetti
Amen

'You could have been more sympathetic,' said Robin reproachfully, half an hour later.

She and Strike were parked in a side road near Tufnell Park station, having just seen Zoe onto the Tube. Zoe was now in possession of the key card for Robin's hotel room and a hundred pounds in cash, given to her by Strike.

'I am sympathetic,' said Strike. 'Why d'you think I just threatened to rip Ashcroft's dick off?'

It had taken them thirty minutes to calm Zoe's grief about Ashcroft's hasty departure, and then to explain how hotels worked, because she'd never stayed in one before. However, she was so frightened that Anomie was going to come and find her that she was finally persuaded nobody would throw her out of the Z Hotel for not looking like Robin and had even accepted Robin's hug of reassurance at the top of the station steps.

'She'll ring Ashcroft the moment she's got reception again,' said Robin.

'If he knows what's good for him, he won't answer,' said Strike. 'Ever again.'

'You realise, if he's Anomie—'

'He isn't,' said Strike. 'I've just ruled him out. Well, ninety per cent.'

'How?' said Robin, taken aback.

'I'll explain after you tell me what happened upstairs.'

'It's all on here.'

Robin took her mobile out of her bag, located the recording and pressed play.

Strike listened, stony-faced, as Zoe said Anomie was going to 'Ledwell and Blay' the two detectives. When they reached a silence broken only by the tapping of laptop keys, Robin said,

'So that's me going into the game. There were two channels open, and Paperwhite – she was *totally* different. She said Morehouse had been a slimy creep and she was well shot of him. And then, after a little while, I noticed it: Anomie and Paperwhite don't type at the same time, and when I pointed that out, across the two channels, I was immediately banned. I'm certain they're—'

'—the same person,' said Strike. He leaned forwards and pressed pause. '*Shit*. Of fucking course: Paperwhite was created to keep an eye on Morehouse. Find out what he was thinking, whether he was considering leaving—'

'—and to try and keep him there,' said Robin, 'because Vikas had grown up since he helped make the game, hadn't he? He was getting more and more successful in the real world, and Anomie would've known he'd be almost impossible to replace. I've just seen Anomie having a real go at the new moderator, BorkledDrek, who clearly isn't up to the job.

'Paperwhite arrived in *Drek's Game* around the time Vikas and Rachel had their falling-out. I don't think that was coincidence. Rachel says Anomie was possessive of Vikas, that they didn't like him and Rachel getting close. Paperwhite was a perfect way of luring Vikas away from Rachel for good.'

'With a bunch of stolen nudes, which Anomie also flashed around at the other men,' said Strike, thinking rapidly. 'What are the odds Oliver Peach was lured to Comic Con on the vague understanding a gorgeous redhead was going to be there to help him locate Anomie?'

He pressed play again.

At the point where Zoe claimed that she'd initiated the sexual relationship with Tim Ashcroft, Strike muttered 'piece of shit,' but when Zoe said the words 'It's Nils,' he said loudly, 'What the fuck?'

'Shh. Listen,' said Robin, pointing at the mobile, from which her own voice now issued.

'*Why d'you think it's Nils?*'

'*Loads of things. I got a shock the first time I saw the window at North Grove. It's got the word "anomie" on it, so that evening, on the mod channel, I said, "You'll never guess, I saw a window with "anomie" on it today, isn't that funny?" or something, and Anomie private-channelled me as soon as I said it, and he said, "Don't ever mention that window again, or I'll ban you. You don't mention it to anyone." He were really weird about it.*'

'*Did Anomie mention North Grove?*'

'*No, but I had a feeling he knew where the window was, and I started to think he must've been there, and maybe that's where he got the idea for the name.*

'*Then one day Nils talked to me about anomie and he explained what it meant. He were telling me you've got to have, like, a purpose in your work and you've got to make sure you stay connected to other people, and about how a commune's the best way to live, because you can't suffer anomie if you're living in a commune, and how I should move out of here and go live at North Grove. Mariam was backing him up. I thought they were being nice. I didn't go, though, because Tim didn't want me to. He said we couldn't be private there.*

'*Then one day I heard Nils and Pez talking about Edie, and I were listening in, because I was always hoping she might come round North Grove one day, and I'd meet her.*

'*But they were both being really nasty about her . . . I thought they'd be proud to know her, after what she did, but they weren't. Pez were talking about this comic book idea he and Edie were working on, before Josh moved in. Pez said Edie would probably sue him now, if he finished it and put it out on his own, because some of the ideas were hers. It were about a time-travelling undertaker, proper dark, travelling in coffins. I thought it were a cool idea. I bet it was all her ideas, it sounded like her kind of story. I bet Pez just drew a few pictures for it.*

'*And then Nils started slagging Edie off and I'd never heard him like that before. He were angry, really angry. Like, Nils doesn't get angry much. He said she'd never mentioned him in a single interview, after he gave her a free place to live and space to make* The Ink Black Heart, *and that she took everything and gave nothing back. He made it sound like if it hadn't been for him, she'd never have been successful, and he were saying she kind of flirted with him to get what she wanted out of him. And he were saying Edie never even mentioned his art or anything, or bothered to turn up at his last show.*

'*And when I were listening to Nils, I thought, that's exactly how Anomie talks about Edie, because one night, not long after I joined the game, Anomie were saying what a bitch Edie were for slagging off the game, when he were keeping the fandom interested and doing her a favour. And then he told me Edie had come on to him, like, in real life, but kind of dumped him when she started making money.*

'*Anomie were drunk when he said that, he told me he'd been drinking. He said he'd had a bad day.*'

'*Why was it bad?*'

'*He didn't tell me – he never says much about his real life. But then, next morning, after he told me all that about Edie, he opened another private channel with me and he said, "You forget what I said last night, if you want to stay in the game." So I never told anyone, because I loved the game so much, back then. I had friends in there – Fiendy1 and Buffypaws – I mean, before you – I used to talk to the other Buffypaws a lot.*

'*But after I heard Nils talking about Edie, I didn't like him as much any more. And I started noticing how much he were on the computer. He does the odd bit of art, but he don't finish many pieces.*'

'*Did you ever see him playing the game?*'

'*No, but someone there had, someone at North Grove, because I saw it on the internet history one time, after I started thinking Anomie might be Nils. I went looking. D'you think that was wrong?*'

'*No, Zoe, I think it was smart.*'

'*And then, when Josh come to stay at North Grove, that month before they were attacked, Nils were suggesting ideas to him for the cartoon. I heard him doing it a couple of times, and that's just like Anomie as well, because he were always slagging off the cartoon – and I never understood that, because he were mad about it really – but Anomie were always saying he could do a far better job than Edie.*

'*So I were getting proper suspicious about Nils, and then, the day – it – happened—*'

'*The attacks?*'

'*Yeah . . . Nils was out. He hardly ever goes out.*'

'*Did he tell you where he went?*'

'*No, I just know he were out, because Bram were off school and Mariam were complaining she'd been trying to do art classes and look after Bram at the same time.*

'*But the worst bit . . . I were so scared, when I found it . . . I were in Nils's studio. He keeps it locked, but he wanted me to get a book out of there for him . . . and I found . . .*'

'What did she find?' said Strike as the silence went on.

'A knife,' said Robin. 'She mouthed it at me.'

'... *a really big one,*' Zoe resumed, now whispering and sounding close to tears. '*It were just there, on the shelf. And it had strange writing on it, like a magic spell or something.*'

Robin pressed pause.

'I've seen that knife. It was Nils's grandfather's. He called it by some Dutch name I can't remember. The "magic spell" was a word in Greek that meant "legacy".'

'It was just lying around, in his studio?'

'Yes, and people clearly knew it was there – or Bram did, because he asked Nils whether he could take it into school with him. Nils said no,' Robin added.

'Thank fuck for that,' said Strike, 'or we'd probably be looking at a school massacre.'

'That's all Zoe had to say about her reasons for suspecting Nils,' said Robin. 'The rest of the conversation was her panicking that Anomie was going to come and kill her, and me persuading her to go to the hotel. So – what do you think of her theory?'

'Honestly?' said Strike, 'Not much.'

He pulled out his vape and took a long drag on it. Having exhaled, he said,

'Edie Ledwell really pissed off a lot of men, didn't she?'

'Yes,' said Robin. 'But I don't believe she flirted with Nils to get things out of him. I don't think she was that type, and anyway—'

'Men are generally predisposed to think they're being flirted with?' said Strike, correctly anticipating what Robin was about to say.

'Some men are,' said Robin as she checked her watch. 'It's always the ones you don't actually like who seem most predisposed to think you're crazy about them.'

She was thinking of Hugh Jacks, but Strike's thoughts darted back to the pavement outside the Ritz.

'Shall we get something to eat?' suggested Strike. 'Still plenty of time before we need to get to the Ledwells.'

So they went to the nearest sandwich bar, to which Strike brought Robin's notes on the four trolls. Once sat at a small table beside the window, each of them supplied with sandwiches, Strike said,

'I've read these notes.'

'And?' asked Robin.

'And I agree.'

'With what?' asked Robin, who hadn't written down her own conclusion, worried that Strike would think she was seeing things that weren't there.

'That they're the same person. I'm talking about Julius, Johnny, Max and Lepine, obviously. Hard to judge with Zoltan and Scaramouche, because we've got no material from them to compare with the others.'

'I think it's possible Zoltan and Scaramouche were banned,' said Robin, relieved that Strike didn't think her theory absurd, 'because I couldn't find any trace of either of them on Twitter. But if Rachel was right, and Zoltan transformed himself into Scaramouche, who also got banned – mightn't Zoltan/Scaramouche have decided to, I don't know, kind of spread the load? Make multiple accounts so they could afford to sacrifice one or two if they crossed the line?'

'Plausible,' said Strike, nodding, 'although there's no shortage of men out there getting a kick out of harassing girls online. They don't all have to be connected.'

'I know,' said Robin, 'but that doesn't explain why Rachel gets so much hate from those four accounts. It breaks the pattern: Edie and Kea had both pissed off Anomie. Rachel never did. And did you see the Ringo Starr reference?'

'Yeah,' said Strike, 'which leads us to the inevitable question, doesn't it? Are we looking at four more online personas of Anomie's? I'm strongly inclined to think we are, and if so, Ashcroft can't be Anomie. I don't know whether you clocked the dates, but Julius and Johnny were tweeting up a storm when you were face to face with Ashcroft in Colchester.'

'*Oh,*' said Robin. 'That's how you've ruled him out?'

'I might be wrong – but I don't think I am.'

'Well, then, *who,*' said Robin, with a trace of desperation, '*is* this person? Could the same individual who wrote those pompous messages to Josh Blay with the Greek in them, and said to Rachel "Edie and I are basically the same person", also be telling young women online they should raped and starved down to breeding weight?'

'Why not?' said Strike robustly. 'You think well-educated, cultured people aren't capable of being as mean and filthy as anyone else? Look at fucking Ashcroft. Anyway, it's not hard to look up a few snippets of Latin and Greek, then copy and paste them. It doesn't necessarily mean we're looking for a brain like Bhardwaj's.'

'If they're all the same person,' said Robin, 'Kea Niven *could* have been telling the truth about Anomie using Kosh lines on her. She's a big catch: pretty, directly connected to *The Ink Black Heart* – Anomie might've thought she deserved the treatment in person, rather than delegating it to one of the trolls.'

'Makes sense,' said Strike, nodding, 'and if Anomie *did* come on to Kea, using Kosh, that points to a man who's not successful with women in real life – or not as successful as he'd like to be. There are plenty of supposedly happily married men who enjoy the hunt for its own sake. Quantity rather than quality, as Kosh put it.

'You know,' said Strike, after a short pause, 'I still keep going back to that first question: what has Anomie got to lose if he's unmasked? I understand why Bhardwaj wanted to stay anonymous. He was a kid wanting to be taken seriously by astrophysicists at Cambridge. I doubt he wanted them to know how much of his life was taken up with the game, or to be associated with Anomie's public persecution of Edie.'

'I still don't understand why Vikas didn't cut ties with Anomie sooner.'

'But you've just found out why, haven't you?' said Strike. 'Paperwhite.'

'But Paperwhite wasn't there from the beginning. Why did Vikas stay, before she appeared?'

'Good question,' said Strike.

'Remember that "joke" Vikas made to Rachel? "Anomie's not my girlfriend. She's my sister." What the hell did *that* mean?'

'Christ knows,' said Strike.

Something in his subconscious was nudging him, but refusing to be explicit.

Once their sandwiches were eaten, and Robin had visited the toilet, she said,

'It isn't that far to Battledean Road, but we should probably get going ... Are you all right?'

'What?' said Strike, who was trying to force the subconscious idea that kept irking him to the surface. 'I'm fine. Just thinking.'

Once back in the BMW, Strike took out his mobile again, with a view to looking up what he now believed to be four pseudonyms of Anomie's. Perversely, given he'd just told Robin that Zoltan might have nothing whatsoever to do with the case, he Googled that name first.

The results were, to say the least, eclectic. Zoltan, he learned, was a Hungarian given name and also the name of a hand gesture, which had originated in a fifteen-year-old movie called *Dude, Where's My Car?*

With a small snort, Strike looked up 'John Baldwin'. The results were numerous and similarly diverse. However, now that he focused on the name, he had a strange feeling he'd seen it somewhere other than Twitter, though his recalcitrant brain refused to divulge where.

The names Lepine's Disciple and Julius Evola were self-explanatory, Strike thought, but as he considered Scaramouche, he heard a phrase of music inside his head. Reflecting that he probably wasn't the only person who thought of 'Bohemian Rhapsody' rather than a sixteenth-century clown when they heard the name Scaramouche.

Finally, he turned his attention to the last name: Max R, also known as @mreger#5.

'We're here,' said Robin, as she turned into Battledean Road, but the words were barely out of her mouth when Strike said loudly,

'*Fuck.*'

'What?' said Robin.

'Give me a minute,' said Strike, hastily entering the name Zoltan into Google again.

Robin continued along the road, which was lined on both sides with solidly built family homes that she guessed, from having house-hunted so recently, were worth well upwards of a million pounds. By luck, a parking space lay right outside the home of Grant and Heather Ledwell. Having parked the BMW, she turned again to Strike, who was still typing onto his phone, scanning the results and wearing an expression that she knew, from long experience, meant deep concentration.

They still had a few minutes before nine o'clock. Robin sat quietly, waiting for Strike to tell her what he was doing. At last he looked up.

'What?' Robin asked, certain, by the look on his face, that Strike had something important to tell her.

'Think I've just cut some wire.'

'What?'

Before Strike could answer, somebody rapped on the window beside Robin, making her jump.

Grant Ledwell was smiling in through the window, a wrapped bottle of wine in his hand, clearly keen to receive his important update.

104

Death's black dust, being blown,
Infiltrated through every secret fold
Of this sealed letter by a puff of fate,
Dried up for ever the fresh-written ink . . .

Elizabeth Barrett Browning
Aurora Leigh

'I'll explain once this is over,' said Strike in an undertone.

'Just been to the off-licence,' said Grant, pointing to the bottle as Strike and Robin got out of the car. His sojourn in Oman had left him with a deep tan that was enhanced by the white shirt he was wearing with his jeans. Without the disguise of a suit jacket, a large paunch was revealed.

'Heather and her mother have got through all my decent red. Oh,' he exclaimed, as Strike moved around the front of the car and came fully into sight, with his crutches and his half-empty trouser leg. 'You've – ah—'

'Lost half a leg, yeah,' said Strike. 'It'll probably turn up.'

Grant laughed uneasily. Robin, whose mind had still been on Strike's peculiar comment about wire, was distracted by Grant's clear discomfort at this obvious evidence of Strike's disability. It made her feel no friendlier to Ledwell, towards whom she was already prejudiced, given what she considered his neglect of his eldest daughter and his niece.

'Got a new addition to the family since I last saw you!' he said, keeping his eyes averted from Strike as the three of them headed towards the front door.

'Oh, has Heather had the baby?' said Robin politely. 'Congratulations!'

'Yep, got my boy at last,' said Grant. 'Third time lucky!'

Apparently, thought Robin, her dislike deepening, Rachel no longer counted as one of Grant's children.

'What have you called him?' she asked.

'Ethan,' said Grant. 'It's always been Heather's favourite name. She's liked it ever since *Mission: Impossible.*'

He opened the door onto a hallway decorated in beige and cream, and through a door into a large sitting and dining area where Heather and her mother were sitting. It was now Strike's turn to avert his eyes, because Heather was feeding her new-born son, nine-tenths of her swollen breast exposed, the baby's head, with its sparse covering of brown hair, cradled in her hand like a large potato. Two little girls in identical pink spotted pyjamas were curled up on the floor, playing with a pair of plastic ponies and riders. They looked up when their father entered with the two strangers, and both their mouths fell open at the sight of Strike's pinned-up trouser leg. Their grandmother, who was short, with aggressively auburn hair, looked rather excited.

'Oh, hello!' said Heather cheerfully. 'Excuse me. When he's hungry, he's hungry!'

'I've read all about you,' said Grant's mother-in-law, drinking Strike in with greedy eyes. 'I've been telling the girls about you. They wanted to stay up to see Daddy's famous visitor!'

'We'll go through to the garden,' said Grant, saving Strike from the necessity of making a response. Strike and Robin followed him into a large and very well-appointed kitchen full of stainless steel fixtures and fittings. The French doors were already open, and Robin saw that the garden was in fact a small paved area dotted with plants in pots, which surrounded a wooden table and chairs.

'Either of you fancy a drink?' Grant asked, getting himself a wine glass out of a wall cupboard. Both declined.

When the three of them had sat down at the table in the garden, and Grant had poured himself wine and taken a sip, Robin said, not particularly sincerely, because she actually thought it rather bland,

'Lovely house.'

'Thanks,' said Grant, 'but we won't be here much longer. We're clearing out. Relief, really, to have decided. We're going back to Oman. Great schools for the kids, good expat community. We've still got friends over there. I can deal with all the film stuff remotely, there's no need to stay in the UK for that. Anyway, Heather's keen to go. She's still worried about Anomie and all the crazy *Ink Black Heart* bastards.'

Plus Oman's a nice fat tax haven, thought Strike.

Grant drank some wine, then said,

'So: you've got an update for me?'

'Yes,' said Strike. 'We're ninety per cent sure who Anomie is.'

We are? thought Robin, glancing at Strike.

'Well, that's bloody good news,' said Grant heartily. 'Who—?'

'Can't say until it's proven,' said Strike. 'We could be had up for defamation. As a matter of fact, we're missing a key bit of evidence, and wondered whether you could help.'

'Me?' said Grant, looking surprised.

'Yeah,' said Strike. 'I've got a couple of questions, if that's OK?'

'Shoot,' said Grant, although Robin thought a trace of wariness passed over the bulldog face, which looked leathery in the evening sun.

'Firstly,' said Strike, 'that phone call with Edie you told me about. The one where she told you Blay wanted to ditch her from *The Ink Black Heart*?'

Grant raised his left hand and brushed something invisible from his nose.

'Yeah?' he said.

'When exactly was that?' asked Strike.

'Er – last year,' said Grant.

'Can you remember exactly when?'

'Must've been . . . June-ish?'

'She had your mobile number?'

Another slight pause followed.

'Yeah,' said Grant.

'And when was the last time you'd spoken, before that call?'

'How's this relevant to Anomie?'

'Oh, it's very relevant,' Strike assured him.

'We – hadn't been in contact for a while before that,' said Grant.

'Would the previous occasion have been when she was homeless and asked you for help?'

Grant's underbite became more pronounced. Before he could attempt a response, both his little daughters came out of the house with the hyper-alert self-consciousness of children curious about strangers, each carrying a plastic pony and rider.

'Daddy,' said the larger of the two, approaching the table, 'look what Gan-Gan gave us.'

She placed the pony and rider on the table. Her younger sister was peering sideways at Strike's pinned-up trouser leg.

'Lovely,' said Grant. 'You run along back inside now. Daddy's busy.'

The older of the two girls now sidled closer to Grant, stood on tiptoes and whispered loudly in his ear,

'*What happened to that man's leg?*'

'The car I was in drove over a bomb, when I was a soldier,' Strike told the girl, more to get rid of her than to spare Grant the embarrassment of having to answer.

'*Oh,*' she said.

Her younger sister now moved in closer, and the two of them stared owlishly at Strike.

'Run along inside,' repeated Grant. 'Go on.'

The girls retreated, whispering to each other.

'Sorry about that,' said Grant stiffly, taking another sip of wine.

'No problem,' said Strike. 'Next question: I wondered whether you'd had any more of those phone calls, telling you to exhume your niece?'

'No,' said Grant. 'Just the two I told you about.'

Strike now took out his notebook for the first time and turned to the notes of his previous interview with Ledwell.

'You only took the second call, is that right? Heather took the first.'

'Yeah,' said Grant. 'I take it Anomie was calling us?'

'No, it wasn't Anomie,' said Strike. 'The caller said, "Dig up Edie and look at the letter", correct?'

'Yeah,' said Grant. He now looked definitely uncomfortable.

'But they didn't specify which letter should be looked at?'

'No,' said Grant.

'Because there are two letters in the coffin, right? One from Ormond, one from Blay?'

'Right,' said Grant, now shading his eyes from the sinking sun. 'Excuse me, I might get some sunglasses. It's bright out here.'

He got up and disappeared into the house.

'He's scared,' murmured Robin.

'So he bloody well should be. Phone call from Edie, my arse. I think we might need to do a bit of good cop, bad cop here.'

'How bad d'you want me to be?' said Robin.

'Ha ha,' said Strike, as footsteps behind them indicated the return of Grant Ledwell, now wearing a pair of Ray-Ban aviators.

'Sorry about that,' he said, retaking his seat and immediately drinking more wine.

'No problem,' said Strike. 'So: returning to the letters in the coffin. There were two, right? We're agreed on that?'

'Cormoran,' murmured Robin, before Grant could answer.

'What?' said Strike, apparently irritated.

'I think,' said Robin, with an apologetic smile at Ledwell, 'we should maybe remember that this is Grant's niece we're talking about.'

'Thank you,' said Grant, rather more loudly than necessary. 'Thank you very much, er—'

But he'd obviously forgotten Robin's name.

'OK,' said Strike, and in a marginally less aggressive voice he said, 'Two letters, yeah?'

'Yes,' said Grant.

'Because when we met at The Gun,' said Strike, 'you talked about *a* letter, rather than two. "The undertaker knew, because I asked him to put *it* in there." I didn't think much about it at the time. I assumed you were talking about a letter you'd personally handed over, and that maybe Ormond took his own to the undertaker's. Is that how it happened?'

Grant's face had become expressionless, and Robin was certain he was reminding himself that Ormond was at liberty and able to expose him if he lied.

'No,' said Grant, 'they both – I had both letters. I was dealing with the undertaker.'

'So why did you tell me you asked the undertaker to put "it" in the coffin?'

'I didn't say that,' lied Grant, adding, 'Or if I did, I misspoke.'

'So you handed over two letters to the undertaker, and if the police go and interview him he'll tell them he put two letters in there, correct?'

'Why the hell would the police want to talk to the undertaker?' asked Grant.

For the second time that evening, Strike had made a man sweat: Grant's forehead was glistening in the ruddy sunlight.

'Because this is a fucking murder case,' said Strike, raising his voice, 'and anyone telling lies about Edie's body, or their relationship with her when she was alive—'

'*Cormoran!*' said Robin. 'You're making it sound as if – sorry,' she

985

said to Grant again. 'This has been an ugly case. I know it's been really tough on you too.'

'Yes, it's been bloody tough,' said Grant forcefully.

He drank more wine, and when he'd set down the glass looked at Strike and said,

'I don't see what difference it makes, how many letters went in the coffin.'

'You're admitting only one went in there, then, are you?'

'No,' said Grant, 'I'm asking how this is relevant.'

'Let's go back to that phone call you told me about. The one where Edie magically had your mobile number and wanted your advice, when you hadn't seen her since bunging her a few hundred quid and chucking her back out on the street.'

'Now wait a bloody—'

'Cormoran, that's not fair,' said Robin heatedly.

'It's an accurate—'

'*You* don't know, and nor do I, what went on in this family,' said Robin.

'I know that bloody phone call never happened. Anyway, it's checkable, now the police have recovered Edie's phone.'

Strike deduced from Grant's frozen expression that he hadn't been aware of this.

'It's not a crime to feel regret that you didn't have more contact with a family member you've lost,' said Robin. '*I* understand why someone might've said there was a phone call when there wasn't. We've all done it. It's human nature.'

'Your partner seems to understand people a damn sight better than you do,' Grant shot across the table at Strike.

'So there wasn't a phone call?' said Strike. 'Is that what you're telling us?'

The buttons of Grant's white shirt were straining across his belly as he breathed in and out.

'No,' he said at last, 'there wasn't. It's like your partner said. I felt – I didn't feel good about not keeping in touch with her.'

'But that non-existent phone call was supposedly the reason you thought Blay wanted Edie ousted from *The Ink Black Heart*.'

'He *did* want her gone,' growled Ledwell, then instantly looked as though he regretted it.

'How d'you know?' said Strike. 'Where are you getting this from?'

When Ledwell said nothing, Strike continued:

'You told me, that night at The Gun, that both Blay and Katya Upcott have the "ethics of alley cats". Strong language. What made you say that?'

Ledwell didn't speak.

'Shall I tell you where I think you got the idea Blay wanted total control?' said Strike.

But before he could do so, the two little pyjamaed girls reappeared, now in the company of their grandmother, who beamed at the group sitting at the table, apparently oblivious to the tension.

'The girls want to say night-night to Daddy.'

Grant suffered each of his daughters to kiss him on the cheek. Instead of leaving immediately, Heather's mother turned to Strike and said,

'Mia wants to ask you a question. I've told her you won't mind.'

'Right ho,' said Strike, inwardly cursing her and the kids.

'Did it hurt, when your leg was bombed?' asked the larger of the two girls.

'It did, yes,' said Strike.

'There you are, Mia,' said their grandmother, beaming. Robin wouldn't have been altogether surprised if she'd asked whether Strike would be happy to be part of Mia's next Show and Tell. 'All right, girls, say night-night to our visitors.'

'Night-night,' said the two little girls in unison, and they returned inside.

The sun had now sunk below the roof of the house, casting the Ledwells' small paved courtyard into shadow, but Grant hadn't removed his sunglasses, which now reflected the ruby glow of the sky. He'd been given a useful interval of thinking time thanks to his mother-in-law, and before either of the others could speak, he said,

'It's just my general impression that Blay wanted her gone.'

'But you can't say where this impression came from?' said Strike.

'Well, they'd fallen out, hadn't they?'

'You said he and Katya had the morals of alley—'

'They thought Edie was Anomie, didn't they?'

'Blay being persuaded Edie was Anomie is exactly the kind of paranoia you'd expect from a perennially stoned bloke in a broken-down relationship,' said Strike, 'but you're the only person who's ever suggested he wanted to take over *The Ink Black Heart* in its entirety. Everything we've been told during this investigation suggests he was barely in a fit state to pick up a spliff, let alone single-handedly write the cartoon and deal with film studios and Netflix. I think you've got a very specific reason for thinking he wanted to take over on his own, and a very specific reason for saying Katya is crooked as well. I think you opened and read the letters you were supposed to be putting into Edie's coffin, and having read them, you chose only to put Ormond's in.'

Whether Grant would have admitted it would for ever remain a moot point, because just then Heather came through the open doors onto the patio, an empty wine glass in her hand, beaming at them all.

'Give me some of that, Grub,' she said, settling down in the fourth chair. 'I've just got Ethan down, and Mum's reading the girls a story.'

As Grant filled her glass, his expression still rigid, Heather said eagerly,

'So, what've I missed? Do we know who Anomie is yet?'

'We will,' said Strike, before Grant could speak, 'once we've seen the letter that didn't go in the coffin.'

'Oh, you've told them,' said Heather, smiling at Grant. 'I *said*—'

'Shut up,' growled Grant.

Heather couldn't have looked more shocked if he'd slapped her. The uncomfortable silence was broken by a dog yapping furiously in an adjoining garden.

'Told him to come clean, did you?' said Strike to Heather. 'Shame he didn't listen. Withholding evidence in a murder case, telling lies about communication with the dead woman—'

Heather now looked panicked.

'Cormoran,' said Robin, for the third time, 'nobody was withholding evidence. Personally,' she continued, turning to address the Ledwells, 'I think you were well within your rights to read those letters. She was *your* niece, and either of the men who wrote them could have been responsible for her death, couldn't they?'

'That's exactly what I said!' said Heather, encouraged. Catching sight of her husband's expression, she added, 'Well, it's true, Grub, I *did* say—'

'I'm not admitting we read the letters and I'm not admitting we didn't put them both in the coffin,' said Grant. He now took off his sunglasses. His heavy-jawed face looked like a primitive carving in the fading light.

'But your wife's just admitted it,' said Strike.

'No, she—'

'Yeah, she did,' said Strike, 'and that's grounds for a search warrant. Of course, if you want to burn the letter before the police get here, that's your choice, but we're both going to be able to testify to what Heather just said. And at a pinch, I expect the Home Office would permit an exhumation.'

With what Strike felt was irritating predictability, Heather's mother now appeared at the French doors and said gaily,

'Room for a little one?'

'No,' snapped Grant. 'I mean, give us a minute, Wendy.'

Clearly disappointed, she retreated. Next door's dog continued to yap.

'I'd advise you both to think hard about the consequences of continuing to deny you've got that letter,' said Strike.

'It'll be fine,' lied Robin, addressing the frightened Heather, 'if you come clean now. Everyone will understand. *Of course* you were worried Ormond or Blay had had something to do with Edie's death. I don't think anyone would be able to resist opening the letters in your position, not given how she died. It's a perfectly understandable thing to do.'

Heather looked slightly reassured.

'Whereas continuing to pretend you haven't got the letter will look pretty bloody fishy when all this comes out,' said Strike, returning Grant's look of hostility with interest. 'It's the kind of thing the papers love. "Why didn't they say?" "Why did they hide it?"'

'Grub,' whispered the now frightened-looking Heather, and Robin was sure she was imagining the gossip at the playground gates, should the papers indeed print such stories. 'I think—'

'We weren't hiding it,' said Ledwell angrily. 'We just didn't put it in the coffin. It was disgusting, what he wrote. I wasn't going to bury her with *that*.'

'Could we see it?' said Strike.

The dog next door continued its frenzied yapping as Grant sat staring at Strike. The detective judged Ledwell to be a stupid man in many ways, but not entirely a fool. At last Grant got slowly to his feet and disappeared into the house, leaving his wife looking extremely anxious.

'D'you get a lot of that?' asked Robin pleasantly, pointing in the direction of the noisy dog.

'Of — of the dog? Oh yes,' said Heather. 'It never stops! It's a Pomeranian. The girls have been *begging* us for a puppy. We've said maybe, once we're back in Oman — the thing is, home help's so cheap over there I could probably cope with a dog and the baby. But it won't be a Pomeranian, that's for sure.'

'No, I don't blame you,' said Robin, smiling while her pulse accelerated at the thought of the evidence that was about to appear.

Grant reappeared, holding an envelope. Before he could sit down, Strike said,

'Have you got a clear plastic bag?'

'What?' said Grant, who still looked angry.

'A clear plastic bag. There'll be DNA evidence on there. I don't want to contaminate it further.'

Grant returned wordlessly to the kitchen and returned with the envelope and a freezer bag.

'If you can open the letter and put it and the envelope in the bag, before we read it,' said Strike. Grant did as he was told, then slid the encased letter across the table.

Robin's heart was now racing. She leaned towards Strike to read a short paragraph written in the purest example of what Pat would have called 'nutter writing' that Strike had ever seen. Small and uneven, with some letters obsessively retraced in dark ink, it looked strangely childlike, or would have seemed so, but for the flawless spelling and the content.

You told me I'm just like you. You made me think you loved me, then dropped me like a piece of shit. If you'd lived, you'd have used and tortured more men for kicks, spitting them out once you were bored. You were an arrogant, hypocritical, despicable cunt and I want these words to rot beside you, your closest, truest epitaph. Look up from Hell and watch while I take control of The Ink Black Heart, forever.

'Katya Upcott gave you this?' said Strike, looking up at Grant.

'Yes.'

'It's disgusting, isn't it?' said Heather hotly. 'Just *disgusting*. And the fact that Katya copied down all that filth and then handed it over to Grub, knowing what was in there — and Allan Yeoman and Richard Elgar saying she's such a nice woman — it honestly made me feel *sick* to hear them, that day at the Arts Club.'

'Except that Katya Upcott didn't write this,' said Strike. 'This isn't her handwriting. *That's* her handwriting,' said Strike, pointing at the envelope, on which was written 'For Edie' in the same neat, square hand as the list of names Katya had given him weeks previously.

'So . . . who wrote that?' asked Grant, pointing a short, thick finger at the letter. He and Heather both looked scared, now.

'Anomie,' said Strike, now taking out his mobile and taking a picture of the letter. He put both phone and notebook back into his pocket and reached for his crutches. 'You should call the police immediately. Ask for Ryan Murphy of the CID. He needs to see that letter. In the meantime, don't take it out of that bag.'

Strike managed to get back up onto his crutches with some difficulty: it was always harder to balance after a long period sitting.

'Good night,' said Robin quietly to the Ledwells, finding it hard to immediately abandon her good cop persona. She followed Strike back into the house, the yaps of the Pomeranian next door punctuating the shocked silence they left behind them.

105

'Right,' said Strike, as they walked down the Ledwells' short front path in the gathering darkness. 'We need to talk to Katya. I want to get to Anomie before he starts smashing up any more hard drives.'

Once they were both back in the BMW and Strike had shoved his crutches onto the back seat, he called Katya, but after a few rings he reached voicemail.

'No answer.'

'It's a quarter to ten,' said Robin, glancing at the dashboard clock. 'Maybe she mutes calls at this time of the evening?'

'Then we'll go to the house,' said Strike.

'Don't think Inigo's going to be happy getting a visit from us this late,' said Robin as she turned on the engine. 'It'll take us a good twenty minutes from here.'

'Hopefully the miserable sod's still in Whitstable.'

As Robin pulled out of the parking space and accelerated up Battledean Road, she said,

'Katya can't have known what she was handing over. She *must* have thought what Josh had dictated was still in the envelope.'

'I agree, which means she let that envelope out of her sight at some point between sealing it at the hospital and handing it over to Grant Ledwell. We need to know exactly the journey it took.'

'There's still the DNA, as long as the Ledwells haven't contaminated it too much.'

'Anomie's not stupid. I'll bet he wore gloves, and if there isn't any DNA on there all we've got is the handwriting and potential access to Katya's handbag.'

As they passed through residential streets, behind whose illuminated windows Robin imagined sane, happy people living, she said quietly,

'We're looking at someone really malign, aren't we? Wanting to put *that* in her coffin?'

'Yeah,' said Strike, deep in thought, his eyes on the road ahead, 'this is a deeply disturbed individual.'

'Who thought Edie loved him.'

'Or kidded himself she did.'

'Can I know what that "wire-cutting" comment meant now?'

'What?' said Strike, who was following his own train of thought. 'Oh – I was talking about cutting through barbed wire to breach the enemy's trenches.'

'And the wire in this case is ...?'

'Those satellite accounts Anomie made on Twitter. The arrogant fucker never thought anyone would get interested in all these minor accounts, so he got a bit slack with the names ... Give me just one more minute, and I'll tell you where I think they're pointing,' said Strike, taking out his mobile again. 'I *know* I've seen the name John Baldwin somewhere other than Twitter ...'

Though feeling both impatient and anxious, Robin obediently fell silent as she turned the car onto the Holloway Road, which would take them north-west, towards Hampstead and Highgate. Beside her, Strike was hunched over his mobile, scowling, intermittently typing and thinking.

'*Got him!*' said Strike so loudly that Robin jumped. 'He's on Reddit, the "Track Criminal Bitches" page and – fuck.'

'What?' said Robin, whose heart was still hammering.

'He reported Marcus Barrett's sister.'

'*What?*'

'"*Lying bitch Darcy Olivia Barrett made false sexual assault accusation against boyfriend. Living at 4b Lancaster Drive, Hoxteth*" ... He gives all her social media accounts ... That'll be why I couldn't find any for her. I bet she wiped the lot once this appeared.'

'Strike, *tell me about the names,*' said Robin. 'What do they give away?'

'Well, for a start, Marc Lépine shot fourteen women. Anomie's favourite number's fourteen. Julius-I-am-Evola tells us Anomie is, or was, at North Grove.'

'I thought you said Evola was the kind of writer the far right—?'

'I was wrong. If Anomie's Lepine's Disciple, he's I am Evola, as well. Then we've got Max Reger, nineteenth-century German composer – I should've spotted that: I saw a book of his music on the bloody keyboard.'

'Wait—'

'John Baldwin, sixteenth-century British composer; Zoltán Kodály, early twentieth-century Hungarian composer. Scaramouche: straight out of "Bohemian Rhapsody" by Queen. Which means somebody who listens to Queen, and the Beatles, possibly because he hasn't got a—'

Strike's mobile rang over the car's Bluetooth: Katya was ringing him back. He answered the call, but had uttered one syllable of 'hello' before a high-pitched scream rang through the speaker.

'*Help us, help us, help—!*'

The call was cut.

Strike jabbed at the number to call it back, but nobody answered. Robin slammed her foot to the floor.

'That wasn't Katya – that was Flavia. Strike, call—'

But he'd already dialled 999.

'Police – there are screams coming out of number eighty-one, Lisburne Road and there's a man in there with a knife ... Because I know there fucking is ... Cormoran Strike ... A family of four ...'

'Shit,' said Robin as Strike hung up. '*Shit* – this is my fault, it's all my fault, I spooked him—'

'It's not your fucking fault,' said Strike, grabbing the sides of his seat as Robin took a corner at speed.

'It is, it is – I should have realised ... Strike, he can draw really, *really* well.'

'How d'you—?'

'There's a self-portrait in the loo at North Grove. I thought it was done by Katya, but then I saw one of hers in Josh and Edie's room and it was rubbish – and—' Robin gasped. 'Strike, *I know why he diverted into trees after stabbing Edie.* Ryan Murphy told me there was an out-of-control Alsatian on the Heath that afternoon—'

'And he's terrified of dogs.'

106

'No police,' said Robin frantically as she braked a few doors from the Upcotts' house.

She threw off her seat belt, leaned across Strike and, before he realised what she was doing, slammed her hand on the button that opened the glove compartment and seized his skeleton keys.

'What the fuck d'you think—?' shouted Strike, grabbing the back of her jacket as she opened the driver's door.

'Let go of me—'

'You're not going in there, you fucking idiot, he's got a fucking machete—'

'*There's a twelve-year-old girl – get OFF ME!*'

Dragging her rape alarm out of her pocket, Robin pulled free of her jacket and half fell out of the car. The rape alarm slipped out of her hand and rolled away; now free of Strike's restraining hand she chased it, snatched it up, then sprinted up the road towards the Upcotts' house.

'Robin! ROBIN!'

Swearing fluently, Strike turned to pull his crutches off the back seat.

'*ROBIN!*'

A silhouetted head appeared at the lit window of the nearest house.

'*Call the police, call the fucking police!*' Strike bellowed at the neighbour, and leaving the door of the BMW open he set off in slow pursuit of Robin on his crutches.

She was already at the Upcotts' front door, trying, with shaking hands, to find a key that worked. The first three were ineffective, and as she tried the fourth she saw the light in Gus's ground-floor bedroom window go out.

On the fifth attempt, she managed to turn a key in the lock. Ignoring Strike's distant bellow of 'ROBIN!' she pushed the front door ajar.

The hall was pitch black. One hand still on the doorknob, she groped on the wall beside her, found the light switch and pressed it. Nothing happened. Somebody, she was certain, had pulled out the main fuse block, doubtless because they'd heard the shouts, the mention of the police, running footsteps and the jangling of keys at the front door.

Leaving the front door open to admit some light, her thumb on the button of her rape alarm, Robin crept towards the stairs.

She was halfway up when she heard the thuds of Strike's crutches and his one foot. Turning, she saw him silhouetted against the street-lights, then something moving in the shadows behind the door.

'STRIKE!'

The dark figure slammed the door behind Strike. Robin saw blue sparks and heard a buzz. Strike fell forwards, limbs jerking, his crutches clattering to the ground, and in the grey ghost light admitted by the glass above the front door Robin saw a raised machete.

She jumped from the fourth step, landing on Gus's back, arms around his throat; she'd expected him to fall, but thin as he was he merely staggered, trying to prise her arms off him. Her nostrils were full of his dank, unwashed smell, and then he'd tripped over Strike's outstretched, motionless leg and both of them tumbled forwards, and as Gus's head hit the opposite wall he let out a roar of rage:

'*I will fucking kill you, you cunt—*'

Somehow, Robin was on her feet again, but as the machete sliced the air in front of her, Gus still half-kneeling, she had no choice but to flee up the stairs, and only then registered that the rape alarm was still clutched in her fist, and activated it. The screech pierced her eardrums.

'Flavia? FLAVIA?'

She couldn't hear a response over the screech of the alarm, but behind her she heard Gus running after, taking two steps at a time on his long legs.

'FLAVIA?'

There was more light up here: the curtains were open and through the door to the sitting room Robin glimpsed a huddled figure on the floor near the window. Thinking only of interposing herself between the girl and her brother – *where were the police?* – Robin sprinted towards what she thought was Flavia, skidded on a dark pool on the polished floor, and only then saw the overturned wheelchair that had been hidden by the sofa, and the crooked glasses on the dead man's face.

'Oh Jesus—'

She turned. The alarm in her hand was still screaming its warning and she threw it from her. Gus was advancing slowly on her, panting, still holding the machete.

'I'm going to rape you before I kill you.'

'The police are on their way,' said Robin.

'That's all right,' said Gus, half panting, half giggling. 'I probably won't last long. It'll be my first time.'

The foot-high marble torso of a woman lay feet away on its table. Robin began to edge towards it.

'Does it make you wet, thinking I'm going to rape you?'

Robin's right foot slipped on more blood. Still she edged towards the table.

'I know women fantasise about being raped,' said Gus, still advancing.

Robin's groping hand found the marble.

'Do you smell of fish?'

In one quick movement, Robin had seized the marble from the table: it was so heavy she could barely hold it, but then, with a strength born of terror, she swung it into the window, which shattered: the marble slipped through her hands and fell with an echoing bang onto the path – if that didn't alert the neighbours, nothing would.

Then Gus was on her, twisting her around, one arm around her throat, the other still holding the machete. Robin stamped hard on his bare foot before both slipped in another puddle of Inigo's blood. As Gus's grip loosened, Robin's found his forearm with her teeth and bit down, hard. He dropped the machete to punch her in the side of the head: she felt dizzy, the room seemed to spin, but terror kept her jaws locked on his flesh and she could taste his blood, and smell the animal sweat on him, and then Gus trod on the fallen machete and with a yelp of pain he slid sideways, releasing her. Robin stamped again on his injured foot and then, somehow, she was free again, skidding and running towards the door.

'*Fucking bitch!*'

'FLAVIA?' Robin bellowed as she reached the landing.

'Here, here, I'm up here!'

Robin sprinted up the second flight of stairs, passing a dropped mobile, but she had no time to pick it up because she could hear Gus running after her again. On the top landing, a door that had already been attacked with the machete opened, and Robin flung herself through it, realised she was in a bathroom, turned and rammed home the bolt on the door seconds before Gus began throwing his weight against it. As the door shuddered, Robin saw, by the dim glow from a skylight, Katya slumped on the floor beside the bath, blood all over the hands she was pressing against her stomach.

'Flavia, help your mum – press that over the wound!' Robin shouted, snatching a towel from the rail and throwing it at the terrified girl. She felt for her own phone, then realised it had been in the jacket Strike had pulled off her.

Gus was now hacking at the bathroom door with the machete. One of the panels splintered and she could see his livid face.

'I'm going to fuck you then kill you – fucking *whore* – fucking *bitch*—'

Robin looked around: a heavy brass pot containing a cactus sat on a washstand. She grabbed it, ready to smash it into his face as he entered, but suddenly he turned away, and with a shock of relief, Robin heard male voices.

'Easy, Gus – easy, son—'

Looking down at white-faced Flavia, she pressed her finger to her lips, then quietly unbolted the door. Gus had his back to her, facing two men, the larger of whom was wearing pyjamas. Gus was slashing the air between them with the machete.

Robin raised the brass pot and brought it down, hard, on the back of Gus's head. He staggered as the cactus and earth showered everywhere, and then the two men had him, one seizing the arm holding the machete and snapping it with his knee, so that the knife fell to the floor, the other grabbing Gus's neck and forcing him face down onto the floor.

'Call an ambulance,' panted Robin. 'He's stabbed his mother—'

'We've already called,' said the pyjamaed man, who was now kneeling on the struggling Gus. 'He stabbed a guy just inside the door.'

'I'm a doctor,' said the other man, and he hurried into the bathroom.

But Robin was now hurtling downstairs, jumping steps, bouncing off walls. The rape alarm continued to wail from the sitting room as she passed the open door, flying towards where Strike was slumped against the wall beside the open front door, a hand pressed to his upper chest, smears of blood on the wall behind him.

'Oh God, Strike—'

As she knelt beside him he gasped,

'. . . think . . . he's punctured . . . m'lung . . .'

Jumping up, Robin opened Gus's bedroom door and ran inside, looking for something to press to Strike's back. The place stank: a place where nobody went, where nobody visited, where filthy clothes lay everywhere on the floor. Grabbing a sweatshirt, she dashed back to Strike, making him lean forwards so that she could press the cloth hard against his upper back.

'What's . . . happened?'

'Inigo dead, Katya stabbed, Flavia OK,' said Robin rapidly. 'Don't talk . . . Did you let those two men in?'

'Thought . . . you didn't want me . . . to talk?'

'You could've nodded!' said Robin furiously. She could feel his warm blood soaking the sweatshirt. 'Oh, thank Christ . . .'

Blue flashing lights had appeared in the street at last, and as more and more neighbours gathered to peer at the house, from which the alarm continued to scream, police and paramedics came running up the path, past the fallen sculpture of the woman's torso lying in broken glass.

CODA

The heart continues increasing in weight,
and also in length, breadth and thickness,
up to an advanced period of life:
this increase is more marked in men than in women.

Henry Gray FRS
Gray's Anatomy

107

Oh foolishest fond folly of a heart
Divided, neither here nor there at rest!
That hankers after Heaven, but clings to earth
That neither here nor there knows thorough mirth,
Half-choosing, wholly missing, the good part: —
Oh fool among the foolish, in thy quest.

Christina Rossetti
Later Life: A Double Sonnet of Sonnets

'Nicotine patches,' said Robin, 'grapes ... bananas ... nuts ... oat bars ...'

'Seriously?'

'You told me you wanted healthy stuff,' said Robin over the top of the open supermarket bag.

'Yeah, I know,' sighed Strike.

Five days had elapsed since Anomie had been dragged, struggling, out of his parents' house in handcuffs, but this was only Robin's second visit to her partner's hospital bed. Strike's sister Lucy and his Uncle Ted had dominated visiting hours, and Robin supposed Madeline must have been in regular attendance too. Robin had been desperate to talk to Strike, but her only previous visit had been unsatisfactory, because he'd been full of morphine, dazed and sleepy. Her guilt and anxiety about his injury hadn't been assuaged by the definite coldness in Lucy's voice when she had called to tell Robin that Strike would like to see her again today. Evidently Robin wasn't the only person blaming herself for what had befallen her partner. She wondered why Madeline or Lucy couldn't have brought Strike the supplies he'd texted her for but, grateful to be permitted to do something for him, she hadn't queried it.

'. . . and also dark chocolate, because I'm not inhumane.'

'Now you're talking . . . Dark, though?'

'Better for you. Antioxidants. Less sugar. And Pat insisted on making you a fruitcake.'

'Always liked that woman,' said Strike, watching Robin put the foil-wrapped, brick-shaped package into his bedside cabinet.

Each of the four men on the small ward had visitors this afternoon. The two elderly patients who were recovering from unspecified operations were talking quietly to their families, but the man who was recovering from a heart attack at the age of thirty-three had just persuaded his girlfriend into a walk where, Strike knew, he was hoping to have a quiet cigarette. The smell of smoke his wardmate trailed in his wake every time he returned from one of these walks was a constant reminder of a habit Strike had now vowed to kick for ever. He'd even advised the young man censoriously that he shouldn't be smoking after a heart attack. Strike was perfectly aware of his own gross hypocrisy, but sanctimony was the only pleasure in which he could currently indulge.

'. . . and these two flasks are strong tea, but before you tell me they taste funny, they've got stevia in them instead of sugar.'

'The fuck's stevia?'

'A calorie-free sweetener. And that,' said Robin, drawing the last item out of the bag, 'is from Flavia and Katya.'

'Why're they giving *me* a card?' said Strike, taking it and examining the picture of a puppy holding balloons. 'You did all the work.'

'If you hadn't managed to open that front door and let the neighbours in,' said Robin, dropping her voice as the wife of one of the old men passed the foot of the bed to refill his water jug, 'we'd all be dead.'

'How are they?'

'Katya's devastated, unsurprisingly. She's still on the ward upstairs. I visited her yesterday, that's when Flavia gave me your card. I don't think Katya had any idea what . . . what Gus *is*. Ryan Murphy told me that when the police searched Gus's room they found terrible drawings everywhere. Women being knifed and hanged and tortured . . . He'd put his foot through his cello, too.'

'Did they find Blay's phone? The dossier?' asked Strike, who was evidently far more mentally alert today than he'd been the last time Robin visited.

'Yes. It was all hidden under a floorboard he'd prised up, with Josh's genuine letter to Edie and the latex masks – everything.'

'So those voice-change calls,' said Strike, who'd had plenty of time to think while lying in bed. 'They were from Flavia, right?'

'God, you're good,' said Robin, impressed. 'They were, yes. She saw Gus replace Josh's letter with his own, in the kitchen, where Katya had left her handbag. He had his back to Flavia and she crept upstairs without Gus realising she'd seen. She told me she got the idea for the voice change from Bram telling her about those noise apps. She's a really clever, observant girl.'

'Well, let's hope her mother keeps her off the internet,' said Strike, reaching for the bar of chocolate. 'We don't need another fucking criminal genius in the family.'

'She wants to be a detective,' said Robin. 'She told me so yesterday.'

'We should offer her an internship. Why didn't she tell her mother what she saw Gus doing with the letter? Fear?'

'Well, she can't say it openly in front of Katya, but yes, I think she was absolutely terrified of Gus. If you ask me, Flavia was the only one in the family who sensed what he really was. You know, she *kind of* tried to tell us, or to hint – remember her saying "Maybe you'll have to come back again" after we went to their house. She told me she saw Elliot Rodger's shooting spree on the news while Gus was in hospital. I checked: that was the day Edie was hospitalised for the suicide attempt, and Anomie disappeared from Twitter and the game over the same couple of days. It was one of the bits of so-called proof that Edie was Anomie, which the Peach brothers put in that dossier.'

'Hm,' said Strike, wincing slightly as he adjusted himself on his pillows, 'well, we could've done with slightly less oblique hints. But next time I say, "How d'you fancy X as our culprit?" let's just stop the investigation right there until we've ruled out X.'

'Duly noted,' said Robin, smiling.

'Get this. Angela Darwish dropped by yesterday,' said Strike, and Robin felt a flicker of resentment that Darwish had been permitted to see Strike ahead of her own second visit, 'and she told me the fucker *was* bugging the upstairs. He's been very busy on the dark web, buying all his kit. He was able to hear everything Josh and Katya were saying to each other, and Edie too, before she stopped going round to their house. But he's been hoist by his own petard, because the bugs picked up what happened before we arrived on the street.

'Apparently the Royal College of Music called that afternoon to say Gus hadn't turned up to talk to his tutor, hadn't submitted any of his agreed work and, basically, that he'd been lying to his parents for most of the year about attending private tuition and was about to get chucked out. After a solid hour of Inigo telling him what a useless little shit he was, Gus went down to his room, grabbed the machete, went back upstairs and stabbed Inigo repeatedly in the chest and neck.'

Robin had already known all of this, because Murphy had told her, but made appropriate noises of interest. She had a feeling Strike needed to know things she didn't right now.

'And he said they've interviewed the Barretts as well, but he didn't tell me how that went.'

'Murphy told me a bit,' said Robin. 'Darcy was three years ahead of Gus at the Royal College of Music, and she felt sorry for him because he was such a loner, so she asked him to a party one weekend.'

'Women's capacity for pity is bloody dangerous,' said Strike through a mouthful of dark chocolate. He'd have preferred a Twix, but it was still a damn sight better than hospital food.

'So Gus told Katya Darcy was his new girlfriend. She was really happy he'd found someone, because he's always been "a bit awkward with girls".'

'No shit.'

'According to the Barretts, Gus turned up at the party and then sat on a sofa fiddling with his phone all evening, not speaking to anyone and looking livid because Darcy had an *actual* boyfriend there. Gus must've hacked Marcus's iCloud that night, because the Barretts never invited him back, due to the fact that he followed Darcy into the bathroom at 2 a.m. and forcibly attempted to kiss her.'

'I'm starting to see why he needed Kosh,' said Strike.

'She shouted and struggled, and her boyfriend and brother chucked him out, but she never reported him to the college or anything. As I say, she felt sorry for him – it was Rachel and Zoltan all over again. Zoltan told Rachel his father was abusive, so she cut him a lot of slack – until the rape and death threats started.'

'Sounds like Gus has been living in a completely delusional world, where every woman who's polite to him wants to screw him.'

'I think that's exactly it,' said Robin soberly. 'Katya told me Edie used to be nice to Gus when she visited the house. When Inigo made the kids go along to North Grove, Edie encouraged Gus about his

drawing and told him she'd been a real introvert when she was a teenager too. I think that was all the contact they ever had, but again, he
built it all up in his head, thinking she was keen on him. Then Edie
criticised the game publicly . . . and he turned.'

'Are his hives even real?'

'Yes,' said Robin, 'but when the police got inside his room they
found all this food he wasn't supposed to be eating, hidden away in
odd corners, because it triggered outbreaks. He didn't want to go back
to college, he just wanted to stay in his room and be Anomie . . . I've
been thinking about Rule 14, you know, too. All that anonymity. I
don't think it was only that he and Morehouse were scared of their
parents and universities finding out what they were up to. I don't think
Gus could stand the idea of creating a game where other people could
flirt with each other. He wanted total control and enforced abstinence
for the players – and meanwhile he was desperately trying Kosh lines
on girls all over Twitter.'

'You know,' said Strike, who'd had time to mentally review the
case as he lay in bed, 'all of this could've been avoided if people had
just *opened their fucking eyes*. Inigo and Katya, not bothering to check
what their son's up to, forever holed up in his room. And Grant
bloody Ledwell – if he'd looked at the handwriting on the envelope
and compared it to the letter, if he'd shown it to the police instead of
deciding Blay must just be a money-grubber, which is the worst bit of
projection I've seen in a while, Vikas Bhardwaj might still be alive.'

'"She's my sister",' quoted Robin. 'From what Murphy told me, I
don't think Vikas's parents were anything like Inigo – they didn't seem
like bullies in the slightest – but Murphy says they were astounded to
learn that Vikas had co-created the game, because they thought all
he cared about was science.'

'All adolescents need something their parents don't know about,'
said Strike. 'Just a pity some of them choose murder.'

'But that explains the initial bond between Gus and Vikas, doesn't
it? They were both so precociously good in their separate fields, and
must've been feeling a lot of pressure, and neither of them were having
any luck with girls . . . you can see how it happened, how they became
friends . . . Shall I put that card up for you?'

He handed it over, but his bedside table was already so crammed
with handmade cards from each of his nephews, and shop-bought
cards from Lucy and Ted, that as Robin attempted to balance Flavia's

there she accidentally knocked a large one to the floor. As she bent to pick it up she saw a long handwritten message, and the signature 'Madeline'.

'Chuck that in the bin,' said Strike, seeing what Robin was holding. 'We've split up.'

'Oh,' said Robin. 'While you've been in here?'

'No. Couple of weeks ago. Wasn't working.'

'Ah,' said Robin, and then, unable to resist the temptation, 'Amicable split?'

'Not really,' said Strike. He broke off and ate a couple more squares of dark chocolate. 'She kicked me.'

Robin didn't mean to laugh but couldn't stop herself. Then Strike started to laugh too, but stopped on feeling a hot pain through his upper chest.

'Oh, shit, are you all right?' said Robin, seeing him grimace.

'I'm fine. Are *you* all right?'

'Of course. *I* didn't get stabbed. I'm great.'

'Are you?' Strike insisted, watching her closely.

'Yes,' said Robin, knowing perfectly well what that piercing look signified. 'I honestly am. The worst thing's been the bruising where he punched me in the head. I can't lie on that side to sleep.'

She didn't want to tell Strike about the sleepless nights since, or the bad dreams, but when he continued to look searchingly at her, she said,

'Look, it was awful, I'm not pretending it wasn't. Seeing Inigo dead – although it wasn't as bad as finding Vikas – but it all happened so fast, and I knew the police were on their way, and I knew if Gus was busy trying to rape me he couldn't be killing Flavia or Katya. And,' Robin tried to repress laughter, a slightly hysterical reflex she'd had to fight over the last few days, 'he *definitely* wanted to rape a live woman rather than a dead one, so that worked in my favour.'

'It's not funny,' said Strike.

'I know it isn't,' said Robin with a sigh. 'I never meant to get you stabbed. Strike, I'm so sorry. I really am. I've been really worried—'

'You didn't get me stabbed. I had a choice. I didn't have to follow ...'

He took as deep a breath as his injured lung would permit, then forced himself to say something he'd have preferred not to.

'You saved Katya and Flavia's lives by going into the house. The bugs recorded it all. The bastard was trying to smash his way into the bathroom when he heard you trying to get in through the front door. He tripped the main fuse then ran downstairs to hide behind the door. And if you hadn't thrown that marble thing out of the window, the neighbours wouldn't have come running to help, so . . . I can't say I wish you hadn't done it.'

'But if you'd died, I'd never have forgiven myself. Ever.'

'Don't *you* start fucking crying,' said Strike as Robin hastily wiped her eyes. 'I've had enough of that from Lucy. I thought the point of visiting people in hospital was to cheer them up. It's been wall-to-wall waterworks every time she looks at me.'

'You can't blame her,' said Robin huskily. 'You nearly died.'

'But I'm alive, aren't I? So she should learn some bloody jokes if she wants to keep coming in.'

'Is she back tonight?'

'No,' said Strike. 'Tonight's Prudence.'

'What, the sister you've never – the therapist?'

'Yeah. Kind of hard to pretend I'm busy right now.'

'Don't give me that,' said Robin, now smiling. 'You'd have found a way to put her off if you'd wanted to.'

'Yeah, maybe,' admitted Strike, but he added, 'do me a favour, though: if Lucy phones the office, don't mention Prudence was here—'

'Why would I?'

'Because she won't like me seeing Prudence.'

The idea of suggesting that Strike stop lying to the women in his life occurred only to be dismissed, on the basis that the resolutions to stop smoking, lose weight and exercise were enough personal improvement to be getting on with.

'How're things at the office?' Strike asked, still eating chocolate.

'Fine, don't worry. We've taken the next two off the waiting list, both extramarital affairs, nice and straightforward. Oh – but something funny happened this morning. Nutley phoned. Now The Halvening have been rounded up, he'll be happy to come back.'

'*Will* he, now?' said Strike dangerously.

'It's OK, Barclay took care of it,' said Robin. 'He took the phone out of Pat's hands. I think the exact words were "get tae fuck, ye cowardly shitstain".'

Strike laughed, winced and stopped.

'Has the glass in the door been fixed?' he asked, again rubbing his chest.

'Yes,' said Robin.

'And?' said Strike.

'And what?'

'Have you looked at it?'

'Looked at what? The glass? Not really. I haven't been into the office much, but Pat hasn't said anything, so I assume it's fine. Why?'

'Pass me my phone,' said Strike impatiently. 'Jesus Christ. Four of you in the office, and nobody's noticed?'

Robin handed him his phone, thoroughly confused. Strike opened photos and found the picture the glazier had sent him at his request.

'There,' he said, passing the phone to Robin.

She looked down at the familiar office door with its frosted glass, which she'd seen for the first time five years previously, when she'd been sent as a temp to an unknown business and realised she'd been sent to work for a man who was doing her dream job, the chance of which she'd thought was gone for ever. Five years previously, the words engraved on the glass had read: 'C. B. Strike, Private Detective', but no longer. She was now looking at 'Strike and Ellacott Detective Agency'.

Without warning, the unshed tears of days poured down upon the screen of the mobile, and she hid her face in her free hand.

'Bloody hell,' muttered Strike, glancing around at the assembled visitors, some of whom were staring at Robin. 'I thought you'd be pleased.'

'I am – I *am* pleased – but why did you have to spring it on me?' said Robin, frantically mopping her eyes.

'Spring it on you? You've been walking past it for the last five bloody days!'

'I *haven't*, I told you, I've been doing sur–surveillance . . .'

She groped on top of Strike's bedside cabinet for tissues, knocking over half his cards in the process. Having blown her nose, she said weakly,

'Thank you. *Thank you*. I just – thank you.'

She didn't dare hug him in case she hurt him, so instead she reached out and clasped the hand lying on the bedcovers.

''S'all right,' said Strike, returning the squeeze of her fingers. In retrospect he was pleased she hadn't noticed, and that he got to witness her reaction in person. 'Long overdue, some might say. You'd better tell Pat to order new business cards as well.'

'That's visiting time over, I'm afraid!' called a nurse from the doorway.

'Any fun plans for this evening?' asked Strike.

A strange qualm passed through Robin as Strike released her hand. She considered lying, but couldn't, not after being so angry at Strike for doing exactly that.

'Well, I've ... I've actually got a date.'

Strike's beard hid some of the dismay he felt, but not all of it. Robin had chosen not to look at him, but had bent down to pick up the handbag beside her chair.

'Who with? Not Pez Pierce?'

'*Pez Pierce?*' said Robin incredulously, looking up. 'You think I'd go out for a date with a *suspect*?'

'Hugh Jacks, then, is it?'

'No, of course not!' said Robin. 'No ... it's Ryan Murphy.'

'Ryan ... what, the CID bloke?'

'Yes,' said Robin.

Strike said nothing at all for a few seconds, because he was struggling to process what he'd just been told.

'When did that happen, then?' he asked, a little more forcefully than he'd intended.

'He asked me out a while back and I couldn't go because I was working, and – now I can. Free weekend.'

'Ah. Right.'

Strike struggled to find something else to say.

'Well ... he seems like a decent bloke.'

'Good to know you think so,' said Robin with a slight smile. 'Well, I'll come back in whenever's convenient, if you—'

'Yeah, do,' said Strike. 'Hopefully I'll be out soon, though.'

She smiled again, got up and walked away, turning back to wave at the door.

Strike was left staring at the place where she'd vanished, until the young heart-attack survivor reappeared and returned to his bed. The detective didn't chide his wardmate for the strong smell of Marlboro now wafting on the hot air, because he was experiencing a clarification of his feelings as irrefutable as it was unwelcome. The thing he'd been trying for years not to look at, and not to name, had stepped out of the dark corner where he'd attempted to keep it, and Strike knew there was no longer any way of denying its existence.

Trapped by the drip and the drains in his chest, confined to the narrow hospital bed, he couldn't follow Robin, couldn't call her back and tell her it was about time they talked about that moment outside the Ritz.

It's one date, Strike told himself, suddenly craving a cigarette more powerfully than at any time since being admitted to hospital. *Anything could go wrong.*

Murphy might get drunk and tell a racist joke. He might patronise Robin, who was a detective with no formal training. He might even make a rough pass – although Strike didn't like the idea of that at all.

He reached out for one of the flasks of strong tea Robin had brought with her and poured himself a cup. The fact that it was precisely the shade of creosote he preferred made him feel, if possible, worse. He drank it without really tasting it, so couldn't have said whether stevia tasted different to sugar. Cormoran Strike had just suffered a blow to the heart that the machete had missed, but this wound, unlike the machete's, was likely to cause him trouble long after the drains were gone and the drip removed.

And the worst of it was, he knew his predicament could have been avoided if only, in his own recently uttered words, he'd opened his fucking eyes.